THE NAKED VIRGIN

or

Muddy gets his corridor

by

Robert H. Smith

Published by:
ANCIENT MARINERS PRESS LLC
1314-F Garden Wall Circle
Reston, VA 20194

Copyright © 2005 by Rober H. Smith—1st edition.

ISBN :　　　Softcover　　　1-59926-292-4

1. The Seventies; the ways of Washington—fiction
2. The Imperfectibility of Government—fiction
3. The U.S. Navy; Follies & Glory—fiction
4. Mysteries of Sound in the Sea—fiction
5. The Present; Triumph of the Submarine—fact

All rights reserved. No part of this book may be reproduced or transmitted in any form or by any means, electronic or mechanical, including photocopying, recording, or by any information storage and retrieval system, without permission in writing from the copyright owner.

This is a work of fiction. Names, characters, places and incidents either are the product of the author's imagination or are used fictitiously, and any resemblance to any actual persons, living or dead, events, or locales is entirely coincidental.

This book was printed in the United States of America.

To order additional copies of this book, contact:
Xlibris Corporation
1-888-795-4274
www.Xlibris.com
Orders@Xlibris.com
29426

BOOKS BY ANCIENT MARINERS PRESS

- BETRAYAL IN APRIL
- THE DOOBERMAN FROM HELL
- SILVER KING
- HELL AT TASSAFARONGA
- HISTORY OF CUBA'S ARMED FORCES
- AUDITING GOD'S BOOKS
- CIA! CUBA AND THE CARRIBEAN
- BIRD OF ONE WING
- THE TAKING OF MIAMI

For the fair Winifred . . .
Sharer in the Voyage

"If you insert a long tube into the water, and put your ear to one end, you may hear ships at great distances . . ."

"I have this knowledge (of the submarine) but I shall not reveal its secret lest wicked men turn it to evil use to destroy ships and send innocent seamen to their deaths."

Leonardo da Vinci

1

The setting sun brightened the cupola of the Maryland State House that George Washington had known, lit the golden spire atop the Naval Academy chapel. But below those familiar eminences the streets of Annapolis were already filling with shadows. Down Cornhill Street a tourist couple paused to admire the little row homes with their fine doorways and knockers of polished brass. Tessa Morgan could hear the woman's voice clearly.

"Such darling little places, I wonder who lives in them."

Relics, my dears, relics, Tessa thought amusedly, rattling a dish of nuts. She set three glasses out on a silver tray and looked around her small living room. Dominating it—in truth overwhelming it—was a full-length portrait of her late husband in the dress blue uniform of a Navy Captain. Binoculars slung around his neck, he was standing upon a warship's deck beneath massive grey turrets elevated towards a dramatically clouded sky. Hidden within the edge of the great portrait's frame, a border of tiny light bulbs cast their glow of honor upon the oil's shiny surface. "Tsk." She noticed that yet another bulb had failed, adding a stroke of darkness to an already disconcerting patchwork of illumination. Tessa's thoughts, however, only vaguely touched Irish, lost so long ago. Her concern was focused upon the living, foremost amongst them her son, David, youngest and the most perplexing of her children. With still greater immediacy she was thinking about Admiral Malcolm Waters, the last of her friends still in touch with power. Whatever age it is when a mother ceases to scheme for her children, Tessa had not reached it.

The room was too dark. Impatiently she switched on more lamps. Accustomed shadows leapt backwards, forcing her to reconsider the ambivalent virtues of abundant illumination. No enemy of dust, neither did Tessa Morgan see any need to advertise it. But *there* . . . a sense of strangeness had touched her again; this renewing wonder at herself, far removed from the western town of her girlhood, so long amongst these Morgans and Boatwrights whose strong flowing lives had swept her up and joined their richer history to her own. The room reinforced that strangeness. The walls were covered with affectionately inscribed photographs of vanished friends, plaques and insignia of ships of forgotten fame, fleets of victory long disbanded. Yellowing ivory, darkling brass, carved glowing woods, oriental rugs of swirling color, told of an age of unhurried travel and easy plunder. The room breathed the fleeting age of U.S. colonialism in rule over distant pleasant islands and last small enclaves of empire. It breathed adventure too.

A Morgan had voyaged with Hanson up the Amazon; an ancient shoebox on a back shelf held a notebook in sepia ink, vague parts of shredded clothing, a snake's fang, a sinister hank of coarse black hair. Abner Boatwright had stood beside Farragut at Mobile Bay, been with Porter bumping his way up the tangle of the Yazoo. Irish's father had made the historic transit to Queenstown with Taussig. Ghosts all. But vigorous ones. She sighed, mistress, she feared, of a coming thinner line. She sighed doubly now at the tapping, unmistakable on this quiet street as Long John Silver's peg leg, of Miriam Gearing's cane along the brick sidewalk. Ah well. Friends no longer so numerous that one could freely choose. Tessa swung open the door to discover Miriam in a state of unaccountable agitation. "Come in, dear," Tessa said briskly, yet not unkindly. Miriam's state of temporary speechlessness was not such a rarity as to be alarming. "Let's not allow all the warm air to rush out." She settled her friend with a glass of sherry. Time had not wrinkled Miriam's face, merely rounded and filled it. Pink from the evening's cold and the exertion of her walk, it looked cherubic. Beautiful eyes, baby doll's eyes still, were wide in perpetual readiness for surprise. A readiness that showed no sign of lessening in some seventy years of encountering it.

"So, very well," Tessa said. "Do go on. There was, I gather, a . . . collision." Necessarily, Tessa had to urge along the pace of Miriam's telling, aware that she could not get on to her own treasured topics until her friend's news had first been sped out of the way. "*Almost* a collision," Miriam corrected. "And it was the *girl*, not the young man. I hate to imagine what . . . ."

"But there now, she didn't bump into you, did she? Just be thankful."

Tugged forth by Tessa's persistence, the little story came out in the fullness of detail that Miriam wished for it. The girl had been clutching a midshipman's cap, evidently having snatched it from the head of the young man chasing after her. *"Her hair was flying and she was laughing and running like the wind."* A Miriam breathless anew with the vividness of recollection. "In our day—"

"Nothing was different" Tessa broke in. At once though she softened. The eternal perplexity of Miriam's expression recalled sunnier years fondly. Thus it was that in a little while Miriam, refilled sherry glass in hand and pillows plumped around her troublesome hip by her solicitous if bossy friend, had been coaxed into that degree of attentiveness that was the only one permitted when Tessa was discussing her children. Yet, vexingly, Miriam fell short of being an ideal audience. Although Tessa felt that her points possessed irresistible logic, and despite the vigor with which she marshaled them into argument, Miriam retained a small but resistant strain of independence. Deferential to Tessa on matters of fact—as was prudent in the case of someone like herself who had never, in near fifty years as a Navy wife, sorted out such details as the difference between a cruiser and a destroyer—Miriam's opinions concerning people were less malleable. She had known David since he was a baby. Her loyalties, if gentle, had fiber. "I believe you are worrying too much, Tessa dear. David is a sweet boy."

"Forty plus years old and going nowhere."

"And his Aliason is so pretty. Beautiful really, many would say."

"But a little sharp-faced, I've begun to notice that lately."

"*Tessa!* It's Aliason's dear face. And it goes with her."

Something, perhaps a spot of mold beneath the glass on one of the old sea prints, seemed to have registered depressingly on Tessa's distant expression. "Tell me truthfully, Miriam, don't you find her a little . . . odd?"

Miriam's stubborn kindliness had her frowning in search of a better word. "She is fey." Her hands moved gropingly. "She seems so vulnerable . . . fragile."

"Why that should be accounted a virtue I'll never know." After a moment of silence, frustration and regret burst forth from Tessa in an old lament. "Why couldn't he have gone to the Naval Academy like his brothers? Life is so much simpler for those who do."

"But, poor David couldn't help that, could he? Wasn't it his eyes?"

"Well, of course. Certainly not his studies. He has a good mind, though it wanders." She shook her head. "But his job does seem to fascinate him."

It was one of Miriam's virtues never to give up searching for sources of cheer. She had noticed a copy of the Naval Institute Proceedings on the coffee table. "You know, Tessa, you are proud of David for those articles. A *writer*, think of it."

"There have been only a handful of articles, when all is said and done. And I gather, poor dear, that he works awfully hard at them." But despite her deprecation, Tessa's heart was plain to read. Her son's writings, even if mystifying—and nothing was more mystifying than this minor flowering of apparently admired literate expression following a long line of men of action—thrilled her more than she could say. The mother has not yet been born who finds it difficult to yield some acknowledgment of a son's virtues against the press of another's admiration.

"I expect that they will be valuable to his career too," Miriam said. Of that Tessa was less sure. "They may be too critical of things, although it's difficult for me to tell. There's a lot of history in them too. And I don't think they really want much of that up there in Washington."

"Some people apparently approve of what they say."

"Not Muddy," Tessa laughed. "He complains that he doesn't even understand them."

"Muddy's just saying *that!*" Miriam's face took on a sudden glow while Tessa's own recomposed itself soberly. She had a hankering for some clouds in the best of her weathers.

"Aliason is holding David back," she declared gloomily. "Why, Tessa, you know that for her the sun rises and sets on your David. And she's given you beautiful grandchildren."

"Whom I too seldom see." "My dear, who ever sees enough of her grandchildren?"

In a balance of moods, which was what Tessa knew of peace, she reached for a cigarette. Elegant long fingers inserted it in her ivory holder and went on to light it in a series of unconscious motions that had become as natural to her as breathing. *Ah*. Inhaling deeply, savoring that first draw, a smoker of old, before the age of guilt and fears, eyes almost closed in ancient transport of her spirit to indefensible realms. It seemed to Miriam that an elusive comradeship had been regained. She came to the gingerly conclusion that she might, without having her head taken off, bring up the more exciting subject of Muddy's visit this very evening.

"For heaven's sake, Miriam . . . I *invited* him. That's all there is to it."

"Still. He's always had a crush on you. He'd take you in a minute."

Tessa whooped with laughter. Such a laugh. Few were left who had heard it in its prime but it had made parties go, knit friendships, touched total strangers with rare intimations of spirit and beauty. "What a man at his stage of life is looking for mostly is a nurse."

"Not Muddy. You're very attractive still, Tessa."

"Miriam, thank you. I still have my teeth. But that's about it."

Miriam was trying hard to think of something she had very much wanted to remember. Now she had it. "I was reading about Muddy the other day in *Time* magazine. He's become the Navy's *Grand Old Man*? Our Muddy. What do you think of *that*?"

"I really don't know." She waited with surprising patience for Miriam's solemn assurance that there was much in that news to think about.

"They say he's at the White House a *great* deal." Tessa's smile was too private to read. Guessing what Irish would have said to all this, she could not resist teasing her forever innocent friend. "Oh, and just what is it he does there?"

"*Do* there? Why . . . goodness . . . all sorts of things. Why . . . ." But any possible telling of those presumptive good things remained stalled on Miriam's lips. "There." Tessa patted her hand. *"Of course he does."* Ringingly. None too soon to put herself in the proper frame of mind for Muddy's arrival. And if Muddy's belated veneration was bound to be something of an oddity, this was not the time to poke at it. Still, she could not deny herself one observation. "Funny though, isn't it, what happens if all you do is live long enough. Muddy is a dear, but he was never the man that Irish was."

Miriam's eyes misted over loyally. "That is so true, Tessa. But Muddy is the one who's here, isn't he? All alone in that big apartment. Right on the Potomac. It still is the Potomac, isn't it? He must be terribly lonely since Grace died."

"So am I at times, God knows. But there are worse things than loneliness."

Miriam though was not ready to abandon the matter. Anything new in the shrinking circle of her awareness was too precious. "Tessa, dear, might I please have another sherry? I don't care what you say. I just have this *feeling*."

Tessa handed Miriam her glass with a glance at the clock. "I poured you only a half. Drink up, then I'm afraid I must shoo you out."

"I can't stay even to say hello to Muddy?"

"Not tonight." At the door, however, Tessa could not entirely withstand her friend's sad look. "Cheer up. I promise that you shall get to see Muddy next time."

"Oh, Tessa, how many more next times are there going to be?"

"None of that kind of talk." Tessa's farewell kiss was fond but no less decisive. She straightened up the room briefly, dabbed on a bit of perfume and, in the few minutes before Muddy was due, enjoyed another cigarette. Last for a while. Muddy did not care for tobacco smoke, and tonight she would give him no cause to fuss. Church bells began to chime, symbol of that other great comfort in her life. By the quiet waters of Spa Creek, across the rooftops of the old town, the notes clanged sweet and strong. In her lifetime the church had changed much, but at least it still offered this glad remembered song.

▲▲▲▲▲

As Tessa was pushing her friend out the door, Admiral Malcolm Waters, U.S.N. (Retired)—"Muddy" Waters to friends of his generation—was striding towards her house. He had a fair distance to walk. After considerable cruising about, the Admiral had to leave his handsome car parked in a region off West Street. Old, but not historic, the Annapolis Historical Society had designated the area, the sort of distinction that Muddy would not have appreciated even had he known it. Yet indisputably he too was old Annapolis, recalling when West Street was not so tawdry. Curly-headed children darted through the dusk, jabbering in unknown tongues. Neon signs winked from darkish bars. The wind, catching an oily smell from a dimly yellow restaurant, flattened a scrap of paper against a sooty wall. From a new and sinister sea, tides of menace seemed to wash against these older shores.

Merely with distaste though and not apprehension he made his transit of this neighborhood. Fear had always been Muddy's least ration and there was to his progress an unhurried grandeur akin to the long ago triumphant sweeps of his destroyer squadron through the phosphorescent seas of the Southwest Pacific. He had reached familiar territory. Along cobbled streets, he might once more know the lift of recognition. A startled midshipman fired off a tidy salute. Not that everyone remembered Muddy, even knew he existed. Yet a stranger encountering him was likely to believe that he should.

A glance at his reflection in the window of a uniform shop along Maryland Avenue provided a look that still pleased. His wavy hair, thick as in his youth, was stunningly silvery. Its waves were like sculptured swells of the sea itself. And that *head!* Historical scholars, students of those factors that have aided the rise of men to prominence have found no shortage of evidence to remark upon the worth of a striking one. Caesar's bald dome is stamped on a million ancient coins. The example still haunts of Danton on the guillotine steps, challenging all to mark well his own mighty head whose like the mob people would not see again. Scholarship has gone further, noting—with ill-spirited envy, to be sure, for the drudging obscurity of such labors tills gardens of resentment—that the success of many a grand head has borne scant relationship to its contents. And although Muddy's roots went back to a rambunctious age, of midshipmen genially cruel in their nicknames—when protuberant teeth won you "Rat," and many an Italian was fated to be "Wop"—it was not alone the jolly workings of tradition that had earned Muddy his own. Teammates on a once renowned Navy football team remembered their stalwart's tendency to find more mystery than most in the O's and X's of the play diagrams on the coach's blackboard.

It had not been a good day. The reasons were, with minor variations, the same teeming ones that had kept the last several decades from being good ones either. While social commentators may philosophize upon the anomaly of the professional military man in democratic America, it was the burden of Muddy to struggle with its paradoxes. Most keenly he felt the *insufficiency* of tribute. In reverie, he cast his imagination back to days when nations were wont to heap protean rewards upon their military winners: Queen Anne's gift of Blenheim Palace to the Duke of Marlborough; Wellington and his own celebrated accretions of grandeur, the iron of his captured cannon remolded into glorious statues in London parks. British naval captains of the Napoleonic wars had returned from their voyages with stunning riches of prize money. One had to be quite old and long in the Navy, and moreover be an intent observer of the seemingly relentless erosion of fringe benefits which once had lent such added glitter to the military career—and Muddy qualified there—not to mark the withdrawal of the rights of prize with a sense of gloomy historicity.

Persistently, in another way, his thoughts kept returning to Britain. Its quaint ways he had long ago embraced her with that uncritical love endemic amongst generations of Americans who know her mainly from afar. He thought of knighthoods generously conferred, the thunder in the ear of those marvelous titles that only monarchy can bestow. *Montgomery of Alamein, Cunningham of the Mediterranean, Maxton of Cape Race and The Western Approaches.* He lingered over that last: Happy Sir Bruce, slaughterer of U-boats. Wondering what the old devil was up to these days. Muddy sighed. It was not enough to be the U.S. Navy's *Grand Old Man.* Nor could he warm to the doubtful dignity of "Big Daddy Destroyer," with its frazzled echoes of rollicking times. Even his White

House pass carried its own freight of disenchantment along with honor. The Washington press, ever inclined to facile flattery towards anyone in whom it encounters nothing to provoke its enmity, made much of his visits to the White House. "State visits," it was pleased to call them. In truth, it had been several administrations since Muddy had spoken with a President, let alone had one incline his ear to those words of wise advice which, as negligently researched folklore had it, the nation's Commander-in-Chief was anxious to hear from one of its grand old warriors.

Fortunately, there remained still a small store of pleasanter things to think about. Fragments of wistfulness. He was summoning recollections of tropic seas and green summits soaked in clouds, while trial phrases rolled majestically through his imagination.

Admiral of Melanesia.

Waters of the Slot (This one his mind's voice repeated several times until, elusively, he sensed reasons to reject it).

Waters of Kolombongara. Ah yes. That one sang. And for a moment, startlingly, so did Muddy. The tune of "Nancy Lee"—to which generations of midshipmen had marched off Worden Field—sprang to those old lips. *"A sailor's wife a sailor's star shall be . . . ."*

He whistled with boatswain's pipe clarity, going on for a minute or more, pleased to form those lilting notes. Alas, the lift did not last. He well knew that, short of the establishment in the U.S. of a British-style monarchy—an idea for whose fulfillment he could have roused himself to counter-revolutionary enthusiasm—any hankerings for a title was a nonsensical dream. Thus it was that his remaining ambition, as well as the fraying cord of his discontent, was tied to a more attainable objective. At least one that *ought* to be attainable, this notion of gaining a short length of one of the long corridors of the Pentagon's E-ring, a small brightened oasis of interest dedicated to himself and set aside for memorabilia, paintings of sea battles, a treasured salted cap, his "steamer", its gold braid turned a coppery green, some sooted flags, and ship models, and other catchy and admirable stuff.

Why the idea could not get off the ground, when every office he visited claimed to regard it favorably, and every individual in the Administration whose approval for it was crucial expressed overwhelmingly warm wishes, was to Muddy a vexatious mystery. One to which, after a typically frustrating day making his familiar rounds, he would retire with his scotch and soda to contemplate in gloomy bafflement. Not long ago the stringy muscles of his ancient arms had actually ached following one of his White House visits. The hearty squeezes rendered to his elbows by the obviously well practiced fingers of various aides lingered like a palpable memory of his frustration. To a man, these young fellows promised not merely support, but also something which it seemed to please them to call Action. Several of them, amazingly, even bore the title: Action Man. *My word.* Little did the world know what Muddy went through. Bearing patiently the diminishing respectfulness and the lengthening waits outside of offices to which he was shuffled about with brisk energy, if seldom discernible purpose.

Yet even in that stout heart hope was dying. Too long approval had teetered on the brink, the business of getting it underway seeming to be only heartbreaking, yet unbridgeable, inches off, perhaps a mere phone call away. It had come to seem a mocking chimera, a grinning mischievous Puck, nimbly uncatchable, destined to hide forever in a murky landscape. Ducking behind boulders of jargon like "fiscal years," "program elements," "joint committee blessing," and all the other impediments to common understanding of a new age. Before Muddy let go of these thoughts for this evening—and periodically he made himself do so, for the good of his digestion—in imagination he revisited once more his completed corridor. Picturing it whole, glowing, a small but appealing museum with people drifting past in pleased flow. He pictured some lowly secretary, papers in hand, her hard heels clacking, suddenly stirred by the sight of what she was hurrying by and feeling a small dart of grander purpose, a remembered flash of patriotism beyond the latest fire drill about the Budget. No siree, Muddy concluded once again emphatically, this was not a mere exercise in vanity but a service of merit. Good Lord, after all the Army had a Marshal Corridor. One for Bradley too, hang it. Meant you didn't *have* to be dead. But then . . . the Army had always done this sort of thing better. Yes, yes, and there was already a display for Arleigh Burke—the sainted Arleigh, admittedly no man deserving it more—but nowhere was it writ in letters of gold that the Navy's allotment of Corridors must be capped at *One.*

Ah well. Yet for Muddy it was always an easy bridge to cross from one source of discontent to another, having at last to give thought to Tessa's requested favor. Not only did he not care to face up to the truth of his own greatly shrunken influence, but he had also to consider the nature of Tessa's son himself for whom he must presumably now expend a bit—*more* than a bit, knowing about such shenanigans—of his last hoarded currency of persuasion. Not that he had anything against young David. In a way he was fond of him, as he was loyal to anything connected with Tessa. But it was the *irony* of the thing. And irony, which carried a whiff of effete associations, was something that Muddy had always viewed with suspicion.

Good heavens. He remembered David since he was a tiny fellow, the lad having to be rigged with glasses right from the start and always running into the furniture, a solemn and obedient child on skinny legs in whom the adult of today had been forecast. The pained love of his father, no surprise, and certainly forgivable, that the baffled Irish had come to the conclusion that there was no hope for it, that son David would be taking up golf as a last resort. Muddy recalled the sadly damming judgment implicit in that decision. Not that Irish held anything against the game *per se*, no more than did Muddy. A pleasant enough diversion for later on in a man's life, but certainly not a sport you *started* a lad off on if you had other choices. Anyway, it probably explained things about David. Amongst the lesser of Muddy's secret convictions was that no man became a writer except for unfortunate reasons.

Those damnable articles: Composed in strange language, the new idiom of technology, replete with awareness of missiles and computers, a whole new age of warfare that had succeeded Muddy. But there were strange ideas in them as well, bizarre notions about the shrinking importance of surface warships. My word! Muddy was sincere when he told Tessa that he did not understand what her son was saying. Except, that is, for his occasional articles that related to history. Now *there,* he conceded, they were pretty good. Thus, happily would he grant to David—indeed, would smooth and hasten the way—total immersion in, or elevation to, whatever success he could carve out in some career dedicated to dim researches which, on the evidence (hard for Muddy to doubt), were distinctly the young man's better bent. Picturing David ensconced in the obscurity of some college as Resident Professor of this or that, Muddy dearly wished that he knew how to make it come about. Or even that, as alternative to some of Tessa's busy notions about her son—the latest and oddest, and yet the most dismayingly persistent, being that David's proper niche was as some sort of highly positioned politico-military thinker—he wished he could summon the nerve to argue with Tessa when she got some such bee in her bonnet. Still, David a *Strategist? God, save us.*

Yet Muddy's concern was merely personal, his worries not institutional. It was not as if David really threatened Muddy's beloved Navy. Nor, Lord knows, had the articles attracted much notice. It was one of Muddy's comforts that articles in the Naval Institute Proceedings—and David Morgan was not its only author to suffer, as Muddy would phrase it, from a few "wild hairs up his ass"—attracted little attention. If someone was aflame with a heretical idea there was no better way to ensure its forgottenness than inter it with full honors in the Naval Institute Proceedings. It was a truth that enabled the Proceedings to enjoy the reputation of being a boiling cauldron of feisty and innovative ideas while, in reality, managing near perfectly the desire of Navy leadership to preserve the Fleet in all its soothing changelessness.

How the Proceedings maintained the dualism of its nature so effectively was no mystery. In a nutshell, few people read it, least of all naval officers. The Proceedings did its good work then, not through the slumberous reaction to its ideas, but in making friends for the Navy, keeping alive colorful images that vividly and appealingly defined the sea service. Graceful grey ships, shining brass, scarlet threads of tradition, deep hues of ocean. Not for the naval officer did the Proceedings live; foremost it reached out to another kind of man, the Navy buff in the hinterlands, the many who hungered (tens of thousands of men, feeling themselves achingly deprived of some vital part of life's feast, had that hunger all their lives) for the sense of trackless seas and ancient ports looming up through morning mists, golden girls waiting. Images made for lives stuck fast in the hard brown earth of America, for the dentist in Pasadena, that hardware dealer in Council Bluffs, your commodities dealer shouting his years away in the pits in Chicago. At bottom, romantics all. Men also like Muddy himself who, if they occasionally did happen to read a Proceedings article, preferred misty-eyed reminiscences about, say, the first four-piper cruiser to pass through the Panama Canal. What right sort of fellow too wouldn't rather read about capping the "T" at Surigao Straits than funereal laments for the dimming future of the destroyer? Now... now that *last,* hurt. A new era of naval warfare might presumably be dawning but Muddy did not believe a word of it. A man who has lived with the roll of the destroyer's deck beneath his feet knows better. He was recalling now one of his old ships, the swoop and dare of her lines. It may only have been the unsteadiness of the antique bricks of Annapolis sidewalks, but he was feeling again the powerful tremble of steel plating underfoot as throttles spun open wide with steam to her turbines.

No, it was not that a few articles—mere words—of young David Morgan's nor anyone else's, froth upon deep flowing currents of time, were the problem. More disturbing was that sense, closing in upon him, of a weakening of faith. An era of spurious rationalism had infected near everything. Right down here at the Naval Academy itself—and the chiming bells, at this moment mournfully bonging out some nautically encrypted hour, were a reminder of what things had come to—astonishingly, midshipmen were no longer required to attend chapel! Now Muddy's own life had not stamped him as a paragon of religious devotion. In truth had he read Samuel Butler, he would have subscribed to that gentleman's view (without, however, endorsing the impropriety of actually *saying* it) that the genuinely civilized man is neither fervent in religion nor indifferent. The former characteristic restraining a man from committing massacres in its name, and the latter insuring that he absorb its graces. A man then ought to be lukewarm, observing the forms but not taking them too seriously either. *Exactly.* Thus it was that generations of midshipmen—like lithe bodied young men everywhere, perpetually starved for sleep—used to be marched into chapel, set down in that inspiring warmth, to feel the rays of rainbowed sunlight through glorious windows, the lulling music, the sermon's droning comfort, and allowed to doze right off, heads lolling *en masse,* in that sweetness of stolen rest sweeter than any other. Arguably, that kind of somnolence was the tribute of a secure piety that trusts the Lord to look down kindly on a basic human need in fallible bodies which are, after all, His own creation. So much for theorizing; the fact was that *by God, they went.* And no lasting harm to anyone, so far as Muddy could see. And even if compulsory attendance did, indeed, represent a violation of one of man's freedoms—and Muddy, even though he had been serving at the time in the cruiser that carried President Roosevelt to his Atlantic Charter meeting with Churchill at Argentia, had lost track of exactly which ones *were* the Four Freedoms—surely it wasn't a dreadfully serious trampling of any one of them.

Ah yes, *Freedom. Damn,* how often Muddy found himself shaking his head over the word. He had been accustomed in his younger days, and actually through most of his naval career, to voices of authority. Today, in place of those former grand *harrumphs* of thunder, there was babble, everywhere a bleating of sheep with the oddest opinions. As if there could be Sea Power without ships! And now here was this latest thing about SEA EAGLE—another pretty kettle!—that fine destroyer program stalled yet again in Congress. It was a commentary on the pokiness of such procurements, the endless gluey labyrinths through which such matters had to wriggle themselves out into the light, that the seeds of SEA EAGLE had been planted in the last years of Muddy's active duty. His feelings towards it were thus paternal and therefore his dismay all the greater to witness this fine offspring of power strangling in endless debate. And now moreover, inescapably aware that at the fringes of all this raging brouhaha (however insignificantly, yet no less incredibly) was Irish Morgan's son himself.... A child of this present age, with his plethora of code names out of mythology, and the oddest notions storm-lashed to shaky spars of unpronounceable acronyms, all atangle in abstruse debate, as to whether one of those new systems with that lady's name—DIANA? Well, no matter who or which—could enable a destroyer to hold its own with a nuclear submarine. Tedious arguments through whose fog Muddy's convictions cleaved sharp as a destroyer's bow.

Technology is damned! His beloved destroyers had killed many a U-boat, ramming them if need be. These young whippersnappers and their electrons! Muddy knew what steel could do. *What hearts could do.* Destroyers had taken on battleships! Yet, for all of the foolishness that abounded, and in which young David Morgan unaccountably partook, he felt for Tessa's son only baffled tenderness. If he did not understand him ... well, a piss-pot full of the current crop of admirals he did not understand either. Said to be a new breed. That they were. But, *oh.* What children became. Tessa's house loomed, its knocker gleaming from the corner streetlight. Yet thoughts of the navy's tribulations, the certainty that that he would not be long through Tessa's door before she would be at it again, laying on him some new point in the burden of her hopes for her precious David ... all were dropping away. A sober sort of fellow, thirsting for a special brand of wit, Muddy Waters had made this journey once again across Maryland's gently rolling countryside. He straightened his shoulders and knocked. He could not say just why—except, by golly, it was high time—but he had managed at last to feel no longer disloyal towards his old pal Irish, blasted to smithereens on the bridge of his battleship in that kamikaze's flash so many years ago. He took a tighter grip on his bouquet as he detected movement within. *Tessa!* Old hearts can pound too.

▲ ▲ ▲ ▲ ▲

Spring again, David Morgan thought, gazing out the window of Dr. Gray's office in Crystal City. He reflected a moment longer on the banality of the thought, let shadows fall away. As they ought. As a Senior Engineer in the Naval Material Command's division of Experimental Acoustic Research—EAR—the world would say that he had much going for him. Things still seemed to await him, problems their solutions, even shining rewards. Rewards of riches beyond and of a different kind than those, say, for which his Aliason assiduously clipped little coupons or licked gummed labels, affixing them in proper slots to be mailed off to contests hither and yon. And if all things in his life were not under control—understatement!—well, of whose life could it be said that they were?

"Are you still with us, David?" Dr. Gray was inquiring pleasantly.

"Sorry. Just drifting off for a moment." Thinking golf. The sweetness of a perfectly struck shot . . . .

"I thought so," Dr. Gray—Tawney—observed tolerantly. He was a florid, white-eyebrowed cherubic man who had good reason for the peace of his countenance.

"I'm all alertness now, "David added impishly.

"Good. I do have one item of importance. My readings from the Pentagon tell me that DIANA is going to move. 'Go', one could say, in a big way." Tawney's look passed from David Morgan and rested, with seeming preferment, upon Julius Baumgarde. There were just the three of them. "You mean," Julius said, seeking clarification, "that there is going to be an acceleration of its progress from research into the acquisition cycle?"

"And thence," Dr. Gray added after a pause commensurate with the unfolding momentousness of his information, "move straight to fleet introduction. The prototype presently in the frigate *Esposito* . . . ." It is a paradox of the world that certain bombshells make no sound. Tawney Gray, looking up at last from his clasped hands upon which his eyes had kept themselves lowered in some inaccessible trance of concentration, looked at David with amusement, "Did I detect a cry of pain?"

"Tawney. You've got to be kidding! It's premature by years." "Unfortunately," Tawney responded with his patented little smile, "that isn't, after all, for us to decide."

"It is up to us though to be the technical conscience of development programs."

"And so we shall be," said Dr. Gray with a glance away, "up to a point."

"We haven't reached that point yet, Tawney. Why, the SLRS numbers in ADAMP"—ADAMP, SLRS, DIANA, and so on, not other than incomprehensible acronyms to the great majority of the world, and yet absorbing to the small community of the knowing—"tell a perfectly godawful story that we haven't yet begun to get across."

"David, you're sputtering. As for ADAMP . . ." Tawney paused, with fastidious distaste. "ADAMP is not part of EAR. It is independent of—"

"Certainly," David interrupted hotly, "because it's to serve the Fleet. But doesn't its very independence serve more to confirm the validity of its data than to refute it?"

Tawney wet his lips. "David. Frankly, I can't see much mileage in your getting close to that funny little maverick who runs that ADAMP outfit. Jencks, is it?"

"I could be mistaken," Julius inserted solemnly, "but actually I don't believe the man ever got his degree. In any event, data banks merely record the history of what has happened. They tell us nothing about the probabilities of future events."

Tawney turned to David as if to say, "now isn't that just the way it is?' It was a reprise of the times that they had seen Julius, armed with his Cambridge doctorate in mathematics, subdue entire fractious rooms with his iron grasp of Laplace, God of Probabilities.

Tawney Gray wanting to get off this. All his life he had been quick to tamp down the lid on any pot aboil. Whatever the bureaucratic clichés for the safety of his career, or the peace of his soul, his nature had clutched them all as instinctively as the squirrel its branches. "Let's just say," he murmured, "the times they are a' changing."

"Changing?" David, of course, would be the one to pick up on that rumination. David Morgan, his younger colleague, fellow sharer of distant times off the Hawaiian Chain and in the Red Sea—though now perhaps, nay *surely*, no longer the friends that once they had been—who could be both acute and obtuse in the same breath. Yet Tawney's gaze was one of sincere regard, even as it was mixed with pity for the ludicrously thick, but manifestly indispensable, glasses that hung on David's prominent ears, and from which the current arts of optometry—lagging the pell mell advances of the sciences towards miniaturization and melioration of such other blatant affronts to vanity—could not spare him a faint, but inescapably cruel, impression of absurdity.

"Changing, yes," Tawney went on, his voice having the fleeting timbre of decisiveness "and we shall sensibly change with them. But now . . . ." Moving away from DIANA. On to the nits and gnats; complaints of poor telephone etiquette by some of the secretaries, the moribund state of the Plowshare Program . . . . Which David had briefly forgotten, while a puzzled Julius had entirely. David offered clarification. "As in electrons into . . ."

Julius stirred uncomfortably. Tawney Gray though clapped his hands.

"I like that, David. Someone the other day—someone, I might add, not always in love with your writings—was saying that you have a nice little wit. Anyway...."

A fair bit of ground to cover yet. Captain Leads, amongst other things. The good Captain retiring soon and no relief in sight. Just as the flag billet of Development itself, which oversaw EAR and other offices within Materiel, had been vacant for some time. No, Tawney said in response to a question from Julius, he did not think that these gaps portended any downgrading of EAR's role. "In fact..." but Tawney now halted himself, a man who always knew more than he spoke. A fact was a coin to be played carefully; the shrewd man in government did not toss one out willy-nilly. So. Moving on some more.

"Now, on the subject of trips, funds are tighter. Strictures more severe, more scrutiny. This may be just a flurry, or it may be a long cold spell. In the meantime, let's ration our overhead travel carefully. For trips, of course, for which project sponsors are willing to put up the dough, well... with my happy manumission, you may jaunt off to Timbuktu." Timbuktu? David's mind caressed the sound. Unfortunately, program sponsors didn't send you to Timbuktu or any other place echoing enchantment. Their funds only dispatched you to Akron or Cedar Rapids, to New London or Syracuse, or to a dozen other lusterless cities of America's industrial heartland where the future of DIANA was being forged. *Forged?* Many words were possible for DIANA's shaky progress, but that was not one of them.

"Yes?" Tawney paying further notice, with mild annoyance, to another blossoming of one of David Morgan's inward smiles. "Don't *tell* me David. This summer's Wolf Lake Oceanographic and Acoustic Symposium is on your mind. The outline of your talk is in hand and I have gone over it carefully"—in truth, as David had no doubt, he had barely skimmed it, just enough to be apprehensive—"and I picture you on the podium proudly dispensing your wisdom and your lovely Aliason out there as well making the rounds of the artsy-crafty shops with my Tiny by day, and happy as a clam with the wind sighing in the pines by night. Your boondoggle is safe."

"*Boondoggle?*"

"No offense. You indeed have worthy things to say. Don't be bothered by my little word. But face it. Boondoggles are a part of every profession. So enjoy." Tawney paused: an idea murkily glimpsed moments earlier was now swimming nearer the surface where he could see it clearly. Yet only part of his idea he now chose to unveil. "As I say, I'll be going over your prospective paper with you in greater detail."

"For changes?" "Mere suggestions," Tawney fended easily, "at this stage."

The idea that had been forming in Tawney's mind, though it had begun vaguely out of a tiny worm of fear, grew more specifically out of his concept of leadership. Yet "concept" was too grand a word. "Style" was closer to it, "means" still closer; these being little more than a grab-bag of notions, an ill-attended sack of rusty tools from which, as the need arose, he would grab one. Lacking feel for the grander foundations of human motivation, his approach was manipulation in lieu of inspiration. And so it was this moment that a particular notion had leapt to the forefront of Tawney's mind. Reminding him of the obvious.... If you controlled something someone else wanted, why, *you had power over him*. The stronger that person's desire, the greater the control. Fact One was David Morgan's pending promotion to GS-14. Overdue, richly deserved, and desperately needed too, if Tawney understood correctly the chronically painful state of David's economic circumstances. Not that David, a proud fellow, would ever plead those. But EAR was a small office and over time Tawney had some clues. Fact two, a lesser one but not trivial, was his subordinate's anxiety to get to Wolf Lake this summer, and confer on his beloved a rare shared vacation. Tawney here pausing to picture again, with mingled lust and recoil, the bewitching Aliason Morgan. Recoil though the stronger feeling, as his mind tolled. *High Maintenance*. With an associated mental check off of gratitude towards his own Tiny, low maintenance as they come. In fact, all Maintenance now taken over by the Lord, and thank you, Lord, for that. Inextricable from the mix of Tawney's thoughts, yet for reasons still so inexplicit as to constitute mere uneasiness, a shadow no bigger than his pink little finger, Tawney Gray was weighing that whatever talk the quirkily rebellious David Morgan was going to deliver must be carefully orchestrated.

"Yes, yes," Tawney was saying, looking down at his hands. But a satisfied smile was rising—a smile that only the means in hand for confident mastery of a situation could bring—on a countenance grown more benign. He could afford to speak soothingly: "We will get to your talk when I return from Paris."

Thus on to Paris! All roads now clear as once they were for Patton and LeClerc after the breakthrough at St. Lo. On past Avranche! The prospect of the trip, pushing aside the niggling vexations of EAR, further boosted his spirits. The glorious oceans that you could talk on about forever and never have to do a thing about. Oceans that would not change, not in the lifetime of even the most dewy-eyed representative to the Women's International Symposium on the Seas—WISOS in short—newest contender in the Ocean Conference sweepstakes. He had the keynote speech dutifully to make, scattered seminars to attend and luncheons and receptions beyond counting. And all to take place in the City of Lights. *Crillon*, stand by!

That such trips came under scrutiny by ill-tempered members of Congress—not to mention squinty-eyed auditors in mean-spirited establishments like the General Accounting Office—had never been troubling to Tawney Gray. He could deflect criticism more surely than the medieval bowman's arrow of old was made to clang harmlessly off the curving surfaces of a knight's armor. Take the metal hot and take it striking. With good reason Tawney Gray was selected by the Director of Naval Laboratories to be spokesman of the Navy's officially prepared defense, the *generic* one as it were, of all such trips undertaken by countless numbers of his colleagues. To be sure, in such defenses Tawney had powerful support. The National Science Foundation and the Office of Naval Research, a multi-thousand cohort of pipe puffers and leather elbow patches—natural allies to a man—were behind him one and all. Before Congressional Committees Tawney's testimony, light and humorous, was a skillful transmutation of technically abstruse objectives into the vernacular of worldly reality. Congressmen, most comfortable with horse traders, recognized a fellow. He was even disarming to those churlish representatives of Peace and Deprivation whose constituents were least inclined to sympathize with battalions of prosperous and educated men regularly traveling far and well on government monies for a variety of purposes having tenuous links to National Security. His patient answers turned away untold floods of wrath. Remembered—indeed kept in mind exceedingly well, for the event was still wholesomely, renewingly alive—were his recurrent performances in behalf of Wolf Lake's annual Symposium.

Nineteen years the Symposium had lasted, growing stronger with each year. This year's session would mark its Twentieth Anniversary, The Big Two-Oh, as its enthusiasts liked to say, already beating the drums for its coming round of summer events. If the original concept had actually been that of Dr. Erik Mundelein of Wolf Lake College, it was nevertheless true that the resourceful Tawney Gray on the Washington scene—Washington, where the all-important spigots of money must be kept turned on to make these things go (no one in his right mind ever attending on his own nickel)—had been critical in guaranteeing its survival. As it had grown sturdier Tawney had seen to its stiffening with ever brawnier grants of money. Eventually it gained the dream of all Programs, the status of *Budget Line Item*. Tawney's shrewd testimony, under many a set of lights, had made it seemingly impregnable. The timing had been opportune. Tawney and his supporters, like a thousand California surfers all at once had caught the same golden wave of the oceans. A dozen other competitive academic symposia, with their mangrove-like roots also more or less in salt water, arrived hard after, thence to eye Wolf Lake's success with envy. Such imitative gatherings waxed and waned; fitful stars, briefest of novae, most enjoyed at best a few years of tepid support and then disappeared from the scene. Some did manage to hang on longer, but sullenly, their survival primarily dependent upon a humbled willingness to meet in the more loveless of America's cities—Waco, Texas, say, or Fort Leavenworth, Kansas—consciously eschewing the uncomfortable visibility of grander locations. Even so, they barely subsisted while Wolf Lake flaunted its prosperity. *Wolf Lake*! All that was needed now. Utter those words and everyone in its special and not so small world knew. As well known as Woods Hole, that heavyweight of the East, now balanced in name recognition by the challenger from the West. Tawney Gray had done it. Triumphing, in the end, with a handful of crucial sentences still quoted from the conclusion of one day of hard-pressed testimony years ago. They were the fondly handled coin of a special realm and shone like much rubbed gold. "Gentlemen," Tawney Gray had declared to the assembled in that hushed, crowded and hot Congressional Hearing Room, "no number can be placed on the value of scientific communication. It is immeasurable. It can also be fateful." He had paused then, making sure that he had them, every one, the cynical staffers and the hard-bitten Congressmen alike secure in the palm of his hand.

"Gentlemen, I conclude. No one can ever predict the outcome of such interchanges. No one can ever know in advance what a scientific man may take away from a meeting with another man of science. It may be nothing. Or it may be momentous. And we must never deny ourselves, for our nation's good, every chance for that spark of some idea indispensable to our nation's security."

People had clapped. Bold and impermissible cheers had to be gaveled down. Nor was there, amongst all the passingly enchanted, a single sour soul to suggest that what most individuals took away from these meetings was a deeper suntan, a sharper golf game, a contented wife, a cheered girlfriend. No matter. Wolf Lake Symposium was secure unto the ages and Tawney Gray's name thereafter inseparable from it.

"I guess that's it," Tawney said. He had not spoken for a minute at least. Nor had his deputies, both of them used to these reveries, said anything to disturb this one. He had been thinking again of Paris. While it was true, as Tawney's graven words had set forth so many years ago, that no one could predict what a man might carry away from these affairs, those who knew Tawney best, and who saw him upon his return, had at least a fair data bank of visible indicators to form predictive judgments on what he would be bringing back from his latest lark. A brighter twinkle in his eye. A few more pounds too. The latter though he would quickly shed through a bit more of his beloved sailing, plus a routine of modest will power he did not save for work. Nor would he carry back from Paris anything unwanted either. If not discriminating as to where he placed his precious pecker, he was assiduous in precautions. There was more to that genial look that he now passed from one face to the other of his principal deputies than either of them would ever know.

"Nothing more? Then, I guess, that indeed is it." Frowning, Tawney himself thought of one thing more. "David, there *is* a further influx of nut letters from the citizens along Wolf Lake. Pick them up from Daisy." He expressed now, with a sigh, that extra measure of distaste that all in government understandably share for one additional nuisance: "'*Congressional Interest*', I fear too that some are stamped."

David spoke, "They are not all from nuts, Tawney. A few are downright bothersome."

"Yes, yes," Tawney said impatiently. No heart, I'm sure, is immune to all those pleas. Which is why I try not to read too many. I truly regret the burden—

obviously a growing one—that answering them places on you. Beyond the letters, I have directed you, David my boy, as you recall, to come up with the long-term solution. Right now we're merely responding to symptoms. When we solve the problem, happily the letters will cease." He added then what David, who fancied himself something of a collector of understatements, deemed a dazzling contender for the Ages. "I realize that I haven't handed you an especially easy task."

"Oh?" David gazed at Tawney with a new awareness; chewing on a bit of further unexpected discovery about this man he had known so long that he did not think that there could still be surprises. "I could propose that we place acoustic baffles around the entire lakeshore. We might be able to install them for under a billion dollars." He appraised Tawney's stony expression before compounding mischievousness. "Of course, that would screw up the loons' nesting. More practically, we could reduce DIANA's peak power." It was Julius' turn to be sternly rebuking. "That we cannot do."

Tawney was even blunter. "David. Stop talking nonsense."

David Morgan hung his head in mock shame. "Henceforth, I shall be good." They had not, of course, jumped on him because he had transgressed against anything sacred in their shared sense of scientific discipline. Rather, and deserving of greater severity, David Morgan had gone off trampling in realms of the non-negotiable. As if he did not know as well as they that, out of a profound skepticism, the Office of the Secretary of Defense had decreed these ongoing protracted full power tests for DIANA. Otherwise, only too eagerly would the Navy and its minions in the Laboratories have done anything to evade requirements that had the mightiest generators at the Wolf Lake Test Station groaning away night and day under loads beyond their design. For months blue smoke had been curling ominously from the giant electrical busses of solid silver, thick around as a young tree, through which DIANA's awesome electrical power was split to the hundred-fold transducer elements pulsing away in the depths of the lake below the moored test barges.

Everyone—even the janitors Tawney Gray mused—knew that. Which was why he was still muttering to himself after David and Julius had departed. "The eyes of the . . ." Quite so. He did not say the rest of it. Tawney, generally a rare practitioner of restraint in language along these salty halls, finished the thought inwardly. *The whole fucking world is watching, my frivolous friend.*

▲ ▲ ▲ ▲ ▲

The selection process to flag rank—Admiral (and, off and on, Commodore) for those who do not grasp the subtleties of the variant terms that designate hierarchical success in the Navy—had become ever more rigidly structured here in the Seventies. Always a formal thing, as any matter so important rightly should be, these days the Selection Boards came forth with ever fewer surprises. Yet how could it be otherwise when there were no worthwhile wars for a man to distinguish himself? Because of World War II—and only *in* World War II—the system *did* undergo upheaval, got its one good shakeup. In 1942, that year of *sertiatim* disasters when the professional Navy of peacetime days was forced to fight the Japanese Navy on even terms, it was touch and go. The clutter of cookie pushers had themselves to be pushed out of the way first, cautious men who cherished the protocol of the quarterdeck and had too long feasted on polished brass and teakwood holystoned to bone white cleanness. It was not that those good but inadequate men, barnacled with their wrongness, were not brave or well intentioned. But the vital spark had been snuffed out in the peacetime Navy that had molded them. Beyond any swift mending, they had to go.

Getting them out of the way did not come easily, was paid for with wasted blood. One Admiral was relieved without ceremony upon the return of his task force from a protean missed opportunity to destroy the Japanese transport fleet waiting at Rabaul to invade Java. The man had not learned that there were more vital concerns than violating the sacred peacetime rule of not allowing destroyers to drop below twenty-five percent of fuel. The scholarly Ghormley had to go, making room for Halsey, after the Savo Island disaster. But all this took time. In the case of submarines, sending them off on patrol and waiting sixty days and then giving them another sixty day patrol, seeing them once again return empty-handed from an ocean full of targets, only then accepting the truth that your skipper was not the tiger you needed but a pussy cat.

The coming need for the right men had at least been recognized by some before Pearl Harbor. There was Ernie King. There was Dick Edwards. There were others. Give the Old Navy credit. Dimly it sensed the future, possessed enough knowing seniors willing to keep aboard some fighters. Men, whose drinking habits were not the best, did not excel in shoeshines. Brawlers destined never to go far in a peacetime Navy, marked for early retirement. Such men even the hidebound Navy of the Thirties nevertheless found ways of saving. Thus, in time, the Mush Mortons and the Creed Burlingames and Freddy Warders, the Butch O'Hare's and the Wade McCluskys, the men who won at Midway, were there to get the job done. "But crap, what have we now?" The utterer of the question, as indeed all the foregoing freewheeling historical perspectives, was Captain Gary Leads.

"But I think too . . . ." The Captain's current listener, hesitantly agreeing, though not sure what to think, was David Morgan. The Captain, on the brink of retirement, had taken to dropping by the office of his subordinate. That David was a Navy junior like himself intensified in the Captain feelings of kinship, stirring him to praise the pre-World War II breed of naval officer. He contrasted their virtues with those of their present successors in blue. The latter bureaucratic hustlers, politicians and poor ones at that. If there was inconsistency between his disparagement of the old Navy, its fussy ways—and such inconsistency was not difficult even for a frequently inattentive David Morgan to detect—Captain Leads eventually explained it. The difference summed up in the ennobling word:

"*Idealism.* Those old timers had their faults. But they were believers."

"I guess they were," David responded cautiously, "I can't really say."

"The heck you can't!" Leads exploded with blunt good-humor. "Weren't we both a couple of ankle biters in those days before the war?" The Captain though was not demanding remembrance. He was focusing now on the young flag officers of today. A subject rendered still sorer by the just published list of the new selectees to Admiral. He kept coming back to the list with its brief individual biographies of each of the new selectees. Rapping offending facts with bony knuckles. "So what's the latest crop?" His question bounced off grubby filing cabinets, faded walls. "The usual collection of executive assistants, prefigured number of nuclear submariners, a handful of attack carrier skippers, the inevitable Chiefs of Staff of the Sixth and Seventh Fleets. And one, and only one—by God, just to pretend that they care about rewarding skills in system acquisition—Program Manager. Finally, the token black guy. Yep. This Roosevelt Jones is bound to be the one. No matter how good he is, he'll carry with him all his days the albatross that he got it only through his color."

"I hope not," David said. Because all too likely it was so.

"Everything is quotas now. The booty of promotion parceled out by the numbers. Look at the top of the list, the most senior guy. Last chance, bound to be a big surprise. Corks popping and the bubbly flowing amongst family and friends. No doubt had his retirement plans all solid. Now everything's upheaval, his wife in a tizzy...."

"I guess." David then ventured what seemed the sensible observation. "But if it's really all that much trauma, can't he just turn the promotion down?" Captain Lead's expression was one of honest amazement. "My boy, you are an innocent still. This guy is obviously one of those who'd slit his throat on the spot if he could be sure of having "Admiral" chiseled on his tombstone. He is his *own* kind of quota. Stands for Hard Work, Plugging Away. Sticking it out to the last day of his thirty years. His is the reward for being one of those lights on in the Pentagon long after everyone else has departed."

"I hadn't pictured that."

"Welcome." Captain Leads then let the unfortunate object of his mockery go with a heavy flourish. Perhaps though, in the swings of his cudgel, he had accidentally given himself a swipe. Not for some time had he been anyone's light in government buildings on nights when sensible men of sound relationships, priorities straight, were heading home to their families. A moment of reflective silence though was enough for him to return to analysis of the anomalies of the selection process. "One measure of effectiveness prevails to tug a man from Ensign right up to Captain. Judged on how well he drives one of just three vehicles, submarine, surface ship, or airplane, and on precious little else beside. Unfortunately, the mesh is not fine and almost every kind of fish imaginable slips through. Truth is, driving a ship or flying a plane isn't difficult. In mechanistic and intellectual terms, frankly it's a snap. Thus, by keeping the paint unscratched on their charger's metal, great numbers of middling talents ooze their way up to senior rank while having done little other than safely transiting from one spot on the globe to another." He galloped on without encouragement, or read David's clearing of his throat for the same. "Yet what other criteria, the system asks plaintively, can there be? We haven't had a worthwhile war for decades and won none of those. For our Navy, Vietnam was a lieutenant's war, all riverine craft, or light attack aviation. The POW's at least had a chance to show guts, but we destroyer types were doing nothing but bombarding outhouses in rice paddies. So the Selection board's process of differentiation comes down to *minutiae*. If your Dad was a well known Admiral, that can be a big help. Selection Boards sometimes get lost in a time warp. Some colorful trait, any gimmick, that separates you from the crowd is also handy. Then find some special horse, no matter whether the Navy needs it or not, and ride it furiously. Each year we select some thirty new admirals—guys who have driven their various ships or planes passably well—and then pitchfork them, ignorant as a Victorian bride on her wedding night, into bewildering new arenas where they thrash about with responsibility for weapons systems costing billions. The results can be read in some *Washington Post* horror story every week. We've created a hybrid naval officer, half-baked technically—Post Grad School can never make him more—and less of a sailor too. Yes?"

"I'm afraid that may be so." David's attention was drifting when the Captain rapped again at the Navy Times and its list of selectees that was so annoying him.

"Sneedon Snowdon. Tsk . . . Head and shoulders type, as they like to say."

"I've never heard of him."

"You will. Count on it. Fits the pattern. Three tours at least as Aide or Executive Assistant. Washington and staff duty up the kazoo."

"Well," David observed, reluctantly inclining towards the opened copy of the Navy Times to pretend interest in the career summary of one more stranger on a list that had nothing to do with him, "at least he's coming from a sea command."

"A bare nine months of it. Half of those in the shipyard. They sent him to the Pacific just long enough for his ticket to be punched and get his feet wet in salt water."

If he did not know what to say, David Morgan most times knew to say nothing.

"So. Where does that leave us?" asketh the Captain, glancing again towards the Navy Times and banking the roll of his eyes upward towards the ceiling in another fascinatingly unbroken motion. The little office was oppressively warm with the government's prodigal outpouring of heat. Down the corridor, the only sound in the world, a secretary's footsteps were moving on an errand of no hurry. David was thinking of work that he ought to be doing and scarcely anything about the Captain's soliloquizing. Yet it was necessary to nudge the latter aside with some sort of response if he was to get to the former.

"*'Unfortunately, the nation that wants to have good warriors',*" he said as best he remembered it, "*must remain constantly at war.'*"

"Napoleon. Yes," the Captain's jaws clicked shut with disappointment, possibly at preemption of the famed quotation. "You know, Morgan, you're an interesting fellow. Easy to underrate. People see first only a quiet professional, even a rather mousy sort...."

Why, damn you.

"Say, I hope I haven't offended."

"I'll be thinking about it." Yet a touch of embarrassment lingered in him over an uncharacteristic bluntness. He did not want to meet the Captain's eyes with their own still lively lights of apology and thus found himself, for want of something more appropriate, noticing Aliason's framed picture. Copies of the *Journal of Underwater Acoustics* had piled up to block sight of the lower portion of her, cutting off her legs at mid thigh. With a recurrent twinge of disloyalty over the photo's casual relegation, he made a belated vow to clear his desk soon and to promote it again. Promote it though to what? The vow, however—indeed the question—was for the future. His had been a practical glance, lacking especial fervency; he was one of those men, supposed to make up the majority, who try to keep their professional and personal lives separate. Compartmentalized, being the dreadful word of the times.

"Your wife?" The Captain, apparently still guilty over wasting his subordinate's time, even as he was prolonging it, seemed to find in the passing attention that David had bestowed on the photograph a means of making amends. "Most attractive. Believe I may have met her at one of Development's picnics. As I recall, we talked books."

"That would be my Aliason." The silence following was one in which the Captain appeared to recognize the topic's absence of a future. "Well . . . good luck, Morgan."

"And good luck to you, Captain." Which stopped the Captain at the door. "Occurs to me. The flag detailer will be hunting for a slot for our newly selected Sneedon Snowdon. Don't be surprised if that hard charger doesn't end up over here. Stranger things have happened. They're upgrading Development to two stars, so, they say."

"I thought you said that he had no Antisubmarine Warfare experience. In fact"—David reached over to confirm certain earlier noted items of Captain Sneedon's career, but the Navy Times had by now slid away unhandily amongst other papers—"I don't recall that he's been associated with Research and Development either." David's restrained note of indignation revived in the Captain another display of owlishness. To it he added an exuberantly toothy smile. "Tut, tut. Our boy, they say, writes a good letter."

▲▲▲▲▲

The old but determinedly erect man was striding again through the twilight of this city that was his truest home. From out of sight, beyond old brick walls, came the scent of early flowers, the ancient pushy magic of Spring. The brass knocker that would have been any battleship's pride gleamed just ahead. His fingers sought it eagerly. The door flung open.

"Muddy." She gave him a hug, not overly long. "Flowers again!"

Muddy stood blinking while Tessa hung up his coat and scarf. He had rehearsed several opening remarks, meaning to be clever but as usual in Tessa's presence he forgot them. "I like your perfume, Tessa. What is its name?"

"Darned if I remember, Muddy," she called cheerily from the kitchen while making their drinks, "a bottle lasts me an age these days."

"Cheers, Tess." She could see though that her friend was a bit down. Nor was it hard to guess the cause. "The Corridor? It's not moving?" She shook her head at herself. *Corridors* did not move. "The usual runaround," Muddy said.

"Oh, dear." She listened to his familiar lament about interchangeable young men at desks guarding outer offices. "Just who *are* these people?", Tessa wanted to know.

"They have many titles, my dear, executive assistants, aides and so forth . . ." His puzzled expression deepened. "Some also are called '*Action Men.*' Not in the least apparent why. Tell me, Tess. Did we all used to have to be smiling all the time?"

"I do believe we were a pretty happy bunch, Muddy. But *tsk*. I know it's frustrating."

"Oh, my dear." He turned sad eyes upon her. But Tessa knew how to lift his spirits. Keep his drink fresh and bend talk around to good times of long ago. "Remember Peking? How each day we were all planning to traipse out to see the Great Wall, and we never once left the hotel. One long party. Sinful, I suppose, that grand chance passed up. What was our Navy doing out there in China anyway, Muddy? I'm afraid I've forgotten."

"Oh, my dear, you remember the *Panay*. Our river patrols were important," Muddy said what he had wanted to for a long time. "I always thought that you were important out there, too, Tess. You were . . . a belle."

"Muddy. What a sweet thing to say. But 'belle' always makes me think of southern girls and that I was not. I only wanted to make a welcoming home for friends dropping by. All of Irish's ships, I think I can claim, had good spirits."

"With your help. The young officers were wild about you."

"I only remember how fine they looked those polo afternoons at Wak-Wak. You never saw whites so glowing as in the Orient. Uniforms starched by beautiful brown hands and pressed, you felt, with love. We found out eventually that those brown hands didn't love us that much, after all, did they? Anyway, so many grand young men, and so many of them lost." Muddy made faint murmurs of regret at an unwanted turning. That was a long time ago, and anyway the price of war. Laughter was the fare he sought. No life is complete without an enemy and Muddy had only to bring up one of Tessa's favorites. A light came on in Muddy's solemn eyes as he lowered his voice to a husky whisper. "You realize, Tess, Alice Navarro once confided to me that no woman's husband was safe with you."

"She said that?" Tessa, who had never disappointed, did not now. "Well, goddammit, Muddy, *her's* was." Muddy roared. That serious man gasped and slid to the floor. Slumping against the couch, helpless against spasms. He recovered, wiping his eyes. "Tell me, Tessa, just what happened between you two?"

"Truly, I can't quite remember. Something silly there in Panama at the Strangers Club." She frowned. "That could hardly have been all of it though. Alice was always full of prunes. Or maybe I'd gotten the idea that she had her eye on Irish."

"I saw Alice some time ago, "Muddy said. "Over on Charles Street. Not the best neighborhood. Pug, I fear, didn't leave her well off, and she didn't appear in the best of health." "I am sorry to hear that." Tessa's old clock was ticking away. "Muddy, you *can* help David?"

"Indeed I have been thinking much about it, Tessa." Reconciled that he would be surrendering to Tessa on this one, he had about settled on the idea of a slot at the Center for Naval Studies. It was not—STUD as it had long been called—the worst of such outfits, not compared to other misbegotten clottings of these study types, and except that they called it *analysis* these days instead of *thinking*, not a bad show. An old friend now running the place should remember a favor or two. At once the idea seemed such a fine one that Muddy, with pardonable unwariness, chose to reveal it. Bringing a reaction that blew him back against the wall, "*No, no, no,* Muddy. Bless you, that's not it at all. That's only more Civil Service, more slogging to nowhere. You see?"

"Oh yes," murmured the bewildered old man, who did not see at all.

Until moments ago, this instant actually, Tessa in the swirl of emotion had no firm notion of what she wanted for her David. Suddenly, like a sail catching a puff of wind, she felt her eager little boat with its cargo of ambition tugging in a sure direction. "The *White House! That's* the place for David. One of those strategic advisers I keep reading about. He ought to be somewhere"—a phrase, a random bit of gold, gathered she no longer knew where, spun its way into the excited lights of her imagination—*"close to the throne."*

My word, Muddy said to himself, *my word*. Tessa was hopping about, positively nimble. "A light like David's shouldn't be hidden under a bushel basket." Poor Muddy. Some time ago having come to the belief that wherever he looked he saw a world blighted by too sparing an application of bushel baskets. "You *can* do something for him, Muddy?" She had maneuvered her face close to his own. He was conscious of winy but pleasing breath. "I dare say I might be able to do something." Tessa seized that reed of ambiguity like a handle of oak. "You *will?* No more than a word from you to the President should do the trick."

Muddy managed to invest his promise with the rumble of authority. "Tessa, my dear, my very next time at the White House I shall bring it up." Not having the foggiest idea how or what he was going to do. No matter. The world forgives a lover small and uncrafted deceits. Preparing to depart, Muddy found prudent a self-protective caution. "You understand, Tess, these things take time." "Muddy, I *do*. The main thing is, let's get the ball rolling!" She thrust upon his lowered cheek a gratifyingly ardent farewell.

He touched his chin, the part kissed. "I thought I might drop down again soon. Call first of course. Not surprise you." She laughed tenderly. "Muddy, *surprise* me."

She found herself deciphering, after Muddy had departed, the nautical chimes of Irish's old clock and punched out a familiar phone number, the notes dancing their own little tune. "Boat, darling. Why are you still up?"

"It's not late, grandmother," Boat, a self-assured seven. "I'm watching a war." The whine of dive-bombers, muffled explosions deep within a wounded aircraft carrier's belly carried to Tessa's ears the simulated sounds of the Battle of Midway.

"When are you coming to see me again?"

"Soon, I sure hope." Fondness for his grandmother was at odds with impatience to get back to these flickerings of destruction. "Daddy's asleep. I'll get Mom. Bye, grandma." Before Tessa could give her account of Muddy's visit, Aliason was pouring out her own story. Characteristically, even their good news in collision. Bullets of information were zinging Tessa's way, jacketed in the confusing vocabulary of the times. "It arrived today," Aliason said, retelling it more slowly, "the latest edition of Who's Who Amongst Electrical Engineers of America."

"Did you have to buy the book to get listed? Isn't it that kind?" "Tessa, it's an *honor* nonetheless. It lists David as one of the top hundred signal processors in America."

"Well that's wonderful. Especially if it speeds up David's promotion."

"That's coming, don't you worry." I worry, Tessa said to herself. About everything. "Are you still spending all that money on Beth's horse?" "Well, King can't very well go out and buy his own feed." A sleepy voice came on the line. "Okay you two, cut it out."

"David, dear. How long have you been on there?"

A yawn delayed his answer. "Long enough. What's up?"

"Well, my darlings . . ." At last Tessa was able to get her news out. But somehow, like the just boated dolphin dying on a boat's deck, the play of its lovely colors was fast fading.

"Mother, I'm an underwater acoustician. I can't make heads or tails of what you're cooking up." "What I make of it is opportunity."

"Oh, I agree with you there, Tessa." Thus spaketh Aliason. Easy to picture visions of White House dinners dancing through her head.

"Jesus." He waited for Tessa's gasp to vent its air. "Nothing . . . ."

"That was certainly *not* nothing, David. But getting back to the point. I hate to see your career bogged down when you clearly have so much . . . ."

"Beautiful talent," Aliason chimed in. One kind of intrusion Tessa could bear.

"Nor do I underestimate your writings. But I sincerely believe that the White House is where they will most appreciate you and your stuff."

"By the way, Mother, I'm not bogged. I'm happy."

"Oh, he's *not* Tessa. He loathes Civil Service. He's *frustrated* where he is. You should hear him sound off at what he sees happening at the office. You just don't know your boy." To that last Tessa said nothing. Taking seconds more before pronouncing: "Well, my dear, happy or no, you two would know best. But bogged, my son, you surely are." From the silence which followed the vehemence of that assertion Tessa decided that, by picking away with other questions—as opposed to frontal assault—that she might best dislodge her son from one of his moods. "So what is your new Admiral Snowdon like? I'll bet I knew his father, Old 'Flakey' Snowdon himself. You ought to march right into his office and introduce yourself. Make clear to him who you are."

"That's one thing I'll not be doing. It's a different world, mother."

"And one you are welcome to, my dear. One more thought though, and then you can get back to your beauty rest. Your father swore that the Navy forgives you almost anything except anonymity." Her son's reminder that he was not in the Navy slowed Tessa not a whit. "Know what else your father said?" It would take someone less fired up with the flame of holy message than Tessa to sense the steeling of her son's nerves in his reply. *"'Hitch your wagon to a star'."*

"Exactly!" David forebore. Bringing kindness, and almost calm, to his mother's, next, "Darlings, my funny bunnies, forgive my lecturings and I shall say a prayer to St. Jude that David makes it to a twelve."

"Actually it's the other way around, Tessa," Aliason inserted timid correction, "he wants to move from thirteen and *become* a *fourteen*, and he will. You move *up* in the numbers, you see." "Well, I leave it to you two to keep those Civil Service things straight. Next time I call, David, I hope that you won't be so grumpy." "I make no promises."

Still not sleepy, Tessa turned on television but its images did not divert. Strange Aliason and touchy David. Yet she felt warmth for her daughter-in-law with her loyalty, as scatter-brained as it was fierce, that you didn't find growing on every tree. Still . . . picturing her David up there in his bedroom alone, and with a rare surmise. Surely that fine old-fashioned cure for the grumps had not been subtracted from the powers of marriage.

▲▲▲▲▲

Donnie Lee Webster, a man of numerous and wayward pursuits, now lately a staffer in the White House, knew the Sixth Precinct Captain in Milwaukee, the Dogcatcher in Sacramento, political friends of the moment, ten thousand faces. Yet lights in his mind shone only a short distance and the objects they illumined were selective ones. Here and there his beam might shine further, but only by narrowing itself, recalling some former ally's waverings in loyalty, vengefully spearing the inflictors of political wounds, keeping bright debts to be repaid in kind. Otherwise, he was like a train in the night rushing down a dark track, with little more visible to the engineer than the road bed reeling in. But Donnie had noticed early on that Sara Jane Whipley was different. Here in the galleys of the Ship of State, full of the shouts of *two-to-go* and *once over lightly*, where all decision was served up rare, beyond the clichés of the political trade, Donnie sensed in Sara Jane . . . other things. The past was not all dark with her. And, no doubt about it, she was handy to have around. Proving it again in the matter of the White House Passes, one of those myriad trivial problems that kept ending up—most unfairly in Donnie's view—on his desk. Too many people possessing these passes, too many strangers able to sail in through the White House gates and thence freely wander these hallowed corridors. One day an alarmingly odd little man actually tugged at the President's sleeve, prelude to asking for a job. Furiously the edict went out: Ruthlessly prune the list of holders. Thus, in yet another role, Donnie the pruner.

A harder job than it first appeared. Many of the holders were from previous administrations, grand names from a misty past. And Donnie was shrewd enough to know the risks. Yank someone from the list whom you shouldn't, and you had a self-inflicted political wound. For these were not ordinary passes. In this City the little red, white and blue plastic doodads with one's picture were *cachet*, fortune to a fellow. Some men in Washington had nothing else of value, either of spirit or coin.

From Donnie's list names leapt out, the favored powerful of the moment, the mighty loyal of yesteryear, claimants not to be denied. Kings of Union and Farm, Southern California liberals whose easy wealth made their consciences ache. Twits, but hearts and wallets in the right place. There were other names he did not recognize; phantom figures, he could only sense, like the dried leaves of autumn, still swirling their way through the White House gates on the dying winds of a once potent past. Between urgent summons to matters of higher priority, Donnie advanced, frowning, down the names. With Sara Jane there to help when she could. "You're getting down to the end," she said encouragingly. "About time." Out the window the shadows of great trees trembled across the White House lawn. Reluctantly he got back to his list. "Paul Watanabe," he read off. "Milk Producers of America."

"That's not hard," Sara Jane said firmly. "You don't touch him."

"Jesus, no. Not until the cows come home. Small joke, Sara baby. Next Admiral Malcolm Hilary Waters III." He pronounced each syllable with mocking emphasis. "Finally an easy one." His pen made a slicing gesture across his throat.

"Not so fast. What's an Admiral worth to you these days?"

He giggled. "Not a heck of a lot." But his pen remained suspended while he tried to read Sara Jane's expression. Then she murmured words she had been trying to recall. "'White Wake Waters.' His nickname. In the war." Donnie's frown deepened into his question, "The Big One?" Her look was one of those noncommittal ones that made him nervous. "That's right Donnie, World War Two. Let's check your file." She pulled the next pasteboard folder from a by now diminished pile and flipped through its disorderly contents, shaking her head. "Scheiss. Who *keeps* your files anyway?"

"Okay, no lectures. They oughta be better, *et cetera*, I agree. But this is sensitive stuff. Not for some blabby secretary's eyes who's gonna quit and write a tell-all book."

"I see he's on the Board of Shipbuilders of America. Correct me, laddie," she teased, "but I don't believe you're doing so dandy in the shipbuilding states."

His laugh was bitter. "Sara Jane, my girl, right now this Administration isn't doing so bleeping red hot anywhere." But something had quieted in Donnie. Shipbuilding had done it. With it was released a whole mudslide of fears, uncovering in the back of his mind the title of a stalled naval program on the Hill and pained recollection of what he was supposed to be doing about it. Get it unstalled, that was all. Sea Otter? Something like that. Sara Jane drew out of the folder a sheet of scribbled notes, turning it this way and that to facilitate decipherment. "What's this, 'Sucking around for a corridor'?"

"Haven't the foggiest." His regathering cloud of gloom brought back with it testiness. Sure as God made little green apples, the Boss was going to be bugging him about Sea Otter. She recognized the inimitable scrawl as well as the elegance of style. "*Your* handwriting, Donnie. Obviously you talked with him."

"Lay off, Sara. I talk to a piss-pot full of yo-yo's every day." Her finger paused alongside her nose as she sifted possibilities. "Might that be a Pentagon corridor?"

"How in the hell do you give someone a corridor?"

"*Confer.* An honor. Like the Eisenhower Corridor. Or the Arleigh Burke."

"Never even been in the Pentagon. Just seen it from outside. On the protest marches. May first, seventy-one. He added, on a rising note of pride, "A great day, Sara."

"I'm sure," she said. "Anyway, lengths of its hallways are dedicated to famous generals. In this case, maybe another Admiral. Commemorates the man with flags, old pictures, war paintings and so on."

"Kind of a spot where he can hang his medals and all that crap?"

"You got it." Watching pleasure color Donnie's round and open face, Sara Jane had the passing thought that there was actually something attractive there.

Something easy to miss that lately she had been missing. "I remember him," Donnie said. White-haired guy with a spiffy cane. Talks so slow you want to jump out the window. Polite though. Not like a lot of jerks wanting something. It's kinda sad though. All he's got on his mind. It's on the project list I tell him, humping along and all that." "It *is?*"

Donnie rolled his eyes. "You kidding?" The phone rang and she noticed how his hand ceased its trembling, reassurance in the feel of the glossy plastic. While he barked his answers, she let her mind play. Amongst an unexciting White House crew, she suspected that he would fill the bill. It was far from deathless love, not even an episode of high passion that Sara Jane was hankering for. Simply a weekend with someone pleasant, reasonably likeable, emphatically *clean*, and Donnie's fussiness in his clothes, the evidence of his nail clippers in frequent if tasteless public use, the aroma of his cologne, all struck her as favorable clues. Yes, he would do for a start. Not only a start, the *whole* of it. Aware of the finiteness of emotion she could spare for a fling, Sara Jane had to guarantee that it could not be anything more. It would not be guessed, but Sara Jane's spirits had not begun with, nor been entirely consumed by the Feminist struggle for women's rights. This woman now so ardently dedicated towards her socially afflicted sisters, who could wield every line in Robert's Rules of Order like a sword, had once been another kind of girl; trustingly inclining her fair brow and soap-scented dark hair to young men's words as if they deserved to be cut in stone. A girl to linger with and to share, over checked tablecloths and candles stuck in waxy bottles, grave undergraduate conversation on the Meaning of Life. And when talking was done, not infrequently eager to crown the dawning day with that winy impulse that may be no answer to Life's mystery but at least is one of its shining pieces. Panties stuffed into her purse for the tidy Sara Jane too.

If no longer that hot and sometimes heedless girl, it was not that she had fundamentally changed. She was merely busier and older. She could not both control, and ride, those storms she had once invited to roar within her. Once she had loved a towering intellectual, a man with a mind capacious as Fermi's and a record of adventure that stood in honored volumes on the most selective of bookshelves. A man who was to Donnie as a lion to a chipmunk. And there were men still, no doubt, capable of changing her life, upsetting its rhythms, dissolving discipline, even—irresistibly as for one of those starry-eyed innocents in a Russian novel, facing the blazing power of a Dostoevskian hero bursting through the doorway of her life, winds at his back and a light blazing behind him not of this world—drawing her off to follow him to perilous ends of the earth. Fortunately for Sara Jane's peace, such men were rare. Unimaginably Donnie. Who at this moment had, with a jab of a button, moved on to another call. While Donnie continued to plead, now whining—apparently his caller was a Congressman Duke who was being difficult—review of her plans for Donnie had become mixed with recollections of a livelier past. She shut her eyes, opened them wide again, startled at a monetarily lustful reverie. *No.* Emphatically she sought no mighty transports of feeling. Merely someone of surpassing ordinariness. Untaxing and bite-size. Donnie to a T.

She gave a private nod, a sense of rightness reconfirmed. For sex—impure and yet wholesome, to apply to it the accurate and encompassing word to what she had in mind—in order to enjoy even a passable bustle of life in the pairing of any members of the White House staff, needed rare circumstances, a putting out of feelers for only the hardiest growth. Mutual excesses of vitality that could be spared were scant. Consuming well-known energies of the spirit, it had to subsist on scraps. It had to thrive in furious if empty winds, strange chills, Saharan heat, mysterious fogs, soarings and dippings of favor, the glare of artificial light, the darkness of cruel neglect, figurative nibblings of unknown little animals, the competition of vanities, interruptions at the worst of times.... For her purposes, then, Sara Jane craved no *sequoia sempervirens,* no growth of grandeur; better a stunted bristle-cone pine, clinging to a crevice, able to suck water from rock. Best, a resilient weed. Donnie. Who was now signing off this latest call with a great deal less than his former air of command. "Yes *sir.* My apologies. Yes I did say Sea Otter when I meant Sea *Eagle.* You realize though, Congressman, I do have a full plate... again, sorry. *My* problem, not yours. But getting back then to the matter, all I ask, all the *Administration* asks, is that these cuts not be rash... oops, forgive me for 'rash' too... yes sir, be *talking.* A nice day to you too." Her intended—sort of—banged down the phone. "Son of a bitch!" "Having a little problem?" she asked mildly.

"Nothing with Ab Duke is little. Appropriations. Sits on a pot of gold though. *Shit.*" Yet Donnie's mood was improved, a vital element restored to his spirits. For minutes he had been plugged into the electricity of power. For a little while at least something was patched up, time bought. His round, not quite sybaritic, face beamed. Yet it annoyed Sara Jane, this latest evidence of the disproportionate sustenance that a colleague could extract from a mere phone connection. Sharply she glanced again at Donnie's folder. Sara who could find an extra arrow in her quiver whenever some balloon could use a puncture. "Your notes also say that on his last visit your Admiral was asking about a spot on the Staff for someone named... let's see... Jesus, Donnie, your *writing....* Didn't you take penmanship? David Morgan, is that it?"

"Haven't the least. This guy Waters asked *that?*" "Who we're talking about, Donnie."

"Okay, lay off." But the request was amiable. "Well who *is* David Morgan?" she persisted. "Nobody. Less than nobody. Never met him. Never will."

"Evidently, again from your notes, the Admiral was pushing him as a Defense expert. Suggesting that he be put to use 'rethinking'—your word—our military posture."

Donnie made a face. "All we need. Like a hole in the head." Sara Jane felt heat rising. "Wait a min. We damn well should be rethinking it. That bunch over there—she jerked her thumb vaguely westward towards the Pentagon—"never will, and besides . . . ."

"*Say-rah*," Donnie wagged his finger, grinning. The caution was memorial but Sara Jane threw up her hands in symbolic reaffirmation of a previous and more publicized surrender. Recalled were the first weeks of the Administration and the heady days when new faces flooded the town and tired governmental clichés were showing their astonishing powers of recuperation. Days of shining tinsel hope and none so bright as those for Women, whose banners Sara Jane bore. No sea anchors of doubt held back Sara Jane's merry barque. There was nothing women couldn't do as well as men and she was going to take Washington apart stone by stone to uncover every possible job. "What about the military?" one reporter had pressed her. A prime target, quoth she. For that whole dreary five-sided pile of stone that was the Pentagon, she added with eager pugnacity, she had no awe. Did this, the reporter went on—deadpan but delighted, sniffing news that he was helping to create—"include the Joint Chiefs of Staff?"

Now, as it happened, antipathy to all things military had deflected Sara Jane from her usual homework. A handful of minutes would have put her in better mind to grasp the distinction between, say, Chief Petty Officers and the Joint Chiefs of Staff. In this instance, zeal overrode details. "I'd fire the whole bungling lot of them." *WHITE HOUSE WOMEN'S ADVOCATE WOULD REPLACE ENTIRE JOINT CHIEFS OF STAFF WITH OWN SEX,*" read the *Washington Post* headline. It was the first brouhaha of the new administration, making Sara Jane Whipley for a few days the best known woman in America. The Left, of course, cheered, but from the ever powerful Right there was gloomy confirmation of its worst fears towards this already demonstrably wayward crew up from the cotton patches to try its hand at governing. One prestigious flag officer sought an audience with the President and the latter (though no causal relation was established) soon thereafter made a speech, which the Soviet Union denounced as "saber rattling", reaffirming U.S. commitments and the power of U.S. arms. Emphatically, *men* at arms. Editorially, it was solemnly affirmed, from Seattle to Miami, that the President had stubbed his toe. That hard cookie, Sara Jane, *stubbee.*

What the President truly felt no one knew. The meeting to which he summoned Sara Jane was just the two of them, and Sara Jane had popped back out of the Oval Office smiling. The papers described her as chastened but unsubdued. Fiercely intelligent, she saw that no objectives need be relinquished, merely tactics modified. Grudgingly conceding now the necessity of at least some training before her sisters were pushed to the fore of driving ships, the drilling of marching men, the business of guns and explosives which—however distasteful and a folly—*was* an activity that required special education to supplement the good sense which (a prime article of her faith) the human female had to a superior degree. Meanwhile she was already able to contemplate with satisfaction the numbers of women entering the Service Academies and their infiltration through varied arms of war. The seeds of social uplift that she was helping to plant would in time be flourishing. Yet she saw clearly too that the process could be hurried only so much, even as human kind plodded on, evolving at a pace that knew no speeding. *Time.* That was the secret, the small dull secret that she was coming to understand. She glanced out Donnie's fine window towards Lafayette Park and took in those great trees, lifetimes older than herself. There stood the very one still under which Dan Sickel had shot his wife's lover. She pictured that outrageous being and his outsized passions, the legs that hustled him to Gettysburg, the one he lost there too still preserved in the lead casket at the Army Medical Museum. Dan Sickel, the ultimate male chauvinist, and all his questing, dust. In passing melancholy it was as if she were in the wilderness and listening to the sound, faint but clear, of a rushing river. Touching her with personal recognition; the knowledge too that the world simply kept rushing on, that nothing ever was truly solved, least of all the ever changing but always ruinous attitudes of men towards women. The cycles of history, the Greeks, the Crusaders, Chinese . . . had she not studied them all? One put things together in one place only to see them go flying off in pieces elsewhere. Not a sigh this time but a stamp of her foot. The practical side of her nature dominating the philosophic. One lived in the present, yes, as the poets told it, and time was indeed a thief; yet if a betrayer of dreams, it could also serve a small but happy scheme. And Sara Jane, face it, you haven't done such a swell job managing your own time lately. Donnie was still frowning over his list. "Sara Jane, I guess you're telling me this guy Waters hangs on to his pass." "My recommendation, Donnie."

He looked searchingly for any sign of sarcasm. "Sara, baby, almost through the W's. Leaves, let's see . . . yeah, X's, Y's and Z's. Could finish up in an hour or so, with you giving me a hand." He added: "I figure too there won't be a heck of a lot of X's."

Good figuring, Donnie. Which she did not say. "It'll be late when we finish," he said, "but when this list is wrapped up we might relax over a bite. Nothing fancy, just be like ordinary citizens. Stroll up Pennsylvania, grab a pizza at one of the GW student hangouts."

"Sounds nice, Donnie." Nearing the end of their by now common task, Sara Jane took a stretch. Donnie's head was still bent in concentration, absorbed in the merits of one Mario Zantorini, raised from Brooklyn skull-cracker to thousand dollar suits and controlling statesman of waterfront unions from Perth Amboy to Red Hook. She found herself studying Donnie's carefully tousled brown hair on which, she suspected, stylists had lavished more care than her own. Maverick strands of silver ran through the still youthful riot of those dense curls. The observation came with poignancy, a clue to the lost exuberance of a campus *machismo* that would never know what hit it. She had the fancy that she could look right through that hair and skull, like a glimpse into bright but flawed crystal, with here and there indecipherable flecks, which she took to be thoughts in embryo. In the peculiar intimacy of its revelation she felt obligation, responsibility conferred. Donnie's shoulders jerked into motion and with his familiar mixture of brisk decision, and yet rightfully haunted uncertainty, he was explaining his reasoning on brother Zantorini. It was like this. So, even *if* the guy's money did come from extortion and murder, etc., etc, on the other hand the guy *had* donated some of his wealth to the more compassionate party. "Bottom line, we keep the guinea on the list."

"Absolutely." Beautiful, Donnie. Poor bunny. Her plans became more explicit. She was recalling an isolated hideaway cottage with a fireplace, enormous stacks of wood, while still gazing down affectionately at that pleasant unknowing head wrestling with the last of his Z's. Sweet bunny. Guessing that she still knew how to make a man happy.

2

Massive, monotonous, the lumpish buildings of National Center were stolid squatters between the blackish spread of Alexandria's railroad tracks and the traffic jolting along the battered roadbed of U.S. 1. It is quitting hour and *en masse* cars are revving up, creeping in lines out of hidden garages, darting into open slots in the traffic. Drivers grasp their wheels tightly, gritting teeth as they maneuver for advantage. Detached critics of Civil Service, scorning its sluggishness, would modify their opinions, or at least rearrange their prejudices, after a few minutes watching on a nearby corner. For like an observer at the edge of Murchison Falls, that thunder of white water feeding the Nile, one here too witnesses explosions of energy, potential into kinetic, that leave no doubt as to the unapplied power resident in thousands of government office cubicles. In this flurry of departure is daily-reenacted unsuspected fierceness, motivation undreamt.

Yet not everyone rushes homeward. There are the oddballs. Along deserted corridors, in quieted offices scattered about hastily abandoned buildings, some people linger. On the east side of NC-3, David Morgan looked out the window towards the airport and the river beyond. The Potomac's brown flow was strong, bearing whole trees torn from distant mountains. He guessed this must be like the Congo in flood, with its storied floating islands sweeping towards the rapids above Matadi. He lifted a heavy compendium of oceanographic data from his routing basket. Not the first man, nor the thousandth, to contend with stray regrets at the beautiful forests felled to make the paper that crossed his desk. He initialed the document and was shoving it towards its certain destiny of leaden obscurity when he was arrested by a photograph relieving pages of monotonous statistics. A cone of light illuminated the ocean floor of the abyssal plain twenty thousand feet beneath the surface of the North Pacific. The brightness, undoubtedly the first in that blackness for a billion years, had startled some sinuous bottom creature which could be glimpsed disappearing down a hole trailing a smoky swirl of silt. Which dreaming glimpse of time unimaginably past was interrupted by the sudden onset of a sharp smell. It needs mentioning that the resident olfactory ambience of his office was a blend of perfume and chewing gum, each of these the copious daily legacy of one Viola Fletch, clerk typist. Yet in his nostrils right now was something else—acrid and unmistakable—conquering the customarily gentler scents. Yet this too was, in its way, an indirect assault by the recently departed Viola upon the air. He reached the burning coffee maker just as Helen, EAR's office supervisor, was pulling the plug on a smoking ruin. The coffee switch, Viola's sole securing responsibility, had been thrown to HIGH instead of OFF.

"*Yuck.*" Glum but unsurprised witnesses to a by now repetitively familiar disaster, they contemplated the last fraction of an inch of viscous residue in the silent pot bubbling away like thick volcanic mud. The burner was cooling from vivid orange to ashy grey, but the glass pot, a goner in any event, was too fragile with its soak of heat to risk moving. Vapors of smoking insulation and poisonously melted plastic joined the bitter richness of murdered coffee. "Helen, can't there be a formal check off list for her?"

"I've tried that." Her hands moved despairingly. He expected that she was going to revive some old Viola story, perhaps her favorite about the time that their girl had managed to entangle her chewing gum in the new IBM electric typewriter. But it was late in the day to muster humor. Nor seemingly was there anything possible new to say about Viola. Except for the hope implicit in Helen's question, "So, how *is* the Cause coming?"

The Cause, his campaign for Viola's dismissal from the Civil Service, a process initiated over two years ago. The relevant papers, a thickening file of forms and justifying addenda, were best pictured in allegorical terms, glimpsed from time to time struggling up the dim slopes of official mountains, only to come tumbling back down again, replete with annotations of newly discovered errors and accompanied as well by bruising rockslides of official reproof for further multiple insufficiencies in procedure by the originator: David Morgan, Immediate Supervisor. The latest problem presumably rectified, the ascent of those papers must once more renew from scratch their tedious upward journey. Each time with renewed hopefulness that this next try would make it to the top. "I think I'm almost there. But I honestly don't know for certain." In a protracted campaign, a man could not follow the tortured course of such matters day by day. The signals that such paperwork sent back in its dim meanderings through unseen worlds were few. "Keep our fingers crossed."

"Oh, yes." Over time, Helen's instinctive loyalty had blazed into palpable admiration. Only someone long within Civil Service could appreciate how rare, bordering on the eccentric, were such tenacious attempts, rarer still prospects of success. Helen whose competence was a stunning counterpoint to Viola's. Her typing comforting to him as the sound of machine guns to an infantry commander recognizing his own. She had started checking over her end of day notes. "Mr. Perrozzi called to get on your calendar. Selling next year's programs, I suppose."

"Ah yes." That time again.

"It won't surprise you that he mentioned Plowshare." "It doesn't surprise." Already another budget year beginning its cycle and claimants reemerging from the same old burrows. With the same things always seeming to be coming around again. "Good night, Helen." The building had grown quiet in a way that only late workers knew, stray sounds magnified. Pipes and invisible structured rods popped and rustled in readjustment to night. A cheap building, every corner cut, its contractors eventually going to prison over its construction, but not before gifting themselves mansions overlooking the Potomac. Only a surpassingly tolerant organization would have accepted such a horror. The Federal Government had embraced it with joy. A toilet flushing some floors away reverberated like a minor explosion. He jumped as the phone rang. "Hi, darling. How's it going?"

"Working away." He readjusted the phone from the awkwardness of his initial grab, hand trembling. Like millions of men, more than the paucity of their tales might indicate, David Morgan had actually married his first love and never gotten over his winning. Recently Dr. Gray had expressed regret that David, once so near his doctorate, had not wrapped up his thesis formalities and been able to put Ph.D. after his name. A damned useful brownie point still, my boy, quoth the good doctor. Tawney Gray though had never walked beside the slenderness of a girl named Aliason O'Neill, seen the autumn wind flattening her dress against the gracefulness of her thighs.

"Any news?" Her question thrust right off, without preliminary. *The* question.

"Not yet." Counseling patience. "Darling. We *need* that promotion."

"Tell me about it." "Oh, my dear. Still, it may all be academic. Tessa's been talking to Admiral Waters again, pushing for that spot in the White House." To this and more David was ever the careful, if skeptical, listener. "Interesting."

"Interesting? The way you put things. Forgive me, but I'm floating in spite of the day's start. Sorry about that one, darling. But that's your girl, right? No matter, I'm bursting into Spring. The Wolf Lake seminar is still on for summer, isn't it? You and I? I've been thinking too that maybe it's getting on time to crack the piggy-bank." The river was no longer so prominent in the scene, blending in with grey twilight and he was indulging himself in a bit of irrelevant wondering about some of the lights coming on, gleaming as if from a distant jungled shore. "Are you still there?" she said.

He answered slowly. "Still here. No, I don't think it's time." Because there was no piggy bank, its modest treasure long since dribbled away. One day when the timing was right, he would break that news. If ever the time would be right.

"I defer to you, my lord and master. But . . ." Other questions to be ducked, thinking how her voice always struck him romantically, like a stream with fine whispers. This evening he kept straining to hear something else too, rills with meaning to which he was acutely tuned. Waiting hopefully with more than an acoustician's ear. "What I was thinking . . ." he began uncertainly. Because, naggingly, he hadn't yet caught that subtle ordering of notes into chimes of pure promise, ardent as a poet's blue sky above the Piazza San Marco.

"You were thinking . . . ?" She said it tenderly.

Awkwardly, he let unfold what it was he had been thinking. Something exceedingly simple, thoughts that were variously, dependent upon one's point of view, romantic, conjugal, or carnal. In truth, all gloriously and brutishly mixed up. Whatever, the lamp that lights the world. Whatever too, the wish that David Morgan now sent along thin copper miles of telephone wire, he did in somewhat more shyly convoluted form than an eavesdropper, should one happen to be listening in, would deem oddly incongruent with the kind of talk that a decade and a half of marriage seemingly ought fairly to call for.

"*Super* idea, darling." Pop of a kiss. "Except I have a meeting. Afterwards? Oh, sweetheart, you're such an early bird and I'm . . . I'm what? Don't tell me." She laughed. "Did I mention the yarn?" She described it again, a special green, luminescent as shallow seas. "It's for your glasses' case. Yes, I'm back to needlepoint." For a moment there was silence, and then she was telling of things she had to do, ironing, supper to get ready, the kids started on their homework . . . . Her words came faster, a jumble of hope and concern. Concern especially for Beth in her schoolwork, an old story. Except, now failing History as well. "You *will* talk to her? And sweet, don't give up on me. How long has it been, you poor dear? Fortunately, you are not one of those husbands who counts." *Who says?*

"If you want something to keep you awake, my checkbook's a mess . . . ."

Yes. Another given. He worked until it was black out, synopsizing the latest reports of DIANA's unsatisfactory tests, making further notes on the dilemma of the beleaguered residents along Wolf Lake. At last his pencil dropped, the fire of the day gone out. He placed his classified material in his safe. The steel drawers shut clangorously and he spun the dial with the habit of years. He felt his way down the darkish corridor, the government thrifty at least with lights. The building quiet as a tomb. He could not make out the name signs he passed but he knew each office by heart: Rizzo, the dour statistician, cynical Hickelson, James of piezoelectric materials, the gentle black man, an early token hire presiding over events as slow moving as the crystals that grew in the vats he funded in Toledo, Ohio; Winston, newly come and hurriedly assigned responsibility for Anomalies in Long Range Propagation. And Romulus, the younger black engineer now James's assistant, too recently aboard to have a sign of his own but already, with his *dashiki* and street talk, making his mark. David Morgan felt the presence of departed friends and fellow workers. A few had died but most had retired, lives shrunken to the dimensions of narrow condominiums in places like Myrtle Beach and Pinehurst. He stayed in touch with them, conscientiously declining invitations to golf at golden courses he could only dream of playing. He recalled with warmth those who had been kind to the young maverick David Morgan in their midst, cautiously amused at his small stands on principle, even then so pathetically rare in government. Yet most of them had at one time felt hotter suns, tasted the salt of distant seas. A distant bond of more vigorous days. There were many good reasons for David Morgan to be dismayed at the ways of this place that paid him, yet only a man who finds much in his work still to love would feel this way.

He rode down in the rustling elevator normally thronged by day. He passed the security guard, solitary and glum in idling watch over glass doors no knowledgeable enemy would find it worthwhile to storm. Outside, a breeze was whipping through the canyons of dark looming buildings. An artificial city, like downtown Dallas, where he sometimes visited, deserted and weirdly barren. Elsewhere human beings must go for shelter, to eat, to love.

Driving the Parkway, traffic thin, he watched the red lights of cars ahead rise and curve and reappear prettily on the twisting hills. He turned on the radio whose static yielded fragments of news. A Congressman from a shipbuilding state was demanding the nation get on with the *Sea Eagle* program. Elections were far off, but the vats of politics were simmering. How great would it not be to borrow even a small bit of the power of that nonsense for uses closer to his heart? He yawned. He would not make it to his study tonight; he had nothing left over for his submarine haunted vision of the seas. Not going to get to Aliason's checkbook either. He remembered then her request and, in the nook of the Golden Needle—less a business than someone's fond hobby⁻catering to the practical dreams of countless good women in the abundance of the warmly tended homes of Northern Virginia, he savored bins of yarn from floor to ceiling, walling a cave of sensuously glowing colors. Amidst such troves of riches a man might know his love in peace.

▲▲▲▲▲

David stopped by at Daisy Ketcham's desk to pick up the latest complaint letters from Wolf Lake. "Also, by the way, Tawney promised my Annual Review right after Paris."

"Our pal promised, did he? Crossed his heart and hoped to die, right?" The springs of Daisy's merriment had been pushed deep but she laughed with the delight of old. "What's another rescheduling?" Her look though was suddenly penetrant. It said, we are something rare in this town. Friends. "I'll do my best." Which was a lot, Daisy's best. Hers was one of those stories which were it to be chronicled would tell much of Washington, more of the times in which she had lived. Her real story could have been one of those romantic digressions in the *chansons de geste,* but her unfair fate was to be painted only in the colors of gossip. Missing was *perspective.* Because those who knew her best, who could have told all the good things and true, never spoke up. Scuttled for cover they did, every one. These days though, mercifully, Daisy was something else, what she had chosen to be: Diminished by time, all but forgotten. Ten years ago that did not seem possible. That she could be forgotten.

She was serving at that time as Senior Secretary to the Deputy Chief of Naval Operations for Air Warfare. She was a woman of surpassing handsomeness;

arguably she was beautiful, though to some her forcefulness chilled. Her talents and energy had already served half a dozen successive incumbents in that office. She had picked up the complex vocabulary of Air Warfare, knew the Chief Operating Officers of a dozen mighty aerospace manufacturers by their first names. Her graceful hands, supple as a hula dancer's, were skilled in graphics as well. And as everyone in Washington learns, sooner or later practically everything comes down to some frantic episode preparing a passel of viewgraphs for some critical briefing due bright and early next morning. In stale post-midnight air she would still be pouring coffee, making fresh, emptying ashtrays, radiating feminine freshness for the weary. At times, seniors would share nervous laughter over what would happen if she ever chose to spill the beans. But then they would reflect reassuringly on her flawless record of discretion. Not our Daisy. For not ambition nor vanity, nothing of frailer motivations, only shining pride and patriotism drove her. Loyalty to her Navy was as constant as the blood that pulsed through those superlative veins. Directors of Air Warfare came and went and Daisy remained, guiding them tactfully in the intricacies of the budget and doing battle with the Congress. Solid men they were, knowing much about the operations of high performance aircraft but seldom wise in the ways of Washington. She was able to teach unobtrusively, curb their jet pilot-bred warrior tendencies towards impetuosity, helping them in countless ways. And, finally, in that one extra way nowhere set forth in her Job Description. Simplest and kindest way of all.

Very well, Cluck. Join the throng. And yet . . . after all have done their wickedly amusing best, let a quiet post-script be added. It was not as it sounds. One had only to have had the good fortune to have seen Daisy Ketcham in her hey-day, glowing with the grace of an Olympic gymnast, caught just one quick smile of that terrific and honest woman, to see the shallowness of any facile assessment. It had all come about naturally, unstoppable as flowers in spring. All of a piece. After all, there she was twelve hours a day, sharing in the tribulations and the triumphs, working side by side with these Directors of Naval Air Warfare in the immensely challenging business of shepherding fighter and attack aircraft along in their lengthy, politically perilous and often snake-bit, journey from designers conceptual sketches to prototypal creations, and finally to whole production squadrons of tail hooks clanking down on some aircraft carrier's greasy flight deck on the far frontiers of U.S. power. It was thrilling to be a part of it. Over time, one felt its majesty too.

Very well. She slept with them, whatever one chooses that silliest of euphemisms to mean. Pale phrase for the sweet and calming marvels bestowed. But still . . . just how many had it been, people wanted to know afterwards. Certain wives, of course, most of all. But also that wider world of the curious, Americans loving their numbers, collectors of stats. So? Did she actually have that kind of relationship with *all* of the Directors of Naval Air Warfare? *Each and every frigging one, for God's sakes?* The more knowledgeable could start working away on their fingers and deduce that Daisy's tenure spanned five full tours for the successive three-star admirals who had occupied that prestigious post. Five and a half, counting Admiral Peter Peller. Six men in all then, tried and true, who had presided over that big desk while Daisy was sitting outside at her smaller one, a smile for every visitor, hopping up from her restless sea of paper to fetch a welcoming cup of coffee dozens of times a day. Well.... In fact, there was no final count. And afterwards, from the only one knowing for sure, red-hot tongs could not have torn forth a word. Yet if anyone had taken the trouble to make intelligent construct of events, the audit trail was clear. For years Navy leaders had tolerated what was going on. With quiet knowing humor, Daisy had come to be referred to as Miss Naval Air Warfare. If a few wise, or more prim, seniors could see eventual painful consequences, their demurrers were overwhelmed by a steady murmur of acceptance. Men responsible for getting things done seldom tamper with successful arrangements. The gallant creations of those times, flaunting their dashing names, were a roll-call of great naval aircraft thundering across the skies. *Vigilante, Crusader, The Phantom!* Try to match those these days—if you can. In Daisy's bedroom, high in a Rosslyn tower close to the Pentagon, hung a grand artistic rendering of the F-14, the fabled *Tomcat*, gift of a grateful Grumman Aerospace. It preserved a professional aura, eased consciences. Was this not, after all, merely the office extended? Good for the nation? *Good for all.*

Not that Daisy gets off free. But if her faults were large, they were inseparable from her virtues. She made the mistake of worshiping her job and, with the same fervor, idealizing her bosses. Between warm sheets, under stars by lonely runways, by moonlight gleaming off the wings of parked aircraft, more than ever then she felt herself a participant in mighty events in the embrace of these muscular middle-aged men, athletes all in their youth, who had proved their nerve in combat missions, walked away from a thousand carrier landings. She believed her men too, taking what they told her at face value. But since when is trustingness a grave sin? Besides, were not those wives the responsibility of the men? Wasn't that a problem quite removed from herself? As it turned out, actually no.

The furor started, as emphatically it ended, with Molly Peller. Up to her time Molly's predecessors had either been ignorant of the situation at their husband's office or quietly endured it. Molly Peller was a different cup of tea. A whole cauldron of teapot, in fact. The moment that she absorbed the rumors of Daisy, she stormed down to the Pentagon. And, after storming Pete's office, charged next into that of the Chief of Naval Operations, following up with the Secretary of the Navy himself. Sending those worthy gentlemen, problems enough, scampering up their grand draperies. Yet it was ironic, because of all of her bosses Daisy cared least for Pete Peller. But irony was the last thing that

Molly Peller was in a mood to appreciate. She was on a Holy Cause, fighting not only for herself but as she was soon pouring it out to a *Washington Post* reporter, for the sake of "also, who could say how many other marriages?" *The Jezebel must go!*

The Secretary and the CNO, as with most men at their level, possessing natures warning them in all sticky matters to proceed cautiously, wished to ponder the matter, avoid precipitate action. "All factors have to be taken into account . . . etc." Amongst the factors were the rights of an esteemed performer, medals up the kazoo for the fair Daisy from the Civil Service to prove it. In regard to which, if Daisy were to gain the aroused backing of the Government Employee's Union, those senior gentlemen were not merely judicially concerned about doing the correct thing. They were scared shitless. For if Molly Peller was already acting the terror, with her raging tears, far worse threats loomed. The U.S. Navy, for all its steel is a startlingly fragile structure; it reacts badly, shriveling like a snail at the touch of salt to adverse publicity. First thing then, *calm* Molly Peller. Sit down please, Molly, if you will. Coffee? Enter now the Guamanian steward in white jacket, a soothing presence, link with tradition. Sugar? No? Cream? No? So be it. Black then. Very well. Let's begin Molly, by lowering our voices. Only then can we start to arrive at reasonable accommodation. Something to be said, gang, for letting the old dust settle first, eh? The difficulty was that Molly Peller was not looking for accommodation, feared not roiling dust. A few more minutes of this and her response was even more succinct. *Out*! Screaming it. *Now*!

Important men scurried about the rest of that day, shoved the Soviets aside. They hunted up a new position for Daisy, labeled it "lateral transfer," gilded it with promotion. They gave her a Ceremony of Appreciation and a testimonial scroll with as many signatures of the Mighty as could be rounded up by senior aides trotting up and down the E-ring. No clotting of sycophants in grave rally at the Kennedy Compound after Chappaquiddick, straining for the right words to save Teddy's tail, labored harder to obfuscate so eloquently. The Best to Our Girl, they repeated to one another late that night over their blackish coffee (Daisy not around to make fresh) amidst stale smoke and unemptied ashtrays. Even more to the point, put most pungently by one of her ambivalent saviors, we make damned sure any peeing Our Girl does afterwards is still inside the tent and not outside all over the flowers. They gave her a large Merit Bonus check, compressing into hours paperwork which government's normal pace would have taken six months to achieve. Not that they had to do any of this to buy her loyal silence. Showing how little they still knew Daisy Ketcham.

And, oh yes, gave her one thing more. Half a day to vacate, a bare four hours to pack away memories of twelve years. Years in which she had known a remarkable variety of experience, been in touch daily with men of power and helping to Get The Big Job Done. She who had known special travel orders to the Paris Air Show, rendezvoused for dawn flights in jet fighters, sneaked into covert hops by romantically stirred aviators who could not resist a dare. Memories, these many a man had to put away too of a girl in an oversized flight suit by windy desert fields, or by narrow runways cut through the silver birch forests of Bodo, Norway, dark hair blowing.... She had known passion, love too; one of her former bosses she had truly loved and he had loved her, loved her still as he drove his distant fleet, for one week of recent crisis gaining the cover of *Time*—so it could be said that she had known it all. Except, one thing shy: Marriage. Never its humdrum peace, the world's conventional approval, security unto age. Anyway, so she kept on, Daisy, tossing things in boxes, the bric-a-brac along with the photographs of the famous signed in flourishes. Thence to arrive at EAR, not trailing clouds of glory, but scarlet threads. For the reporter to whom Molly Peller continued to spill her guts obligingly spread them over the Style pages of the *Post*. Story of Larger Meaning. But that, as it turned out, was pretty much that. Excitement lasted for a few days in EAR, and curiosity's initial white heat swiftly cooled. Washington, City of swift forgetting and outsize forgiveness. Speculation about the infamous new secretary did not outlast EAR's pleased discovery of her competence and good humor.

To David, himself then not long at EAR, the surprising thing was how energetically she took up her new duties. Giving no sign of having come down in the world. Like some admirably adaptable general, once commanding brigades but now reduced to platoon leader, she assumed her new responsibilities with the zest of the old. Patriotism, pride—whatever, still a mystery—propelled her in the funny little world of EAR no less than in the grand one she had left. To a younger Dr. Tawney Gray then, acoustician and comer, she gave too no less than what she had conferred upon the exciting warriors who used to zoom through her life. Doing her damnedest too to make Dr. Gray's measurement programs prosper in oceans that she would never sail. Some years back though, Daisy broke off the affair with Tawney. One kind of service coming to an end. Clear only that Daisy was the one who ended it. She may have grown bored, or seen through him finally, last thing ordinarily she seemed able to do with a man. Perhaps too, still attuned to the continual periodic changes in the Directorship of Air Warfare, subconsciously she had been expecting the system to generate a replacement for Tawney. A rhythm set, presumably there ought to be Tawney Gray's *seriatim* too. But faces change slowly in Research; a Director may wear out many a leather elbow patch before hanging it up. She and EAR were stuck with one another, platonically, at least, for aye. Yet Daisy's cutting Tawney off had been evidence, in David's gradually focusing view of the event, of something profound. She had figured out at last what had hit her. The corners of her mouth had more lines, criss-crossing ones that once came only from smiling. She had grown wry. But when something genuinely amused her—in this instance, aware that David was still utterly committed to getting Viola fired—she was transformed by the radiant mirth of old that had won more hearts than she never knew. "Good luck, my boy." Nerve she knew. Her hand touched him, as it had men more important, with affection and strength.

He felt, not with conceit, merely the beneficiary of chance, that he might be the last recipient of her magic. He judged her—even with her present looks, drying mouth too much turned down, an aging princess in severe Chanel suits—something terrific still. A woman of another age, at most a transitional figure in this one. There were new mores and laws to protect women such as she, of high heart and innocent faith, but she had come along too late though for those officially mandated fairer shakes. What her life was like outside the office, what loyal friends she had, what joy, if any, David had no idea. It was enough to be aware of Daisy's history. Her life's journey, the adventures she had known along the way, the presumed fascinating confidences she had once shared on misty and vanished upslopes amongst the clouds, he allowed himself to picture like the view the eagle has as it soars cant-winged against the ice face of a mighty mountain. A sight like the gift of rare knowledge. It had to be a plus, special value brought to this shared business of creating the Navy's replies to the agitated folk out at Wolf Lake. He and Daisy had come up with a series of preordained responses tailored to the specific category of complaint and the deduced background and seeming sophistication of the complainer. Standard stuff, such simple "profiling", but Daisy gave it enrichment. Her word processor, the newest thing in the mass production of government paper, conferred the flexibility to handle the growing volume of mail. "Too bad," she mused, hefting the latest bundle of complaint letters, "time out of your technical work."

"Your time too."

She shrugged. "What I'm here for." She gazed down pensively at the top envelope. The handwriting was childish and it was weirdly addressed and yet it had found its way by circuitous route to the very place it ought to be. Letters born of painful sincerity, the awkward product of people who seldom in their lifetimes picked up a pen. "Sad, isn't it? I came from a small town myself, probably not so different." Her memorial mood now vanished under a rain of questions from the unseen Tawney calling from within his office. Final travel arrangements for Paris not yet firm. His questions came interspersed with advice. ". . . *Then*, if you can't get me a room at the Lotti—and it must be on the courtyard, away from street noises—try say . . . the Vendome . . . ." His voice turned plaintive. "Daisy, are you *getting* all this?" "Every blessed word, Doctor." "Very well." He recovered his magisterial tone. "The Vendome is a smaller place but it's come up, I hear. It's located right by the Place Vendome and—."

Daisy called back softly. "Tawney, I know the Vendome." Lightest of razor flicks. Whether Tawney even felt it was doubtful. His flesh was firm, bursting with blood and health, and his nerve endings were tucked away safe within that soft barrel of confidence. Besides, he had had all the care he needed of the kind that gives a man the highest heart, had women uncounted since. An understandable forgetting.

*   *   *

David Morgan picked up again the letter from Mrs. Samuel Nordvedt of Wolf Lake, written on plain white paper with a pen that spread an erratically thick blue line.

> *Dear Sirs of Government,*
> *I am writing about these funny sounds coming up from the lake. Only they're not funny. They keep my husband, who has the emphysema, from sleeping good. Of course, its cigarettes that done that the doctor says, so I'm not blaming anyone there. I'm not a complainer and didn't sign that petition. People tell me it's important to our Navy and if that's so I reckon you got to keep banging away. We got our country's interests at heart too. My husband done his part in Viet-Nam, fortunately coming back unscathed. There's other things. Our little boy is four now, but not trained. It's them sounds coming up the pipe into you know what. He just won't go. At least not where he should! People say, why don't you move, but that's not easy for folks in our means. Well, I'm running on.*
> *I'd sure appreciate it tho if someone back in Washington would write my family personally that it's real necessary. Willing to do our part.*
>
> *Sincerely yours,*
>
> *Amelia Nordvedt,*
Box 32—High Pine Road,
Wolf Lake Country

He had written a reply out in longhand as he did occasionally, and it would go out in the mail that way. His own stamp he would put on it too because it looked less governmental than a metered envelope. Having a few minutes more, he reread what he had written.

"Dear Ms. Nordvedt . . . ." He altered a few words. His aim for each of these letters was to put himself sympathetically into the mind of the troubled person, otherwise unknown, who would be its recipient. Okay, done. No, not quite. Ms.? Change *that*. They hadn't yet heard of Ms. out that way. He was not proud of his reply, but neither was it dishonest. In spite of his instincts, an organization man's normal conflict in loyalties forbade saying a number of other things he would have liked. He took a deep breath. That's enough fellow. Just get on with it.

▲▲▲▲▲

The phone was ringing. Ringing on and on. Viola Fletch, clerk-typist extraordinaire, must have been down the hall at the Ladies Room, a favored spot. It rang a number of times more before it struck him to pick up and it was Billy Jencks.

"Davey! I can hardly hear you." "This better?", David asked.

"Yeah, but you still sound kinda quiet." "Merely thoughtful."

"Too much so, I'll bet. About DIANA no doubt, and SEA EAGLE, and lies and . . . ."

Billy went on in this vein for several minutes more. Talk of the kind David Morgan shared with no one else. Embarrassing but not displeasing. A hero to Billy, if no one else. "Come on, Billy. Anyway, got to run to a meeting." "More cheerleading for DIANA? Skip the meeting. Come on down and relax. Everybody's heard enough of you anyway."

Relax, yes. He liked the sound of that, deciding that it was indeed a meeting that he could pass up after all. He got himself a cup of coffee, letting it bound this small vista of free time that he had just made for himself. Not so much thinking, as letting ghosts steal in.

In the beginning, as they say—that beginning that came soon after the world was merely darkness and void—was the sea. It begat its primitive creatures and eventually, out of its great warm prehistoric puddle, up onto the land wriggled that life which became man. Then came man's return to the sea, tentatively at first, for the perils were great, but with ever-bolder heart. The sea was a broad highway for roaming, it unbound man from the tyranny of land, the hard travel of waterless sands, impassable mountains, the rut of valleys where for a lifetime entire villages might never see anything more of the world than the top of the next hill. Ships tugged threads of meaning across the unmarked expanses of the seas; ships drew the first maps. Ships for trade and soon after, hot in their wake, ships for war. Ships for a man to love and loving them pouring into their creation his strength and ingenuity, shaping them with his feel of beauty, the promise of romance. All that men felt for the sea, its strangeness and peril, he built into his ships. From the gilded triremes to the dragon-prowed Viking long boats, to the flying clipper ships with their lusty female figureheads, to a modern destroyer's sleek lines, they joined grace and purpose and the best of the things that man liked to believe about himself. An old deep thing, this love of ships.

On the walls of his office were copies of ship paintings. They were part of David Morgan's heritage; reflecting an unfulfilled yearning which his disastrous eyes had denied him. Disappointment had faded, but nevertheless he was conscious of bearing within himself ungerminated seeds of the family's pride and glad that he could stay in touch with ships, keep fresh his fond regard for naval history. Late in the day, when there was no sound from the deserted building but little clinks and pops of stressful readjustment to the departure of the sun's warmth, he would look up towards storied warships and colorfully portrayed naval battles of old. *Constitution vs. Java, Bon Homme Richard vs. Serapis,* and think how it might have been to talk over ships with his father. He wondered though about this fancy. For warships had changed so much. No longer bristling with guns and most of their payload consisting of electronics, computers, all massed into complex systems, which would have been a revelation to his father. Even as their paucity of guns been a stranger mystery still.

Serving these modern naval ships, were the sensor products of EAR, designed to exploit underwater sound for the detection of submarines. Inevitably then, scattered amongst antique sea prints were also the latest classes of antisubmarine frigates. EAR's "babies," those who worked here liked to feel. The most prominent amongst his gallery, of dimensions disproportionate for his small office, had been presented him by a Gulf Coast shipbuilding company. An artist's conception of *Sea Eagle*, the work was of heroic size by the standards of most such efforts, the original surely hanging in the corporate boardroom, or on the paneled wall of some highly placed individual who could influence the contracts for SEA EAGLE'S construction. That there was even a copy of this picture in the undistinguished office of one toiling so far down in the grass as David Morgan told something of how far afield shrewd marketers would choose to roam in dispensing their goodies. Some obscure and hitherto ignored voice might suddenly become a critical one. You could never tell . . . . Cover all the bases.

But . . . back to the artwork and its subject. Five hundred feet *Sea Eagle* was going to be, so it stated in the inset box which listed other vital statistics and prominent weapons systems, including the marvelous new sonar DIANA. There was also the prideful boast (not entirely accurate) that it would be the largest warship ever built solely for ASW. That last being an ambivalent claim too, size not always a virtue, though publicists of SEA EAGLE flourished best unburdened either by history or fact. Curbs on such poetically inspired inscriptions were few. The view of the ship was from ahead, a sleek grey form racing across a glassy blue sea, bow wave peeling away in classic fashion. Torpedoes were spitting from her, caught hot and smoking in mid-air by the artist. Yet the colors were soft and dream-like. The sky held vague puffs of clouds and visible through them was a great sea bird, of fierce beak and glossy talons, which had seized the sinister darkish hull of a submarine of obligingly crumpled metal. Nor was Lady DIANA neglected. Within heraldic borders, glowing in filmy gown, she stood regally poised with quiver of arrows and mighty bow. Harmless art of its kind, David paid it no more attention than other minor gifts of advocacy from contractors that did not rise to levels of defined impropriety. Lately though he could not help glancing up at the picture with increased interest, a man increasingly dismayed by the prematurity of optimism over the intertwined destinies of DIANA and her prospective consort SEA EAGLE. An odd mating, an odder pair. Seduction of this sort can be a mysterious process, going a long way back, certainly beyond David Morgan's knowing, and where it began, and how mere flirting drifts into dalliance, and in turn becomes corruption—all of the usual and seldom ennobled features of defense acquisition—are usually beyond recall. The faces keep changing. These are matters too more of maneuver than intellect. There is little of true passion to burn and scar; it is more fumbling than fondling. Squads of the most zealous investigators, sensitive as bloodhounds, could never pick up but a fraction of the trails. Memory is writ on air, history swiftly turns ancient. Soon it makes no difference how it all began, whether the beady-eyed raptor is bringing the Goddess of the hunt low, or the other way around. But like many an illicit affair, this one too could be coming to a sad pass.

Ah, well, thinking too much again. Now standing by his one window, viewing only a panorama of sooty rail yards under misty rain, buildings long familiar, a hole in the ground out of which more offices were going to rise. Then suddenly, just in time to halt a further slide in his mood, he was thinking again of Billy Jencks. Picturing that funny face, the rat grin, legacy of teeth from sharecropper parents who never knew of such frills as orthodonture. But denial of cosmetic dentistry was its own gift too, making possible looks of devilish merriment rare and wondrous. Indeed, he was overdue in dropping down again to see his friend. Many things seemed to be joining: DIANA's darkly rising prospects, Tawney's ambiguity, Tessa's hectoring him to give Admiral Waters a call, how to speed up the dismissal actions on Viola, Wolf Lake, the Navy and its machinations, and Aliason . . . always Al.

In imagination he was already on his way, descending grubbier levels to the unfashionable southwestern corner of the building. To noisier environs and unpainted concrete walls, to spaces without the enrichment of a view. To Billy's cluttered mini-empire of computers serving the Acoustic Data Management Program—the soddenly christened ADAMP. To the comfortable obscurity of this center of realistic fleet data that everyone was collecting and that no wanted. To hear again Billy's lament—the perennial one of all those who play with computers—that his machines lacked sufficient "memory". Even as did his City itself. But anyway, on to shared laughter and easy talk. To Billy's quick optimism, always some new source of cheer. This month it seemed Billy was getting his dreamed-of larger computer at last. To process even faster numbers no one asked to see. "I'm going down to ADAMP," he told Viola. The motion of her jaws slowed. "Mr. Jencks' office," he said, trying more familiar syllables.

"Oh, right." Ruminatively, yet the act surprisingly not devoid of grace, Viola Fletch drew a portion of her gum out between her teeth in a sagging tendril of strengthless thread. He ought to have kept on going but was trapped; seeing her tongue, swift as a flycatcher's in retrieval. She drew the last of its thread in quick little nibbles, rabbit-like, the way she must have sucked in blades of sweet grass in those high apple meadows of her girlhood. *Four years*, he murmured to himself. That long since Viola had arrived at EAR through the intervention of one of those periodic government programs of social uplift, borne on tides of morality and compassion, though never entirely pure ones, that ever and anon surged through the marble halls of Congress. Mandating that the great creaking and putatively under-employed mechanism of Defense must be put to nobler uses than merely inflicting the destruction of war. Amongst these uses was providing menial clerical jobs to tens of thousands of citizens which the private sector, through less merciful Darwinian processes, had found unqualified. Such well meant tides swelled and receded but their flood-borne baggage, lifted to various floors of governmental Washington remained there stranded, adding to the clogging *detritus* of good intentions. Viola. He found himself further distracted, attention drawn away from the daring acrobatics of her gum to her ankles loosely crossed. To make plausible a few trance-like seconds to Viola, who was regarding him curiously, he affected a still deeper concentration as he leaned over to check on his memorandum to Dr. Gray, which he had given her first thing this morning. "I had to start over," she said. "I messed it up."

"That happens." He held his breath so as not to take in too strong a whiff of her perfume. "So, how's it coming?" he asked cheeringly. On the sheet of smudged bond paper one erasure had resulted in her rubbing the paper through to the grey see-through thinness of damp toilet tissue. Viola's shoulders heaved with the start of familiar sobs.

"Oh not good, I'm afraid," she wailed. "In fact, lousy."

Now, decently, he had to delay departure, let emotion run its course. He stood by uncomfortably, never good at such moments. "There," he offered, "there, it's okay."

How fair skinned she was. Full bodied, hers seemed a rosy fruit's perfect ripeness that could not last but the briefest part of a season. Her lips were full— too full, the aesthete would condemn—her teeth (except for lipstick smears) white as milk. Her eyes large and blue, vivid with bright mineral clarity. A luxuriance of glowing red hair fell in breaking waves. Yet it was all amiss, a squandered bounty of indiscriminate Gods. Her nose with its too flaring nostrils, a brow reflecting millennia of intellectual deprivation, were in unkindly disharmony. She was a vulgarity of abundance, a rich red apple from a distant and unsung Eden. Her perfume, now that he thought about it—at the moment he could not *not* think about it—actually did bear in it the fragrance of apple blossoms. Unfortunately, no subtly haunting evocation of golden Shenandoah uplands. More like stuff that came in jugs from roadside stands, stacked between cider and the watermelons, so heavy that it was miasma; the kind of scent that

Nature herself conjures up only in the stillness of warm moist meadows, making even the bees dizzy. Great Gods! She must bathe in it, store it in kegs. He pictured her stepping out of the tub dripping, skin slippery with aromatic oils, drying herself. And because any male naturally looks further, he pictured other hair, wire stiff, bright as new copper. But that was fantasy. In that forever sunless cleft all colors turned somber. Redheads betrayed their dreamers. Not the fieriness of a new-minted coin then; merely the dark of an old penny. "There." Spoken once again to the inconsolable Viola.

"But you wanted it right away. It's *important*." It was a theme, once found, not to be relinquished, . . . "about finding enemy submarines and all. It's important to"—she concluded now a vigorous, if not coherent, paean to the worth of his judgment with a burst of tear drying, giggling enthusiasm—"to our country!" "Hmm. All right, keep on. However"—the old saying had just popped into mind—*"Don't let perfect become the enemy of good."* Which improbable enmity he left her to ponder as he headed down to Billy Jencks. To soothing changelessness, where Billy's Bicentennial souvenir straw boater, jaunty with its red, white and blue cloth band, bought one recent fine day of rousing patriotic music, sat in disuse, dusty and fading, on top of the same old file cabinet with its clutter of yellowing data sheets. To the most genuine of welcomes, with Billy putting down his book on mathematics, a new one and evidently, from its bold dust jacket, one of those varieties of popularization that were his favorite. A mathematician by avocation, if not by training, and at bottom a bad one. Billy, who skirted the labor of reasoning and went for flashes of insight. His mathematics had a romantic strain too, like that of the Reverend Charles Dodgson, creator of *Alice in Wonderland,* in whom an elegantly honed intellect was joined to ethereal concepts of love, visions of maidens in silver mists. Billy Jencks to a T. A yearner, rather than a chaser. Making his knowledge of women mostly theoretical, giving him innocently exaggerated notions of the delights of living with them. Imagining boons of propinquity that make for a continual feast rather than, as many a married man could enlighten him—David Morgan nearest at hand—more likely to be quirkily episodic. "Hey, I'm into fuzzy sets now," Billy said, tapping his new book.

"Referring, I presume, to categories of objects defined by the quality of fuzziness. Peaches, for example. And short-haired animals." David stroked his chin. "Though most animals are glossy rather than fuzzy. But possibly the koala bear . . . ."

"What?" Throughout David's speculations, Billy's initial expression, that look of quivering alertness that might be termed basic Billy, seemed to undergo a form of suffering in which disbelief was the cruelest part. But he was still intently watching David's face (the protective hand having pulled away) whose expression could not be kept deadpan.

"Hey, you *do* know what I'm getting at, don't you?" His grin reflected David's own. "You like rattling my cage, I know Davey. Now let's take beautiful women."

"Fine with me."

"As a *category*. They're a set, at the same time ill defined. Come in many forms and colors. So, as a set, they're fuzzy. But mathematics has gotten around to handling this sort of thing. Fuzzy sets are important too. In the real world, most things fall into them."

"I'll buy that." It was pleasant listening, like a quick little stream over rocks, without trying to catch it all. Billy's interest in David's professional advancement, always keen, was acute today. Emphatically he did not want to hear—in reply to his question how the White House thing (just whatever it was, exactly) was coming—that nothing was happening. "Hey, Davey, *Make* it happen." Abruptly Billy's mood turned memorial. "Remember old Main Navy. The Mall close by, all that grass. Nice stuff to lie on; nothing but concrete and asphalt around here. Sure, old Main Navy was god-awful, WWI temporary, bare pipes and always too hot or too cold, but I liked it there. The technical desks were close together and they still used to talk to one other, didn't they Davey?" That they did. David thought of the obscure plaque, close by the tiny lockkeeper's cottage of stone marking the terminus of the Chesapeake and Potomac Canal at 17th and Constitution, inviting remembrance of the men and women who had worked in those now vanished buildings of War and Navy. Humble as the marker is, probably there was not another like it, requesting from the random passer-by kindly feelings—more, a concession of honor—towards thousands of unknown government workers. In the directness of its call were daring words from an age of faith in government. Nothing else so surely dividing the past from the present.

But Billy's recall could not stay memorial though. He loved the excitement of the present. Though in theory isolated from the daily ebb and flow of events he was more in tune with the news of the matters that touched their lives than David was himself. He picked up—David could never figure quite where or how, but was a sponge nevertheless—stray items of information, bits of gossip, hard little pieces of fact, and wove them into a coherent pattern of surmise on matters which, by all rights, David Morgan ought to be the more richly knowledgeable. A David unable to confirm the most obvious items about the new Admiral's doings that presumably ought to be his bread and butter.

"He's a dynamo, Davey. That's what they say. You can bet too he's not unaware of the maverick David Morgan. And, you know better than I, that he's already picking up on that daffy Plowshare idea of Artie Perrozi's. Going to push it, they say." Which, David had only recently found out himself, was true. But quietly amazed that Billy had heard. "Well, I'll be doing my best," David said, "to head Artie's latest off at the pass."

"Good luck there. But in the luck department, I do gather you've at least gotten through to your next to last hurdle in Viola's termination."

"Ah, my Billy," David said, his admiration more real than mocking, "is there nothing you don't pick up on? But what's this 'next to last' hurdle? Aren't I home free?"

Billy whooped. *"No way José.* You've got a final session coming with the Honorable Anthony J. Cringhlo. Count on it."

"The top dog? Come on Billy. That's absurd." Billy shook his head and then launched into explanation of where "El Cringhlo" was coming from. A former Montgomery County Congressman, defeated for not heeding the needs of his largest constituency, the governmental work force at the Surface Warfare Center at White Oak and, aiming to return to Congress, he was not going to make that mistake again. "Going to prove ever after the best friend that those in Civil Service ever had or could have. How can you not know these things?"

"Just asleep at the switch, I guess."

"Ah, Davey. You really do live in a dream world." Billy wrapping up with notes both fond and wistful. "Truly. EAR is a special place. You don't know what it's like outside your cocoon. You may loathe Civil Service, but the fact is you don't know the worst of it."

Billy rattled on. More news. Or rumors, at least, of the forthcoming Agonizing Reappraisal on DIANA. That Grand Meeting, far off to be sure, not until the Fall, and inevitably to be more of the 'same old Show-Biz', but still an indication that there was a lot of opposition out there. Otherwise, it would not be taking place at all. David smiled. Knowing a few things that Billy did not. Declaring quietly, but happily: "No. We are *not* alone." Thinking of the admirable Admiral Tommy Blue out there in the Pacific and his band of skeptics. Tommy Blue too, however infrequently heard from, a fan of his writings as well.

"No." Billy's face scrunched expressively with rumination, as only Billy's face could, digesting the truth that, of course, they were far from alone in their knowledge of DIANA's terminal hopelessness. But now extracting from that fact less satisfaction than a source of caution. "But things are different now. You've been insulated up to now, Davey. Able to fire off your memos"—Billy's lips curled with the imminence of a phrase, plainly wrestled with but, at last, pleasing—"your little Missiles of Truth."

"So, what are you telling me now, Billy?" He could not help grinning. "Lay off?"

"All I'm saying is, it's not a game anymore." It was odd, but David felt a momentary chill, as of a cloud speeding across the sun. He rid himself of it with teasing.

"Come on, Billy. I'm the only one in the whole darned world who reads your ADAMP summaries. Let alone takes them to heart. I'm the one carrying the water for ADAMP." He did not stress the obvious. If Billy was his fan, he was also Billy's champion.

David did not pursue his advantage, nor did Billy revive his own arguments. That was not the way of these get-togethers. It was right, sufficient and natural, that Billy should return to his underlying state of admiration for his friend

David Morgan, the excellence and unassailability of his central Message, embodied in numberless memoranda, as numerous as they were cogent, that was going to find a much wider and more receptive audience in its concisely presented story at the Wolf Lake Symposium this coming summer. To Billy's runaway enthusiasm David felt it necessary to insist upon a demurrer.

"We'll see, Billy. But I'm afraid it's all but inevitable that my message may get trimmed by the time it has Tawney's final blessing." He added, "Plus, no doubt, now our new Admiral's as well." "Don't put up with that," Billy said, once again all scrapper.

"Sounds good, Billy," David said soberly, "but that's the price I may have to pay to attend. I hate to tell you how much Al's counting on the vacation."

"And *deserved*," Billy said fervently, one of the last of that once large number of those half in love with Aliason Morgan from times before she had mostly slipped away from the eyes of men. A Billy though, if momentarily balked at the seemingly irreconcilable objective of the accuracy of David's forcefully delivered message, and Aliason Morgan's dreams of a getaway from her kids, who was now able to console himself with David's latest status report on his book. *The book*. A work beyond, *far beyond*, the games and deceits and follies of DIANA. Testament for the ages. Which was, no more and no less, than the enduring Ascendancy of the Submarine in Control of the Seas. "Is that what you're really going to call it, Davey?" Billy, seeming to balk over its awkward length.

"No," David reassured him, "that's just a working title. How about '*The Shadow of the Submarine*'?" "Oh *yeah*." Billy's grin said definitely, "*much* better."

It was fun to daydream with Billy. And that was what mostly this was, a dream, so far was he from creating this imagined master work that was going to track the history of man's undersea adventures from their very primitive beginnings, through wars and adventures down to the present day's patent supremacy of the nuclear submarine as the ultimate determinant of just what, and whose, ships were going to thrive on the seas. One David Morgan going to put his arms around the whole shebang, building a world of such overpowering logic and substance that it was going to sweep the field of argument clean.

"Blow them," enthused Billy, "right off the court."

"Ah yes." There it would be, as he saw it, standing up in his imagination, like one of those great rocks of the West along the Oregon Trail, giving heart and direction to the toiling pioneers who carved their names upon its face, inscribing the dates of those who had died along the way, scratchings of faith that could use all the help it could get. Yet even as he contemplated his masterpiece in finished form he drew back from it. Knowing something of dreams and their mischief and how, like flowers, they could wilt in too much light or premature exposure. Sometimes he felt, as he made his notes there at odd moments, working away in those evenings when he could summon the spirit and alertness to do so, that he was like one of those heroic midgets at the foot of the North Face of the

Eiger. So much to be gotten out of the way first. More time to be made for the kids. Wrestles with finances, those eternal. And Al. Always Al.

* * *

Tawney Gray looked up from David's memorandum on DIANA to confront its author. "Your latest, my David?" Tawney looking these days ever more like the wise old owl. White tufts and all. One whose last mouse had not agreed. "I imagine so."

"You imagine. You ought to serialize them. On the other hand, you might make it easier by not creating them at all. They read much the same."

"Not really. Each one is variant bad news from a fresh perspective."

"Somehow I don't catch the freshness part. Nor does the Admiral."

"If all that's wanted is good news, let's make more use of Materiels' cheery Public Affairs Officer upstairs." The day had begun meanly—Al at her early morning worst—his nerve ends on fire. Tawney Gray simply stared as David went on. "Do you remember, Tawney, the old SQS-26 sonar, DIANA's grandfather?"

"Of course," he snapped, "not all that long ago."

"And how, at Admiral Martell's direction, the only copies of the Operational Test and Evaluation Force's negative test report were locked away in the Admiral's personal safe."

"That's the kind of folklore you do hoard, David. But many people would consider that a good move. The Navy, after all, got its sonar."

"Which still won't do shit. Least of all what it was designed for." An odd expression flitted across Tawney's face, the look of the wary administrator when confronted with genuine moral outrage. Something rare, and beyond the usual abstractions of paper and hot air, and Tawney's was the reaction to that kind of harsh music to which Washington unfailingly executes its own special dance; a mincing step forward, a swift one back. He shook his head mournfully, "My dear David, sometimes I fear that you have a death wish."

David found himself executing his own Washington shuffle, one of obliquity. He was tired, although it was early in the day. Enough on his hands right now. "I don't think I've heard that pop psychology phrase in a long time."

Tawney's mouth twitched with unwanted tugs, wearyingly offering his upturned palms. "Only trying to help you, my friend."

▲▲▲▲▲

The view from Admiral Snowdon's corner office, as from Dr. Gray's own, was a grand one, including a fair bit of the Potomac's flow and, beyond, familiar edifices of Washington's power and historic glory. The Admiral had no time though to moon over views. Only a few months in his new job, he was excited rather than awed. That his professional background included nothing of anti-submarine warfare, not a smidgeon, did not faze him. The U.S. Navy had pioneered the notion of the preeminent virtues of the versatile generalist, and junior officers did not mature into senior ones by committing themselves against myth. There was consoling manumission in the notion that above a certain level all challenges were not technical but managerial. Admiral Rickover, the old man still at it, was a holdout to that consensus, deeming it nonsense. But he ruled only part of the Navy.

From where Admiral Snowdon sat, there was much to manage. Lines of power from more than one great program now wound their way into his office. With his first minted stars he had guessed well where to head in his first Flag Job. Far reaching decisions trembled in the air above that polished desk. Circumstances, the good luck of timing, far more than lines on organization charts, had created the whirlpool of EAR's present dynamism. The Russian Bear had given another growl and a U.S. Navy, too long becalmed in some eyes, was stirring. Ship construction was the renewing lifeblood of the Navy and stalled procurements were beginning to move. *Ah.* The Admiral's sigh at this moment was inward, even as his most important view was equally an interior one, and the landscape of opportunity that his imagination roamed was more beguiling than the drab Potomac. Amidst the wayward and treacherous currents of man's power, more mysterious than the forces of nature, better than most men the Admiral glimpsed one of those tides in the affairs of man meant to be taken at the flood. *Ah*. Once again, that *ah*. Since first his tiny hands had clutched the crib slats, even then in his baby blue eyes twin glints of ambition had been inextinguishable. Quick eyes seeing early what many men, otherwise wise, never learn in a lifetime: That Washington is a city not of ideas but of power. And like every new flag that ever was, compellingly motivated by one central thought. How best to gain his next star. Feeling his youth—no Admiral ever looking younger—he could not fully contain the energies seething within that trimly muscled body. Pleased with his reflection in one of the windows, he engaged in a brief flurry of shadow boxing with his energetic phantom self, in the midst of which his Technical Director appeared. Quite unbothered by being caught, perhaps elusively pleased, the Admiral's smile was secure. "Keeping the blood moving. Come in, Doctor. *Entre, entre* . . . ."

Tawney Gray sat down with deliberate ease, took out his pipe. He was the old timer, the corporate memory, an impression he wished to enhance. His own drumbeat would be the slower one, more muffled. Young admirals came and went, they were as grass; he could handle this one too. "This Morgan thing," the Admiral began, "is bubbling up a bit higher. I'm seeing his papers hither and yon. Old articles even being dusted off. Quoted in the latest *Jane's*. He's even had some notice taken of him at the Upper levels of OPNAV. There's nothing that we can do about critics outside of our own organization, except counter them with solid argument, but *inside* . . . ." A goodly fist slapped a goodly palm.

"A very different situation." Tawney responded agreeably. "Actually, I'm not sure I can place your Morgan. Though I guess I've met him. Skinny fellow, thick glasses?" Something eased in the Admiral. Target identified. "He appears pleasant enough though."

"He is very capable. Also he's very"—here Dr. Gray's hesitation was not over his choice of word but whether to utter it might be a mistake—"idealistic." It was a mistake.

The Admiral's inner spring instantly tightened. "Not a nut, I hope?"

"Far from it. Some of his points are valid." The Admiral shook his head as if an insect were buzzing it. "*Doctor*, everyone on God's green earth has valid points. Comes a time though when everyone has to put aside his private doubts and . . . ." "Hop aboard."

"Exactly!" The Admiral's expression of gratitude was beatific. But clouds, as well as sunshine, were alternating in swift succession—like a changeling day in Norwegian Spring—across that boyishly mobile face. "The Brits, you are aware, will be over here before too long. A delegation, including Sir Bruce Maxton, the legend himself, will be getting the pitch on DIANA. Needless to say, we don't want our visitors exposed to premature bad news. DIANA's are no more than the usual teething troubles." Occasionally, and unaccountably, Tawney Gray would sight down the stem of his pipe at nothing apparent. Sighting down it now.

"Well." The Admiral clapped his hands. "Leave it to you. I gather you've been Morgan's mentor. If mentor is the right word." In Tawney Gray's slight shift of position an observer of nuances would sense discomfort. Unfortunately, it was almost precisely the word. Sneedon Snowdon contemplated the personage of his technical director. A wise old bird. How much the system needed such types too. Even if their fires sometimes did need relighting. No sooner had he savored a moment's relaxation than the Admiral frowned again. Reaching in his basket, he took out a sheaf of papers. "Coincidence, same gent, but this hit my desk yesterday. The business of this secretary . . . let's see, one Viola Fletch."

"Actually she's only a clerk-typist." "*Whatever.* Your Morgan is most anxious to be rid of her. And evidently, according to what I'm seeing, succeeding. Or just about." Whistling softly, the Admiral paused, reading. "'*Gross incompetence,*' that's *it?*"

"That," Tawney shifted again, "Morgan feels ought to be enough."

"Don't you ordinarily require more than that to hang your hat on? Things can't have changed in Civil Service that much since I went off to sea." The Admiral looked up sharply. "Is she that bad?" Tawney Gray took a deep breath. "Pretty bad." Realizing that he was venturing another risky word. "I fear it's a matter of principle with our lad."

"Principles are dandy, but a person learns not to act on each and every one." Fingers drummed. But that quick mind had already moved on and away from the fate of some unknown munchkin down in the grass and on to business closer to his heart.

"Plowshare?" Tawney repeated the momentarily elusive phase, one he had been only too glad to put out of mind, while racking his brain for a response that would not embarrass.

"Frankly, Admiral, I must tell you, Plowshare is a pretty dead program on all fronts."

"We shall give it life. It will be our Lazarus. Incidentally, your Morgan, to give him his due, appears to have one contractor in his stable who has ideas. Amongst them I noted something about harvesting fishponds out there in the Hawaiian Islands."

"You ought to know that our David Morgan is not an enthusiast for Plowshare either. That fishpond idea is one that leaves him especially cold. To his credit, he's tight with Uncle's money." Amusement for a moment relaxed the Admiral. "Encourage then a bit of looseness. Might rid him of some of his wild hairs. And speaking of such, I've been over Morgan's pending talk at that . . . Wolf Lake shindig coming up. Fortunately, it seems a closed affair where a bit of academic freedom, may not be amiss. Still, I count on you for extra guidance for our maverick."

The office had grown quieter with the end of the day's mass exodus from the building.

"One thing more, Doctor. My wife, Ginger, lets me know that not all of EAR's wives are responding as she had hoped with her volunteer campaign at the Handicapped Children's Hospital. There's a bit of foot-dragging." The Admiral paused. "Morgan's wife, sorry to say, though far from alone, seems to be one of the foot draggers. Perhaps you can do a little needling there. Your Tiny, I might add, is a real trooper Ginger tells me."

Damned well better be . . . .

"Our lad, Morgan, "the Admiral said, "seems to be in our gunsights a great deal today. I trust this is just a passing phase." Tawney Gray gestured vague assent to a trust he wished he could share. The Admiral rose, signaling Tawney's own rise. He took Tawney's arm, giving it a squeeze. The Admiral stretched, moved his arms in an end-of-the-day gesture. "You know, Doctor—Tawney— there's a great deal happening. Big things. We must talk more."

The Admiral's arms continued their movement, making larger arcs, suggesting a world that no mere human limbs could encompass. "Giant programs, you know," he murmured. But what it was that he wanted to say further about them—what compelling thoughts could illuminate facets of their mightiness and which ought, in some way, to unite the two men in a deep and common bond—presumably must await another day. "They're something . . . ." Perhaps, though it could not be known, he wanted to express how it was that giant programs ground on like speeded-up glaciers. Grinding up not only mountains of dollars but whole communities of men and their dreams. Whatever got in their way.

* * *

Sexist to think it, denigrating to say, it was nevertheless true that in responding to a ringing telephone Aliason Morgan was a woman of her time. Aliason lunged for hers, upsetting a basket of needlepoint, knocking her book to the floor, dragging a skein of tangled yarn with a slippered foot. In instinct, she was a sensate embodiment of the outer range of Gaussian probabilities. For it just *could* be good news, some contest won, a rewarding chance to name a tune . . . . And even though the effects of her last call, one from Cynthia Snowdon—only lately, but painfully, had she become acquainted with the wife of David's new Admiral—were still atremble, her eagerness in responding to her new caller was undiminished.

"Aliason, Tiny Gray." A soft collection of words followed, not all of which Aliason caught except to gather that it was some sort of prayerful blessing. "How are you, dear?"

"Oh, I'm *fine*, I guess." But hell's bells, she didn't want it to be mere guess. She added more positively. "Coming along just great."

"For myself, God has brought joy through knowing."

"Ah," Aliason shifted her grip bracing for a long call, sure too that she would have to get to the bathroom before it ended. "That's wonderful, Tiny."

"The secret of happiness," Tiny went on, though not without first a disclaimer before unveiling her secret, "not that I feel that I have the answer for everyone, but—".

"Then just *your* secret, Tiny," Aliason urged her on.

"Certainty." She let the resonance die. "A beautiful word."

"Oh." It was, though Aliason disguised it, a cry of dismay.

"Or is it certitude?" Tiny mused, "a more elegant word. My minister says—".

"Oh, Tiny," she wailed. "Whatever, I'm afraid I have little of either."

"You're talking now about the gift of faith, I imagine, and—".

"*Tiny, I don't know in the least what I'm talking about!*" The quiet along the wires after this outburst was a tribute to Ma Bell's miraculous abilities in noise suppression. It could have been that Tiny had simply vanished, fading back into infinite silence. But that was a forlorn hope. Aliason an expert on portentous silences, David's, Tessa's . . . . The world saved up theirs for her. "Aliason, dear," Tiny Gray came at last to the point of her call. "Cynthia Snowdon asked if I might persuade you to reconsider your reluctance to help."

How the simplest phrase drew blood. Even as it missed truth by miles. *First Tiny—though, dear God, she could not say it—before helping them, I must save myself.*

"We're only talking a few hours a week. If you could see those poor children—".

Too well. How could anyone not see those unfortunate children, cruelly damned by random blows of nature, and not be torn in two? The trouble was—well, *one* of the troubles—that she wore her skin inside out. Nerves placed all wrong, sensitivity amounting to paralysis. She saw endless lines of afflicted little beings with brittle bones and twisted limbs and patient pain-glazed eyes.... If she could, she would hug them to her heart until her arms ached and they dissolved into her flesh. "Tiny...." She stopped herself. Never complain, never explain. Remembered from somewhere, perhaps no further away than her David, but like other fine rules of life easier said than done. "Aliason." Tiny ever so gentle. "Only thinking of you both."

"Both?" Another alarm sounding. "Did Dr. Gray also ask you to call me?"

Tiny's reply was one betraying second too long. "He did suggest—".

"Damn." Her heart was like a small animal trying wildly to escape the cage of her ribs. "Tiny, how well do you know Mrs. Snowdon?" Her question was practical, vaguely a starting point for action. But at once the impulse of purpose fled, dissolved by Tiny's sweetness. "We've met a few times and have talked by phone." Gradually Tiny seemed to circle in towards Aliason's question within a question. "She seems very nice. But no doubt, I would say, she feels that she has to push a little. Few good things in the world get moving without a prod of some kind. Heaven knows, I'm no leader."

Nor I!

"Did I hear you dear? I thought I detected a whisper, or something."

"A whisper it was." Hardly able to muster the strength for that. She pictured herself as an antique barque in failed winds, sails limp as Kleenex, putt-putting along on a one-lunged auxiliary motor and touch and go if she was going to make it to an imagined deserted harbor and some lonely waiting pier haunting her mind like a vision of salvation.

"I owe her a call. May I tell Cynthia that at least you'll be thinking about it?"

"Dear God, yes." Her need for the bathroom was acute. "Say that." *Too* much, *too.* much.

▲ ▲ ▲ ▲ ▲

David Morgan was off to meet with the Civil Service Commissioner, but couldn't refrain from checking first with Billy Jencks. Wishing at once that he had not. Billy too full of additional cautions. "Be on time. Be *early*. Late is one thing you don't want to be. The guy'll use any excuse. Do you remember what Sir Thomas More wrote of King Richard the Third? You don't Davey? Funny I thought you would. Okay: *Where his advantage grew he spared no man's death who stood against his purpose."*

"Pretty strong stuff, Billy." But David's laugh only deepened Billy's seriousness. "Take care. This meeting isn't for nothing. He's going to make *you* the shit."

"I'm not worried about him working on me. I'll just stay with the facts."

"Davey. For God's sakes!" throwing up his hands, "You still don't get it."

However much he was inclined to discount Billy's forebodings, as soon as he was ushered into the inner office of the Honorable Anthony J. Cringhlo, David could not help recalling something else Billy had said. Asserting that Washington was run for the most part by small men situated in overly large corner offices. Men who could look out upon the beguiling scenes their windows offered, of majestic trees, silenced traffic, people in constant flow, but men who deep down lived in mortal fear of what they saw out there. Men whose deepest anxiety was of having ever to return to that turbulent anonymity.

Anyway, here he was, the man himself—and it struck him as movingly odd, downright prescient of Billy—in a large corner office altogether too much like the one that had been pictured for him. Testimonials and degrees were numerous on the walls, but a little too far away for David to make out the print. The message was in their framing. A broad polished desk sat at an angle in the room's center and was bare except for a thick folder with a bright yellow cover. Vivid upon the yellowness in perfect red letters—neither block nor gothic, but with a calligraphically skilled hand's compromise of style—VIOLA FLETCH was written in Magic Marker large and bold. Attached to the folder's exterior and beneath her name was a color photograph, larger than passport size and in the smeary tints of the kind of pictures taken in a booth in an amusement park arcade. Viola to the V. Thick carmine lips, eyes wide and solemn as if in bewildered victimization. But whatever his unnervingly accurate prediction about the location and dimensions of the office, Billy's imagination was thereafter less successful. In the voice that now addressed him, preliminary and hastened courtesies out of the way, there was nothing betraying fear. Streaks of silver conferred added dignity to a head of hair otherwise too shiny. "I am," Anthony Cringhlo said, "the Court of the Last Resort. Or, let us say, *we* are that Court. Let's talk man to man." He motioned towards a chair, taking its mate close by. They were alone, the aides who had ushered him in melting away.

"You may ask why I'm taking so much time on one individual." He made a grand sweep of his arm that said: *Weighed against all this.* "Ever been fired, Mr. Morgan?"

"No sir. Fortunately."

"'Fortunately'. Apt word. Terminated? RIFFED? Hit the bricks? Quotaed out? Gotten the pink slip? I note a smile playing about the corners of your mouth. Uh . . . uh . . . make *no* apology. It is a normal reaction. Especially amongst the secure. I use those trivial expressions to emphasize how we cloak one of the most destructive events in a human life in ways meant to render the whole event comfortably bearable."

"None of those." David swallowed. "But I believe I'm capable of feeling it in others." "Ah." There was a change of tone, from near sarcasm to a gentle, almost afflicted, sincerity. "Very good. I too never lose sight of the truth that we're dealing with a real human being." "I haven't forgotten that either," David said firmly.

"Hey, my good man"—heartily—"I'm sure you haven't. But shift gears for a moment now. Things are not always what they appear. It can be a tricky world out there"—a gesture towards the window—"and alas, a cruel one. Many times the reasons people are let go never show up on Form ABC or XYZ or the like. "Reasons for which I must serve as a final shield of protection . . . you know? Our girl here"—he waggled a finger at Viola's picture, frozen in her cheaply colored gaze of surprise directed at the distant grand ceiling of the kind of office she would never see—is moderately attractive, right? Her record informs us, under Extracurricular, that she was a Pom-Pom girl at her local high school back in East Gungywump, or wherever. They don't pick the ugly ones for that, right? Hey, my friend, I'm not looking for a Miss America judge's evaluation number. Let's just say, attractive enough. Okay?"

"Okay."

"Now maybe, in the case of an attractive female—it happens all the time—some supervisor has had designs but can't get to first base. And, in typical male fashion—"

"*That's not me.*"

Anthony Cringhlo threw both palms up. "Not *suggesting*. Merely recounting the kinds of things I've got a duty to explore. "You see?" Anthony Cringhlo was, by turns, professional, hearty, stern, folksy, sophisticated (just-between-us-two-men-of-the-world-ish), softly persuasive, rhetorical . . . eventually seemingly merely sad. "You realize that she is through in Civil Service forever. Dead as a doornail. Record to Central Files. The iron bars are up." But that note was too high, it strained at the top; it could only be sustained by more, and even more implausible dramatic fare. Off it an odd and silly harmonic vibrated in David's own suppressed consciousness. Images of Viola barred from the Elysian Fields. Fated to be locked out forever, gazing wistfully at some fair green land through forbidding bars. A small and interiorly mirthful reverie was broken into by the strengthened return of the Commissioner's voice. David seized on the one clear word, standing in isolation, that now seemed to be topical. "Coordination?"

"Exactly, '*Coordination*', the important man repeating it with pleasure. "There is a hierarchy of such in all human beings. It all comes down to hand-eye. What sets the great athlete apart. Why Bill Bradley could shoot the basketball in the Princeton gym and know after one shot that the rim of the hoop was mounted an eighth of an inch too high. Why Emlen Tunnell—before your time, but a football teammate of mine in High School and later on a Hall of Famer—could control dice rolled on a blanket as well as he could break a tackle."

"Sir—"

"Just a moment, I'm talking about basic attributes, the hookup of nerve and muscle that makes certain skills a snap for one human being and a trial to the next. The fate that has some girls born to be great typists and others like your Miss . . . ." "Fletch."

"Check. Who sure as shit wasn't endowed with that magic. Back to her record, our Pom-Pom girl. Now obviously—we agree, she's pretty enough—if she'd had what it takes she'd have been a *cheerleader*. Way it goes. The liveliest and best become the cheerleaders. If you got lesser bounce and rhythm you're stuck at Pom-Pom. Natural selection conspires to place us all in some foreordained niche of talent."

"But—"

"No '*buts*' about it, my exacting friend. Chekov warned us of the folly of judging ordinary people by the impossible standards of great men."

"It's not only about typing." David said with mild heat, "there's filing, ordinary office skills, simpler things, just remembering to turn off a coffee pot . . . ."

"Were coffee mess duties in her Job Description?" The Honorable Cringhlo asked this with seeming seriousness. David equally seriously, with a stiffening of confidence, refused to reply. Anthony Cringhlo, who knew a loser when he saw it, shifted tack. "Do you have any idea what she's going to do now?" "I really don't know."

"No?" He smiled triumphantly. Having lost a point a moment ago, clearly he felt that he had gotten one back. "Not your affair, right? How she puts bread on her table?" David's tongue went to his lips, a tell-tale reflexive act that an old pro like Cringhlo would never miss. "Even as with one word from you, Mr. Morgan, an X changed from one box to another on a simple form, and Miss Fletch keeps a gainful life. Nor would she have to remain in your organization. There are certainly jobs she can do elsewhere satisfactorily. Perhaps even apply her . . . typing abilities to offices where requirements are not so stringent."

"I hardly think that it's in the best interests of the U.S. Government just to foist a problem off on someone else. That's done far too much already."

"'The U.S. Government,'" Anthony Cringhlo repeated 'solemnly, "the *entire* U.S. Federal system. Wherein you, as an individual, have taken it upon *yourself* to decide what's best for it. Tell me, Mr. Morgan, do you seriously believe that this young woman"—he gestured at the folder on his desk, keeping one eye on David—"can truly be the most incompetent GS-5 in the entire Civil Service?" David shook his head. "I can't say."

"*Or GS-3?*" She could even revert to that. There's precedent. *Come*, Mr. Morgan. You're an old hand in Civil Service. Also an expert in statistics. Oh yes, I've looked you up. You know better than anyone to be prepared to insist that in all this vast governmental system that there cannot be a single clerk typist *more* incompetent. Your gods of probabilities know better." Anthony Cringhlo waited for a response, got none. "And so do you. Fact is likely there are dozens, hundreds worse. A long way from superstars, granted, but doing a job. And yet it seems that one young woman, amongst all that number, has had the bad luck to find herself victim of one man's Holy Cause. Mere chance did it. Is that fair?" David cleared his throat. "Mr. Cringhlo. There are a lot of things I could say to that. But as to the specifics of Miss Fletch—and I assure you I'm on no 'Holy Cause'—I have taken action I feel is appropriate and have made my recommendation accordingly. And, yes, I'm aware that probably there are talents even inferior to Miss Fletch's widely distributed throughout the Federal Government. But it's beside the point. Lots of people run stoplights too, but that doesn't deter the system from taking action against the handful who are caught—"

Anthony Cringhlo threw up his hands. "That old tired analogy! I expected somewhat better of you, Mr. Morgan. Judging you had a more subtle mind." The Civil Service Commissioner walked away, strode around the room. He came back and sat down staring dramatically for some seconds. "Let the decision be on your conscience."

David did not flinch. On my conscience then it must be. Abruptly their meeting seemed at end. Coldly and silently, without further pretense at courtesy, Anthony Cringhlo, Adjudicator, rose and turned his back, hands clasped stiffly behind him. There would be no farewell handshake. An invisible buzzer must have been sounded because the door opened and an aide entered. Without a word more being spoken David found himself being escorted through the wide ornate doorway and past the steely mannered secretary guarding the outer office. A genteel bum's rush. "Just a minute," he remembered, "I've got to sign myself out."

"I'll get it sir. There's only the time of departure to be entered in the Visitor's Log Book." Had he detected added chill, or was it merely only another manifestation of the same but less noticed efficiency that had greeted his arrival? The midafternoon sunlight and the traffic noises smote him following the dim and cool quiet that had held him for the last hour. At times like these, with his reactions uncertain, instinct told him that a long walk was the right thing. He thought too that he would just as soon arrive back sufficiently late and not have to face a relentlessly curious and no doubt gloating Billy until tomorrow. The stoplight changed simultaneously to green and to WALK. The latter blinking insistently. So be it. It had not been, when all was said and done, your ordinary civil servant's every day kind of encounter. Still, more grist for the mill, he said to himself. Whatever grist, whatever mill.

▲▲▲▲▲

It must have been a Wednesday because Helen, creator of small traditions, had brought in her customary donuts. Treating the gang. "One more?" she offered, "before I set them out for the mob." She bore David's own before her reverently, set on a folded napkin, like a lady of ancient times with a votive lamp. "Thanks, Helen, I think one will be it."

"Discipline," she commended. For a moment she shared the view. The sun was low in the East, shining across the earth's fresh new green turning it into fire. It burned on the flood-swollen Potomac, the color of chocolate gold. The red-tinged city of Washington was touched by the rawness of that power. The phone rang and it was Billy Jencks, calling to confirm lunch. David replied he was too busy, but Billy was a wheedler. David Morgan looked regretfully over his cluttered desk, which was not going to regain its lost order this day either. "All right, Billy. Lunch in the usual spot." The pile of correspondence in his IN basket though did drop satisfying inches this morning. The heavy data compendia, stiff with their fresh and lasting unreadability, obscurely born and destined for a deeper obscurity, were handled with a simple flourish of his initials on the routing slip. Other items were less readily sent on their way. There were more troublesome reports on DIANA, then something fresh to be learned about the vexing resonances of the swim bladders of wrasse, new profiles of sound velocity off the *Nord Kop* . . . . Here were results of bottom cores from the Atlantic's Abyssal Plain, millennia compressed into inches. Because low frequency sound reflected off ocean bottoms, there were also men ready to satisfy curiosity as to the absorption characteristics of those prehistoric muds. Gentle, decent men they were, with murmurous voices like the sea itself; wasteful, academically inclined men too, on to a good thing, a quiet and prosperous living. The oceans an unending mystery, but also a feast for many.

The next piece of correspondence that he took out of his basket was a letter from the Technical Director of the Wolf Lake Test Facility. But . . . ah, David's sigh just for a moment was wholly pleasurable. Picturing Wolf Lake not as one of DIANA's battlegrounds, but as he had beheld it once on a perfect day, bluer than any ocean, deeper than Loch Ness, the steep cradling mountains like a setting for a jewel of stunning beauty. The Naval Test Facility set all alone at one remote end of the lake on its private point of land and its buildings hidden amongst the pines. Moored offshore, hundreds of yards out, were the great yellow test barges. Coming back from that trip he had described Wolf Lake to Aliason and rashly, carried away by that ever renewing optimism that at one time unfailingly blossomed in him after every trip, speculated that the prize of Technical Director out there ought not be beyond his reach. With the right fall of the cards . . . . Wolf Lake thus joining that longish list of Aliason's golden places. Not quite supplanting fondly remembered Hawaii in her pantheon, but another bit of heaven shining far from Annandale. Helen put her head in the door following the phone's ringing. "A Miss Lisa Alverez." She wagged her finger. "Mysterious females who won't state their business."

"Be tolerant. They can't help themselves." He yawned, feigning disinterest. But his dampening palm was slippery on the phone's glossy plastic as Helen tactfully shut the door behind her. No matter how many times before he had fenced with these steely women working the sullen frontiers of Delinquency. "Mr. David Morgan? I am with the Credit Department of Sears and our records show you behind in your payments on the Easy Payment Plan."

"Ah. The Easy Payment Plain." Yes, indeed, that one too. But not in the worst shape. With relief he felt passing silliness. "Tell me, Miss, why is it called the Easy Payment Plan? Never mind. Perhaps my payment has gone astray in the mail."

"Our records, sir, have you *two* payments behind."

"That many?" He shifted the receiver to his other hand where it did not feel so hot. He tried to picture Miss Alvarez, doing it ever more with these women of the telephone, strangers yet armed with plausible rights of aggression.

"It is, sir. And we must have both payments within five working days or—"

"My credit rating is jeopardized. And the American dream goes poof."

"Sir. One's credit rating is a very serious matter." "Indeed it is." In his mind he quickly juggled a few numbers. Reconciled to another visit to good old Household Finance, lender of last resort. "Payment will be in the mail today."

"Thank you, sir." A cold and puzzled lady. Must be a lot of nuts each day for Miss Alvarez and he was sorry that he had added one more. He sat unmoving, letting die what had to die within him first—shame, no other word—before he could function again. No matter how many such calls he had to take he never got used to them. The knock on the door came too soon but he had restored his expression to one of sufficient composure that would reassure Helen. It wasn't Helen though but Viola. "I've finished this here latest memorandum, Mr. Morgan." She shifted her gum again to make room for more words. "Got all the mistakes out this time too, I think." Her thighs pressed against the front of his desk. He looked up again into that well-meaning frown, a poignant addition to an expression of permanent perplexity. "I appreciate your letting me know how my dismissal papers stand", she said. Her reddened eyes were actually sympathetic. "So you're trying it again, huh?" He evaded her look. Viola, as usual, behind the power curve. Not aware how far along things were, that she was on the brink.

"Yes, I feel . . . that I must." *Stupid* words. He could think of nothing though to add.

At the edge of his desk were miniature ship models, presumptive beneficiaries of EAR's technology. The bulge of Viola's lower abdomen had just capsized a plastic Charles Francis Adam's class destroyer. He raised his own eyes again to an unavoidable encounter with those depths of baffled earnestness. "It's mainly a case of where your . . . talents might be better applied." "Hey, Mr. Morgan. Don't look so sad. Like, it's *okay*."

Time to be meeting Billy. The government's green paint recently applied upon the wooden slats of the outside benches in Crystal City was soaked in the sun's direct heat and its shininess was warming his legs and back with a thoroughness that equaled the strong light pouring over his face and chest. It felt good, for the air was cool. He was enjoying this moment's taste of aloneness, letting his thoughts find lazy drift, when Billy's familiar figure came trotting. Billy Jencks, all five foot-two inches of him, with that boyish face which ever and anon—and patently today—mild ravages of post-pubescent acne seemingly must still revisit, but glowing his usual happiness to be with his friend. His checked sports jacket flared colors that would have shamed a racetrack tout at nearby Bowie. "Your jacket, Billy, proclaims well . . . youth!" "Do you like it?" David avoided his reply in the involved mechanics of unwrapping a sandwich. But there was something else about Billy. Unaccountably he was taller. David took only a moment before glancing down towards Billy's feet, which made the unaccountable accountable. Though platform shoes were the usual wear for Billy, today's boots were something special. Their high heels were of stacked leather, hard and shiny as laminated wood, and a complex design was stitched in them with twine of bright reds and blues. From absurd heights, inches beyond good taste, millimeters this side of perilous instability, Billy cast a warily proud eye at unaccustomed vistas. David had not meant Billy to detect his scrutiny, but it was the kind his friend was quick to catch. "Yes, David, I *know*. But unless you're born my size no one can understand."

"No reason to explain. Enjoy your lunch." Which Billy was soon doing. Showing off some of the latest dainties, glazed orange slices and ginger marmalade, prepared by his Vietnamese girlfriend. Far cry from his usual slabs of cheese and baloney. Things apparently moving ahead with his favored, she of the glossy black hair whom David as yet knew only by the photographs Billy kept pulling out of his wallet in accompaniment of his praise of his Shin. Praise though that was shadowed by Billy's doubts, as if there were something subtly amiss, wrongful in its easiness, this courting and winning a girl from a country so gravely wounded and diminished by war. Instead of—as ought to be the way—winning, as presumably David had done, a full-fledged American golden girl in competition against varsity squads of American males. Billy's nagging worry found explicit expression. Out here in what ought to be exculpating sunlight. "Davey, tell me I'm doing *right*. That I'm not taking unfair advantage of . . . circumstances." David's reassurance was hearty as he could make it. "Don't be silly, my friend." From his frequent trips to Saigon, back in the days when he had been analyzing the complex locating acoustics of the porpoises that the Navy Labs were training to hunt down and kill underwater swimmers threatening Navy ships, he now drew on memory to confirm the abundance of female beauty that was the joy and wonder of Saigon. Broad boulevards alive with astounding numbers of young Vietnamese women, slender, tiny, delicate, ethereal in flowing silks, a wave of loveliness billowing down the streets and alighting like flocks of butterflies. Just what Billy wanted to hear, David's confirming that the young women of Saigon were the most beautiful in the world, and that he would be a fool to let his suit be clouded by useless fret over his good fortune. *Carpe diem.*

* * *

An ordinary office morning, but he realized he had not seen Viola in some days. It seemed that even the last steps of disassociation from Civil Service, were no small affair. Not that he should be surprised. "Just come to say goodbye," she said. "So soon? All checked out?"

"All the papers signed, I guess." Again the crooked smile. "Least, I hope." There was a silence in which he noticed that she had on a dress he had not seen before. It was too brightly florid and the taut silken material accentuated the lush slackness of her figure. He had the feeling that on it, and new accessories, she must have blown a sizeable portion of her terminal paycheck. Her handbag was large, woven through with thick threads to make a busy pattern of birds, trees, flowers. A country idyll on rough straw fiber. Her shoes were white and strawberry red pumps, modeled upon some discarded style of the Fifties.

"Well. So. What are your plans?" A bit too heartily. "Plans?" The long eyelashes blinked. "For starters, reckon I'll go stay with my sister out near Berryville." Except that she pronounced it Burrville. "Off route 7. Hit's kind of small and she's got two kids.... I'll be looking for something." The moment drew on, "I know that you'll find it," he said.

She mustered a mournful smile. "You do? You don't know country. Anyway, sure wish. I don't want to go back to McDonalds." There was little more to say and Viola, unusual in his experience, seemed to realize it. She tightened her grip on her handbag and upon the official brown severance envelope tucked beneath her other arm, "Anyway, want you to know that I don't have hard feelings."

"Good luck Viola."

"Yep. Good luck to you, Mr. Morgan, and all your ideas. I hope Mrs. Morgan has good luck too. With her . . . affliction."

He didn't see the tears but the flood was coming and her head was down like someone crying as she went out. For a few seconds more he was listening to her footsteps. Irredeemable gracelessness clacking down the corridor, fading into the noise of the building, as of the sea. Listening on, even though by then there was nothing to hear and wondering why, at the denouement of his small but not unworthy triumph, he felt like such an utter shit.

▲▲▲▲▲

David Morgan reached down for Boat's small bicycle; one wheel sprawled skyward, and set it on its kickstand. For seconds he gazed at his home and at the light shining out the window onto the lawn. The word came unbidden. *Volcano.* Odd, as if not even his own voice, yet a true one. Only fifteen months ago, after another tumultuous relocation move and their first Autumn in the new neighborhood, the leaves dropping from the trees had exposed the truth that their house was little different from others in this tract. Winter once more had starkly bared, nor had Spring yet fully concealed, the artifices of the developer's game, the cunning in the superficial variations by which the buyer is lured into believing that he is purchasing uniqueness. At the front door he detected Al's hurrying steps and before he tried his key the door was flung open. "You *didn't* forget the yarn." She kissed him warmly, holding the fine and fluffy material up to the light where it glowed in multiple rings of shining color. A magical beauty, like a streetlamp in haloing mist. He followed her into the kitchen, setting his briefcase down. "New dress?"

She twirled. "Stop looking like that. It was on sale. Don't ruin things." Tears brimmed. "Now please call the children." Yet it was a peaceful meal, able to turn merry. The topic was Daddy's job, subject of recurrent mystery and mirth. "What is it you *do*, Dad?" Beth asked. "I mean really do. I know it has to do with submarines, but still I can't figure it. Because every day you go to an office just like lots of other guys."

"Just like lots of other guys." "Your father does experiments in ways of detecting submarines," Aliason volunteered with tutorial dignity and passable accuracy.

"You gotta find *every* submarine?" Boat getting into the act.

"Sure. Found one in Lake Fairfax. Popped up first thing this morning." There were seconds of amazement on the little boy's face that he would treasure. Treasuring no less a delighted dawning. "Aw, come on, Dad. You're kidding, aren't you Dad?"

Along the flow of nonsense Aliason grew wistful. "You remember my grandparents, David? Of course, you children never knew them at all. Well, they had this little store in Alton and they ran it for more than fifty years, grandmother and granddad, heart and soul in it together. All the children, among them my father, helped. The ups and downs of the business were talked about at the table. Everyone knew every nail sold, every penny brought in, the whole family sharing in the ... *destiny* of it. Wouldn't it be wonderful if people could get back to that kind of life?" His laugh was sharper than he wished. "Just tell me how."

After supper she hurried to get ready. He was reading the news when she came into the living room and leaned over to bestow him a newspaper-crumpling kiss. "I do know, do do *do*, darling, that money is a problem. And that we must have a real talk."

"And after talking, perhaps do something about it?"

"Dear, how much I know that too. *Choices. Decisions.* Which reminds me. Would you go over my checkbook? On the kitchen table. I can add it up, but you do it faster." Her voice softened. "You'll probably be sound asleep when I get back." "Such are the odds."

"I envy you your deep sleeps. You won't believe, but I really do sometimes give you a nudge, hoping to wake you." With a tickled funny bone he walked her out to the car. Moonlight caught his grin too, refusing to go away even out in the evening's chill. He felt her mystification through his hold on her arm. "What's so funny?", she wanted to know.

"Trying to recall when last I found my ribs bruised from your nudges." She threw her arms around him. "Oh, my darling. My patient husband."

She clung to him hard, like farewell on the eve of a great voyage. She drove slowly, not confident of her night driving, taking back roads that, for all of the towns and villages sprinkled across this part of Northern Virginia—a civilization of endlessly strewn clusters of dwellings—nevertheless cut through patches of forest. Animal eyes, bright as reflector glass, stared back fixedly at the headlights and disappeared with the abruptness of magic. Families of foxes were out this way. She halted her car at a stop sign and turned towards lighted storefronts and the winking colored signs of franchised urban civilization. Glad to be free of the dark woods. A city girl, for all her yearnings. So many cars, all these comings and goings. Once, if she had thought at all about the astonishing levels of American nighttime traffic it was to take for granted that all these other people were also heading to the warmth of friends, to conviviality and refilling glasses, to wit and laughter. Her life too had embraced a party time. They too had been a Golden Couple. Or so it had pleased her once to believe.

She had learned by now to attach a very different meaning to this particular hour, comforting in its constancy. For along these same streets moved cars, more than the world knew, with the tug of its own special but powerful migration, invisible because unimagined. Towards destinations unguessed, a flow apart from the general consciousness of man. Yet many of these cars too had also just backed out of suburban driveways just as ordinary as her own. Having only in common that their drivers were drawn, more straightway than moths to a flame, to the spartan basements of neighborhood churches and salvation of a different kind from that heralded in the stained glass windows of the sacred spaces of the floor above.

"Aliason, my dear."

"*Marty.*" She could never match the strength of that bear hug. Messiahs come in many guises but Aliason's own was packed in the squarish figure of a sixty-five year old woman in shapeless slacks and a black vest flopping over a pale cheap blouse. A face wrinkled as a prune and puffy slits through which the kindest pair of eyes on earth probed you. Holding her hand with a grip of iron. "How you doing, love? Keep it simple."

"Oh, *yes.* I'm doing that." Not yet actually. Promising herself though that the time was coming. She saw Marty move on to greet someone new, make another bestowal of her inexhaustible gift. Aliason had heard Marty's story only once, but in this community of grim stories hers was the most terrible. Remembering her own first visit here, she was watching Marty talking to an overweight pale young woman in a stained smock. The woman's trembling hands could not hold her coffee cup and she set it back down clattering and sloshing. Aliason looked away, not wanting the woman to feel that anyone was noticing. Aliason had worlds yet to learn about the fellowship, but one thing she knew well; that was its raw material. The portable chairs had been set up once again, also the podium, and the electric urn with its little red welcoming light that meant the coffee was ready. To this bare and comforting place she had journeyed through other moonlit nights, faithfully also through snowstorms, and in the suffocating hotness of many a summer evening. To companionable air thickened with tobacco smoke, sign of that universal, if infinitely milder, addiction that was like another part of the bargain struck, seemingly an inescapable trade. To friends she would meet nowhere else, but friendships that were like loves. Tony, the former radio broadcaster, Fred who wore sinister dark glasses and who had broken arms for the Teamsters, and the beautiful Sara, bones delicate as a bird's and her grave model's face, sorrowful as a Madonna's and with fine white wrists roughly circled with scar tissue from slashings with shards of broken china that were the nearest tool handy on the floor where she had lain sprawled in despair. And Helen, ancient Helen, fingers sprouting diamonds and who had tottered into the program on her cane at seventy-five because it mattered to her what Cause of Death her grandchildren were going to read on her Certificate and who would settle for—indeed craved—the blessed obscurity of 'Natural'. Here too gentle John who had yielded all but the last marginal functioning of his liver to the dutiful sociability of the Foreign Service . . . . And always more, the unending straggling in of the fresh wounded, an ever-renewing muster of vivid lives without last names and stories beside which her own was pale.

To the diversity of human life and the commonness of its afflictions, to the mystery of self and a forever uncompleted voyage of discovery. To clichés that never became tedious, their gold keeping them bright. *"One day at a time."* The much passed around coin of salvation. Worn and precious. Before the signal for the meeting to begin, she listened in on conversations. It was like at a cocktail party, but this was not one of her nights to feel amusement at the irony. She was restless, she and her styrofoam cup of coffee kept moving on. It was late April and therefore Fourth Step time again and her palms were damp. Fourth Step rolled around too often, so quickly in fact that she thought that they must be tampering with the regular plan of rotation. And yet they couldn't be speeding up the orbit of earth itself around the sun, now could they? *Damn.* The place was buzzing and there was no escape from the swarm of words and she stood beside John, whom she liked, while Mark talked on. Mark was young, burly, the blackness of his beard just touched by gray. He had been a Jesuit and she took his brilliance for granted. Mere nuns had been her teachers and in the Catholic hierarchy of her childhood Jesuits were Gods. Mark went to prodigious numbers of meetings, knew the Big Book as well as he knew Albertus Magnus. As once he had been aiming to be a great classicist, now he was going to be the preeminent theologian of the fellowship. He was expounding on why Fairfax County had so many in the program, *why* the rich abundance of the stricken in this particular territory. It was not simply the affluence of the county—though obviously people had more money to buy booze—but the key was the fact that so many of the people here were in Civil Service. "It's the infinite tolerance of the federal government towards drunks. It coddles them; let's them get hooked, whereas industry is quicker to fire. People there hit bottom much sooner." Mark went on, loving his theories as much as he detested government.

John was cupping a bad ear, the best he had. He had known seventeen stays at rehab houses and uncountable trips through detox. He was early old, with lusterless hair and a face that was an unrestored battlefield of shattered capillaries; he had heard no end of theories. His voice was a roughened whisper. "Perhaps so, Mark. But why bother with whys and wherefores? All that matters is what are we going *to do* about it." Yards away she could hear Marty's smoke-worn voice, but unlike John's making no effort to lower itself. It was a shovel digging into familiar strong earth and tossing out its wisdom in brute chunks. Breaking into Aliason's listening was their leader's rap on the table telling them to take their seats. Her heart jumped as if at a pistol shot. *Step Four*. For a few minutes though there was reprieve in the form of drama. Floyd had shown up. He was barely out of his teens and his hard thin face bore the pustules of drug addiction on top of the ravages of alcoholism. Floyd was forever dropping out of the program and coming back, seemingly to no purpose except to make plain that he wasn't buying a word of it. Sometimes he defiantly slammed his boots on the table and cut away at his dirty fingernails with a murderous knife. His black leather jacket was adorned with swastikas and other puerile symbols in studs of gleaming steel. He shouted wild things, but there were signs of a mind behind his punk's face, his pathetic bravado.

Tonight he was venomously hostile, plainly drunk, and he started with an incoherent harangue. What did these fat smiling faces really know about trouble . . . ? He turned on Sara sneering at her refinement, the folly of her beauty, the pretentiousness of her sitting there on her . . . . Sara flinched, turning even paler, if that were possible for her ghostly skin. Getting no reaction from the group, which was deadly quiet, Floyd shouted polluted invective, at Sara's body, its intimate places . . . . Aliason sat frozen, terrified he was going to turn his vicious assault on her next. She had been at sessions before when someone became outrageous, but never this bad. Several men made a move towards Floyd who was screaming, foam dribbling from his mouth, but Marty raised her hand for restraint. Marty and her boxer's face, Marty who could outstare lions. Letting

Floyd run down like a broken toy . . . "so party-ass Sara, with her gold bracelets and expensive dresses and her airs, thinks she can preach about booze . . . ."

Sara swallowed, but that was all. Aliason admired her this moment, unsuspected steel. "You finished, Floyd?" Marty said evenly.

"Hell no. I'm not finished." Waving his arms. "Yeah . . . I'm done forever with you sad sacks." A Floyd unsettled as to whether he was finished or not. It was comical and sad, but the comical only deepened the sadness.

Marty's eyes never left his distorted face. "Let me say this. Sara won't mind, and she's too much of a lady to tell it herself." Marty's tone was matter-of-fact. "Let's just put it that Sara has peed away more booze in a week than you've poured down your throat in a lifetime." As if struck, Floyd lurched to his feet, making a gesture of strengthless hatred. Marty's words followed after him gently. "Floyd, stay. You have only to behave to be welcome." Her voice rose after his retreating figure. "Help is here. Keep coming back."

The quiet at the table lasted through the sound of a motorcycle starting up out in the parking lot, a snarl and then a mutter dying away and there was no mention of Floyd after. He had been only a brief diversion before getting on with the business at hand, now advancing relentlessly around the table. Floyd had scattered Aliason's nerves, her carefully rehearsed words, even as now bearing down upon her was the whole inescapable matter of the Fourth Step. Absurdity overwhelmed. As if *anyone* on earth were truly capable of making a Fearless Moral Inventory. Yet apparently many members of the fellowship did so routinely, easily as you took count of your flatware. Now the man right next to her was speaking. He was Harry, dear companion of these evenings, but might as well have been a stranger talking a lost language. *Her turn.* Her mouth moved like a landed fish, opening and closing in silent gasps. Patient eyes were upon her. "I can't . . . ." Tears were pouring and she was blacking out. *"I'm sorry."* Still, they did not have to put a paper bag over her head, not this time. Marty's beefy arms were around her. "Don't worry. Some of us wait for years. Let the time come."

She nodded, blew her nose. "You going to be okay? Sure you will be." Surprisingly, she was. On the drive home feeling peace. In hollows, mists were forming. Spring's air meeting the still cold-soaked earth of winter. She was thinking of the Wolf Lake Symposium this summer and looking forward to its vacation and vowing to herself all the good things that were going to be hers to bestow on her beloved David.

* * *

The house had grown exceedingly quiet. Its structure, an even cheaper one in this latest downward progression of the Junior Morgans, strained and rustled in all but undetectable night airs. He found himself listening for the sounds of Al's car returning. He was both restless and weary and not going to get to the business of submarines tonight and reluctantly he picked up Al's checkbook sitting on the kitchen table. With suspicions he had long held and long put aside could no longer. *Jesus Al, Jesus. My darling you can neither add nor subtract.* Putting aside the checkbook, at once affecting and hopeless, he made himself a nightcap, sipping it as he made the rounds, turning out lights. On Al's chair her latest needlepoint, its pattern just emergent in the glory of its colors, was splayed like a miniature pelt of some mythological beast in the circle of her lamp. He left that one light on and mounted the stairs. On the bedside table there was the usual topple of books and the by now familiar, *Recipes of Royalty: Favorites of Kings and Queens down through History*, crumpled tissue, other scat of Al. He undressed, flopped down, and reached over to pick up a fresh title noticed uncovered in the slide of the pile of books. Intrigued by the jacket of this new one, *Early African Explorers*, with a dark river winding away into green jungle. Checking out the back cover and tempted to try its pages and chastising himself for even wondering whether the book was library or if it had been purchased. Not the kind of questioning he ought to be asking while getting another covert glimpse of his girl. Guilty over such innocent probing, not because it was wrong but for what was withheld, what ought to be his cheers, huzzahs for her progress. At least in her taking better hold of the precious structure of ordinary existence; each day her grasp upon its rude but satisfying iron seemingly stronger. A *wanderer*, after long absence, embracing again the things of home.

She was not, to be sure, Alison Morgan, a wanderer in epic mold, no kin to Conrad's young man of ragged harlequin clothes in *Heart of Darkness*, that classic burning spirit of pure romance. No Mungo Park, of which her newest book was telling, that restless doomed soul stepping forth on Gambia's shore to discover the two thousand mile twistings of the jungled Niger. She was, his Al, of a commoner tribe, of whom no golden tales are spun. These, the stricken and infinitely the more numerous, nomads without camels to carry them, never knowing the comfort of gilded tents. Hounded through wildernesses of the imagination more lonely and terrible by far, nevertheless they must negotiate strange wastelands with less resources; they carry merely the small backpacks of sustenance and courage that are passed out to the average samples of mankind. Physically they travel only minor distances, across the anonymity and swift forgetfulness of modern suburbs. Amongst the new real estate developments rising up out of bulldozed and burning stumps, the vexatious red mud and new earth around each new clotting of houses becoming the green lawns and flowers of Springs to come—from Azalea Heights to Spirit of Verona, from Dogwood Estates to Military Heights—they belong to families forever on the move. Not moving onward and upward, as may first appear, but sidewise at best. Not *towards* anything so much as *away* from something else, shaking the dust of communities where former names quickly fade and reaching out for those places of newly broken ground, ever numerous, where there is scant curiosity to learn the names of the new. No historical signs mark their trails, no monuments commemorate. It is no mighty *hegira*, nothing to conjure images of the granite chiseled face of Pioneer Woman, chin thrust forward and gaze distant and stoic as she jolts and rocks along at two knots on the front boards of her Conestoga wagon toward the plains of buffalo beyond the wide Missouri. This lady is different. Al Morgan having made her own forced marches carrying unpacked lamps with trailing electric cords bobbing behind on the sidewalk and lugging laundry bags overly stuffed with things tossed hurriedly into them. Journeys not of hope but of flight. The vehicle the family car, augmented perhaps by a Ryder van, because such moves are short ones and paid for out of the family's pocket. No packing specialists for such, no ordered piles of labeled cartons and masses of soft guarding materials here for precious things to be borne away in eighteen-wheel trucks with those familiar emblems of mighty enterprises on their sides. Preciousness wears away with too frequent moves. All the family pitches in, Beth and even little Boat, carrying what they can, clutching battered and loved toys, and it seems that there must be a hundred trips back and forth between the old community and the new one before the deed—the dirty deed—is done. And in the hopes, but mostly the anonymity, of the new neighborhood there is little remembrance of the old. The light and sullen pollen winds carry few whispers and a handful of miles can be a voyage of forgetfulness wide as the oceans.

She had come, Aliason Morgan, from—had fled—fires in kitchens of her making, blackened roasts in smoking ovens, demon screams in the night, sirens and flashing lights of local rescue squads, explanations that wouldn't wash, parked official vehicles in front of her home strangely often, the kind of excuses that run out, and an altogether too great knowledge of the firemen and policemen of Annandale and Springfield and Fairfax who, if not become her friends, were at least by now sympathetic and puzzled acquaintances. Put behind her was the curiosity and the kindness—painful kindness too—of former neighbors, the indelible recollections of the little clots of them that used to gather on the sidewalks in front of their houses, quiet in their speculations and respectful before the unaccountable and possibly the tragic. Eventually to disband and drift back inside the aluminum-sided walls of their own opaque and fragile fortresses, to the ordinariness of meal preparations and the colored flickerings of their televisions. To any number of better things that Aliason Morgan too was determined to reclaim as her own and which it was her David's hope. A hope which, if not necessarily springing eternal, defying the odds, once again was back.

▲▲▲▲▲

In her frequent, and seldom nourishing, musings on her husband's professional activity, it might have pleased Aliason Morgan to discover that with reasonable simultaneity the attention of others was similarly focused upon her

David. She would have found it flattering to discover that the *locus* of this attention was not in the office of his immediate superior, Dr. Tawney Gray, but was taking place in one of the exalted offices of the U.S. Navy's shore establishment. Yet had she also been granted the marvelous senses of Superman, making the stone of the Pentagon walls both acoustically, as well as visually, transparent she would have been the recipient of revelations more disturbing than heart warming.

For instance . . . . Well, no matter the 'for instance'. Let an imaginary camera zoom in on a husky middle-aged man in the Navy blue uniform of a Rear Admiral. The print on the bakelite name tag, which regrettably even these days admirals were now required to wear, overturning custom, and to the detriment of dignity, was faded and askew just enough to be unreadable. Just as its wearer would have it. For amongst the knowledgeable no one could fail to recognize the redoubtable Marshall, "Smoke", Madden. He was leaning back on a leather couch in an outer office of the Chief of Naval Operations and smoking a cigarette while waiting to be given the word that he could now see the boss. Smoke Madden's own reaction to these familiar surroundings was relaxed. But in the imaginings of Aliason Morgan the *ambience* would all be excitingly new, making a scene on which her eyes were bound to feast as upon a kind of glory. Here beige carpets, temptingly soft enough to lie down upon, glowed as if they had had a visit from Mr. Sunshine Cleaners only yesterday. Mahogany desks looked as thunkingly heavy as automobiles. The secretaries were matchingly handsome, ladies whose hands ought to be more at home with silver tea services than electric typewriters. This was a place reverential in its calm certitudes and the gravity of its decisions. A Filipino mess man in stiff white jacket with a blue and gold crest set down a cup of coffee. Smoke Madden said thanks in a humorous Tagalog phrase—souvenir of a dozen Western Pacific deployments—and the mess man flashed a smile of unexpectedly awakened memory of home and family so long and cruelly far away.

Smoke Madden had, of course, himself known this sort of beguiling grandeur and obeisance as a carrier task force commander and it rolled off him with an ease instinctive to the man. He was thinking instead of the retirement cabin he was building with his own hands in Western Maryland by the shores of a fine remote lake. Smoke, a standard if excellent product of a demanding system— Right Stuff and all that—that accommodated only small tolerances in deviation from it, was nevertheless, within the limits of his molding, an unusual man. It was not any protean attributes of performance, no record of accomplishment beyond that of the best of his fellows—that is to say, the count of so many MIG's shot down in scattered wars, his thousand plus carrier landings, etc.— but rather an unusualness to be perceived against the background in which he was serving this last year of his final tour of active duty. Amongst the large but vaguely organized personal staff of the Chief of Naval Operations of that era, men of shifting responsibilities but constant busyness, he stood out by his absence of ambition. He contrasted with the young hot shots, the eager junior rear admirals, the bright new captains with papers constantly in hand, all alike ceaselessly striving for extra lights of recognition, however fleeting and elusively marketable. His pride was elsewhere, being able to do well the kind of things that few men did at all; landing on a carrier's pitching deck; to have found his way a hundred times to targets in black night through the mist-shrouded humps of the Viet-Nam Highlands . . . . Where others must scrape and bow, turning themselves into one of Scott Fitzgerald's "high bouncing lovers," Smoke Madden was simply himself. Authentic. A rare thing in Washington.

Nothing more to prove, he waited close to dozing. Others, his fellow gofers, would have been jiggling a nervous foot, reviewing notes. Smoke Madden's notes were in his head. Idly wondering if this fellow David Morgan—a GS-13 located in some outfit called EAR—could be related to the man the destroyer *Morgan* had been named for. A long while ago, that old hull, surely razor blades by now, but still . . . . At the start of his naval career Smoke had been sentenced— that is how the man who passionately wishes to escape the poky world of the Navy's ships in order to fly looks upon it—to serve a year in the surface Navy before receiving his orders to flight training. *Morgan* happened to have been his ship. On the wardroom bulkhead a photograph of the long deceased Captain Morgan, face pinched atop his high-collared, old-fashioned blues, had gazed out sternly over latter generations of destroyer men. Part of the intelligence Smoke had already picked up on this assignment included his learning that this particular David Morgan was a Navy Junior. So, just maybe . . . .

The Assignment. Every day new ones were passed out, and from this golden office squads of these special men went forth to do their dynamic Chief's bidding. Swiftly generated tasks, meant to be solved with corresponding swiftness. The solutions, symbolically to be pictured like scalps of triumph dangling from a brave's belt, were brought back and delivered to that softly gleaming desk. If usually concerning something as easy, say, as a balky Commander sitting at some obscure desk in Materiel holding up dollars for some favored project, they also could include, on some stormier day, an entire shipbuilding program costing billions and some ship class that perhaps must instantly be redesigned into a new and more saleable profile. New escorts, amongst them the infamously inadequate 1052 class, had been redrawn by the nimble at this sort of thing on the back of an envelope at midnight. A not untypical mission might require an urgent trip to Norfolk on Piedmont Airline's early morning "milk run," and discreet conferring with the Commander of the Operational Test and Evaluation Force as a forerunner to certain creative tampering—"correction" the preferred word of these vigorous CNO messengers with their inexplicit portfolios—with, say, unacceptably low figures of hit probability for some new torpedo under evaluation and now under the procurement gun.

That sort of thing happening ever more often. The frazzled rectitude of the Operational Test and Evaluation Command, seldom distinguished by stands on principle, nevertheless had a way ever and anon of popping up in annoying acts of independence. With stiffened spine OPTEVFOR would take some vexing position that, if allowed to stand, could jeopardize the acquisition of, say, hundreds of sonars, bring smoky factories to a cold shutdown, upset Congressmen . . . in short, cause an impermissible state of affairs. Fortunately—fortunate in terms of expediting procurement, if not for those in the fleet counting on systems to do their job—any renegade feistiness of OPTEVFOR would seldom outlive a visit by a representative of the CNO. Transitorily stiff spines would prove accommodatingly frangible.

Now critics of this approach, disbelievers in the merits of platoons of hot shots with their rough riding ways, had a case. That the ill design of ships, the hardness of steel already poured, the poor concepts of years, and barrenness of imagination, the follies of acquisition going back for decades, could be cured in a jiffy, was illusion. *And yet* . . . . This kinetic Chief of Naval Operations, new in the job, committed, younger than a hundred of the admirals under him, could not help being haunted by the briefness of his tenure. Pressingly a whole mighty Navy needed to be turned around. Great limbs of deadwood lopped off to make the great trunk healthy again. Early on he saw that one of the great impediments to his leadership—perhaps the greatest—was the sheer impossibility of getting the bureaucracy to move. Inevitably this driven individual, to so many a shining hope, must choose other means, "out of channel routes," as it was said, to get the job done. Not the first CNO then, and not the dozenth, to be so frustrated, he must then make his own way, soar right over the gluey labyrinths—their thick fluids scarcely meeting minimum criteria for liquids at all, congealing towards unmovable solid a little more each day—of National Center. And if the methods of a leader cut from such cloth were often punishingly direct, well . . . that is the kind of thing generally forgiven. The Borgia Pope, Alexander VI, with his murderous peccadilloes and skirt lifting ways, Rome cheered for advancing skillfully the interests and the glory of Holy Mother Church. So might not the nation too, won by the results of this particular reign of naval leadership, eventually applaud its practitioners? Arguably things ought not to be this way. Indisputably they were.

Today it was not the Chief of Naval Operations but the Vice-Chief, Admiral Bernard Worth, with whom Smoke Madden was meeting. Yet it made not a particle's difference whether the CNO or the VCNO was passing out the assignments. Barney Worth was the CNO's alter ego. One of a pair of golden peas in a golden pod. Coxswain sized, charged with the crisp combativeness frequently observed in men wherein small stature and enlarged ambition are too tautly bound, the broad gold stripe and the three narrower ones on his sleeve seemed ludicrously disproportionate to his personal dimensions. As if all that gold out there at the end of his sleeves must make those diminutive arms difficult to raise. Yet the instant he moved, any sense of excessive burden was dramatically dispelled in the flick of a single taut gesture. The description "Napoleonic", not always unflattering, popped into minds. The voice was much stronger, more reverberant, than one expected. Not surprisingly, at the sound of her husband's name (keep in mind that it is Aliason Morgan's ears and eyes that we have presumed as witness to this private conversation between the Vice-Chief and Smoke Madden) her heart skips a beat. That her husband was indeed a remarkable man was, of course, a truth justifying her innocently loyal voyeurism. But, having sampled now this initial evidence of attention by the mighty focused upon her David, it would be better at this point that she withdraw from further witness. Slip away with dreams and illusions intact.

"What exactly do I do about this guy?", Smoke Madden asked. He liked his instructions explicit. In carrier Ready Rooms he was accustomed to pre-flight briefings providing his precise flight profile, telling him what targets to attack, what sequence of weapons to pickle to take them out. "Exactly?" Barney Worth winced. Perhaps he was additionally annoyed at the sight of this mere Rear Admiral—though older than himself—sprawling too comfortably on the expensive leather cushions, another cigarette newly and unapologetically lit dangling between his fingers. But Barney Worth checked his temper. In the mushy, democratically compromised, U.S. Navy, the hold over someone on the brink of retirement was slight. With a deeper breath than usual, Barney Worth was wishing to hell he had someone else for this task. But the challenges, large and small, kept piling up too fast to be fussily selective. "Keep your eye on him," he said striving for patience. "Let's be ready." Smoke Madden blew smoke ceilingward and watched it swirl. "Is he worth the bother, Barney?" In private, just the two, Barney. Smoke had known him *when*. The familiarity was another thorn prick that the now Number Two man in the Navy had to put up with. "Where's our sense of balance, Barn?"

The question, however, was one that others, even those of less skeptical inclination than Smoke Madden, might reasonably ask. If good marks might fairly attend some features of the U.S. Navy's administration of this period, a disinterested observer might equally ascribe to it the besetting weakness of an unwillingness to leave any matter, however trivial, quite alone. But Barney Worth, whose extraordinarily successful career had not known a setback thus far, with a *modus operandi* foretold as an ensign when he had encountered a single crushed cigarette butt on his quarterdeck and had tracked down the miscreant in a fit of maniacally zealous detective work, was sure as shit not about to be lectured on the virtues of balance. Goddammit, imbalance was Barney Worth's strongest suit. Had taken him far.

"Bet your ass. We may not be able to do anything when some A-hole like Congressman Duke shoots off his mouth, but we sure as hell don't have to take it when one of our own people stray off the reservation. Sea Eagle is shaky. One shove from the wrong jerk could topple it." Smoke Madden shrugged, not sure that fifty or sixty frigates really were all that important. Those tight little circling rings of escorts, allegedly there to protect the carrier, really had in fact always struck him as being survivable themselves only *because of the carrier's protection*. The tacticians had it bass ackwards.

"Find out, for one thing" Barney Worth went on, "if there are going to be any more of Morgan's articles. Those guys in the Institute don't have to be so fancily independent. Their building sits free on Academy land and we can yank it out from under them. What was that last thing of his, *Destroyer Attributes in a Changing Atlantic*? What is changing about the Atlantic Ocean? Barney's irritation, fed upon itself, "And what in hell does he know about tin cans?"

"Could be the guy's just writing what he believes." "Free country, and all that."

Barney Worth shook his head in emphatic negative. "Find out his game plan." In Barney Worth's Washington, no man was without a game plan. "Get this too. The guy actually busted his ass to fire a *secretary*. And for incompetence, for Christ's sake."

"From what I've seen, a lot of those types could use some firing." Barney Worth continued to restrain impatience, not bothering to explain the obvious to an amused face that refused to understand the thickets of this unique city. Smoke's next question confirmed his hopelessness. "Why not let Morgan's own people handle him? They've got a new hotshot boss. Someone named Sneedon." "*Snowdon*," Barney Worth almost shouted it.

"Anyway, they must have pinned that broad stripe on him for something."

"Don't you worry about him." Barney Worth cocked his head sagely, but then his voice lowered huskily to impart a mistrustful knowledge of newly frocked flags. "He's sharp, but he's still new. Solution to this one he isn't going to find in the book. There's more here, Smoke, than meets the eye." He turned his gaze away for a second, avoiding the eye of someone who saw *less* meeting his own eye. "Got a theory on this Morgan." The small man's shoulders hunched forward and his voice lowered. "His old man was a naval officer. Doesn't always mean anything, but they named a tin can after him."

"Yes, I know." Barney Worth regarded Smoke Madden with the surprise that any knowledge of a surface warship revealed by a naval aviator was bound to occasion. He recovered with fleeting reminiscence. "Still afloat, the *Morgan*. Twenty-two hundred, tonner, short hull, recently palmed off on the Taiwan Chinese. Anyway, the way I figure, the son couldn't make it into the Navy himself and he has to piss-ant his life away as a simple servant in some building down in Materiel. Now he's trying to *prove* himself."

"Could be." He had flown with enough Navy juniors to have an opinion there.

"Give it the *Gestalt*. I want recommendations. I can have his ass hijacked out of Materiel as fast as he can dream up his next critical adjective and he won't have a pit-stop short of East Gungywump or the Northwest Cape of Australia."

For a man such as Barney Worth, irritably prepared to detect the slightest signs of foot-dragging in a subordinate, there was no challenge in reading in Smoke's stroking of his chin a revisit of earlier misgivings. Barney Worth said exasperatedly: "*Smoke.* Have you read this guy's stuff?"

"Yes." Truthfully, the only way Smoke Madden knew how to answer. At least he had given the offending articles as much attention as he paid to most specimens of the printed word. But their very nature, encompassing grand strategy, discourse upon classes of ships, all fell outside the compass of his interests. His professional fascination had always been with technical practicalities, how you got a Sidewinder missile to lock on to the "cat's eye" of a jet target, the physics that enabled a plane to fly . . . . One night he had taken off in his F-8 Crusader with the wings folded—as the airman knows, that particular aircraft actually *will* fly, though recognizably not dandily, in such a mode—and then, discovering his forgetfulness, reasoned how to put his aircraft into a precisely timed zero "g" maneuver in order to gain the mandatory unstressful seconds for proper unfolding of the wings in flight. The kind of man successful in that caper was forgivably indifferent to tedious argument about the kinds of escorts to shepherd poky convoys. Gripped in a reverie of flight, Smoke had not noticed that the session was at an end until Barney Worth's peremptory throat clearing recalled him to the present. "I'll get on it, Barn," Smoke said.

"And right away." Testily. The meeting, from Barney's view, had not gone well. There was a nagging insufficiency, like a protracted session with too chewy a steak. What set Smoke Madden apart from an otherwise homogenized group of eager-beavers darting around the twin thrones of the CNO and his Deputy had never struck a sharper contrast. Remnants of earlier exchanges with Smoke were running loose in Barney Worth's mind. Irish pennants flying in an ill wind. *Damn.* His eyes fastened again on Smoke's ribbons which conveyed the splendor of his medals: the Navy Cross with gold star designating a second award, the royal blue Distinguished Flying Cross, its pattern almost invisible beneath a prodigal cluster of stars . . . . Aviators!

Now, there was very little in Barney Worth's still reasonably young life that furious ambition had not already earned him nor, plausibly, that he might not seize before his race was run. Such awards though were not amongst them. Yet neither was it Barney Worth's fault that fate had served him up no worthwhile wars. Vietnam, with its sluggish canals and tiny riverine craft, had mostly called for a "brown water" Navy. A lieutenant's war . . . or an *aviator's,* drat them. Now Barney's destroyer might have bombarded the Asian shore till kingdom come (and it had), pouring five-inch shells into the paddies and jungles, but the land was a sponge. Herman Melville had his own caustic description of similar shellings by French gunboats off West Africa a hundred years before. Barney Worth's problem was plain. The cleverest word manipulation could not conjure up images of heroism against an enemy not shooting back. Old resentments flared fresh in

Barney Worth. And right now, observing the state of Smoke Madden's uniform, he writhed inwardly. *Jesus, that uniform was an insult!* Shapeless, shiny with age, wearing grey smudges of ash, in its negligence was the blatant ease of an owner secure with his own identity. And yet . . . that miserable jacket happened to carry—with maddening irreverence—bits of decorative cloth for which Barney Worth yearned with an unappeasable hunger. Anger rose like steam in a kettle and boiled over. "Goddamn it Smoke! That uniform is a disgrace. You're a flag. Can't you wear a better one?" Smoke Madden was not immune to the outburst. He had a second of shock, his eyes narrowing. But this man who had ejected with runaway turbine blades exploding in his F-4's engine, who had spent six days in a rubber life raft and eaten seagulls raw, was—in the best sense, before the word's corruption into the trivial—cool. His smile returned.

"Sure thing. I'll be working on it, Barn."

* * *

David Morgan had detected Daisy's heels, orders of magnitude finer than his Viola's, clicking down the corridor before she arrived summoning him down to Dr. Gray's. Such calls to the good Doctor's presence rarer all the time. "*Right now,*" she added, *"tout suite."*

"Ah," he said with a wink, teasing of old, "for my Annual Review no doubt."

Daisy eyed him. No one better at dead pan. "You should live so long."

He popped in to Tawney's mockingly smart. "Morgan, aye. Ready, willing, and able. My Review, of course." Tawney blinked with lack of appreciation of the attempt at humor. "I have only minutes. Due at an urgent appraisal meeting on DIANA."

"I'm sorry I'm not invited." "I'm not," Tawney said. Shed, tossed aside for the moment in the seeming need for haste, was the comforting suavity Tawney ordinarily wore like a velvet cloak. "The Admiral has reviewed your talk. *Proposed* talk. Bluntly, he doesn't care for some things."

"Oh." He acknowledged the judgment with a seeming casualness but his throat was dry. "I gather that you feel the same way."

"Well, yes . . . I do." Lending energetic motion as a spur to what appeared to be less than total conviction. Tawney was now flipping rapidly through the draft pages of the talk liberally marked with red. "There are a number of . . . items . . . ."

The lazy *rascal* still hasn't read it, David said to himself, certainly not with care. Knowing his man. Even as David was equally sure that the Admiral had gone over the text with a fine tooth comb. Marching through it word by dangerous word. "David, before you get too crestfallen, it happens that the Admiral is actually yielding just a bit. Given the collegiate atmosphere of Wolf Lake, and so forth, he believes that it's best not to have us all in lockstep. Fortunately too,

Wolf Lake is off the beaten track. The affair is, as I've explained to him, sort of . . . *family*. What's said out there, even what's shouted—and you'll not be the first renegade to stand up at that podium—travels no further."

"I'm relieved to hear what you're saying, David said. "Because, believe me . . . ."

Tawney held up a hand against premature effusions of gratitude. "What I'm saying David, my boy, I'm actually not quite finished saying. Will this be"—he rapped the edited sheets of David's speech with pinkish knuckles—"exactly the talk you give?"

"Pretty much, I suppose. Though I'll obviously have to look it over again and—"

"*David*" Tawney's smile was strainingly sweet. "Once more. *Exactly?*"

"What you're saying is that Admiral Snowdon buys the text you have there."

"Bingo! Without a pfennig's worth of any other changes, David. Not a comma's insertion, the fact is"—Tawney interrupted himself to look at his watch, schedule impinging upon rhetoric—"the Admiral's being darn decent about this, going against his wishes in leaving a few of your precious jewels intact. He's skittish as hell about one David Morgan." Tawney paused. It was unconscious, but he was beaming like a politician at one of those hopeful junctures in a speech where applause ought to be irresistible. The pause drew on though until David found it uncomfortable. "I do thank you for . . . ."

"David." Tawney picked up his briefcase, touched him with the other hand. "You'll be able to get some things off your chest. And no one will have reason to believe that you've retreated excessively, sold out, or whatever silly phrase some people may choose to apply to a presentation of good sense and discretion. You will disappoint a few, those looking for fire and brimstone. So be it. Let 'em sniff their sulfur elsewhere."

"In short. Take it or leave it." Tawney winced, recovered. "*Take* it! Enjoy. Your girl Aliason has been talking to Tiny. I gather that she's counting on the trip."

"So be it." David's voice small. Taken. Well afterwards, when much had happened, become an item in a small and special history, all that water having flowed over the dam, David wondered if even then he had not been entertaining deep within a secret spark of betrayal. If "betrayal" it was. Not his word. Though that of others. Yet all along, he could tell himself truthfully, he had been thinking mostly of Al and the vacation she was counting on.

Just as Tawney, edging towards the door, the strain of hurry tightening on his face, unavoidably was thinking of his Tiny and certain distinctly glum prospects. For Tiny Gray, who these days never traveled with her husband to any of his usual happy places, not fair Lisbon nor sweet, sweet London, a man's town more than Paris ever was, was nevertheless an insistently loyal adjunct at every one of the Wolf Lake seminars. Long ago, in a different marital clime, she had accompanied Tawney to the first one, sharing in its uncertainties and initial triumph that had pointed the way to decades of success. Thus seemingly some dim instinct, carried forward from that time to this, unfailing as whatever keeps the high-hearted salmon fighting its way back up the stream of its birth, had graven in stone that this one particular trip must be Tiny's in perpetuity. It was not any sentiment resident in this fact though that was now revealed as the animating force in Tawney's currently spinning thoughts. He had in mind matters more practical—disturbingly, it had almost sounded to David, as if it were part of a deal struck—which was how Aliason's presence could pleasingly alter Tawney's own circumstances. In plain terms, add to the peace of his days by lifting from him a portion of the burden of Tiny's not unnatural demands for attention. Even confer, he could dream, tots of freedom. Granted that Wolf Lake's perennial handful of attending lady analysts were not the kind to set a man's chromosomes to boiling, still . . . . Gold was where you found it. "Tiny is always at loose ends at this affair," he explained, "rattles around all day and then drags me off to shops after the sessions are over. Now she'll have a playmate. Aliason likes to buy too, I recall. Together they can hit every one of the Indian curio places, stock up on turquoise, moccasins and so on . . . ." Other notions, pulled out of similar air, brightened Tawney's contemplation of prospects heretofore drear. "They'll get along splendidly. Old friends pick right up. Though Tiny has gone heavy on religion lately, regret to say. Nothing much to be done there except tune out. Come to think of it, isn't Aliason strong on it herself?"

"News to me." "No? Funny, I somehow thought that she was always heading off to some sort of inspirational gatherings. Anyway, best to let the women settle their own agenda." David's agreement there was drowned out in exclamation. *"Shit and damn!* Late already, and have to get to the E-wing of the Pentagon. But I hope you agree our talk was worth it. My vehicle waiting, Daisy? Super." Tawney swore heartily again. Yet, withal, one of those men not really meant to swear. There being a mismatch between his visible nature and the coarseness of words seeming too much borrowed. His swinging briefcase was shiny, like the rest of him. Life had rolled off him, rolling happily still. He flung back over his shoulder, "Got to rush." Do not hurry, David addressing himself to Tawney's fading footsteps in a curious, yet clear-eyed, neutrality of mood: DIANA will keep on its anointed course, whether you show up at this meeting or any other one.

▲ ▲ ▲ ▲ ▲

David and Admiral Waters had concluded their long promised luncheon meeting and after it the slender civil servant—shy of grace through conscientiously trying for it—and the distinguished old man, tall and erect in black coat and banded homburg, started walking. It was the heart of downtown. Street vendors with carts were out and hawking. Washington becoming ever more like a mid-Eastern city with countless junky bazaars. "I suggest we head south," the Admiral decided with vestigial manner of command, the unforgotten confidence in compass directions of one long on the sea. "Your generation probably finds it quaint, this habit of a walk after a meal." *No sir.* Not at all." David Morgan, given to irreverence behind Muddy's back, especially when around his mother, nevertheless unable to subdue feelings of awe at actually finding himself the focus of the famed old Admiral's attention.

"Good. Has its purpose. Used to call it a constitutional. Maybe what's wrong with our young people." David assented to that, more than half honestly. The luncheon had stimulated him, the Admiral's conversation giving surprising gratification and bringing an afterglow that matched the light of this crisp early afternoon. The Admiral had reminisced about distant events, names now dimming into history. Recollection of battles, their distant receding thunder, was a stirring accompaniment to the excellence of the meal, the darkened sunlight of their sherry, all of it a contrast to brown bag lunches with Billy. Those stories, David was thinking, should be taken from the lips of these old timers before they passed on. Especially he was fascinated by the year 1942, "the year of the naval professionals," as the Admiral put it. For better or worse, the Navy had to fight with whom and what it had when the war started. Muddy told of staff officers crying and jumping on their caps when that one prodigiously disappointing Admiral gave the order to turn away from striking at the Japanese transports in Rabaul. David recalled Captain Lead's acid perspectives; the difference was that Muddy had been there. So much of this must vanish when these men were gone, a wealth of stuff that would never find its way into the printed record. For a moment David had the fine tempting idea that he himself might become the preserver of some of it . . . but no. There lay another lifetime to pursue. His own magnum opus on the submarine was still waiting in the wings. Meanwhile he had missed something the Admiral said about Butch O'Hare. "The one they named that damnable airport after in Chicago . . . ." Muddy's pause went on until David felt it okay to say it. "O'Hare?"

"That's the one. Anyway, I spent some months on a carrier before the war and I picked up a lot I wouldn't have otherwise. Butch, who was in the Air Group, wasn't a first class airman, not as his comrades told it. But one thing he was, a masterful gunner. In practice shoots he tore the sleeves to shreds. A point to be made there." A point though left behind as Muddy stepped off the curb crossing Sixteenth Street. Like an old ship, seeking calmer waters after buffeting weather, the Admiral commanded their transit to Lafayette Park with its teeming squirrels and tranquil walkways and then led them around the splendid curve of the ellipse. The large but graceful bulk of the White House was a baroque of Grecian grandeur floating upon the greenest sea of grass. The Admiral was describing that small piece of history in which Admiral Joseph Richardson had opposed President Roosevelt's wish to deploy the Fleet from the West Coast to Pearl Harbor. "Oh no," his voice was suddenly strong. "Uncle Joe didn't want to do that. Told that to Roosevelt, who didn't like hearing that one bit. Fancied himself a naval strategist. So he got rid of Joe Richardson. You don't see men standing up often, but when you do it's a wonderful thing." "Yes sir."

"But FDR was right about a lot of things too. Couldn't let the Brits go under." Listening to the Admiral's words—with their certitude of dates and colorful asides to set matters in context, told without stumbling, ringing true—David felt transported, magically across time and space, so that his face was pressed right up to an imagined window that let him observe what passed between the two men of power. Gripped, he was watching the old sea-dog of an Admiral setting forth in no-nonsense fashion the perils of basing the Fleet in the Hawaiian Islands and the President, alternately solemn and jollying in his politician's way, vainly trying his fabled charm on a man possessed of vexingly too much backbone.

"The President wanted a 'yes' man." Muddy chuckled by way of postscript, "and he got him." He shook his head. "Though that's not fair. Kimmel was a solid professional who did his best. Washington kept him in the dark and sold him down the river. Our Navy's great for doing that, by the way. Yet for old Doug Macarthur, whose failure at Clark Field in the Philippines was shameful, letting the Japs catch all his planes on the ground, the nation poured medals. So how about that, young fellow?" By now David was barely listening to the old man's story. But he kept on looking at the White House, hypnotized by the strength of its face, the purity and grace of its columns. He pictured, against continually shifting images of offices and corridors, the drama and tension of its daily business, people striding swiftly this way and that, handling telephones with skill and panache. Good people, he told himself earnestly. He pictured himself too—that was the idea, after all—David Morgan, Defense Expert, drafting memos that a President might read, some kernel of wisdom insinuated that could result in an aircraft carrier churning off to the Indian Ocean, or perhaps one more submarine bought or, better still, one whole class of dopey frigates less. He guessed too at the unpleasant kind of things that went on there too, the scramble for status, dirty fingerprints smudging the chalice of splendid ideals . . . . But such reflections—and he was still holding onto the graceful iron of that curving fence, feeling its rough strength in his fingers, clinging boy-like—were not so much discounted as subsumed. The White House misted in his eyes, floating above that fine sea of pampered lawn, an ice-cream castle of enchanted hope.

His feelings, naïve as they were transitory, rose and then fell off—as such emotion must—a high steep peak. But a glow lingered. It is a familiar phenomenon, indeed the hallmark of Washington, that allegedly cynical town, whose cynicism is, in truth, only millimeters deep. Not its corruption, for cynicism is not to be confused with corruption, the latter being a different matter and, Washington's own, taken all in all, rivaling in depth the Marianas Trench. Unbelievers can never sell themselves so completely. A man might be carting away a million heisted, or otherwise noxious, dollars from his Government in a shabby suitcase and yet still pause in his fleeing, yanked up short in salute, hat pressed to his heart, to honor with wetted eyes Old Glory descending at the Iwo Jima Memorial. The people of Washington, those who scheme so and prosper so greatly did not come to make themselves rich, to assuage vanity—not consciously anyway—but with awe. Wishing just to touch, at the outset so reverently, that shining power *to do good*. Power to assure peace, Honesty in government, Long Life to harp seals, banish Hunger; in short, to change all the multitudinous things that burningly need changing. Into Congress, into the massive Executive buildings, it sucks decent ambition as irresistibly as an Alnico magnet scraps of iron. Arriving with an ever renewing hope and innocence and a still free-swinging view of the world. Born of that inexhaustible soil of American faith, rich as Iowa's loam that shoots cornstalks thirty feet into the pale prairie sky, upon a town that merely imagines itself knowing and disbelieving, they descend like starving birds to a bursting feeder. For one David Morgan, closer to home but kin to the many come from afar, it was the temptation to believe that he too could have a little say, even—dare he dream?—*clout* (favorite word of the time) in choosing the best ways of defeating submarines by the energy of sound. "So, my young friend," the Admiral said as David turned away from his rapt contemplation, "still think you'd like a try there?"

"Absolutely, Admiral, I *do* want it." Tessa would be proud of that resolute affirmation. Perhaps though he would have roused himself to it even without her spur. A man with many bills due and up to his ham hocks in debt, has mundane temptations as well as inspired ones. He had gotten so far as to wonder at the sort of salaries the exaltedly fortunate in there were receiving. "In that event David, my boy," came the heartily resonant, if curiously delayed, promise, "I shall do what I can." They were coming up on Seventeenth Street, river of roaring traffic. It sped in swift flow between banks of shade trees that had seen it all, past monuments to valorous dead. "Thank you. Admiral. I must be heading back now." Muddy was moved by the huskiness in Irish Morgan's son, a slim and boyish likeness of his long vanished friend; he felt the surprising strength of that handshake adding its own measure of faith. At the same time he was asking himself how an old man with faded stars was supposed to land a slot in the White House for some young acquaintance of shaky credentials. Muddy Waters, a by-passed island of history, getting nowhere in planting his own flags. "You must be patient, you know, David."

"Oh, yes sir. I realize how Washington works." Looking into those trusting eyes Muddy thought of Tessa. Not as today but when first stunningly encountered, long ago. Yet the images, past and present, were the same. A mercy of aging, also its torment, that eyes do not see the changes in those they love. Nor science explain how across great voids of space and time human desire transmits itself unattenuated, not a micro-erg lost, as for seconds now he felt everything all over again in its fervency of old, the iron of his long quest still hot fired.

For, as noted, seconds. The feeling itself was mere phantom; what mattered was its warmth. Muddy was a practical fellow, the limits of his imagination were his strength, but at that moment it struck him that something dear might actually be attainable. Thus his thoughts were spinning rather faster than usual. Faster than those of David Morgan who, even as he was feeling a fondness for the old man, should he have tried to picture what was going on inside Muddy's head would not have reached out first for images of say, speeding motorcycles in a cage. Yet things really were going around, even if clanking, rust and a few teeth flying off those old gear teeth, the apparatus just a bit out of control, like ancient mining machinery going berserk. Metal popping off even as it grinds away. Muddy sighed then mightily, and it was like a switch turning it off, letting it rumble down to silence. Still . . . Tessa. In pulling his silk scarf firmly about his throat, the gesture unconsciously symbolic, was reenactment of the naval commander's role; tightening cloth against the chill of a ship's bridge while weighing lonely tactical decisions. David only sensed the resolution and was buoyed. Trust, a wafted return of fresh hopes for himself, was expressed in a final surmise, "I daresay you get over there quite a bit." Lightly, but with respect, David waved towards the White House now hidden.

Muddy's reply, with its gesture of graceful depreciation, just the right twinkle in his eyes, was masterful. "Often enough, my boy." Thus hinteth one Muddy Waters whose name had been quite forgotten by a whole generation hustling away since in the White House, and whose visitor's pass, token of grander days, hung by an even slenderer chain than the old man in his gloomiest moments could imagine. "You shall hear." Clasping his hand on David's thin shoulder. "Yes sir." A David Morgan now hastening back to his world of Crystal City on winged feet. Yet he would have been genuinely disturbed had he realized the distressed state of Muddy's mind, the agitated beating of that sturdy heart. It would have saddened him that his own desires, more ambivalent than his robust affirmation might convey, were responsible for putting that decently antique gentlemen in a quandary. It was the *lying*, more than the difficult, nay near impossible, challenge posed by David that was bothering Muddy. In fairness, indeed in tribute, the gentleman had little experience with lies, even of the thin and indirect sort that, without his intending it, were by now a Byzantine carpet setting its own weave. Even in this city, where falsity was its meat and potatoes, his conscience could not take a lie for granted. Yet there are all kinds of deceits, and surely poor Muddy's, minor truly and meant only for the furtherance of romance, had to rank amongst the most forgivable.

* * *

He found Aliason, as he did too many afternoons, napping. So called naps, anyway, this late afternoon hour before Boat was called in from play and the start of preparations for the evening meal. Perhaps they really were just "naps." Hoping so. He didn't always want to know. The bedroom was silent and his girl was lying face down on the bed, her long hair flung like that of the tendrils of a sea creature across the whiteness of crumpled pillow. He sat on the edge of the bed and laid his hand down on the back of her head, across the part, its whiteness of skull a neat line of order cutting across a primitive wildness. She stirred, but barely. He watched her breathe, her shoulders rise beneath her thin blouse. How many times across the years had he not rubbed that head, kneaded that skull. For consolation, for migraines, to assuage sorrow, real and imagined, for comfort, for kindness . . . with feelings, sometimes honest as they come and at other times, as now, weighted with ambivalence. How warm her skull was. Feeling almost hot to his fingers probing with gentle intimacy. The medical books all said that the blood exiting the human's head was warmer than when it entered the skull and his fingers confirmed it to be true. *Good Lord!* It felt not merely that supposed fraction of a degree warmer but downright hot, aboil with all that was going on up there. . . . *Four billion years,* he murmured to himself, to make that skull and the little he would ever know of what was teeming up there. Four billion years, plus or minus half a bill, and here he was . . . . "Peace, my little one," he murmured, "we're *going.*"

It was all that it took for her to roll over and spring to sitting bolt upright. *"Really?"* A pale face, red-creased, confronted him with delight. Wide eyes, labeled 'raccoon eyes,' with their framing circles of darkness, description never more apt. "Really and truly?"

"Would I kid on that one?" "No," she said, "you never would." She was suddenly grave. Hand over her heart. "You didn't, I hope," she said, "have to . . . *compromise?"*

"No, no," he said, "hardly at all." Which even that shading, that last, he would have eased if necessary, but her gladness at the prospect he had released overtook all other questions. Instead he picked up the book lying face down beside her, half way open. Its jacket, glossy and askew, had a montage of pioneer aviation and aircraft on its back and on its front was the depiction of a painting, probably of Bleriot's gallant aircraft, first to cross the English Channel, banking with the Eiffel Tower in the background. He slid the cover back onto the volume, heavy and new, and read off the title aloud. *"Principles of Flight."*

"Oh yes, darling. And as you can tell, it's expensive too. But please say nothing about that. Because this book will be with me for a long time. I know you're skeptical. But you needn't be. Because it's an indispensable starting point. No one should try to fly a plane without mastering first the *theory* of flight, you have to agree. And that's what this book is all about. For instance, it really gets right down into things like Bernoulli's Theorem. You've heard of Bernoulli . . . ."

"Never."

"Oh, David, *of course* you have. I can see that you know all about him. And you'll be able to help me as I go along. As you help me in everything else."

She hopped up. Energized by happiness. "I'll make *you* a drink. Tonight we'll celebrate." "You call it," he said.

"*Wolf Lake. Here we come.*"

3

The registration line for the Twentieth Wolf Lake Symposium backed out of the hotel's Jim Bridger Room and wound into the lobby. The line moved slowly and David Morgan's business of picking up his badge, along with the bulky envelope containing schedules and banquet tickets and brochures of local lore, was some indefinite number of minutes away. The line lurched, stopped cold again. A briefcase in the hand of the man behind jolted into the back of David's knee almost collapsing it. A voice uttered hoarse apology. "Scuse me." The line made more jerky advances to the point where David could see the cause of the delay. Ahead, the line divided into a number of shorter lines defined by the initial of the attendee's last name. Cardboard signs, in the Symposium's thematic colors, announced the particular letters served by each desk. Unfortunately, due to the absence of the S to U registrar, the lady handling David's line, M to R, had double duty, having continually to hop over to handle the S to U types who otherwise would have no one. The man behind David uttered an oath. "Same-o, same—o. Like this every goddamn year." David agreed amiably, in truth enjoying the pokiness. Like many another attendee, it gave him a chance to collect his thoughts, spot old friends. Many faces were familiar but grown older, caricatures of youth dimly remembered, names forgotten. He had left Aliason in their room contentedly going through the amenity basket with its plunder of lotions and sewing kit and he wasn't in a hurry to depart this murmurous lobby with its comfortable feeling of a place where anonymity might prosper.

"Shit and corruption," his fellow in this bogged down business behind him went on. "Think about it. Arranging this show are the very guys who somewhere else are running big buck programs. Yet what you have are always the same slow lines, fucked up nametags, rehashed papers from years ago. What does that tell you about government?" "A fair bit, I suppose." Surprisingly, that neutral comment had a calming effect on his windy neighbor. The man's briefcase gave David's legs another buckle. "Scuse me again."

"No prob," David said again. "Say, you're a nice guy." A hiccup was like a form of punctuation, releasing another flood of voluble monologue, on the subject of GIANTS. How once they bestrode this special earth of theirs in numbers. David was listening with only half an ear but not a displeased one. The man's rough wit was humorous, even if his theme was an oldie. How even in Symposia such as this, GIANTS actually used to attend. Guys who truly *knew* something.

Had put their smarts to winning the Big One. Like Morse and Kimball. Yet you could reach out and touch them. "You know?" David felt a tug of a hand on his arm that told him that he could not entirely escape the man's personally directed attention.

"I believe I do." "Yeah?" Pugnacity receded, in swift collapse, to wistful suspicion. "Say, you're not a GIANT yourself?"

"Afraid I'm not." "Hey, don't be afraid. Doubt if it's easy. You know the kind I mean," the man's yearning was pure, distilled to essence, "guys like *Koopman.*"

"Koopman's here actually." David could not resist turning around full to enjoy the amazement on the man's face with its likeable sagging jowls of an aging iris setter. His jaw did not recover from its descended position for some seconds.

"Attending? Our high guru of Search Theory? *That* Koopman? Alive?"

"He certainly looked it to me." The line speeded up and soon David was picking up his material. The man behind him still muttering. "Be a son-of-a-bitch . . . *Koopman.*"

Back in their hotel room, Aliason greeted him excitedly. Everything was new, stimulating about this adventure. "Registered and all?"

"And all. Something brand new in my life too. A fellow in the checking line wanted to know if I was a GIANT. Practically accused me of it. "Confirmed it, of course. What else? Nothing but the truth spoken out here."

"Oh my darling you *are* one too." She touched him with tender respect. "My own GIANT. What a silly grin. I suppose you'll explain it all to me. I do want to enter into the mood and challenges and, oh . . . everything else that concerns you and this place."

"Well, you might look over some of the stuff for openers. Some of it's for wives too."

"I thought that this was called the Underwater Acoustics Symposium," she said, drawing out documentation from the thick welcoming envelope.

"They've partially re-christened it to appease the Oceanographers." He had settled back in an easy chair of the fine large room, sipping a drink, dawdling. "It's complicated." Wishing that he wasn't always saying that. "Finding submarines is mostly acoustics, ninety-nine percent in fact, but oceanographers like to peddle the notion that by more research, exploitation of special phenomena—'fronts and eddies' being one recurrent buzz phrase—that it's possible to make marvelous strides in the business." He watched her frown deepen. "But . . . ."

"Their baloney recycles in fashion. Like the locusts, which keep coming back, except that they afflict us much more frequently than every seventeen years. It doesn't take long for faces in Washington to change and with their departure memory goes too. Conditions are always ripe for old ideas in new dress to be pounced upon by each fresh young crop of naval officers who arrive with more enthusiasm than knowledge and are eager to make their mark. Shrewd old Beltway Bandits, like our imaginative Artie Perrozi, find a fine living regurgitating what was obvious, or what was bullcrap, twenty years ago." "I see...." But doubtfully so.

"Though the oceanographers are shy on smarts and though oceanography is amongst the least of academic degrees, they're long on purple prose. Fact is we've gone about as far as greater knowledge of the oceans can take us. But, though oceanographers contribute little, they have a lot of clout."

"And so they must be appeased. Oh, but darling, I hope that you're not becoming cynical." Why did it seem of late that others as well had that hope for him?

"At this moment, let's say, liberated." Possibly a little dangerous too, he murmured to himself without knowing for sure what he meant. Facing moods, still mixed, unsorted, forming within him. Taking a last swallow of his drink he debated fetching another. She started to ready herself for dinner. Rubbing her face vigorously with some potion, eyes wide open and reflected in her brightly lighted portable makeup mirror. A fighter on this front to the end. She who would go down with all flags flying.

"Humph." Impossible to tell whether, upon mirror or husband, that amusedly grumbled judgment was based. "I'm disillusioned," she teased, not ceasing the vigorous circularity of both of her hands' motion, "Here I'm picturing the oceanographers going on about the wonders of the waves, and the whales singing away and experts like you discoursing learnedly on your own little pulses of sound zipping wisely through their depths. All one big happy family." He grinned, raising his empty glass in salute. "Picture again, sweetheart."

▲▲▲▲▲

She had not accompanied David on one of his professional trips before and it seemed that everything she encountered was surrounded by question marks. The scene had changed too abruptly from the familiar every day impressions that clothed her life. From cluttered suburbs, gas stations and grocery stores she knew, she had been deposited amidst awesome beauty. Beauty that could frighten, as much as stir.

At the same time, the regular business of her life has been lopped off as with an axe. The number of new faces she was introduced to was both startling and intimidating. At home, the addition of a single acquaintance to her small and precious hoard was an event. She wore, like the other wives, a badge with her name handsomely penned beneath the symbol of the conference, a cartoon wolf with paw cupped to its ear, the creature depicted as pleased to be receiving waves of sound. Once she would have been self-conscious at such trappings, however innocent; here they provided reassuring identity. Many people, she was discovering knew her David. It gilded her pride. Mornings she awoke lazily. She had coffee sent up and began her day reading one of the Albigensian novels by Zoe Oldenborg, a heavy volume lugged all this way. Its tale was densely rich, crowded with semi-barbaric kings and queens, the march of brightly caparisoned armies, savagery that she could not bear. Yet she idealized the faith that drove these people and avoided thinking how little she shared in it. Each day she hoped that David would come back to the hotel to share a romantic lunch, but he was always busy. Lunch then had to be with some of the other wives, usually including Tiny Gray.

"I hope you're enjoying yourself," Tiny remarked this day. Tiny herself was discovering and making the rounds of abandoned rural churches, basking in the warm memory of their Good. "Every single minute, truly," Aliason responded. After lunch she wandered through bookshops and artsy little places, picking up things for the children. A ski shop banner proclaimed Sale and she wandered in. Though no one in her family skied she was drawn to the grace and gloss of the skis, the brightness and the rich feel of the clothing. There was a tall young man, burnished by suns of both winter and summer and she wondered if he was what they called a "ski bum," though it seemed too facile and mean a label for anyone so beautiful. His easy confidence made her nervous. "Now's the time to buy," he urged.

"Heavens, I don't even ski." "Got to begin sometime, miss," said the young god. *Miss*! Boldly he raised her arms level, did his measuring. She clomped around in chunky red boots seemingly better meant for the surface of the moon. "Feel right?"

She felt merely helpless. "Oh, yes." She noticed that his eyes were glacier blue.

"Well, my lady . . . ." She couldn't disappoint that smile. Some day, after all, one of the family at least was bound to put these marvels to good use. But a few minutes later, charge card exercised, while passing a window and glimpsing her reflection with its weird cargo of skis and boots, she felt sick. She hid her purchases in the closet, skis set upright behind her dresses on their hangers. Explanation for David would come later. Yet remorse did not last. She read more, dozed. When she woke the sky had softened. Time for David. But each afternoon, like this one, he returned to their room subdued. After an early supper, she felt him stretched out straight beside her in bed, wide awake. "Still brooding on your speech?"

"Hardly. Not for a talk that's all cut and dried."

She gave a cry, sat up. "Oh, my darling. You're supposed to enjoy this affair. Why don't you sneak off and play golf like I see so many of these men doing."

"Well, now there's a thought." More reflective words floated through the silver darkness. "Tomorrow actually nothing special," he mused. She sensed her man mentally reviewing the program, making choices. Here, the lecture maybe not to be missed. There, a workshop that might be foregone. "David? Here's an *idea. Don't* play golf. Let's play hooky, take the whole day off. We'll rent a car. I know it's an unplanned expense, but . . . . There are beautiful drives around here. I've heard wives talking." Her head was on his shoulder. The wind in the great pines stirred them like their own special song. Like surf, calling. Starting early, they followed a route that went close around the lake, a narrowing way against the face of plunging mountains. Clusters of cottages became fewer, stands of timber thicker. They glimpsed shining water, wooded islets, clumps of worn gray rocks. Hand lettered signs offered boats, bait. The signs gave out and there was only the wilderness road, which veered inland and climbed through stands of towering spruce filtering sunlight. They stopped for a herd of mule deer sauntering across the road. Abruptly they exited onto an open plateau, into dazzling cool. Far below a point of land jutted into the lake. Amidst its trees were low buildings and a flagpole flying Old Glory. All was tiny, a child's play village. He had slowed and now pulled off to the side. Announcing with a flourish: "There it is, my girl, Wolf Lake's Naval Test facility."

"So that's it. At last. It is still on your preference card, isn't it? Long shot though you tell me it must be." "For a twilight tour," he said. "When the hurly burly's done."

"Pooh to that." They got out of the car, she taking his hand, and they found a pleasing grassy spot and a boulder to lean against. With a box of crackers and a chocolate bar they made a picnic. Close by a sunning chipmunk quivered. A light plane droned overhead and she exclaimed. She *was* going to fly. She truly was. She vowed it and he let pass what he might have said. He lay with his head in her lap, looking up in at the sky, which was so blue that vision penetrated to the darkening recesses of space as she talked about Zoe Oldenburg's books and the Crusades. "I want to *go* there. The Tarsus Gate, Antioch . . . ."

"Someday, perhaps . . . ." She punched him playfully. "*Promise*, my prince."

He was shielding his eyes against that stunning blue; it made them ache. She popped another square of chocolate in his mouth. He watched strands of hair drift across her face.

"I keep thinking of Godfrey and Bohemund and Tancred, those first ones over the walls of Jerusalem. And what *drove* them" "Not religion, so they tell. Not a Christian in the lot, according to St. Bernard of Clairvaux."

"Oh, I know," she said impatiently. "Everyone knows *that.*" A bird was soaring in his field of view. A larger bird than ordinary, an eagle perhaps, a black form of lordly grace. "David? Don't think it silly of me, but reading that book I found myself thinking of you and your battles." He laughed. Laughter surprisingly soft and easy. "None near so grand." Yet the grandeur of the scene drew feelings out, gave them scale. "Nor is your guy all that marvelous either." "You *are* marvelous! Darling, please do tell me all about Electra. It is time."

"*Electra*? In this case, I'm afraid, it's DIANA whom mourning becomes."

"Don't condescend. You know who I mean. Or what." He told the story then, the part of it least that he knew, compressing a long tale, choosing a layman's language, but doing no injustice to the truth by simplifying it lying there looking up at the sky. Speaking steadily, not moving except to stir slightly at intervals to readjust his head. Going back to Langevin and his Swiss lake, not so different from this one, measuring the speed of sound in water with admirable precision. Afterwards they asked themselves why they had to journey so far for this unlocking here in the warm grass and the scented mountains. "Dear . . . ." Feelings of the moment rose in her chokingly. Such an awful lot depending, it seemed; the security of free peoples, treasures of nations, the future direction of navies, dreams of men; all concentrated here, distilled in the essence of this gorgeous air. He took her hand. After his stroking it she grew calmer, her voice natural again. "I realize yours is a special and mysterious world. But I can't bear your fighting battles alone."

"Not all that alone." He sat up. The ground had grown hard under him.

"You mean Artie Perozzi and that Pacific bunch," she said scornfully. "How much can you count on them?" Well now, there was a question. Not for the first time wondering that himself. He stood up, faintly dizzy. Out on the lake, far below, a moored barge was bright yellow against the blue. Suspended from it was DIANA's acoustic array. On the barge's deck men were moving about. Aliason and he walked back to the car hand in hand while she sang a childhood song, sweet and clear. The road descended, winding down the mountain face. The Facility came in and out of view and he was explaining how the Navy's test purposes demanded such a lake, acoustically pure, scoured deep by ice-age glaciers.

"They're testing now. Listen." He downshifted, for safety, on the steep slope. Between the gears grinding noisily and the wind swirling through the open windows she couldn't hear a thing. He stopped the car by a gate where a blue and gold sign announced: *U.S. Navy, Wolf Lake Test Facility*. "Now try listening." Faint squeaks, like new chicks, reverberated in the air, seemed to sing, bouncing off distant rocky walls. Gradually the attentive ear could discern a rhythm, periodicity to the chirps from the bowels of the lake. "Oh, yes I do hear," she said. Her eyes glistened. "I thought they were crickets. How can it be that such silly little clicks have all these people living by the lake in such a snit?"

"That isn't," he murmured amusedly, "the only mode that they experience."

"Whatever you mean by that," she said. He started the car. The guard in his little shack was staring. "Let's *do* look around," she urged. "Your I.D. card, I'll bet, would get us through. I'd love to see the Director's quarters."

"Afraid you would. Anyway we've still got a long ways to drive." The side of the lake where they were heading was emptier still. Marshes stretched away to grey eminences, bony crags. "Sweetheart, I'm starving," she said. "You must be hungry too."

"Daresay I could be persuaded to have a bite."

"Persuaded? *God.* Why can't a man just plain admit it when he's hungry?"

They noticed a thin pier far off stretching out into the water, then a sign, *McPhee's Crossing.* Eventually a restaurant and general store of weathered brown boards came into clear view. Both structures appeared unmanned, deserted. An antique gasoline pump, surmounted by a glass vessel of clouded yellow fluid, stood like a gawky sentinel. A faded sign advertised guide services and a seemingly newer one proclaimed the largest lake trout ever taken on four-pound monofilament line. From their halted car two visitors from another world peered out at the unwelcoming scene. "Wait, hold it," Aliason said, "I spotted a light on inside." The front door was unlocked. A bell, dangling from a strip of cloth, tinkled away at their entry. In dimness they passed into a small room with wooden tables, bare except for chunky cellars of salt and pepper. A woman appeared with a look of surprise. "No, not open, my dear," she said softly, "it's in-between seasons, no hunting nor fishing." She was grey haired and she read the disappointment on these strangers' faces. "I could, she offered, "make you something though, if you'd not mind fish the way we enjoy it. Simple-fixed."

"We'd love it. Simple is best, isn't it?"

In back, Leon McPhee was splitting firewood. A task of old, yet it was a decidedly recent evolution, the manner, that is—his having to use one arm, the other being in a cast—in which he was going about it. Yet even a casual observer would have been inclined to perceive an extraordinary resourcefulness. The traditions of the area, a father before him who had been a comrade of Ben Lilly, the legendary hunter who had guided Teddy Roosevelt through these heavens of high forest, would have reinforced admiration. His own younger days had included a hand-to-hand battle with a mountain lion. Ever since he was known locally as *Lion* McPhee. Yet looking beyond the obviously injured arm, one could spot as well an odd glint in those clear woodsman's eyes. For with every difficult, yet crisply sure, stroke of his axe, and in the new kind of artificial sounds that his keen ears detected from the water, from the normally silent and comforting earth itself, there was persistent reminder of the darndest kind of accident that had ever befallen a man. Mrs. McPhee was beaming over her guests devouring her savory fish. Mr. McPhee, she allowed, had in his creel the secrets of bringing summer trout to hook. "It's delicious," gushed Aliason. "I must get your recipe."

"Why, just butter and garlic and heat."

"Oh, David, now *do* get some white wine for yourself."

"Don't have no wine, I'm afraid," said Mrs. McPhee, "only beer."

"Beer will be wonderful. For my husband."

Mrs. McPhee had poked up the fire and now her husband bore in a load of wood mightier in one arm than an ordinary man could carry with two. Firelight enriched the spartan room, flickering over the large mounted trout above the mantel, honored loser to the four-pound monofilament. There were browning pictures of satisfied hunters and a tinted photograph of a boyish soldier with the features of Mrs. McPhee. "Howdy." Mr. McPhee shook their hands and got a beer for himself and another for David. He drew his chair close. Keen eyes knowing a couple of strange birds. "You with that gadget down lake?"

"Actually, we're just out here visiting," David said, deciding not to get into the Symposium, *et al* and sundry, about which his questioner could care less.

"But we are from Washington, Aliason added proudly. Touchingly too, grasping at her sense of place. Even such. Mr. McPhee looked his visitors over with friendly but shrewd eyes. Game pinned down. His voice had a rough rolling sound. Judgment, formidable but mysterious, seemed to await later refinement. "Reckon then you know what they're up to." He pulled out his pipe. "Catching submarines, hear tell."

Mrs. McPhee, bringing out coffee and cake, gave her husband a warning glance. "This young fellow maybe oughtn't be telling about such things."

"Ah." Mr. McPhee had no trouble accepting David's reticence. Reminiscing on his military experience. "In the Army." He spoke of North Africa, Tobruk . . . . "Hard on that, the bloody Salerno landing and marching on up Italy's boot into Germany. Son was in the service too later. Korea." He gestured to the picture. "Lost him out there."

"Oh." Aliason's eyes misted. "I'm terribly sorry." The fire crackled softly. In between crackles David detected, exceedingly faint, but unmistakable, signals generated from his special world. The power of DIANA's pulses increasing. The room was very quiet, an ideal low ambient against which to discriminate a subtle code.

"Pardon me," Aliason blurted into the quietness, more loudly no doubt than she intended. "If you don't mind my asking, Mr. McPhee, how did you injure your arm?"

Mr. McPhee rose abruptly and prodded the fire to vigorous life. Mrs. McPhee whispered quickly. *"My husband don't like to talk about it."*

"Please do forgive me," Aliason said. Mr. McPhee turned from the fire. He asked, "You don't suppose what's going on down lake could start troubling the fish none?"

"I believe the possibility was studied exhaustively beforehand, and a complete Environmental Statement filed and . . . ." But *ah shit*, David cut himself off. Mr. McPhee deserved better than bureaucratic verbiage of doubtful validity. Yet Mr. McPhee had a genially reflective side. "Fishermen are great figurers, of course, blaming anything real quick if fish don't bite. Seems to me they actually struck harder last season. But whether the Dolly Varden are going to taste so good, or grow so big, will take time to tell."

"Dolly Varden," Aliason murmured dreamily. "So anyway, you hear those funny noises up here too." Mrs. McPhee rolled her dyes. *"Do we?"* A smile awoke on Mr. McPhee's wonderfully creased face. "In the weirdest places. Well...." Time to be off and doing. He held out his mighty hand to the office-bred hand of his visitor. "Don't think we fret too much about the funny music they're putting out down lake. Some people up in arms, but most of us lakesiders figure you folk know what you're doing."

"Why that's a *wonderful* attitude, Mr. McPhee." Aliason sure that she would treasure this day, new friends quickly grown dear. Emotion quavered as she asked Mrs. McPhee directions to the Ladies Room. A stray note of concern had sounded in David's mind, but like a tune only vaguely familiar. Scattered clues, the folklore of his profession, the reticence of Mr. McPhee, buried knowledge of physics he was at the moment too lazy to dust off, the interval between these accelerating pulses of acoustic energy, plus half a lifetime sorting out the vagaries of underwater propagation.... Somewhere was an answer only languidly sought. Beer had relaxed him, the fire lulled. Also, divertingly, the image of Aliason going off lingered with fond specificity. Her cashmere sweater, her high red stockings were a revival of a fine feminine style that used to flourish before the onslaught of jeans. She swished off, graceful survivor from an age of romantic desire. A minute had elapsed since Aliason disappeared into the Ladies. Abruptly DIANA's notes peaked strongly. Simultaneously a scream, extreme but unmistakably human—unmistakably Al's—announced that it was too late for any warning. Amidst the screeching of a hook tearing from wood, the door banging open—her original scream not dying either—she burst forth, escaping with an expression of terror in a state of disorder and acutely embarrassing undress. Mr. McPhee hurrying in from the back gallantly turned away. *"Oh, oh...."* Sobbing out horrors. At once Mrs. McPhee was beside her, pulling her up, tucking her in. More or less. "Now, now... don't you cry. Reaction is only just *natural*." After other soothing words, the good woman drew Aliason back into the privacy of the space just exited. And minutes later, head held stiffly high with artificial dignity, pale but passably neatened, she reappeared.

Goodbyes were swift and fond. Aliason regained her voice, though still trembling with its recent enrichment of emotion. The McPhees would accept nothing for their hospitality. Voices were lost in the crunch of gravel. Hands kept on waving, figures grew smaller. "We'll never see them again," Aliason said sadly. Return seemed swifter, the road straighter. Aliason stared ahead. "Stop smirking," she said at last, "it was frightening."

"In time you'll be chuckling at the memory of it."

"You can be philosophical. It didn't happen to you. *I'd sure as heck* be signing petitions." Miles of dark road spun away in steady but not monotonous song. They ceased pointing out to each other scenery, endless variations of beauty. Her eyelids drooped and her head fell on his shoulder. She sat up yawning as they halted at the town's first stoplight. "Goodness," she said, "I didn't even know Wolf Lake had a newspaper." A structure of unpainted cinderblock, obviously originally built for more humble commercial purposes, announced its present identity by a crude lettered sign: *Home of Mountain Calls, Serving the Newspaper Needs of Plantagenet and Wolf Lake and Duke Counties.*

"Can't be much of a paper," David commented, "I haven't even noticed copies for sale." The towers of the college loomed. "Almost there." It had been an extraordinary day. More like a voyage, they agreed. Natural then that such a day must make room for promise, draw itself together in resolution. She snuggled closer. "I want so much to be of help."

▲▲▲▲▲

That simplest and best form of Aliason's help had been uppermost in his mind for some time. Happily, for sure, she had the same idea. "We don't *have* to go out to supper tonight, do we?" she said as they got out of the car. "I think all that trout will keep us."

Then, "What *ever* are you doing? Why bother even locking a rental car?"

Why indeed? As they walked rapidly across the parking lot, she skipping on ahead, there came music, faint and clear from a mile away. The orchestra at the college of music was starting its regular evening rehearsal. "Listen." He stopped with recognition, "*Marriage of Figaro*. Do you know why sound travels so well across water, hon?"

"You've explained it a dozen times, darling. Git!" Clicking to him like a horse and propelling him towards the hotel. A woman when she wants to—she was giving fresh reason to believe—could undress faster than a man. No ties to unravel, no shirts to unbutton. In seconds she had slipped herself gloriously naked. A moment when the usually excessive warmth of the American hotel room could be most appreciated. No unkindly draft touched her skin; the soft carpet was reassuring on bare feet. The room was toasty, private as a womb. "Stop fidgeting," she commanded." "Just getting my socks off," he protested.

"Why bother?" She laughed gaily. "Turn around. You can be so shy."

"I always feel I look silly." "Silly? It's beautiful." She gave a quick kiss in proof.

"Just a min'." He broke away and darted into the closet. "Got to get . . ."

"Come back here. You don't need *anything*, darling."

Muttering to himself that mostly what he didn't need, *they didn't need*, was another baby, he hurriedly pushed past hanging clothes; on hands and knees, an interesting sight, no one's best angle, groping through the furthest recesses of the closet. He flung several of her bags aside and had just got his fingers on the zipper of his own in whose side pocket he remembered tucking away the coarse, passingly effective implements sought when he felt a menacing rush of air. Something hit him on the head. With curses he scuttled back dragging the offending object which was long and smooth. He touched his forehead, fingered a lump, an ooze of blood. He looked at what he had extracted from the closet, strange as if it were a rock from the moon. "Some former guest evidently left a damned *ski* in there."

"Actually," she said, "two of them."

He stared. *"You?* Why?" Then, the more pressing question. "How?"

"Credit card." She waved her hands helplessly." "Our Visa, maybe. Don't ask."

"Hell's bells. *We're up to the limit on our credit there already."* He shut his eyes, his head spinning. He felt her take his hand. "Darling, *a suggestion.* Let's not talk any more right now." Her voice was soothing, sensibly in charge. "I'll get a washcloth and a Band-aid. Then let's back to that wonderful time we started out to have."

"Oh, yeah. *Great.*" But after some moments, and a few more surly points made, he saw the merit. With pettings and, as it turned out, *two* Band-aids crisscrossed, her wounded man was repaired. Hand in hand they walked over to the glass doors of their balcony. Against grey-black mountains, behind which the sun had just disappeared, the trail of a jet high up glowed like fiery snow. She glanced down. "Oh, dear, we're going to have to start over."

"Surprise, surprise." But those were David Morgan's last notes of petulance.

Wolf Lake Hotel would some day cease to be, its foundations buried far below the probings of archeology to come. The occupants of Room 306 on this night would be restored to atoms and all records of their existence have vanished in a mere wink of eternity. But for a little while those ordinary walls were witness to the power, delight, and mystery of man's creation. Happy animal lusts that marriage calls upon God to bless. No matter that the man was an unhandsome fellow with rounded shoulders and glasses that reflected the lamplight like orange suns. The crawl of life up out of the ooze, the prolongation of the human race, has never demanded perfect beauty to fuel the fire. There was curiosity, experiment, touching entwinements, eager teamwork, tender freedom; all the earlier dreams and hot fumbling of youth, it seemed, had been but a trembling on the brink of this new hotter age arrived. Afterwards she pulled his arm under her head. *"There.* What's that saying, *After . . . ?"* He said it for her in Latin. "But you're not sad now," she said anxiously. "I can't imagine that."

Later, in their robes, she insisted he rehearse his talk for her. He dug into his briefcase and handed over a wealth of notes, apologizing for the confusion of several versions. He delivered his pitch standing, his arm a pointer, gesturing towards imaginary slides. Sometimes she lowered her head, frowning over his text, "What about some of those other terrific sounding things you told me?"

"Scrubbed. This is the text blessed by Tawney back there in Washington."

"Sounds awfully like *censorship* to me." He gazed down upon his ardently loyal audience of one. All the while thinking, thinking . . . . Thoughts that came and fled and returned. Whispers of temptation. Like *what the hell.*

"Darling, you must have had a reason for bringing your older versions. I say, do what you must do. And devil takes the hindmost. Oh that funny smile. I know, you're going to tell me I don't even know what that phrase means." "Actually, I don't either," he said.

But then she was urging him onto still another rehearsal and encouraging him to add some of the thoughts he had told her before, and parenthetically he was inserting old forbidden phrases, and even buttressing his statistics with some of Billy Jenck's latest data, the numbers bleakly tolling DIANA's performance that he could reel off without even going back to his notes. "Oh, I *knew* it. You still know all that old speech by heart."

By heart. That he did. Well before he had finished the next go around, her eyelids were drooping. He lifted her, her heartbreaking skinniness, bore her to bed over drowsy protests. For a long time he stood at the window, looking out towards the cozy lights of the little town, winking with innocent appeal through the trees. Then to his pleasure there was something close by, and better, to contemplate in the moon's bright rising through the pines than mere endlessly recycling images of his ambivalent self.

▲ ▲ ▲ ▲ ▲

Lights were on late in the offices of the *Mountain Calls* with another strategy session. Amidst tobacco smoke and the stale oily smell of pizza remnants, the three officers of the Weekly—except for printer and layout man, the paper's sole employees—had been shouting. Passions reawaken in a family with a terminally ill loved one and, irrefutably, their baby was very sick. Indeed it was dying. Just a moment though they were silent—Andy Wirth, the bearded one; Mark Pacek, of black flashing eyes and ceaseless movement; Mary Burt, straight short hair and, like the men, wearing worn jeans—arguments spent, each touching gloom in his own way. They had been the Protesting Young of the early Seventies. Only a few years back a mighty wave of tumult had risen beneath them and their lives, like surfers, had caught its sweepingly collapsing slope at a speed too fast for reflection. Rushing shoreward from turbulent seas, it cast its children up on many a strange shore, its force exhausted but with hunger for a more beautiful world, for doing good deeds, intact.

Many escaped to drugs, others to doing pottery, some to molding candles. These three comrades pooled their monies and brought forth a newspaper where there had been none before and for a little while had it thriving. Novelty buoyed it. Collaborators in a new adventure, they immersed themselves in the region's lore, ran articles on rising costs of feed, features on apples, news of square dances and weddings, on fishing and hunting and adventuring in these dramatic mountains and steep valleys. A Wolf Lake College professor wrote a history column, serving up tales of French settlers whose loyalties banished many an Indian name and conferred upon remote prominences ancient titles of Burgundy and the Loire.

Yet in spite of their best efforts, circulation dwindled. The team, for all its ardor, had no enduring *raison d'etre*. No Cause. Yet it was not for lack of trying. They took up the problems of the local Indians, but the tribes' capacity for passion had grown soft on the Reservation, been numbed by alcohol. The paper anointed itself Protector of the Coyote, but the local ranchers were only amused, and the dubiously benefited animals bought no papers. Ditto for the eagles. Gun control was the next Issue, but this was a region where the young had rifles pressed to their plump little shoulders as tots. The paper took on the Federal Government, stupid regulations, the prodigal waste of tax dollars, bombers whose wings fell off. . . . Alas, its fiery scorn was like a match thrust in a bucket of water and dismay dawned on the trio that they had cast their lot amidst a last refuge of primitive patriotism. Flags flew before many a humble home; no war was so mean or muddled that it was not remembered with pride. In ten thousand square miles, thinly populated by ranchers and hunters, no human voice seemed able to raise itself to appreciable volume. Geological mightiness walled in, diminished, human plaints. City bred, sentimentalizing nature, the newcomers could not comprehend those who had known it for generations as a brutal adversary. Amidst grand mountains, a matching nobility of spirit ought to flourish, right? Instead, these baffled crusaders encountered humdrum people, lives narrow and accepting. *"Stones,"* Mark Pacek said bitterly—borrowing words from Ché Guevara's despairing diary entry there amongst the Andean peasantry—"it *is* like trying to rouse stones."

"Yep," Andy Wirth agreed. Yet he was different, as Mary too was different, from Mark who was the true and fierce revolutionary. The other two were not, as they were discovering, three peas in a pod. All week Mark had been keeping watch on the scientists here for the Symposium, discerning a majority of the attendees skipping sessions wholesale, availing themselves of the golf course, playing tennis, lazing in canoes. Mark had skulked behind trees, observed jolly picnics, listened in on chatter, gotten careful count of idling truants, thence taken his evidence to the Man in the Street for samplings of presumably matching outrage. The reaction of one Albert Thatcher was typical. A beefy unhurried sort, he pushed his expensively proud Stetson back to listen amiably. Eventually he broke the flow of Mark's indignation, but still regarding his intense young questioner, indeed the whole errant world, tolerantly. "Cain't blame those visiting folk wantin' to relax. Why a few years ago I took the wife and the kids back there to Washington. Seen all them cars and breathed that smoke. *Ooo-ee*. Sure can understand a fellow enjoying skipping out on all that."

"Yes, Mr. Thatcher, *yes*. But do you realize that every one of these hundreds of persons in alleged attendance is out here screwing off at government expense?"

"That a fact?" Scratching away at a head, which had pondered not at all on such matters and was loath to still. He chuckled. "Well, don't reckon I'm any poorer 'cause of it."

In the offices of *Mountain Calls* it had grown quiet again. *"Jesus!"* suddenly burst forth in frustration from Mark Pacek. Seeing what he had come to. He pictured the revered Ché, riddled corpse naked on a slab while militia figures gawked. Mark's eyes misted. Not for Ché but the living Mark. Himself one of the East Lansing Five who, this shrunken latter day, had spent hours in petty trail of government goldbricks ducking their responsibilities. His fingers drummed while Mary and Andy braced for some new form of fury that was about to come forth. He was their flame. "It comes to this. We've *got* our Cause if we play our cards right." It was all there in Mark's mind, swirling around. Abruptly, with a broad magic marker he dashed off a bold headline: *"WOLF LAKE NAVAL TEST FACILITY—MENACE IN OUR MIDST!"* He returned his gaze to the skeptical eyes of his colleagues. Saying to himself, you two are changing. He shoved aside that depressing thought; blood hot, the Mark Pacek again whose voice one spring had pied-pipered four thousand fellow students out of classes not to return until fall. *"Okay guys. Think.* It adds up. The woman in Antlers Town who bumped her head. *Six* stitches, man. That guy, McPhee, on the West Shore who broke his arm. How about that old lady out in whatsitsname who was flown to a psychiatrist in Laramie? For Christ's sake. No one ever has had to visit a shrink up here before. *No one. Yes*, Andy?" "These events are widely scattered. Dramatically, they don't add up to much."

"That's why we are their voice. *Andy baby, Mary*, what's a newspaper for? To find the pattern, knit it together. How about the distracted school kids? The toddlers growing up afraid to poop. The rainbow trout losing its colors. Wild geese shunning the place. Okay, maybe it's not happening quite that way. But people *are* bothered. Putting up with it only because they believe The Great Father back in Washington knows best. But what if they find out the beast doesn't work so hot? That the fucker never will."

Mary wet her lips. "And how do we know that?" Mark slapped his surreptitiously procured material down, spread it out with the flourish of a Las Vegas dealer, cards, folders, schedules . . . . "It's called, I've learned," he purred, 'DIANA'."

"Okay. And it *doesn't* work?"

"Not as it's supposed to. Those anyway are the vibes I pick up." Mark pushed a folder over and, part way down one listing, tapped his finger. Whose title Andy obediently read aloud. *"Non-Linear Acoustics In Classic Vortices of an Ideal Fluid'."*

"No, numb nuts, the one *below. 'DIANA, An Appreciation.'"*

Andy rubbed his chin. "Maybe he likes it. After all, it's an appreciation."

Mark's eyebrows shot up. "I hear otherwise. That this guy is an oddball, has a way of straying off the reservation. But we won't know unless someone attends, will we?"

"And that someone is to be me," said Andy Wirth wearily.

"Hey, pal. My face is too well known," said Mark. "You got the beard."

For a moment Andy's and Mary's eyes met. She put her hand on his arm. *What?*" Mark, a tiger ready to spring. "It . . . it bothers him. Sneaking in."

Andy raised his head, the picture of a troubled man. "It just strikes me as wrong."

"It would be a bigger wrong if this region had no newspaper and none of us had a job." It grew very quiet. A car passed and not another. From up the street came the burst of a bar's revelry, giving way to a mournful ballad of the High Plains. Out past filling stations and darkened hamburger places, a coyote howled. As if it were a poker chip, Mark casually flipped to Andy a rectangle of cardboard reading "*Underwater Acoustics Symposium.*" "I picked this up off one of the tables outside the entrance. Just fill in your name and clip it on."

Andy kept turning it over. "It's that easy? What name do I use?"

"Shit, pal, think up one. With that bunch, weirder the better."

▲▲▲▲▲

The rest of this night David Morgan hardly slept a wink. Moonlight flared off the snowy flanks of mountains, set the glossy needles of pine trees alight. It glittered off the lake, a lively sword of silver pointed at his heart. Brightness beat upon his eyelids like the wakefulness of day and merged insensibly into the paleness of dawn and he was touching again the crossed band-aids on his forehead. Early, a cock crowing, Aliason sensed his restlessness. Sensed it from the depths of perfect relaxation and conferred additional blessings of calm. Her eyes still shut, murmuring kindness, her hand giving it. One hour's rest conferred anyway, this late last scrap of night, and when he had showered and slipped out of their room he felt strangely marvelously buoyant. Too keyed up for breakfast he went straight to the auditorium and was, as he had hoped, first to arrive. He ran through his slides and waved thanks to the projectionist in the booth. He could not describe his own mood, did not try—borne on a magic carpet of confidence, perhaps merely a mood of mindless daring—but it had its beginnings in yesterday's trip and, early this morning, the feeling had reached a crest now carrying him along at a marvelous and yet seemingly not dangerous clip. It was more than the peace of satiety. Faint but sweet music was playing; words of praise rode the waves of its melody. Remembered words, strong and specific towards that male event, however indiscriminate and, for all the lost numbers of its reenactment, like unto the grains of the sandy shore—that could still carry with it more than a touch of wonder, the force of life's mystery. Size, texture, mighty root—adjectives for both sword and velvet—had been summed in his mate's dreamy description with a clinician's precision, an artist's passion. Not that he dwelled upon the details, simply absorbed their glow, the recall of a special respect.

It is private knowledge and history does not record its effect on the lives of men. Yet the beginnings of countless acts noble, as well as impulses quixotic, may lie untraceably in the warmth of such hidden memory. Alexander the Great apparently did not need its spur, nor Napoleon, but many an ordinary man it has catapulted onto the stars. David was still at the lectern, lost in his daydream of worthy rebellion, when attendees for the morning session began drifting in with their styrofoam cups of coffee and licking their lips over just gobbled doughnuts. The senior entourage, the Admiral and Dr. Gray, entered followed closely by Julius Baumgarde who asked David about his bandages. "Small wound."

"Not so small, I'd say." Julius staring with undue thoughtfulness.

"Don't be alarmed, Julius. There's no sked change. Just finishing a quick rehearsal." Julius looked relieved. His recent days had not been easy. He appeared run ragged by details. Tawney Gray, true to form, having dumped the whole show upon his shoulders. Julius mustered a weak smile. Something here, at least, presumably under control. "Good luck." His blessing almost lordly. "Don't try to change the world, eh?"

"*Jaime.* Nothing but the facts. You know me, Julius."

But Julius possibly had noticed numerous penned markings on David's copy of his talk, inexplicable for a presumably rigidly approved text. He may also have observed David's head momentarily bent in some shared communication with that renegade pal of his, Billy Jencks, their exchange of winks. Whatever, Julius taking his seat looked more glum than before. The abiding discomfort of ambition. David settled himself into a seat well off to one side. Long morning yet. Awareness of impending folly, of possible consequences, touched him but only lightly. He was beyond that. He was still floating with righteousness predominating. *These things have to be said. Overdue.* The Emperor and his absent clothes and all that. Telling himself other things to stiffen his spine should it give signs of wavering.

Out in the lobby, bathed in low slanting light and slashed by angular shadows, the long tables set up at the conference's beginning were still there. Piles of schedules, stacks of extra blank name tags, other paraphernalia of worthy organization, were there as well. Coffee urns and the trays of doughnuts were set out too just as at the start of each day. But whereas on that bright opening day near a week ago, with its jolly start and imposing machinery of administration created for a gathering seemingly scarcely short of eternal, now the ravages of thousands of careless grabbings were plain. Stacks of folders had toppled into disarray, tablecloths were stained. Tobacco ash from unemptied trays swirled across surfaces like grey ghostly spiders with each opening of the outside door by hurrying latecomers. A doughnut was mashed into the carpet like a flattened beast on the highway.

Noticeable too by their absence were the generous numbers of ladies who in the conference's early days had graced these tables. Beaming eager smiles, colorful in their tasteful best, they had put Wolf Lake's best foot forward. Courteous, efficient, attentive to security—women who truly believed in dire consequences to their country if one single unauthorized visitor were to slip in—they were the admirable bloom of pre-liberated womanhood. The same kind of women who make golf tournaments go, dressing alike in cutesy theme skirts and carrying players' scorecards. Exuding warmth, a wise jollity, the strengths of reasonably happy marriages, and conveying a sense of possessing greater talents than these limited ones on display. The cream of Wolf Lake College's small society, faculty wives brimming hospitality to the outlanders. But there are cycles in enthusiasm and, the first flush of excitement passing, these worthy ladies were less to be seen. Remembering they had houses to clean, children needing attention, groceries to be gotten in. Inexorably their numbers dwindled and this morning, symptomatic of élan's decline, what with one excuse or another by all these good volunteers feeling the tug of elsewhere, Millie Doss found herself alone in charge. Millie, secretary to the Department of Social Sciences, had no family, felt no tug of elsewhere. Millie was not first team.

Not that she wasn't trying, was not willingness personified. But the numbers of attendees were great; they surged, swarmed messily over the trays of doughnuts, clogged the working area, ignoring Millie's gentle ministrations about showing their badges. Against such a crowd, whose flood the increasingly panicky lady imagined might be carrying in with it dozens of unidentified agents of hostile foreign powers, poor Millie was reduced to fluttery movements and peeps of feeble protest. Now lights in the lobby were blinking and like a suddenly unclogging drain the mass of people was swiftly sucked inside and there was silence, as after a tub's climactic gurgle in the wake of its water's vanishing. Ah. Anway, *gone*. Millie contemplated the empty lobby, more trampled doughnuts. And with her sigh, a core of exquisitely good sense, which even unto this day many women work to hide, whispered to her the truth that it didn't matter a hoot in hell who sneaked in. Another straggler appeared striding swiftly for the entrance, looking neither right nor left. "Oh, *sir*," Millie calling out not peremptorily though, not harshly; more than anything actually grateful for the man's loneness. This stranger representing the possibilities of conscience's redemption, the chance to prove—if only to herself—that she could handle this sort of thing properly.

"Oh?" The man looked startled. Andy Wirth's heart had flipped. Not having thought this caper through very far. Barely at all in fact. Brass alone meant to carry the day.

"Sir, I must see your badge," Millie said.

"*Forgive* me. Here." Turning its blank shiny face, which was pinned to his jacket, fleetingly her way. But Millie was too alert. "Sir, you haven't got your name on it."

"I haven't?" As the trapped so often do, he smiled. Shaking his head over such forgetfulness. "*Mea culpa.*" An ordinary smile, with extra ingredients of charm, still he could not realize how it saved. For if one part of Millie's motivation was to be recognized for conscientiousness, her stronger companion was a chronic sense of unfulfilled romance. And all these men of the Symposium, gobbling away at their donuts, surpassingly indifferent to her existence, bore the golden gleams of distant travels, exciting lives. Now leaning contritely over her table was this nice looking young man paying Millie more personal attention in seconds than she had received the whole week. "You've managed to get in each day with your pass like *this*?" she said with exaggerated disbelief.

"Ridiculous, isn't it,?" Andy said. "But then no one else has been so sharp-eyed. I guess the thing to do is for me to sign it right away."

"Better late than never, I always say," Millie said gaily.

Giddy with attention, she watched him sign. "What an unusual name. 'Fomalhaut O'Higgins' . . . ." She started down her list of authorized attendees, but half-heartedly, not wanting to forfeit precious seconds available for looking into those dark sincere eyes. "I suppose you're a 'Doctor' too." Modestly, Andy lowered his eyelids and gently corrected her pronunciation of his borrowed name. "It's the name of a star."

"There are so many strange, excuse me, I should say *interesting*, names among you. There's another one about a star. Let's see. Yes. Here we are. Antares Antonescu. And, oh, here's a dilly . . . Tanaquil Iandello."

"And Telemachus Agammemnon," Andy volunteered inventively.

"You know so many, I'm sure, that I've never heard of. Of course we all know of Athelstan Spilhaus. His little tutorials are all in the funny papers."

"Good old Athelstan." She was transported. "You know, I don't actually recall you. But then so many of you do look alike, if you'll pardon. So many beards."

"Yes, well, shaving can be a problem out there at sea," said Andy Wirth, whose closest exposure to any body of water resembling a sea was a glimpse of Lake Michigan during the 1968 student riots in Chicago's Grant Park. *Out there.* For a moment, through the detached spaces of Millie's mind, a blade-winged albatross soared across the face of a mighty swell. The mysterious seas! Her morning was fulfilled. "Oh dear, I'm detaining you. I'm sure things have begun. But do get yourself coffee first."

Andy Wirth pointed obediently to the hand-lettered sign, obviously prepared in some haste and dismay, forbidding persons to take food into the auditorium. "Oh *that.*" Millie's wave was spirited manumission. "My goodness. They're *all* doing it."

He took a place in the back where there were many empty seats. A person announced as Dr. Baumgarde came to the podium to pass on various administrative items. The next coffee break would be last chance to sign up for tonight's farewell cocktail party. Also, reference documents on today's talks were available in the Lobo Room. Finally, Lost and Found had an unclaimed five iron picked up on the fairway of Wolf Creek Country Club. Julius' voice now turned somber. Admiral Snowdon had a few remarks to make. A murmur swept through the audience at the unexpected. "What's the story?" Andy whispered to the small man who had just plopped into the seat beside him. Billy Jencks' smile gleamed with an insider's special delight. "*Pissed.* That's the story . . . ." The Admiral, splendid in uniform, spoke without notes, a microphone amplified clearing of his throat preceding. "I am disappointed in many of you gentlemen. At great trouble the Office of Naval Research has arranged this Symposium in order that the members of the ASW community—its very cream—can enable our Navy to advance. Yet regrettably many of you persist in treating this event as a *lark*. You start off well enough, bright-eyed and bushy-tailed, but as the day wears on more and more of you seem to . . . melt away. To the tennis courts and to other hedonistic pursuits, and also, I gather, drifting off to an establishment I have learned of only lately known as the 'Grizzly Bear' . . . ." To a ripple of laughter the Admiral's response was stony. No one in the audience moved. The lives of most, measured in dollars, stood on that stage.

"Values." He gave them time to ponder values. "They are why we are strong. And yet, without discipline we will weaken. Lift your imaginations. Picture the Atlantic Ocean, once an American lake. Long our protective moat. Today, that moat is filled with prowling sharks of an unfriendly power whose values are abhorrent." The Admiral's right hand rested casually in the right hip pocket of his blouse. Unafraid of a pause.

Billy Jencks felt a thrill of shared professionalism. However different their circles, the Admiral was, like himself, a Toastmaster. Good speaking techniques were not accidental. "Those sharks are nuclear submarines. We have made great strides in controlling them and in your products, such as DIANA, you have opened up new worlds of promise. Between us, the Navy and the private sector team, is a tremendous store of talent that can make the future happen. Enough said." Well, not quite enough. "Congress looks closely at affairs such as this one, demands we justify the taxpayer's money. Frankly, this could be the very last Symposium of Underwater Acoustics." The Admiral let that thought sink in. "Let us, this final full day, set an example of which we can be proud."

Andy Wirth let out a low whistle. Wow. *Good stuff,* an unexpected bonus. He leaned over to his neighbor. "That 'DIANA' he mentioned, is the same one that's—"

"Making all the ruckus?" Billy chimed in happily. "Stick around," he confided warmly. "You ain't heard nothing yet." But Billy had glanced at his questioner with surprise. Assuming the whole world must know of DIANA. Of course, this guy might be into submerged structures and borers and such. Worm types never knew anything but their worms. "What's going to happen?" Andy wanted to know. "With the people? What are they going to do?," Billy waved rhetorically. "Why, thay'll keep right on melting away. Hey, golf is still winning." Billy's cynicism, mere molecules deep, never cheerier. Truth to tell, at this, his first Symposium, attending to countless details, arranging limousines for the important and contending with multiple foul-ups in room reservations—all cutting into his chances to make it to many of the sessions—his spirits nevertheless remained high. Though it would have wounded him to hear it, Billy was the perfect "gopher." And by next time, when that kind of crap duty was passed on to some other willing munchkin, Billy might have earned the right to deliver a paper himself. Thus there doggone well had better be a *next* time. No more rumors of cancellation! Such concern though was mere shadow. For however unexalted his role, buoying him along were high and secret expectations shared only with his special friend whom Billy had been prodding all along to herald ADAMP's utterly damning numbers. Even if his friend David had been doing a bit of waffling, things at last seemed on track. Billy's nerves twitched with excitement. Truth, with banners, was going to fly.

At first, Andy Wirth paid dutiful attention. A credit to the journalistic profession, doing his best to understand *Improvements in Barium Titanate Transducer Elements.* He grasped momentarily, and then quite lost, just what was happening in *Low Frequency Propagation in the Arabian Sea Basin.* For the papers came too fast, one every twenty minutes, and relentlessly the moderator hustled the presenters onward. Even the wise grew numb, weary of squinting at dense graphs, straining to make out ordinate designations too tiny to read. In the darkness and steady rain of droning voices Andy Wirth felt little men dancing gently on his eyelids. He roused himself for *Skull Structure of Acoustic Sensing in the Porpoise,* charmed by strange squeaks and beautiful photos of our slippery grinning friends, before going down for the long count. He woke up conscience-stricken, picturing himself letting his paper down, and started copious notes on *Wave Coherence in Bottom Interactions.* "No notes," his new acquaintance reminded. "*Classified.*"

"Oh, sorry." He snapped his notebook shut. "Right. Forgot."

"Don't worry," said Billy consolingly. Feeling that he may have been a bit short with his unknown colleague, though it was odd that the man did not know better. "All tired stuff."

"You're kind," Andy Wirth had grown to like it here in this dim murmurous auditorium, having an inkling of what many a long time devotee of the Wolf Lake Symposium comes to feel; that one could doze contentedly forever in this untaxing embryonic darkness.

"Hey. *Now.*" It seemed that not an hour, only seconds had slipped away before Andy Wirth heard urgent whispers and felt a light touch on his shoulder. In this dream he had been drifting down a strange jungle river on an odd grey warship, bumping into slithery creatures. The awakening hand shook him again. Now firmly, Billy determined that this fellow not miss the *piece de resistance*. "Here's the baby you've been waiting for."

▲ ▲ ▲ ▲ ▲

Even in the immediate aftermath of the morning's presentation, signals reached Aliason. Invisible current coursed through the quiet artsy lanes of Wolf Lake village where she was shopping with Tiny Gray. Something Had Happened. It showed itself in the expression of the attendees, a resurgent, if transitory, vitality on faces sated with golf and tennis. Some men that passed her she knew, and yet it seemed that when they waved to her it was with surprise and then, reflectively, a kind of salute. They were laughing, clapping one another on the back. Maddeningly she could not tell what they were saying.

The event showed itself in paradoxical ways, which Aliason could not sort out. At the farewell luncheon for the wives women came over to her to talk to her, making a point of it, women whom she had barely known before. Perhaps to touch an instant celebrityhood not yet clear. Other women, some women Aliason knew moderately well, hung back. As if unwilling to trespass on some newfound respect, not wishing to touch, and possibly dispel, an aura which mysteriously she had just acquired. While other women sipped their sherries, feeling gay and liberated, Aliason felt *unique*. All through lunch, and the speeches afterwards and Tiny's final words of warmth (they were *all* participants, that the theme) and the slide show of the history of Wolf Lake and Duke County, Aliason was dying to know more. She squirmed through the last of the talk before making hurried exit. Even though realizing that David's last afternoon session wouldn't be over for hours she headed straight for the hotel to await his arrival. To her delight, she found him already back. "Darling!" She flung herself into his arms. Her eyes moistened and she saw that his own were having trouble too. "I want to hear all about your success." Which she did and was warmed by its glow. Not in a long time had she seen him so pleased, lights of gaiety in his eyes, rare playfulness shining through the enduring seriousness of his manner. "But," it struck her, "shouldn't you be back at the auditorium?" He smiled at her concern, pulling out his schedule, flipping through the final afternoon's copious bill of fare. "Don't you think," say, I can pass up *Resurgence Phenomena of TEREDINUS LIMNIUM with Salinity?*"

"What's that?"

"The boring worm. Not to scorn it. In the Twenties the rainfall diminished over San Francisco Bay and in the saltier waters *teredo* flourished and brought the waterfront crumbling down. Anyway, I doubt that there's much new there that I can't afford to miss."

"Oh, I *guess*." Trying to be judicious but feeling only fluttery. "They schedule those types last" he said "because interest is least. A lot of people have to dash to planes early this afternoon." She thought that over. "That's not fair. Their big moment and everyone skips."

"They're used to it. Actually, I might have gone but there's an early get-together at the *Grizzly Bear* and I thought we'd drop over." "A kind of final celebration, is it?", she said. Lighting up, figuring it. "It's *you* they're celebrating. Should I change?"

"You look great. Of course, we don't have to go. It'll be mostly noisy nonsense."

"No." Firmly. "You've *earned* it." Walking over she fretted some more about being dressed correctly. What was right for a luncheon was not necessarily right for this occasion. She went on, out of nervousness, yet not unhappily, full of anticipation for this afternoon's fun. Then observing those entering, and especially the condition of those departing—hearing as well the din emanating from within—she was prepared to accept that a protean tolerance in its customers' dress was one of the Grizzly's characteristics. David shouldered open the heavy brown oaken door over which a mangy elk head with massive antlers was mounted askew. Fumes working on it too. "Here we are."

Here they were. From early times man has sought out his taverns and, where not existing, worked swiftly to erect them. In the Pacific war the Navy's Seabees hammered Officer's Clubs together on embattled beachheads, Japanese bullets smacking raw lumber. Poets have their Mermaid Taverns and cowboys their saloons, of which this was the lineal descendant. Salesmen of aluminum siding their hangouts too to tell their tales, bemoan the recalcitrant who lack the vision of their products, boast of their coups. Acousticians and ocean scientists too, no wonder. Not so different, their vanities and miseries, from other trades. From the Symposium's opening day the bored and restless had begun their trickle here, sneaking away to enjoy the taste of local beers, relief from the droning march of indecipherable slides. Here shadows comfortably wrapped a man telling harmless lies, indulging technical dreams. The trickle had become a steady flow. In a few days it had gone from random visits by renegades to custom for the general. Today a buoyantly jolly flood. Everyone was here except, it seemed, that pitifully small number still anxious, or merely dutiful, to hear about barnacle encrustation at a thousand fathoms. Out of the dimness, the darkly beamed ceiling hung with mournful heads of game, David and Aliason were welcomed by an eruption of shouts. As their eyes adjusted they saw a table *seem* to rise—no, *actually* rise. Everyone at this one table, palms spread, lifting it shoulder high to more cheers. Yet for all its oddness, it seemed to David, the pleased honoree, just about right. The table thence let down, free hands that had lifted it now led the clapping. They were all here, his friends, many others he could not yet recognize, but with broadly smiling teeth that were like lights to this dark jumping place. Not all tables applauded, but he felt their eyes upon him.

Many of them mystified, having passed up his presento, sensing only that some deed had been done.

"Make room fellows," Billy Jencks was beside himself with delight. He grabbed empty chairs from an adjacent table where, from the looks he got, its people were not ready to part with them. Nuances, and more, lost on the oblivious Billy now waving for fresh pitchers. Next boisterously proposing a toast. "Okay," David said at last, "enough, that'll do."

"No *siree*," said Billy, who now, hopping out of his chair again—busy as a flea on a dog's back—came around to David's side of the table and leaned to deliver a whisper that could be heard several tables away. "This is freedom, David, like Truth is Freedom." Billy's response to David's demurrer was another toast. *"Liberation Day!"* Thus leadeth Billy, a dozen massed heavy glass mugs raised on high. Boys again. Boys all.

People dropped over to tell David what they thought of what he had done. Words of admiration which, as they became more fervent, were correspondingly less coherent. Artie Perrozzi spoke with the greatest emotion. "I'm telling you, David, as a taxpayer and an analyst too, that a great thing has happened. It's the beginning of the end for DIANA." His hand sought David's again in further affirmation, that varsity swimmer's big hand a clasp of warmth and strength. "With you, all the way, pal."

Their table grew raucous. Other tables were dragged over to join it. And if in the inevitable diffusion of the gaiety, away from David's specific act of rebellion and towards a general silliness, there nevertheless remained unifying elements which from time to time would trigger a resurgence of emotion that, like a wave rippling, evoked more bursts of contagious laughter, conspirational vows, dire prophecies brave with beer. "The bastards finally heard it!" To the tune of Farewell Pamplona they sang "Farewell DIANA." Revolution in the air. Heady stuff. Aliason, the only woman at the table, a novelty, receiving an extraordinary share of attention and, and though located some seats away from David, courtesy of the socially directive Billy, wore a softly glowing expression of unshadowed pleasure. Giving her David frequent shy waves whenever she caught his eye. If he was the hero of the party, she was its belle. Artie was bending her ear now concerning the Hawaiian Islands, their loveliness and the passionate hold they had upon his family. His wife could not live anywhere else; neither, he vowed, could he. He had a toehold, by God, in the Islands and his great little company, Pacific Ocean Research, was going to grow as surely as the Islands were green and the Pacific remained blue. David detected that much anyway and smiled inwardly. Then he realized, feeling foolish, that he was also smiling outwardly. The inward and the outward smile though not in conflict. Feeling passingly warm again towards Artie, his friendship, the quality of his ideas, for having ideas at all, so rare in this business. At the moment even able to forgive him for the nuttiness of his Plowshare proposal, even for his pushing it with the Admiral behind his back, while swearing on a stack of Bibles that he would never do such a thing. A David full of beer able to feel even more kindly disposed towards Artie for the luminous effect he was having on Al. Her gaze was far away, her lips parted. Through the marvelous discriminative properties of the human ear, which can distinguish lesser signals amidst a din of louder ones, he heard her sigh. He saw her shining with remembrance of their long ago sojourn in the Islands, the months when he was deep in the stimulus of measuring long-range propagation across the vast stretch of the Pacific Ocean from Kaneohe up to Kodiak Alaska. Project PARKA. Months of rare professional excitement and fulfillment for himself. Months of pure bliss for Aliason, drifting and dreaming through blue Hawaiian days. A spell of pure romance, before the children, before a world of things good and bad. And, never so acutely, a time of the young David Morgan smitten with the wonder of winning this girl he had won. Realizing, a part of him now drifting off, that the wonder was still there and then, having drifted too far, aware that he had missed something that Charlie Wicker, Artie's colleague, had said and he was apologizing to Charlie and asking him to say it again. Whatever Charlie had to say always worth hearing.

For already, through several hours of this noisy afternoon, they had done a lot of talking, and even through all the spurts of communal silliness Charlie's thoughts had been a continuous thread of quiet good sense. An engineer's engineer, believer in voltages and acoustic aperture and proven performance in the blue water and in little beyond that. A young sonar man in WWII, he knew the old searchlight sonars like a historian, had sat beside Eddie Duchin at Sonar School off Key West and read doppler notes together, yielding to the call of the famed jazz man's ears of perfect pitch, sensitive unto legend. Today, Charlie was more relaxed than usual, mirthfully wry. His yellowed fingers held one cigarette after another, smoke curling up through wiry eyebrows, overgrown into briars of permanent questioning. Charlie Wicker had always seemed to exist, in the corporate sense, somewhere off in Artie's shadow, yet as the corporation's Senior Scientist he was a steady grey presence and a useful counterweight to his volatile partner. There was this directness about him, a removal from the vast fraud of the world, at least the ASW analysis part of that world, that was to David—for all the foul tobacco air that wreathed him—refreshing. But Charlie had more than skepticism; in his stubbornly competent way he had made balky underwater systems succeed, done his engineer's best to squeeze out every last decibel of signal excess, had spent time on ice islands, knew the gradients of the Chukchi Sea. His civilian medals of achievement were a Pacific Ocean Research asset no less than Artie's pizzazz. David was grateful for the hand that clasped his shoulder, telling him that he had done right. "Will it do any good?" A David Morgan growing contrarily more sober. "Well, got to start somewhere." He gazed around. Past and future seemed to pull at him. "I may not be around much longer, you know. Artie frets about me, the kinds of things I may let slip, that can upset the Navy bosses. So maybe I've maybe got another good year or two. But I'll be sorry to leave the business. I would like to have *solved* something first, gotten my arms around . . . ."

"ASW?" He looked at David first with surprise and then with seeming forgiveness for his not seeing more precisely. "The mystery of acoustic detection. The signal processing that may ultimately do it. I *know* . . . wise old birds insist the wet end is crucial. But I still have faith in circuits. I don't believe that even the matched filter is the end." He brightened slightly. "Anyway, so it goes. Artie's spinning his web." Smoke rose past his reddened eyes, rising from a deep-ashed ashtray in front of him as from a damped fireplace. His vitality all in his slow smile. He got up and David rose to shake his hand.

"My best to . . . your wife. Sorry there was not the chance to know her better." His farewell was tugged by an odd wistfulness. "Perhaps, in the future . . . ."

David watched his figure, tall and stooped, probably once strong in the way of Lincoln's bony kind of strong, move towards the door. Over bobbing heads and through corrupted air David's eyes followed until the door was flung open to reveal, against a twilight sky, Tawney Gray and Admiral Snowdon and Jules Baumgarde standing in the entrance. The trio poking just their heads in, faces impassive, joyless, but by themselves at last; duty done, right down to the final presentation on erosion of steel rods in submerged concrete, concluding what was bound to have been a soured and wearying day. Their dignified dress was a further contrast, and likely felt by them to be a mocking one, with the gross informality glimpsed inside. They peered in for a few more seconds and then with shrugs expressing the hopelessness of getting a table turned away. David doubted that they even noticed him, let alone could discriminate against the noise of his own table's continuum of puerile mutiny. But for a moment he was moved, conscious of the prosperity of his own feelings as contrasted with the discouragement visible on those well-known faces. He had an impulse to run after them with an invitation to join his table. Deterred by the seeming hypocrisy of the gesture, also its futility. Billy hopped up once again, running around to his side of the table. "See *that*?" he exulted. "Not so different from us, Billy. Just tired guys wanting a beer."

"*Baloney.* We got 'em on the run. Don't turn nice. Get 'em down and stomp on them." Billy, a tiger tousling raw meat. David Morgan realizing that perhaps he had no true killer in himself, that his passion was fitful, and he was still feeling the glow of his talk with Charlie Wicker and this part of his professional life that was its own best and pure kind of love. Eventually the Morgans departed. Not slipping away quietly, but bombarded with more nonsense, final toasts. "Wow," said Aliason once they were outside, and now the silence, and the dark and the cold of the mountains, much colder, as if that great dark loomingness had let out a silent exhalation of winter, had her shivering. But if she had gone to the *Grizzly* with trepidation, she exited skipping. "So that's what you all are like by yourselves. I can see that it would be fun sometimes to be a man." His own mood was a restraint on her skippingness.

"Well, there are other facets to it too," he said. The stars were bright as the gravel of the walkway crunched underfoot like the hard iron filings grittiness of frozen snow.

"Guess what Artie had to say?", she teased.

"Let me guess. That fate arranges that I end up at Pacific Ocean Research. With high pay and a fine title. And we all live happily in the Islands ever after."

"Poo." Her step took a disappointed hop. Through the tall and tamed pines, dark borrowed sentinels from the high wilderness, the lights of their hotel shone warm and yellow. "Anyway," her voice had an edge, "what's wrong with the idea?"

"A whole piss-pot full of things. Starting with all the years we have already sunk in Civil Service. The golden handcuffs." Sorry to have tacked on that oldie. Hating it for its very truth. But she wasn't listening. "Anyway, Artie thinks the sun rises and sets on you."

"God love him." Artie who, when the zest of this nutty afternoon had subsided, was going to dope out soon enough that one David Morgan was no longer to be touched with a ten foot pole. They had passed through the pines onto an openness of lawn illuminated by the hotel lobby. They could feel its brimming hubbub, see people restlessly passing to and fro. Directly above the grand rococo entranceway was the window of their room several floors up, a single light on, dim with their absence. He sensed her stiffness and then their hands brushed and she caught his tightly. No vacation this fine to be spoiled so easily, nor was she going to let it be. "Oh my gosh," she said as soon as she caught sight of the clock in their room, "hardly time to change. Where is it we are supposed to be meeting with the Grays and the Snowdons and the others?"

"I have a hunch that's become academic," he said, gesturing towards the little red flashing light on their telephone, indicating a message waiting. "Oh? Think it means anything?" she said, suddenly all concern when he put down the phone to announce that the Grays and the Snowdons *et al* would not be joining them this evening after all.

"*Mean anything?*" Ah my love. *Al, Al*. . . .

▲ ▲ ▲ ▲ ▲

The day of their return was one that makes of Washington's Augusts a legend. The sky dirty purple, gritty with stagnant exhaust; the humid air, smelling of bubbling tar and gasoline, swirls up from the asphalt runways like a foul belch. Grit scurries and stings. Beyond the grey concrete of National Center, dark sooty clouds are piled, promising less relief of rain than violent storms. Anger at all *this*. Their rumble penetrates buildings, a hundred times more powerful than the horns of the automobiles stuck in front of the airport.

Airports, so it is told, are fascinating places to watch people. The strangeness and variety of human kind. Joyous faces, faces contorted with sadness, confident faces and timid. Bold hands hold briefcases with the sureness of years, small feminine hands clasp knitting bags in order that up in the air, whatever befalls, to the last those hands can be busy at something nice. Tonsured young men in robes, girls with poppies, solicit with out-thrust tin cans. Stylish women stand apart in unconscious mystery, faces composed over their secret lives. But better than they, healthy good-humored hurrying girls after whose naturalness the heart trots like a puppy. American women, in droves, over whose thunderous walk a gloomy Camus voiced wonder and lament. People unceasing, pouring through the terminal with their tourist treasures, pineapples from Hawaii, palm hats from the Bahamas, French shopping bags. More than ever this particular day, sky-caps on strike, every traveler, no matter how lordly, is inseparable from his luggage which, as he mutters curses at its awkward haulings, likely tells more than he wishes. But whether tapestried Gucci's or scarred fiberboard held with twine, each person must wrestle his own out to the curb.

But for a moment our hypothetical watcher, though he has seen many an arresting sight, is focusing his attention on a slender woman struggling with a bulky bag and a pair of skis and floppy poles. Still in her thirties, barely blondish, uncommonly attractive in a yellow shirtwaist dress, its stylishness rumpled from hours of cramped flight and the sullen heat of this day against which the airport's air-conditioning is feeble protest. But it is not the oddness of the skis that strikes one; skis pass through National by the thousands. Even right now in South America the Beautiful People were making the most of an Andean winter, zipping down thrilling slopes, pausing to watch the great condor glide. Yet unmistakably this woman has not just returned from a southern hemispherical adventure. No joy of memory touches the corners of her pressed lips. In the uncertainty of her movements, her fine-boned and somehow vulnerable china prettiness, above all, the pained evidence of current discovery that being five-foot two and continually jostled, there is *no* good way to get skis through this mob; out of all of this there arises a counterbalancing conviction that close by there must be someone on the verge of her rescue. Or surely, instincts of symmetry insist, there *ought* to be. Such women draw protectors like bees to honey. And actually, as our sharp-eyed observer shortly notes, there *is* someone else—yards ahead, to be sure, a man himself burdened by two heavy bags and a cosmetic case—and upon whose bobbing head her eyes keep concentratingly fixed, like a saving buoy periodically glimpsed in a cruel sea. Her look at her husband's head is not one, however, that conveys grateful awareness of help near at hand. Closer is it a wish to kill. The skis are awkward, slapping against her thigh. There is no way to maneuver them handily, let along gracefully, through this madhouse. Abruptly she stops trying. Letting skis and poles fall to the hard shiny terrazzo floor with a clatter that in addition to the stares of strangers recaptures the attention of husband David who up until this point is acting as if his is a single-minded journey through the crowd without a mate. The crash brings him back—as quickly as reversing direction with his burden against the flow permits—to share one of those tautly whispered exchanges to which likely, given sufficiently provocative circumstances, no marriage is immune. She stands with her arms folded, a small but steadfast rock in a perspiration-wetted dress around which traffic irritably divides. "What in *hell* are you doing?"

"Dropping skis." Her bared teeth are not a smile. "*That* is what I am doing."

"Al, *please, f*or God's sake. Who bought the goddamned things?"

"Right. And, you're teaching me a lesson. Very well. Consider me taught."

A deep breath from David. "My only objective, Al, is to get us a taxi before they're all gone. Most of them too, I've heard, are also out on strike in sympathy." Her stance of icy dignity starts to melt. "You didn't tell me that. But admit it, you don't want to be lugging those skis either. Dragging them through the airport embarrasses you." He shakes his head. "This is crazy." So very true. She reads his face. A moment longer they just stand there. Then, decisively as she dropped the skis, she picks them up. "Let's move it."

Luck, at least, on the taxi front. A shared ride but worth it. Jammed suitcases on laps, their company includes a distinguished looking gentlemen plainly suffering shock to his world and a fat voluble black women. *Lawdy, it is hot.* A tedious wandering trip through the snarl of rush hour, winding through Rock Creek Park and thence into the menacing dreariness of Northeast, past the fronts of row homes that had their fine day in Lincoln's time, next into favored Georgetown, a fair portion of its residents sensibly, prosperously, having deserted it this month. Finally, they cross Key Bridge into Northern Virginia. Rain starts to fall, the rain that had been so ominously rolling in from the West. Big drops plop from out of that sulfurous sky, raising hot vapors from smoldering asphalt. Her hand slides across the glossy hot sweat-slippery surface of the leatherette seat cover. "Thank you, darling." For a moment, the smell of cool pine forest is back. But once home—out of the sweaty taxi at last, the fare so large it has to be paid with a check, sullenly accepted by their Afghan driver with all his own numerous reasons to be sullen—after being deposited in front of their sealed-up house, quiet as every other house in this quiet neighborhood, barred against summer as if the plague, and after being greeted with whoops by the children, after too the treats and the souvenir gifts have been distributed, the bear's claw, bits of polished rocks and the sitter driven home, and kind and watchful neighbors thanked, shadows—not gone after all, not even strayed far, merely held at bay—return. At the bedroom window, looking beyond his thickly uncut lawn, he reflects that Monday he will be gazing out again at the familiar railroad yards of northern Alexandria. She is humming an old cowboy tune that caught their fancy on the trip and is still bubbling with homecoming and memory, "What are you looking at?" she breaks off. "Reality," he says.

"You chill me." But her spirits of the trip raised high refuse to depart. "Maybe you *won't* pay. Maybe something marvelous will happen. People will say, *my God, that man is right*. And the wheel of fortune will swoop you up to who knows what grand destiny." She waves her arm. A thin girlish arm for such a grand arc. "So, who knows?"

"We shall see." In spite of himself—knowing better, only the details yet to be revealed—she had coaxed more than a crooked smile. Smiles, he could reflect, had saved before. Then it came back. Over and over. *What have I done?, what have I done* . . . . ?

▲ ▲ ▲ ▲ ▲

NAVY EXPERT DECLARES GIANT SONAR DEVICE VEXING LAKESIDE RESIDENTS WON'T WORK!"—was the headline in *Rocky Mountain Calls*, *"A STINKEROO!"* The text was set off in a thickened border for prominence. Adjacent was a cartoon of a sulking trout curling its fins to protect its ears from assaulting waves of sound.

"*This servant of your paper was a "fly-on-the-wall" at the Navy's recent Symposium on the Oceans and Underwater Acoustics held at Wolf Lake. Amongst many talks—both esoteric and classified—one presentation had this observer suddenly sitting up bolt upright. A Dr. Morgan of the Naval Sea Systems Command presented a paper whose theme was twofold; the first being that these modern long range sonar devices, not only the one called DIANA, but the whole family of these belles, were incapable of living up to their 'grandiose' (Dr. Morgan's word) promises. The other theme was that surface ships—read 'Destroyers', you old Navy veterans—can no longer hack it in anti-submarine warfare (ASW) against very capable advanced nuclear-powered submarines. Dr. Morgan declared it a costly delusion to persist in creating a fleet of ships woefully incapable of meeting the challenge of the future. In Dr. Morgan's phrase, the destroyer is . . . a victim of history whose bell has tolled. Modern technology has transformed sea power, which is now dominated by those systems that can speed fast above the seas or hide within them. The surface ship, striving vainly to prevail at the interface of the two great media, air and water, suffering the disadvantages of both and the advantages of neither, unable to travel fast in the one, nor to conceal itself in the other, is fated to be . . . well folks, face it . . . a target.*

There followed a surprisingly accurate summary of the speaker's remarks. There were minor technical errors and, a trivial one, mainly David's elevation to 'Doctor.' But on the whole the reporter—whoever he was (prudently, in view of his covertly breaching Security, providing no clue to his identity)—displayed excellent retentivity of much material bound to be foreign to him. Towards the article's end offering his own assessment.

"That Doctor Morgan concluded his talk to silence did not per se have special meaning since little applause followed any of the talks. However, in this case it struck me that the silence was particularly frozen, and there seemed an edge of sarcasm to the moderator, a Dr. Baumgarde, thanking Dr. Morgan for his 'most interesting remarks.' It is emphasized that your uninvited witness to these proceedings cannot evaluate their technical merit. Possibly too, some of the coldness of the audience, particularly amongst the naval officers, arose from resentment at a civilian scientist's trespassing on areas where such types are not supposed to venture. Certainly, no other speakers wandered so far afield, engaging in no editorializing but rather concentrating on the "nuts and bolts" of the trade, plankton migrations, swim bladder resonances (I didn't dream any of these up, honest!) . . . etc. Dr. Morgan definitely strayed off the reservation.

"It is possible, of course, that this speaker could have been an eccentric—every symposium has its share—the fellow who fanatically propounds 'far out' ideas, or tiresomely repeats old discredited ones ad nauseam year after year. "But Dr. Morgan doesn't fill that bill. To begin with, there are his credentials as recounted in the program brochures. One notes too that he belongs to the Experimental Acoustic Research office, whose efforts, one gathers, are crucial to the development of our bedeviling DIANA sonar. This reporter's gut feeling is that the good Doctor knew exactly what he was talking about, and that the shock greeting his words was that of knowledgeable professionals listening to what they know is all too true, and yet which they are reluctant— for reasons this observer can only speculate—to face squarely. Dr. Morgan, I suspect, was the one fated to tell the assembled that the emperor has no clothes. And, by some, to be unforgiven for that overdue and obvious news."

At this point the reporter lapsed into cuteness, for a moment reverting to the small town newsman, boyishly proud of his scoop. His maturer tones returned in wrap-up.

"What does this mean for Wolf Lake? We will not dwell on the phenomena of the bizarre squeaks that afflict the lake front residents, as well as our entire community, which enjoys this marvelous gift of nature. There are tales enough of the severe effects of some emanations striking people engaged (we will forego intimate description, ours being a family newspaper!) in that private act best accomplished serenely, free of alarm. Surely, not much to ask. One down-lake resident, not known for blinking at fear, carries a slinged arm which is all that he chooses to reveal of one particular startling intrusion of our Lady of the Lake! It remains to be seen whether this region may not be witness to—not funny, folks—a whole generation traumatized by spooked recollections of the 'troll in the well.'

"As for the glorious Rainbow trout, the official Environmental Impact Statement tells us not to worry. Response frequencies of our treasured fish are, we are assured, much higher than those of the reverberant DIANA. But a government that repeatedly violates the trust of its citizens does not inspire confidence. Which brings us to the relationship of Wolf Lake's citizens to their federal masters. For some time we have seen how cheerfully, at least stoically, our good people have borne the nuisance of their Navy's booming monster. Enduring it out of the same faith with which, ever and anon, they loyally send their sons off to war.

"It remains to pose the urgent question: WHAT NOW? How much longer will our people put up with this affliction even though their sacrifice only serves to advance a manifestly misguided project that ought not to be pursued further? There is one more thing to think about. This mischief-making contraption down at the end of the lake is hideously expensive. Budget figures foretell it costing hundreds of millions of dollars annually and eventually—if DIANA is installed in all the warships planned—billions. Think then about your hard earned tax dollars grooming this discredited monster each time you rise before dawn to milk those cows, or must ride fence on the high pastures in blizzard winds.

"Up to you, good folk. Whatever.... 'THE CAT IS NOW OUT OF THE BAG!"

▲▲▲▲▲

Yes indeed, as they say (Billy Jencks saying it everywhere), "the cat *is* out of the bag"—more explicitly truth, or one man's version of it at least—but... perhaps the timing was wrong, or circumstances, or whatever.... In any event, an imagined wildcat spitting—howling!—defiance and exultation in its freedom after angry captivity was off the mark. Wryly, David bethought an image closer to his experience. One day while taking out the trash and, just before dumping it in the garbage can, he caught sight of something pinkish and furry. Inspection revealed it to be a possum that obviously had been snooping around and gotten trapped. It was seemingly lifeless but then he detected that it was breathing... "playing possum." Like many in the suburbs he sentimentalized raccoons and other creatures that scattered his trash and he would do them no harm. He carried the can to the wood's edge and gently turned it on its side, expecting the animal to move out briskly. It did not twitch a muscle. Gradually he tilted the can more steeply, until finally it was upside down. The plump body slid out on the grass and he touched its warm bristly sides coaxingly. He did not persist in his prods, however, noticing the teeth set in a powerful jaw informing why possums had survived some millions of years. After a moment more of wary inertness, the possum—abruptly ending its game—righted itself and trotted away composedly. Making for an old tree with which it was evidently familiar and ducking into a hollow at its base and he never met Mr. Possum again.

* * *

Thus, not the *processes* of communication, then, that are one of the modern world's greatest wonders. Not even if, every second, nanobits of information zip through space at the speed of light and thence, decoded at a million different ground stations, make a fair portion of humankind recipients of its intelligence. A bombardment rivaling cosmic rays. But boggling the imagination does not alone confer the quality of miracle. More amazing is what is dumped in man's lap and ignored. Hidden, so to speak not *from*, but *in*, the public eye. Knowledge that sits like lumps for people to stub their toes on and yet which, for all the frightened confusion they ought to cause—like firecrackers sizzling on a busy sidewalk—is ignored. People blankly step around. Perhaps they can only absorb so much.

The article, given maximum prominence within the limited typesetting capabilities and distribution resources of Wolf Lake's little newspaper, ought to have exploded in the world's face. On the world's face, there was . . . nothing. The wire services did not pick it up, possibly no local stringer had sent it on, or its significance was missed by the night watch on the clattering teletypes at New York or Washington. Yet, if there were billions of people who could not care less, credibly there were at least many, beyond the ringing mountains of Duke County, who would have been a respectably sized readership for such news; numbers of Congressmen, foremost, detesting all military expenditures and forever scrabbling for rocks to throw; close to home, Congressman Abner Duke himself. And, as well, the nation's shipbuilders ready to fall on their swords at any impediment to creation of the nation's warships. There was too the manufacturer of DIANA, and all its corporate in-laws, already rich on Super Long Range Sonar and its predecessors—a whole northern tier of cities first lit by the genius of Proteus Steinmetz—whose prosperous feudal benignity would have been sorely tried were the word to leak out that, in a respectable forum, conviction was expressed that their goose of golden eggs would never remotely perform according to the hyperventilating prose of its advertising brochures. Careerists in laboratories, sponsors in the Pentagon, whole battalions of scattered ambitions on the line. There were . . . ah, but indeed beyond count, all the participants and onlookers, voyagers and voyeurs, who would have been extraordinarily attentive had such news come into their ken.

But this baby wildcat, born to scream, died a kitten. Some copies were cut out locally and mailed off. David received his own from a colleague at the Wolf Lake Test Center, flecked with exclamations. Likely Tawney Gray and the Admiral saw copies too, though neither of them, through all that was to come, made reference to it afterwards. Beside the point. Possibly too right now just holding their breath. News of the event survived mostly by personal contact, spread amongst a thin network of those who treasure such juicy arcana. There were rumors, scraps of phrases, borne on the light corridor winds of EAR, but these did not carry. Even though Billy Jencks circulated extra copies, choice bits circled in red. Billy, the unflagging orchestrator still of this Holy Cause. Not that David held it to be even a Cause. Explaining this to Billy, trying to rein him in. "I was never intending this to spill over. All along I worked to keep arguments in-house." He was thinking—as if with the imagined opening of some improbably favorable dialogue—of Tawney and the Admiral, wherein their gratitude for his post-Wolf Lake restraint ought to play a meliorating part in their calculations. Those yet to be learned. "How that reporter sneaked in I have no idea," David was still musing. "Nope." A momentarily thoughtful Billy, making no connection with the stranger who had plopped down beside him that morning. But then he was off again. "The point is it happened. And now it's ticking away. You'll see."

Aliason carried around her own Xeroxed copy. With pride and affection showing it to her next-door pal Tony Ghezzi and a handful of other friends. Kept in her purse, refolded from a hundred readings, the cheap paper softened, eventually thence to crumble along the creases. Even so she scotch-taped it and long afterwards it found its way into her bureau drawer beside a ribboned packet of David's steamy love letters from his voyage to the Red Sea.

4

It had been, all things considered, a surprising length of time since his returning from Wolf Lake. Days turning into weeks. Routine going on as usual. Correspondence basket filling and emptying in familiar tidal rhythms. Now, at last, here it was. Daisy coming to fetch him. Making it down the long corridor, past all the usual many doors, to pop her head in, hailing him to follow her with a silent wave. Fingers to her lips too in silent drama. David put down his coffee and rose with as much of a smile as he could summon. "This is it, eh?"

"Seems so. I gather you were quite the bad boy out there at Wolf Lake."

"Something anyway." Her eyes widened, keeping her expression grave. Still able to rise to the theatricality of governmental moments in which she no longer believed. But then she could not sustain it. She winked. It lightened something in him just enough.

"Our man is waiting?" "Oh yes. He and the Admiral have just had themselves a session behind closed doors. Wish I could tell you more." "Thanks, Daisy." Squaring his shoulders, he liked to think manfully, outside Tawney's office and getting from Daisy a blown kiss and her silently mouthed *Good Luck,* as she shut the door behind him.

Tawney was standing behind his desk. He did not sit down and made it plain that David was not invited to sit either. For seconds Tawney simply glared.

"Well, David, don't you have anything to say?" "I was thinking," he replied, wishing his throat was not so dry, "that perhaps I'd already said it all."

Tawney glanced down at his desk. Bare but for several sheets of spread paper. He's rehearsed this, David thought, an insight not without amusement. Well, of course. Waiting for Tawney to launch into his little speech which went on for some minutes in recapitulation of the awful thing that had occurred. At the end Tawney's voice rose, his words bit.

"You let me, the Admiral, and all your colleagues down. You were disloyal. I will let pass entirely the childish celebration afterwards. I can scarcely express how disappointed in you the Admiral is. It was a shameful performance. It was *betrayal.*"

David nodded to each of these, and others, of Tawney's words. Accepting some of them, most perhaps, but not all. "Surely you're not *proud* of what you did?"

Well, there was a question. He let out his breath. "I'm still working on that."

The answer seemed to surprise Tawney Gray. This seemingly as far as rehearsal had taken him. He shook his head. "Tell me David, why that silly smile? I can't for the life of me imagine what's behind it."

Just nerves, David wanted to confess, but then instead, still out of nervousness, could not resist repeating the latest from the Pacific. "Maybe you haven't heard this one yet. But Admiral Blue declared that sending a destroyer banging away with DIANA in search of a nuclear submarine is like dispatching a naked virgin with bells on out into a black forest at midnight in order to apprehend a rapist." Tawney Gray's jaw clamped down hard. His face, that cherubic face, turned beet red. His lips quivered. He turned away to the scene outside his window. When his gaze returned to his offending subordinate his voice was almost sorrowful. Perhaps even genuinely so. Tawney still able to surprise.

"You could have done a lot for this program, you know, David. You have . . . talents that could have contributed much. Still could, perhaps, though I don't know how."

Wondering how himself, David made an insignificant gesture that Taney cut off before it became words. "I have to run off to a meeting, David. But don't take it that this is the end of the matter." "No." Assuredly he did not.

Every evening since they had arrived home from Wolf Lake Aliason was on him for news. *What was happening?* At least now he had something to tell her. Giving a full account, withholding nothing, at the same time conveying his own bafflement at the encounter, its fateful insufficiency. Al's own expression fell with her own unsatisfied excitement.

"That's it? That's *all?*" Stroking that small delicate chin. Her mind going around busily. Sober, these past days, as far so he could tell; grateful and strengthened for that not small succor. If mystery was the cause, or whatever was the reason, so be it. Glad for whatever did it. "Have you talked this over with . . . your little friend, Billy Jencks? I think you should, you know. He often has good insight. You've said that yourself."

His smile grew. With credit for her being on precisely the same track as his own. He told her so, "You see, sweet," she said, "I *do* have ideas."

His get-together with Billy, took place barely a day later. Out there in September's mid-day sunshine, eating their bag lunches and with the shiny green wooden slats of their favorite bench warming their rears. Billy all rapt attention, sometimes halting his chewing, concentrating on the details of David's recounting of his session with Tawney Gray. Repeatedly interrupting to demand that David go back over some particular portion of what Tawney had said. "So Davey, when he said *that,* just what was his expression, his tone of voice?"

With David conscientiously complying, indulging in none of his customary teasing. Genuinely anxious for Billy's opinion on this one. A Billy nodding, his eyes narrowing, repeating certain phrases, sifting nuance, Billy who in the end did not disappoint. *"Got it.* At bottom very simple, Davey. They're playing games. Testing you. It's part of their plan."

"Games? *Plan*? Come on, Billy. That's no help."

Billy held up his hand. A sure Billy. A patient one, too with his friend who, for all his smarts, could sometimes be pretty dense. "You see, they're really not through with you. Giving you time to ponder before they're convinced you're going to keep your neck in the noose."

"It doesn't add up," David said. "I can't picture what you're telling me."

Billy could. It had nothing to do with any fondness or remnants of loyalty toward one David Morgan. *"Shit no.* Not a milligram's worth. *But*, the fact is you could still be worth a whole lot. With a valuable role yet to play. It's called "Seeing the Light." Letting the world know the error of your ways, that DIANA's problems are fixable, that it's going to turn out to be all that the Navy is counting upon. Hey, Dave, don't look at me like that. Think about it. The heretic who comes back into the fold, who recants and gives witness to his wrongness, carries ten times the credibility of all those types in the chorus cheering things on without having really *studied* this thing" Billy now bringing up well known examples of other big programs vexed by their own black sheep who, after spells of wandering about in the wilderness, were heralded for rejoining the team.

"It still strikes me still as awfully far fetched, Billy."

"So what's your take then?" Billy challenged him. But David Morgan had none. And as still more weeks went by and things went on mostly as before and his IN basket kept filling and while, if not ever called down to Dr. Gray's office, he nevertheless caught at least passing nods of neutral recognition from the good Doctor in the corridor, Billy's interpretation, however far-fetched, remained the only one at hand. Meanwhile, staying busy readying his talk for the big get-together on the future of DIANA. No longer mirthfully labeled The Agonizing Reappraisal, having gotten itself a grander and more optimistic title, yet with himself still scheduled to talk; Billy on the program too. Amazingly Billy and all his drear numbers. Encouraging David to believe that perhaps letting Billy be the main bearer of bad news that one David Morgan, maverick but presumably still in the fold, might deliver a more muted message. Not kicking them so hard in the nuts. Clinging to that thought, for whatever hope was there.

▲ ▲ ▲ ▲ ▲

In the office of the Vice Chief of Naval Operations the sea prints on the walls were darkened originals from the romantic age of Navies. Here phones rang softly. And even if people responded swiftly, there was a soothing economy to their gestures; the paper came and went with scarcely a rustle. *The Paper.* Which was, of course, the reason for these well-integrated human beings gathered here. Masses of it teetered high in routing baskets. Yet this was not your ordinary paper dully addressing routine matters. Here was sharply wrought text cut on bond embossed with radiant blue and gold logos heralding offices of prestige. For all its thinness, the vital lifeblood of the Navy in Washington. Study and rebuttal, *posit* and *reclama*, the surging flow of an unrefreshing and yet eternal tide.

The paper was about money. Neither wars nor strategy animated this place. An officer who ventured to question how a certain new weapon might fare in a threat environment did so at peril. Aversion to such probings was deep, endemic, logical. Only a handful of eccentric true believers expected the U.S. Navy some day actually to ever fight a major war at sea again. A new time had succeeded. Measures of effectiveness—MOE's in Pentagon shorthand—for either a system or an individual had scant connection with combat and everything to do with prevailing in the fiscal jungle with its special vocabulary, full of CPAM's, DSARC's, POM cycle, HASC . . . other mysterious clottings of initials. At once challenge and tool, means and objective, by them men shepherding systems along knew victory or licked wounds of defeat. And yet, paradoxically, the language of war was the one used most frequently to describe how the paper was coming along. For if men's concerns were far removed from how their favored plane or torpedo— or whatever—might be able to perform in some hypothetical conflict, and even if their constant diet was paper, their talk was more colorfully that of tigers, tearers of red meat. Exchanges had the bitter tautness of unrelenting siege. Amidst all this menacing paper, emotion was high and at its storm center, as it were, was Admiral Barney Worth still. Ambition and temperament cast him in this role which, for all its power, was not a happy one. Seldom did there come into his once acute sailor's consciousness a memory of ships, images of the albatross skimming the wave . . . least of all the consolations that the feel of a warship's deck under foot gave a man, reassuring him that he is honorably engaged in his nation's worthy business, nobly guarding the world's last and best hope of freedom upon the earth and . . . "the rest of the *et cetera* shit," as Barney inimitably would put it.

Anyway. No more the tang of salt water. True, the Atlantic Ocean, coming past Cape Henry and up the Chesapeake, did sometimes affect the Potomac's flow—retarding it a mite in its surges—and ocean fish actually did struggle up it to spawn. There were sea birds too, and on foggy days one noticed the grey and white lumps of them stolidly aligned in wetted grasses by the Pentagon's North Parking. But even at its best the river was poor substitute, its gulls wards of man, less fishers of oceans than scavengers of shopping malls. Yet even if the sea had been driven from Barney Worth's consciousness, there were times when he could still savor some sense of professional accomplishment. All ambitious lives have their ways of keeping score and Barney's was the count of the Navy's ships. On this day its Order of Battle, as it is spoken of ships—in being, and prospective ones—then at five hundred and eighty, had by a House subcommittee vote, made a decent advance in the likelihood of reaching the Navy's goal of Six Hundred ships, a number currently enshrined as sacred, through approval for eight new minesweepers. Even humble minesweepers, customarily neglected, to the Navy's recurrent surprise and dismay, eagerly honored in today's count.

Thus, a plus for the day so far in Barney Worth's eyes. But other contests were going on. In the budget were many systems and classes of ships, with every one at constant risk; threatened by liberals, nit-picked by defense intellectuals; or even in trouble due to ignoble squabbling amongst the staunchest of conservative friends over the spoils of procurement. The Vice-Chief's phone rang continually. Runners came and went, bringing news on how some key vote might be leaning, assessing what a frowning brow of a senior House staffer portended, or conjuring up some new strategy on how to by-pass yet one more know nothing "wise ass" in the Office of the Secretary of Defense . . . and so on. Unsurprisingly, Barney's days were wearing, with everywhere looming walls of Jericho ready to crumble at the wail of a hundred uncertain trumpets, never an unalloyed triumph whose half-life could safely be measured in more than a handful of days. Things allegedly stitched together one day unraveled overnight as maddeningly as Penelope's web.

This day a typical one, including an especially busy afternoon that had taken Barney Worth to the "Tank" for a meeting of the Joint Chiefs of Staff (filling in for the CNO, who was on travel), and then a dash up to the Hill to testify on the matter of sexual harassment of female sailors in a destroyer tender based in Norfolk, the majority of those aboard being pregnant. Having to respond once again to the whines and needles of Representative Pat Schroeder. A flaming A-hole, but a powerful one. Later he had worked in dutiful attendance at the funeral of a classmate at Arlington. Thus Barney Worth was burdened additionally with a sense of mortality, not the best of armors to absorb the news—crack out of the box as he hustled back into his office—that *Sea Eagle* was . . . "in trouble again."

Sea Eagle! Beside any threat there, bits of good news about mine sweeps, that handful of mere spikits, was nothing. The Admiral heard his aide out impatiently because he had heard it all before, the whispers against Sea Eagle's predicted effectiveness, opponents bringing up the disappointment of, God forbid, the unlamented SQS-26 sonar, the melancholy record of the old *Wilkinson* and the *Willy Lee*—as if history had any bearing!—the press leaks, the wavering members of the House Armed Services Committee (on which he kept a dossier, every slippery one), and so on. Enough to see that all of this was once again going to coalesce into the demand for more testimony on the Hill, and the Navy's further (and ever more difficult) twisting of the truth, sweeping facts under the rug . . . all of the painful usual. Not that consciously he thought of it that way.

Oh? That last could bring smiles to the knowing. Even Barney Worth, in rare moments of introspection, might have trouble with it. But damn it, in practical terms of what had to be done and *how*, the nitty-gritty of building a Navy, did anyone but Barney Worth realize all that was involved? With greater understanding, and greater wistfulness, than most men, he would occasionally recall Mark Twain's admonition always to tell the truth. That way you had much less to remember. Oh yes, very cute! Nice work if you could get it! But did anyone but Barney Worth—having ever more of these attacks of self-pity lately—truly grasp how difficult that was? The sheer mechanics of deception! No single lie did the trick; you needed whole seamless strongholds of them. The most maddening part of it all—beyond the dreary sense of *déjà* vu that came from lugging the same tired vugraphs (refurbished, of course, in fresh colors) up to the Hill for yet another try—was his inability to pin down his opposition. Veering phantoms, bats in perpetual dusk, forever flitting just beyond his ability to fix them clear in his sights. It was unfortunate that Smoke Madden should show up in the midst of this precipitately deteriorating afternoon. But Smoke was conscientious about his updates, more so than Barney Worth had expected him to be. A good citizen, Smoke, Barney would reflect grudgingly. Smoke's dump this afternoon covered a number of fire drills, but this one, coincidentally, concerned *Sea Eagle* and the offending, if temporarily out of mind, munchkin of a David Morgan.

Now the Admiral was sophisticated, knowing well that in the whole balky, gluey sequence of actions by which iron ore from the Mesabi eventually, across decades, is transformed into the steel of a finished warship, the notion that a minor civil servant could play any measurable role in preventing the Navy's gaining some major shipbuilding prize was absurd. Whatever advanced *Sea Eagle*, whatever halted it, was intertwined with countless forces shifting through the murk of Washington's grubby light—the ambitions of powerful men, the wealth of states, the survival of a thousand industrial vendors—and thus relationships of cause and effect, so direct and clear in classical physics, were untraceable in this detestable city. Indeed, the Admiral knew it better than anyone, which accounted for his chronic frustration at all the stinging burrs in his saddle that nothing could remove. Accounting too for the perking up of his ears, all angry alertness—metaphorically continuing the imagery of tormented horse and rider—at something as explicit as a particular human being. Human beings by God, were *not* phantoms. Identifiable people you could do something about. Kick their Asses. "That fink Morgan again?" The Admiral's fingers drummed. "Apparently," Smoke said cautiously, growing a little worried about Barney Worth. Knowing his man. He moved on from the matter of Morgan's latest article to mention of some evidently bothersome presentation at a recent symposium. Place called Wolf Lake. And *where in shit* is that?, Barney wanted to know, his color changing as visibly and dramatically as a chameleon pausing upon a rose. Smoke told him, conveying a bit more, as much anyway as Smoke himself understood of the setting and the purpose of the Wolf Lake Symposium and its conclave of obscure experts. While Barney Worth, throughout Smoke's description, waving these details aside like a man brushing away cobwebs, could barely hold back his impatience to get to the heart of the matter. "And just what the hell are this guy Morgan's bosses doing about him?" Barney's eyes narrowed, trying to recall, in summoning the name sought. "That new Boy Admiral, whatsisname . . . has got to be taking action, right?"

Well, as best Smoke was able to pick up on the matter—emphasizing the scraps of rumor and secondhand information upon which he was relying—the apparent strategy in handling Brother Morgan seemed to be one of subtle pressure, letting time and reflection work away on him, waiting for him to recant, the program thereby gaining for itself a heralded return of the prodigal to the fold.

"You know, Barney," Smoke said, "like in the Bible, that shepherd who's allegedly all the happier for getting back the one animal that's strayed than he's glad for his whole flock of sheep still with him . . . ." Smoke did not continue. He had gone farther than he wished, revealing more knowledge, however thin and fading, of the Bible than he cared to advertise. Even as he was more decisively slowed by the expression on Barney Worth's face, one far removed from the solemnity he professed at the countless Prayer Breakfasts that duty compelled him to attend and towards which the sum of his true beliefs was to be read in inverse proportion to the seeming reverence of his scrunched features.

"*Kid gloves*, Smoke?", Barney Worth murmured in wondering disbelief. "*That's it?*"

Barney Worth leaned back in his chair, gazing up at the uncommunicative ceiling.

"Tell me, Smoke, just what are they teaching the mids back at old Canoe U?"

"Got me, Barn." For a further moment of hushed silence the two men were one, or at least were sharing a point of tangency, the unspoken doubts about how well the U.S. Naval Academy was doing its job. On Barney Worth's part, having observed, year after year, the fresh crop of newly minted ensigns coming aboard his various ships for duty, that the ROTC graduates from the nation's premier colleges were superior in performance to their Naval Academy counterparts. The sense of this truth hit Barney again but with no better way to cope with it than at other times. His response therefore was oddly timid, peripheral. "Smoke," Barney's voice was small. "I hear they actually do have a Leadership course down there now. Or they are supposed to."

"So I hear," Smoke assented. With little interest, being one of those skeptics that Leadership could be taught at all. "Then, Smoke, *what the hell are they learning?*"

"Good question. But maybe they hadn't started it up when our Boy Wonder was there." Barney Worth stroked his chin for an answer that was no more yielding than the previously interrogated and featureless ceiling of his office. Barney Worth for a moment oddly dreaming. "Smoke, what do you figure you yourself ever learned from that place?"

Poor Barney. His question was at least semi-serious. Smoke gave a laugh. A Smoke having his own answer to that one long ago. "I took away just two things, Barn. How to tie a bowline and how to tie a Windsor knot." Yet that wasn't wholly true, Smoke thought. He could have added the knowledge on how to cover up and counter punch from Spike Webb, his old boxing coach. And, as a halfback on a pretty fair Navy football team, how to take a handoff and to plunge straightway into the line without waiting to see the hole. Just have faith that it was there. He had also, even then, picked up a sense of the hollowness in human affairs . . . but no, consciously Smoke put aside such thoughts. Anyway, that came later and besides, this bleakness of vision he felt was not something to be put into words. Not by Smoke Madden anyway.

"Why," Barney Worth said, "did I bother to ask?"

Smoke shook his head calmingly, still bothered by Barney's funny little smile. "Getting back to our boy Morgan. He's not that much of a factor."

"A factor *nonetheless*." Words bit off like nails. Smoke rounded out his picture with other information, stressing the truth that Morgan was hardly alone. There were major pockets of resistance elsewhere, especially in Naval Laboratories where, of course, oddballs were numerous and tolerated as institutional assets. Then there was the Pacific Fleet. Tommy Blue and his cohorts. They did have a free swinging way of looking at things in Pearl, Smoke added, tiptoeing around Barney on that one, concealing a residue of secret fondness. The Pacific Fleet was the grander Fleet, had higher hearts. The Pacific Ocean was the Navy's own by God, a battlefield won and never relinquished.

"Too fucking independent," muttered Barney Worth, himself an Atlantic sailor. He diagnosed the cause. "Just plain distance, the inverse square law of attenuation. Hard to make Washington's influence felt out there." He dwelled wistfully on the Atlantic, whose obedient naval forces were conveniently based. Just down the Chesapeake and you reached Norfolk's mighty port. Not so long ago, when the charismatic Admiral Charles Martell had been the ASW Czar, there was none of this chaotic Babel. "Why Charlie"—and here the tip of some instructive reminiscence from that irrecapturable time of dynamism broke through—"ran the Atlantic Fleet like his own boat pool . . . . Anyway," Barney concluded, "Tommy Blue won't be a problem much longer. We'll be dumping him."

"Firing Tommy Blue?" Tommy who had won Navy crosses in two wars and shot down seven Jap planes and flown with Wade McLusky?

"Why the hell not?" Barney glared, ramming his unlit cigar back in his mouth. One of many men lately constantly with a cigar, not for pleasure but effect. "He's had his day."

Now the world, as Smoke Madden saw it, was a battlefield and life was a journey lit with few things worth a man getting truly excited about. The responsiveness of a high performance aircraft. The cunt of a beautiful woman. The scent of wet autumn woods while waiting for a deer to glide down to a misty pond. Loyalty to rare men who had earned it. Smoke Madden better attuned to the Middle Ages. In the Fourteenth Century he would have followed the Black Prince, envied the survivors of the legendary Combat of Thirty. Knights who in dull times cooked up their own battles to the death just for the hell of it. This particular afternoon of the late Twentieth Century, however, looking past the diminutive figure of the Vice Chief of Naval Operations against the window to the sky sullen above Arlington, Smoke had no adequate response. But his thoughts were swirling in outrage: *Tommy Blue was at Midway!* And to be sent packing by a man of an age that had never known a winning war. No war at all, in fact, worth ten cents. A man for God's sakes who hadn't experienced the pucker factor. Toss that in too.

"Okay," Barney Worth said almost complacently, "what else?" Without further interest Smoke Madden finished up. Carelessly, beginning to repeat himself, and Barney was about to motion him shut when Smoke mentioned a certain oddly named little shop over in Materiel called ADAMP with which the Vice-Chief was making late and unwilling acquaintance. Barney Worth picking up on the name scowling. "Jencks?"

"Yes sir, Billy Jencks. Another bit player." "That's his whole name? A southerner?" Barney hunched forward, figuring it out. "Only down in grits country anyone lays on names like that." It was Smoke Madden's shrug that did it. Set Barney Worth off. *"What in hell does he do?"* The return of the senior Admiral's former choleric color, briefly fled, was swifter than an arctic gale. His face went from red to strangled purple.

Soothingly as he could—at best, imperfectly too, for Smoke seldom ventured across the borders of the arcane world of computers—he provided his understanding of what a certain obscure Billy Jencks was up to. Helpfully deciphering the acronym of Billy's work. Which Barney Worth jumped on. "Poor tin can sailors wasting time filling out goddamned forms and mailing data to Washington and never hearing anything back for their trouble. Pouring their stuff into a black hole. Thought we'd killed that stinking program." Smoke Madden smiled with the fun of a small needle. "Evidently parts of the beast survived."

"He's a computer puke, eh?" It was not a derogation to which Smoke Madden demurred. If they had further tangency, these dissimilar men, it was their attitude towards the digital computer. Of a transitional generation, resenting the instrument and destined—coming upon it too late in their careers—properly to mistrust it. Out of Smoke's combat experience came the suspicion that those bits of dancing binary code could bollix human judgment, betray instincts, at crucial moments let you down. Leaving a man without the compensating analog of his senses (these having atrophied) fully up and ably working to save him. Computers hid the plain truth that war came down to placing an ordnance package alongside the other fellow and making sure it exploded. And the man who could keep nerve and eye steady on old-fashioned cross hairs might prove to be the dominant warrior yet. "What's the relationship between these guys?" Barney said. "Relationship?" Smoke read the world distastefully. In addition to computers, Smoke and Barney shared convictions concerning the role of the sexes. Men and women *fit*. Men didn't. "Nothing like that, so far as I can see."

"No . . . *organizationally*. On the wiring diagram." The Admiral a connoisseur of organization charts. No neurosurgeon could direct a scalpel more skillfully at severing undesirable networks of communication. "Nothing," Smoke assessed, "I guess just friends."

Perhaps it was the word's simplicity, its harmlessness in juxtaposition with the nefariousness of the activities that Barney Worth surveyed. *"Friends?"* A grotesquerie to apply that word when more accurate and stronger ones—not the least, but including "traitors"—leapt raging through the Admiral's mind. If "friends" was the most that Smoke could come up with, words themselves were out of control. Suddenly it struck Barney Worth's frenzied consciousness that Smoke Madden was, in his own alarming way, also out of control. That still basically relaxed warrior, the same incurable slouch that bespoke the powerful athlete of long ago, was a maddening affront to all the unavailing past reminders which Barney had flung at this casually detached man. The worn uniform in which Admiral Worth had last dressed down the offending warrior was today at least pressed, but that only emphasized its threadbareness. The colors of its coveted ribbons had not weathered their final cleaning but run together in a mélange of pale streaks. Korea melded with the yellow of 'Nam', Purple Heart and Distinguished Flying Cross mixed with the surpassingly trivial National Defense Ribbon. Fraying threads cried out for snipping. Smoke Madden sure as shit out of control.

Barney Worth too, scarce wonder. Conflagration so swift that the chemist knows it only by the imprecise but satisfyingly vivid designation of explosion. Everything combustible in his nature going up at once. Friends *indeed*. "A couple of *piss-ants*."

Earlier the prevailing sense of order in the Vice Chief's office was noted, the smooth flow of its paper. What happened now could be viewed in several ways, either: *One*, evidence that the impression was illusion, a seemingly solid structure but of precarious imbalance forever on the verge of toppling, or; *Two*, evidence that the office could also handle its thunderstorms with the same cool professionalism that kept its paper moving in other climes. The actions now occurring amongst the staff, smoothly efficient as an Indy winner's pit crew hopping to change a tire in seconds flat, supported the latter interpretation. At a telltale rise in the Admiral's voice, an aide—one of the nimble and favored—

sped from his desk to shut the door on the tumultuous polluted stream pouring forth. But even the heavy door, the very walls themselves, could not totally bar the outrage emanating from the overwrought boss. Thus a waiting visitor—in the queue for his own moments with the mighty gentleman—would even as he pretended not to hear, observe a quickening in office activity. The secretaries, dignified ladies upon whose ears such language decently ought not to impinge, were typing away with extra clatter. Burying the signal, as the acoustician describes it, in white noise.

In defense of such outbursts, it is possible to rationalize them as not in disharmony with the naval scheme of things. A warship's propulsion plant is a marvel of balanced flow processes; demand for power and steaming rates linked in a complex continuum of pumps and regulating valves. Yet in recognition of the fallibility and the perils of the best of man's systems, safety valves are provided to send steam roaring harmlessly into the atmosphere before pressure can build to blow up boilers and kill people. Admiral Barney Worth himself now a boiler popping safeties. Ugly words issuing in a stream that if at first they had a crude logic—that is, the terms related more or less to the object being vilified—now were losing even that rudimentary grip on obscenity's conventions. To Smoke, though certainly not surprised to hear a high-ranking flag officer talk in such a manner, the deterioration in language was nevertheless marked. What struck him most was the *oddness*. Phrases starting out ordinary and springing to the bizarre. Cogent old words, proud since Shakespeare was a pup, split and recombined nonsensically. "Bullpricks!" Scatological terms were joining sacred ones, clinical words mating with the commonplace. Female parts were wildly imputed to male locations and vice-versa in weird anatomical confusion. Humorless hybrids out of Kraft-Ebbing and Dr. Seuss. And was that actually foam appearing at the corners of the Admiral's mouth? Smoke, who up until this moment had only heard of Barney's tantrums, never witnessed one up close, had to make sure. More seconds passed in which last shreds of rationality dissolved in a sea of vicious incoherence. Smoke strode around the desk and shook the little Admiral. "Barney, settle down." The Admiral's eyes, which had gone glazed—fixed on distant peaks of rage—began to clear. He looked around dazedly, regaining awareness. The objects of his fury had not departed, only now they seemed rejoined to some sense of proportion. "Wimps." "Okay, Barney, okay. I'll buy that. But easy, fellow."

"A pair of *wimps*. Goddamned nothings, holding up a whole ship class."

"Barney, they're hardly doing it by themselves."

"No?" Barney Worth was like a sad little boy, desperate to accept offered hope. "Still," shaking his head, "it shouldn't be that way, Smoke." Tears welled, his voice cracked. "Smoke. Did you know that that guy Morgan is actually quoted in *Morskoi Sbornik?* The Soviets, for Christ sakes. How do you build a Navy with creeps like that gumming up the works?" "Yes," Smoke said very softly. Some truth there.

In the strained quietness, Admiral Bernard Worth groaned. A hard day. A hard year as well. As gloomily forecast, this was proving the year for the Navy to take its lumps from the latest crop of second guessers. Could *no one*, he cried out, clutching his pounding head, lift from him the burden of his affliction? It was scarcely a cry worthy of King Henry, yearning to be free of the nagging conscience of Becket, nor was Smoke Madden his man for the deed. But later, gleams of night stars gathering across Arlington's hillside, in the presence of others more receptive, the Admiral's cry was uttered again, however plaintive and elliptical the form, and soon enough other barons were galloping off towards new Canterburys, swords sharpened, to make sure that whatever had to be done would be taken care of.

▲▲▲▲▲

Looking forward to this morning of the big show on DIANA even more than he had thought he would. Still on, he and Billy, to give their scheduled talks. David mentally reviewing his intended presentation as he drove in to work. Having entitled it "Grand Truth," and as it was listed on the Program, nevertheless, in keeping with his hopes for the continued sufferance of his tenure at EAR, he had crafted it less abrasively than his infamous rabble rouser at Wolf Lake. That Admiral Tommy Blue's people from the Headquarters of the Pacific ASW Forces were also appearing on the program reassured him that there would be no shortage of buttressing voices telling it like it was.

Moving along on crowded old Glebe Road, the road every commuter loved to hate, and then turning on to good old U.S. 1, David Morgan, mind and spirits in a balance of careful calculation, was a construct of courage and fear. A precarious equilibrium which, after only a few hundred yards of progress northward on Jefferson Davis Highway, was rudely ruptured with his right front tire blowing. *Bang.* The steering wheel almost jerked out of his grip, and his car veering sharply over onto the shoulder in a clatter of gravel and a roil of a century's roadside dust. Sitting there only a moment though, letting his trembling limbs steady themselves, just long enough to remember an auto repair shop a quarter of a mile up the road. Getting his old heap underway again, listing and thumping along on a flapping carcass of rubber and dropping his car off with a minimum of formality and looking for a taxi. *No taxis.* Thus hoofing it while traffic thundered on by him too close for comfort. Then looking at his watch and calculating his time, realizing that he still had to get over to the Pentagon, never mind how, he started running, briefcase slapping against his thigh. Thoughts about his presento mingling with a hundred stray thoughts, one of them the vow not mention to Al this latest fiasco, needing no more safety lectures on the importance of tires. It wasn't a hot day, not become one yet anyway, but running had made him sweat and Daisy, who spotted him as soon as he made it up to EAR, was clucking. "My goodness. You look god-awful. What happened?"

"No time to . . . tell," he said, still out of breath, "just time to pick up my view-graphs."

"Well", she said, "but surely a minute too to get you presentable." Which Daisy, with her sharply appraising eyes and efficient hands, helped achieve, brushing the dust from his trousers and shoes, smoothing his wilted collar, straightening his skewed necktie and, lastly, pressing her car keys into his hand to expedite getting him over to the Pentagon. "You've done enough rushing already this morning. Now you can make it there in plenty of time and be *calm*."

"Thanks a bunch, Daisy."

"Oh, by the way," she said, where did you leave your car?" He told her. "Oh God," she laughed, "Max Interrer's shop does good work but, I hate to tell you, he's a bandit."

* * *

"So whadda you know, whadda you know . . . . We're gonna have another say." Setting aside mystification and yielding to pleasure. Billy in spite of himself. "Yes, indeed," David said, "wonders never cease. But come on, Billy. Let's hustle. We don't want to miss a word."

"Yep, yep . . . ." Billy slapping his palms as they trotted on to the auditorium. Where they were brought up short by a line well removed, and in fact around the corner, from the auditorium entrance. "What the . . . heck?" "Probably just checking badges more carefully," David judged, "what with the full crush of late arriving attendees showing up all at once."

There seemed to be more to it than that. The line was lengthening and the administrative help at the tables located just outside the entrance and checking off names were taking extra time. Also, as Billy and David drew closer, they could see that, along with checking off names, the checkers were passing out a special kind of badge, plainly recognizable as such by its having boldly different colors. "So what's this?", Billy said, at once twitchingly alert.

"Nothing special, I suspect," David said.

"Not *nothing*," Billy pronounced. Raising his head alertly, like a bird dog sniffing a new scent. Adding slow postscript. "Something's up for sure." What was up became clearer in a few minutes when they had advanced to the young man with the list. Neither David's nor Billy's names were on it for attendance at the coming session. "I'm sorry, I don't understand," David's voice rose. The young man let David scan the list of names himself. Neatly typed, alphabetized, the sheet he looked at held both the J's and M's and it was plain that there was neither a Jencks nor a Morgan authorized. "I think there's been a mistake," David said, "is there no supplemental list here attached?" Yes, there actually was a supplemental list of authorized attendees, lately delivered, the young man said, and he flipped to the back of another stapled list and obligingly let David confirm for himself the absence of both their names. Meanwhile Admiral Snowdon and Tawney Gray had just shown up and were moving by in some sort of Expedited Access for the Important, who were evidently to be spared the pokiness and indignity of the regular check-in procedures. "I don't understand," David persisted, "there's definitely been a mistake."

The young man shook his head with a helpless half smile. His province a small one, not the correctness of lists, merely to check people in. Now looking back at the line of people which was growing longer, held up by this unknown but courteously obstinate individual who refused to bow to the finality of an approved list. David Morgan still protesting even as a hand was pulling him away. "What . . . *what* . . . . ?" David not realizing who or what had pulled him away until he was some yards down the corridor and realizing that it was Billy sparing him further humiliation. A Billy breathless with his certainty as to what had just happened. Thrusting a revised program at him. "Look. No ADAMP presento. No David Morgan. None of those guys from the Pacific either. "Jesus, Davey, can't you *get* it?" Billy's arm propelling him along as if he were in a trance. "*That's it*. The sign you've been looking for. *We've* been looking for."

"What are you saying, Billy?" Billy's exasperation grew with his impatience. "That's how they do it. Simple as you please. They don't have the guts to look you straight in the eye. But this is it. In letters ten feet high. We're out of it. Kaput. ADAMP is history and so are you and we're both going to be hijacked off to somewhere else."

Yes, David thought, feeling as if he had been kicked in the gut. Yet he couldn't get over how quietly—skillfully, looked at one way too—it had been done. No more of a sound than of scissors snipping a thread. They were walking briskly, but also as if to nowhere. He became aware of a clacking sound and realized that it was Billy's boots. Clack, clack, clack . . . the loudest sound in this Pentagon corridor, sharp over the murmur and rustle of people's to and fro. Which sound was a kind of punctuation to Billy's running commentary on the event that had just transpired. Billy's voice gaining further timbre in outrage.

"Fools, Davey, that's what we are. Now they're just going through the motions. Going to be nothing but a Pep Rally. No more Bad news, just convincing each other how they're going to fix everything, cure all problems, pulling new decibels of signal excess for DIANA, gain, signal processing, better dome coating . . . all right out from where the sun don't shine."

"Yep." Finding himself gritting his teeth against the acid rain of Billy's assessment. For all its accuracy, or perhaps, paradoxically, *because* of it, wanting to hear it less. "*Davey.*" There was a new plaint in Billy's voice. "Just where *in shit* are we heading?"

"Now there's a good question." Which David Morgan, without attempting to answer it, now simply deflected their steady, but heretofore directionless tramp over towards the broad corridor of the A-ring. The windows on this inner corridor overlooked the expansive central inner courtyard, itself pentagonal, an area of calm pleasantness unsuspected by the passing motorist on the speedy roads that encircle the Pentagon. It was the kind of warm day that Washington confers until well into October and which makes Fall, if any season there is loved, the favorite of many. The grass in the courtyard had kept the vividness of early summer, leaves had only half turned, and their colors were bright. More people than usual had been drawn out for their noon hour. They were lying on the grass, sitting at tables under colored umbrellas; some were strolling along the geometric walkways that radiated out from the center. In no hurry to return to their cubicles. There were couples arm in arm. Two not so young men in shirtsleeves were tossing a Frisbee. All of this under a heart-breakingly blue sky. But if there was gentleness to the scene, there was also strength, with its sweetness a quiet defiance. The wooden kiosk was out of another time. David thought of a pointillist painting, quivering with life like one of Seurat's holiday views of a park by the Seine. Wounded as he was, the whole business unimaginably demeaning, some part of him was still capable of surprise, reminding him of his innocence. Yet he was not yet ready to massage his wound, even to think ahead. He merely felt—the bruised spirit in him perhaps unconsciously shutting out the morning that had been—some dim but linking common awareness, and out of it tenderness towards all those in the courtyard. Harmless companions, unknown thousands of accomplices, trapped in this familiar prison; in its simplicity a small and winning glory. These people too had their file cabinets, their safes and desks, seniors to please, their own little pieces of paper, red hot for a day, knowing each one their own moments in the light .... He and Billy gazing out the window. Billy's eyes on the secretaries down there, small figures against the high tawny concrete walls. From here all were fair. "I see that the kiosk is still open," David said.

"The *what*?" "The lunch stand," David said. "Let's get a bite."

"Why *here*? No point in sticking around old Fort Fumble. I'm not even hungry. I lost my appetite in there. If you want to, okay .... " More anguish burst forth. "*Davey. They don't even want to hear.*" Billy's reluctance notwithstanding, they descended to the courtyard and each bought a hamburger, a coke, and chips and carried them to a bench. The pre-cooked hamburgers were wrapped in wax paper sealed with scotch tape. The hamburgers were tepid. Billy took the top half off of his own to examine the flattened circle of grey bloodless meat, looking as if advanced to some form of early decay, lopsidedly framed in the catsup reddened sog of the mashed bun. "*Aagh*. How do you begin to bite into that thing?" His disgust over the conference must have been nauseous as well. "Just don't look," David said, "that's the key."

"*God!*" Billy. More than usually full of high horse judgments. "You married to a gourmet cook too." Becoming glummer with each crunch of his potato chips, all he was willing to eat. David was feeling the sun upon his face, soaking through the fibers of his jacket too, deliciously warm. Perhaps meaning its last kindness he would know for some while. Take it. Billy's next words—a continuation of his rant—deferred to appreciation of a tall girl in red slacks walking by. Gloriously trim, a creature not of this sodden place, a shining representative of all the hungers of Billy's life. "*Dee-feat,*" he said dramatically. "We're totally out of it, forever, you realize. And don't give me any more of that business about how they're going to find out the truth eventually."

Billy jumped up. "Jesus, David. In the *long* run, some smart guy once said, we're all going to be dead. Stop thinking of the Navy and start worrying about yourself. They're not thinking about *you*. They're going on to fame and glory, riding DIANA for all she's worth . . . ." A crumb of potato chip hung to one lip despite his agitation. Though unwillingly, David found himself listening attentively. "Your rival Julius will be riding high. Tawney Gray will stay on, of course, making pretty speeches and screwing his way round the world. With old Sneedon *Whodon, young* I guess I should say, going to get his third star and, as I hear it, heading off one of these days to put down what's left of the Pacific rebels."

"Quite a picture, Billy."

"You've got your patented little smile, Davey, but it isn't funny." Billy still doing one of his little dances. Unable to stand still if he wanted. The sticking chips doggedly clinging. "So beat 'em' to the punch, Davey, find a new home if you can. Try Mines. You know mines. Me, I'm just a doink. Probably end up over in Human Services. Or worse. If anything is worse . . . ." Muttering on. *Mines*, David murmured, lessening its strangeness. It might turn out he could be comfortable with them again. Weapons that wait, their friends called them. And, after all, he was something of a waiter himself, in spite of his grand impatience. And the men who nurtured mines were not uncongenial. Men too of enduring passion, fellow seekers in dimness. If their flame did not burn high for the world to see, it was steady. There was challenge too. Year by year mines— at least on paper—grew trickier, did their listening and counting with ever-greater subtlety. Mine men were basically happy too. Frustrated, deprived, but quietly sure their time would come. Old Lassen, forty years studying the phenomenology of mines burying themselves, establishing, *reestablishing,* the obvious, lugging his tired fluttery time lapsed murky underwater movies of mines snuggling down in the sand, showing them to all who would sit still for them. Hair grey as winter, Lassen still keeping his smile.

Billy though had already reconsidered. "Nope. Not mines. They'll be afraid you haven't put your whistle away. Mine programs are too fragile to tolerate a Davey Morgan. Mine folk rightly figuring most of the world out there is plotting to put them out of business. If a mine doesn't blow up one of our ships once every six months—the Navy's half life of memory—it forgets they exist." The door to mines barred, Billy had a good idea what the alternative would be. "One of the 'Ilites'." A sentence dolefully pronounced.

"Jesus." David said involuntarily, "I hope not." Sadistically teasing, Billy ticked each one off," . . . Maintainability, Reliability . . . even Operability, maybe." A giggling Billy. David folded his wrappers and stuffed them into the overflowing trash basket and minutes later they were proceeding down the A-ring towards the Concourse. Billy had not stopped talking. The clacking sound, odd but familiar, seemed intensified in its renewed accompaniment. "I *got* it. Supportability . . . *there's* the living death." "Okay, Billy, that'll do."

"I remember Aliason telling me at the EAR picnic about the trip to France she was planning to celebrate your getting your Fourteen. A long while now until that happens. You may work your way up again, knowing you, but it will be extra slow in any of the 'Ilites'. The worst of it is what they do in those shops: *Nothing.*" The clacking was louder, too obviously emanating from Billy himself. People were noticing. Here in these corridors where people lived out whole lives never looking twice at a passing soul. "How will you break all this to Aliason?"

"That's *my* problem, Billy."

"Sorry. Forgive me for living." Abruptly they halted. This morning's experience had gotten to them, done more mischief; the years had taken their toll and a full sum of frustration was due. One of those balloon payments in which America specializes and which lie in wait for its strivers. Friendship was staggering under the load of disappointments shared. In the middle of the broad corridor, with pedestrian traffic, and even a slowly pumping bicycle mail messenger wending his way around them, they were quarreling. During a moment when Billy had reduced himself to mere sputtering, David decided that he was going to have to be the source of whatever calm that might be applied to this eruption of nuttiness. Drawing out his handkerchief, he removed from Billy's face a spot of foam dribbling out of the side of his mouth. *"What are you doing?"* Billy shrieked. "Billy, for God's sakes," flicking away that last stubborn bit of chip. "There. You've got to take care how you look. Forgive me, but it costs you. Sometimes you can look ridiculous." *"Me?* For ridiculousness, you leave me in the dust." Belatedly David had identified the source of the clacking. Nailed it down. Loosening layers of hard wood lamination in the structure that constituted Billy's footwear had gained a rhythmic acoustic life of their own. "And Billy, I hate to tell you this too, but you're making a racket like a Dutchman in clogs. My friend, trust me, you don't *need* those stilts."

"Don't *need?"* Billy lowered his voice momentarily for the passing by of a pair of distinguished looking generals, gravely conveying perfection in the fit of their uniforms. His reddened eyes glared at David through pools of wetness. "And what the hell do you know about shoe construction? Fact is, engineers have investigated a whole variety of materials, metal, reinforced plastics, the works, and found that for these platforms wood is still the best. Old fashioned, beautiful, American . . . *wood.*"

"Billy, I'm only saying—" "*What do you know about anything?*" Billy sneered. "Nowheresville, that's your destiny, Davey. Not even the Beltway Bandits will touch you. You'll rot in National Center. And your family will pay. *Rot.*"

"Billy . . . ." But his hurt friend was stomping off. Then, seemingly conscious of the impression he was radiating, Billy altered his gait to lessen his afflicting sound. Taking his steps with care, self-consciously, like a man trying to glide across a floor of eggs. Remorsefully David ran after his friend and caught up with him at the ramp sloping down to the Concourse. "Billy, please . . . ." Billy jerked his arm away and kept on, and now, after a moment, David realized that he too was walking without an objective. Arriving at the Concourse, moving generally towards the stairs that led to the busses spitting smoke, but heading there circuitously. He felt himself in a giant eddy, a chip of humanity drifting in aimless circularity. As always, the Concourse thronged. It could be midmorning or three in the afternoon, times which should be the quietest, yet this vast and odd openness was heavily murmurous, like restless tides. For it was not in sinister offices, where—as the world imagined—the presumed monstrous plotting of various forms of destruction was taking place, that the Pentagon existed most truly. Right here in the Pentagon's public Concourse, at its threshold, beat its true pulsing heart; human, distracted, paradoxically innocent. An indefinable city unto itself, perpetually dim, neither day nor night, a single unchanging season like a subterranean cave of earth. The lights of the shops shone alluringly, creating a Midway of desire. David found himself looking at individual faces and it came to him easily what it was that he read on their faces. Dreams. And that was why most of them were here longer than they had to be, dawdling on errands beyond their original purpose . . . drifting fishlike, unalarmed, in a dreaming sea. Clothing store displays helped people imagine how they would look living their dreams. Travel agencies—mounting posters of castles and sunny beaches and Macchu Picchu in the clouds—promised the magic of rapid transportation and to confer upon the fortunate all arrangements for serene voyages. Banks were there to help the saver, for the spender as well, with loans for those to whom thrift perhaps came hard. A drugstore shone with its massed creams and lotions, compressing the hopes of human transformation. Aspirin to banish headaches, contraceptives to make joy safe. Book stores to fuel dreams—had he not picked up many there for Al?—to concentrate their sparkle. Posters heralded the boons of education and listed extension courses; pasteboard color photographs showed ivied towers that presumably anyone might scale. A man in a blue blazer with brass buttons was helping someone fill an application for the fruits of knowledge, the magic wand of its power. Stands of flowers were here too, lending sweetness and glory to the shadows.

Protesters had planted themselves, a half dozen young adults in sheets, long hair spilling; their hands were smeared with the thickness of simulated gore. Crude signs in black told of death and bombs and their bearers were chanting words indecipherable against the reverberance of thousands of shuffling feet. It made no difference. No one was listening. People glanced incuriously and eased around them, the questing lights in unheeding eyes not changing, nor their fixity either of grave and distant longings. Occasionally someone looked away guiltily—not about the message, they could care less, their lives had nothing to do with bloodshed, were only of paper, of dollars and car pools, groceries and furniture, of promotions and lust, the countless worms of small cravings—but some were sensitive to proprieties, brought up to revere politeness. Bothered that these sad young in their pathetic sheets were trying to get something across and no one cared.

David had been thinking himself about dreams. Asking if it was true that people must have them to live. He had been toying with the idea of bringing a small gift home for Al. It might make things go down more easily, breaking the news. Consciously, he decided against buying anything. Seeing them both at the brink of a bleak period where they must live without dreams. For a while anyway. Though that last modifier—the temptation to cling to it—might be, in its own way, the biggest dream of all. The fact was that the looming situation could prolong itself forever, and Billy, pain in the butt that he was, was right as rain, and true austerity had to start somewhere. With direction decided, briskly he headed towards the busses, fifty smoking elephants at least, all in a line. Thinking: Have I done this to myself? Or was it fated, inescapable? Conscience wanting to believe the latter. Anyway, a world of time for sorting that one out. Only then, about to board one of the busses back to Crystal City did he remember the business of his car and its flat tire on the morning drive in and finally, bless Daisy, realizing that her car was sitting right here in South Parking waiting for him.

▲ ▲ ▲ ▲ ▲

Back at his office, there was a note. Al had called; he was to contact Interrer's Garage. The note was from Daisy, doing double duty today, Helen off and no replacement for Viola yet having been found. Not that, in regard to the latter, had there been much looking either. The voice at the garage was sharp, hard, partaking of the sounds of clangorous iron that was its background. "Max Interrer here."

"Yes, Mr. Interrer. I'm Mr. Morgan who—"

"Yep, fellow who came limping in with the flat this morning. Just wanted me to give it a patch. Tried that, but it wouldn't hold no air. Carcass too bruised.

You have to get a new tire, mister. Called your home. Didn't have your office number."

"I see. Well, if that's the extent of the bad news, just go ahead—" A harsh laugh broke in. "Mister. That ain't all. Your wheel rim's shot. How far did you drive on that flat?"

"Too far I guess."

"You got that right." He took aboard the man's figures. An exact number for the new wheel. But only an approximate dollar figure for the new tire which, David told the man, sounded higher than he would have thought. Again that laugh. Sharp and hard as a tire iron. "Sure it's high, mister. You got a radial on the other front and they gotta match. Gimme me a ring towards end of the day and I'll let you know when she's ready."

Daisy happened by his doorway when he put down the phone. "Just making sure you got your phone message. By the way, if you like I'll drive you over to Interrer's after work."

He took Daisy up on her offer. He was beat. The day which had begun so long ago, nothing good in it from its very start, with detection of the tell-tale sweetly sour exudation seeping through Al's soft white cool morning skin. Breath fresheners, the odorlessness of vodka, other stratagems, all together had their own varied success rates at concealment, but this betrayal was sure, bouquet beyond the conquest of artifice. Saying nothing, nothing new to say, making coffee and slipping away. When late afternoon came and the office turned quiet he was grateful for Daisy's matter-of-fact kindness, the efficiency of her mind, her accurate assessment of the situation a la Interrer's. "I'll just sit a minute and wait right here," she said, pulling up in front of the begrimed cinder block structure of Interrer's garage, "until you make sure that your car's ready."

The garage interior was grimmer, grayer, oilier, mustier, more cavernous than he remembered from this morning. Day's light had shifted and the place was contrastingly dark from the remembered bright hardness of morning. Max Interrer in begrimed T-shirt, wrench in hand, wiggled his leanness out from under a car that was not David Morgan's. Shaking his head. "Nope. Not ready. You should of called first. Still waiting on those tires. Had to scout around for a set. So, maybe an hour. Give me a ring."

David was struck by something—like how did a *tire* become a *set* of tires?— but as he was about to ask, from somewhere, unseen within the depressing spaces of the garage, came a rapid banging of metal in whose thunderous reverberations all possible conversation was obliterated. He watched and then something in him said let it go and he went back out to Daisy's car and gave her a thumbs down sign. She reached over and pushed the passenger door open. "Hop in. No point in your hanging around that dreariness for an hour. You can relax up at my place. Okay?" Okay.

He had not known the location of Daisy's apartment building, only that it was in downtown Rosslyn, but he was to discover it as pleasantly luxurious, discreetly expensive. A mirrored and paneled elevator propelled them swiftly, up thirty plus floors. Whatever the mixed bag of Daisy's personal history, she had obviously seen to the strength of her finances. In the pictures on the wall, in one grand painting especially in colors of blue and gold, with a military jet visible and yet small over a sunlit mountain, and in a simple silver frame an inscribed photograph of a man in a naval uniform, David was seeing a tastefully set forth tribute to fond memory. She led him to a balcony whose view she urged him to enjoy while she took a moment to do a little fiddling around in the kitchen.

"Fiddle away," he called back, taking a gingerly downward glance towards an abyss of empty space overlooking a parking lot and neat massings of cars sickeningly far below. But it was a good place from which to gaze across the rooftops and flora of Washington's far-flung suburbs and take in the still sunny late afternoon view of the best of its monuments, their stone pale and strong for the grandest of its men that the city had served up to history. Daisy called from within, "I'm not deserting you. Just fixing a little something."

"Doing fine," he called back, "this is a great place to get one's red, white, and blue pumped up." Her laugh was soft. "Tell me about it. I step out there often."

He could hear Daisy rustling things, an oven door thunking shut, and in between Daisy humming a tune. She joined him now out on the balcony, tray in hand. "Fixed us some of these little cheezit things. Nothing fancy, just heat and serve, the best I have I'm afraid."

"The best," he bowed, taking several, "is good enough."

The light was too bright out here, harsh for Daisy's years, and as if she felt it she led him by the hand back inside, asking him how the conference had gone. Knowing more than she pretended, nodding to his recounting of the barring of himself and Billy.

"So," she said, "you're still twisting in the wind."

"That's the in-vogue phrase." She clicked her tongue in sympathy, touched him. "Well," she said, how about a margarita? You could use something."

"I think you're right there." A margarita? How long since he had one?

"Say. I'm sorry," Daisy said, "slipped my mind. Your wife called earlier this afternoon when you were down the hall and she wanted you to call. Apologies."

"No problem." Picturing Al and her small and yet endless urgencies. "I should give her a ring though. Let her know I'll be late and so on."

"Absolutely." Daisy gestured him towards the privacy of her bedroom. The room was large, dim, winningly feminine, pale in its pearl décor, soft with a lounge chair and silken cushions, a brocade canopy of muted but not inconspicuous design whose abundant folds might have seemed too much, but somehow did not. There were many more pictures on the wall, a fighter plane doing its stuff, scenes of far off lands, both painted and photographed, more trove of Daisy's memory, but none of them could be made out clearly and he did not want to be caught wandering away from Daisy's bedside phone to conduct serious inspection.

"*Darling,*" Al's voice was breathless, "At last. Anyway, the important thing is that Mr. Interior called about your repairs. He had to call home, he said, because you didn't leave your office number. But I'm so relieved he was able to get hold of someone about all of your awful tires." "*Tires?*" His hand was sweating, growing slippery on the plastic.

"Well yes, of course, *tires*. Well, anyhow, it seems that your two rear tires are also in awful shape too and need replacing, and while I know it was no fun having your blowout, you'll have to agree that it was a lucky break that Mr. *Interior* got a good look at all your tires...."

"*Interrer.*"

"What? Okay, *Interrer*. What diff? The important thing is that—"

"I'm on the hook for four new tires." "Actually five. The spare, of course."

"*Al.*" "David. I don't know what that little peep was about. *Of course* you have to have a spare. If you'd had one this morning, you'd have just propped up your car and put on your good old trusty spare and been zipping on your way." His hand was unable to crush the receiver into pink plastic bits. The balked pressure radiated down to his gut, twisted viscera over the leaden donut that had been breakfast, squeezed darkness. "Al. *How much?*"

"Just a minute. I have it all written down. I know you may be a little shocked, but Mr. Interrer and I had quite a long talk about tires. I learned an awful lot that I didn't know before. And you probably didn't either, my poet and dreamer. He was quite patient with me and though he's on the rough side I would say that he's really an awfully nice man. Anyway, according to Mr. Interrer, it seems that if you have one radial you have to have all radials."

So it is written in letters of gold.

"Darling, am I hearing music?", she said.

He froze. "You may be." "*May?* I *know* I am. It's Mozart. His Twenty-First. The Elvira Madigan.... Where on earth are you?"

"Just some bar." "Well, I must say it's a lovely one. It makes me want to get back to playing. Oh why oh why did we ever sell our lovely Baldwin?"

"You really want me to tell?" "No, no. I *know*. Too well. But listen, darling. Please now, you take all the time in the world to be sure that your car is absolutely right before you drive off." A kiss smacked down the wire.

Daisy was still playing when he came out from his call. She rose from the ivory colored bench that matched her ivory baby grand with its polished reflective surfaces. "Don't stop."

"That's it. Don't know any more. Just showing off." She gave him an inquiring look, not intrusive but sympathetic, expressing only the concern.

Curiosity she would keep to herself. "Now for your overdue drink. I held off the blender part just so it would be fresh."

"Thanks, but I really can't figure on staying very long, Daisy."

"Lean back and relax. Old Max Interrer takes his time." He obeyed, sinking back against soft cushions. Surrendering to the comfort of the cushions, finding himself adapted to the atmosphere of Daisy's roomy apartment with its perfectly ordered décor. To its neatness, its foreignness to him, its seamless melding with the easy efficiency and practicality of its solitary inhabitant, no longer striking him as intimidating. Daisy declaring that she would pass up her classical tapes, that the hour called for lightness, did it not? Treating him to Caribbean music, island tunes, reggae and calypso, but not any of the standards of Belafonte *et al*, but older singers Daisy said she liked even better, names like Trinidad Tiger and Blind Blake and he was shutting his eyes to take in *Mary Ann* and *Yellow Bird* and *Dolly Dawn* and the full soft flow of all that go-to-hell music from places easy to picture, steel drums and waving palms presiding over the loneliness of tropic sands. Then he was leaning back still further, deeper into those welcoming cushions, opening and then shutting his eyes again to the sounds of an old Sinatra tape, the voice unmistakable, the songs marvelous, ingeniously phrased, out of the recent times of America and resonant with wry and saddened nostalgia. The man hit every note, slurring not one, and any listener could forget that modulating that clear and glorious resonance of acoustic energy was the soul of a pig. From hidden speakers, loveliness. This was *America* wafting, America distilled. His country's inventiveness, its pleasures in array, its endless possibilities, the beguiling sense of all good things awaiting, the blessings of its land, whatever.

He opened his eyes to the clinking of ice and the scent of lime and tequila in his nostrils. The goblet she put in his hand was graceful and frosted and its fluid, green as early spring, was at his first sip all that he remembered a margarita to be. Tart, fruity, with a meliorating suggestion of healthfulness. "Thank you, Daisy." She hovered over him a moment longer, coaxing from him his opinion, which he preceded by licking his lips thoughtfully. She backed off, satisfied, cautioning, "Take it slowly. They go down just a bit too easily. And now, I know you'll forgive this working gal for not changing her evening's routine. Which is kick off her shoes and relax. I'll disappear for just a minute to shed my uniform."

Daisy emerged from her bedroom wearing a long, full length loosely belted gown of light tannish color printed with the primitive design of a South Seas tapa cloth, dark brown and the deep reds of old blood. She was barefoot. The gown softened her lean severity, took years off, and it seemed she had done something with her hair too. Perhaps though merely loosened it.

"Get you another?" He had not realized that he had almost finished it, and much too quickly, but so he had. He looked at his watch. "I guess I have a little time still."

He leaned back again, deeply, almost languorously. Not sleepy but something better than sleepy. Frankie was singing on, a laudation of love and honesty. The orchestration rose climactically with his voice, its thunder though never drowning him, as the singer batted out his concluding paean for primal virtues, the beauty and grandeur of human existence. The voice rolled on and away, ceased to be exhortation and retreated to soothing whisper, each listener's alone. America herself seemed summoned upon some great stage while one imagined the spotlight shifting away from mere Frankie and his much lifted pumpkin face, and one was seeing only purple mountains and small towns and Stars and Stripes Forever and good wars won. "Here you *are*," she said, handing him his second drink and sitting down beside him with her own.

"Cheers."

"Cheers," he returned. They chatted a little then of the office, the life they shared, of Tawney's quirks, other challenges and personalities. Yet only a moment later it *hit* him, a sharp insertion of pain throbbing along the skull's path behind his eyes. He waited, pausing in a moment of suspended but genuine fright, for the pain to get worse. To become overwhelming, fatal, if that it was going to be. Instead the pain merely became less focused, settling into dull heavy throb. At the same time he felt it traveling downward, reradiating into the pit of his stomach with the beginnings of nausea. He leaned forward carefully to set his drink down on the coffee table but the act, which he judged was performed with deceptive self-control, nevertheless betrayed. "You all right?"

"A bit of a headache."

"Aspirin? Or maybe one of those sinus pills? I've got a full medicine chest."

With his eyes shut and his fingers to his temple, he was aware of her departing only in the sense of diminished pressure beside him on the couch. She was back with a glass and pills, white and pink, lying on her open palm. "Gobble them all, but with lots of water."

He did as he was told, wiped his lips on the back of his hand. "Thanks." "Now lean back again," she ordered, "way back, let me help you." She started rubbing his head.

"Sorry about all this, Daisy," he said, yielding to her massaging fingers. "My apologies."

"Relax. Going to take more than a few minutes."

He breathed deeply, surrendering to command of her fingers manipulating his temples in slow circular motion, the skin sliding across hard bone just above his eyes. Surrendering too to the scent of an unfamiliar perfume seeming somewhat closer, surrendering at last, languorously and strangely—enormously tired, but alert too, not drifting completely—to awareness of the arousal of his loins. The pressure of an erection building which she could scarcely avoid noticing and which now, with her other hand—even as the rubbing of his head underwent no slighting—she was helping him gently with another kind of caress. "Daisy...."

"Shh... here now. Let me help our boy out so he'll be more comfortable." Lazily he observed, languidly he helped with the fumbling of an awkward unzipping. Wonderingly too. *So how in hell... ?* The dumbness of such questioning. Because they all knew, of course, and why shouldn't they? Fingers thoughtful and knowing. But that sort of mulling was *ex post facto*, not of the moment, which latter was pure pleasure and mindless, the urgent spike of sensation that for millions of years has energized the human race. *Ah. Yes! Yes! Yes!*

"My goodness." She sounded genuinely surprised. Perhaps at how soon it happened. Or perhaps at the volume she was witnessing. For which its offeror felt he had to explain.

"Sorry. But it's been a while."

"I would say." With which no doubt well founded judgment, missing not a beat, she was reaching for a tissue. Which tissue, located on a side table and encased in a finely painted decorator's box studded with colored pseudo gemstones, no doubt not even to be judged semi-precious, perhaps mere bits of glass, but awink with gathered light of the fading day and not without their own prettiness, seemed to be sitting right there in readiness, as if waiting for just such a purpose. Even as Daisy Ketcham, herself quick as a minute, was applying those tissues as efficiently as she did those same supple fingers to her keyboard, as if continually poised for just such an event. Whisk, whisk, and a couple of sheets of tissue had served their purpose. She kept her hand on him there for wordless moments longer, thoughtfully, his hand companionably pressed atop hers, until there was no longer any point and she was tucking his shrunken self back in efficiently. Her face had crept nearer. "Been a while for me too, David Morgan."

He didn't reply. He was appalled. At himself. With regret, guilt, fear pulsing through him like the standard three phases of alternating currents that he understood so well. All of them repetitiously energizing the looming question in one David Morgan who had never known, hardly ever imagined, a single instance of marital infidelity in his life. Who thus neither by experience nor temperament, nor from knowledge, had the foggiest, the *least*, resources to decipher the conundrum hammering through his brain. Did it *count*? But who was he kidding? Knowing all too well that it did, by the only count that mattered. Al's. He had an overwhelming desire, near frantic, to get away but now here was Daisy's face pressing close upon his own. "*I want more.*" He smelled her breath, faintly sour like sourdough bread, above all natural, the sense of a fellow human body leaning too close. Another breath descended heavily. Her eyes were hooded. *"Much more."* Perhaps it was only her breath, its visceral hints inviting deeper knowledge, threatening perilous intimacies from which it might be much harder to withdraw. She made a quick, almost imperceptible shift of her position on the couch and her hand went under her gown. Wordlessly she thrust her fingers to his nostrils. Essence of Daisy. Strong but not rank, its oily moistness a powerful refutation of any false image of our Daisy as all papery dryness of pressed flowers.

"Ah, Daisy." In the slow measured way of removing her fingers from their gentle but firm aggression, conveying both courtesy and infinite regrets. Following up with a sigh.

"Afraid I best be checking on my car." "Drat your car." She moved back a few but critical inches, a pale blur of disappointment. "Why don't you first give them a call?"

She waved him towards her bedroom phone but did not follow. With a deliberately loud voice, meant to be overheard, he faked conversation. "Yes, Mr. Morgan . . . here. Ready? She is for sure . . . ? He rang off curtly, putting the receiver down hard with feigned annoyance.

"I'll take you," Daisy offered, slipping on some low shoes.

"Tell you what. I'll walk," he said, "it's not over ten minutes. Not worth the nuisance of getting your car out of the parking garage only to get stuck in the slows of what is still rush hour traffic. The walk will do me good."

"I thought I had done you good," she smiled mournfully.

The walk, as Daisy had forecast, was a dreadful one. Trucks rumbled by, spewing gasses in noisy pauses at intersections ruled by lights designed to guarantee any rare and oddball pedestrian a risky crossing. In the shortness of his transit emotions flitted, refused to alight; inescapable wraiths of feelings that were less guilt and closer to shame. Atop all was the sense that Daisy had been diminished, and there was no way to make that right.

Reaching the garage, its proprietor emerged from the grimy lights of its greasy cinder block spaces, dust and oil suspended in the dim and surreal air. Work toughened, mean-eyed, the black wrench in Max Interrer's hand was like an extension of slender but wiry forearms whose strength would endure into age. As would rudeness. "Car's been ready a good while. Would'a been closed up 'cept for a late job." Glad for that, you A-hole.

"You say something, mister?"

"I said, I trust you'll take a check."

"What? For nine hunnert some dollars. You don't have no credit cards?"

"Not with me." Take it or leave it you son of a bitch.

The hour was late and Max Interrer was tired too and he had, in his own time and in his own way, faced and held his own with meanly glaring men holding tire irons. Right now, one David Morgan, a slight bookish fellow in a suit and with twitching lips stared him down. Writing out the check and thinking, David Morgan, with bleak amusement. *Absurd.* Not Camus kind of absurd, but a smaller included piece of it, the wonder and the nuttiness of the human condition, the American part anyway, that had not David Morgan alone, but millions like him—Al more on target than she knew—spending ever more money that they didn't have and going ever deeper in debt, juggling withdrawals and deposits in multiple bank accounts and plundering no end of easy lines of credit, in that tawdry game he played so nimbly and whose catastrophic ending he used to foresee in many a wakeful nightmare, until at last, over time, it began to seem that Armageddon, at least his own small one with a small *a*, managed to keep receding into the indefinite future, his mechanical rabbit somehow staying ahead of that pack of dogs yelping after it. He was smiling now, thinking of Al and her man still pulling rabbits out of his hat, maybe not so crazy a notion after all, and still smiling goofily, thoughts far away, and it was not until Max Interrer was lifting the check from his abstracted fingers and regarding him with a puzzled look that David Morgan recovered and realigned himself with the present moment and remembered to ask where the men's room was located. "All the way back and right," Max Interrer said, recovering his own brand of charm after a momentary lapse into bemusement at his check-writing customer's drifting off into some never-never land, "but don't be taking lots of time there. Gonna be locking up soon."

"I shall not tarry." But he did, having made it to the very rear of the cavernous garage and latching himself into the begrimed filthiness of Max Interrer's washroom, easy to believe its setting some sort of new low even by the drear standards of such industrial spaces. Groping for a greasy light switch firing up the single bare hanging bulb, illumination both dim and harsh. Revealing a floor littered with crumpled paper towels, a begrimed washbasin and a toilet bowl that even a thirsty dog would pass up lapping from. To which David Morgan paid no attention, splashing water and grabbing the gritty blackened fragment of workmen's soap and rubbing its chlorine rich sandpaperiness across his fingers, over his face, with the vigor and panic of the damned. Banishing, he trusted, all residue of *eau de Daisy* to whose scent, just as David Morgan was one to detect a single lingering molecule of Gallo's best in a rinsed glass, his Al, no less with a wrinkle of her delicate nose he was hauntedly sure, could bring comparably matching alertness to a rival. Ablutions done, finding no clean towels left in the battered dispenser, making do with dry and passably clean pieces torn from the paper littering the floor.

He drove homeward through lessened traffic in the last light of day. Confident of the severity of his measures in Max Interrer's dainty washroom and soothed by the extra smoothness of his old heap rolling along on its grand new rubber, orders of magnitude too good for it. His mind quieted at last too, mental gymnastics and rationalizations having run their course. Internal arguments that could only be recycled so long. Just past Tysons Corner an historical marker told of when those converging roads were wilderness trails and gave the date when Stonewall Jackson's Brigade had tramped by. A man sat waiting on a folding chair beside a roadside stand offering bunches of flowers. Pulling over, David Morgan guessing that this tiny business had served the needs of other tormented consciences. "Flowers, you want flowers, mister?" The man was old, wiry, but not decrepit. His voice was sharp, mirthful, pure country. The strength of better times was in him. Someone content to be sitting breathing foul roadside air and trading his hours away for small change beneath a sooty sky's last light. "I was just wondering"—well, plausibly, just what ought a reasonable man to be wondering?—"how long these flowers will last."

"Forever!" the seller called out uproariously. Slapping his knee. A card. He snipped the stems of the bunch chosen and with bony hands spun a conical wrapping of wax paper around the mass of blossoms. He thrust their softness towards David's nose, the damp richness of their scent. He handed over David's change but did not at the same time let go his sense of humor. "*Guaranteed.* Anything ever happens, you bring 'em' right on back."

"I just may do that." Working up half a smile, and in that diminished mood arriving home glad that he wouldn't have to be presenting his flowers to Al after all. The house greeting him with added quietness. Reading the signs, the usually faithful front light not on, the upstairs lights on in the children's bedrooms that spoke of their toiling away on their homework; most tellingly, the master bedroom dark. One of the children—in this case, Beth—crept downstairs softly to inform him that Mother was napping. Oh, right. Even so, unable to press upon himself a compensating sense of manumission . . . .

He placed the flowers in water and looked into the oven where, as a scrawled note on the kitchen table promised, a lightly warmed and yet far from ruined dinner was waiting. He was moved by a sense of something admirable, always trying. He wrapped the untouched plate in foil and put it in the refrigerator and went up to his study bringing a cup of tea where he managed to work for several clear-headed hours. The ordinariness of the long day's ending, on the heels of much that had not been ordinary, made it easier to put it behind him. Here he lived. Towards the end of those hours of work both the children came quietly to him amidst his books, the scatter of his notes. Holding back though, anxious not to interrupt, until he drew them to him. Realizing that he had neglected them this evening, ought somehow to have done better. Making up for it, he hoped with a shadow of caring. "Hey, aren't you guys up a bit late?"

Nodding agreement that they were. Unsaid, they were lonely. Wanting their Dad.

"I should have checked," he said, "but I'm hoping you guys got yourself some supper."

"We did, Pops," Beth said, "not that stuff though Mom had waiting for you. We worked up something else." In silence he squeezed both of their young thin shoulders.

"It was pretty good though. Nourishing, Mom would say."

"Atta way, gang." Gang. Liking that. "Well, okay, fair enough. You guys better hit the sack now. And don't be whining that old Dad has to read you a bedtime story."

Collectively they shook their heads in register of small amusement for times past. He pulled those warm heads towards him. "Be kind of quiet though. Don't be waking your mother."

"Oh no." Beth. Not giving him a wink, but as if she had. On to the game.

He went back to his reading. The final pages were rumpled, much used. Lines etched in memory, burnt upon the soul . . . . "*The beaten foe emerged* . . . .

All over the broad Atlantic, wherever they had been working or lying hid, the U-boats surfaced, confessing the war's end. A few of them, prompted by determination or struck by guilt, scuttled or destroyed themselves, or ran for shelter, not knowing that there was none; but mostly they did what they had been told to do, mostly they hoisted their black surrender flags, and said where they were, and waited for orders. They rose, dripping and silent, in the Irish Sea, and on the mouth of the Clyde, and off the Lizard in the English Channel, and at the top of the Minches where the tides raced; they rose near Iceland, where Compass Rose was sunk, and off the northwest tip of Ireland, and close to the Faroes, and on the Gibraltar run where the sunk ships lay so thick, and near St. John's and Halifax, and in the deep of the Atlantic, with three thousand fathoms of water beneath their keels. They surfaced in secret places, betraying themselves and their frustrated plans; they rose within sight of land, they rose far away in mortal waters where, on the map of the battle, the crosses that were sunken ships were etched so many and so close that the ink ran together. They surfaced above their handiwork, in hatred or in fear: sometimes snarling their continued rage, sometimes accepting thankfully a truce they had never offered to other ships, other sailors. They rose, and lay wherever they were on the battlefield waiting for the victors to claim their victory. Two rose to Saltash, off Rockall."

He stopped for several deep breaths. Not again, he was thinking. Not ending that way. He paused a moment longer, testing that thought sparingly.

So their battle ended, and so, all over the Atlantic, the fighting died—a strangely tame finish, after five and a half years of bitter struggle. There was no eleventh-hour, death or glory assault on shipping. . . . But no anti-climax, no quiet end, could obscure the triumph and the pride inherent in this victory, with its huge cost—thirty thousand seamen killed, three thousand ships sent to the bottom in this one ocean—and seven hundred and eighty U-boats sunk to even the balance. It would live in history, because of its length and unremitting ferocity: it would live in men's minds for what it did to themselves and to their friends, and to the ships they often loved. Above all, it would live in naval tradition, and become legend, because of its crucial service . . . its price in sailor's lives, and its golden prize—the uncut lifeline to the sustaining outer world."

He put it down and looked off through the window at the dark suburban street. Shaking his head with admiration and regrets. He couldn't do that well, couldn't match it, but he was not totally put in the shade. He would, he promised himself, add something to that, do it justice. Till the future writes a codicil to that story. A different tale. A very different ending.

▲▲▲▲▲

Still after many further weeks, nothing. Even though there was no longer any doubt that matters were wending their way towards those vague but certain ends forecast by Billy. Billy himself already departed, so it appeared. Getting the news second hand, Billy not dropping by to say goodbye. No surprise, but depressing all the same. With each night Al greeting him with the same eager questions. "So what's new?" until at last he had to reply, *Sweet, don't ask.*

"But I am asking" she cried out, "that's what I'm here for." Flying up the stairs in tears and not to be seen again that evening. Anyway, now come to this, last summons to Tawney's office. Postscript to an already revealed certainty. For weeks he had not received any new documents, no correspondence to answer. His IN basket stayed empty, a skeletal structure of wire mesh. He was surprised at how much he had depended upon that flow of heavy useless paper. Missing that ponderous symbol of presumptive activity.

Came the time when there was, literally, nothing to do. Since then he had sat at his empty desk, slurped too much coffee, kept busy with too many trips to the head. Consolingly thinking of it as exercise, staying in shape for battles to come. Knowing better. He had joined the ranks of the permanently unassigned. Those ranks huge, dismaying in magnitude if one were to contemplate them whole, a melancholy reflection on man and government. The citizen's dismay would be rationed, however, because no one could take all these people in at a single glance. These were not numbers that would ever muster in broad array on the Mall. If so, they would stretch from the Reflecting Pool to the steps of the Capitol, a milling crowd, visible all the way from the White House to the Congress and surely a frightening thing to whomever had a hand in creating this sullen monster. But such men did not gather. Seldom did they venture into light of day. These soldiers of passive legions became ever quieter men, their lives matching the stale peace of their offices. Blending back into walls and depleted desks that shared their diminuendo into meaninglessness. Which was why an unknowing visitor to a federal building, some person who could not read the signs, might not realize that there were such people about at all. Yet even though one did not notice them, could go years without their existence registering, once you grasped the truth it was like a curtain lifting on a huge and silent tableau of uncomplaining wounded. Once you knew how to identify them, they were everywhere. Every floor harbored dozens. Men, who had lost their funding, lost their will. Former Project Managers, shorn of their projects, men through whose fingers millions of dollars used to trickle easy as quicksilver. Hard to forget that, adapt to being without. Their numbers included victims of pique and politics as well as budget cuts. Many were victims of themselves. Done in by their own natures, by ineptitude beyond the call, or, more rarely, by uttering a bold and honest word. Men who had grown prematurely tired in their jobs, tired of the drab walls that held them, tired of life. But—this the saddest part—they included giants too. Men whom once anyone would proudly have followed. Now *former* giants. Geldel, shelved, bottled, not to be uncorked again.

The unfired and unfireable, all were to be found here. Too young to die, but too old to tear their lips away from the bounteous teats of Civil Service. Suckled eternally as if by unbreakable glue, the overspilled milk now hardened and keeping lips stuck, impossible to remove except by too painful ripping of joined flesh. An uncounted and uncountable multitude. But making no difference to a government which did not wish to count them. Knowing no way of counting if it *should* care. For government, it was simply enough to *be*. From that sprawled and sprawling jellyfish like figure, infinitely maternal and infinitely bountiful, issued millionfold fingerless of flow. As from the queen in those enormous African anthills, surrounded by her masses of wriggling grubs, nourishment for all. One more, or a million, equally welcome. There was, easy to believe, a sustaining connection for everyone in the entire world from that boundlessly expansible source.

One of them now myself, David thought. Not a whit worthier. He saw himself, as he saw all his companions in idleness, marooned on by-passed islands of shrinking vitality, useless energies still to burn. Stranded, each one standing alone in shallow seas, but with no way to get back to the near yet so far solid mainland of purpose and accomplishment. Cursed alike with excess of time, he spotted his new kin everywhere. Keen to the signs, spoor of a special kind. Men who had all the time in the world to listen, to collect the latest jokes; full of remembrance and gossip, with endless amusing tales of deeds done, or the folly of it all. Cynics, but even their cynicism grown mild as themselves. Like himself, wandering the halls, shyly peeping into other doors, seeking new recruits in idleness. Once you cracked the code you sniffed them out with ludicrous ease. They dwelled in offices too neat, depressingly clean, stayed busy with irrelevance. Their present shrunk to nothing, they played with things of the past. Time for the placement of decorative souvenirs, educational testimonials, growing plants. The offices of such men were greener, their plants more robust, leaves oiled and shiny. Time to water. Their offices even smelled differently. Better. Staleness banished. Or, rather, cherished in scents of furniture polish. In a small barter market, they traded around the duty can of Pledge. Speculating amongst themselves, whether some of that lemony Old English stuff might not be superior. David had polished his own desk, its bare surface inviting it, borrowing a can from Carlson down the hall. The all but forgotten Carlson who had inherited the Red Sea Saline Measurement Program (RESAM) from Tawney himself at least a dozen years ago, and who hadn't tallied a molecule of sodium chloride since. Not in the Red Sea nor anywhere else.

What Carlson did now instead was to *plan* saline measurements. Unfortunately, his grandiose program—a line element of zeros on budget printout sheets—was as unrevivably dead as King Tut. With not a soul in the world pining for any of Carlson's results, understandably his planning was languid, leisurely unto the ends of time. He puttered, read endlessly on varied subjects, attended obscure symposia. Periodically he segmented sheets of paper with his draftsman's triangular rules, drawing black lines at perfect right angles to one another in precise creation of embryonic schedules. Listings of Action Items with spaces left for dates destined to remain forever blank. Yet frustration, if he felt any, did not show. His smile was sweet with apology. He handed over his can of furniture polish to David with a flourish, jiggling it to test contents remaining. "Shake it first. Distributes it better. An emulsion, you know."

David had absorbed this information and somewhat more about optimizing the functioning of furniture polish cans, when he managed to break in with a promise to pay him back with a new full can. Carlson's kindness touched him. "Hey, no big deal." Carlson's free hand serving up another grand gesture. "Keep it. You do me a favor some time."

Harry Kirkman was a gentleman of comparable courtesy and good cheer. Wearing his niceness like an insulating cloak, visibly anxious to prevent any further thrusts into that bruised core of him that never lost its sensitivity to the possibilities of some new wounding. And just as niceness was one safeguard against any fresh touching of their shame, so did heartiness of manner and a jauntiness in dress serve as other coats of mail. Many of these lost souls became the best of dressers, impeccably groomed. It never struck any of them how this proclamation (for that was exactly what it was) set them off vividly from harried and indifferently dressed colleagues who had no time to polish their shoes. Excessive neatness communicated their state more boldly than would signs in six-inch letters above their doors. Sartorial excellence, another mixed gift of time. Lately, before departing for work, David would find himself checking over his own small collection of ties to make the best match. That solitary little act, ordinary as it must be, he had not indulged in before. Harry Kirkman, actually *Dr.* Kirkman, had once been in charge of Project Coliseum, a grandiose scheme to plant on the bottoms of the ocean's abyssal plains huge transmitters radiating acoustic energy through all the six hundred million cubic miles of the world's seawater. Returning sound energy would be received at vast distributed bottom arrays and its staggering amount of sonic information be discriminated, filtered, and what not else, to the end that all the prodigious numbers of false echoes and reverberations would be identified and unerringly labeled and cast aside. Then all that was left, the small residue of that computer processed vat of information, would be—what else?—Lo! *Valid Submarine Contacts!* All of the submarines of the entire world. Friend and foe alike. From brodiggnagian Soviet TYPHOONS to the two man civilian jobbies nuzzling the oil platforms in the Norwegian Sea. Such the dream.

A hare-brained idea then, hare-brained still, unimproved by time, it had nevertheless not died, dried, and been blown away in winds of good sense. Rather, it had undergone standard Washington metamorphosis. Coliseum had simply become *something else*. It remained in deep hibernation, a state of animation not quite suspended, but with vital signs as feeble as life can keep, like one of those patients whom modern surgery packs in ice in order to retard the metabolic rates to their uttermost bearable minimums. Coliseum had lost even its name, receded to the status of "Study". Not any of your small and chintzy study programs though, but gifted with a fair-sized line budget each year nevertheless, and over which, faint as the impress of a Pleistocene fern in a lump of coal, Harry putatively retained vestigial rights. Once a year its melon would be cut into variously shaped chunks and passed on to naval laboratories in beneficent ration. The week that that was done, usually in October at the beginning of the fiscal year, was Harry's one flurry of activity. A kind of ceremonious occasion, a chance to affix his signature obediently a number of times, for Harry Kirkman had not the slightest say over how the funds were allocated. But still . . . . Harry's week. His only duty, like a docile prisoner, to be violated at will. The remaining fifty-one weeks of the year he was allegedly monitoring the progress of the laboratories. In fact, there was no monitoring, no progress, and Harry Kirkman, loving home and fearing airplanes in equal degree, never visited the laboratories. Poor Harry, people would say, is no manager. As if one were wanted.

Yet Harry understood the game. Shrewdness lingers when the will is gone. *Old* Harry, people would say with a smile. But it was in Harry's own smile, too accommodating, that David read horror. For Harry Kirkman had been a brilliant physicist—spent four years at Cambridge—perhaps was brilliant still. No way of knowing. David had met Harry's wife at one of EAR's annual picnics, a sweetly lovely woman, feminine mirror of Harry, sharing his quiet passion for roses. Wondering himself, David Morgan, if that's going to be me, puttering nights away at flowers . . . . Damn, rebuking himself for the lazy randomness of his thoughts, but thoughts, without any feel for the future, bound to slip away to the past. Thinking now how these days could be other ones if he just heard from Billy Jencks. But Billy didn't call and there would be no more lunches nor laughs. Aliason's own calls, so often in the past a nuisance, potentially always a heartstopping concern too, had themselves tapered off. He wasn't even seeing her as much lately. If that made sense for two people living together. She was off on another kick, archeology, and when on one of these she would read consecutively every library book that she could check out. But at least not buying them. Six, ten, at a time, lugging home the legal limit. On the dining room table rested heavy tomes with colorful covers bearing titles like *Gold of the Chaldees*. They were now like two ships passing. Yet indisputably she was a caring ship, conferring many an anxiously sympathetic look. Better than nothing. He shook his head, dismissing fragments of a man's simple lusts. *Too much damned sitting lately*. Still another thing wrong with this present dummy situation. Beyond his idly clasped hands he spotted motes of dust on the broad and empty surface of his formica-topped imitation walnut desk. Immediately he thought of Carlson and his full can of furniture polish and he actually started down the corridor towards that comparably undernourished office to make a borrowing. *Whoa!* Stopping himself just in time. *Hold on!* Enough of this nonsense.

With a gesture of resolution he placed on the desk a pad of ruled paper and took a volume down from his bookshelf. It was his college freshmen text on mathematics, *Beginning Calculus*, and he was going to go through it again from page one. That done, he would start on another of his reference books, renewing acquaintanceship with every volume on his shelves. He had a goodly collection of technical books, tables of integrals, logarithms, formulae, and so on, all of the engineer's usual—they occupied four shelves of his spartan government-issue bookcase—containing the concentrated knowledge of great names of science and mathematics, from Galileo to Maxwell, LaPlace and Poisson. Heroes all. Still. Yet even as his fingers had worked the volume out from his tightly pressed, little exercised, array of books, he detected mocking echoes. Was this not the familiar brave vow of most men abruptly deprived of responsibility, but not yet health? Commonest of promises, the kind every exile makes to himself. More vain groping for self-esteem. At *last*, so temptation beckoned, the chance to go back, to delve once more into the roots of that fine store of scientific and engineering knowledge which (standard lament of every single Washington desk-bound engineer) unfortunately he never has time to apply here in these shallow mills of churning paper and vue-graph engineering. He would return then, David Morgan, *would* by golly get back, unlike those other slugs, to the eternal verities of science. Resharpen those rusting tools! Back to the pristine beauty of calculus, those building blocks of the modern world, the beauteous precision that in a mere three hundred years had overthrown the untidiness of a million years of superstition and religion. He would immerse himself again—with a youth's excitement, a youth's heart—in the transforms of Laplace, the distributions of Poisson, penetrate the mystery of binomial expansions. He would . . . why he would learn again to derive natural logarithms. Why not? That admirable Admiral Stockdale had done just that in a Vietnam prison. Simple but worthy drill. But even as he started through the pages of his freshman *calculus*—an old fashioned book, it had the elegant thin line drawings that went out of style long ago, and was written by an author entranced by the grace of Newton and Liebnitz's original proofs, lovingly treating the shrinking values, the vanishing delta symbols smaller than any microbe, speeding away from the mind faster than the electron, receding before the eye to the infinitesimal—he knew better. And knowing, he shook his head at himself, the naiveté and the folly of middle-aged men. In real life you did not go back again. Like an interested patient, patient and doctor in one, he was analytically fascinated at the phenomena of what he felt as a slowly unfolding doom. Phases of wastage. First the mind, limbs to come. He looked up imploringly at the clock, relieved that it was only minutes until he was due at Tawney's office. Gratifyingly one event today without option.

Though he had not been told the purpose, it had to be to learn his fate. Where they were sending him. Already he was thus in a kind of transitional state, neither here nor there. His journey already begun, like a leaf dislodged from the bank and drifting out into a stream. Yet between him and the Carlsons and the Kirkmans—though the symptoms were identical—a canyon yawned. Their sins were merely of omission, and for such the system's great and sloppy heart had infinite tolerance. The condemnations of passivity surpassingly gentle. Remain forever, the system whispered soothingly, all you have to do is just keep showing up. . . . Heading out the door he noticed something different. *Something*. Keen to the slightest change in his virtually changeless office, still he could not at first figure it out. Accustomed to seeing through the bare mesh of his empty IN basket to the scratched imitation walnut surface of his desk underneath, he realized that he could not now see its surface. A sheet of paper had actually found its way into his basket, a flyer for a farewell luncheon. In the style of such notices, this one was enlivened by someone with a flair. Tipsy champagne glasses, bubbles, masques of gaiety, flourishes of beckoning jollity. . . .

"HELP US GIVE A GREAT SENDOFF TO OUR GAL DAISY AFTER 11 YEARS!
THE PLACE: PANCHO'S PALACE, AT 3323 WEST COLUMBIA PIKE
THE DATE: THURSDAY, 29 OCTOBER, 1200 HOURS
P.S. Maybe enough Margaritas will loosen Daisy's tongue and she will tell us where she's going. She's keeping that a mystery."

He took it with him down to Tawney's office. Daisy seemed to be finishing up straightening of her desk. Her bag was slung and her lips were pressed together in abstracted concentration. "Hi there," she said, without immediate warmth, "right on time."

"Not hard to be on time these days."

"I daresay." She looked younger as she smiled. She looked at him sympathetically but added nothing false or foolish. "The Man will be ready for you in a moment."

"I see you're going *hiyaku* as well." "Thanks for not asking where," she said.

As if his look had sought further explanation, she went on with one. "High time. I need replanting. Anyway, basically it's nowhere. A quiet five and a half years over there and that will be that. So. Now you know my age."

Nodding to that. With the simplest of calculations, the generous rules of early Civil Service retirement told it as firmly as an affidavit of one's birth. "But maybe, on the other hand you can tell me where I'm heading." Surprised, she looked him in the eye. "Could, but can't."

"Okay." He did not press her, admiring as ever. The loyal keeper of secrets. True to the system to the end. More likely, true to some ideal of herself.

"I can say this much. You're sure as shit not going to like it."

"Well . . . ." Their talk flagged. She seemed anxious to get away. Yet her eyes were wet. He gave her a kiss. Her cheek felt smooth but papery. He had an inkling of how she would let go of the world. Growing gradually dryer and dryer, groomed to the end, not a hair out of place. One day a powerful wind would carry her off, her dandelion wispiness, with a whoosh.

"Daisy." Steeling himself. This thing which was overdue. Owed to a friend. Since that evening, so many weeks ago, he had hardly seen Daisy. In truth avoiding her. And yet, for all the time that had gone by, and much as he had thought of what he might say, regret came out haltingly. "Let's just say—I'm sorry."

She gave a little wave that said let it go. Still, his apology muddled onward. "We were . . . sort of like a couple of . . . teenagers fumbling away in a car."

"Oh?" Cocking her head. "Well, what's so bad about that? Anyway, promise you'll be coming to my farewell luncheon." He gave his promise, one not to be kept. "Good luck." "You too." She was one of those rare people, who put sincere feeling into the second person. *You.* Tawney called out as Daisy departed. "David, my boy. Good morning."

"Good morning to you, Doctor. I presume you've called me in for my Annual Review."

"What?" For a moment Tawney looked disconcerted, as if David were truly serious. Tawney, one of those legions trampling wholesale over Civil Services' substance and ever fretful of being found out scamping on its forms.

"Actually, I'm afraid we never did get around to that, did we?", Tawney wetting his lips. "Relax, Doctor. Joke." In spite of himself, David felt a minimal twinge of admiration. Tawney didn't after all, have to do this. An underling in Admin could easily manage what dirty work had to be done. Yet neither did Tawney look David quite in the eye when he spoke. "No doubt, you're aware of the new assignment. I expect Daisy told you."

"She didn't tell me anything. She said that she was supposed not to. I have a good idea though. One of Materiel's very own elephant burial grounds, no doubt."

"You're over dramatizing things, David. As usual. It's not the end of the world. You should look upon it as a . . . a chance to—" "Catch up?"

"Well, yes." Tawney nevertheless seemed annoyed at the words furnished him. "All right. What's wrong with that? To . . . take stock." David waited. "There is another thing. You are asked to . . . please vacate soon as practicable." "Fair enough. How soon?" A week David had been thinking. That ought to be enough time. No point in hanging on. "Today, actually." Tawney hastened on soothingly. "You have the morning left, and the entire afternoon."

"*Tawney.* Do you have any idea of the magnitude of what I have to go through? Whole file cabinets. Bookcases to empty . . . ."

"You may leave all the classified material here. Indeed you must leave it."

He's afraid I'll be using it to write a book with. In a flash, David said, "I am insulted."

Tawney's hands moved vaguely, more in helplessness than apology. "It's been decided. I . . . *we* think it's for the best."

"*I don't even have boxes.* I'm to make a hundred trips lugging stuff in my arms?"

"David, take it easy. You'll burst a vessel. Arrangements have been made."

"Arrangements?" Still incredulous, he was ready to stalk out when Tawney, looking up at the clock, seemed to make a conscious effort to detain him. "David. Over by the window. Behold." Reluctantly David followed the grand sweep of Tawney's arm. Out there the City, the monument, shapes of grandeur and inspiration. Tawney's voice was solemn. Theatrically saddened. "*Tibidabo.* Remember? The mountain looking down on Barcelona, one of the grand views of earth. The Oceanic Conference there in '73."

"All I remember is that you didn't invite me to accompany you." Tawney waved away that detail. "You know the legend. The Devil tempting Christ with all the kingdoms of the earth."

"This nearly was *mine.*" Grinning in spite of all. Giving away to giggles. "Hains Point too? An entire golf course to myself?" "The principle," Tawney said tersely. "I'm afraid, David, that you are hopeless." Despite his sour mood, Tawney nevertheless still seemed oddly desirous of drawing out the time. Glancing at the clock repeatedly. Insistently his manner implied that he had something more to impart but, as it was turning out, there was nothing of any content. The minutes grew strained with their lengthening.

"Tawney. Cut the B.S. Where the hell am I going? I don't need even the title of the organization, if it's too painful to utter it." Tawney thrust out his hand to reveal a pink piece of paper like a folded telephone message form. It was dampish from the number of minutes it had been pressed into his palm. David absorbed at a glance its scanty information. "That's it?" The System, so rife with paperwork, on occasion could greatly abbreviate it too. A room number, a scrawled name without initials. When, somehow, one felt there surely must be a government form even for such sentencing. "That's all, I'm afraid. Anyway . . . ."

There were reviving tones of final sentiments in Tawney's voice. There may also have been an outstretched hand, but David turned from that possibility and strode away headlong down the corridor, almost passing his office. With good reason not recognizing its entrance. Stacked boxes obscured the doorway. These, the "arrangements." The whole thing orchestrated. Timing, people's actions, all fit. Daisy must have been in on it too and he regretted it from her standpoint, sorry that she had to do something she was bound to have detested. Boxes were piled inside his office as well. The government's standard best, two dollars apiece in the GSA Catalogue. No castaway crates for this royal firing. These were brown paperboard but admirably sturdy, with a handsome label for recording contents, niftily fitting tops. David was startled to find someone in his chair. A young man popped to his feet, introduced himself with a name sounding like Cutter. "Here to help in any way I can, sir." Cutter casual as his sport shirt, bright-eyed, a pleasant country twang. At the bottom of the government heap, but evidently a specialist in crash moves. "That's all right, thank you. I'll manage it myself."

"Okey doke, sir. Be here if you need me." And so he was, sitting just outside in Viola's old chair, poised in readiness through the rest of that morning and the afternoon. From time to time Cutter's inane but cheerful whistling burst forth.

David Morgan selected, chose, threw away, labeled for retention, marked for BURN, stuffed in boxes . . . working away. Not pausing for lunch or a cup of coffee. A compressed journey through eighteen years of his life. He raised dust, tore through canyons of cabinets, attacking thick hills of paper, never slowing lest reflection or sentiment disrupt him. His guts and blood and anger in that paper. Pale paper bits clung to his clothes, his arms were sore with lifting. A little after four o'clock two stoically uninterested black men, but with the beef and overtime authority for their task, showed up pushing heavy moving carts. He took down the last of his pictures, the big one of Sea Eagle working its taloned fierceness on a helpless submarine, and was truly done. He thanked the young man. "Heck, didn't do nothing. Anyway," said the ever-spirited Cutter, "I take it from here." He waited for Cutter to take it from here. He watched the loading, listened to the squeak of the carts wheeling away. At once it was very quiet. His office, shorn of the paper and the artifacts that had supported its life, had never seemed so small.

About to leave, he noticed on a vacant desk, a comically postured miniature figure of a colonial soldier. Viola's desk, long bare except for a scattering of pencils and paper clips amongst the dust, plus the silly enduring figure that evidently had been there all this time. Viola unreplaced, the sum value of her contribution expressed by the vacant expanse of scratched gray composition surface. His eye had passed over the figure for months without its registering. It was carnival prize quality, the strutting soldier in moth-eaten red felt with brass buttons, standing aslant and imminently ready to topple. Its cheap buttons were tarnished near black and the soldier had lost his rifle but the sun-faded dusty figure still had its arms stretched out in pathetic appeal. Yet Viola must have found pleasure in it. He picked it up and was about to take it away with him and then he asked himself why.

▲ ▲ ▲ ▲ ▲ ▲

When things got too hot, that is to say when the rising tide of problems threatened to lap his shoes, Tawney Gray was never in doubt. Responsibility having a way of flowing around the desks of the absent, he made it a point to be gone. Foreign travel was favored, of course, but setting up some grand trips on short notice was not always practical. Crises came not on any schedule. To meet them there was *Wanderer*. A private love, he kept her down Calvert County at Solomon's Island. She was thirty feet, a trim and lovely sloop, easy to sail alone.

Her winches gleamed, her varnished mahogany glowed like deep brown fire, her brass had the depth of gold. She was all wood, a creation of grace and glory, an anachronism braving on in an age of fiberglass and plastic. She was always waiting, sitting moored in lightly lapping waters, her leisurely pitching making her seem to nod in agreeableness at the fineness of many a day. He would disappear for a week. He would visit St. Michaels, the Big and the Little Choptank, and run further south to remote crabbing and oyster ports where the slow beat of life changed not from decade to decade, where patterns of speech pleased with a unique and ancient sound. He anchored in small inlets with impenetrable vegetation tumbling down to the shore, by marshes where the white heron delicately stalked. The Lower Chesapeake was his *querencia*, Marlowe's dark land, all the adventure close at hand that a man sensibly could ever wish.

Alone, his city chest bare to breeze and sun, he sailed a lazy man's sail, tiller atremble with life. He trolled for bluefish in its bounteous season and watched for the daring flashes of silver, ever thrilling, to rise struggling up out of darkish green depths. He cadged oysters from passing fishermen, made lavish sandwiches, sipped his beer at a man's own sweet pace. Lying on deck for long periods of time he looked up at kindly skies. *Thinking.* For yes, even here, eventually thoughts would pursue. But it was a languid pursuit, a languid struggle too when they overtook. Of late he was thinking more about Tiny. Presumably long ago, and depressing to recall, something there had charmed, been *desired*. The metamorphosis from shy petite pretty young girl into the chunky, vigorous horse of today, an assertive, cheerful scold with a fine, maddening moustache blooming above her upper lip—mocking the achievements of a billion dollar industry that flourished to take care of such afflictions—was complete; the latter woman had sponged up all traces of the earlier one. Yet if impossible to desire, she was equally impossible to ignore. It was her late arriving and growing solicitude that alarmed him the most. While unresting in her attempts to have him join her at church on Sunday mornings, other means of helpfulness had also lately come into her mind. Wondering, for instance, if she ought not to accompany him sailing.

"You have no companion, dear. It must be lonely for you out there." Her eyes shone at her mate who bore separation so gallantly; small lips began to move with big vows. Swiftly Tawney would remind her of the horrors she used to experience out on the water, the fright and the nausea that she had known repeatedly and—he bore down hard on this point—*incurably*, in her attempts to become a sailor. "I know." Her eyes misted with vivid recollection of frustration and failure. "I did try to be a good sailor for you though, didn't I? Of course, you could have been nicer about it all."

"I can't remake the sea, sweet. Nor alter those many things demanded to make a boat sail well and safely upon it." He had said such things before. Discoursed upon the cruel wisdom of the sea, the demanding mistress that a boat must be and so forth. But it was also true that gradually, even as his original romantic desire to have Tiny share life with him on their first boat had long ago vanished, realization had dawned that it was possible, quite on his own, to increase the level of unpleasantness to achieve what the sea, left to its own strictly unaided resources, just might *not* be able to do. Augment its terrors, so to speak. Thus it was that he had raised his harsh standards notches higher, shouted and cursed, been as unforgiving as Bligh, relentless as an eighteenth century sailing master. In the end accomplished his objective. Peace won. *His* peace. "Maybe I should try again," she had offered recently, "take lessons and really learn to swim, for instance. Then I wouldn't be so terrified." Tawney shook his head with a smile of sad wisdom. "It won't do it, I'm afraid. There are people who really shouldn't ever go on the water."

"*Pshaw.*" Antique expressions, snatched from the air had become a feature of her speech in recent years. Somewhere along a crumbling line it had also become something else to set his teeth on edge. "It's true, however," he went on, nevertheless composedly, "the Navy, *my* business, after all, has statistics on its chronically sea sick sailors."

"Fiddlesticks." He had stared at her for a moment, his best stare. Without effect. "Tawney, I have sympathy for all those poor sailor boys. But I couldn't give a tinker's darn."

"Dam. *Dam.*"

She shook her head, her mouth fell open, a genuinely bewildered lady. "What? What on earth are you swearing about?" Tawney, rolling his eyes, outlasted the moment by saying nothing more. Yet with fascinated horror he seemed to be observing in slow motion an awful solemnity of events reaching towards him out of dim swamps of the past. Palliative fingers, lending cures for spirits that did not wish cure, exorcising ills he did not feel. *Tiny.* There were many strains of refinement in Tawney Gray. All had shuddered in unison.

Golden haze burned on a pearly horizon. Tawney, stretched out on the teak decking, scrubbed clean to soft bone whiteness, opened his eyes and in a twinkling all thoughts of Tiny vanished, clearing the decks for concerns of higher priority. He needed to plan. More specifically, he needed a *Plan*. His central thought— more profound than mere thought, it was his very motivation—was a most simple one. And shared by many. *By damn, he wanted to live forever.* Freeze these splendid years. More than most men, he had abundant reason for feeling that way. In the modern age—with the swift rise of technological progress compressing the rise and the flourishing of some whole new area of science into as little as a handful of decades—a new and specially groomed kind of man was possible. Starting on the ground floor, and with a bit of luck, within the experience of only a part of his own lifetime, a man's glance could take it all in, seem even to *know* it all, the whole sandpile, genesis, history, present, future . . . . ! With good fortune, as in the case of Tawney, he could be the Grand Old Man of his ocean sciences field even while owning a head scarcely flecked with grey, every tooth still stuck solid. He loved being that Grand man—yes, forget the "Old"—seigneur of his profession, elevated to a lasting Nirvana, while the *man* in him was still young enough to enjoy. The trips, the glowing introductions, the applause welling up out of cavernous auditoriums (welling up basically for *nothing*, to be sure, demanding nothing except that he be standing up there to take a bow), were a steady succession of golden moments. And if that obeisance fundamentally grew not out of his accomplishments, or his wisdom, but derived from the protean sums of federal money and grants—unfettered and negligently monitored—that it was his power to dispense to those in the audience clapping most loudly... well, no matter. Hollandaise and sauce Béarnaise, taken often enough, dull the palate, and conscience numbs to pinpricks. It was a world, blending hedonism and respect (or the glittering simulacrum of it, even better, demanding therefore nothing from its recipient) to which many have aspired though few have gained it. Only a matter of time until Tawney Gray was going to have his very own sea mount named after himself. He had one already picked out. Reserved, so to speak (such arriving honors do not take place in a vacuum). And ... other things too.

    Multitudes of lovely women out there, no seaport or academic haven so small nor distant that it did not nurture them, intelligent yet unhappy—unfulfilled!—wide-eyed, compliant, endlessly willing to give themselves to this special piece of History passing through. So it had been in Mombasa, and in Mauritius... so it might be, with luck, in the Ibiza's and Tutuila's and Auckland's of symposia yet to come. Tawney Gray kept no count, men successful in that mode never do, but he had screwed a dozen races. Well before the burgeoning of the world's conscience in regard to color, Tawney had proved himself commendably without prejudice. *Ah.* All very well, but reminiscence was not the order of the day. The challenge was to insure that this good thing continued. But *how*?

    Truth was that lately he had rather botched things. Foremost, of course, Wolf Lake. Even if its damage was contained, still, another egg on his face. He did not shrink from repeating to himself other standard Washington phrases of events gone askew. So, lost a bit of skin out there, our Tawney. Yet in his City's environment, as well as the spiritual poverty of that life as conveyed by the worn aridity of its language, such phrases were paradoxically reassuring. Had he not said the same of others, and worse? Probably (he could smile to himself wryly) *they*—his enemies, that is, the trampled on and the discarded and those left behind in his upward rise, but some, now lately rejuvenated and emerging from their grubby cubicles, reviving *pupae*, one might say, warmed by the heat of his discomfort—were even now dragging out and dusting off the ultimate derogation to an individual in the scientific community. He could imagine them whispering it as, in an older and quainter age, suspicions of a woman's damning lapse from virtue were passed around. "*Old Tawney, I'm afraid, has grown technically a bit insecure.*" He could even force himself to feel that one. Even as he twisted with its sting. *Touché.* For as yet only pride, and not the impregnability of his position, had been bruised. In a town built on words, words were cheap. It was a cruel and unforgiving town but also, consolingly—compensatingly!—a forgetful one. It rushed on, towards new crises, challenges and *gaffes*, rushing headlong, a hungry hound forever pell-mell on the trail of fresh meat. And yet, if it was a vengeful town it was also, paradoxically, an undemanding one; not perfection but a passably mediocre batting average sufficed to keep one snugly secure on the team. The same safeguards that existed to protect the Viola Fletch's had thrown up for men like Tawney Gray mighty battlements against which the hurled thunder of Presidents (assuming any President would bother) could not dislodge a grain of their stone. No, truly it was not the security of his position troubling him most. It was *pride*. He craved not safety, but redemption.

He sighed. For, whichever way he turned, he must come back to it again. *DIANA*. The bitch. Nevertheless, key to all, DIANA and her retinue, SLRS, MINERVA, APHRODITE, and VENUS—the whole family of those projects named for belles of mythology—that the spotlight was shining on, the richest core of the Navy's hopes. Success there would recoup all. If these wayward females were the cause of his wounds, they could be the source of his salvation.

The ripples, the long reverberations from the unfortunate business—the debacle! to give it its right name—of the previous summer at Wolf Lake were at last dying down; it was the kind of mistake that, obviously, must not be repeated. As for those who had caused him his grief—the mavericks, the aberrant and otherwise troublesome—these would be handled in due course. *Were* being handled. A picture of David Morgan now passed through his musings; it paused, came into clear focus. He saw once again—and for the last time; the last, that is, in any meaningful human sense—those large glasses, earnest eyes, the mouth twisting itself almost into a stammer whenever he was excited, which was entirely too frequently for his own good. *For anyone's good, for shit's sake!* Yet, for all of those concerned, for David alone did he still feel twinges of regret, above all, for the worse that must lie ahead. A fair talent, at least, and a lovely wife too—in lustful daydreams Tawney used to covet her—the latter so pathetically valuing the fruits of ambition, the good things and nice life it could win. No fault of hers she had a husband stuck with a fateful squeamishness towards government. He did not dwell on the fate of his former protégé though. Nor did the possibility linger in Tawney's mind that David Morgan might actually be right. Tawney Gray, for all his manipulation of the system, was paradoxically a believer in it. Subscribing to the power of consensus, the wisdom of mass. A giant program, with megabucks, as they like to say, behind it and all those dozens of Admirals believing and *wanting* . . . all that commotion *had* to be right. America could do anything it wanted, put wings on the Pentagon. When pigs could fly, the Old Russian proverb . . . . Well fuck the Russkis. The U.S., if it had to, could have whole pens of porkers flying. To accept a contrary possibility was to invite chaos. DIANA *must* work.

But the foregoing musings—just what and *who* must fall by the wayside and so on—concerned mere details. And Tawney Gray was not a detail man. He believed in backing off and surveying events, so to speak, from one of those lordly yet literal heights that Plato encouraged man ever and anon to climb in order to set perspective aright. That Tawney and Plato were thinking different things, the latter meaning to provide a sense of scale in the affairs of man, and thereby a useful humility, the former knew very well. Also beside the point. What Tawney craved was the *view*. The "Big Picture." And, in those terms, things were actually moving along fairly nicely, thank you.

For however slow the Navy might be to perceive, let alone accept something, when it finally chose to move it could do so with that admirable dispatch and single track momentum that still justify the ever ailing, and yet unique, virtues of military organizations. At his own level, Tawney could feel electric currents coursing through those higher levels of decision above him. A giant magnet was being drawn invisibly along, polarizing to a single direction countless scattered filings, which heretofore were scattered every which way. The word was out, like a sinisterly whispered decree from an ancient and tyrannical king. "The debate is over, we *like* DIANA." The royal We. That last supposed to have come from the CNO personally. And now the impending transfer of Sneedon Snowdon seemed again a calculated masterstroke by those at the highest levels of the Navy's leadership. Another star for Sneedon, of course, a comer still if he had ever spotted one. The whispers, seeming to be true, were that Sneedon was actually "in a holding pattern," waiting to take over the Anti-Submarine Warfare Forces, Pacific. Tawney pictured Sneedon as not unlike one of those dependably loyal Roman generals who from time to time had to be dispatched from the Eternal City to put down rebellious provinces on the frontier. Correcting, by means as harsh as necessary, mutinous spirits in surly legions. None too soon in the case of those renegades in the Pacific.

With so many favorable auguries, and so few and minor the loose ends that still dangled, it might be asked why Tawney continued to feel dissatisfied. For cautious good sense, all the experience of his Washington years, indicated that this was a time when he could afford to do nothing. Let the remnants of the opposition simply be attritted by the grinding of the system and retirement. Lick one's scratches and let be.

The trouble was that this poky route to DIANA's acceptance did not banish what rankled most. Wounds to pride are slowest to heal. What Tawney wanted was symbolically akin to a statue of himself set up somewhere near important Navy offices and periodically, on some anniversary date, to be garlanded with flowers. On the pedestal imperishable words graven as to Dr. Gray's rightness in the matter of all those mighty low frequency sonars. Vindication total. *Let all those skulking bastards look on my works and despair.* Ever more distinctly, like a ship looming through fog, the shape of an old idea was reforming. Already broached to Sneedon Snowdon, and still going to take a bit more selling, it was an even grander thing, no less than a full evaluation of DIANA's capabilities, an undertaking both mighty and intricate, multiphased and realistic (his mind actually phrased his intent in just such words, the inescapable language of government), to erase all lingering doubts. Tests that would pour forth convincing numbers with the volume and irresistible power of a tidal wave. *Tawney redemptus!*

Ah . . . . If typical of Tawney to be vague on the details, scamping the means of attainment, it was also characteristic to leap ahead to confer upon the operation a title. Names were important, as Winston Churchill himself had taken pains to point out, admonishing commanders to choose ones of impressive gravity such that no grieving mother must be mocked by the knowledge that her son had perished in some frivolously named military assault. Tawney knew too from his own experience how important it was to choose a name that, out of the welter of limp acronyms that the Pentagon spawned daily, was certain to capture attention. Partly by inclination and partly by education, he had long been noted as one of the more inspired inventors of code names. From the lips of this specialized poet, as it were, could be counted upon names from legend, a march of mythological titans lighting man's way down into the darkness of the oceans. Restless, Tawney broke off lazing in the sun and got underway. His eye roamed the airfoil of his bellied mainsail, the sharp curved blade of the tautened jib, his engineer's knowledge and an artist's sensitivity blending in keen awareness of beauty and function. All the while seeking the one word that would carry with it that same haunting feeling of perfection. Names of islands, dim rivers disappearing into the mysterious lowlands of the Eastern Shore, drifted through his mind, all alike fetching up short. This one must sing.

HUNTRESS? DIANA *WAS* A HUNTRESS, WAS SHE NOT? Reluctantly, he dropped it. It rumbled of conflict and blood. Naval laboratories were being renamed right and left to expunge any sense of war; best their names had to ring with a feel for the government's benignity, less about killing submarines and more about kindly intentions towards the fishies. Late afternoon he anchored to watch the day's end, a flame in the western sky. SUNSET? But SUNSET had the sound of finality, lacked zip. He slept out on deck and the moon rose and he tossed in its flooding whiteness. MOONGLOW? His ear tested it at intervals throughout a tormented night until his sensitive antenna detected notes of weirdness. Just before dawn he dozed off only to waken minutes later to gulls' cries and to watch a red sun arriving much too soon. It rose through mists, turning orange, climbing out of some marshy island's piney groves. It became a yellow disc, blazingly transformed into the day's heat, yet soaring; irresistible, in spite of all that is known better, with its gift of morning that is the recurring optimism of man. *Yes.* All week it had been right there burning his eyes out. What else?

SUNRISE!

5

"So *tell* me," Al would ask, striving valiantly, prodded by loyalty, "is Supportability *interesting?* What is it like? Truly?" Trying. Al. Even as her man was watching her more than she knew. David Morgan, master of decibels and the sonar equation, also keeper of lesser special skills, able to sniff out a handful of residual molecules of Gallo's best wine in a rinsed glass. She was losing once again, he would have to say. Not dramatically, no fall yet off the cliff. But wanings of Hope not her cup of tea. To be fair, the cup of few.

"*Truly?*" Always he would fend her off. Tiptoeing around the worst of it. Yes, yes, there was much to tell his beloved, just give him a little while longer, okay? And Al, surprisingly, would be patient, bought off; wanting to be bought off, sighing over yet another Spring come her way. And David would revert to his holding pattern, his tale in suspension. Sparing her. At bottom, he didn't want to tell it. Or even know *how* to tell it. That Supportability was all he had anticipated, feared it would be, that it contained, in microcosm, in its poisoned cup, all that he or anyone else ought to detest in one's Federal Government, was, of course, obvious. Blatant. Supportability all that Billy had predicted, a swamp, a pit, a cesspool of dying spirits, a quiet horror, a disgrace, an enclave of awfulness, a torment to conscience, a bad joke, a corner of rot, yet another black hole down which the oblivious citizen was pouring his wealth, his life's blood . . . . All those things too true and too easy to say, phrases dark and true without number. But he did not want to utter them to Al, to set her fragile self fretting over him even more, even as there was yet *more* to it. The harsh and dreary words, for all their truth, still fell naggingly short of what somehow must be conveyed. There had to be *other* words, whole stories within stories, to encapsulate the reality, the origin and improbable survival, of such an aggregation of human beings and an assemblage of desks and file cabinets, clotted high up and taking over near a full floor of National Center. *There must be.* At the core of it, in its awesome improbability, there was mystery, a preposterousness that fascinated. And it was this *mystery*, rather than the negligible sum of work he was supposed to accomplish each day, that kept David Morgan making his way each morning to his assigned place of work that provided the monies to keep his family fed and a roof over their heads. In pondering this shipwreck of an organization in looking for clues . . . there was the belief that at least a part of him was engaged in something worthwhile, keeping a heart alive otherwise fated to grow old too fast. Yep.

When brother David Morgan here had his own answers, then Aliason Morgan would get hers.

Waiting for him after lunch this day was a pink slip saying that Aliason had called. There was no reason not to call back, no appointments nor conferences, nothing. There never were in Supportability. "I'm not interrupting anything, am I dear?" He detected an effort for control of her voice. "I called Dr. Wilson's office for a dental appointment. The receptionist said they wouldn't schedule one until we paid our bill. It was most embarrassing."

He performed the kind of swift calculation that, with frequent practice, he did so well. "Go ahead. Write a check." "David? I've been good, haven't I? I'm holding off getting my yarn for the turtle rug until next month. Isn't that budgeting?" "Sounds like it to me."

"I hope you mean that. Because just yesterday I told Beth *no* to silver jumping stirrups. Those heavy sterling kind that make it easy for her toe to regain a stirrup."

Marvelous, sweetheart.

Abruptly her emotions veered. "Oh, how I *wish* you were still golfing."

"Stop worrying about such. I don't need it."

"I'm not talking *need*. But you can, can't you, keep up your game on a driving range—" "Yes, yes. Now easy does it . . . ."

He heard, in another kind of sigh, his counsel working. "But I will have to find another dentist. I couldn't go back to him now, though he's very nice."

"Well, scout around for someone else. We can just as well make another one rich."

"I doubt that they're all getting rich. You're not the only one struggling." At one time he would have worried acutely about their conversation or, more accurately, its aftermath. Concerned with all kinds of imagined events that might follow his putting down the phone. But no longer. *Let go,* they said, and that this Grand Enabler was beginning to do. It was something else though, an idea removed from personal worry that was stuck up there in his brain. Though she had flung it out lightly, her mention of struggling had him thinking. Certainly he was still struggling financially—more than ever, that seemed eternal, an ineluctable given fact of existence—but it had not occurred to him that he was struggling otherwise. But there were all kinds of struggles, weren't there? Battles within and without, psychic and real. Why, even up here in the offices of Supportability—contained in a single large space with many desks, half of them unoccupied, the place all the quieter for its semi-emptiness—there was struggle. Even if partaking less of fang and claw, and more kin to the grapplings of the gelatinous creatures of the warm puddle of pre-Cambrian seas. Here too there were things, in spite of knowing better, he was fighting to change. Simply a quieter struggle, lesser roils in a slower stream.

The idea of struggle widened within him. He had a sense of the enormous and endless struggle of all the earth's creatures, in darkness and light, seen and unseen—in his mind a gigantic, hazy, Darwinian vision swirled—everywhere life grappling. Aliason and her battles he knew (at least he assumed so), Billy's he could only guess at imperfectly, even Tawney Gray's and Admiral Snowdon's he glimpsed from a distance with unexpected tolerance. As for his own struggles . . . he was just sitting at his desk smiling foolishly. Picturing the lives of dentists, those white-coated professionals for whom Aliason had such sympathy and who were making out very well, thank you, in the crevices of her pretty but cursedly soft teeth.

These were philosophic thoughts—there was time for them up here in Supportability; *that* maybe had to be counted one good thing at least about the place—and they brought him a thin kind of comfort. Yet however plausible these intimations of the universality of human struggle, there was contrary evidence compellingly near at hand. In Mason, Supportability's Director, whose desk was located only a few desks away from his own it was not possible to read the slightest sign of struggle. Nor despite David's close and accumulating observation, to discern anything that Mason did; whatever, that is, of use to Navy or nation. Unlike David's own desk, Mason's was entirely and permanently bare, surface harshly exposed, which—apart from the implications of the level of activity it served—was doubly unfortunate in a way peculiar to Supportability. For Supportability's desks were wooden, almost antiques, stained, battered, carved upon by the bored, burned by generations of smokers . . . . Nakedness can be an embarrassment at the best of times, but if the beauty is not svelte, if it is old, wattled, mottled, harried, stained, humiliation is that much more acute. Supportability did not experience, would never know, periodic changes in its organization, the uplift of the notice of seniors, occasional winds of vitality that in other offices here in Crystal City brought an influx of at least transitory newness, fresh blinds, shiny file cabinets, pristine desks, matching brightness of hope. The scandals of GSA and its Art Metalcraft Desks, the streaming procurement of cheap furniture beyond the power of governmental man to turn off, did not touch this floor. Supportability was ancient, enduring, uncared for, like its desks a relic, a holdover; neither faces nor furnishings changed here. Yet if its desks were eyesores, at their best mercifully scattered with papers, they were also just right for putting one's feet upon. Feet positively belonged upon them. An attraction like that of the magnet and iron filings, and one which David's boss gave no more sign than an iron filing of resisting. Mason flung his own up there with defiant good cheer, a total naturalness unfeigned. His feet, except when he used them to wander about his office, or to go down the hall to the head, were always there.

Most of Mason's morning hours it was his habit to spend reading the *Washington Post* in detail, missing nothing, not even the obituaries, daily demises of strangers from eight months to ninety-eight years. His reading done, he would fold up the paper, perhaps having cut an article out of it first (purpose unknown), and then get up and walk around, at first gingerly, seemingly testing his muscles for their continued utility. This led to his most active period. He would come over to various desks, visit, chat, ask how things were going—though not listening particularly for the answers—move about some more, and verbally review, almost animatedly, some topic such as how the prospective acquisition of another two hundred and seventy pounds of beef for the Redskins offensive line might alter the team's lately dreary prospects. He would look out the window for some time. A moment might come when he even talked business, complaining about how "they" did not appreciate Supportability, all the good things it was doing. About this time restlessness regularly grew in him, mounting unaccountably, to a pitch which it had taken David some weeks to decipher. He would pace about with increasing rapidity and then abruptly, late each morning and always at the same time, dart out the door. He would disappear for ten minutes or so and return with the early edition of the evening paper, the good old *Washington Star*. He was waiting, David eventually figured it out, down at the street edge for the delivery truck. Paper in hand, he grew calm again. His feet resettled themselves and, for hours to come, this later offering of news did what the *Post* had done for his mornings. An afternoon fix. He was hooked, a newspaper junkie. At bottom, a painless addiction. Twice a day, for twenty-five cents, taken care of. The riches, variety, and turbulence of the world trickling into his veins, a sea of printer's ink mainlined.

Wrapping up his day, Mason's last hour was preparing for departure. In contrast to the wakeful languor of his preceding hours, this period was all-purpose and method. He turned on his portable radio and listened to traffic reports; he looked at the sky and read the clouds, assessed the portents of rain. No wise skipper ever read better shadows on the sea, more keenly integrated in his mind the diurnal effects on sound velocity and gradients, than did this man of offices now testing in his mind the options in his various routes of escape. No move was wasted, no gesture squandered, in his controlled race downward. No poky elevators for him, only the breezy freedom of the dusty stairs, reverberating with the feet of the most energetic, those greediest for the advantage of seconds. Down, down, into the dim, thunderous recesses of the underground parking garage, hopping into his car with an agility any bank robber would envy, and zipping out into the light of day. No pausing for any such frills as fastening seat belts. Out of all this, precious fractions of time gained over the thunderous herds that soon after would be clogging the highways in homeward crawl. David, who carpooled with Mason when his car was again having its troubles—which was ever more frequently—had added reason to appreciate his resourcefulness. Mason knew shortcuts, alternative routes when familiar areas were jammed, could assess the traffic helicopter's radioed reports of flow and impedance with a battlefield commander's quick sense and knack for instant decision. He knew what a fender-bender on the westbound ramp to Little River Turnpike meant to the flow in

Gallows Road miles away, spasms of slowing that could occur as far away as the Lee-Jackson Memorial Highway. He could predict the impact of a dusting of snow on the exits from Braddock Road. In case of real snowstorms, those rare but greatly afflicting manifestations of natural distemper to Washington, he was a wonder of his kind. He knew each hazard, every treacherous hill, the schedules of the snowplows, where caches of sand and chemicals were stockpiled; he knew the folklore of plowing, how it helped, where it hindered, remembered whence had fled the snows of yesteryear. They had not fled; they were unmelted, right up there in Mason's noodle.

Mason brought more to the voyage than mere knowledge of negotiating traffic. That he regarded as a comparatively minor skill. He was the informed conversationalist of their pool; all those hours seemingly wasted reading newspapers now flowed in golden minutes within the speeding car that held his passengers captive. He was greatly exercised by inefficiencies in Defense, waxed indignant over the daily ration of its follies, had a host of seemingly well thought out ideas and intelligent suggestions for the rectification of all this deplorableness. Mason read his newspapers *deeply*, remembered what he read no less well. His time was not, one saw, squandered; misdirected perhaps, but applied with remarkable attentiveness. All this kind of talk was a long ways from the neglected knobby little asteroid that was Supportability, but that never slowed Mason. Seeing his country chock full of good intention but without staying power. "Afraid my boys, we've lost it." Such pronouncement might come while he waited, tapping his fingers at a stoplight or while zipping through a stretch of more open traffic, dodging trucks. Here too, a nimble Mason. His words fell on trapped ears. Their imposing host was possibly right on many things, but when David considered the source, the Truth seemed diminished; the brightest commentary did not dazzle, it depressed. It was Captain Leads all over again. Mason a fount of melancholy wisdom. But shit! Consider the source. When all was said and done. *Mason*. Towards David, Mason had been from the beginning pleasant, elusively sympathetic. If he was curious about, and even perhaps fully knowing of, the story of David's coming into his shop he did not reveal it. No doubt used to people slipping into Supportability by devious routes, never trailing clouds of glory as they came. Mason expected it, as he had to accept everything that came his way. Long ago choice had been taken away from Supportability; not even last rights of refusal. One of the permanently sidelined himself, Mason was used to the company of third team benchers.

* * *

The word at first came into David's consciousness so quietly that it did not register. Not surprising. All ideas, or concepts, or new notions, certainly anything like a fresh government acronym, slipped into Supportability's collective awareness sideways with muffled obliquity. Things of a hard nature, like a baseball, or even a ping-pong ball, that if hurled into many an office would bounce about noisily, cause eyes to fly open and minds to get turning over, underwent a different fate. Up here they did not bounce, they were absorbed. Disappearing softly as the tiny fish is taken and disappears into the circlet of waving tentacles of the sea anemone. Thus David Morgan one morning, catching in someone's chatter by the coffee urn mention of sunrise, was impelled to no more reaction than to glance out the window at the sun climbing out of the fiery gold of the distant Potomac. So. Well, yes. Sunrise to be sure. But so what? The only thing unusual was the mention of it at all up here where notice of, let alone curious reference to, worlds beyond Supportability were rare. A blizzard, if giant enough, might intrude, but scarcely the *sun*. The *sun*?

Yet he was hearing it again. Sunrise. From various lips, off and on, conveying a sense of *something*—hard to imagine what—yet seemingly having some augmented influence, a stirring of languid eddies, on stranded lives beyond its age-old meanings of mankind getting itself cracking on its day of toil. And, then—it must have been weeks later—he heard it spoken again. But this time not as natural daily phenomenon, this time as artifact of man. SUNRISE. All in caps. And then, still later, he heard someone named Diana mentioned—a Diana in these offices where there were Joans and Millies and Graces and Allies, but nary one Diana—making him wonder had he heard it right? and yes, he *had* heard it right, DIANA too in caps and SUNRISE linked, and David Morgan, from far off and far out of it, at once had a hunch he knew what was up. Saying to himself, I'll be damned. Several times. Be damned. Repeating it with mirth and wonder. Billy, of course, would know. Billy no doubt keeping up as he had in days of yore. But he hadn't heard from Billy since that day he strode off, clacking away down the Pentagon corridor and David didn't know his phone number and he had a pang for days that were gone.

Winston crossed his mind, Winston who had taken over for him in EAR, Winston who in technical terms couldn't carry his pencil box, but Winston too who had made his offer to give him a call whenever David should desire an update. What was the point? Whatever was up with DIANA was presumably far removed from Supportability and leagues farther still from one David Morgan, formerly there at the center of things.

▲▲▲▲▲

Fall gone and winter slogged on past and now already well into another Spring and half a year and more gone by since he had been hijacked out of EAR and dumped in Supportability. Boat seemed subdued on the ride down to Annapolis to visit his grandmother. His father meanwhile kept up commentary on the beauties of springtime as displayed in the countryside passing by out the window, the rich green grass carpeting, rolling hillsides, the dogwood trees with their jewels of white and pink blossoms luxurious against dark shadowed woods. "Oh yeah." Boat looking briefly but then going back to humming some monotonous tune known only to himself. Moving his father to comment on his quietness. "Something bothering my boy?"

"You and Mom fight."

He wrestled with that one for some seconds. "You should realize that your father and mother don't actually . . . *disagree*, if you will, necessarily more than other parents. Yes, I know you heard us . . . discussing your mother's concerns about the impact of our latest move on your schooling . . . and friends. But interestingly . . . ." He would have gone on but Boat's expression, more bored than anything else, said enough. Boat yawned. "Don't worry, Dad, I'll be talking a lot when we get to grandmother's." And so he was. The two of them, grandson and grandmother, right from their initial hug launching into animated chatter from which, both because of its spirit and special content, the father was effectively shut out. After a few minutes more of gentle teasing, however, Tessa took notice of the exclusive nature of the gaiety that was skipping right over the apparently superfluous member of the middle generation.

"Since you're just mooning about, why not trot on out and try to find some light bulbs for this border of your father's portrait. One more of those pesky little things has failed."

"Well, I can do the trotting part. You realize though, I've looked before."

"I'm not sure how stalwart a searcher you are. Have you tried the boat supply houses by the waterfront? Muddy is sure one of those places down there will have them."

"So old Muddy is sure is he? That is a clue, mother," he said, removing one of the bulbs, "that up to now has been withheld from me. Relax. Just taking one as a sample."

"Now you must get . . . yes, that makes seven. *Seven* new bulbs. I see you double-checking. You needn't. I can still count. You don't look especially happy about this errand, dear. You weren't planning to hurry home, were you? I thought that we might have a little visit before you shoved off." "I think we can give it a try." He planted a kiss to prove it.

"Good. Boat and I will be making fudge. How about that, Boat?"

One member of the family at least, David reflected, in accord with Tessa's program for the afternoon. He walked down the streets of the city that had been home to him for most of his childhood years and made his way across the harbor square to the weathered structure that he remembered as Hennessy's. It was high ceilinged yet dim, jammed with stacked wooden bins. It had uneven dusty wooden floors and its air was rich with the calming smell of tar. An elderly man, the look of a beached sailor about him, squinted at the tiny bulb held in his shaking hand. Muttering over it like a dimly remembered jewel. "Yep, seen these, come from Germany...." A younger man came up and plucked it off the old man's palm impatiently, holding it up to the light. "Rare, all right. But never saw a bulb we couldn't locate. It might take a check with our international sources." Gratingly knowledgeable, he smiled with his own kind of pleasure. "And we have to ask a small deposit."

"For a *light bulb?*"

"For querying our computerized databases worldwide. What's your boat?"

Confessing that he had none, David explained the bulb's purpose, the man nodding in affirmative snaps of his head. Able to tell right off a gent who did not own a boat from one who did. His advice was quick before he sped off to more promising customers. "Rewire it, resocket, then you can pick up your bulbs at any five and dime." "*That* could cost money, too." The man's farewell laugh was short. "Doesn't everything?"

The bulb trembled again atop the old man's horny palm, its matedness, if ever to be, an even more uncertain prospect. He shook his head, his baffled desire to be helpful in conflict with everything that experience had him knowing better. "Thanks for your time." David repocketed the bulb. "I'll think it over." And think it over carefully too was what he advised Tessa to do. "Think it over!" she said indignantly. "What I want is simply illumination for your father's portrait." She regarded his empty-handed return as yet another example of his varied ingenuity in failure. "David failures," they used to be called in the family, coming in sizes large and small, and once the object of considerable clucking disapproval amongst his older siblings who used to sit *in loco parentis* for his vanished father. "I don't believe you really try hard enough...." Her voice quavered. "Any one of your brothers...." She did not follow through on comparison with his patently more resolute, but always distantly deployed, older brothers in the Navy.

"Very likely," he agreed soothingly. Not the moment to prolong pointless argument. It was a critically tense time in the fudge making. He joined Boat in watching the dark viscous fluid in heavily graceful flow, father and son united in breathing the richness of its mouth-watering smell. Peril past, he uttered the small additional thought which (fair to himself) his mother ought to understand. "Those little bulbs aren't exactly growing on trees. You see—" Her unexpected tenderness shut off his excuses. "I realize that, dear." She touched him with a hot damp hand trembling from its exertions in wrestling with the heaviness of the iron pan. A bit later, things calming and cooling further, he promised that he would continue to look for the bulbs in Washington. "Darned little things." Tessa said. "But somewhere in your great city I have faith that anything can be found if one really looks. It sounds like a good plan." His mother had an unusually strong faith in plans, he had observed, for a person of ordinarily such high good sense. Unfortunately for the moment, bits of their conversation, like filings straying too close to lines of magnetic force, irresistibly veered towards *The* Plan. *Her* Plan. Still alive in Tessa's mind, anyway, if nowhere else. "Because, you know," she said, "Muddy's still working away on your behalf." "God love him," David said.

"Don't affect that weary tone, dear. You will, count on it, continue to hear from him."

"To deduce, after all his kindly harrumphs, that nothing is happening."

"My dear, Muddy Waters *knows* Washington. As, sadly, you never will."

"True. But down in the grass one also picks up a few things."

"Down in the *grass*?" She let that pass, peevishness returning. "You know what Emerson said.... Very well, smirk all you like, but getting out of the trap of Civil Service life ought to be your foremost objective." It was a recurrent hope, if another vain one, of David Morgan's days that if he did not pick up on one of his women's topics that it might go away.

"This lateral transfer of yours," she said, "is it going to be helping you?"

He smiled in spite of himself. "Where on earth did you pick that one up?"

"Your Aliason. Last time we talked. One of our rare times, by the way. 'Lateral transfer'", Tessa pursed her lips over it musingly, "more of the odd vocabulary of your life. Now I gather you're in something called Supportability. Well, I guess it's no more odd than your old EAR. We never had to put up with such in your father's day. Navy language was straight forward. You were promoted or, God forbid, you were passed over. To be fair to Aliason, she sounded as if she was, no more than I, able to make heads or tails of it. Though maybe, she was trying to shield me from some sort of bad news."

Good for you there, Al. "Don't be worrying about your David."

But Tessa's fretfulness was feeding on itself. Her thin lips trembled with what he had hoped she had forgotten and then knew what was coming. "And your *priorities*. Giving up your membership in Army-Navy. Where you never could have belonged if it weren't for your father's long ago joining. To Aliason's credit she did regret telling me that news, sounding as sad as I to be hearing it. I do believe she was crying."

"Mother It's not the end of the world. It's not as if I'm giving up playing golf."

"I fear it is." Her lips quivered. "Sixty years the family has belonged and now that tradition is no more. When we first joined, the main Club was only a little old farmhouse and the golf course had just been built but everyone, your father included, loved his golf. We were young and your father was just a junior officer but still we felt we were important too, just like those famous founders. And there was the head professional there for a few years, and he was a well known name too and ... have I told you all this before?"

"Yes."

"That ... marvelous man ... they called him the ... the *Silver* ... don't look at me that way, dear ... help me." "The Silver Scot," David said.

"*Yes!* I knew you'd know. It's the sort of thing you're good at. History anyway."

"Thank you, mother. His name was Tommy Armour."

"Yes. He had just one eye. Lost the other in the War. Even so he was better than everyone else with both their eyes. Your father played with him once. Important pros did that with ordinary golfers in those days. Your father loved that, you know."

"As would I."

"Funny, but I somehow think that your father's association with that splendid man may have started you off on the right track towards the marvelous game that eventually came your way." My *marvelous* game. *Ah Tessa.*

"And now all for naught." He watched his mother's glasses slip down her nose. "And I suppose you've still got that dratted horse." He was still framing a reply when Boat piped up. Boat whom he had forgotten in the midst of this latest inquisition but who was now finishing up the fudge bowl with a flourish, having licked it as shiny clean as if it had just been pulled from out of the dishwasher. "Oh yeah," deepening his voice with some new found comical instincts, "gotta keep that dummy horse, grandma. It's *sacred.*"

"Well, my boy," David said, "you're quite the little mine of information."

"And don't you stop being one either," Tessa said, "Boat, dear. It's the only way I'll learn what goes on in your house. Or understand your dear father."

Understand me? Ah, mother, that is nothing. The key is to identify me.

I am a gambler.

But not as conventionally portrayed in popular mythology of the Old West, a flamboyant and daring fellow. In bold dress and sporting a vaquero moustache— with maybe too a diamond stickpin in his tie—he would coolly turn a card on a table aswarm with blue chips or watch his horse thunder down the stretch with no flicker of an eyelid telling how he hopes the race turns out. On a single hand of poker he tosses into the pot the deed to the family plantation. The storied gambler of old, however, has in fact modern counterparts that neither attire nor manner proclaim. Unseen because it does not pay them to advertise, they too are the real thing and a hundredfold—nay thousands—more numerous than their rivals of legend. They are me for Christ's sake!! They drudge at ordinary jobs and wear the muted shades of quiet agony. Shame does not show on their everyday faces, no more than the churning of their guts inside. Yet these men, and they are the anonymous legions of America, risk all. As the farmer of old once bet his life on rain and sun, more perilously still do these modern urban men bet on themselves, right up to the hilt, on the sum of whatever modest talents and energies nature has stuffed into their trembling skins. Foolishly—foolishly, that is, by any coldly objective standards—they do it out of emotion. Do it for Love. Going for the long shots! For children of the middle percentiles on whose frail shoulders and insecure minds the future has to be the shakiest of bets. For colleges of their young's choice, unhesitatingly they shove into the pot second mortgages on tract houses that hold all the pitiful equity they will ever possess on earth.

At Christmas time, for the rich ceremony of a neo-pagan age, they pour out their modest treasure, go still deeper into debt. For the straightening of a daughter's teeth, a daughter's nose, for the banishment of mere zits—for daughters who, even thus unzitted, a trifle straighter now of nose and teeth, are never going to launch any ships with their sails set for some new Troy—their eager hands leap to sign notes that will demand half their working lives to repay. Taking for granted that they will be safely employed, go onward and upward, for all the years ahead that it will take to recover. For the care of the family dog, the slobber of its ambivalent affection, or in taking on the gargantuan thrice-daily feedings of a child's beloved horse, they toss their money upon confused waters not known to carry bread back to the thrower.

A madness, this, yet one which helps keep the American economy roaring on, making for a civilization the likes of which thousands of years of man's civilizations have never seen. Ordinary men, small talents, ludicrously and repetitively bet to win the world.

Bet their lives.

From far off it seemed he was hearing his mother and Boat discussing fudge, how long you let it cool, the kind of knife best to cut it, how large the pieces should be. Tessa rebuking herself for not having buttered the pan more.... Abruptly her voice was sharper, nearer. "David, are you talking to yourself again?"

"Who better?," he asked.

She shook her head. Reaching for something farther back. She touched him. "Forgive me. It's not fair of me to single you out for understanding. After all, you two are a *pair*. You and your Aliason."

He was thinking again—his mind a collection of stray sensitivities—that no one could pronounce Aliason's name, hitting every syllable like song, half so well as Tessa. It would have been recognized perfectly, willing to bet, in the courts of medieval France, from Angers to Chinon, clear as the bells along the Vienne. He did not understand how it could be, only that Tessa's tiny grammar school in a primitive West, grounding her in fundamentals better than present college graduates, had instilled in her a lifelong reverence for words. Beyond explanation, however, he chose at this moment to confer to the uncompromised elegance of his mother's pronunciation intimations of civility overarching the wrangles of the moment.

"That we are. Can't get away from that."

"I know my dear that I should get off this. Yet I just hope that dear Muddy never learns of the ways of you and your Aliason. I'd hate to hear what he'd think about someone who can't manage his own finances scolding our Navy about the kind of ships it's spending its money on." She flitted from topic to topic. Some alightings could sting.

"Au revoir, Mother." She scanned his face. In her searchingness she looked fragile. He bent down to say goodbye to Boat. "Take care, young fellow. Be down to get you late tomorrow afternoon. Unless, that is, you keep yapping family secrets. In which case, I may just leave you here."

"Don't worry about those dratted bulbs, dear." Tessa hugging him tighter. It will be as Muddy predicts. They can be found in a dozen spots in Washington." *Super. Let the old boy dig them out himself.*

▲▲▲▲▲

He had picked up Beth one afternoon at the stables after work, this duty going on unchanged, but pleasure still just as before the Great Banishment, as he chose to call it these days. By this hour, the homeward leg was night time and the road was dark as only winding back country roads can be. To the dusty scent of his car's ancient upholstery, dry with time, was added the fresh day's richness of stable smell from Beth's boots, her horse sweat smelling jeans. As they progressed out of the country and approached the suburbs the traffic thickened. Before long they were creeping in a long line of cars, rear lights blinking, a winking necklace of stalled red lights climbing hills and disappearing around curves. The traffic would speed up and there would be a momentarily exhilarating spurt of hope that somewhere ahead the mysterious clog had been broken. Then once again the long line of cars would lurch to squealing and disappointed halt upon the rusting iron of antiquated bridges, their pounded concrete reverting to powder and pebbles. With each stopping he was reminded of the squeak of worn brake linings, rattle of loose rods like a dance of old bones, the wheeze of ebbing energy, hints of ills both trivial and terminal.

"What a night," he muttered, "what a wreck of a car too, kiddo, your Dad has you risking your life in." She giggled. "Except for those four marvelous tires. At least we're safe there. Can't forget them, can we?" He shook his head, but with a smile the darkness would not let her see. "You're a card, my girl, a regular card."

"Well," she said, "*well*", drawing out the 'well' in theatrical tones, "how could I forget after the big pissing contest you and Mom had over buying those tires?"

"Don't talk that way, hon," he said. "Well, Pop, that's just what the heck it was."

"If you must then," he said, "the proper phrase is 'peeing' contest. Peeing. Get it right." He became aware of an unusual amount of talk on the radio and remembered that Aliason had taken his car to a Meeting the evening before because her own, their so called good car, was low on gas, and evidently she had changed his regular radio station. A police officer was giving a helicopter traffic report of trouble spots, counseling sensibly, advising alternate routes for those lucky to have choices, patience for those without. He sounded like a black man and there was something fine in his quiet good spirits, one of those citizens truly and unaccountably loving his city of Washington still. News followed with a brief report on the travails of *Sea Eagle* and the latest verbal attack by Congressman Duke. A commercial followed in which two bugs were talking, their chirping conversational tone sliding rapidly from bravado to terror at the arrival of the Terminex man. He would have changed back to his regular station but for a certain bored curiosity. More voices followed, doleful Marge and happy Jane, the former constipated and the latter offering patent remedy. Next heard from was a bouncy Marge, her mornings now rainbowed, tubes clear as a whistle. The station fell quiet but with expectant rustling, like low cracklings of a radio telescope picking up faint signals from the stars. The suspenseful noise gave way to a dull rhythm, accelerating in strength and tempo. It built into a complete beat, African in vigor, like urgent tribal drums. Abruptly, the sound retracted to allow the portentous announcement: *"Presenting—and Taking Washington each night by Storm—the New Rome in Review with Rich and Lark Bright."* The storm (plain now that this was what the drums had been building up to) came with a roar, playing in rolls of thunder. Made up of recorded moments of fearsome storms and compressed into seconds, it became a shrieking devil before dissolving into an orgiastic crescendo. Leading in to a quiet, "Good evening. This is Rich Bright."

"And *Lark* Bright." Lark's voice was soft, swift, insinuating. The listener would not find it hard to imagine what the simultaneous television presentation to the watcher at home could confirm, an image of a poised, wide-eyed blonde, with a smile alternately sweet and sly, in a zippered satin jump suit, matching her husband's own uniform for the show. Coming out of nowhere, the Brights had soared to prominence on the soiled wings of Washington news. Politics, legislative up-dates, bits of gossip, bounced back and forth between them with astonishing speed. Yet, "bounce" didn't even seem to be the word. David pictured them like *jai alai* players who caught the *pelota* in their great curved *cestas* and, with no slackening in the graceful arc of their motion, hurled it back in a blur. A perfect circularity of motion, the ball never truly in one court or another.

There was more to the Brights, it was said, than met the eye. Embedded in their news, their elliptical references to events, were barbs of innuendo, dirt fused into diamonds, allusion to dark events, sexual misadventures of the mighty, bribes taken, all shaped and sharpened into a living spear as tight and dangerous as the rhino's horn. Aficionados of the show—and Aliason had tried vainly to turn him into one—likened their words to colored anagrams flung into the searching light. If you were quick enough, supposedly you could catch their glitter in mid-air and find patterns of meaning. Their patter went sailing right on over his head tonight as well. Along with a multitude of new fans, the Brights had gained serious critics. Amongst them the National Review, where lately it had been written; *". . . the Brights are the perfect flower of our audio-visual age, the ultimate product for, and purveyors of, all human events. The mighty flow of history is trivialized into entertainment, the anti-apotheosis of thought. All is there for the mincing and dicing—'digitizing' in the god awful word of today—into extraordinary forms for jaded palates....*" Such stuff rolled off the Brights like water off their scotch guarded satin sheen. Better than anyone, knowing an idea whose time has come.

Yet the Brights were changing, even as allegedly they grew. At one time they had been relentlessly naughty but, like some revered comedian of prime time whose wholesome humor bears no hint of the sleazy clubs and the bathroom jokes from which he sprung, the Brights too were distancing themselves from a coarser past. The Brights had *matured*, in the eyes of their admirers, *deepened*. Indicators were subtle and overt, a delight for the aficionado. Both forms of evidence were showing now in the particular feature—the Bright's name was "Featurette"—coming up. Weekly, out of the teeming Washington scene—its "simmering vats" said Lark—they placed an individual of importance in the spotlight. "Time for PIP," Rich announced.

A roll of drums. *"Personality in Power,"* Lark followed up. "Tonight, unusually, we salute a military man. Unusual, because the military has been in eclipse ever since our recent debacle in Viet-Nam—" She stopped herself. "Would you call it a 'debacle', Rich?"

"I'm afraid I would, Lark. A debacle if ever there was one."

"Tonight is doubly unusual because our guest doesn't fit the pattern of the typical military leader with his inflexible and, regrettably, insensitive attributes, gaze so fixed on his goal that he never pauses to reflect on the kind of world that may follow after victory."

"Too often a hollow victory," Rich intoned mournfully. Lark's sigh, thousands of amplified watts of it, floated into the Virginia countryside, drifted out of car windows and through screened porches of homes where people were looking at the fireflies rising. Lark roused herself from murmurousness. "Thus we hail Admiral Sneedon Snowdon, *United States Navy.*" A tinny burst of martial music included bits of *Anchors Away*.

"I'll be damned," David reaching to turn the volume up. "Good evening, Lark and Rich. Thanks for the kind words." The Admiral's voice was eerily distinct, yet elusively something was different. It had borrowed the rhythms, the timbre, of his hosts. "Now for *vitae*." Lark sped through the Admiral's biography, starting with colonial forbearers, zipping through boyhood hobbies, early dreams of becoming a naval officer. Another blur of words covered academic excellence, captaining the fencing team, June Week parades, his own beloved Ginger becoming the Color Girl, and a wedding in the Naval Academy Chapel . . . *the gallant bones of John Paul Jones in the crypt below.* "All coming together," Rich Bright added, "ensign's stripe, romance fulfilled, the whole nine yards."

"All nine," the Admiral confirmed agreeably. Lark brought the Admiral's career up to the present day, mentioning destroyers, deployments to the Mediterranean, and shore duty tours interspersed with those at sea in the traditional patterns of a naval officer's rotation. Her voice took on girlishly honey tones. "May I toss you a teeny curve ball, Admiral?"

"Toss away, Lark."

"I can't help noting that you've spent a lot more time on land than on ships."

The Admiral responded affably. "Lark, let me say to that—"

But Rich Bright was right in there with help of his own. "Isn't it fair to say that today's complicated Navy demands considerable time ashore in study?"

"That's certainly a part of it, Rich."

"I believe I've seen it written that the modern flag officer must be far more than simply a mariner and a warrior. He must also be, so they say, something of an economist, technocrat, psychologist and, let's not shrink from it, even something of a politician."

The Admiral gave no sign of shrinking. "A bit of all those are necessary." Lark concluded her summary of the Admiral's career by highlighting studies at Oxford. Executive Assistant to the Secretary of the Navy . . . extra jewels in the crown of one so young. Smoothly, Rich Bright's voice filled in the seconds of Lark's next pause for breath.

"Early he was spotted as a comer. And today is the Navy's youngest Admiral." Lark now described the Admiral's present job. But in trying to make clear the concreteness of his functions through the changing, continually reorganizing, swirl of the Navy's technical commands, she faltered. The Admiral coming to her rescue tactfully.

"Good. *Thank* you, Admiral, for your corrections." The listener could picture grateful nods. Lark never stronger than in bouncing back from her rare bobbles. "But is it not safe to say that upon you rests much of the Navy's future in coping with the submarine?"

"But again, Lark, my own role is perhaps overstated." Having to dispute flattery did not, however, put the Admiral in ill humor. "Let's say a team effort."

"Spoken," commented Lark Bright, "with the modesty of this remarkable man. But it's time to move from talk of qualifications in warfare and destruction of submarines. The phrase actually is *'killing'* them. But that does personalize the matter rather dreadfully, don't you think?" "I confess we military types are sometimes guilty of that, Lark," the Admiral said.

"Anyway, moving on from the horrors of war . . ."

"Not that we don't want to win wars," added Rich, "if they come our way."

"Heavens, yes." A note of annoyance was detectable in the purity of Lark's wish to distance herself from the uses of war. A hint too of the possibility of something less than the perfection of the Bright's professional relationship carrying over seamlessly into the personal one. "*Of course*, we want to win our wars," Lark went on, "but it's another side of the Admiral we want to talk about. It concerns simple kindness, and one man's dream to apply the huge resources of the Pentagon also to *help* people." There was a fervent pause to match words which themselves had grown fervent. "Let the Admiral himself now tell us about these wonderful things." The Admiral spent several minutes describing the aims of Project Plowshare, and David waited, somehow not in surprise, for the Admiral to get around to mentioning an apparently promising project in the Hawaiian Islands. Through the harvesting of fishponds, abundant protein could be made available to large numbers of poorer people while, at the same time, useful therapy provided for the handicapped.

"And many of the skills that the Navy uses in hunting submarines, I gather"—there was the sound of notes being shuffled by Lark—"for instance, telling whales from submarines, are transferable to the aquaculture of these ponds."

"Correct, Lark. It is our theory, and our hope, that by the same techniques that these unfortunates can learn to separate the edible from the so-called trash fish."

"A footnote here will appeal to our listeners, especially those who have visited Hawaii and who remember how, all along the coasts, one sees stone breakwaters walling off a portion of the sea. Regrettably, however, those ponds were not for the benefit of the Hawaiian people. They belonged to royalty—the *alii*, so called—and ordinary people, though they toiled to stock them, had no access. So it's nice to think that their riches will at last revert back to the use of all citizens, however humble." "Absolutely, Lark. Just as it ought to be in a democracy."

"Now, as I understand it, Admiral, you are not only working to broaden the usefulness of military research funds. You have also taken the lead in helping the disadvantaged right here through volunteer labor from personnel of your own command."

The Admiral told what was going on in the Hospital for the Handicapped, taking a moment more to explain his own concept of volunteerism. "Once the fineness of the purpose is made clear to people, and they become aware of the satisfaction that comes from helping others, they respond cheerfully." "I call that," said Lark, "inspirational leadership." The Admiral remained true to his earlier touches of modesty. "Leadership isn't the word I normally apply to a voluntary program. But it's true that seldom are there any totally spontaneous wild fires of enthusiasm. There always must be some fanning of the flames."

"Hail, then, a premier fanner. Tonight we recognize too your wife, Ginger. Rather than frittering her time at the bridge table or on the golf course—the prototypal pampered high military wife—she works right alongside her husband, faithfully carrying out his policies."

"In many ways, way ahead of me, Lark."

"We honor you both," Rich Bright came back in nicely. March music grew and then fell away to a soft beat of the same earlier drums. "Honor *is* the word, not used lightly. Not everyone singled out as a PIP wins that accolade. Thus again, a salute and thanks to Admiral Snowdon, military man *extraordinaire* and humanitarian. For a new age, a new kind of warrior...." "Oh, my goodness," Lark coming back in," something we almost missed. A most notable omission.

Our honoree was too modest himself to mention it, but in the *Post* yesterday was a brief announcement of those Admirals scheduled to receive another star and there was Rear Admiral Snowdon, leading the list of those soon to be *Vice-Admiral*. Do we have that right, Admiral?" "Indeed, Lark, I am most pleased to confirm that you do."

"Isn't it awfully *soon* to be getting another star? I mean, hot on the heels of your recent selection to Rear Admiral." "But not unprecedented," the Admiral said. "Let me add, on a personal note, that I was bowled over by the news. I feel very humble. I am a most lucky man."

"Humble we buy, Admiral. But not the lucky part. Luck we doubt. By the way, the announcement of your extra star also indicated your next assignment. It said that before many months are out, you will apparently be on your way to Command of the Anti-Submarine Warfare Forces in the Pacific and be headquartered in Pearl Harbor."

"Indeed, Lark, that is yet another piece of my good fortune."

"Hmm." The 'Hmm' from Rich Bright. "I wonder, Admiral, heading off to where you are, if it is not too far a flight of fancy to suppose that both your posting, and your proximity to those fish ponds of the Hawaiian Royalty, will place you in an ideal position to further advance the Plowshare Project that is so close to your heart?"

"Come on, Admiral," Lark Bright added teasingly, "now surely a *teensy-weensy* bit?" The Admiral cleared his throat." Let it suffice to say, Lark, that will be on my agenda."

"Spoken," Lark said, "with no doubt proper discretion from this remarkable man." Several seconds of scratchy, breathy noise from a mike seemingly held as close to her lips as a toothbrush, foretold that Lark was not quite done. "Since you mention your agendas, Admiral, I hope it is not amiss to bring up Project Sunset, which is also in the works, and will be taking place on your watch out there in the Pacific."

"Sunset?" The Admiral sounded momentarily puzzled. "Oh, I think, Lark, you are probably referring to *Project Sunrise*." There was a small sound, as of feminine hands slapping a forehead. "Indeed I am! *Poco cabeza*, as they say, a thousand pardons."

"None are necessary, Lark."

"But isn't safe to say, Admiral, that this *Sunrise* is evidently going to be a mighty evaluation of great significance to the U.S. Navy in its ability to meet the threat of enemy submarines? I mean, are not all sorts of marvelous new systems going to be tried out there to prove themselves and pave the way for new ships and all?" "Well, Lark," the Admiral said with a chuckle, "let me commend you for the excellence of your homework. Would that some of my Navy compatriots were so thorough. But let me insert one small correction. These marvelous systems to which you allude do not have to *prove* themselves. They are *already* proving themselves in the fleet. Rather, sad to say, Lark, we're still trying to bring aboard the laggards, the doubters, who find it so hard to grasp the obvious...."

"As in," Lark said, "the case of none so blind as those who will not see."

"You got it, Lark," the Admiral said with a sigh, "I'm afraid that oldie says it all."

"Oh dear, we're running over. But not so late that we haven't a handful of seconds of our time to wish you all success in your grand cause. And to you, personally, Admiral, all good things." "Thank you, Lark. Thank you Rich."

"Indeed. Until tomorrow then, Rich Bright for New Rome signing off." "And Lark Bright as well. With beautiful thoughts of you all." A pause and another beautiful thought arrived. "Tomorrow is Good Friday. So let's wish everyone a *good* Friday."

"My gosh, yes, Lark. To everyone then, make it a good, Good Friday."

"Not quite *everyone*, Rich, we must remember. Let's amend it, rather...."

"Right. A little gaffe, please forgive us, those of you who are not—"

"Lark Bright again." And to all a breathy good night. The background drums powered up in driving rhythm. Unlike thirty minutes earlier, when they had dissolved into a heraldic cacophony of sound, now one was reminded of a jet plane. It seemed to roar overhead and then recede into vague but powerful destinies of the night, imagined lights twinkling and growing swiftly smaller. It was difficult to picture that a few miles away, in a Wisconsin Avenue studio in Northwest, D.C., existed an over-lighted room, basically prosaic despite its booths and cameras, where a pair of Brights were putting away papers and shaking hands with their departing guest of the evening. A natural scene of dissolution of one of modern man's sessions of inventive entertainment. It was much easier to imagine a phantasmagoric rocket ship, hurtling off dizzyingly into the early evening stars and then, that intelligent machine having slung itself far out into black cold oblivion, curving back in some prodigious arc of Einsteinian space to reappear—first making one thunderous orbit of Washington—alighting at the same spot the very next evening.

"I'll be a son-of-a-bitch," David said aloud, forgetting that Beth was in the car beside him. "Amazing." "Daddy, how about *your* language?"

"You're right, Princess. Sorry about that."

"But what's amazing? You know all about what you were hearing, don't you?" "Not all," he said, "but enough. Let's say there's a lot to file away."

"I don't suppose you'd want to try to explain it all to me." "Too much, daughter, I'm afraid," he said, reaching across and touching her hand, "too much."

"That's just what you always say to Mom." "'Tis true," he conceded, "though not always."

Preoccupied with the program's conclusion, David failed to notice that traffic had freed itself and that formerly creeping cars were now hustling, seeming in their speeded up motion to scent the freedom of hills beyond. The honk of a horn behind him rectified his lapse and at the same time lightened something in him. Al, if she were up to it, and had not succumbed, would probably meet him with more than her usual greeting at the door kind of enthusiasm. She would pump him on his reaction and he, in turn, would have special fun responding. Kind of fun they had too little of lately. He was wishing for Billy, wherever his friend was, who would love to kick this one around. Well, well . . . . Anyway, another Washington day ending, with not even imaginative fiction able to replace what many an ordinary man found touching his own life every day.

▲▲▲▲▲

The silvery wispy man with jerky limbs in thin shapeless suit strode through the muggy clouded grey of this early evening along the Gulf Coast. A step behind was the nuclear submarine officer accompanying him. The famed Admiral was walking in the familiar stooped gait, chin out-thrust, as if his head—(that *amazing* head), with the startled raptor's darting eyes, missing nothing, wide pitiless eyes too—was determined to get there first, intellect tugging where the rest of him was going. Their two swiftly moving figures were the only signs of vitality in the worker-deserted shipyard. Cranes, their steel framework standing out stark against unmoving sky, were like skeletons of prehistoric creatures, tiny-headed giants frozen in a moment of lowering their long necks to tear off clumps of marsh grass at some misted pond's edge millions of years ago.

The Admiral's workday had begun at seven that morning and the eleven hours since had been filled with conferences and inspections. He had been up and down a dozen submarine hatches and to the bottom of deep dry-docks, their floors foul with the silty muck of southern rivers, their close air rich with the swift dying of barnacles and sea growth that still clung wetly to the great cylindrical black hulls under which he roamed restlessly, scrutinizing every inch of the rarely glimpsed curving undersides of the giants he had fathered. All day he had examined technical papers, peppered individuals—managers, welders of alloy steel, seamen, shipyard workers—with questions. Executives in the shipyard's corporate structure had all day felt his sarcasm like the rasp of a file on steel. Through his power ran, woven—flesh of his flesh—the *fear. What he was capable of doing.* To lives, careers, corporations, whole economic regions. Behind it was the drive for the theoretically impossible, nevertheless often astonishingly attained, perfection that was his goal. His edge was not remarkable intelligence, nor greatness as an engineer, but singleness of attention, forty unbroken years of days such as this one. There was pride also and idealism, vengeance too, the itch to settle scores, the rankle of a race with five thousand years of pain and anger under its skin. A part of him was mere style too;

show biz, the tricks of any leader. Long as the day had been it had not yet consumed the energies of this remarkable man. The Admiral and his briefcase carrier were passing a dry-dock holding a Navy destroyer and abruptly he turned towards the handsome grey hull sitting on its blocks. The accompanying Commander in uniform took away from the petty officer of the watch apprehension over the unknown civilian striding up the gangway with clear intent to visit. Also, the old gentleman's manner disarmed. "We would like to take a walk around topside, if that is all right."

"Yes sir." In minutes more, their tour of the topside area barely begun, the Command Duty Officer—"Lieutenant Agnew," introducing himself with a casually cheerful salute—appeared and offered to escort this mixed duo who had invaded the lazy peace of an in port evening. "Thank you, Lieutenant. That will be appreciated."

"My pleasure. Welcome, gentlemen, to the fair destroyer *Esposito*. The foremost ASW ship, as many will aver, in the whole dad—burned U.S. Navy." The Lieutenant was at ease with himself. The evening meal was concluded and he patted his ample stomach with an air of accomplishment. He did not know his extraordinary visitor from Adam. The Commander had taken in the Lieutenant's flourish of welcome without expression. But with a private and vague surmise about a type of naval officer largely unknown to him. There were no such Lieutenants in his nuclear submarine Navy.

The tour took them past gun mounts, life rafts, anchor chains, vents pushing out warm air with the heavenly smell of baking bread . . . the standard and appealing impressions of a destroyer's topside. He took them next to the O1 level where they stood beside the external plating of a great stack that jutted, slanting rakishly, out of the midships portion of the deck. "Each stack takes the uptakes of one fire room."

"Pressure fired boilers?" It was the Admiral's first question. Their guide turned around with an expression of amiable surprise. "Search me. I'm Ops. I'll take you up to the bridge now." Following a steep climb up the close dark passageway of an interior ladder, the trio entered the spaciousness of the deserted pilothouse. Last of daylight, palely bright, flooded through the round battle ports to give passable illumination for a sketchily informative tour of its basic equipment. "Wheel, of course. Ship is steered from here." "Ah."

"Gyro repeater," Lieutenant Agnew touched each item as he went along. "Over here's the magnetic compass." He stroked the large spheres of black iron mounted either side of the binnacle. "Called the 'navigator's balls', he said with a grin. "It's easy to see why, Lieutenant. But tell me," the Admiral wanted to know, "what is their purpose?"

"Why . . . it's to help reduce errors. Compensate, you know—"

"For induced magnetism? Permanent? Or . . . ?" Lt. Agnew frowned; disconcerted for a moment until his likeable grin came back. "Like I say, the navigator's babies. Now—" But the Admiral insisted on knowing more about the ship's magnetism. Were not degaussing coils also a part of the compensating system? "Yes indeedy." The Lieutenant stepped to the after bulkhead of the pilothouse and rapped his knuckles against a panel, which turned out to be the switches for navigation lights. Then rapping his head at his error. "Nope. Over *here.* Yep. Degaussing settings for "I" Coil, "Q" Coil, and so on."

"And which coil is meant to do what?"

"Haven't the slightest. We just follow the gouge." Lieutenant Agnew was indefatigably good humored. He was, as any student of naval types would recognize, part of an older and inexorably shrinking breed. He belonged to that last band of men who genuinely loved ships and enjoyed going to sea. Technology was slowly killing them off, poisoning their ardor, but not yet this genial fellow who now clasped both hands upon the shiny brass handles of the engine order telegraph, the final item described amongst the pilot house's moderately fascinating inventory. Decisively he yanked the handles towards himself until the engine indicators read "Back Full." Immediately he pushed them forward to "Flank." Old-fashioned bells rang out from within the sturdy upright device with its aura of antique tradition.

"This is how we give the word to the engineers what speed we want."

"And presently, I gather, you are indicating demand for maximum speed?" With a nod from Lt. Agnew, the Admiral went on. "Please tell me then why you initially pulled the handles back when the intention was to signal speed ahead?"

"Tradition, I'd say," Lieutenant Agnew replied with unabating geniality. "Mostly a way of getting the snipes' max attention. The bells really zing out in the engineering space. Actually that particular mode is telling them to throw away the normal acceleration tables. You got to kick her in the ass, you know, when heading off for plane guarding, or whatever. Maneuvering with dash."

"Ah. And what does it do to the engines," the Admiral asked still purring, "when habitually the engineers must ignore sound engineering practice?"

A faint shadow, not of comprehension but of annoyance, crossed Lieutenant Agnew's face. A fly had perhaps alighted on him but he wasn't sure where. Then with a laugh and a wave the fly was gone. "All I can say is, those babies are still humming." By unspoken consent the three exceedingly dissimilar men, a clotting of humanity for a few minutes out of eternity, drifted out onto the open bridge where the suffocating humidity of a Gulf Coast summer evening wrapped itself around them. The sun-soaked metal of the ship giving its heat back to evening, rising in waves from the gray-painted steel. The sour smell of stagnant waters enclosed by the piers rose on the same uplift of humid heat. Sunset had occurred and with it the ceremony of colors and in the bow a young sailor in whites was folding the starred blue cloth of the Union Jack. They watched him come aft, stepping across the cluttered forecastle deck with its stopped anchor chains.

Then, with nothing else to watch, their gaze lifted across the roofs of low-sooted brick machine shops and beyond to a small squared view of the slate surface of the Gulf of Mexico, uninteresting as a featureless plain leading away to grey mountains of unmoving clouds on the darkling horizon. Perhaps Lieutenant Agnew was conscious of the oppressive silence and feeling his faltering duties as host and he spoke about this view from the bridge, describing how at sea going into heavy swells the bow rose and fell and how, in its swift falling, it cleaved the blue water, cutting a foaming furrow through the newness of seas that were just as if they had never known a ship before. He went on haltingly yet not unpoetically, telling how the ship would shudder to meet the great walls of water which would be whipped back by the wind to smite the ports and blur the vision, swirling over the heavy glass in such volume that the whole ship seemed to be swimming, struggling up from under the weight of seas.... Sometimes the water caught you too—that is *you*, the officer of the deck—stinging the eyes and dripping salt on the tongue, but that was okay too, a fellow didn't mind it because in savoring such action, in its surprise and violence, one had the taste (and with it the *power)* of tasting the eternal sea itself....

There was a girl (he did not speak of her though she was a part of this reverie) a few years younger than himself—but also of romantic disposition, nurtured on good literature and soon to graduate from college—who came from his home town and to whom not long ago he talked in similar words of fervor. In the town's one cafe—its atmosphere scant, with A-1 sauce bottles and napkin dispensers the main permanent adornments to its booths—the girl listened to him talk as he was talking now. She did not know it yet for certain, still only sensed that because of what she was hearing, that it was going to happen that she would follow this likeable man; bear his children and cook his meals and make a home for him in varied ports around the world. And somehow along the line not necessarily "too late", because not necessarily would she have chosen differently, she would stop and wonder about it all.

The Admiral was a different kind of listener. Prowling restlessly along the wooden deck gratings of the open bridge, stopping and sniffing like a hungry mouse, he did not seem to be listening. But he was, every word. And when he came back over to Lieutenant Agnew, head cocked, the Commander read the signs and stiffened at what was to come. "Mind if I ask you about your antennas?" The Admiral was squinting up at the varied metal shapes and strung wires that climbed dizzyingly to the top of the cluttered mainmast where a gull perched with lordly disinterest. "Not in the least," came the cheerful reply from one of the world's innocents, knowing no more than a bowling pin does why it is being set up. "Shoot." A pin (and, in shape, the good living, amiably hedonistic, lieutenant somewhat resembled it) with no sense of the ball rumbling down the alley. "That one, for instance." The Admiral's voice was deceptively soft. "That's the surface search radar, sir," said Lt. Agnew.

"And the larger one above it?" Lieutenant Agnew could identify the air search radar too but that was the limit of his knowledge of the metal flora of the mast. Of the various electronic countermeasure equipments, the fanciful forms of the various intercept receivers and, finally, of the various communication antennas—the stubby ones of the UHF transmitters, the powerful whips of the single sideband radios—he knew not one. The Admiral's questions climbed the mast platform by platform, until reaching the bulbous bulk of the tactical aircraft navigation homing device where the seagull was taking its ease. The Admiral bored in, inquired about frequency bands, the challenge of lubrication for the most inaccessible of these antennas, how one handled corrosion in metals that must sit up there for years, baking in the sulfurous stack gasses, dripping spray, crusted with blackened salt . . . . Abruptly the Admiral stopped in mock surprise. "I heard you say that you are the Operations Officer. Aren't electronic countermeasures in your department?"

"You betcha."

Ah." An acid question hung unspoken in the thickening twilight.

"I've got an ECM Officer you see, to take care of that stuff."

"And no doubt a Communications Officer to worry about communications?"

"Uh . . . huh." Faint notes of weariness were making their appearance in the Lieutenant's voice. The questions were becoming a nuisance. Who *is* this little fuck? But now over the loudspeaker came the tweet of the boatswain's pipe, the immemorial call for sweepers to commence "a full sweep down fore and aft," its ancient sounding language comfort and symbol. It was the music of quiet days in port, the languor of routine. Soon it would be time for the eight o'clock reports, the setting up of the movie in the wardroom, perhaps gin rummy with someone afterwards, the coffee pot ever fresh and sea stories going on into the machinery humming night. Such were the small pearls strung out along his days.

A moment later the Admiral was saying, "Lieutenant, when rounding the inboard edge of the dry-dock, I noted your sonar dome there in the bow. An unusually large one, it would appear." "None bigger," Lieutenant Agnew's voice perked up, his shoulders squared with pride. "It houses the transducer for DIANA, the most advanced sonar in the world, the main reason this here otherwise humble old tin can keeps busy with all eyes upon her."

"There seems to be," the Admiral said, "considerable yard activity taking place around the dome. I observed several yard workers at work with grinding wheels."

"You got it right, sir. You got an eye, mister. It's the reason we're dry-docked for the special availability. Yard birds up forward are working away round the clock under floodlights to grind away all the barnacles and nicks and crapola on the face of the dome. Take it down to bright metal smooth as a baby's butt. Down to microns of finish."

"Microns?" the Admiral said. "Well, maybe it's millimeters. Pug could tell us. Likely he's down there on the dry-dock floor eyeballing how it's going."

"Pug?"

"Yes sir. Senior Chief Sonar man Puglaski. He's the man."

"And all this . . . unusual activity is no doubt to some special purpose?"

"You got it, sir. Soon as our baby's done its refurbishing, we flood this old dry-dock and zip on down to the Canal and out to Pearl . . . ." "Pearl?," the Admiral asked.

"Pearl Harbor, Hawaiian Islands. Going to be a part of Project SUNRISE. The big shebang." "Ah," the Admiral repeated softly, "the big shebang. Good luck to you there. Now if I may ask . . . ." But even as Lt. Agnew sought to edge his persistent visitors towards the ladder, the Admiral's questions came more rapidly. They hopped all over, a boxer's quick jabs; they hearkened back to words and phrases from minutes before. They touched, brushed up against, and then hooked hard, like a hawk's talons, into that whole body of things about his ship, the tactics of war, that the Lieutenant did not know.

What is the range of those guns up forward? No, no. Their effective range? And what is the ship's maximum speed, when you demand of those engineer's down there in their hole that they, as you say, "kick it in the ass?" And what does it do to feed water consumption?

The Commander, whose attentiveness to the Admiral's interrogations seemed never to stray into independent curiosity, moved closer to his mentor. He put his face next to the Admiral's, keeping his head inclined—from one angle theirs could have been two heads in a frieze on a coin—to miss nothing, dutifully anxious to catch it all. His expression was impassive, but a muscle could occasionally be seen to twitch along a tautened jaw line.

Lt. Agnew was able to answer few questions, none at all completely. But the ambiguously negligent quality of his nature did not alter throughout the increasing, and yet still unfelt, heat of the interrogation. "Feed water?" he repeated, seeming to turn the phrase over like a gem of appealing but unfamiliar quality. "Yes, *feed water*, for Christ's sake!" The explosion was so sudden that the young officer could only stand there and blink. With a gesture of disgust the Admiral darted towards the exit ladder, leaving the Commander and the Lieutenant to hurry after him. Even so, those younger legs losing distance all the way down. Mixed with the reverberation of feet on iron, came back to them a spewing of profanity for which the Admiral was famous. They caught up with him at the quarterdeck where, all impatience and ginger, he was bouncing around like a jerky marionette, petulantly anxious to get away. He left it to the Commander to take care of the minimal amenities of farewell. "Thank you for the tour, Lieutenant." "My pleasure." Lieutenant Agnew gave a languid salute. If faint lights of puzzled wounding could be detected in those clear but unseeing eyes they did not last. The wardroom movie beckoned. A western he had selected himself, privilege of the Command Duty Officer. Another shit-kicker, but never scorned.

Admiral and Commander strode away through the dusk; the ship, with its warm lights, receding at their backs. The Commander broke the silence; clearly he felt that it was up to him to do so. "Admiral. I am ashamed for my Navy after that performance." The Admiral made no reply and the Commander went on. He spoke emotionally sincerely . . . well, perhaps not altogether sincerely. Some degree of calculation had to be woven through his words. The Admiral had controlled his naval career since its infancy, could break the Commander—one of the system's honed but interchangeable parts—and send him packing into the outer darkness of his profession with a wave of his hand. Submariners who were three and four star Admirals today had first been selected by him into nuclear power training as ensigns. As in the times of Queen Victoria when men grew up from babyhood, fought wars, raised families, and grew old, knowing no other monarch, so it was with this breed of naval officers, who turned their faces to no other sun. This particular Commander was one of the anointed, but even so the competition was keen and his world a fickle one. The Admiral toppled the favored, often for the slightest transgression, swiftly and brutally, though—as noted—less for failings in performance than for lapses in loyalty. Nuclear submariners had crashed into cliffs, rammed merchantmen, bounced off the continental shelf at high speed, dopily exceeded test depth, returned from patrols with periscopes inexplicably curled, ascribing it to whales, but whales somehow shedding paint, and yet, so long as the skipper's hair remained fair, the Admiral could be counted upon to intervene before investigation turned sticky. Generous manumission vouchsafed only to the Navy's special few. And perhaps that was the way indeed it ought to be.

For behind the Commander was a decade and a half of unbroken eighteen-hour days, years of relentlessly demanding command, continuous weeks of close covert trail of Soviet submarines—the semi-blind following the blind—which only the elite who partook in them could know what ball busters they truly were. There had been special operations, "SPECOPS", around the Nord Kap to the Kola Peninsula where he had kept his submarine squatting just above the mud for weeks, observing the Soviet Northern Fleet stream out of the mighty naval base complex at Murmansk, the screws of a hundred hostile ships thumping as they passed overhead. He had taken his submarine to the North Pole too, dodging the ice-keels that thrust down far below the underside of the heavy arctic ice, and had punched the ice-hardened sail of his submarine through ten feet of emerald ice, and then he and his men had climbed out on the ice and stood blinking in the strange half light, awkward in their unfamiliar arctic gear like astronauts testing another moon, feeling the gigantic cold of space itself, looking around with comic nervousness for polar bears. Even now, assigned to the Reactor Division of the Naval Sea Command, his eighty hour weeks did not abate. A half dozen Sunday picnics he had planned this summer with his family, and had to scrub every one. Yet competition was ferociously keen and only a handful out of these hard driving submarine Commanders could ever make flag. The choices of the navy's submarine rulers were still tightly constrained by law and tradition; the horse trades of the past still governing the present. The quotas were set in iron and in no branch of the service was the culling of the excellent so severe. Nowhere but in the submarine service did the pyramid narrow so cruelly. Thus even a nuclear submarine Commander of such quality as this one could not relax a minute if he were to touch his dreams... if, indeed, such a softly rounded and glowing word as 'dreams' could even be properly applied in conjunction with these steely haunted old young men with natures as tightly integrated as the sleek hulls and masses of gleaming machinery they mastered.

The pair walked on. It grew dark but no less warm nor moist. They passed dimly lighted shapes of nuclear submarines, squatting low and shadowy beside deserted wooden piers. Because the Admiral was saying nothing, the Commander felt that he must speak more. To what extent he was sincere, as noted before, is impossible to judge. Men of less abilities have brown-nosed much harder for lesser reward. Some things are ambition's necessity. Thus necessity too that had the Commander, after his last voyage to the Arctic, presenting the Admiral a chunk of ice from the North Pole. The gesture, so fine and impulsive as it began in the glittering arctic sunshine, the hacking out of a piece of bluish ice with a fire axe and carrying it down in a bucket to store in the ship's food reefer, turned into something frustratingly else the day of delivery. He had flown all the way back from Pearl Harbor with the wondrous chunk in the plane's baggage compartment, souvenir ice and bucket packed in dry ice, but by the time he arrived the dry ice had evaporated and the non-arctic temperature of a Washington summer was doing mischief. The day was broilingly hot and the ice was melting rapidly, a shrinking berg sloshing around in a sea of grainy slime. He had to walk further through Crystal City than he had planned and he felt the fool with his unwieldy and improbable bucket. The civil servants crowding the elevator, clerk-typists carrying their cardboard boxes of doughnuts, glanced at him curiously. Maneuvering himself and bucket out of the elevator he splashed some of the liquid over his uniform trousers and shined shoes; cursing silently, he went into the nearest men's room and paper toweled it off.

He had a lengthy wait outside the Admiral's office, although he had a firm appointment. He heard the Admiral shouting his usual threats and obscenities through a series of phone calls. One man's style of leadership. When he finally got in, the once grand piece of the frozen Arctic had shrunk to the size of a baseball, a rough globule of grainy ice swimming in a cloudy pool smelling of decaying Arctic micro biologics. The Admiral took the crumbling aggregate in both his hands, water streaming through his fingers. Seizing it greedily, like treasure. His normally cold eyes were bird bright. He smiled delightedly; he acted incredulous, as if humbled by this arduously implemented tribute of honor. "You did this for me?" he kept repeating, "you took all this trouble to bring this to *me?*"

The Commander guessed that he had been very close actually to saying "little me." He thought *that*—he was sure of it, in fact—because for once in his life he was staring at his mentor with pure hatred, his senses chiseled preternaturally sharp. He was dead tired; twenty-four hours of sleepless travel had been grafted directly onto many weeks of draining arctic operations. He had nothing left in him but exhausted clarity, the ability to see plainly an act of painful hypocrisy, a phony boyishness right down to the phony smile, the phony glee, a normally good actor's very bad performance. Watching a batch of pure shit. He stared at the little Admiral for a moment longer, answered his questions as briefly as possible, accepted his spuriously tainted fulsome praise, and departed as soon as he could escape the man's presence. He had seen something that he had not expected to see, seen it up too close, and he was shaken. But nothing happened. He returned to his submarine in Pearl and took it away from the pier times again and drove it far and well. Which is to say, primarily he maintained his reactor perfectly. He pushed the incident to a corner of his mind and did not revisit it. Few men seeking much have ever allowed a lone jolt to their illusions to knock them from their course. The focussed man does not let self-knowledge grow out of hand, let cynicism corrode the hard metal of his ambition. Applied right, it only polishes, makes a man see better.

"Anyway, Admiral," he concluded, turning to the thin shadowy figure bouncing alongside beside him, "I am truly ashamed for my profession." A thrill of fearful doubt immediately went through him; uneasily, it struck him that he had already said that. Still the Admiral said nothing. Hoping that he had not laid it on too thick, the Commander offered nothing more. They walked on and on, the Admiral turning at whim up one industrial street, down another. Exercise or madness? It did not matter, not to his solitary striding purposes. Neither did it matter that the Commander, still with one foot in the normal world, was hungry. But it would be up to the Admiral when and where they ate tonight. If eating was even part of the program. Yet as usually happened, they would end up at some greasy spoon picked at random at some late hour, some neon-lurid place of heavy dishes and strong coffee, for which the Commander would have to be glad. He would wait for the Admiral to decide. His role was to carry the briefcase; for what else he was not sure. Possibly the Admiral was weighing the Commander's words, testing the worth of their substance. Likely not. Men in high places do not expect the whole truth from anyone, least of all an ambitious subordinate. In the Admiral's case, he was seldom interested in other people's words. He had heard them all long ago. Thus probably what made him stop at last—halting in the middle of darkness now beginning to lighten with a moon rising over the roof of a great silent machine shop—came from a different set of data entirely. The Admiral turned and spoke, as the Commander had not heard him speak. Softly, actually calling him by his first name, getting it right more or less, and his voice had an ordinary human quality. As from some vanished world of traditional courtesies, from a time before the Admiral had mounted the world's stage. In his voice was a kind of pleading, hoping that the Commander was going to get this right because he was only going to say it once. The mask truly off, if only for a moment.

"Don't you see?" He repeated the Commander's first name, getting it slightly wrong again, and yet in another way, but close enough. What mattered was a father's kind of caring, the kindly teacher's voice. "What I've been saying?" Moonlight was in the old man's silver hair; a light breeze, coming up from the sea, finding its way around all the buildings, was ruffling it. He looked forlorn, enormously old, heartbreakingly fragile. His years about up. "My message." He actually touched the Commander. "What it's all been about. No mystery. What I've been telling them all along. *These goddamned naval officers simply don't know their own business.*"

* * *

David had lately taken note of his boss's, Mason's, altered behavior. Time and opportunity to notice, of course. How some new kind of feverishness, competing with Mason's addiction to his newspapers, seemed to be bollixing his routine. New gestures, more than his usual gazing off into space, sudden and unusually intense, if unaccountable, periods of activity. Striding about, more than ordinarily voluble, yet with much of the time his lips moving but with no apparent listener but himself. Talking to himself, David observed amusedly. This going on for some days. Mason in a state of mysterious, but no more productive, agitation. Then all at once the mystery explained. With Mason one day sidling over to him, DIANA and SUNRISE linked in his questioning. Covering his embarrassment with a cough, hating to ask. "Just touching base here, you could say. Recalling that you're sort of our resident expert on the subject."

"Well," David said, slinging his own feet up along side Mason's on his desk—making a statement but not sure what—"I do know something about DIANA. About SUNRISE I know nothing. Just the rumors floating around here."

"*Big,*" Mason declared, looking away to distances, possibly mountains in his imagination which alone could convey any proper sense of the awesome dimensions of the operation, *"real big my boy."* With Mason then recovering from his reverie to describe, for David, his understanding of SUNRISE's purposes and methods. Mason getting them pretty well out of focus, David was able to deduce, but inserting no correction. Listening on with only half an ear until catching something that had him blurting out his surprise. Something weird.

"You're kidding. How's that again? Supportability's going to be fielding a whole *team* out there?"

Perhaps it was his subordinate's tone more than his surprise, but Mason drew back. Offended. His outfit just kicked in the balls again. And by one of its own. Clamping his jaw. Mason, keeper of Supportability's pride. Who else?

"Goddamned right we are. Bet your ass." Mason dragging his heels off his subordinate's desk with a show of, well . . . something, abruptly backing off this session sooner perhaps than he intended. "We *should* be there. This is, I'm telling you, the biggest gang bang of the year." Mason paused. Needing more. "Make that the biggest one in a decade."

Amazing. To which David did not utter a sound, beginning to have a hunch that it just might be the case. Picking up then more about the project over the next week or so from his office mates. And waiting. Not with hope especially; hope being a quality that for some time he had kept on a tight ration. Just waiting. Living with Mason's Silent Treatment of him. Not all bad when all was said and done. Then one afternoon, several weeks at least having gone by, Mason barged right up to his desk. A Mason clearly in a hurry. Near quitting time. The old familiar energies of departure revving up in him. "Morgan!"

"Morgan aye."

"It's all set. You're *going*." Mason's sweeping gesture of his arm was lordly in keeping with its generosity. "You're on the team," Mason the A-hole, but a not unkindly one. At least not meaning to be. "Well," David said, "I thank you—"

But Mason cut short David's thanks, time's imperative of departure too keenly vibrant in him. Also needing additional seconds, not to be allowed to infringe on his countdown, in order to get across the remainder of what his memory had been saving up.

"Yep, yep . . . . I'm taking you even with your attitude. Because I'm trusting that you can contribute." David nodded. Putting aside the many things he might have said to volunteer the one piece of information that his boss fairly ought to have.

"I've got to tell you that the powers that are behind this huge caper will not be happy to see my name on your Team's listing. I didn't land over here exactly trailing clouds of glory."

Mason's shrug said, who does? "Screw 'em." Brandishing his unlit cigar, a recently acquired prop of executive toughness, with as much pathetic defiance of the system as Supportability could muster. "I don't have to provide names. You'll just be stuck in there as Data Taker number three." David repeated it. "Data Taker."

"Best I can do," Mason said apologetically, something of his well meant kindness returning, and with it a return of lordly manumission. "But, hey, my boy, it's a *deal*. Enjoy. Latch on to that *per diem*. Take the little woman along. Bring the whole family." Ah yes. You bet . . . David Morgan thus able this afternoon to bring home for a change something different, something nice, to his family. News greeted with whoops and hollers, all cheerled by Aliason, whose enthusiasm for this news was as large as was her perception of its cause whackily but endearingly askew.

"You see, sweet. You *see*? It's as I've said right along," something marvelous is going to come along and sweep you right up back to where you ought to be."

"Well," he said, unwilling to tamper seriously with anything that could bring such color back to his girl's cheeks, "it's not actually quite that way."

She brushed aside all demurrers. Exulting in the prospective dollar figure of the *per diem* he had unwarily mentioned and which now, in metaphysical terms, she brandished like a beacon of salvation. "Can you *believe* it?"

As a matter of fact, he barely could himself. This odd gift out of the government's blue making it all possible. Even if barely. Which misgivings, amidst the family's jubilation, he still had to get out. "I really still don't know how we're going to handle it financially."

"Oh, we'll figure a way. *We'll figure it*," bucking him up. Of course, having no least idea herself. But wasn't that exactly what he had always wanted, that heedless optimism of heart? Supper too was happy chaos, salad forgotten, grace skipped, rolls burnt. Their leverage never to be higher, parents extracting impossible promises from the children. Of relentless scholarship, prodigies of neatness and discipline... worlds never to be. Peace did not come this night until late and with not a detail settled. In the dark, late, she went on talking, but with a strange calmness and clarity. "Oh, darling, don't keep poking the gift horse in the mouth. It's salvation."

"Reprieve, Sweet, a better word."

"You and your words. But you know what I think? Truly believe." She did not finish what she believed, but not because of sleepiness. A great blue swell, cresting, glittering with sunlight, was bearing down upon her... about to overwhelm. She watched its massy approach, fascinated. *Hawaii!* Only weeks away and so much to be done.

Tessa sounded, as she picked up the phone, as if she were in a sinking spell. Her voice though roused to delight at David's news of Hawaii. "You'll have a chance to see your brother Sean, your paths crossing at last. He's at the Headquarters of the Pacific Fleet, or whatever they're calling it these days. You'll get to know Betty. They'll both be dying to see you."

"Mother. Be realistic. Truth is that Sean and I hardly know each other. By the time I had my first memory of him he was already away at the Naval Academy and thereafter I've only seen him as a passing stranger."

"Well, darling. I suppose I should be sorry that you had to come along so late. But I won't apologize for the awkward spacing of my children. We took them as God sent them, the way it still ought to be, but don't get me going on that. Anyway, Aliason will have a taste of her beloved islands again. I can't fault her dreaminess there. Before the war your father and I lived in a cottage right on Waikiki. It cost sixty dollars a month and that included our little Japanese maid Suki."

The excitement at David's news kept Tessa energized for days to come. "Forgive me for calling so often, my darlings. But I've neglected to ask. Is your being out there going to . . . *help*? Your career, that is. I was talking to Muddy about it and he said it certainly sounded like you're 'back on the team.'"

Ah Mother, Muddy . . . Al. All. The whole sweet dippy lot of you.

"David, are you still there? My goodness, your silence. "Still here," he said. "No. Afraid not. Not my former team, at any rate. This whole thing is an aberration."

"A *what?*" She did not though slow down to learn. "Anyway I can still pray. Now promise me that you will call Sean as soon as you arrive. You can learn much from him too, whether you believe so or not. If you will just listen. You often don't, you know."

"Thanks, Mom."

"He will roll out the red carpet of welcome for you," Tessa said, "I guarantee. His Betty, too. Now *there's* a girl. I do hear that Hawaii remains that kind of place. Everyone wanting the visitor to love it as much as they." "That's the way we recall it," David said.

"I hope it stays that way. A rare and beautiful touch of life like that should not be allowed to fade." Nope. Taking longer himself this night to fall asleep. Whacky. But whacky as it all was, he would take it, embrace the life lifting power of the unexpected.

6

Tessa's confidence in his brother's welcoming hospitality turned out closer to the mark than David's doubts. Sean and Betty learned from Tessa the flight on which the younger Morgans were arriving and surprised them at the airport. Meeting them traditionally, with an abundance of *leis*, the richness of plumeria stronger than the oily smells that rose from the dark asphalt shimmering in the sun. Beyond, the airfield's wide runways stretched to the sea, blue as the sky. The mountains rose steep and green and the white clouds were moving over them just as Aliason had long treasured them in memory. Betty Morgan proved extraordinarily thoughtful, rescuing Aliason from the frequent immobility of their having only one car, and that one mostly tied to David and the demands of his work. She drove Aliason about, up to the North Shore, bringing reacquaintance with Chinaman's Hat and Laie Point and other loved places. Al's sighs joined Betty's at the feast of beauty. Her chest would heave as if it might crack, and at a certain sight here or there—simple as a sliver of glittering sea framed by palms—she would give a cry, a heart being squeezed.

Tessa had made it her urgent duty to prepare David for renewal of relations with his older brother. Stressing that Sean was an intelligent man who obviously also thought much about war and such. The very kind of person David could discuss such matters with enjoyably.

"Mother, I'm looking *forward* to seeing him."

"I hope you are." Tenderness as well as sternness was in her caution. "Just don't undervalue Sean. You have that fault, you know, doubting the brains of others and taking no pains to hide it. Ah, but you do, my dear." In spite of deeming his mother's judgment an unfair one, it had stuck in his mind. And still there when, several weeks after their arrival in the Islands, he responded to Sean's invitation to drop by his office at the Commander-in-Chief Pacific Fleet Headquarters.

"Welcome, little brother," Sean greeted him, waving towards Pearl Harbor and the brownish distant Waianae mountains beyond. Sean was Operations Officer, one of the handful of so-called "king-maker" billets, only it hadn't made him a king. David had not seen him in uniform before and, although he was wearing simply a short sleeve khaki shirt and khaki trousers, standard working uniform of the tropics, unadorned except for silver eagles for rank and the gold wings of the naval aviator—nary a ribbon, though he had many decorations—

Sean's trimness and grace made him stand out in splendor. A saddening splendor, for his ambition was going no further. Shining only for itself. Sean Morgan burned with a sense of lost wars, comrades dead in futile battles. He spoke of Korea, a shadow pointing to that future when wars would no longer be fought to be won. Scorn poured forth for a certain senior Admiral up at Camp Smith, head of all the Pacific Ocean Area who for five years had lived up high on that hill, luxuriating in the grandeur of his quarters and pampered with his stewards mates, presiding in silence over the mess that was Viet-Nam, never uttering a peep of protest. Now, well out of there, having authored a book bemoaning about how goldarned awful it had been.

Sean could not contain his amusement at David's ideas, their intricate reasoning or their *naiveté*. Amounting to a concocted structure of frailty that the storms of war would sweep away—Sean's arguments were saying—like a house of twigs in a roaring canyon of flood. "That ship, that frigate, younger brother, that you don't want because—I have actually read some of your articles, by the way—you say won't hack the job...." "*Sea Eagle*?", David said.

"Right, that's the one, and maybe it *won't* do the job so dandily. But each one of those ships will, if we ever get them, have some weapons aboard, at least a couple of guns. *Numbers count*." Their talk went on against the background of that sweet blue sky. The whitest of clouds, sailing swiftly before the trades, were visible out the broad window that also gave such a fine operator's view of the harbor, the ships of Sean's fleet coming and going.

"It's never been my objective to do away with ships," David responded hotly, "I've just sounded a small trumpet for the Navy to get itself better ones."

"I hear you, little brother. But because this DIANE, *or whatever*—" "DIANA."

"—won't do its job, what we'll probably end up with is no *Sea Eagle* at all. No new class of ships, nothing to take its place. And our Navy will be smaller. What the Navy loses in ships for a few years, it loses for decades. Now it's the aircraft carrier the arm chair experts are telling us is vulnerable, that we shouldn't be making any more of those dinosaurs. And, hell yes, it doesn't take much to turn the flight deck into a streaking fireball. Christ, haven't I seen it? Yep, the old carrier *can* be had, by your submarines and their cruise missiles. So pretty soon then it's to be no more carriers either?" Sean paced as he talked. A beam of sun caught him and he looked like a God, bronzed from a thousand noontime tennis games. Abruptly, his voice lowered furiously and both his arms flew up in exasperation. "*Paralysis by analysis!*" Staring down at his audience of one. "You've heard of it little brother?", Sean said.

"Only a hundred fucking times."

Amusement lightened Sean's expression. "And," he said, "fair to say, you've been accused of it." Abruptly the tension went out of that taut body. Sean laughed in prelude to his apologies. "Hey, so why don't I let up? Pummeled you about the head and shoulders for now. We'll have many a hot session before you head back to the mainland. So, how are you doing?" The question suddenly a personal one, acute and perhaps knowing.

"Doing okay."

"You're sure? Because I gather from Mother that you may have gotten yourself in deep kim-chee a while back. And you're still in sort of limbo now. Got that right? "Obviously too you know that your old boss, Sneedon Snowdon, has taken over from Tommy Blue. Bumped into him yet?"

"No. But, we don't move in the same circles."

"Anyway," Sean said, "our Boy Wonder has his hands full with that SUNRISE operation that he dreamed up while back there in Washington." A residue of feeling, perhaps envy or resentment seemed to linger in the wake of Sean's mention of the young Admiral. Perhaps recalling that the Selection Board that had vaulted Snowdon over a thousand of Captains senior to him was the same one that had spelled the end forever to Sean's own chances. Brooding over that injustice though for only a moment. "So, small world, eh?"

About which, vexations of small worlds or large, Sean conveyed his inability to do much except to promise, for both himself and Betty, to do their own part to make the younger Morgans' Hawaiian sojourn a pleasant one. Which promise David took away gratefully, thinking of Al and the children, otherwise destined to be stuck too much in their small apartment on the slopes of the Punchbowl. But mostly from this meeting David carrying away a hunger for more talks. Bearing in his heart of hearts, and never so much as out here at one of the world's mightiest naval bases, rubbing elbows every day with men of action, a worm of doubt that his act of defiance last year might have been more bravado than some epic stand on principle. Yet despite Sean's promise of all those good talks to come, and though thereafter there were a number of occasions when he and Sean were together, they were always social ones. He felt more acutely than ever a sense of isolation since cut off from his professional associations in EAR; missing as well these lighter bondings of the spirit with Daisy and Billy Jencks and a handful of others of his old pals. He even missed—was it *possible*?—Viola, her driftiness, her friendly softness, her quirky grit, as well. His loneliness was all the greater out here in all this sunshine, this beauty that could mock the spirit. SUNRISE, and planning for its forthcoming showpiece, CORRIDA, sustained him only so far. With the best of his conscientious professionalism, melded to the patriotism of the good citizen that he was, fortified by the admirable record of his family's wars and its journeys, he could still not—not for all his trying—pretend beyond a point that the current business that he was engaged in was not simply a . . . *crock*. What else?

Everything else clamping down, he was turning more to Al. His lone bright spot. In spite of his fears, and with all his acute, if covert, scrutiny of her behavior, suffering no lapses. For all that it was true that there was no such thing as a "geographical cure," could there not be at least the transitory blessing of a geographical *remission*? His Al. Brightening in mood and spirits daily, with Betty Morgan, true to her promises, contributing. A Betty whose help went beyond treating Al to luncheons, chauffeuring her on shopping expeditions, the kids to the pool and stable. The energy, competence, wit and humor with which Betty lived her own life casting a trail of sparks, light and glorious, in her merry wake. Aliason was charmed, was yearning to borrow a tithe of that talent and pizzazz.

Like many a Navy wife in the Islands Betty had taken hula lessons, but wanted to know hula better; not just the *hapa-haole* stuff of the officer's wives' Tuesday morning lessons with Mary Lou. To learn the traditions of the true hula that survived, she regularly drove far up the Waianae Coast to meet an ancient woman named Alikea Kahawahanna. Aliikea had parchment skin and the small fluid bones of a cat and performed the hula as she had been taught it by her grandmother, a lady who had known the sons and daughters of Kamehameha himself. One time Betty took Aliason along to her practice session in this lonely place, a sun-faded cottage with chickens pecking in the dusty yard. It was an area Aliason knew about from her time before in the Islands but would never have come up here except the way she and David used to do it, in the strengthened company of a group to watch the giant surf at Makaha. This was a poor, bony kind of land, steep and cruelly rocky, dry as a desert, and here native Hawaiians had retreated in poverty and bitterness, nursing brutally dangerous resentments. It was a place of brawls, unsolved disappearances. Dark faces watched you pass and not with love. No prudent *haole* came this way alone, and not other than warily. Betty sailed in like a queen, pulling up in her big car in a cloud of dust and squeal of brakes, past rusting hulks of cars hunkered down in starving brown grasses. Aliason watched Betty dance while her ancient teacher chanted Hawaiian in accompaniment of difficult melodies wailing from a hand-wound victrola. For minutes the old woman would be swaying in a trance and then pop out of it to advise Betty briskly how to improve her movements, to refine subtlety. Betty always brought presents, clothes for younger members of the family, toys for brown children in ragged shorts. For Aliikea she brought medicines, once paid for her hospitalization.

One Saturday afternoon the Morgans, junior and senior, picnicked by the tennis courts of Makalapa. On the court Betty flew, the mass of her dark hair bouncing in colored ribbons. To any bystander, a mere dozen yards away, she could not be many times a grandmother. Aliason ached to be able to play such tennis herself. No, simply to *look* like that playing. Betty would trot over to the sidelines for a towel and in the momentary expressionlessness of the act of sipping lemonade the lines around her eyes and her mouth, normally hidden in the creases of smiles, were vivid. Pale radial tracks against the fine brown of her tan. Then her smile returned and it was another plus to see that she spent no time brooding on anything as unimportant as growing older. David, keeping it hidden, in his own way noticed Betty—her slender shinily muscled girlish legs—more than could be guessed. More at least, he hoped, than Al guessed. But Al guessed. Later on subdued with thoughtfulness. "There's the kind of woman you deserve," she said to David with quiet matter-of-factness, "someone who is whole. No telling what you might have done."

"Come on Al. Cut that out."

Such shadows did not linger. If they came they blew by as fast as the trade winds drove puffs of white clouds over the mountain peaks. The very next week, when they rendezvoused for the polo matches at Mokuleia on the North Shore, no day could have been lovelier, nor freer of stress. By the old white fence where their cars were parked the Australian pines swayed and whispered and they feasted on the spread that Betty had set upon the hood of their car, formal and yet casually appealing with silver candelabra, while out on the field the ponies thundered by with their muscled beauty, the daring of their riders. After the game they strolled over to the little airfield where the gliders congregated and Sean, proud for having qualified at mastery of yet one more kind of aircraft, rented a glider and took Aliason up for a brief flight. Able to soar, Sean said, if need be forever, in the updrafts created by the trade winds hitting the cliffs. The frigate birds kept aloft, too, tiny and motionless high up on their blade wings, along with toys of men. As soon as the glider stopped its bumpity roll along the broken grey-black macadam of the old field, Al flung open her side door and came running. Calling out her triumph. "I had the controls, darling . . . I truly did." She turned to Sean, following some yards back, for confirmation.

"That you did." With an instructor's thumbs up. "Quick hands. A born fighter pilot." He winked, but it was not a mocking one. "Next flight we'll be tackling acrobatics." "You *see*, darling, you *see*." Yet after that special polo day at Makuleia such congenial times with the senior Morgans grew less. There seemed no special reason for the falling off of such occasions, and neither he nor Aliason had the feeling of being dropped. Because henceforth, whenever they did get together, the warmth from Betty and Sean was there intact. David and Aliason reviewed the facts, speculated on signs that might reveal clues; in the end concluding that nothing was amiss. It was only natural. SUNRISE perhaps dragging on too long, having multiple extensions, and it seemed that most of the good things, the fine shining pieces that the Islands heaped up on its plate, had all been done, with the irrecapturable freshness of first times best not to be repeated. David and Aliason and their kids were no longer novelty, had become habit. They could see too that Sean and Betty had their own busy lives, social and otherwise, at the upper level of rank of CINCPACFLT, living the favored life of senior officers of Makalapa. David and Aliason accepted, found themselves glad for time to do things on their own. Drawn again and again to the powerful and endless blue flame of the North Shore. Once they rented for the day a four wheel drive vehicle and jolted their way around Kaena Point at the northwest tip of Oahu upon whose bleak shores the giant Pacific swells rolled in and boomed across the lonely quiet with few to hear. There were invitations too to drop by Artie Perozzi's home and the pleasure the children found in these visits overcame Aliason's reluctance. In quiet moments though, up there on the cramped lanai of their spartan apartment, Al would ask why Artie Perozzi was even bothering with the Morgans.

"I mean," she would go on vexedly, "what's *Artie* getting out of it? Out of *you*, who can no longer dig up money for his darned contracts. Isn't that why he used to bug you so much?"

David had done his own thinking about Artie's possible motives. But less compellingly. Even languidly, as it was bound to be, with Artie's *mai tai's* repeatedly pressed into his hand and looking over at the blue sparkle of Artie's pool and at his Boat out there joyfully splashing away. The fruit of which thoughts, he offered up to the skeptical Al. Perhaps no more than simple friendship on Artie's part, a shared mutual professional respect. Debt to the past. "Or maybe just the spirit of aloha. Some of that out here still."

Al bit her lip for what was surely true. Aloha did survive. Still. "There's condescension there, too," she insisted. "Secretly he's lording it over you."

Disagreement though did not fester. The Islands' lulling breezes saw to that. Meaning only kindness. In any event, the matter took care of itself. The times that they stopped by Artie's, as if by unspoken agreement, grew less, and ever more the little clutch of Morgans, transitorily lodged here in the vastness of the blue Pacific, were on their own. Each weekend getting up and going. Heading out to the thunder of the surf, beaches for themselves alone. David lying in the sun, drugged on the hot sands, thinking neither of past nor future and glad not asking himself why.

▲ ▲ ▲ ▲ ▲

Despite her stunningly refreshed fondness for the Islands, there were many days when Aliason could manage no better by their loveliness than sigh over distant views of the sea. Each day there was Boat to be entertained. With that lively little boy removed from his adventurous buddies of the old neighborhood, the task laid a strain upon her imagination. Visits to Paradise Park and its blue macaws could only take one so far. Then there was Beth too to be gotten to and back from her stable sessions. For those days when she had to have their rented car that meant driving David into the Naval Station early through rush-hour traffic. And sometimes (too often, because it was bound to be David, if anyone, working late on Ford Island and finding himself alone in those analysis lofts on the top floor of the ASW command) she had to drive back to pick him up. Usually it was the most inconvenient hour of twilight, interrupting supper's preparation, and too late by then for David to bum a ride home. There were any number of SUNRISE analysts with whom he could have shared a ride if he had chosen to depart at the routine hour of four o'clock, joining the exodus of the less dedicated. The mass of them jamming the great seventy-five foot launches with the press of their bodies, shoulder-to-shoulder, gunwale-to-gunwale, rides aplenty waiting on the other side.

At the same time, she would think of her David proudly as she sat by the landing in the greenish light under the palms, reading her book and keeping her eyes on Boat as he threw pebbles or stooped to gaze at the little fish playing in the clear water around the furry sea growth on the pilings. She watched as the gray motor launch chugged smokily towards the landing, across the glassy waters mirroring the sky's rosy end of day, seeing David's standing figure silhouetted, in the all but deserted launch. There was something romantic in the sight, and in regarding her own self too, a picturesquely imagined figure of quiet destiny on an empty pier by this pale tropic sea. No matter, as David stressed to her, that he was returning from having done nothing memorable, or even useful. The implicit virtue of his solitariness, a host of worthy reasons she clung to, triumphed over inconvenience. She hoped too that her feelings, which she kept turning into fervent words for his benefit, helped banish any sense of failure or diminution of his self-esteem. David Morgan sunk to mere *Data Taker*! For something as dreary too as Supportability! She burned with that. Yet she grew fond of this oasis of seclusion towards the harbor entrance, where ships passed dramatically close. One sunset she saw a submarine gliding by, the latter all sinister purpose, black and graceful and silent as a shark's fin cutting the green and red tinged water, calm as a sea painting's surface. Improbably, as David told her, the army of analysts was still growing—their numbers of his fellows eventually to peak with CORRIDA—threatening, he claimed, to submerge Ford Island under their weight, causing the Arizona Club, Ford Island's own greasy spoon, to run out of hamburgers and potato chips at lunch time. Yet all this analytic talent gathered to pursue—David's sense of wonder was inextinguishable even as his motivation waxed and waned—the putative virtues of the quixotic DIANA. A protean assembly of presumptive talent chartered to sift out rare scraps of favorable news while shoveling out dumpster loads of data contrarily laden with unpleasant truths.

* * *

David had not intended to be rude towards his desk mate on Ford Island. Yet through concentration on his own tasks he discouraged talk. The result was that Carter, a pleasant enough fellow—the Naval Laboratory System's ad hoc representative on Supportability's team—was intimidated. The Lab rep was envious that David could manage to find so much to do when he himself was *not* unwilling to work but, "doggone it," he would stress plaintively, simply waiting" ... for these overseeing naval powers in charge to get off their 'rusty-dusties'" and assign him something concrete to do. To be fair to the man, there was no one to tell Carter what to do; productive management in any sort of loosely cobbled together government undertaking such as SUNRISE being rarer than diamonds. His questions to David about what *he* was finding to do were politely curious, but with his cubicle mate's answers not expansively opening towards further revelations, Carter lapsed into baffled silence. From other offices talk bubbled; the noise of congenial types who were at peace with their idleness. Typically there would be the voice of a raconteur with some good story, followed by laughter echoing through the cardboard thin partitions. In David and Carter's own location there was mainly the scratch of the former's pencil, or the rustle of the latter's magazine being turned.

It was not, David judged, that Carter was basically unenergetic. Actually Carter reminded David somewhat of his Washington boss (Mason, of course, out here too but never seen and said to be serving on another, and much higher, team; Policy, or something of the kind). Undeniably Carter did take action on anything placed before him. He emptied his correspondence basket with the alacrity of the genuinely deprived. Once in a while there would come happily into Carter's basket a seemingly finer prize, one of those large new publications, covers shiny with disinterest, so chunky that its several volumes had to be bound with tightly applied wrappings of rubber bands. The mass would make its leaden way, pristinely unread (even rubber bands unslipped) from basket to basket on its poky descent to oblivion. On an occasional correspondence slip, in the Remarks section, there might be a scrawled request from some senior: *Carter: Give this a once over and let us know if there's anything of interest.* There never was. Not in these stolid publications dense with impossible formulae, appendices thick with tabulated numbers. Such matter, not quite stone but less than vegetable, born obsolete and dedicated to dimness, was headed with slow and yet irresistible ballistic momentum, like a jungle river gliding towards darkness beyond the knowledge of man; in this instance for the forgottenness of the shelves of the Technical Library. Yet large numbers of good people had paid for this stillborn creation with their toil. Such suspect massings of paper George Bernard Shaw had in mind when he urged mankind to look back with dry eyes upon the presumed tragedy in the fiery destruction of all those ancient manuscripts once moldering away in the great library of Alexandria, unmissed and unmourned.

The low regard in which the designated objects of his attention were held did not bother Carter. He went at his review tasks humming, wending his way through pages stiff with disuse with a thoroughness possible only to a man experiencing the calm of true contentment. Afterwards, he prepared a memorandum in a looping longhand of grace, full of conscientious comments. Details no one else would have unearthed, extracting judgments where others would only skim, and returned it to the querying senior from whom he would never hear again. There were a number of naval laboratory men on the staff, usually come to Pearl Harbor for just a year. Longer could create an imputation of permanence and risk upsetting legal myths of transience by which generous *per diem* grants were sustained. Their tours ending, these men would then return to their parent sites in various parts of the mainland, to San Diego or New London, or Panama City, Florida . . . Going back to wherever had spawned them in the far-flung and prodigally wasteful Naval Laboratory System that an insufficiently mobilized handful of wise men would long ago have strangled, if they but could, for the little it accomplished for the muchness of treasure that the nation poured into it.

Carter, the quintessential Lab man, had his family with him too. David had met Carter's wife Doris, cheerful and plump, at the Ford Island Officer's Club. Their children too carried in their baby fat the finer sustenance of many locations, reradiating their parents' understandable domestic happiness. Lively northern batteries recharging in the Hawaiian sun. David did not go to the pool often, then only at the noon hour, but whenever he did, the Carters were there. The "bunch"—as Carter called them—evidently came over daily on the grubbily humble but cheery Ford Island ferry, lugging a picnic basket and sharing with Dad the pleasure of his unoffending day. Once David spotted Mason at the pool too and got a friendly wave. A thumbs up too, presumably conveying a wry and secret comradeship. At the same time Mason obviously holding back from closer contact. Perhaps he had picked up alarming items about the maverick, trailers of his subordinate's mischievous history. Yet, at bottom, such bound to be untroublesome. No blame could attach to David's boss, now breathing finer airs than Supportability's native ones.

For Carter's family, as for Carter himself—indeed, as for all of the Lab people—it was a perfect vacation. A vacation paid by others and having few and unirksome restrictions. Savoring the contents of their generously filled basket, which Doris Carter pressed upon him, David was struck by how closely both parents employed the same agreeable voice. Not an insect's shadow of conflict crossed their sun-splashed idyll. Waves of enthusiasm bowled over every object of their attention. They conveyed the flavor of people whose enviable experience it has been to feel themselves welcomed visitors to planet earth lifelong, cheerfully fated to go on sampling spots around the world forever and yet not compelled to devour more than they wished. David absorbed tales of past Carter journeys along with family homilies upon the uplift of travel upon the children. At first he listened with impatience, then with envy. The Carters were connoisseurs of vacations, revelers in the varieties of lovely and folklore locations which the workings of their beneficent government employer made bounteously available. Best of all, it seemed that they did not have to plot to scheme to live this dream. It arrived with the naturalness of sunrise, richness of choice lubricated by generous *per diem* flowing into their life on a perpetually generous stream. Mere *willingness* to go was enough. Receding in time, but not in vividness, were recollections of the little test facility at Lake *Pend Oreille* amidst the grandeur of Idaho's Cour d'Alene region. Romance tinged their recollections of Key West on the one hand, the chill salmon waters of the Straits of Juan de Fuca on the other. All of America their oyster. This land was their land.

Now bearing down upon the Carters on their unceasing river of goodies, like a tall pure white sail looming slowly up over shining horizons, was the best yet, the prospect of a tour at the NATO Underwater Acoustics Laboratory at La Spezia, Italy. This, the prize of prizes for the luckiest of Lab men. For *all that*, great God!"—Doris Carter laughed infectiously—"she was willing" . . . to be stuck for a *couple* of years." She shared packets of postcards by which she kept family appetites whetted. Drawing out of her large straw bag photos of the NATO laboratory, nearby stony little towns, folk dancers, and the charm of Lerici. Ancient castles tawny against the blue Ligurian Sea, steep mountains plunging to the sea. Shelley's last home. She already had them using Italian table phrases across the lunchtime spread. Only one glitch. "Worst case . . . ." Conceivably the family might have to wait another year before this super assignment came to be. Doris wrinkled her nose at that with fetching humor—ever the good sport—rolling her eyes to her friendly heaven again. *So.* Just possibly then they might have to endure one more dreadful New London winter. But *then* . . . Cheerfulness returned to Doris Carter with the swiftness that the trades blew wisps of gauzy clouds away from the face of the sun. "Because La Spezia *is* coming. In the bag. Lordie, yes," she assured one and all, "it's *coming*." The system delivering. Rattling on, Doris Carter had them all rooting for her. In some funny way, David Morgan no less. Even as he would never torment Al with this tale, hopes of enchanted travel for which she would die.

▲▲▲▲▲

CORRIDA.

At *last*. For David Morgan, who couldn't wait for it to come. Doing his best, but lately his spirits feeling return of the old nibblings of darkness.

They *would* give it a snappy name David reflected, but then not intolerantly. CORRIDA caught the aim and the spirit of this force of destroyers. The latter to be thought of like *toreros*, seeking to contain the torment, within the arena of their naval maneuvers, of the sleek black muscular bull that (also not difficult to imagine) was the nuclear submarine. David was outside in the fresh air on the main deck of the frigate *ESPOSITO*, Charlie Wicker beside him. The sea was calm, ruffled by light winds, and it was gorgeous blue in three quarters of the directions in which their eyes roamed. In the quarter towards the morning sun the sea glittered, wearing a blinding yellow blaze of light. Standing up there between test runs, with Charlie puffing away on his cigarette, these were sweet moments of peace. Just taking in the sea enough. Not even thinking much either, though that was harder not to do.

For David could not help picturing great circles drawn upon the surface of this blue sea. Slender drawn, insubstantial as they existed on the charts of the planners of the exercise, and transferred by the mind to the surface of this sea, they were—whatever the foolishness or the optimism resident in them—indispensable in understanding what the exercise was all about. The circles represented presumed submarine detectability, their radius equal to the range of probable detection computed for each ship's particular sonar and for the oceanographic environment of the day. David had not been a party to the development of the tactics but he had, from guess and knowledge, a pretty good idea what was taking place and the rationale as well. In purely hierarchical terms, however, he ranked near the bottom of CORRIDA's augmenting crew of engineers and analysts whose numbers were now cramming the sonar spaces and overflowing the spare bunks of every ship in the exercise. As lowly Data Taker, shoved well back, as befit his status, from the battery of cathode ray scopes, with his clipboard in hand he was supposed to create for each run such fragmentary narratives as were possible from the snatches of information to be picked up above the hum of blowers and the squeakings of the sonar. As for the grander picture, the higher vision where Objective and Method merged in Understanding, what he did not glean from glimpses over huddled shoulders, Charlie Wicker filled him in. Well up in the pecking order, a contributor to Experiment Design itself, Charlie knew every parameter that went into each circle. Essentially there were three main sets, one for the SQS sonars, one for SLRS, and one, and only one—swelling grander than any of the others—representing *ESPOSITO'S* prototypal DIANA. In quiet moments such as the present one, Charlie, using notebook and pen, would sketch in various arrangements of the circles to amplify his explanations. Sometimes the circles would be conventionally placed around the submarine, sometimes strewn randomly like soap bubbles. Phantoms to be moved at will. There was also a pattern, created by taking all the circles and spreading them peripherally, each tangent to another that made a circumference of circles that amounted to a single gigantic one some hundred miles in diameter. In one pattern the circles overlapped, like chain links, creating a look not dissimilar to the colorful circles of the logo of the Olympic Games. Not surprisingly, that particular series of barrier exercises was termed OLYMPUS. Seated on the frigate's deck, leaning back against a gun mount, feeling its sun-warmed and somehow not very hard steel flank upon their backs, Charlie Wicker drew the latest series of circles with one hand, waving his cigarette around with the other. Throughout his explanations David had spared him, right up to the present, until he asked his friend his final question deadpan. The one that screamed to be asked. "Afraid that I don't quite understand these circles, Charlie. Just how do they protect? Do the submarines just bounce off them?"

Charlie gave a sidelong apologetic grin. "Come, David. Please." Actually they seldom talked much about CORRIDDA. These intervals in fresh air were too precious compared to the hours in the overheated darkness of DIANA's sonar spaces below. Even here in the cleansing sunshine, the permeating smell of all the extra bodies below remained in his clothes. It had been a hard week. Hard not merely because of round-the-clock operations, but difficult in terms of living conditions. The riders had overtaxed the ship's facilities; extras in anything, whether space or amenities, always in short supply in the tight design of any destroyer. Charlie Wicker had been granted a bunk in junior wardroom country, but those in David's category were relegated to "hot-bunking" it in Chief's Quarters. Meals for all the technicians were surrounded by steel. Hustling in with their metallic trays were hairy young mess cooks with sweat pouring down their arms and soaking their white T-shirts.

The sailors were good-humored and hospitable towards their visitors at first, but welcome was wearing thin. At first, the engineers and the scientists were regarded by the sailors—in the way of men less educated in the presence of those more so—with exaggerated respect. Such attitudes though wear off in the close confines of a ship when the natives discover, as natives quickly do in enforced proximity, that their Gods have all too human attributes. A series of rough days had intensified the tendencies of the landlubbers toward seasickness. Long periods below decks worsened the situation and many a suffering observer failed to make it to the head or topside rail in time. Stomachs perpetually queasy, their interior plumbing stopping up, most of the scientists and engineers were perpetually tired. They carried packets of saltines, nibbling what was easiest to keep down—discarded cellophane cracker wrappings becoming a clutter underfoot—and they traveled like sleepwalkers between Bunk and Sonar. A puff of dark smoke was visible from the after part of the ship. Simultaneously, in the sparkling air—tiny flakes of gold dancing through it—came the whine of forced draft blowers speeding up. Perceptibly the ship was gliding faster, rustling through the dark blue mass of a gently heaving sea. The hull shook beneath their feet with the stress of power. From an unknown but linking past David felt a thrill at these tremblings of vitality. "About now," he said.

"Yep," Charlie Wicker at the same time flipping his cigarette out over the water. It was invisible for a second in the generous wind-aided arc, and then suddenly sharply visible again, a tumbling speck of white matter against thousands of fathoms of royal blue. Yet neither was anxious to hurry below, out of the caressing air. The whole effort, CORRIDA—the showpiece of SUNRISE—had gone steeply downhill. No matter how ingeniously the tacticians arranged the phantom circles, shifting them about in imaginative patterns, the submarine kept getting away. Like a ghost of the depths it would vanish, surfacing hours later in some unlooked for location several horizons away. From there, communicating its presence and telling in code exactly what maneuvers had abetted its escape. Yet in spite of the professional tone of these repetitively predictable messages, there gradually built up something ineffably comic. The parallel was bound to assert itself between the cartoon character *Bugs Bunny*, carrot in paw, popping up from some hole ludicrously far removed from the one where plausibly the pursuer judged him he to be. Posing over and over the same insolent question to his dim-witted but lovable hunter. *"So, what's up, Doc?"*

They did not however, neither David nor Wicker, spend much time discussing the unraveling fiasco. Free time was too sweet to squander in going over the painful events they were witnessing below. CORRIDA was a party gone bust. A week ago twelve destroyers had steamed out of Pearl Harbor's channel with flags flying. Each gray ship in the force had hoisted to its masthead an identically sewn pennant of brave identity and *esprit d'corp*: A crimson circle ringed a black mythical figure, especially created, that was a horned bull in front joined to the streamlined hindquarters of a nuclear submarine. Around the ring's circumference, in unendorsed Latin, was the inscription: *"Taurum de mare matamus."* Past Hospital Point, past the place where battleship Nevada ran aground, past a million memories of sadness and glory, they steamed by in closed up column, a fine sight as they accelerated past the mangrove shores of Iroquois Point, bows beginning to rise with slow grace at the first feel of the sea's swell. The Pacific Fleet band was playing lively music at Charlie Landing as they sped by. No Crusader host set forth from Vezelay more colorfully caparisoned, weapons brightly glinting, than did those ships resplendent with their flags and their hopes. Festivities ashore, a pre-CORRIDA build-up of spirits, had been held the night before sailing in the Pearl Harbor Officer's Club. Billed as the CORRIDA Bash, the bull and the ring motif contained in the exercise flag had been duplicated atop the ceremonial cake. By all accounts it had been a rip-snorter of a party. There were the usual pre-exercise exhortatory messages too, the longest and most eloquent—here and there alight with downright purple phrases—being from Admiral Snowdon, the senior most immediately responsible for carrying out SUNRISE.

Messages had arrived as well from commands more senior. Unusually, there was one from the Chief-of-Naval Operations in Washington, reprinted in Esposito's Plan of the Day: The CNO wishing the participants fair winds and following seas and not shrinking, in characterizing CORRIDA's tests, from calling them "historic." That was the unusual part, Washington edging itself out on a limb. Because it was right for military leaders, commanding real forces of men and steel upon the sea, to speak only of success in forthcoming exercises, just as the worthy warrior admits no possibility other than victory in battle. But that was not Washington's way, could not be. For defeat is too much a commonplace, in battles by the Potomac, for those who wage it not to be prepared for it constantly. Imperative that something can always be nimbly transposed into something else. Thus the rashness of CORRIDA's blessing could make it awkward to have to explain to Congress how historic tests might overnight have turned *un*historic.

"Tsk. Would you not say that the Navy is pushing all its chips to the middle of the table?" The Plan of the Day in Wicker's hands fluttered, seeking to tear itself away in the sea breeze. Yet even though acutely conscious of the politics of CORRIDA, they were less inclined to cynicism out here. Seeing so much effort and spirit coming to naught, however predictably, was not an occasion to gloat. Mostly it was to be made sad. One could not scorn such earnest trying! First of all, David Morgan and Charles Wicker were Americans. So they mostly talked of other things. Awaiting the start of the countdown for the next run, borrowing from the same general overlay of sadness, Charlie Wicker spoke of his wife, dead now for seven years. Not a waking hour went by, he said, that in some way or another she did not come to mind. Not broodingly, but still adding up to his missing her. Wanting to reassure that evidently insecure spirit that she had done well.

"Run Forty-X. Two minutes and counting. Check clocks. Time is . . . . Mark!" The word blared over the speakers of the ship's announcing system. Radarmen in Combat Information Center and the sonarmen in Underwater Battery Plot reset their clock's hands to the second. The Jack O' the Dust deep in the close confines of the bulk storeroom passing out sacks of flour to a mess cook, he too cocking his head to this announcement having nothing to do with him before getting back to his count of flour.

David could not say exactly why, but what was bothering him most was the effect, whether perceived or imagined, of CORRIDA's empty results upon the people around him. His concern had shrunk to the length of the ship and the steel shell cupping its people. Anxious that it go well mainly for the sake of the crew. America's great bargain, the Navy's enlisted man, putting up with so much for so little. All this steaming about for these young sailors with their scrapers and brass polish, not having the foggiest idea about what was going on, it only being enough for them to keep the metal clean and bright. He thought of the radarman in Combat, hunched over their plots, playing with the Circles; the firemen before their furnaces, tending their blazing oil burners, spinning their great burning hot valve handles as if life depended . . . . All this striving, these flags bright in the sunshine, deserved to add up to *something*. He wanted it to go well for the skipper too, the fair-haired—literally—young Herbert Lance II whom he was watching now on the starboard wing of the bridge, locks lively in the breeze, turning his head to shout an order to the wheel, easing his ship into position for start of the run. Yet on the surface of things Herb Lance, fleetingly renowned as the youngest Commander in the U.S. Navy, was not an obvious figure to generate sympathy. Indeed, a classic type to raise instant hackles of hostility amongst the knowing, he came straight from Washington to command of *Esposito*, plucked from the ranks of Executive Assistants to take this currently most favored of frigate commands. Hopping, as it were, symbolically, onto the sleek back of DIANA, his latest steed to speed him onwards to his next accelerated promotion. But how he had gotten here did not alter the reality of these present twenty-two hour days on the bridge, doing his damnedest to meet the challenge of the here and now, to *make this mother go.*

A vignette witnessed earlier conferred upon Herb Lance an appealing human dimension. The morning they sailed David had just stepped aboard himself and he was waiting, suitcase in hand, to be directed further by the quarterdeck watch, when a shrill note on the boatswain's pipe preceded the announcement, "*Esposito* arriving!" Archaic but right. The captain as living embodiment of the ship. A station wagon was easing down the pier and as he stood at attention, along with everyone else topside, David noticed a blonde woman driving. Youthful, strikingly pretty even at this gray dawn hour, inevitably she was a veteran of that elite army of heart stopping girls that used to pour, no doubt were pouring still, down to the Naval Academy on sparkling Fall weekends, floating out of chapel on Sunday morning, aglow with the final hymn, part of the glow too of the golden leaves on the trees towering over those old brick walkways. David had watched Herb Lance hop out and come around to get his farewell kiss, read his wife's lips forming "good luck," saw kids in back wave, and then the Captain, was bounding up the gangway to carry aboard a buoyant mood that caught them all up in it that first morning. In early coordination meetings in the wardroom, Herb Lance's enthusiasm was such as to suspend all doubts. So eagerly anxious for things to go right, exhorting everyone serving the operation, sonar crew, key engineers, humble brewers of coffee, right on down to the lowliest of the data takers crammed into the wardroom, scrunching their butts down on the leatherette couches, the overflow pressing itself layers deep back against the metal bulkheads, rousing them all to do their damnedest. The Captain into every detail. Try, *concentrate*, each one give it his all, he urged. Ending each meeting always asking if there was anything else anyone might suggest to make things go better? He drew the query out, conscious of dramatic effect.

David had been looking at a mounted photograph of *Miguel Esposito*, Corporal U.S. Marine Corps, dead long ago on a South Sea Island of the hand grenade he had thrown himself on to save a buddy. He seemed scarcely twelve years old, but for his high necked marine uniform with the symbol orbs on his collar. "Anything at all?" the Captain repeated his plea and David, startled, taking his gaze away from young Esposito's solemn eyes found his own locked onto the Captain's stare. The challenge not hostile, but rebuke nevertheless for one of his Team drifting off. Blue patrician eyes held David until he shook his head, his lips forming a soft "no." The Captain was still offering suggestions as he sprang to his feet. "You data takers, have plenty of pencils. Don't be having to dart off in the middle of a run to sharpen one and miss something." Pencils important. *For the want of a nail the battle* . . . . As the old poem had it. The ship had glided into position, was now keeping bare steerageway. Over the General Announcing System came "*One* Minute Warning." The seconds remaining were being counted off. "Let's do it," Charlie Wicker said.

"Righto. Got my sharp pencils too." Facetiousness lost in the thunder of Charlie's feet hammering down the iron ladder. David took a final glance around. Hull down, yet with each detail of their superstructures sharp in the superlatively clear air, was a line of ships strung out on an arc embracing fully a quarter of the horizon. Beyond that line, and far below the next horizon, steamed yet another formation of patrolling ships. A multiple barrier, this would be the most ambitious test yet conducted. Regardless of lack of results on preceding tests, CORRIDA's original Test Plan, hewed to undeviatingly, called for a steady dimensional expansion and a relentless advance into complexity and magnitude of challenge.

The transition from sunshine to Sonar Control intensified the impression of stygian gloom, a darkness in which dim figures crouched over glowing cathode ray tubes. Eyes not adjusted, latecomers like David found themselves bumping into fellow observers, stepping on toes, murmuring apologies. Stronger than the smell of sweaty bodies was the acrid bite of electrical insulation. Earlier runs had brought smoke curling from heavy copper wires, never to be thick enough for DIANA's awesome currents. DIANA let loose another monumental pulse of acoustic energy, reverberations dying away in a protracted wail. A small flat sound seconds later was the returning echo of the still docile target submarine. Sonar control's speaker came on for the last of the seconds counting down. ". . . three . . . two . . . one . . . Mark. COMEX!" Simultaneously those in Sonar Control heard, though muffled through many decks of steel, the ship's whistle giving a prolonged blast. One of those vestigial adjuncts to naval spirit, bursting with a jubilant roar. Steam knowing not tentativeness, incapable of depression.

"Okay, mother fuckers!" The voice of Puglaski, the Senior Chief Sonarman was now dominant. "I want your eyeballs sucked right into those scopes."

If David's lowering mood over CORRIDA's proceedings had contracted primarily to human terms, it was Chief Puglaski upon whom the heart of his feelings was concentrated. For practically everyone else involved, the engineers and scientists, while anxious for things to go well, nevertheless possessed a variety of other interests and aspirations. Whatever befell DIANA, there lived in them the core of technical successes known before and the reasonable expectation of other stimulating programs coming their way again. Win some, lose some. So it was, in a not dissimilar way either, for Herb Lance to whom David's sympathies had also been drawn. Because, for all the dedication the skipper brought to this particular effort, the totality of his being was only transitorily engaged. Whichever way CORRIDA went, he would still have his ship, could look forward to bonnie voyages to come. The wrinkles in that aristocratically formed brow would not furrow into permanence. If he had hoped to sprint DIANA straight to flag . . . not to weep. Other sleek steeds would come his way.

For Ernest Puglaski—"Pug"—there were no other consolations. Glowing scopes were his all. No fallback for Pug, no future beyond CORRIDA in these dwindling numbers of months of a thirty-year career now ending. A legend in a trade that had made few, Pug had earned a medal for manning his sonar for ninety-six hours straight while his destroyer tracked a Soviet diesel submarine in the Mediterranean, eventually forcing it to surface. Fueled by coffee, breathing overheated and foul air, he had stayed glued in his metal-backed operator's chair through the roll and pitch of a winter gale such as stout Odysseus had known. His headset had stuck to his sweating ears, the rotting rubber smearing like black grease. Pug. A famed set of ears, hanging on into an age of acoustic processing that no longer wanted ears. A throwback, a terror to the smooth-faced junior sonarmen under him enduring the lash of his old-fashioned sailor obscenities. For those baby-faced initiates to Pug's raw and quirky world were a different breed, going on liberty carrying briefcases. Pug had no briefcase, but owned lurid tattoos on his hairy forearms and bore a knife scar zigzagging down from below one eye. No true blue woman had ever driven him down to his ship. Pug's women had crabs. None of which mattered, only that right now, in this dim and taut world, he was one hell of a sonarman. His voice into the bridge was firmly professional. *"Tracking!"*

And so they were, DIANA, Pug, the fair frigate *Esposito*. A *team*. Locked on. Every run thus far had started out this way actually, but repeated disappointment never dampened initially renascent moods of optimism. Fingers kept crossed. *Maybe this will be the one.* Every minute or so, came a burst of sound energy and then for seconds afterwards trailed a diminuendo of reverberation. The wailing dying away to the rustle of the background noise of the sea itself, out of that clear void of sound came to the straining listeners that flat hard note sought. What all this massing of electronic cabinets was for: *A submarine echo.* Another pulse, another echo . . . . Piece of cake, my boys. "Okay," Pug said tautly, *"okay baby."* He was at the master control console and on either side of him, omni-directional active console to his left, passive to his right, were the two assistant sonar operators. "Easy does it," murmuring encouragement, gesturing inspiration. "Atta boy . . ." Every few seconds his arm reached to adjust the companion scopes as well, touching the Brightness knob on one, Gain Control on the other. "There we are . . . ." Soothingly. Three bent figures, faces pressed close. David could see, at the instant that he heard each returning echo, a brightening on the scope, the glowing blob of electronic energy being the visual representation of the submarine echo. But even as they strained to see, to hear, the echo was growing smaller, its sound less audible. On the next ping the echo's visual display faded away almost to nothing. Whether the submarine was going deep or its aspect had changed from the favorable beam one at the outset that had maximized its target strength, could not be known. Pug's mutters grew louder, his hands busier, near frantic, reaching out simultaneously to grasp the knobs sought. Pug's shoulders twitched with the powerlessness of his frustration. His head jerked left then right with unfair condemnatory rage at his helpless fellow operators, *"Jesus Christ. You'd a thunk their mothers would a' drowned them!"* The circle on the omni display marched again towards the edge of the scope, spiraling outward in representation of the range of DIANA's latest pulse of sound, moving away at a mile a second from *Esposito*. The circle passed where the last echo had been. Nothing. But on the passive scope, down on its lower face, many degrees of bearing removed from where the echo had been, there was an abrupt brightening. Like a thin piece of pie it covered the scope from its center, widening on the way to the outer edge. "There she is!" Pug yelled, "she's speeding up. Gimme a bearing."

The electronic bearing cursor slewed and halted, quivering, bisecting the bright wedge of sound. "One-six-zero!" They could feel the tremble of power as steam valves spun open wide. The ship heeled as it swung with full rudder to the bearing of the submarine racing away. Sonar's speakers roared, the radiated energy of the submarines propulsion masking even DIANA's transmissions. Over another speaker, mounted on the bulkhead above Pug's main console, came the Captain's voice. A red light fluttering provided accompaniment to the excited tremor of his voice. "Bridge, aye! Coming to one-six-zero. We're after him, Pug, at flank speed!" Without taking his eyes off the scope Pug reached up to depress the speaker switch. "Sonar, aye. Bearing steady. Lots of cavitation, skipper."

"Bridge, aye. Let's hang on to the bastard this time." And so it seemed they might. The ship's speed imparted to the decks beneath their feet an exhilarating instability, like balancing on the back of a racing steed, pulsing muscles rippling through their feet. South by southeast, they sped. Across the South Pacific, two thousand miles of empty ocean away, lay the Marquesas. "There are fast submarines my boys, and there are quiet ones," Pug gloated "but there are *no fast quiet* ones." In his concentration on all three scopes, ceaselessly reaching for the controls of the adjacent consoles, he seemed unaware that he had taken over from the other operators. Shrugging, the two sailors removed their headsets and slipped out of their chairs. Screw it. All Pug now. Pug in personal combat. The ship seemed to be flying in turbulent air, in reckless chase. Moments that thrilled.

Abruptly the wedge of sound energy faded. Vanished in the seconds between a single held breath. There was a strangled cry of pain as Pug called mournfully into the squawk box. "Bridge, masking has faded." "Bridge, aye. Slowing." The ship began to roll softly, released from the grip of its power. DIANA's transmissions, unheard during the minutes of noisy pursuit, came back loud. Mockingly so, for scopes bare of contact. "Sonar, Bridge." The Captain's voice was flat. "Any recommendations?" *"Captain,"* all of the anguish was Pug's, *"the son of a bitch is gone. Hiyaku."* A *cri de couer.* Pug tore off his headset and hurled it to the deck, stomping each earpiece. The sound of overpriced plastic crushing. Nothing intruded into the embarrassed silence. Ernest Puglaski a silhouette of despair against the sickly glow of scopes that had lost their meaning. The son-of-a-bitch indeed gone. Gone, if it wished, unhindered to those green Marquesas of men's dreams. Even unto the ends of the earth, to the gray-blue seas of Antarctica and the islands of emerald ice that Captain Cook first met in *Resolution* two hundred years before. To return only of its own volition, to inflict such mischief and violence, as it must, at times of its own choosing.

* * *

They were out on the main deck again, the two colleagues—David and Charlie Wicker—perhaps on their way to becoming fast friends. The hour was the same as when yesterday's run had started. The same sun glittering and the caressing breeze still tickling the hairs on their bare arms resting on the lifeline. One thing different though was the lack of urgency. Excitement had fled and eloped with Interest. After yesterday's run, CORRIDA's tests had at last been redesignated, all references to CORRIDA being expunged from the Operation Order. Out in the sunshine Charlie and David read a copy of the message from the senior officer conducting the exercise. Its theme was that the best interests of the tests called now for primary emphasis to be on the fundamentals of detection and tracking, training which was, after all ". . . the key to success." All hands were cautioned on the necessity of not discussing the tests with unauthorized persons. Stressed was the "extreme sensitivity" of the results. Charlie Wicker shook his craggy honest engineer's head. "What results?"

They continued to dawdle on the main deck. Nothing was to be learned by going below. The submarine, now located smack in the center of the twelve circling destroyers, was not moving at all, except when hovering grew difficult and a minimal speed of a knot or so was necessary to keep at the designated depth in the shallow isothermal layer most favorable for its detection. The transmissions from every other ship arrived through *Esposito's* underwater hull, passing through steel and reradiating out into the sparkling air as a virtually continuous, squeaky irritation. "Ping time," this sort of drill was called. The destroyers were in tight formation, creeping round at a lazy six knots. Not quite so close to one another that the impression was strictly comparable, say, to a ring of circus elephants, with tails linked. Still that was the image that came to mind.

The forecastle deck with its cargo of scientists and engineers had taken on the look of a raffish and overcrowded cruise ship; bored passengers in colorful sport shirts sprawled in the sun. Yet it wasn't hedonism that had most of them up here, but escape. Given the constant assault of reverberant sound energy, rest below decks was impossible. But now that they were all gathered up here, communal proximity joining with release from responsibility, there was a festive mood. Some sat on blankets, insulating rears from the scalding hot decks, playing cards. If the racket was bad here aboard *Esposito*, the delighted consensus was that things had to be ten times worse aboard the submarine. Like being in a hardhat diving suit with someone pounding on one's metal helmet with a sledge. Those submariners had to be going *bonkers* down there. Let those smug S.O.B.'s suffer, was the childish mood. Just for their being submariners, punishment just. David too stretched out to doze. The deck was gritty with sooty debris from the stacks, but the steel itself in the shadow of a gun mount was like the warm flank of a great and not unkindly beast.

Ah . . . . The last thing he was thinking of, before he slipped off, was what he was going to tell Al. She was bound to want to hear everything. She would want a story. Deserved one. The lilting rhythms, wry and humorous, if possible, of success. However his own success, in personal terms, was to be scored in these days at sea. But the sun soaked deck was spreading its heat through his back, suffusing it through his body . . . luxuriously enervating, and his last thought before dropping off was the old fear for the kids, the hope that Al was driving safely, that that madness, its challenge all too soon to be gotten back to, stayed in check.

▲ ▲ ▲ ▲ ▲

At the Department of Human Resources in downtown Honolulu, shooting skyward its high modern buildings all around, Joseph Kanakanui was himself—like DHR's own nearby faded wooden headquarters, protean friend to termites—an anachronism. Unlike his younger subordinates, no advanced degrees in the sociology of deprivation trailed after his name. A dropout from his Kalihi high school, he had risen to Director of Handicapped Services for essentially the same reasons that, many years ago, he had gotten his first job at the Waipahu Home for the Hopelessly Insane. Few wanted it, even in those poorer times. From the start the amiable youth had brought to it the qualities evident in the bulky graying man of today, gentleness, common sense, and the considerable strength to handle his feeble-witted but occasionally obstreperous charges. It had been a long time though since he had had to follow sad naked patients around with a bucket, or to go searching for unfortunates who had wandered off into the forested gorges near the Home. And to spot, usually fairly quickly, yet another of those big-eared mongoloid faces grinning down at some lively little stream he was muddying with the play of his bare feet. Always he would find them near water, as if they must seek it; both need and comfort. It was his practical knowledge of such people, the conviction born of experience that nothing could be done for them except to take care of their basic needs that made Joe Kanaka—as universally he was known—suspicious of ideas contrary to his experience. He was wary of bright young college fellows with their enthusiastic talk of "rehabilitation" and of sociological progress, presumably moving ever onward and upward away from the traditional, supposedly outmoded, "shelter concept." Ya, ya . . . all kinds of good and innovative things could presumably be done for these people. Joe Kanaka had listened to too many of such promises, knew better. Yet such was his good nature that it did not bother him that his fast-talking haole friend, Artie Perrozzi, was also spending time cultivating his more progressive colleagues and was, in fact, taking their side—in ideological terms so to speak (a way that one Joe Kanaka emphatically did not speak)—against him. With a beer in his thick-fingered hand, looking out through the broad windows of Artie's office at the seas and mountains, he found it as easy to tolerate Artie's energetic seeking of business as it was to resist the assault of his friend's wild and one-a-minute ideas. "Hey, Artie," shaking that brown wrinkled face, "slow down, brudda. You don't know."

"That could be. You have worlds more knowledge." Artie's mobile face would fall, so expressive of disappointment, humility, rejection—all a beautiful ploy—before rebounding with its usual shine of optimism. "So, how about another beer? Shaka, brother. A *good* beer?" And Artie would gesture with humorous imperiousness to David Morgan, lately importuned into some undefined form of helpfulness to Artie's scheming, showing up mostly out of boredom, to . . . "bring our distinguished friend a Michelob."

Joe's brown gunnysack of a face would crease with a beautiful smile, happy to be teased. "'Nuther one, yep, but I'll stick with the best. Toss me a Primo." And he would take the familiar silver can with the plumed Hawaiian warrior on it in his large fist as he had grasped ten thousands of those cans before. His beer, beer of his time and of his race. There were better beers—truth to tell, a man had to search far and wide to find a worse one—tangy Sam Miguel from the Philippines, princely Heineken from Holland, fancy diet ones from the mainland, and the newer generations of the islands, those young fellows who went to the Kamehameha Schools and who would never pump gas or wait on tables in Waikiki, had eagerly taken to the taste of these invaders. Not Joe Kanaka. For as shadows grew longer, falling across the little tumbleacious white homes in Palama, under the spreading monkey pod trees, on the cloudy heights of Kaimuki, in tough Waimanalo and the dry lowlands of the Waianae Coast, Joe Kanaka was secure in knowing that on a thousand shabby lanais men like himself, kindred spirits, were in their undershirts leaning back in their battered chairs, round brown bellies overhanging their belts, clasping their cans of Primo, looking towards blocked views of the sea and the beaches their ancestors had owned. In a world overburdened with pretentious absurdities such as Identity Crisis, Joe Kanaka owned the kind of certainty that made it easy to resist Artie's enthusiasms *cum* calculation that had stampeded less steady men.

Over several late afternoon visits to Artie's office, invited to share Happy Hour with the two, David glimpsed Artie's strategy. No matter where conversation roamed, from island politics to who was making it with the new Tahitian dancer at Duke Kahanamoku's, a thread of purpose knit together Artie's bonhomie. He kept returning to Project Plowshare, extolling its benefits to the "unfortunates"— Artie's word—pointing out the shining thing that it would be for the particular State that first embraced it and, "hey brudda," not to be forgotten, the professional esteem, going to attach to that particular pioneering Director of the Handicapped (guess who?) astute enough to grasp its potential . . . fame and virtue combining. The only beneficiary of all this whom Artie left out was himself. Once again, David felt the power of Artie's enthusiasm, finding himself drawn along, half believing. Artie once more describing for Joe this "Demonstration Project", as he called it, that he had in mind. Yet, like a shady diamond of doubtful antecedents, Artie kept changing its facets so that it always dazzled and yet could never be seen whole. Artie stressing the economic benefits in lowered food costs, the inmates' delight, better than any therapy, et cetera . . . . Pulling out all stops. Dramatically he gestured towards David.

"Our pal David Morgan right here can tell you! He understands the analogy between fishermen and the submarine detection process, telling false contacts, the separation of the edible fish from the trash, better than anyone. He knew all about it back in Washington where he headed Plowshare." Artie's hand went out again in some grand offering, like the God of Michelangelo to Adam there in the Sistine. David Morgan, shorn of power, presumably his pride lifted from him as well. "He is one of the foremost experts on the processes of classifying submarines!" Some day too, Artie added, this paragon was going to be working for him at Pacific Ocean Research. Oh, *right*, David said to himself. Joe Kanaka turned upon David a lingering beer-sleepy look, eyes narrowed to slits in folds of copper wrinkles. His gaze lingering because, well, maybe . . . if you were with Artie, did not that make you another sort of Artie? A chip off the shining rogue himself. Perhaps too it was curiosity flickering at a life tied up in something as bizarre and useless as finding submarines.

"Ya, that's good, Artie. If I ever want to find submarines in some fish pond I'll go hunt up your akamai guy." Joe roared with laughter and winked at David. But Artie kept boring in, passing another beer. While Joe merely kept nodding, a little sleepier with each generous lip licking swallow. "I dunno, Artie. Seriously." So easy to read Joe, that transparent face, that good heart. Thinking what's the point? In a few years he could retire. Not imagination but loyalty he was being paid for. Just keep his little show that no one gave a rat's ass about on the road, and never, *never,* rock the governor's outrigger canoe.

"Think about it, Joe." Artie urged with soft fervor. It was twilight, the distant ocean blue turning gray. David had known a number of these needlessly late days recently, lengthened not by work but, seductively, by curiosity. Lately he felt adrift; CORRIDA behind him, everything was anti-climax. "I just dunno, Artie." Joe's face showed the torment of indecision. "Gee, I gotta tell you. I'm afraid of it. There's just something . . . I dunno." But David knew. The Hawaiian's curse had always been friendship, a self-betraying warmth. Never so foreordained as at such moments as these in the company of the relentless Artie Perrozzi, who could talk the cat down off the fish wagon. Artie now turning those wide, boyishly irresistible, eyes upon the transiently useful David Morgan. "Hey fellow," Artie said, "you'll be coming too, of course. Hope a' hope." "*Moi?*"

"Hey. Don't give me that, old buddy." Artie conferred a squeeze, strong and meant to be true. "*Of course* you'll be there, my friend. This baby was hatched in your shop."

David just stared. When Mr. Keith in *South Wind* proclaimed the most precious of all gifts being the ability to believe one's own lies, he had to be heralding Artie's to come, armies of ardent salesmen as yet unborn. Artie pressing on, trampling upon all doubts and hesitations, stirring in David the oddness of regrets for this man so enthusiastically squandering prodigal gifts of persuasion on something as thin and tawdry as the pretenses of ASW analysis. When all the while peddling real estate in Southern California would have been his *querencia,* orders of magnitude more rewarding.

"Sure you will," enthusiasm feeding enthusiasm, flames joining flames— leaping upward, from treetop to treetop like an unstoppable forest fire in trees dry as tinder—"you *got* to, pal." Matter of life and death. Of loyalty and love . . . . All good things. "Atta boy!" Those big brown eyes shone.

"Artie, relax," David said, "I wouldn't miss it for the world."

"Super! I'll keep you posted. Where and when. Day and time et al. Everyone's going to be there. The governor maybe. Admiral, for sure. His baby too, after all."

To which David Morgan thought of many replies and made not a one. Not to those shining eyes that could only reflect, but not absorb, irony.

▲ ▲ ▲ ▲ ▲

"What are you doing up so early? Al calling out sleep drugged surprise to David moving quietly about their small bedroom filling with grey dawn. "Ah, yes, good question."

"None of that 'good question' stuff," propping herself up on one elbow. Dressed and ready to go, he sat down on the edge of the bed.

"A demonstration? *Plowshare?*" Recollection dawning in her from what he had revealed to her from what seemed times long ago. "That dopey idea of Artie Perrozzi's about recruiting the poor retarded patients to harvest the fishies?"

"Please. Let's show some respect. Wipe away that smile."

"You're grinning too, for heaven's sakes." "Can that be?", looking off to early morning's tender pale lightening to blue. "Well, got to be running, sweet."

Young Tim Fowler, Pacific Ocean Research's star acoustician, not to be working the Sonar Equation this day, had also risen early, putting aside thoughts of his own love, to drive out here. Tim though unlike David no mere spectator but a participant, having gofer responsibilities assigned by Artie. A Tim now sitting beside David on the grassy hillside, these idle minutes before there was anything happening except to observe the gathering of the clan. Now it was the Admiral and his Ginger, Artie leading the way, taking the latter's hand down the somewhat steep slope, slippery with dewy grass. David pointed out some of the more prominent of the other attendees, Tawney Gray and, of course, his right hand man Dr. Julius Baumgarde. "Oh, yes," Tim said, "I met Dr. Gray once." His voice breathed reverence as at mention of one of the Gods. Inwardly David smiled. Tawney earlier had actually passed close by, his glance going right over and beyond David Morgan. Yet, if there actually was something such as subconscious surprise, the good Doctor's head had given the slightest jerk, as if a bug had alighted on the back of his neck. But for so brief an interval as not even to bring a hand around to swat it. Tawney bobbing and shaking hands and moving on. One David Morgan all long ago and far away.

The reporters from the Star-Bulletin were evidently to be one of Tim's primary responsibilities and after the pair had introduced themselves to Artie, they were escorted over to Tim. "You're in Tim Fowler's good hands now," Artie said, turning them over. For the first time this morning Artie seemed to notice David, but with a muted gladness, somehow less than the effusiveness of his invitation of a few weeks before. But still, troweling it on for the reporters. "This gentleman knows more about this project than anyone else." Those sincere eyes now regarding David with as much plea as bravado. "You'll help too, I trust, Davey, to make this thing clear, fill in the blanks, as it were, to these distinguished members of the press." "Do my best," David said.

"*Super.*" Then Artie with a wave like a salute was off again, skipping down the slope, resuming the role of host, squatting down beside the Snowdon's, working their ears.

From the first David had been struck by the quietness. Now, standing on the hillside, the reporters positioned between himself and Tim, he was impressed by the *scale*, the expanse of the scene that had the effect of diminishing its wide scattering of human figures. He felt the restlessness of the reporters beside him. Artie had, according to Tim, dithered about whether to seek media attention, pondering aloud which was better, publicity or no, which the higher morality, and so forth. In the end satisfying himself that even though he risked the accusation of being self-serving, he was yielding to The Greater Good by not denying a noble endeavor exposure to the full light of day. They were looking down to where a thin line of dark rocks curved out from the shore to enclose a small calm part of the sea. So neat was the arc of rocks that it was as if a modern contractor, with all the latest tools of his trade, crane's, backhoes, *et al*, had placed them there instead of unknown

Hawaiian royalty of centuries ago. The pond's surface was a mirror, holding blue sky and puffs of clouds. Across distant grasslands spotted with cattle shadows of clouds moved slowly. Beyond were green mountains topped with mists. A kona day, meaning a hot one, Tim remarked, still learning the subtleties, and the language, of Hawaiian weather. "That's Admiral Sneedon there?" Kuru, one of the reporters asked. Kuru was slim, a constant smoker, with darting eyes.

"Snowdon." Tim corrected, volunteering further identification. "The next gentleman is Mr. Perrozzi, President of Pacific Ocean Research. Beside him is Mr. Kanakanui of Vocational Rehabilitation. The lady is Ginger Snowdon."

"Ginger." The reporter had a way of repeating words without inflection, but still disconcertingly. Perhaps a way of remembering, for he took no notes. Artie, down the slope, was pointing, explaining. Fragments of phrases floated up the hillside. Miss Abe, the other reporter, was tiny, black-haired, with a long-lensed camera flopping around her neck. Unlike Kuru, she held a pen at the ready. Her voice was soft but not sweet. "The idea is that the patients are going to *catch* the fish?"

"*Drive* them." A Tim Fowler, who had no experience in dealing with the press, deciding that he had best strive for precision. Subtly the day had changed, lost its pristineness from when he had first arrived. Then all had been the pinkness of early morning, the Island's alluring soft young babe quality. "Drive them where?" Miss Abe asked.

Tim looked away "To its extremity." Down the slope Artie's voice rose. Singing words with waving banners. "Are you Pacific Ocean's P.R. man?, Kuru asked.

"No. I'm just an analyst with the company."

"Private outfit?" Kuru said. "Yes, except that this particular sponsoring subsidiary of the company"—Tim gave the name of Artie's latest creation—"is a non-profit one."

Kuru flicked away a butt, lit another. Tim's explanations got only a little further because things were starting to happen. Down a dirt road by the pond rumbled a column of busses. There was a squeak of brakes. Kuru let the squeaks and rumbles die away.

"But then, is Pacific Ocean Research actually profiting from this event?"

"Absolutely not!" Kuru was unflappable. "Easy, man, just getting the picture."

"The picture to see is fortunate people doing good for the less fortunate," David interjected, surprising himself. Spurred by no love of Artie, but sympathetic to the beleaguered Tim. Miss Abe kept writing away. Busy Miss Abe. "How does the Admiral fit in?"

"He's very interested in the well being of the civilian community. Sort of a sponsor, one could say." Kuru's might not have been the prototypal impassive Oriental face but it would do. On it was overlaid sharpened curiosity against any premature enthusiasm for the goodly aims of man. "What kind of research is it your company does?"

"Mainly oceanographic."

"Military related?" Some, Tim acknowledged. Kuru kept boring in. "Most?"

"Yes, most." Tim, with sweaty palms, thinking how much more smoothly Artie would have been at handling this. "With the Admiral's command?" Kuru, Tim decided, would be a whiz at twenty questions. "Some, yes." Kuru closed in, "Most?"

"Yes! Though I don't see what's to be made of that." To which Kuru gave a shrug. The unloading of the busses was going slowly. After each inmate stepped down warily, the man stood by the door of the bus, blocking the way for the next individual exiting until an attendant with a prod shoved him aside. Even then the inmates stayed close to the busses, huddling unnaturally against their dusty metal sides. When all had disembarked, the attendants worked them away from the reassurance of their busses, moving them about like dummy pieces on a board of mysterious maneuver. The dislocated residents of Waimanalo Home wore a colorful mix of shirts and shorts. Some had on flopping tennis shoes but most were barefoot. Their faces were expressionless oval moons. Artie and his group had moved closer to the pond's edge, standing on a bluff a little above it. Another of Artie's gofers was bringing them a thermos of coffee and little cakes on a tray. Night showers had soaked the ground and the Admiral's wife was having to stand tippy-toed to keep the heels of her white shoes from sinking. She was wearing a pale linen suit, gloves, and a broad hat of dreamy elegance. Watching her picking her way further down the steep slope, accepting Artie's hand, Tim had found the picture affectingly picturesque. "Oh, it's *starting*," Ginger tootled gaily.

Along the shore the patients were distributed in an extended line. They stood unmoving, staring down at the water which, in some wondrous way presumably having been explained to them, was going to prove a source of exciting interest.

Joseph Kanakanui, Joe Kanaka at his suffering best, was mopping his face, the muggy day exacting a toll. "Hey, Joe." Artie's euphoric expression was the opposite of Joe's. The great day arrived. Artie flung Joe's way the Hawaiian hand sign with élan. "Shaka brother."

"Well, yah . . . I hope so. These people . . . well, you know . . . ." Joe mopped his face once more and then, looking down at his soaked handkerchief, gave up. "Mr. Kanakanui," Ginger Snowdon a sliver flute calling amongst the basses. A different kind of party, but redeemingly full of worthy purpose. "Could you tell us these people's level?"

"Ah . . . ."

"Their *mental* level." Raising her eyebrows in further helpfulness. Now, eyebrows thus raised are nothing unusual. With many they are unconscious habit, at the worst mere social artifice. Upon Joe Kanakanui, however—who did not encounter this trick amongst the ladies of his Kalihi neighborhood—the effect was severe. Those eyebrows of the Admiral's wife had the fixity of a baffling question on some humiliatingly failed examination of long ago. He seemed to sweat even more profusely. "Jeez. . . ." He waved a brown beefy hand. "All kinds. Some pretty bad, eh?" You better believe it lady. Miss Abe moved down the hill, slipping closer to Joe. "Would you say they include a spectrum of attainment levels?" Tim Fowler decided he preferred Miss Abe over Kuru, if only by a narrow margin. Her account of this disaster would at least be factual. 'Disaster'? Had his mind actually uttered the word? Only then did he realize how strong was the premonition. "Yah. That's right." Joe Kanaka bestowed a glance of gratitude that was lost upon the busily writing Miss Abe. A tug on his sleeve by Kuru now caused Tim to turn. Artie's mouth was moving exaggeratedly, but soundlessly. The chairs . . . Jesus! Tim had completely forgotten them.

It was the damned imposition of these multiple additive duties as keeper of the reporters that had caused him to drop the ball, Tim forgave himself as he trotted panting up the hill. Fortunately the chairs were light and he came back down pell-mell, the thin metal contraptions clattering rhythmically against his thighs. "Atta-boy," said Artie, snatching them from his hands. Tim retreated back up the hill, from which vantage he and David Morgan and the reporters were again gazing at the backs of the seated Important. David murmured to himself: Xerxes at Salamis. That gloomy benediction gave way to a more immediate concern. Miss Abe had again positioned her relentlessly questioning self at the ear of the fidgeting Joe. Her questions were reasonable but Joe, visibly struggling with inward turmoil, was not a lucid source. "For instance, Joe—if I may—what is the expected harvest? The pond's yield."

"The yield," Joe repeated vaguely, but seeming at least able to live with the sound of it, "yah . . . ." "Yes, the *yield.*" Crossness shadowed Miss Abe's oval doll face. Joe cast a helpless look towards Artie whose silver tongue, for reasons Joe could not for the life of him right now remember, had conned him to this instant's befogged present. Miss Abe moved smartly, swung her camera aside as she stooped down, avoiding obstructing the Admiral's view, to address herself directly to the horse's mouth. Artie did not lose his look of glowingly boyish happiness that he had been bestowing upon Ginger Snowdon; his smile did not alter either, so much as that a glaze seen to fall across it. Artie waggled his finger back over his shoulder with his best display of good-humored command. "Timmy, Davey, our little lady here has some awfully darned good questions. How about you wise men fielding them?"

Miss Abe repositioned herself beside Tim, but less contentedly. For a few minutes happenings down at the pond stayed further questions. Solemnity shadowed the scene, even as action began to animate it. The patients had entered the water. The pond was shallow at the start, not more than ankle deep, yet the line advanced haltingly. Some patients stopped completely, bemused by unexpected sensation. Some slid their hands down their legs until they touched water, the feel of strangeness. In response to yells from the attendants—yells without words, drovers' cries—the line got moving. The water was deeper now, up to waists. Strangeness wearing off, the liberated inmates splashed, kicked the stuff, tasted muddy essence.

"Look at that one," said Miss Abe, "what on earth is he doing?" Exhilarated, one of them was taking off with some speed, as much anyway as the resistance of water permits. The impression not unlike that of an outboard skiff, wake and all, that has lost its driver, rudder stuck hard over. Round and round he churned in tight, meaningless circles. "What are the economics? I've heard too that there's supposed to be a tie-in with naval technology, how you tell submarines from whales and so forth, helping these people to select only edible fish . . . ." Mercifully, to Tim, Miss Abe's sense of what she was groping for ran out and she reverted to one of her more basic questions. "How many fish do you expect on a drive?"

Holding binoculars to one's eyes, like the classic pipe in the mouth for the ill-prepared professor, made it possible, Tim realized, to fuddle one's answers judiciously. Learning fast. "As for the catch, we'll have to see. You know how it is with fishing." Plainly the beaverish Miss Abe did not know how it was with fishing. Nor care. "What about availability? Aren't most ponds privately owned? And as I recall reading, those old Hawaiian kings had flunkies catch the fish and put them in there in the first place."

"These are all things," Tim answered soothingly and in suitably overdue time, "to be studied. Look at this first effort as . . . a feasibility demonstration." For a moment Tim felt better about his own performance, not for happenings down in the pond. In his binoculars was the image of one patient, a giant of a man with protruding ears. The man was clapping his hands, which were covered with gray muck from the bottom of the pond. Gobs were in his hair and strings of waterweeds draped his arms, dangled from his ears. A slack grin hung lopsidedly from a pumpkin face. His trousers had fallen, exposing red polka dot shorts. They too, soggily drooping, seemed sure to drop much further shortly. From Artie, a few yards away, there was an exultant cry. "A fish! I just saw it jump." Yes, indeed. Others had glimpsed the same small silver fish too. There were nods of satisfaction. Ginger Snowdon herself nodding too; knowing a fish when she saw one. Yet a student of nods might have judged the Admiral's own nod a longer one, restrained by thoughtfulness. Even as Tawney Gray's expression was distant and perhaps even gloomy, removed in spirit, as it seemed he would like to be in fact. For the line had collapsed, lost all order. The unconstrained residents of the Waimano Home were slapping the water, running heavily, stirring muddy wakes. From the bank the attendants were frantically shouting unheeded directions even as a wild contagious joy afflicted everyone in the pond. Now there could be detected a fairly high level, dully joined, animal roar. Above it Joe Kanaka's anguished voice could be heard. "Oh boy. Jeez. We got problems." Not from books, from years in the pits, this he knew. The sagging polka-dot shorts made good their promise, came slithering down the massive legs. The man looked at himself and threw his head back and laughed at the sky. He looked down again, fingering in surprise and mounting pleasure the parts of his crotch that was his original impetus of glee. Miss Abe expressed irritated puzzlement. "Do I understand correctly that some of these people are actually almost normal?"

"One male type I observe," David stuck in, his funny bone tickled, "appears completely normal." But Miss Abe's funny bone was out of reach. "*I beg your pardon.*"

Artie was shouting ecstatically. Seeing things with different eyes. Someone had actually caught a fish. Artie seemed oblivious to the sounds from the pond, palpable with the swelling sense of power perilously caged, insufficiently contained. Now he was gesturing towards Tim, making motions to hand over the binoculars. "Quick, Tim. Ginger's missing some of this." Ginger now. Ginger baby, next? The noise from the pond became a frightening roar. The guards had chucked whatever restraint in language presumably characterized their normal communications. Tim heard "Dumbo" being screamed. The patients were climbing up out of the pond and the guards were pushing them back in, exhorting them towards the far end of the pond where the busses, having driven around, were waiting. Once, as a boy, Tim had gathered tadpoles in a bowl but they wouldn't stay; testing out their emergent legs, they would slither up the sides, frantically wriggling to escape. There were too quick, and some got away. He thought of those creatures now.

Joe Kanaka was moaning. "Jeez." Over and over, helplessly. Nothing though could dim Artie's spirits. "Joe, don't worry. It's not perfect, but it's a good start." The Admiral glanced over at Artie. A look as fixed as stone. Tim saw Ginger Snowdon's lips tremble, a person whose serenity perhaps derived less from inherent qualities of control than from a well kept but fragile façade which had never been seriously assaulted.

Chaos was exploding from the scene. Yells and laughter were overflowing from the pond. People overflowing too. Crawling up the pond's slippery sides, emerging panting, soaking, charged with weird energy. As soon as legs tested the earth's firmness, they started running. Up the hillsides they scattered, primordial creatures spilling up out from the amazing sea, cauldron of life, staggering, but still propelled with raw power, charging towards cattle pastures inland. In those tranquil expanses distant cows, knowing no perturbation from one day to the next began to moo in mournful protest. In minutes every cow was bellowing. Suddenly one escapee appeared close to the spectators, head rising above a near clump of rocks like a sinisterly stalking Indian in an Old West movie. Ginger Snowdon noticed him first, her mouth twitching in gasps of fright. He seemed to be the one who had achieved earlier prominence in the losing of his red polka-dot shorts, but it was hard to be sure. The man's mouth held crossways, like a child's rubber dagger, a small fish. Clamped in teeth that were themselves, at least, whole and sound, the fish's head and tail were flapping spasmodically.

"Hey, here's one with a fish." If no longer exactly exultant, Artie conveyed determination to extract some last morsel of success. "How about that?" Sports fans. While Artie was still beaming around to one in particular, Ginger Snowdon let out a scream. The man was coming towards them and there was no doubt left that it was he of the former polka dot shorts. Far off a voice of lost authority was still calling "Dumbo! . . . ." Dumbo, naked as God had wronged him, charging, short legs pumping straight at Ginger. The fish was out of his mouth now and he was thrusting it out in front of him, its little silvery form still twitching, still bloody, a gift meant for the lady. Ginger screamed again in pure and reasonable terror, she and her chair toppling over sideways in that flimsy chair made for easy toppling. Artie flung himself protectively in front of her, a blocking lineman's quick solid move, and at the last second Dumbo swerved and the lady was spared whatever it was she was to be spared from, and seconds later Artie was helping the lady rise to her feet as she gasped her thanks while brushing away bits of grass and Hawaii's red earth. And now, where earlier the scene had been quiet, it was quieter still as, with nothing more to hold them, people slowly trudged back up the hill to their parked cars. Except, in the Admiral's case, to his waiting official car, purring away and with its rear door held open by his Navy driver in white uniform. From many paces back David could hear Artie speaking to the Admiral. Voice eternally buoyant.

"Well, Admiral, sir, at least we can say that anyway it's a start." To which the Admiral made no reply. But his head did incline in some sort of slight motion from which only such an optimist as Artie Perrozzi could extract some morsel of cheer in possible affirmation that, well yes, it was a start. That much could be concluded. Artie still talking away through the Admiral's closed window even as the car's wheels were crunching gravel in its pulling away, a motion whose slowness defined the limits of the Admiral's courtesy. As its withdrawing sound faded back into the rustle of the ear's blood, from far and ever fainter could be heard the calls of Dumbo, dumbo, dumbo . . . for that single minded fellow—or perhaps even that 'single' flattering—who, when deflected from presenting his gift to the lady, had charged straight on unheeding and away and, when last seen, was still tearing across some tawny upland until at last, courtesy of a Marine helicopter called in from Kaneohe, so it was recounted later, which aircraft served to track his demented run and eventually to lift his exhausted self meekly homeward.

Artie did not waste a second after the Admiral's departure in making a beeline back to ask about the reporters. Tim informing him that they had gone. "Where, for shit's sake?"

"I don't know," Tim said, "back to their newspaper, I suppose."

"Go down there after them, Tim. Down to the Star-Bulletin's office. Find out what they're going to say. Make sure we can live with it." Tim's mouth fell open. He looked over helplessly at David. His voice was sensible, anguished. "I can't do that, Artie. Nobody can tell reporters what to write." Artie's look was one of mournful command. "Got to, young fellow. Too important. For all of us. Go. Catch them."

Tim Fowler looked dumbfounded. But he went. Artie turned to David, as seemingly he would have turned to whatever face was nearest. He might have been talking to himself. "Tim boy, I'm afraid," Artie said, "still has a lot to learn."

"Don't we all," David murmured, conscious of a meaninglessness to match.

Artie's face was pale, stark. Drained of its boyishness. Too much writ on it of late. Things crowding in. From riding high, riding no more, tumbled from his steed. Things trivial and mighty cascading in. Brooding, as Artie could brood on so many things, but anguish serving up mainly the image of Charlie Wicker in his poisoned cup. For no more than Charlie being himself. Doing nothing, but simply being still at large, a free spirit there in the halls of the ASW Command. Honesty run amok. Not that Charlie ever volunteered an adverse word. But . . . if *asked* . . . well, woe betides those who did not wish for his answer. But, for all of Charlie's vexing candor, it was nothing compared to the fallout from CORRIDA. Its failure a dark stain still spreading, even if unacknowledged, tainting all. For which Artie, a mere player, after all, and not responsible for what had befallen it, need in theory share no blame. Yet an Artie too who was one of those, along with senior Naval Laboratory personnel, and the seagoing Test Director, assigned to give the Admiral a private briefing on *L'Affaire CORRIDA*, as it was mockingly christened in the irreverent lofts of ASW. It was, by all accounts—the few and fragmentary accounts gleaned from it, that is—an oddly stiff briefing there in the presumably informal setting of the Admiral's office. A very private briefing too, and for which there were no notes, no record of what was imparted to the Admiral and which, however much the young admiral didn't want to hear it, he apparently took aboard with good humor and a resolute smile for this dose of bad news which, however sanitized and muted, no man with his aspirations would fairly wish to hear. But up there amongst the grubby desks of SUNRISE's low life analytic legions, where candor and mirth could flourish, there were, in the general assessments of the Admiral's reactions, a dusting off of variants of the hoary tales of those Chinese Emperors whose style included beheading the bearers of bad news. Despite the Admiral's seeming graciousness, dismissing his briefers with thanks for their efforts, there was something in the air that had those present fingering their own necks tenderly. Even the favored Artie. And, of course, now *this*. The latest, Ghost of Dumbo. Shit and damn.

Moving on and away from Artie and his helping of sorrows, David almost bumped into Tawney Gray in the clog of the multitude straggling towards their cars. And yet somehow not accidental. David had sensed his old boss earlier angling over towards him with puzzled drift, if less than definite intent. As if that glance of an hour or so ago had been a mysterious and unaccountable seed, needing a bit of time and germination to have acquired the characteristics of recognition. "Ah David. David Morgan is it? My impetuous colleague?"

"The same." Awkwardly, but without unfriendliness, they shook hands.

"I had heard you were out here, David," Tawney said, "and with your lovely family. And I gather then that you must have been on that . . . CORRIDA operation?" Tawney seemed to have difficulty recalling its name, or making a good show of a prudent distancing.

"One of a cast of thousand."

Briefly a shadow crossed Tawney's elegant brow, as if weighing the circumstance of David's somehow vaguely disturbing presence out here. Tawney's hand, freed from an oddly long handshake caressed the other as his expression blossomed more brightly. Nothing evidently coming to mind that should, taken all in all, be worrisome. No more than it crossed David's own as to what that could possibly be, time of his mischief making past. The mutuality of the unspoken realization brought release. The grandeur of the sky's great blue enclosed them. The benignity of Hawaii's soft airs drew forth from Tawney that bounce of joviality that was part of his charm.

"So," he said, twinkle of old, his arms encompassing worlds that were new, "what did you think of today's show, that is?" "Educational," David answering with a bow.

"Come, come, David," the good doctor craving more, *"entre nous."* Looking back over his shoulder though nonetheless, "No great harm done, eh?" Whole worlds of words that David Morgan might have uttered were compressed to a shrug. "Except perhaps," Tawney added with a wink, "to some added shut-eye which we both had to forego to join the throng." They were far away. Out here on this Pacific island. Anything goes, right?

"Add, as well," David said, "pissing away more of the taxpayers' money." That did it. Tore the fragile mesh of renewal, this moment out here in the gold and the blue of the Hawaii morning. Not all that far, after all, from the grit of Crystal City. Tawney, ducking back into his lair, perhaps forced to think again of things he did not wish to think about, the settled glumness of the Admiral's look, Ginger Snowdon's pale stricken expression, the ambivalence of CORRIDA's results (ambivalent anyway, at best, with suitable manipulation), the many things beside which Plowshare was but a trivial sideshow. A rare sliver of fear had settled itself in those bright eyes. Not feeling so differently, Tawney Gray perhaps, than the Duke of Norfolk who had set up the young and beautiful Catherine Howard with Henry the Eighth, and after catastrophe had enveloped the whole business, little as it had been Norfolk's fault that the aging king was not able to hack it; still just as Norfolk, scuttling away, had also cherishingly been rubbing his own neck.

"Anyway, my best to your fair bride," Tawney said, recovering with his own bow, extending his hand, yet not quite so far as meant to be taken, "Aliason, as I recall?"

"Still Aliason. And regards to Tiny."

"Those I shall convey." But backing off, as if even now glad for the excuse of that small duty. Exeunt then to these small actors under the giganticness of this Pacific sky. To Tawney, antsy now to head off to a private North Shore picnic rendezvous with a junior analyst, one of the few females in CORRIDA's stable of hundreds of analysts and who, even if not one to get Tawney's chromosomes, even with their low threshold, to boil, had nevertheless shown him welcoming lights of reverence melded with promise. Gold, or even let it be iron pyrites, was where you found it. For to David Morgan too, anxious to hurry back to Al and the family and one of those last days of full appreciation of Hawaii, but first, above all, to pour out the tale of this morning. Al's sense of humor, sweet always, sometimes grand, did not disappoint. "Oh darling, I don't believe it!"

"Believe you must." "I do, I do," she enthused, "and you must do something about it."

"Oh?" Regarding her with genuine curiosity. Because he had had something of that same notion, but without focus. "Give me some guidance."

"I will, I will." Inspiration such as hers not to be contained. She hopped up, moved around the room. "*Tell* it. The whole nuttiness of it. The wonder, the beautiful futility of it, what couldn't be invented, the nonsense...." He held up a hand. "I suspect love, you could do it better." Saying it more than half seriously.

"No, no. I'm not the writer. But here's my last good word. Just put aside for a bit your articles, your histories, you magnum opus on the submarine... and all that—"

"All of which are pretty much," he broke in softly, "gathering dust on the shelf already." "All the better," she said, her excitement sailing right on over those notes of regret," all that much the easier, am I right, to tackle something else?"

Something else, he repeated to himself, all the more appealing for the vagueness of its call to arms. Ah yes, *something else.* Fiction of course. Against a flood of systematic nonsense, only a reprisal of hyperbolic nonsense would do. From far off came the siren song of old. Faint but clear. Fiction always the queen, was she not? But.... That note in his head came on stronger and then in its silveriness became visual embodiment of sweetly wayward music and, like a brittle dance, seemed to break and splinter against the broad pale sheen of the Pacific Ocean out the window going on and on. Smithereens of irrelevance against the unwanted facts of his life, but not unhappily so, not with this shining day a long ways to run. A horse show to take in for Beth and sometime afterwards an exhilarating tumble for all in the thunderous waves of the North Shore, with maybe another carefully supervised leap for Boat from that famous high rock sitting out there at Waimea, sure to be the last such fling for a while. Maybe last one, period. But he did not let that thought oppress.

* * *

No surprise, and barely worth recording, the fool's errand that Artie had dispatched Tim Fowler on came to naught. Never a mission so doomed as this one pressed upon Kuru and Miss Abe. With that dynamic duo's article appearing under a joint byline, being everything and more that Artie feared it would be. All the more wounding for its straight forwardness, the predictable host of pointed and unanswered questions hovering over it. David did not see Artie afterwards, his anguish hence only to be imagined, and from Admiral Snowdon, hunkering down in his moated kingdom of Ford island, whatever his response to the article's insinuations did not find its way into the pages of the Honolulu Star-Bulletin. Yet, if at the moment, Artie's creaky barque of dreams was more than usually storm-tossed, it did not automatically follow that it was going to end hard up on the rocks. And however it turned out for Artie, for good or ill, was remote from David's concerns. Unlikely in any event, that he was going to learn how it all turned out. But before putting curiosity entirely aside, Artie too for that matter, an appropriate image popped into his mind. Of Artie, in his own way, distant kin to the great John Unitas, at this time still playing out the last games of his incomparable career. Unitas and his Colts on their own twenty and two minutes and eighty yards to go to win the game. Unitas to Raymond Berry, eating up the yards. Unitas, if it had to be, throwing the bomb! Not so admirable a man as Unitas, Artie and his cause, indeed as tawdrily unenobled as Unitas' arm was golden, but still . . . . Artie Perrozzi, ASW analyst extraordinaire, at least a match in resourcefulness. Artie too who could still throw the bomb from his own end zone.

▲ ▲ ▲ ▲ ▲

Because of many things, starting with Plowshare's fish pond fiasco and, at the last, a load of analytic work (flurry predictable, a dozing system awakening to deadlines) which required him to work nights—the only hours abundant computer time was available—David's final weeks in the Islands lost their sense of order. Everything seemed to speed up and to fall apart, spinning away in a progressive disintegration accelerating towards departure. As in old movies the torn off dates of a calendar, a cliché meant to show, like falling leaves in autumn, the whirling away of time in the wind. With only a few days before their flight home, realizing that Betty and Sean didn't even know that the family was leaving, he called to tell them. The elder Morgans, true to form, insisted on having them over for farewell cocktails. "We would have scheduled you a dinner party and a proper aloha if I'd had more notice." Betty's voice with faint, but fair, notes of complaint. "Unfortunately we have obligations later in the evening that can't be skipped. Still, you may count on heavy puu-puus to fortify you for the journey." There was a *lei* too, not bought at any of the customary shops but created by Betty herself, strung of orchid, pikake, plumeria, and maile leaf. Out of those skilled slender tennis-tanned hands, enchantment. She had already made a second lei for a guest who had not yet arrived but who herself was coming to the Islands in a few days. "So, a pair of alohas," Betty proclaimed. Too much class to say: Two birds with one stone. Even if, forgivingly, bound to be thinking just that.

There were, as Betty had promised, ample puu-puus. There was soft music and drinks and Sean, as ever, was the warm host. It was a relaxing hour, a silver one too, looking out at the palms and the calm surface of Pearl Harbor while the large overhead fans, suspended from the high ceilings of these old fashioned Makalapa dwellings, rotated with unobtrusive dignity and reflected slow but periodic flashing rhythms of vitality upon the polished hardwood floors. Sean advanced on Aliason with his crystal pitcher of mai tais, frosty and blue, which she declined with soft plaints of apology. "Just ginger ale, thanks . . . or soda . . . *anything really.*" Sitting on the edge of her chair, too pale for her months out here, too slender, eyes dark circled, haggard and beautiful at the same time. David put down a spark of irritation at his brother upon whom—after, by now, a fair sample size of social occasions—Al's tastes, without any deciphering of the cause of her abstinence, ought to have registered.

"Well, of course," Sean responded with graciousness, stronger than any surprise. But it was Betty who trotted back, part of this impeccable team, with a tall glass of ginger ale chunky with ice and a cherry added saucily. At the same time observing her sister-law with a new sharpness, and yet instinctive sympathy. Perhaps spotting something, but uncertain as yet of the full impact of what she had discovered. Sure only of one part of her surmise. "Actually, sweet, you don't drink at all do you?"

More on edge than he need be, David watched Al turn and lift those dark eyes solemnly upward with the expressive sincerity, the form of those regrets, perfected through a hundred similar apologies. "I really *do* like drinks. But liquor gives me the most dreadful *headaches.*"

Betty laughed softly. "Well, I wish it did for me too. Who needs really to be pouring all that stuff into one's body? I feel it slowing me down when I could be more energetic."

"*You*, Betty? But I do feel guilty, Sean, not partaking of your beautiful mai tais." Al going on. Typically, overdoing it. But the moment which seemed uncomfortably suspended moved on, bird with a bent wing. The music came up stronger. Betty asked: "Do you remember Nina Kealiiwahamana?" Aliason nodded gravely. Oh so well.

"She's coming on next, after the Kui Lee songs." Aliason had her own old Hawaiian records somewhere at home at the bottom of a pile and there they would stay. They caressed extra dimensions of sadness, unbridgeable vastness of oceans. Shadowed with the knowledge of how many of the Island's beautiful voices had died young. The music swelled and sighed, filling the evening air with no sense or rustle of its mechanical origin. Alfred Apaka was singing Beyond the Reef and was not more than a minute into it when Betty noticed, stopping the music. "Oh dear. Damn. I am overdoing it with these tearjerkers."

"That's all right," Aliason responded in a brave whisper. "I'm truly sorry."

"I'm the one should be sorry," said Betty who sat down beside Aliason and put an arm around her. "I'll feel the same way when we leave." Handing a tissue for Aliason as if she were a child. "Buckets of tears for us all."

"Oh yes." Al's voice stayed small, a lost little girl's. Betty, who had kept much more together then they knew, could save this. Motes swam in a last golden band of sunlight, penetrating clouds above the Waianaes and finding their dust-sparkled way onto the lanai with its warm woods. "Tell you what. I'll put Gabby Pahanui on to pep things up," Betty said. A little later she danced for them a lively hula with mildly naughty words. David and Betty exchanged glances, confirming something done right, lightening this farewell.

Then Sean stepped in with his own contribution to lightening, pulling conversation away from the lugubriousness of departure's imminence. Giving David a wink bringing up the Honolulu Star-Bulletin take on Plowshare's noble experiment. "People here on the staff get a chuckle. Not fans, most, of our Boy Admiral."

"Full disclosure, Sean. I was there."

"Ah, were you?" looking not so much surprised as keenly interested. "Did the reporters tell it fairly? Ws it really as nutty as they told it?" Shaking his head at David's telling of it, feeding some freshly expanded and mirthfully renewed sense of his beloved Navy's ability to wrap itself around the axle. A prelude to reflecting, drawing on long observation of the vagaries of naval careers, that while Sneedon Snowdon had lost a bit of skin on this one that most likely he would weather this small tempest, go onward and upward without any serious hitch. "Our boy has his protectors."

Sean took a long sip of his mai-tai, gazing across the top of his glass to the harbor where a gray warship, tiny at this distance, did not move. Betty's own glass came down with a rap on the polished monkey pod table, unreconciled to what Sean had seemingly come to grips with. "And just where in hell," she said, "were your protectors, my man, when your carrier bumped that buoy in San Francisco Bay?" Her bitterness flowed on, salted with other stored up injustices, the pain of which was to be read on Sean's face, at last holding up his hand. The embers of his own anger stirred. "All so very true, baby, but . . . ." Giving salute with his empty mai-tai goblet on the way to refilling it. David marveling at a marriage wherein even its differences were part of its strengths.

Something was happening. Something simple and excellent. Sean's excursion into anecdote and Betty's anger, now subsided, was a door opening onto a brief but mellow interlude of general conversation, of stories from them all. Even from Al, with her sense of humor that was, even now at its best, small and sweet. For a little while, they seemed to be united, were *family*, with the muchness that families reveal to each other naturally. Even Sean and Betty, with their fine control that was like an admirable armor. With Sean, as a part of that shedding of armor, pronouncing a valedictory on his naval career before readying himself to shepherd them all out the door.

"It's easier, you know, to say goodbye to it all when you see the Navy for what it is. A great leaden bureaucracy in which we naval officers have become almost like our civil service opposite numbers. Or worse. Administrators in uniform. With here and there nuggets of gold in the grey mastic that, you like to think, sets us apart. Tom Hudner crash-landing his plane to try to save that black pilot with the flames coming up all around him. Don't know that one? You should. Even if before your time. Look it up. And, here and there some of your own moments that you hold tight and that the world will never know but that can keep you going in front of the fire. Taking the lead flight on a strike into the Laotian mountains on a crappy soupy night off Yankee Station when, as Carrier Air Group Commander, you needn't have gone at all . . . ."

"Sean." Betty's voice had regained softness. "Right you are, light of my life. Let's get this show on the road." Sean looking at his complicated aviator's watch with its multiplicity of dial faces in which something as simple and basic as time itself might easily be lost. Not for Sean, deducing that he could still work in a scenic drive around the waterfront.

As they cruised through the quiet naval base, looking over the ships at the piers, closeness was intensified. One hand lazily on the wheel, driving so slowly that he sometimes actually turned all the way around, Sean resumed talking about himself. The boyish strain was in his reminiscences as they crept past the enormous bulk of an aircraft carrier at the Supply Center's fuel pier. "That plane up on the flight deck with the long needle nose, that's the Vigilante. My old baby. As they tell it, last of the beautiful airplanes. Telling it right." He spoke with the realization of what was passing. No more this colorful life of grace and ceremony. "Used up my last chance at flag with last year's selection board. Guess I zigged when I should have zagged. Anyway, I hang it up next June 30th."

"*We* hang it up," said Betty.

He spoke of comrades gone. "What was the point? In Korea even, towards the last of it, we were actually announcing our strikes and the gooks were waiting with searchlights spearing us and groundfire floating up like you wouldn't believe. So much for political wars and learning nothing. All a waste."

"You didn't think it a waste," Betty said, "not then."

"What do you think you might do when you retire?" David asked.

"One thing for sure," he laughed, "I won't become a damned consultant selling the same crap back to my Navy that I turned down when on active duty. Fortunately we have property on the Eastern Shore down by the Choptank. I'll be the handyman and Betty can raise pups and we'll listen to the geese honking."

"Betty, won't you find it dull?" Aliason asked. Her laugh was short. "Try me."

Sean had both hands back on the steering wheel, keeping within the low speed limits of the base. Lean hands, guiding his crew with the long-lived flyer's prudence. "We'll take a swing by your submarines, David." They moved past old weapons on display, the black and white Polaris missile aiming at the sky, the sun-faded blue Regulus—argued by some the symbol of a whole generation's long delayed exercise of imagination—poised at take-off angle. There were torpedoes and further on they crept by the superstructure of an old Fleet boat set up on the grass under the palm trees memorializing the men of submarines that did not come back. On the tiny bridge men had stood on steel gratings scanning horizons for wisps of smoke, and navigators had climbed up the hatch to take star sights at dawn or midnight too, if it must be . . . a mass of gray metal that had risen and dipped millions of times to Pacific swells, now eternally fixed beneath the evening-stilled palms from which came the screech of a mynah bird. Sean steered slowly past submarines at their finger piers with a soundlessness matching the evening's quiet. "Hey, is that one of ours still?" Sean asked.

David couldn't believe it. Twenty yards away, a living black ghost, was a U.S. Fleet submarine. "It can't be." And was not. From another angle opening up, just aft of the sail could be glimpsed the red maple leaf of Canada. "There are a number still around that we sold to foreign navies," David said, "The Turks and others are using them too."

Sean halted the car and herded them out, a loose huddle of friendliness in the warm twilight, taking in the tarry waterfront smells. "You're the one, little brother, who knows all about these critters. Give us a tour." He was not sure if he was being teased. "I'll try." Contending too against conversation that Betty and Aliason had begun, their low voices following up on this and that. Warm with reassurances. They were sisters. David cleared his throat more with hope than command.

"That Canadian submarine is a good place to start; except for no deck gun, it's still pretty much the same submarine that won the underseas campaign against the Japanese. By the end of the war, it had forged an iron blockade around the home islands." A ponderous, he hoped not pompous, way to begin. "Imagine this waterfront in World War II. Machine shops working around the clock, night skies lit up like summer lightning from the flash of arc welder's torches. Bare-chested sailors glistening sweat in the hot sun as they swing their greasy torpedoes on portable cranes and work them down the finger-smashing loading hatches. They've been back from patrol only a few weeks and heading out again in days more. Yet their morale is sky high—if, that is, they've got a skipper they trust. Picture, across that glassy water a submarine, returning from patrol, a broom in its mast head signaling a clean sweep and hand sewn flags flying, not unlike the charter boatmen at Kewalo basin boasting their catch. Instead of tuna or mahi-mahi though, the flags would proclaim warships, cargo carriers.... Come on ladies, tell the truth, anybody listening?"

"Oh yes. We *are*." Both female voices rushed at him in unison. "Don't stop."

"Over there in Lockwood Hall, mostly hidden, is the Clean Sweep bar. If we had time we could drop in. Around its walls are photographs of submarines and torpedoed ships with their backs broken seen sinking through periscope cross hairs. Also pictured is practically every officer who skippered a submarine in the Pacific in World War II. Not New London, but in there is the true shrine of Subdom. It's darkish and mostly deserted, like a medieval church where now come only the wandering tourist and too seldom the worshiper."

"David, my lad," Sean said, "you see, you're telling it better than many a fellow who was there." "Hardly." He added unsatisfyingly, embarrassed, "I've read a lot, but... no." Historian perhaps, never the warrior. It was the quietest hour at any naval base. Liberty sections had departed and the evening meal was finished. Topside on each submarine there was only a lone gangway watch, a slack-postured petty officer in whites with a pistol belt who looked up incuriously from his logbook as this little band of Morgans straggled by. Otherwise not a human being was to be seen along the length of the waterfront. For all the quiet—even seeming to accentuate it—there was a deep faint rhythm thumping through the evening dulled harbor waters. From the destroyer piers, from the shipyard, the invisible blended heartbeats of many ships.

"David, do go on," said Betty, "please do." Aliason moved up beside him and her hand closing tightly over his. "Interestingly, these submarines are moored in rough chronology. There's a Barbel, last of our diesels. Lots of virtue there still, but Admiral Rickover has blocked any further development of conventional power. So these fine and special subs are passing soon. Yet perhaps he's right, a man who sees far into the future and has the toughness to let no small virtues stand in the way of mightier ones." David nodded to himself, less sure on the last item than he was once. The quiet flowed back. The bark of a dog, angry perhaps simply at day's departure, was clear from Makalapa's height a mile away. The mutter of a base security police truck seemed unduly menacing. Surely the guard must find their group suspiciously odd, a frivolous counterpoint of Hawaii's colorful evening plumage to the seriousness of man's black shapes of war. But he putt-putted on by in his gray government vehicle as if they were a most natural part of the scene. Nothing disturbed the peace; one was witness to the faiths of democracy. The air was limp, without expectancy. Atop the little pole of one submarine's stern light—a moment before switched on at sunset to the darting warble of an unseen boatswain's whistle—a sea bird perched, motionless as if mounted there, not a feather stirring. The harbor water was glassy, mirroring the rose of the dull sunset sky. Its surface bore a thin glaze of oil striations, molecules thick, making for a brilliant snaky iridescence that borrowed from the glory of the sunset. For all the modernity of the massed black hulls, space ships of the sea, David believed that Conrad himself would read it romantically, finding more right than amiss. The air had a sea smell, gulls cawed. Out past the dense mangrove shores and through man's cut in the white breaking reef, waited still the wild sea.

"Over there is one of our latest, the Los Angeles class . . . ." Its hull numbers had been painted out and it was totally black. Some morning soon would find it gone, disappearing on special operations. Closest held of all the submarine's secrets. Absorbedly, gaze was drawn to the black hull curving descending into the dark-shadowed water and the accumulation of the thread-fine sea grasses a few inches below the waterline. Oxygen rich, the vivid green tendrils, thickly massed as a woman's proud hair, waved in simple rhythmic grace with the feel of distant swells. Incongruous, it was an unexpectedly natural touch of the sea on this marvel of smooth steel that seemed less a ship than a shape designed to go to the moon. Soon it would descend into blackness, journey to cold and sunless seas, accelerating to fifty feet per second. Still, these frail grasses would flatten and cling, slippery as fish slime, holding faster than any limpet. Remora to their chosen shark.

Sean lit a cigarette. "Still listening." His smile was remote but respectful. David went on. "The submarine will not lose again. Across the water there, all your gray surface ships banded together are no longer its master. No more the great convoys then with their plodding merchantman, lifelines of salvation and destiny creeping towards the shores of Europe. Did I say no more? That's far from saying that we will not. Victors always start out as they fought their last war and thus we could well see the convoys marshalling yet again. Damned and doomed. And charging through the ponderous merchantmen—if new adversaries have their Priens and their Kretchmers too and, of course, they will; nerve and the killer heart being found everywhere, they'll bring forth their Mush Mortons and Burlingames, just as we, their lions dozing, in peacetime—the attackers will light up the skies with their fires. Sharks slashing amongst the floundering cattle.

"The dilemma of the surface ship is profound, historic. Sean, your beloved aircraft carrier—yes, it too, now in the twilight of its long and esteemed life—suffers from the same intractable problem. Outranged, outsped, detectable by the submarine at ranges tenfold those at which the submarine can itself be detected, its plight is inescapable. It exists—even as vainly, we still demand that it thrive—in two great mediums, suffering the disadvantages of both, able neither to hide in the one nor to go fast in the other. Now Rickover . . . ." Sean's concussion damaged ear made him keep the other one inclined with extra fixity of attention. "You are persuasive little brother," he said, "though some good replies can be made."

Betty nodded impatiently, speaking for the first time in minutes. "Yes, I'm sure there can be, dear. But let David finish." On one of the 688's the lone topside watch, yet another bright young sailor likely recruited from the innocence of lofty academic standing in some small town high school, was pretending to write in his logbook but actually reading a paperback. Anyway, his sub secure. The time of the terrorists, as was the crumbling of the Soviet Union, yet to come. The somber black of the great sail rose, like a sinister piece of modern iron sculpture, dwarfing the white uniformed figure at its base who paid not a glance at the small band of sightseers pausing by his gangway.

"The setting is askew, our vehicle here tied up by all these mooring lines. Like a lassoed whale, temporarily docile. One might almost expect to see her give us a wink of complicity from some giant closed eye that says we both understand that she doesn't belong in the crowded milieu, not in this air and light. Even now she is tugging to be away, like a turtle that briefly warms its shell before slipping into the dark waters of its pond. Picture it running fast on the surface, the glossy water piling up in rippling folds across its bow, great whorls sucking away on the sides like ropy green crystal. Hypnotically it captures the eye, demands we acknowledge the future, even as those good gray ships across the way plead for our affections from the past. Yet in reality it is impossible to visualize the submarine in its own medium. The familiar movie images are false, tiny models gliding through shallow translucent depths. In fact, you cannot see an inch down there, it's all black, invisible against the black.

"Which is the story of the submarine, the opacity of seawater, its awesome resistance, even in these days of high tech and exotic forms of energy—lasers, neutrinos, the rest of the bull shit dream stuff—that defy penetration by all forms of energy that we know. It is the submarine's priceless gift. Even as its opponents rage against the seeming unfairness of that awesome advantage...." He paused in embarrassment, too much of himself revealed.

"Here we are, at the end of things." His hand rested on a concrete shape barely distinguished from other sturdy appurtenances of the pier. It was still warm, soaked with the day's sun, and the passer-by could easily miss the plaque informing that in August 1958 Nautilus had departed from this spot upon its historic transit to the North Pole. "That voyage dramatized that the seas are a continuum. Block off the Iceland-Faeroes gap, and the Soviet's submarines can make it into the Atlantic or Pacific under the Arctic ice"—he paused, seeing attention stray—"well, enough...." "Time to wrap up. Your submarines are the lances, challenging the frontiers of sea power. Their adventures the great untold stories. Some day there will be novels worthy of their people and their ball busting operations, not that crappy nonsense that the Tom Clancys et al are serving up now. For the time we know only for now the occasional mashed bow, the curled sail that cannot be hid . . . souvenir of some crazy Ivan maneuver . . . . Apologies, almost missed it. Over there, along that pier with the security fence, is a ballistic missile submarine. A 'Boomer,' as the submariners call her. Under that level area aft of the sail the missiles are housed and above them the doors pop up open for their vertical emergence. This is also something profoundly new in naval warfare. One Trident submarine, two hundred and forty nuclear warheads, could destroy Europe." Aliason shivered, drew her Indian silk shawl around here. "I wish you wouldn't sound so exultant."

"I don't believe David is exulting," Betty said. In the utter stillness her breathing could be clearly heard. Irrelevantly he thought of parts of his brother's wife he had not pictured before, the shiny red vessels of her lungs, free of tar, sucking in oxygen on a tennis court across which those tan limbs raced. Other parts as well.

"So much for the submarine. Its problems are only those of opportunity. Neither the narrowness of the politics that would hobble its enormous potential, nor the follies of men, can long impede—no more than they could hold back the airplane—its destiny. The submarine is the risen queen of the seas and hers will be a long reign."

Almost dark. The mountains towards Waianae losing their outline. Sean glanced at his watch. "Holy smoke! We've gotta rush!" They dashed to the car and Sean set records driving to the airport, fortunately close to the Naval Station. Fortunately too, the good lady who had been taking care of Beth and Boat, by now an anxious pair, had them waiting at the check-in counter. Aliason ducked into a Ladies Room and set her own record for slipping out of a muumuu and into blouse and slacks. Two minutes more went to picking up a tourist's quota of fresh pineapple and macadamia nuts, and then they were running, out of breath, the gift cartons a flopping burden and the soft damp leis bouncing around their necks, to join the line of passengers in final stages of boarding. This hurrying to the good, getting departure down to essentials, jostling out excesses of sentiment. Only seconds remaining for ardent hugs, vows for the future. Betty's arms held David tightly. That superior lady, and then Sean was shaking his hand. A thoughtfulness from their waterfront stroll clung to him. "I hope it all works out. Your crusade, if that's what it is, takes you where you want to go."

David laughed, a little embarrassed still. "Whatever it is. Wherever that may be." Betty took a flash Polaroid picture of the family and handed it to Boat. Sean's handshake tightened. "Anything I can ever do for you, little brother, just let me know."

You might stop calling me 'little brother.' Not saying that, seeing a future of true friendship. In minutes more, with the stowing of hand luggage, the fastening of seat belts, and his family's collective obedience to the blinking little lights with their word messages restless early minutes were behind them.

Honolulu said good-bye to in a blur of misty lights as they rose with a roar. Soon behind too was their packaged meal, the usual cramped fiddlings with plastic. Then the movie was over and the cabin lights were turned down and the stewardesses ceased their scurrying along the aisles and flight settled into something more. Became voyage. Either by airline computer miscalculation, or the vagaries of human choice, defying the distributions of Gauss, the great plane was uncrowded and they had seized an entire row, these lucky Morgans, and in that aircraft's capacious beam, and under skimpy airline blankets, his loved ones were stretched out in line. Boat's feet in his father's lap, his boy's head, surprisingly big, surely meant for something, sunk in a tiny pillow. Aliason was over on the row's far side of the plane and when he rose to go to the restroom he saw her sleeping the slack-mouthed sleep of the exhausted. In the dim light she looked coarsely old, beyond the reach of her daily miracle of beauty's restoration. He stayed up long reading, feeling a momentous and yet unburdensome responsibility, his loved ones' happiness dependent upon his wakefulness, willing the engines to keep pushing their ship of space onward.

He thought of the dark submarines to which but a few hours ago he had consecrated farewell. Thinking what he might have put better. A blazing moon shone off the plane's wing like moonlight across a lake. Lines of rivets ran towards the wing's tip, smooth little circles of them in perfect array, each rivet a skilled act of man. He mused on the success that commercial aviation had become, beauty in the sweep and dare of its forms. Nothing like birds, indisputably brave creations of man. Dawn broke over Southern California's coast, miles of it sliding beneath the wing, in the interval between each sleepily marveling breath. He had sampled misty mornings down there, the nostalgic tang of wet eucalyptus like the smell of a lost home. In those pale buildings of aerospace manufacture, friends from college had gone to work and to thrive. Deeper than envy, but envy a part of it, and with many things coalescing, the sense of a great technical team working away so beaverishly on something as useful and good as an airplane, he yearned for worlds with the freedom for feats. Engineering, not analysis, the latter a sickly Washington word, ingredients paper and hot air. Not a sharp pang this, duller, more lasting, wound of his own choosing. He stretched and yawned at dawn's grayness, which now filled the cabin. Across the far aisle Aliason slid her fingertips over her face exploringly. "Didn't you sleep?", she called, her voice grazing the heads of strangers. Dozed, he answered, about all.

"You need more than dozing." She smiled then said a few other things, ordinary words but intimate. Rather, to the ear tuned to the talk of married people—language within language—intimate precisely because it was ordinary. "I slept like a log. What were you thinking about?" It seemed that, having to speak loudly above the engine's drone, baring his answer to the world, should yank every passenger bolt upright with astonishment. Not a sleepy soul stirred. "Wondering how I got tied up with such a loser as anti-submarine warfare."

Her smile in response, seemingly of vague but kind wishes, made him doubt that she even heard. Her lips making a lazy girl's kiss, she settled herself back with a drowsily companionable wave. Sharers in this voyage, nothing to do for a while longer but see their little crew steered safely home. But before she let her eyes fall shut again she told him what it was that *she* had been thinking. That school was soon restarting, clothes to buy, a new pencil box for Boat.... Some stores actually sold them still she said, under that very name, and, first thing after arriving home, she would seek them out with one mother's haunted drive for connection with something old and fine and not to be lost. And the life that they had left behind would be picked up with unkindly swiftness, as if they had never been away.

How awfully true, he thought bleakly, that last. Because, with nothing to look forward to but austerity, not as far as the eye could see, it was going to get worse. To be sure, he felt himself stronger. But whether that growing strength would suffice for challenges themselves sure to grow, he could only hope. His own eyes now shutting over a soft cry within.

Al. Come on, baby.

7

Time... Often David Morgan would say the word, but silently. He had read about men in prison camps, and those who fared best in lifeboats, who likewise seemed not to think too much about time's passing. Passivity then the ticket? *Supportability*.... In the same way as *time*, he would say the word. And, in the same way, manage not to brood upon it. Supportability a virtual call to passivity. If that wasn't too dippy a metaphor. Now another spell of miserable heat. Under miasmic skies each noon he would sit on the low stone wall, reading a book between bites of a sandwich from a paper bag. More and more just the classics. Why not? Socrates and Marcus Aurelius saying it all when it came to government and political man.

Today something was happening though. Out of sight came the sound of drumming and a ragged, wind-torn musical march, notes scattering. Around a building appeared a small but strung-out parade of marchers. There had been a number of such parades lately, federal workers protesting delays in their heretofore automatic pay raises. This one had set out from L'Enfant Plaza, over in the great pools of Agriculture and Transportation, teeming vats of resentment overflowing the federal buildings of Southwest, and proceeding down Independence Avenue and thence swinging around the inspiring circle of the Lincoln Memorial and down the grasses of the George Washington Parkway. These marchings took somewhat longer than the nominally allotted lunch hour of the federal worker, but it was recognized by seniors in Civil Service that circumstances were unusual. The marchers were fighting *their* battle too .... For men in tailored suits who would not be caught dead with a placard in their hands. The marches were outside of the usual patterns of worker behavior. They arose out of new dimensions of frustration. Something extraordinary in that already stuffed tote bag where government workers stored their grievances. Psychologists were busy explaining this keenly felt bitterness, lately so sharp, arising out of that chronic dull ache over lack of appreciation. And, in the way of such parades, dedicated to the gain of the living as opposed to the honor of the dead, there were catcalls in addition to cheers as this one wended by. A twisty column of human ants, following the banging of an angry drum. None had come to Crystal City before, but it was expected that there would be more of them as these noontime excursions kept swinging in ever-wider orbits. Planets of formerly dependable docility getting out of control.

The parade passed close to where David was sitting, heading around the awkwardly combined bulk of National Center Buildings Two and Three, and now was coming back. Up past Arthur Treacher's Fish and Chips, by the Rutherford B. Hayes Building . . . a weary bunch of paraders, its band thinned to a handful of trumpet players and one screechy horn. The music bounced off walls, skinned itself on drab concrete faces and then, concentrating in a borrowed swirl of gritty wind, surged back momentarily strong. David thought he recognized a small figure, almost dandyish, yet concentrating conscientiously upon staying in step with the music and the uprightness of his placard. With his resolute dignity, a person possibly absurd to some, indubitably dear to a few. David's heart quickened. The parade halted and its members fell out, heading for water fountains, lining up at the lunch wagons, trotting off towards rest rooms in the interior of buildings. A group of black girls, their hilarious high spirits belying the grimly fierce sentiments of their placards, rushed by on a wind of laughter. Behind them, somewhat more slowly, came a familiar figure. He looked even shorter, although that could hardly be possible. Still, the impression had David checking his memory. It had been more than a year. Getting on two. "Hello, David." Billy set his sign down carefully, out of harm's way. He looked embarrassed, eyes dropping. "Guess you don't have to ask what brings me this way."

"Evidently a good cause." But he meant only kindness to Billy and he hoped that he sounded so. Billy's expression lightened but he still spoke sadly. "I doubt if you believe that, David, and I'm not sure I do either . . . ." David looked at him understandingly. In the next few minutes, rather quickly and a bit more impersonally, for words still separated them and needed to be hurdled they brought each other up to date. "So. It turned out to be Supportability, after all," Billy nodded soberly.

"As you called it, Billy." With a generous gesture conceding to Billy the gift of small prophesy that was one of his prides. Billy told what he was doing. "It didn't turn out to be Human Services after all. Worse even. Housing and Urban Development, the pits, *right*? HUD . . ." He made the last sound like an obscenity. "I'm working in their Special Projects office, PUMP. You've probably heard of it?" "Right," David lied. "*Program* for the *Uplift of Human Potential.* Not the worst of acronyms, I guess. Anyway it doesn't look as if that exposé in the *Post* last winter about corruption in PUMP hurt too much. They got rid of that consultant psychologist who was an ass hole buddy of the Secretary and maybe sticking her. The part of PUMP I'm working on has to do with the potential conversion of military technology and hardware to civilian purposes."

"Swords into plowshares." David had spoken the ancient phrase casually, irresistibly tempted. Yet care taken to purge it of irony. No one more easily wounded than Billy. But his sensitive friend's eyes only darkened with extra depths of trust. "Yeah, I'd say that. Sort of. Actually, it's pretty interesting." Some words can have no trailers but silence. They could hear the traffic out on U.S. 1, that rumbling ruin of a highway, all horns and grinding gears, a thunderous and scornful continuum of irreverence towards the quieter wheels turning away in these buildings of government. Billy could not hold back a great sigh. "No it's not. Who am I kidding? It's the same old shit." He waved his arm in a great circle of disgust. "But I'm kind of a star over there. Crazy. I open my mouth and they listen. You know how we always suspected that, terrible as Defense is, the other departments are probably worse. Yep. Compared to the outfits I see, Defense is a miracle of efficiency. But how about you Davey?"

"In good health." Billy had always smiled respectfully at David's dry humor. Memorially, his smile flashed now. "No. Something about you is . . . quieter."

"More, I guess, to be quiet about." He picked at the last crumbs of his lunch. Fewer people to talk to, for one thing, he explained. His fellows in Supportability were pleasant enough but he still hadn't gotten to know them well. Most days he came out here to eat his lunch and to read. A man adapted. Billy picked up David's book. Not the *Phaedo*—he put that quickly aside—but the one underneath, *Critical Convoy Battles of the Atlantic*. "How is it?"

"Disappointing. It's just all track charts and chronology. No interpretation."

"So you do keep on thinking about it some, eh? Well, so do I. Though, knowing me, I confess to thinking less about the big picture and recalling more our own battles from the far end of those long green tables. I helped with those fights, didn't I? Some guys were basket cases, but we had smart enemies too. Anyway, after those sessions, you and I'd talk it over. Feeling good with our little victories, points made, or lick our wounds after our defeats. But all part of the fun. Eating our sandwiches, leaning up against the tombstones."

"It was fun, Billy. In retrospect." The succeeding silence threatened to deepen into awkwardness. "Guess what?", Billy said. "Not wearing those crazy support shoes any more."

"It's was none of my business, Billy. I'm sorry about that day."

"But you were absolutely right, Davey." David's one fresh bit of news, that he had been a participant in Project SUNRISE, brought from Billy whoops of delight. Billy having heard more about SUNRISE than David would have guessed. "So you were actually a part of that show? Out there in the Islands? And riding good old *Esposito*?"

David was quick to tether Billy's balloon with caution. "Billy. Don't make anything of it. Hundred of analysts traipsed out there. And I was the least of them."

"Still. Did Tawney Grey actually know that you were going to be nominated as a part of DIANA's team?" "Billy, pay attention. I was never a part of DIANA's team. I was just a minor bit player, a lowly data taker, in a sideshow. Supportability would never have been invited if it didn't happen to be one of last year's buzzwords in OPNAV."

"Ah. But, tell me, did the good doctor *even know* you were there until he saw you show up?" "I confess," David said, feeling a revisit of the amusement he had felt at the look on Tawney's face when he first bumped into his former subordinate on Ford Island, "he seemed quite unaware."

"Hmm." Billy's expression underwent a further swift transformation. Taking away the hand that had been rubbing his chin, he looked like a sly gargoyle. Full of surmises. "I'd think the old boy would have been paying closer attention. He can't afford to blow another one."

"Frankly, I don't see what's to blow. Or who gives a rat's ass."

Billy lit a rare cigarette, shook the match out flamboyantly. He blew smoke out like a dragon, through nostrils and mouth. A small but alert dragon. *"Still, then he has made a mistake."* A mistake obviously pleasing Billy mightily. His face mirrored a shifting series of delicious possibilities. His forefinger stabbed the humid air. Seeing importance where David saw none. "Tawney has been careless." For Billy, a pessimistic faith confirmed. The screw-ups continued. The beat went on. "You're the last fellow they should let have a glimpse at that charade. Because you were actually out there on *CORRIDA* too, right?"

"That I was." But now the reassembled musicians of the parade were tootling to rejoin. Billy hopped down from his seat on the wall. But before he rejoined his fellow marchers he had his own post-scripts to crowd in. Part of SUNRISE's aftermath. Scraps, lively rumors. Artie Perozzi riding high again. His Pacific Ocean Research dominant on Ford Island. "And, oh yeah," Billy breathless with more news that still had to be crowded in. "Charlie Wicker's gone. Out of there. Gone for good. Hiyaku. The Admiral all smiles. A happy camper, they tell. Now how do you suppose Artie got the bucks to buy him out? Artie who never had two nickels to rub together?" Billy's eyes rolled and he held his nose, but at last he was truly out of time. The marchers' music, strong and urgent, cymbals clanging, was tugging Billy back into ranks. He shook David's hand fervently. "Great getting together. We'll talk again, uh?"

"Let's. Missed you too, Billy." He watched his friend rejoin ranks and he waved towards the mass of people and Billy jiggled his sign in return. The parade got itself off to a shuffling start, those in back marking time, while the front ranks opened out like an accordion. Then the disorderly business roused itself, feeding on its lively music. Brasses blared, bounced off the planar faces of glass and stone, buildings that craved—and yet for seconds seeming to be touched by—grander destiny. David watched until the form of the march was lost amongst the bobbing heads of passers-by. Thinking about Charlie Wicker and other things Billy had said. Even so, surprised at how little it touched him, how faint and far off it all seemed.

What mattered was that his friend was back.

▲ ▲ ▲ ▲ ▲

    Even from a distance it was recognizable as one of life's familiar scenes. The small boy would keep running ahead along the walkways of the Naval Academy, sometimes taking an erratic excursion to chase after a squirrel. Then deciding that he was getting too far ahead of the toiling pace of his grandmother he would race back too her on flying legs, an olympic spirit out of control, and rush into her arms, the softness of her overcoat, the whole of her a target.

    "Goodness, Boat you nearly knocked me down."

    "I did?" His head inclined upward to be sure if on that wrinkled face seriousness was to be read. Between them most everything was a great tease. Her bony hand tightened on his small one. "Am I walking too fast, grandmother?," he wanted to know.

    "Certainly not! I can walk very well. I simply don't choose to run." Boat entered into a tactful silence beyond his imagination to picture his grandmother running. That silence grew into a pleasant quietness from which he was only dislodged by a return of the not especially interesting subject—expanded upon this time by someone who ordinarily had less capacity to bore him than any grown-up of his acquaintance—of whether he might not wish to follow in the gapped footsteps of his grandfather and great-grandfather, and *himself* attend this splendid institution. Bancroft Hall, Flagg's excellent work, loomed, its grey bulk massive and yet entrancingly graceful. Boat squinted towards that impenetrable shape with curiosity and his usual supply of doubts. Not sure about it, no more than he was on those other occasions when the subject was brought up by adults who pleasantly, but with mysterious persistence, kept working on him. Somehow he could not take to the idea of being locked up in there. "I just don't know, grandmother." He watched his foot scraping the mossed brick of the walk, moving back and forth self-consciously. Not wanting to disappoint her. "Well, the Navy certainly made your grandfather very happy."

    "It did?" At such an age, enjoying the moment, it was difficult to place undue value on happiness. It came with life's territory—free as the air a fellow breathed—not to be pictured as something one had to plan and scheme to secure. Chafing in the grip of his grandmother's earnest good intentions, he fell back on a reply that lately was proving useful when he felt himself cornered. "I guess I got lots of time to decide."

    His grandmother laughed. "You do, my darling, but I don't."

    "Think you oughta be stopping 'bout now, needing a cigarette?"

    "As a matter of fact, I *will* have a cigarette. However, not because I need it. I'd simply like one." Not the kind of subtle distinction Boat was inclined to sort out. And with energies still to dissipate whose overflow could not be handled sitting on a dumb bench he hopped off and ran across the grass to the appealingly deserted bandstand. It reverberated with pleasant hollowness, encouraging a mad scampering in which almost any age might contentedly relinquish all temptation to thought. Returning to where Tessa sat in amiable communion with her cigarette, he zigzagged off again, setting a waddle of pigeons to flight and made it back out of breath and willing to rest for a minute or two. And to contemplate anew the exceedingly familiar, yet always puzzling, figure of his grandmother. "I don't want to get old," he said.

"I can sympathize with that. But if you stick around long enough you have to put up with it." Tessa's smoke hung not unpleasantly in the grey air. Nothing moved in the placid scene except Boat's sturdy bare legs, red from the cold and swinging in ceaseless motion. She was looking at those swinging legs with thoughts far away.

"Let's go grandma." His hand tugged. "In a moment. Don't rush me."
"We going to get that ice cream cone now?" "Shucks. Hoping you'd forgotten."
Deep young eyes looked up at her reproachfully. *"You promised."*
"So I did, so we will," and she took his hand for the walk to the harbor square. They licked their cones and strolled the waterfront. Where once, she remembered, there were only rough work boats of fishermen, now there was a leafless forest of aluminum masts far as the eye could see; in every creek and cove the white and tan and blue hulls of massing yachts. A lone crabber was coming in, engine cut, his long boat gliding across the calm slate water from hundreds of yards out. Silently, gracefully, with perfect purpose through the twilight, its low side lights were like one green eye and as eye of red. They watched the man unload his cargo, white and blue hardshells, fiercely clinging to anything and everything, angrily fighting this fate which was to be shaken from traps and dumped into a metal bin. The hard claws clacked, striking other shells, snapping air. A steely sound, like swords clashing. Later, after supper prepared to Boat's special liking, they shared a television program and then, this being custom too, she took down the bulky cardboard box from the closet shelf. *The* box, its collection of strange and unsorted shells, fine pen drawings of unknown coasts, a necklace of yellowed boar's teeth, a slender crumpled commission pennant, cloth darkened by stack gasses and breathing still the smoke and oils of an antique steamship . . . a leather bound notebook he could not read.

"So what are we going to do tomorrow, grandmother?" he called. He was in his pajamas, on the floor surrounded by a clutter of treasurers. His bed was made up on the living room couch but he was not quite ready for sleep. His head appeared around the corner to find his grandmother sitting up in bed reading, an ashtray upon her lap. "The first thing we do is to go to Mass."

His face contracted into a scowl. "I don't want to go to *church*." "Too bad. On Sundays in *this* household everyone, including guests, attends Mass." The boy contemplated his grandmother with a sense of one kind of battle that he was not yet ready to win. Wide eyes searched Tessa's face. "You're gonna get married, Mom says." "That is true. Not for the first time, however, let me point out."

"What'cha gonna get married for? That Admiral guy ask you?"

"Assuredly I didn't ask him. And yes," answering his next question," I shall be moving."

"Why do you have to go away from here?" "Well," she said, "when people get married they live together. And, as you will discover, Admiral Waters' Washington place is larger and nicer than mine." She looked around. "Anyway, high time I left this funny little den. Shuffle up my things and put all this dust behind." "I like it here. We have good times."

She read the upset on that serious little face. "We have *great* times. Oh, Boat. Come here." Hugging his reluctant figure to her. "We'll have other ones. Goodness, that's no way to be," drying his tears with the edge of the sheet. "There."

"I"m all *right*."

"Now a goodnight kiss. And I've made up my mind. I'm giving you that box."

"The *whole* box?"

"What do I want with that old junk anyway? When your father comes to pick you up you may cart it away." It was not, in more than one sense, a small gift. Museums coveted some of its items. There was going to be noisy hell with numbers of her children when they found out. Well, to heck with them. Later on when Boat—the precious box beside him—was fast asleep the phone rang. "Hello Aliason. You are calling rather late, dear. But no, you didn't wake me."

"With David sound asleep and Boat gone the house is too quiet. Thought I'd check."

"Well, dear, we're getting along fine. Why shouldn't we be?" Afterwards, Tessa listened. Even with ears that now missed much she relished her grandson's breathing deep and strong.

* * *

David tried to keep his voice normal, not an easy thing when he called his mother. "You're really going to get married?"

"I am. And I'm not inviting you to the wedding unless you drop that tone. Though Aliason and my dear Boat and Beth will, of course, be welcome to attend."

"But why? And old *Muddy* at that?"

"That is, after all, my business. I hoped that you would be pleased. All my other children called to congratulate me rather than to hector." "Mother. I only want you to be happy."

"Well, my pet, I haven't heard of any marriage that sets out to be otherwise. Did you just mutter something? You do make the oddest little noises."

Conversation bumped along this way for more minutes, until he heard himself as he must sound to his mother. At that point he apologized graciously and promised behavior sufficient to earn him a place at the wedding. Evidently not far off. Still, he could not entirely keep out of his parting words a faint echo of a distasteful suspicion. "I just want to feel sure you're doing this for all the right reasons." Perhaps Tessa had caught that echo. In her impish mood impossible to tell.

"And just what might those be?"

▲▲▲▲▲

"Yes... well...." Reply, sort of, to one of Billy's involved speculations. A not unappealing silence followed. Ever so faintly a hurt one on Billy's side. "You say that kind of thing quite often these days, Davey. You really do."

"What?" He heard a rustle, pictured Billy's head turning, sensed reproachful eyes. Companions once again, a pair of casual picnickers, escapees from their offices, they were lying flat on their backs in Arlington cemetery's soft and tended ground. It had not rained lately and in the shadows of great oaks the grass was comfortingly dry. "What you just said," said Billy, failing to obey David's hope that he drop the matter. They had slipped unobtrusively into their favorite part of Arlington, wrongly, but doing no harm. Here the gravestones were small, gathered in multiple rows, but unlike those of Vietnam's dead; the latter in their newness were white granite, sparkling pure, painfully glinting sunlight across wide expanses of treeless lawn. These older stones were grey, lichened, stained with the turnings of five hundred seasons, marking the obscure dead, along with concealing the illegal living. Hunkered down as the two of them were, invisible from the winding cemetery roads, barred by trees and shrubs, were it not for periodic mowings of the grass they could remain discreetly encamped forever. Arrayed here were no graves of renown to draw either the curious tourist or the scholarly antiquarian. Not for a century had one of these stones with their crumbling names felt the gaze of loving kin. City sounds were far away. Let a breeze touch the branches overhead, or a single insect drone, and one lost the murmur of man's works entirely. "Well...?" It was the persistent Billy who alone carried the city in with him, its harsh winds and strident alarms, disturbing the gentle airs circulating over men long forgotten. "Oops." David had just glanced at his watch.

"What do you mean, 'oops'?", Billy said, watching his friend hop to his feet and start brushing himself off. "I mean, almost *forgot*. *We* almost forgot, Let's get moving, Billy."

Mystified at first but obedient, Billy followed his fast striding friend who soon was trotting. Then hopping the cemetery's low stone wall, old as the graves it surrounded, David had them running in the direction of the Pentagon. Along gritty sidewalks, past a line of taxi drivers dozing, busses spitting smoke. David led Billy into sunlight, dashing across a highway and down a grassy bank, moving with the prod of special desire. Above them heraldic music burst, drums and the blare of trumpets rattling the air. They were hurrying now through the shadowed dimness of a road that briefly became a tunnel. Its narrow earth border, giving only a few feet of clearance from the rushing cars that paralleled their progress, was damp, sour with its sunlessness. Ahead, sharp against expanding daylight and drooping in black silhouette from the curve of the tunnel's stone archway, stalactites of congealed mud and minerals hung in clusters of long unlovely daggers. "Sure you know where you're heading?", called the panting Billy.

"Trust me." A hundred yards more and they were trotting a seldom used walkway of crumbling concrete which rose alongside a wall thick with neglected ivy. The Pentagon would make an admirable ruin and was further along than the world knew. The height of the wall beside them diminished as the walkways ascended and suddenly, halting, their heads were above the wall and two pairs of hands were cautiously parting a scraggly hedge of bushes. Like kids who had maneuvered themselves to a view of a sporting event for which they had no tickets. "Wow," said Billy. "How did you know this?"

"Shh . . . ." Yet he understood Billy's awe. It *was* a terrific spot. They would be able to view the entire ceremony, its focal center of podium and marine guard and colors scarcely yards away. It was a point of vantage—allowing for having to view mostly the backs and sides of the principals instead of their faces—superior to that of all the hundreds of guests and spectators who had to watch events from a greater distance. The rear view, so to speak, had as well a philosophical virtue, inducing irreverent reflections that in other circumstances David would have been inclined to pursue. Right now the hero-worshipper. Rows of chairs were covered in white cloth for the guests of importance. Amongst the latter, bringing him a sense of fond affinity to these proceedings—thinking of his mother and her widow friends—were ladies in white gloves and broad hats. Beyond the invited guests, held back by security guards, was the usual Pentagon crowd, mostly clerks and enlisted personnel who made up the randomly curious drawn to these noon time shows. From the asphalt of the River Entrance parking lot rose waves of heat in which the watchers appeared to float, unreal for all their bags of munchies and moving jaws.

The color guard marched by, British and U.S. flags dipping in salute. Speeches followed and this proved to be the one disadvantage of their location; yet only perhaps so, for they could not tell what they were missing. Because the loudspeakers were aimed away from their direction, they were fated to hear mostly squawks, a duck language in which the tepid wind, summer weary like the city from which it had wandered, would abruptly expire, leaving hollows of quiet in which they could take aboard an occasional grand phrase. David by now in a trance of concentration, eyes fixed on Admiral Sir Bruce Maxton, the focus of honor. Shorter than I imagined, David murmured to himself, but the broad back, the thick reddish neck, confirmed a powerful man. Once the Admiral half-turned and his pressed mouth, eyes squinting against the sun, revealed themselves fleetingly. David noticed little hairs, counted moles, soaked in knowledge of a winner. In full dress uniform, standing with rock-like steadiness. Sir Bruce now shifted, ever so slightly, his weight from one foot to another. David guessed that this was the sort of thing that he bore rather than enjoyed. In minutes more the event was ended and, to a softly wistful march of farewell, the official party trailed by the ladies in their wide hats, was guiding Sir Bruce off toward no doubt a celebratory luncheon. David let the parted bushes close like a curtain on a stage.

A sense of mirthfulness, enhanced by relief at their not getting caught, rose in Billy. "That's it? Racing over here to look at the back of a guy's head?" But David was soberly satisfied. "Yep. That's it." Billy was also, in his own way, pleased. Later, out in the open at Crystal City, finishing up their lunch, he told a few stories he had picked up about Sir Bruce, some recent lore of this visit. Billy keeping up still. Belatedly, a Billy hit with delighted discovery. "I *got* it. Why the red carpet treatment. He's supposed to talk his compatriots into buying DIANA in order to lower our own production costs. Billy's indignation flared brighter with understanding, "They don't give a crap about the old guy himself."

"Tsk. You and your dirty mind, Billy."

"But that's it, of course. Because, I gather, they still pay attention to him over there in the U.K." Billy bouncing with spirits of old. "From what I hear though, the Brits aren't buying. But listen, Davey. I heard something else." Billy breathless with amused recall of another item of gossip. "The official reason for Admiral Maxton's presence is the annual grand ASW strategy review. With Admiral Snowdon, of course, representing the Pacific Fleet. A gathering of the clan. I'm told our boy Sneedon was giving a talk—nobody talks a better game with a pointer, you remember—going on about barrier operations in the Faeroes-Iceland gap. Suddenly Sir Bruce hops up and grabs the pointer away and raps the chart. '*I fear my young colleague is a victim of the Mercator illusion*'. He went on from there, straightening Sneedon out on great circle distances, how an inch on the chart north of the Arctic circle is not nearly so many miles as at the Equator. Nice about it, talking with a twinkle, but letting the air out of Sneedon's balloon all the same." David chuckled too. A moment to treasure, echo of old times. A companionable silence grew which Billy eventually, and on a note of thoughtfulness, gently broke. "Our boy shouldn't have risked that, should he?" With David's nod Billy went on. "That's the British Navy's world up there. When the U.S. Navy thinks of the oceans it pictures mostly the South Pacific.

Blue seas and shirt sleeves. For the British it's always the North Atlantic, isn't it? Greyness and fogs and icebergs and hellacious storms." David had cocked his ear to Billy, a not displeasing echo of himself. "Stepped into it all right."

But the second arousal of their laughter was the less spontaneous. What did it matter that two former and decisively fired underlings could enjoy an unrecognized moment of fun at the brimmingly successful Admiral's expense? Yet it was, despite this late arriving cloud, a pleasant interlude with Billy out in the sun. Intriguingly, something in his friend was changing. Happiness in marriage doing it. His Shin a wonder, perhaps another little one on the way. "I'm not sure how it will all turn out, David. In the long run. I have hopes that it will become—please, no smiles at my presumptuousness—like you and Aliason." It was not the moment for contrapuntal notes and David let nothing get in the way of unstinting warm wishes. "Been thinking again," Billy said, "about our racing over there. Crazy, if you look at it one way." "Or maybe, Billy, it's the way it's meant to be for two characters consigned to permanent exile."

"Exile? Is that what you call it?"

"You got a better word, Billy?" Billy did not. Shaking his head soberly and calling forth from David extra words of warmth and reassurance before dispatching his friend back to the no doubt equally depressing concrete of HUD. True, it had been a good day, as was any day in Supportability when he could wrest from it the smallest gem. Even so, it was necessary for him to ponder again that figure of Sir Bruce, planted sturdily in the government's fine rich grass, take from it what he could, before he could wrench himself back around passably to what he wanted to feel. Still not willing to hurry back to his office, avoiding the elevator, making himself plod the many flights of dusty reverberant stairwells of concrete, finding in this ascending hike, even without the company of trees or anything green, value that would not be waiting for him when he reached Supportability's floor.

▲ ▲ ▲ ▲ ▲

The secretary at the desk guarding Supportability's offices—spaces never besieged and indeed to which any visitor was a novelty—came to tell him that a Mr. Madden was here. "A contractor?" Improbable. There was no money to be mined in Supportability. Barely enough for paper clips. "I asked him. He said no. He didn't want to leave a card though."

"Well, I sure have time to talk." David said, curious about anyone new up here. He guessed at first that his visitor might be an agent for the Naval Investigative Service, checking up on someone's security clearance renewal, but by the time he had led his visitor back to his desk he realized, something clicking, who this husky, diffident, grey—suited man had to be. "You are Admiral Madden, aren't you?"

"For one more day," he said, "then I'm Joe Civilian."

David pulled over the best that Supportability could muster as a visitor's chair, remembering something that seemed, in conversational terms, appropriate. "Once, a contractor came to see me—not here but in another office—and I said to him, 'Excuse me sir, but weren't you a Vice-Admiral?' He had been retired for some years and I had meant no offense. 'I *am* one still', he puffed up to let me know. *'I'll always be a Vice-Admiral.'*"

"Well, relax, at least I'm not a contractor." The Admiral-for-one-more-day followed that up with a shrug that said: To each his own. A moment lengthened in which Smoke Madden might have explained the purpose of his visit but that was not his motive. This instance though, his dropping by to introduce himself to an obscure civil servant he probably could not have explained anyway. Yet explanation was there, lodged however dimly. It came from histories he had read. Histories that taught him that men in power had always done terrible things to their fellow man. In wars had he not himself, with fire and steel, done the same? Good rulers as well as bad, to preserve the structure of things, had sent victims in a long line to racks and flayings, to dungeons, and to cages swung from towers. . . . But something else set some of these rulers—princes, doges, proconsuls or whatever—apart from most of their kind. A certain few would choose to look upon their victim in his agony. Wishing to see straight into his eyes without flinching. It was the opposite of sadism, a deed of respect, curiosity melded with awe.

The age of officially sanctioned torture was past—at least supposedly in favored parts of the world—but American life had other ways to destroy a man, or make him obedient as a zombie amounting to the same thing. Leave him with ample food, a solid roof, car and television nearby; simply take away some pitiful square yards of office, shrink his title, make it harder to send a favored son to the college of his choice, have to deny a daughter the orthodontia that could transform her dreams. The American most acutely vulnerable through his children.

Smoke Madden had seen plenitudes of bold stands shriveling when men glimpsed the consequences of their puny rebellions. The Russians had figured this too. Well before perestroika, their Gulag only a shadow of what it had been. The labor camps of the frozen *taiga* no longer needed. Just threaten a Muscovite's apartment—all drear concrete and clattering pipes and stained ceiling though it might be—or hint that the bellyacher's name might be removed from the list of citizens waiting for a new *Zis* automobile . . . enough to turn a man's nights sleepless, his pitiful metal crumpling like tinfoil. In the real world Solzenhitsyns rare and as endangered as the Siberian tiger.

Smoke Madden had come here wanting to meet the man behind the name. A kind of amends, a purgative, an act of decency—parts of all these—he too looking into his man's eyes, making himself pay attention. Yet how this fellow was *going on!* Starved for a listener. Those eyes too—Smoke was reading David Morgan's eyes with fascination—innocent, in spite of all. His thick glasses, weirdly so, conveyed their own kind of revelation that had to surpass anything that those lenses could confer in enhancement of the wearer's own vision. This poor guy spilling his guts about his profession, his pathetic stands. Pouring out acronyms latched to the propagation of sound in the sea of which Smoke Madden—prince of speed and of the jewel blue sky of high altitudes with stars to be seen at noon—knew nothing.

Yet the words were pouring too fast, a torrent. For here David Morgan was quintessentially the American, and Smoke was akin to those stolid Russians drudging away in the grim basements of Soviet Intelligence, trying to make something of this prodigality of information. Even as Russia was touted to be the ultimate mystery and enigma amongst nations, the greater truth being that there was ample precedent for old fashioned tyrannies such as the Soviet Union, while none at all for the uniqueness of America, supremely the unbelievable nation. Therein lay the Soviets' trouble. Their Byzantine minds, all twists and turns, could not believe any of it, neither the glories nor the protean follies of freedom. Smoke Madden did not, however, disbelieve in David Morgan. Just trying to make heads or tails of him.

Smoke Madden though was not one of your great thinkers on mankind's nature. His knowledge was pragmatic, behavioral, useful rather than theoretical. As Squadron Commander, he used to embark aggregations of men and planes in an aircraft carrier and deploy from homeport and family for nine months or more. It was a time when one in five of his pilots did not come home but left their fire-blackened bones unmarked in the jungle or were lost somewhere in vast wastes of blue ocean. He had motivated men to fly in sleety nights off Iceland, to maneuver at low altitude through the fog-shrouded hummocks of the Vietnam highlands. That he always went first, proving that many a hairy flight was feasible, went without saying. Other forms of Smoke Madden's leadership were even more important in getting pilots to perform their missions. There was quiet counseling, in which some juniors might unburden his heart. Other sessions were short, severe. While some men needed stroking, others responded only to a boot in the rear. Even in a group seemingly as homogenized as young naval aviators, there was evidence of the variety of man's nature. Smoke's squadrons contained the usual preponderance of daring, gung-ho, extroverted aggressives, but had thoughtful types too, straight arrows and teetotalers. Even, occasionally, a coward. Sometimes a poet's heart beat amongst those roistering spirits. None of this mattering except insofar as Smoke's grasp of the truth was related to the man's having respect for the multi-million dollar piece of the taxpayer's machinery that enclosed him in flight. The coward he cajoled into heroism: he himself knew about fear, but understanding that what the world called bravery amounted mostly to the conquest of imagination.

One other thing Smoke knew—something that any number of expensive federal studies funded for psychologists to research the obvious answer, which nevertheless they could not ever quite reach (even at their best spiraling in towards that elemental truth on a sluice of dense and slippery words)—which was what men mostly lived for. A sense of their own worth. How they attained that self-esteem, that was where the diversity came in. Some men found it in medals, others in bedding down the maximum number of women that chance and endurance made possible. Some needed applause, worldly approval. Fortunately, for the hope of what good sense and peace survived in the world, there were many people for whom a spark of inner pride sufficed. Pride perhaps only in seeing . . . . "So, I guess I saw early . . . ." David Morgan stopped himself.

"You saw . . . ?"—Smoke Madden repeated encouragingly, guiltily, his attention wandering: he was thinking of his retirement house in the forested mountains to the west, the sweet smell of fresh cut wood—". . . that it wasn't going to work," Smoke going on in a braking murmur, wondering: *What* in hell exactly wasn't going to work? Fortunately, David Morgan winding down. For by now Smoke pretty much had learned what he came for. Though a variant of the type, David Morgan was a messiah, in an age that had no use for such. Smoke had known others, men out of his own aviation trade, who had taken stands against buying bad planes, dumb weapons, and been vindicated by time. And for what? The bones of their broken careers whitened the Navy's past as regularly as crucifixion markers once lined the Apian Way. Smoke Madden made an involuntary stir, a tug to be away that David Morgan could not miss, and yet who was still pressing on to an obviously abbreviated conclusion.

"You see, the concept, the oceans themselves, are all wrong, cannot sustain . . . the technology is not *there*. Only recently there was this big operation meant to justify their high power, low frequency, sonars. It was called CORRIDA . . . ."

"CORRIDA", Smoke Madden repeated courteously, blankly. But David Morgan, his face furrowed, had at last run down. His eyes though still held mute plea.

It was Smoke Madden's turn to convey apology. "You realize that I don't know much about these things. Perhaps you're right." No 'perhaps' about it. He knew squat about decibels in the sea, but he knew men. He rose. Yet, because David Morgan's eyes, those absurd eyes, were fastened upon him still with a kind of dumb hopefulness—not for himself, but for oceans that could not be made right, for honesty in government acquisition, for worlds of Impossible Causes, for God only knew what else—and because now, at this last, Smoke wanted to do something cheeringly, he turned talk to his woodland house. Never having met anyone not interested in the challenge of building one's own home. David Morgan no exception. But at the same time he was not losing sight of his objective to break himself loose. A keg of special order nails was waiting to be picked up at a nearby lumberyard. "Not too likely we'll be meeting again," Smoke moved talk along, "But then you just might get out our way."

"Always possible," David responded. "My wife and I do take trips to the Blue Ridge to see the Fall colors. We visit old inns and—" "*There* you are. Just drop on by whenever you're in the neighborhood. Let's have a piece of paper." Lending plausibility, Smoke Madden's pen drew directions, starting with where Route 66 left the Beltway and headed west towards Front Royal. A succession of by-ways, finally came down to the words, ". . . you'll be looking for a stream and a small bridge and then you'll see my mailbox. I'm back in the woods another half mile. It's the only red mail box out that way."

"Red," David repeated, "and, thank you Admiral."

"So *make* it happen, fellow," Smoke Madden urged. "And good luck." After shaking hands in farewell, each knowing well that there was going to be no visit, not a chance, the image of David Morgan's questing face stayed with Smoke Madden. Minutes more than ordinarily he looked back towards anything. It was the trust straining in those eyes that he did not wish to contemplate; a deeper mystification there too, and it would go beyond his unanswered puzzlement over Smoke's visit. The guy would never know what had hit him. Wouldn't believe if it were diagrammed out for him on a blackboard. He was touched with doom, even as were a percentage each year of those novices whose repetitive mistakes in Basic Flight Training rendered them historically high probability candidates for self-destruction after they got their wings. There were statistical patterns to these things. Fate was in the man. Naval aviation keeping better numbers on its screw-ups than the world did on such as David Morgan, but the principle was the same. A rare shadow of depressions stayed with Smoke Madden until he got his nails. At once there was something so solidly heavy, so forgivingly useful, in the keg on his shoulder as he bore it out to his car that he gave little thought further to David Morgan. And once out in the woodlands his heart sought, none at all.

* * *

It was the familiar ride home from the stable, the strong smell of horse in Beth's jeans permeating the interior of the car. There was the usual talk of school and marks and then, out of quietness. The Question. "Things declining again, Dad?"

"Things, darling?" He pulled out to pass a trailer compartmented for transporting horses and after executing that maneuver he had the hope that her question might have gone away. Vain hope.

"Da . . . ahd?

"I wouldn't say so. Everything considered, we're doing okay."

"I'm not talking about *your* reverses, Dad. I gather though," she said, "they're just bothersome, not fatal." He waited. "Not fatal. That about sums it up." His life, he considered, perhaps composed of matter able to sustain more fatal wounds than most. She shook her head. "Dad, I'm talking about *Mom*." "Know you are, hon." There had not been anything more to say about that for some time and there was not now. He told her a funny story from the office, a good news and a bad news one, about the carrot and the tomato, the latter gravely injured in an accident yet going to live—that the good news—the bad news being that she was going to be a vegetable for the rest of her life. He waited for a chuckle at least but there was nothing. "My riding instructor told me you'd been getting her opinion on what King would fetch if we had to sell him."

"Yes," he said, letting out his breath, "but it was a casual conversation. Just exploratory, you could call it. I'm a little disturbed, that she passed that on to you."

"Well, it's not like she rushed up to me and said, 'Hey Beth, your Dad's thinking of selling your horse. It just kind of came up in our leaning together up against the fence by the ring. She happened to mention that were a couple of months behind on our board for King and asked if I'd say something to you about it. She was real nice about it. Not like being angry or anything. But she's got to make a living too."

"That she does."

"Still, I wish you'd told me. 'Cause it was sort of a shock. But also if it's not already too late, there are things I can do to help." He did not ask what they might be and she went on. "Like it's not sacred really, I mean end of the world stuff and all of that, if King drops back to two feedings a day. It'll be okay." She giggled. "Course, he might kick a few slats out of his stall, not liking it, but he won't die. I'm thinking too, though I can work some, lots of girls my age are doing it. There are jobs in MacDonalds that are part time, late in the afternoon, a few hours each day, that would make me enough to pay for King's board."

"That's a thoughtful offer, hon."

"But Mom would be the toughie on that one, wouldn't she, figures it'd be a real comedown to have a daughter flipping burgers."

"Well, that's a part of it."

She did not take long to pick upon the other part, the main one. "Because, Dad," she said, "it's not like it's the monthly board, is it? It's what King is *worth*."

"Yes, hon," he said, "I'm afraid it is that."

Out of the corner of his eye he watched her head go up and down.

"It's what I figured. Soon as Barb told me what she thought King would fetch, I mean, like *thousands*. I never would have guessed it, him being such an oaf in dressage, but she said there are riders in the Blue Ridge and Fauquier Hunt who would buy him in a minute." She stopped at a catch in her voice.

"Well, maybe it's not going to have to come to that."

"Don't you be feeling too bad, Dad. Barb told me too not to feel too bad either. That she sees it often, young girls having to give up their loved horse, but then, like it happened to her too, good things come along and you get yourself another big old brute."

"Those are words to keep in mind." She said nothing for so long that he glanced over at her. In the sweep of passing headlights he caught the glisten of tears. He touched her hand lying on the seat between them. It did not move.

"You did did tell me once, Dad, that no matter what, I'd always have King."

"That I did, hon...."

"But, I'm not blaming you ... Dad. I know that things ... well, they happen.... I see that."

They were held up by traffic. It was a longer ride home than usual. He started singing. Old Western songs that she had always liked. *Streets of Laredo. Red River Valley. Home on the Range.* Not responding at first. Now joining in.

"*Never a horse couldn't be rode. Never a rider couldn't be throwed.*"

Enough then of song. Dad calling another tune.

"Okay. School time. Let's get with it. First the easy one. Robert E. Lee's horse?"

"*Traveler.*" With a sigh of the suffering.

"Napoleon?"

"*Marengo.*"

"Alexander the Great?"

That sigh again. *Bucephalus.*"

"General Custer?"

"*Comanche.*"

"Here's a new one. Are you ready for a new one?"

"I guess."

"Stonewall Jackson?"

Out of the quiet. "You gotta tell me, Dad. Remember?"

"*Little Sorrel.*" She did not repeat it. "You know," he said, "I'm thinking of you and your History. Why Stonewall Jackson is a heck of a good guy for you to get interested in. Right along these very roads, through all these dark hills and valleys he and his Brigade used to ride on his Valley Campaign."

"They did?" Her voice was flat. "*Absolutely.* You could, you know, do some research on it. Maybe work it in that next paper that you have to do...."

Her own hand reaching over to his brought him to a halt.

"Hey Pop," she said softly, "can we maybe like give it a rest?"

▲▲▲▲▲

Fabled in story, steeped in legend, its very facts exciting enough, the Oval Office of the White House is deserving of its fame. Here Presidents have pondered the risks of war, groped for paths to peace. Here signed many a proclamation, scribbled phrases, kernels of speeches one day to be cut in marble. Here Presidents have looked out the window at the changing seasons, seen dusty Washington summers, sleety winters, glimpsed too the placards of posters jiggling above the iron fences around the grounds, hear the chanting of Protesters, the oftimes terrible voice of the People.

To the Oval Office have come countless of the mighty, yet awed too. They advance into the room a mite tentatively, looking down at the Great Seal woven into that carpet, reluctant to step upon it, as if that would be a profanation of something holy. There are many other persons, those of the President's staff, for instance, who are summoned there almost as a matter of routine. But they too will admit that, for all that they pass in and out, not a one does not experience each time a little extra pounding of the heart. Donnie Lee Webster's own heart was racing harder too, for he was running late as he trotted in from his office in the West Wing. Since everyone else had already gathered, and the President's reputation for esteeming punctuality was well known, an extra degree of nervousness attended Donnie's entrance and some awkward reshufflings of chairs. The President's face was a mask of irritated impatience. "Now that the Special Assistant to the President has arrived, perhaps we may begin," he said.

There were snickers, but only a few. The occasion was too serious for any of that taut, never quite so light-hearted, banter that passes for humor amongst the White House inner circle. For, as may be surmised, and even such an eternal innocent as old Muddy Waters himself got glimmerings from afar, there are many kinds of meetings in the Oval Office. Not all freighted with history. For Presidents, when they glance out their window are sometimes moved by thoughts other than the transitoriness of human existence or dangers to the Republic. Oftimes, that grandness of vision, which they would persuade the citizenry is their abiding view of the world, contracts to the temporal and the immediate. Then the sight of those falling leaves triggers not only philosophic musings but is directly a reminder of November and coming elections and the fickleness of voters. Acutely, the occupant of the White House is made aware of the precariousness of his own residency and the clamor of other potential aspirants to his fair columned residence. Knowledge grips that yesterday's campaigns, yesterday's promises, are worthless currency and if a man wants to assure himself another four years in the White House steps must be taken with that end unceasingly in sight. A man had better—in language not unknown to the Oval Office—get his ass in gear. In fact, looking over the worried faces of his trusted aides, noting dryly the common interest of each of them in continuing employment in this exciting place (not without its perks, by the way too), the President himself kicked the meeting off in almost exactly the same words. A year and more to the next Presidential Election, but still. "We'd all best get our collective asses in gear."

Recent months had not been happy ones for Donnie. He was ill at ease, abysmally uninformed in these meetings concerning a stream of problems in distant and mysterious realms. Only fragmentarily could he absorb daily evidence of a world in torment, the loosening grip everywhere of the United States. True enough, he sat there just like the others, note pad on his knee, expression suitably grave—none, indeed, more judicially concerned amongst those intent expressions written upon all those straining faces—seeming to belong. Inside he was a blank. How was a guy supposed to know where in hell Kurdistan was, which dissident tribes were threatening rebellion in the Etosha Pan, what the ancient rivalry of the Shiite and Sunni Moslem sects portended for peace in the Mid-East, the meaning of falling chicken prices in the Common Market . . . Others, he was sure, must be faking it too, pretending actually to grasp, say, how Section 189 of GATT affected the sales of General Motors sub-compacts in California. Even closer to home, in his own field, which had become, embracingly, Defense, it was impossible to keep straight all the things that he must. So many fucking kinds of Navy ship types alone! All those obscure hulls used for amphibious warfare and mine-sweeping—varieties of ships, indeed, that he had never seen or even heard of in that mercifully brief boot seaman's stint of active duty whose bare record, in the natural course of things, had conferred upon his own White House desk special responsibility for Navy matters—well, Jesus, on a crutch; crazy to expect anyone to know them all. Not that he wasn't trying. The miniature plastic models of ships that sat upon the forward edge of his desk—some of them given by hopeful builders, others which he had put together from those specialized little kits that are prevalent in the better model shops (and whose parts, only fair to record, Donnie had glued together quite well)—were there for appropriate decoration, and also to emphasize his Navy responsibilities with a certain uneasy pridefulness. But mainly they were there for a sneakier reason. To constantly refresh his knowledge.

In quiet moments—admittedly few—he would look at them hard, focus on their silhouettes, picture them full size proceeding across great blue seas, or lying anchored in some golden lagoon. He had gotten to the point where he was confident of some of them. The aircraft carrier, of course. "The Flattop" (he would repeat the phrase to himself with small, secret pleasure) being unmistakable, and the great cruisers and yes, Sea Eagle too, what it was going to become, he could also tell but it was a pain to keep the others straight. He would have them pretty well set, and then he would get embroiled in other things and when he came back to his little fleet all certainty of ship identities would have faded. In meetings, damn high meetings they were too—the National Security Council itself, on the Hill—he could scarcely listen to what was being said, so fearful was he that he might get asked a question. Against the tightly held edges of his chair, his palms oozed. There were limits to which a "C" minus average in Sociology, the humbly suffered disdain of campus queens, and a superlative willingness to carry luggage for the important, could take a fellow. Donnie bumping up hard against those limits.

Ah, but this meeting, by God, was different. Familiar phrases sang in his ear, the rat-tat-tat of the good old words of campaign, as predictable, vacant, and yet as tasty too, as a holster of French fries from Roy Rogers. They set him off again in reverie—Donnie, veteran of a thousand campaign stops—through a sentimental journey of the happiest times of his life. Where a Donnie Lee Webster counted for something. For not everyone was made for Campaign. Took a special guy. From afar it seemed he could hear a band, the thumping of march music, see the waving banners, ten thousand pictures stapled to ten thousand flimsy wooden poles, imagine the high-stepping strut of the girls, rhythms to which the pulse of the dead ought to leap with joy. It was coming, oh, by shit, it was coming. With Donnie Lee Webster in the thick of it.

"Sir?" In his good spirits, indeed an understandable euphoria, Donnie let himself stop following the President's words and found himself mentally scrambling to retrieve a question which, from the glare of his Chief, was unmistakably directed at himself. Fortunately, one word he had caught. "The South, Mr. President?" "Yes, Donnie." There was a steely patience in the President's voice. "That geographic region of this nation for which you, in your politically operative role, are responsible. You know, places like Alabama, Louisiana...."

"Yes, sir. The good old South." Donnie grinned. Did he know the South!

The President shook his head slowly sideways. The burdens of his office had swiftly aged him. But his voice was strong. "No. Donnie. Not the 'old' South of Spanish moss and moonlight on the bayou and sweet darky voices humming lullabies. The South of today, the South of shipyards, where forty-thousand hard hats will be taking revenge upon this Administration if we don't get them some Navy ship-building contracts." Donnie was no longer smiling. He swallowed hard. "Well, as you know in that regard, Congressman Duke...."

He got no further than a roar from the President. Such a roar as would, had it been heard all across the country, have caused an American people, which had already formed a damning judgment that their Chief Executive was too flaccid a fellow for the job, to revise that opinion. Lambs do not roar thus. On the other hand, no one, save perhaps a rare shepherd in some snowy Tibetan fastness, could have been completely surprised at the words that followed. Indiscreet contemporary history has made the ordinary citizen aware that, for all the mighty decisions that flow from Oval Office, there is not necessarily a matching grandeur of language. "That flaming ass hole!" Donnie swallowed again. "Yes sir. But there's the problem."

The President rubbed his face wearily. This last run of rage had depleted him. "Donnie. We all know the problem. It's not diagnosis we need but solutions. When those workers down there are all out on the street it's upon this office that they'll be heaping their blame, not on some jackass Congressman from Wyoming who luckily doesn't have to give a damn because the nation doesn't build warships out there in his horseshit meadows."

"Montana, sir." The correction, though whispered, was an act of courage. Particularly so inasmuch as Donnie wasn't entirely sure. One of those states, anyway, of vast territory and skimpy electoral fodder.

"Wherever." The President smiled icily adding, "No matter where he's from. I know where I'd like to see him *go*." On a nervous note of laughter the focus of discussion shifted, at last mercifully, from the South. Moving on to other regions—one more creaking caravan of an Administration underway at last on its own predetermined multi-year journey of salvation, carrying such hopes and challenges and assorted baggage of promises as only the truly political know—to strategic considerations of each in turn. To the Northwest, to the Rocky Mountain States, to the Northeast, to those crucial empires unto themselves, California and New York and Texas. The review rolled on, stirring hope and imagination, across a vast renegade land, perhaps only barely governable, inhabited by a people more wayward and violent than America was ready to admit. It was a long meeting, wiping out lunch, the frivolities of eating and other forms of relaxation such as stretching and coffee and even head breaks. Grinding on as befitted a gathering of such life and death purpose. Donnie took it in carefully, yet feeling wistfulness too for regions not his own and those fortunate political operatives who did not have such thorny problems as he. Through a long day and for a time afterwards, he felt, as not before in his lifetime, the deepening chill of a despairing aloneness. Settling upon his spirits the way that the grey gloom outside was gathering and sifting through the darkening limbs of massive trees. Because it was a dogonned long time still before those campaign drums would be starting to pound in earnest.

The new White House Chief of Staff for Personnel, Alvin Boffert, was a worried man. Disappointingly, he was getting nowhere in his challenge of staffing positions with individuals of skill. A man of probity, brilliance (a resumé that was a densely packed five pages) and patriotic sense of mission, he was balked at every turn by his inability to upgrade performance in the teeming White House staff. An insightful and logical man, he deduced early that upgrading was achievable only through getting rid of the incompetent. A lifetime of educational neglect could not be rectified in a pressured cram course of "learning on the job." Yet the reasons against firing anyone in the White House through were proving to be many, some extraordinary, others merely colorful. Let a person have done anything during the last campaign—opened a door, fetched coffee— and he was apparently beyond plausible reach of effective replacement. In his bafflement, Alvin Boffert went to the President himself, offering as documented example Numero Uno no small fry, but that individual he judged epitomized the heights to which mediocrity could rise and the harm he could do. The

President listened with seeming respect. Not changing expression even as his Personnel Chief pulled out the stops on one Donnie Lee Webster. "Mr. President, I urge that he leave." "You do seriously, Alvin?"

"*Sir.*" Poor Alvin Boffert's frustration overflowed. "He's an ignoramus!" And instantly knew that he was defeated. Read it in the President's fabled ice blue eyes. Even so, it was a surprise to hear from the President's lips—though heard from a dozen others in the White House—the same maddening word. Voices would lower reverently, as at the sight of a druidial circle drawn in the earth within whose magic circumference an individual was sequestered beyond all hazards of dismissal. The President fixed his petitioner with the coldness of Arctic night. And if, however, the President brought added magisterial sorrowfulness to his reply, there was even more of defiant incredulity in his invocation of that talisman beyond appeal. "Donnie was *Campaign*. I thought you knew."

Soon after, Alvin Boffert departed. An amicable parting, false words on both sides, and Dr. Boffert resumed his Deanship of the famed School of Personnel Management. He never referred to his White House stint and his lecture course on the theory of mega scale human organizations was accounted one of the best in the world.

Yet another drive out to Serenity Farms. Aliason's suitcase, simply packed, in the back of the car. The narrow road passed through barren fields of stubble corn, grey woods, meadows of wet and flattened brown grasses. The walnut trees on either side of the long entrance lane—some forgotten farm family's fine and satisfying try for elegance—sent their black branches stark, like thin starved fingers, into the grey sky. He had not realized before that it was possible to see the main building from the road but it stood out clearly, flanked by great hundred year oaks, on top of the hill. "We haven't been here," it occurred to him, "in winter before." He had meant it only conversationally, after the long quiet of the drive, but then wished he had not said anything.

"That's right," she said, staring straight ahead, "made all the seasons now, by God, haven't I?

8

It had taken a while, seasons uncounted, in the way that many things waiting to happen—some startling and violent, others quietly profound—can lie hidden. Some, the most, do not hatch at all and so it is that the stories that are never known, compared to those we learn—the mother unearthed, say, clasping her child, heartbreakingly molded in her fleeing for two thousand years beneath the ashes of Pompeii—are few compared to the millions of stories that have vanished prior to our time without trace.

Such thoughts though are mere kernels of philosophy, and philosophy was the last thing on the minds of two men—Congressman Abner Duke and Allan Marks, his staff assistant—who were this moment huddled together in the Congressman's private office going over a handful of newspaper clippings, starting with the original Andy Wirth article in *Mountain Calls*. The most recent was an abbreviated summary lifted from the wire services and reprinted only the day before, obviously—given the absence of additional commentary—as filler on a back page in the *Washington Post*, "Amazing," the young staffer said again, "this business percolating away all this time, unknown. It's fate."

"I don't know anything about that, Allan. Just please hand me that first article again." While the Congressman savored it once more, the young staffer was fidgeting with the special joy of his kind. Unable to resist exultation, "So *how* about that? Happiness found right here in our own backyard." Yet even Abner Duke, skeptical of happiness in backyards or, for that matter, anywhere else, let his lips purse in a rare silent whistle of awe, "The *timing*," Allan Marks purring on into his boss's ear, "my God. Falling into our lap this way." These were golden minutes; the stuff staffers live for, precious time alone with the Boss.

"I've done some added homework too," Allan said. A staff is family; bragging is permitted. "This guy Morgan also took part in that CORRIDA operation that flopped. The one the Navy clammed up so tight on we haven't been able to get anything out of them since." This, Allan's day. "I'm sure we can get hold of him. The guy does live close by and . . . ."

Abner Duke said nothing but his eyes, sunk deep in the crinkles of age and the sun of the high western plains, bore a steady gleam like a frog's in focus upon some bug tremblingly alighted on its lily pad. He held up his hand now against the superfluous flow of his voluble assistant. "He and I must have a chat."

"You realize that we may have to subpoena him and—" Abner Duke's look silenced his assistant. Not an everyday look, no part in it of the compromises and trivial theatricality of the politician's life. It came out of a raw past and possibilities of the blood's heat that the Ivy League recipient of that look had no points of reference by which to imagine them. Abner Duke's grandfather had fought in range wars, ridden ninety miles to a doctor with a Cheyenne arrowhead in his shoulder. Right now Abner Duke's cold blue eyes were those of his forbearers, before the age of electrons and easy words, men who blinked only the human physiological minimum. "Allan. Cease. Just get the gent over here."

* * *

Billy Jencks called his friend, excited as could be. "Did you *see it*, David?"

"Not yet. But I've heard. I'll catch it tonight if Aliason hasn't thrown the paper out."

"This thing really spills the beans. Page 17. It has your name all through it. *The Authority.*" "Billy, slow down. It will register on the seismograph around Washington for a day or so and then be forgotten."

"Ordinarily I'd agree, but it's the middle of the Defense budget wrangles, Sea Eagle taking more flack. Anyway Dave, my boy, watch your tail!" He genuinely wished, for Billy's sake, to be able to respond with at least a portion of his friend's enthusiasm for this tiny new comet in his sky. He could only laugh. As he had not in some time. "Come on Billy. Supportability is the bottom of the pit. What more can they do to me?" But before Billy could answer there was another phone call and he was excusing himself and picking up on a name he had missed, but who was apparently from some Congressman's office.

▲ ▲ ▲ ▲ ▲

He had allotted himself extra time because he was not familiar with these segmented streets in the vicinity of the Capitol with their handsome old brick row homes that had echoed the racing hooves of the horse carrying John Wilkes Booth away from Ford's theater. The trees here were thick with age, gentling these streets with dignity. He had called Al before setting off from his office, letting her know he might be late getting home. Explaining the reason, at least as much as he understood of it himself. He had caught her at a good time, not napping—with all the shadowy connotations that "napping" carried in the freightedly special vocabulary of their lives—and the tone of their conversation, brief as it had been, had heartened. She had been excited, alert, Al of old. Questions, too many, of course, though he could hardly blame her, being full of the same questions himself—pouring forth.

"I wish I could tell you what it all means. I wish I knew, hon. Have to let it unfold." Which, that last, he should not have said. She never could buy, not in former days or now, the fatalism implied in acceptance of "unfolding." He was her man; meant to lead her out of the wilderness. "Anyway, you'll be telling me all about it. And, darling. Good luck!"

David Morgan, claiming at least a standard quota of cynicism towards his elected representatives, nevertheless had the citizen's usual feelings of awe at venturing with serious purpose into the unfamiliar territory where politicians actually held forth. His instructions were the "Old" House Office Building, entering a world of worn marble, an abundance of grand brass and heavy dark woods. Stepping inside Congressman Duke's office, he was struck by the contrast between the dim and quiet corridor down which he had been strolling seconds before with such calm and yet curious expectancy. In the brightness of overhead fluorescent lights, desks pushed together so closely that a person could barely slither between them, a great many people, mostly young, were furiously busy. The atmosphere was tense, gestures were quick faces strained; yet oddly, voices were in whispers. Perhaps not odd after all, simply a necessity; with everyone using merely a normal voice a place this crowded would be noisy as a boiler factory. An arrangement of visual signals, white and red lights on the wall, was blinking in unaccountable urgent rhythm. A stocky older man rushed past him with legs in churning stride. David waited behind a family seeking tickets for a visit to the House galleries.

"Yes?" The receptionist raised her eyebrows. It was late in the day and her depleted ration of greetings had little left of welcome for a stranger with an accent not of her parts of the West. David gave his name. "I believe Congressman Duke is expecting me." There was a blur of movement off to one side, the rasp of a chair being scraped in haste. "*Darned* right you are expected, Mr. Morgan." David shook the hand of a young man with a narrow, classically handsome face. He was wearing a three-piece dark suit, conservatively elegant. "Allan Marks. Military affairs specialist." He smiled deferentially, an almost sweet smile. "Mr. Duke was called to the House floor. Just a small fire drill." He motioned towards a corner where David assumed that they were going to sit. There were no chairs though, only a bit of space by a window, with a sill where rears could scrunch.

"Okay my friend." Again the disarming smile. "So what have you got for the Old Man?" Surprisingly, although it was old ground, as David got going his excitement was rising. It was all moving through his mind again with a fine flow, effect and cause linked in an unbroken chain. He was sure that he had never told it better, the dreams, the follies, the deceits, across the years.... Yet years too not without fine moments; even in the offices of EAR, a repository of world-class acousticians, give it that at least, passions flaring like loves. He wanted to get that across too. It was starting to hit him what maybe he had the chance to do. Because, hey David Morgan, *you're here!* "*You see,*" coming to the crux of this thing and having to catch his breath, *"It goes way back to the SQS-26, right on down to DIANA, each successive sonar, the heir, so to speak, of all the flaws of its predecessor, failure of concept a common thread, the inescapable consequences of Snell's Law...."*

"Whoa. But all *right!*" Allan Mark's eyes shone. "No, man, *don't* stop. Like your style." Perhaps appraising the quality of David's convictions by measures of effectiveness detached from the content that inspired it.

"Afraid I really am... steamed." Embarrassed. Not the place, he suspected, to put your heart upon your sleeve. Looking out at the lifeless sky, his gaze dipped to the broad expanse of the winter-yellowed grasses upon the Mall. A gaze that followed openness westward towards the burnt-blood gothic spires of the old Smithsonian, strange and full of grace. Nothing sinister in those crenellated towers; it took perfervid romantic imagination to read in them the least menace. Only a folksy fake of a fortress that spoke hearteningly of man's quests, his pride and decent curiosity. Contrarily, it was the other government buildings in view, the countless new ones, bare of history, in the very blandness of all those massings of grey concrete, where mistrust might lodge.

"Hey now. Don't worry," Allan counseled, 'steamed' is good. Really *neat.*"

David realized that Allan Mark's self-control was misleading. His hands were in restless motion, gestures of vaguely shepherding invisible people along by the elbow. "Anyway, you'll be passing all this on to the Boss. *Okay?"* A silence extended itself until David asked which particular areas of naval affairs Allan had made his specialty

The question seemed to puzzle. Then that likeable smile returned in full radiance. "Cover the waterfront. Army, Navy, Air Force, you name it. Whole ball of wax. We'd like another staffer to share the load but"—he spread his arms helplessly—"money won't allow. Heck, have to handle Fish and Wildlife too. Mr. Duke, happening to have a fine rainbow stream running through his ranch back there, keeps me humping. Seeing that nothing happens to God's little fishies. I can see you thinking I've a lot of ground to cover."

"It perhaps strikes you the same way."

Allan Marks coughed politely. "I confess, I do have to be pretty much 'big picture.'"

At the front door a group entered noisily, seeming to burst through all at once. A smallish figure—the same energetic man David had seen leave earlier—detached himself from a clotting of these around him and disappeared. "Our leader returneth." Allan Marks sounded relieved. David expected some further sequence of events, a formal journeying upward through some hierarchy of advisors and assistants before actually meeting the Congressman himself. He had pictured too their getting together as more of a general conference, joined by numbers of other intent young staffers writing furiously into their notebooks, *getting it all down.* Yet almost before he realized it, he was in the Congressman's office where, after a granite handshake of introduction, the door was shut on just the two of them. The Congressman moved about detachedly, performing small acts of domestic ordering. "Excuse me, young fellow. Got to poke up the fire. This old stone holds in the chill."

The room was large, dark, paneled, set with leather furniture capable of outlasting a succession of incumbents. Soft lamps and the flickering fire made it warmish. Abner Duke opened a cabinet door. "Care for a snort?"

"No thank you." Rethinking that insipid reply. "Yes, please. I think I will." "Attaboy. It's the hour." Up to this moment, David had felt himself to be merely a presence, even a distraction, one more individual amongst many in the stream of faces that the Congressman met each day. People to be "handled", not allowed to take up more than brief apportioned minutes of his valuable time. But as the Congressman hoisted his glass, his gaze rested upon his visitor with amiable concentration. "Cheers." David echoed the toast. Lots of ice promised eventual dilution of a burning slug of bourbon. Abner Duke shut his eyes. Firelight deepened the crevices in the Congressman's face, made him look even older. "Listen." Something tickling him. "Hear it?" David strained his ears, confessed that he did not.

"You got it. Nothing. Outside the bees buzz and go bump up against that door. Built it thick, those old builders." He took another long depleting sip "Good, this. We can love it too much and for a long time it's great and then it can rear up and bite. Did it to my sister after her husband's death. But that's neither here nor there. This is my sanctum. Anyway, getting on. We may not have long. That durned light will start blinking and I'll have to hightail it back to the floor." He cleared his throat, a gravelly one. "Just want you to realize that maybe the little time I can give you is not a measure of the importance I attach to this matter." He leaned forward, poked David's knee. "Okay. Make me a speech."

David had not gone on more than a few minutes when Abner Duke waved him to a stop. "You're losing me. Going to lose those others on the committee even quicker." He paused. "But maybe that's okay. Make us strain to comprehend. Hell, this is the sub-committee that's actually supposed to know this stuff. Our fault that we're too busy with useless shit to learn what we ought. We had a congressman . . . well, no matter his name, from San Diego, who was the big Godhead of the whole ASW subcommittee. He went to Pearl Harbor, spent a week out there in the Islands with his doxie, wasting the time of Admiral Tommy Blue with briefings and actually asked at the end of it all, now just *what* was doing the detecting of the submarines . . . was it *sound*? He actually asked *that*. Shameful even by our standards. Christ, I at least knew that. Still, what the hell do I know about naval matters? My service was infantry. Just a scared teenage grunt hoofing it all the way from St. Lo to the Vosges Mountains with a rifle on my shoulder."

He took another swallow. "This, my chance. I've fought those guys in the Pentagon on a dozen programs, and they've beaten me down to parade rest on every one. Every budget year they troop up to the Hill with their flipcharts and vu-graphs and weave a cloud of smoke with their special vocabularies. By the time they're through they've persuaded the majority that all those missiles of ours that fizzle, all the black boxes that go haywire, can still be fixed. Worse, if you don't give them the money to get on with fixing that junk, they try to frighten you into believing that the Russkis will be camping soon on the Capitol steps. Well, maybe we will have to fight them some day, even if Communism is supposedly crumbling. They're still Russians. Probably in '45' we should have kept going right on to Moscow, just like Patton wanted. I'm no candy-ass and I could . . . but hell's bells, you didn't come here for war stories. The point is, I've been waiting a long time for a case against some system that is so overwhelmingly strong that it can't miss. One that'll send those bright young guys and their lying incompetent admirals reeling back across the Potomac with their giant fumble and force them to get the job done right. In daydreams I catch them in a whopper so big they can't wriggle out. Some plane, maybe, they're bragging about that can't even get up in the air; just sits there at the end of the runway, flopping like an old goose with too much lead in its ass. Maybe now at last . . . ." He stopped. There might have been almost a pleading light in his eyes, but likely only the fire's reflection. He said softly: "You understand . . . ?"

He seemed to consider something else before going on. "Anyway, Ab Duke has made a lot of noise in his time, hollering wolf, gotten people tired of him. But gradually a lot of guys, people you'd never imagine, some with real brains, who went to the kind of schools that I never saw the inside of, are listening. Conservatives, with solid credentials in support of Defense. Thinking, maybe the old maverick isn't so loco on this one after all. "Yep," he nodded enjoyably. "Though it's taken a bit of luck, that article about Wolf Lake and all . . . . Anyway, a by-God certified loser in hand at last. Or *winner*, depending on your view." There was a lot of small boy in his pleased expression.

"You do have a winner, believe me." David said. Boldness, even a fervent combativeness, had grown from one fiery glass. Abner Duke grinned confidentially. "Been counting votes. In committee, on the floor. It's *close*, but to the undecided I say only, *hold on*, stay on the fence if you please, but wait until you hear what I've got. They're curious. *What's Ab got up his sleeve?* Not talking about Sea Eagle's hard-core support, of course, not the guys from shipbuilding states. They don't give a rat's ass if I prove, all the angels on my side, that their baby will duck right under and go straight to the bottom soon as it slides off the building ways. Navy League types. Never saw a Navy ship so lousy they didn't love it. This time I don't need them. I should be at least five votes to the good to kill it. So. You're an *important* guy, Mr. Morgan." David suddenly did not feel as secure about himself as he wished. "Is there anything special I should be preparing myself for?"

"I sure hope not." Ab Duke chuckled. "Late to be doing any boning up. Just be ready for nasty stuff. Hard balls thrown right at your head. They'll go after every piece of you. Hope you're clean. Nothing going on with some cutie pie secretary itching to tell all. No tax trouble with the IRS. I've quietly billed your testimony as the biggest thing since Buffalo Bill's Circus, said you're the expert on DIANA, Sea Eagle; more, the *Historian* of the whole shmear. Mr. Facts." The warm fire flickering on David's face felt as if it added to his flush of embarrassment. "I feel it's only fair to let you know that you could be overstating my qualifications. On some facets, I may not be the expert you are heralding—"

Abner Duke waved such modesty away good-humouredly. "This town, read two pieces of paper on the same subject, you're an expert. Just tell it straight."

"Yes." Wondering, as Washington made you wonder, how he would regard Abner Duke in a week, a month . . . a year from now. Things had happened too often before, altering first impressions radically, for David to trust his uncritical instincts. History too much in his veins. This City—just as the miasma of old steel towns did it to the flowers, blackening the trees—made an ambience in which heroes shriveled fast. An aching wish that it wasn't so. Not with this man. The Congressman's voice, nothing of reverie in it, woke him from his own. "While I've got you, clear up something for me. This dad-blamed word 'sonar'. One kind, as I get it, *listens*. The sub's got to make some noise to let you find him. That's . . . ."

"Passive sonar." "The other kind sends out pings—that what you call them?—then cocks its ear for the echo and figures out how far away the sub is. That's—?"

"An active sonar." "And that's DIANA?" Abner Duke rubbed his chin. "But apparently that mother couldn't find a submarine if the two of them were locked in the same barn?"

"Well, I wouldn't put it quite that way, Congressman."

Ab Duke roared, slapped his knee. "Of course, *you* wouldn't." David noticed that Abner Duke was wearing boots with his standard business suit. His crossed legs and hiked trousers revealed an expanse of old leather with the sense of some pleasant worn and subtle design. Poignantly, David thought of Billy and his foolish boots; shiny pieces of borrowed life. The whiskey, the fire, the relaxed kind of feeling that everything was set, that there was nothing much more even to talk about were working on him pleasantly. The Congressman's voice, cutting through a mix of thoughts far afield, startled him. "Sizing me up?"

"Oh no. Not that at all," replying with the swiftness of untruth.

"Why not?" Abner Duke said affably. "I size up lots of people every day. Get it wrong lots too. Take a crack at what makes me tick."

"Hatred of government?" Surprising himself at what liquor had him saying.

The older man shook his head and David knew that he had chosen poorly. At once too big a word, and too mean. "No, no. You're on track though." He glanced down at his hands for a moment. "But don't go spreading that one around. My Big Sky constituents are hooked on federal handouts, just like people everywhere else crave its goodies. Wouldn't understand. Even though Madison and some of those other early guys saw very well that there could be other tyrants than kings." Warmly, perfectly, the Congressman quoted several apt paragraphs from that great mind of long ago. "Surprise you? Sure it does. But what about yourself, young fellow?" David had been thinking ahead to that one. "Maybe I'd just like to see the Navy have ships better able to do the job." He was still lingering over the general unsatisfactoriness of that, considering adding something but not knowing what, when there was a knock on the door.

"Fair enough. Maybe, young fellow, together we can make it happen." The Congressman stood up, took David's hand in his own stubby strong one. "Counting on you." He paused with an afterthought. "I can't reward you. Can't even protect you. I'm not big enough in this town. The wolves will be baying. But you know all this."

"Yes." How much really did he know though, he wondered. Abner Duke's smile was tender, sad. "Not that they'll fire you. Not in Civil Service. You'd have to cut the balls off the American Eagle, pee on the Great Seal in the Oval Office. Still, you won't get off Scot free. Though I gather from Allan you're stuck in some Siberia already." He paused, shaking off another insistent knock. "But once in a while, a man has to . . . ."

"Excuse me, sir. It's a detail, but—"

"*What?*" Sharply. The door had opened and members of his staff were massed.

"I just want to know whether I should show up here first. Or go straight to the Committee room?" Ab Duke's patience returned, accompanied by amusement. "Don't bother being early. These circuses always get underway late. Al Marks will recognize you outside the Committee room and slip you in quietly. Does that well. Best not to arrive with a brass band. *Adios.* Take care now crossing streets." Staff personnel, they of the young anxious faces, were swarming. Shunted aside, David watched the scene detachedly for a moment, saying to himself, I guess that's that. He had almost reached the far end of the long corridor when a breathless Al Marks caught up with him. "Almost forgot." David's fingers appraised the heft of a white envelope pressed into his hand. "Subpoena. Just a formality."

Al Marks remembered something else. "Here's the receipt that goes with it. This little piece of paper has to be signed."

"Verifying that I've received it, right?" David doped out. Funny how that stung. "Actually," Al Marks explained, "it's only a *consent* subpoena. Just a bit of legal folderol. Say, hope you don't mind." David supposed that he really didn't greatly mind. All the same, a glow began to fade. He made his way out past the guards still inspecting the briefcases of those entering, The blue of early evening was all around. A few stars were already out, winking diamonds, remote and yet not untender. They too seemed not totally beyond reach, hanging not so far above man's buildings.

Feeling the cold, he pulled his coat closer about him and was aware, in the unnatural tug on his shoulders, of the subpoena envelope tucked in an inside pocket. It made him smile ruefully, thinking I'm a true Washingtonian. Reconfirmed by the realization that he was unlikely to look at the subpoena again; least of all seriously read it. Washington merely churned out its mountains of paper. Sensibly, and with self-mercy, its folk seldom chose to read it. He pictured a date and a place and a time typed in the blanks of some standard form. His own name too, and the signature of someone official. The rest of it would be thicknesses of "boilerplate", excerpts from laws, a recapitulation of the dire penalties that awaited failure to comply, masses of fine and useless words. Nothing sealed so well his kinship with the city, a reluctant but enduring partnership, than his confident neglect of the bulk stuffed there in his coat pocket. Ah well. Walked enough, getting tired. The Monument loomed up, illuminated whitely to its full height, glowing, too bright, gaudy. The floodlights were searingly strong, reflecting off the pale stone, making a glowing haze up there high, destroying the sky for a fair arc around, swallowing up the lovely stars, millions of light years of nebulae vanishing in its garishly blazing halo. Washington, the man—George, that is—deserved better. He too, like ordinary men, ought occasionally to be left to the peace of night, some benign inattention there in the shadows.

Time to be thinking about getting on home, catching a taxi to take him over to Crystal City where his car was parked. But still he held back, shortening his steps, not ready for the abrupt test of home. Al would want to know all—why not? faith and loyalty commanding no less—press him with questions. He pictured waiting for him a grander meal than usual, but in her eagerness likely prepared too soon, simmering away on burner tops, other portions growing dry in the oven. Al already judging nervously that he was *late*. The picture fond and natural.

It was not that he was unwilling to share the event. But there was too much there in it—behind it—it had gone on too long, piling up in him over the years, like cells aggregating until they had made a spirited and complex life of their own; a private life too, for all that it concerned something as public as the oceans and sound in the sea. But more than a private world, a lonely love. Not one all at once to be bared in some simple rush of convivial gaiety; not susceptible to conveying in a single flash of revelation. He had already pictured the committee hearing a dozen times over, imagined the questions, envisioned himself fielding all the hard bouncy ones banged at him. Hostile committee members would be primed by their staffs, loaded with additional ammunition furnished by the Navy itself. The shipbuilders thundering in full cannonade. The new Admiral at EAR and Tawney Grey would be doing their own bit; perhaps even now they had caught early signals of fresh menace and were scurrying about, calling in the TRW's and all the other toadying support contractors. Grand old personages, too, men with rows of ribbons blanketing their chests, would be dusted off and called in from afar. Even if not knowing shit from shinola about the matter. Whatever it took. *General Quarters!* Lights on late these nights in the offices of the Beltway Bandits to help them prepare. No easy thing to rewrite History in a hurry, though many have tried. David was sure though—in spite of all the efforts at obfuscation—that he would prevail. *Because he had the goods.* History, CORRIDA, all! In imagination he felt the camera lights, their sun-like glare. The thing to do, he told himself, was to be controlled, not to lose his temper no matter what the provocation. Keep in check too any of his wise-ass tendencies. Be calm, regal . . . yep, *regal.* Liking that, that beautiful word, and for a moment desire fastened on it as intensely as if it were a glittering jewel in a dream. Did not every man deep down wish *that,* saying only what was needed? To be like Ben Hogan, let one's sticks do the talking. Cool as Meade at Gettysburg. Well . . . . He shook his head at that highly unattainable picture of himself. Shaking it there in the darkness. No matter. *He had the goods.* He breathed in the exhaust-warmed air at the edge of Fourteenth Street. Were vacant cabs those with the light on or *off?* Hadn't caught one so long he had forgotten.

The cab was old, rattly. The seat covers, though plastic, were worn and supple, like leather that had aged well. They exhaled the stale and sour smells of years of human cargo. Yet a not unpleasant blend either, tobacco's acridness, cologne, the juices of the female, sweat, perfume . . . there was something relaxing in the awareness of that composite humanity, as he settled back against the rustling plastic. Even the subpoena envelope—and newly sensed stresses in his jacket due to his sitting down were causing it to jab him again gently, but with telling stiffness, in his armpit—now felt in a different way. Shed were its irritating aspects, the bureaucratic formalism, the demeaning lack of trust. Shrunk simply to reminder. Bringing associated notions how it must be that this ordinary taxicab, which had borne so many people to and fro, many of them—he could fairly guess, given the laws of chance; Gaussian distributions governing the complexity of human motion as surely too as only statistics could express the immense number of encounters of a low frequency sound wave with the molecules of water in its long travels through the sea—well known, famous, or the invisibly powerful, to appointments of urgency, loaning something of its busy history to enrich this trip of David Morgan's own, first leg of a journey which, for the next few days (and who could say how many more beyond?) were bound to be like no others in his life before. So, okay, then, maybe the famed heart surgeon come from Houston to testify that his fees were only proper when weighed against his nerve and skills; the scientist with his message (back in the Sixties) that the *orbital approach* was the only right way for the astronauts to end up safely landing on the moon; and hell yes, too, some shipbuilder hustling in to lobby for more subsidized ships . . . had not each of them sat in such a cab, looking out at rain or sun, spirits buoyed by the surpassing importance of their own convictions borne through these seas of traffic. To this city you brought your faith, your power, and what you had piled up in you over a lifetime you might expend here in an hour. No matter. For some buoyant trifle of time, a man might validly figure that he *counted*. Even as David Morgan, bound by similar intimations of destiny, was reaching for his own waving threads of power blowing loose in these vagrant and wild capitol winds.

The cab driver slammed on his brakes as a car swerved in front of him, a tearing of fenders missing by inches. The driver, black haired, smallish and by the evidence of the multisyllabic name printed on his cabbing license and his photograph, both items of identification encased in grimy plastic, from the Asian subcontinent—another probable spawn of some U.S. defeat or betrayal— spat out an oath in his native language. Then adding seeming translation. *"Foohking bass-tard."* Already well up on the ways of his adopted land.

"Take it easy. In no hurry." Calmly spaketh the man of destiny.

Reaching home he found his love even more excited than foreseen. There had been an announcement on the early news: From the office of Congressman Abner Duke the promise of a witness whose expert testimony was going to" . . . blow the Navy's ill-conceived Sea Eagle class frigate right out of the water." She served him his late and solitary supper hoveringly. Over dessert, having saved her own to share with him, her eyes glistened in the light of candles specially lit. "This is your . . . big chance then. Sort of a *dream*, isn't it?" Her hand went across the table to his. "Your chance to . . . *enlighten* them."

"Sweetheart, it's my chance," his laugh harsh, "to stick it to them."

She drew back shocked. "I've never heard you talk that way before." Which wasn't true, of course. In the heat and the height of passion he had said coarser things, chanted all the short blunt words, she cheering him on. But those didn't count, that was different, back then in the jungle Eden of yore where anything goes.

"I guess," he said, "you've never seen me feeling this way." But the realization that he had spoken in a way not worthy of him hung on. "I think I've found a sort of remarkable man in this Congressman Duke." He felt better saying that. "He could become one of my heroes."

"*A Congressman?*

"Too strong that, maybe. But a champion at least." "Oh darling," she said, her spirits bouncing back, "I do like hero better. But champion will do."

"We shall see," he said, more cautiously He had the fear that she was equating fleeting notoriety with prosperity. Yet at the moment he had no wish to dwell either upon the drab hues of that continuing sullen and featureless landscape that was bound to be their lasting future. Beth's King soon to be history. Professionally, no more the gulls' cry, the fascination of the depths, not again fine whiffs of the sea. Not on the government's nickel, for sure, and to it he was hooked for practical purposes, forever. Lashed to a great loggy spar going nowhere. But now back to Al again. Always Al. But then suddenly in a flash of vision, like lightning baring bones, it seemed that he had seen something surprising, glimpsed in her strengths that could survive, beyond charms that might not. *Al, Al, Al* . . . .

Tonight so keyed up that paradoxically her excitement foreclosed upon a slew of questions she might have asked. Early broadcasts referred to David only as a "mystery witness" but, by the time of the late news—to which she stayed glued for every nuance and tidbit—there was more on the story, with the actual date furnished only a few days off, when his testimony was to be given. By midnight, with its further surfeit of news for insomniacs, David had been identified as formerly associated with the ". . . Navy's super-secret office of experimental acoustic research." This she poured out as she plopped into bed beside him, abandoning all usual pretense of gentle moves towards her pillow in respect of his sleep. "How about *that*? Let me give my 'mystery witness' a kiss." He felt her blood pumping, hot springs of her youngness still.

"Well, yes, how about that?" Mystery witness inclined towards excitement of another kind. But she was too fired up and more of her delayed questions bombarded in earnest, *rat-tat-tat*. What suit was he going to be wearing to the hearing? Better be his *best*—maybe she'd go out and buy him a *new* one—and so on and so on and there was no bridge from her celebratory mood to his own.

▲▲▲▲▲

All this month, and never so acutely as today, Donnie Webster had been in a bad state. It was all coming together—or, still metaphorically, falling apart—the once redeeming hopes of Campaign, the crucial re-election strategy, inseparable from the well-being of that most important of the shipbuilding states. The Duke Investigations, so called, had been a running sideshow for weeks, titillating and outraging Washington by turns, embarrassing mighty organizations and important people near and far. But up to this point Donnie had not felt the cruelest cuts of their wind. By God, they were coming now. Sure as he had known as a small boy that special roaring across steamy fields of cotton and peanuts and his Daddy's teaching, soon as he could toddle, how to whip open the storm cellar doors and hunker inside just ahead of the tornado. This was no tornado, of course, merely some shitbird Congressman from a giant half ass western state of useless trees and cows. More cows than voters. But the aggravating thing was that, unlike the case of the dark destructive funnel about to touch down, Donnie had not the least idea how to react. Even as doom was approaching in slow motion, he could only watch the days dwindle away in a kind of frozen trance of depression. Vacantly he gazed at his little ship models whose names, so arduously learned, he had mostly forgotten. They mocked an idle fleet motionless as he. And *oh yeah*, there was another thing.

Competence was in the air, an issue raising its leering head. Now, of course, the conscientiousness of a hundred Alvin Bofflers, peddling their own brand of Public Good, Donnie could weather easily as a turtle the pelting of rain. But what was one to make of rumors that the President himself was displeased at the performance of his staff. Learned columnists were nodding their wise heads together over rediscovered Truth: As Presidents painfully had to keep relearning from Grant to Truman to . . . whoever, you couldn't run a country relying on your pals from the folksy days of county elections. Not very well, that for sure.

It would have been better, for Donnie's outlook, if he had been able to see the President more often. Lately though those necessary Presidential contacts for the more insecure, a habit that requires a daily fix, even a mere nod sufficing— were too few. There was nothing that Donnie could put his finger on; much indeed was ascribable simply to the President's more frequent foreign trips, the tonic of bands and uniforms in distant welcomes as opposed to the loveless seasons that had set in for him at home. But that did not change the fact. *Donnie could no longer be sure what The Man was thinking.* It was in this state of brooding frustration that Sara Jane, a comparatively rare visitor these days, found her afflicted colleague anxious to unburden his heart. To which outpouring she listened loyally. Indeed, with such sober attentiveness that Donnie could not bear her unnerving silence indefinitely. "Sara Jane. Stop looking at me like that. I know doggoned well just what you're thinking." *That*, Sara Jane had an instant's reflection, she doubted. "Donnie, I'm sorry that I'm bothering you. Truly. I'm only trying to help." A groan, followed by a diminuendo of muttering, issued from Donnie's lips until it shrank to a level suitable for interruption. "Donnie. Get off it. Now, back to this mystery witness who is supposedly about to blow the whistle on your little ship."

"*Ships*, Sara Jane, *ships*. A whole fucking class of them. Not a whistle either. A great big horn."

"Stop acting so weary. You can't be licked yet. It strikes me that everything may come down to this witness for Congressman Duke. Can't you set your little spies to poking around to find out who—" Donnie's mournfully shaking head stopped her, "He's no *mystery*, Sara Jane. That's all media B.S. Don't you watch the news, dang it, girl? He's just one more yo-yo in this town dreaming of a chance to spill his guts."

On Donnie's desk lay one of those broad pads of white paper, a virtual acreage of it for a busy man, suitable for all kinds of hasty jottings. Sara Jane was noticing as well how the bareness of Donnie's desk confirmed his lament on the diminishing level of activity flowing across it. She was struck by the near blankness of the top sheet of his desk pad, which, in happier times would, in addition to the usual coffee stains, bear dozens of scrawled names and cryptic notations. To Donnie, however, Sara Jane seemed to be staring at something upon its otherwise almost pristine surface that had to be obvious. Bold, in the red letters of a Magic Marker, was a name in Donnie's inimitable hand followed by an exclamation point. "Yep. That's him, baby," Donnie said with a sickly grin. "Him?" An annoyed Sara Jane. *"Who him?"*

"Right there. What I thought you were looking at. Big as life. Ab Duke's effing witness." "Sara Jane was indeed now focusing intently. "Actually Donnie, I believe you know him, or *of* him," she said quietly.

"Not from Adam, baby. This guy's from nowhere."

Sara Jane's expression was that disconcerting one, where she appeared to be staring but, actually was focussing with great concentration. Murmuring... "there's a connection...." At last, *remembering....* "Someone trying to finagle him a job here in the West Wing... that old Admiral...." She went on softly as if in a trance. "Something about a Corridor...." Donnie's jaw dropped. "Quick." Sara Jane's voice quick. "Get your file."

Donnie bounded over to a cabinet, pulling open two drawers at a time. Yanking out bulky overflowing folders right and left. *"Yessiree."* Lugging over an armful and letting them thud down on his desk in a loosening pile and, starting to go through their sprawl, both hands flying. "Well, anyway, Donnie. *So.* If the guy actually wants... and...." She did not care to finish. Did not have to. Knowing too well what was to happen next. The ruthless putting of two and two together. Even as she could concede the occasional necessity of it in practice, detesting such with every fiber of her being. This way of business, this immense dark side of the ceaseless to and fro of government that, once you saw it over and over, *was* government. "So...."

"Say no more, my Sara Jane," grinned an ebullient Donnie. In a minute he had found what he was looking for, made a phone call. In another minute he had departed, trotting off somewhere. Returning still trotting. Grinning unstoppably. Charged up. In his element. "Like I say, baby, I *got* it." A bit later Sara Jane wasn't sure that Donnie even noticed when she left his office. Or had not already forgotten that discovery was not entirely his own.

* * *

The television was full of news of David. This evening's man of the hour. The Mystery Witness stripped of his anonymity. "Such a hullabaloo," said Tessa.

"The very word, my dear."

Tessa contemplated her TV's swiftly changing sequence of submarines diving, destroyers dashing about. Standard footage, but ever appealing. "It's funny. I don't think we used to think about submarines all that much. I don't recall Irish ever fretting about them."

Muddy tapped his chin thoughtfully. Yet in truth not trying very hard, choosing the mere simulation of recall. He was a bit low. The Corridor had never seemed so far from attainment. Last he had checked, the White House people were still studying the matter. *Studying?* How long could one possibly study anything so simple? Nor were even his Navy pals doing much. Full of the same old soft soap, but obviously having other fish to fry. In contrast to Muddy's shadowed spirits, Tessa's were aglow. Supper tonight was on trays across their laps, while she stayed glued to the TV. Why . . . *her* David. "Goodness. Seems he's going to stand them all on their ears." Muddy sighed. Kolombongara, its distinctive shape and jungled slopes, loomed wistfully in his imagination with the same vividness that it had first struck him long ago. Then as happens with tropic islands its haunting green was swallowed up in a gray rain cloud. "Daresay," Muddy murmured gloomily, "his business, after all . . . ."

"Well," Tessa took another excited sip of her wine. Not knowing what to make of it all. Except, lurking at the edges of her heart, making tugs at it like a nibbling fish, were feelings suspiciously like maternal pride. Perhaps after a long dry spell, her youngest was at last getting *somewhere*. The phone rang, a passingly rare sound in their lives. Yet Tessa hopped to its summons with all the vague and undeparted hopes of old. "*What* . . . ." Unable at first to make out a word of what some rapidly talking young man was saying.

"It's for you, Muddy, dear." She did not add her belief that she had heard, through the rush of the speaker's breath, the magical words "White House." No point in getting her man prematurely worked up. With those poor old ears of hers, she could also be quite mistaken.

▲ ▲ ▲ ▲ ▲

Coming to be a strange sort of day. Sensed from the beginning, when David Morgan went jogging. Before dawn he saw low grey clouds scudding towards the City. Out of the west thunderstorms, giants grinding their teeth. Soon they would be blowing down trees, putting limbs over power lines, flooding roads, violently registering just disapproval. But it would be all too brief—like everything else it would not stay—and Washington would pick itself up and shake off all that water like an old dog and resume its ways.

There was a real question whether he would make it home before the black clouds got him. Already a few drops had fallen, big, wet, warm, splattering ones. Raising steam on the sidewalks. A weird roiling day for late March. Two opposite seasons in collision, spring trying to shoulder winter aside too soon. His had to be a shorter route, therefore, not the bicycle path but through the neighborhood.

And because it was a residential area, he must definitely keep jogging. A walker these days, whatever the innocence of his intent, in the territory of young children was always suspect. Thus keeping hard at it, the plop of his athletic shoes reverberating lightly off aluminum-sided homes, stirring up the dogs he passed. He knew them by their barks, a restlessness behind the pale fronts of these homes for which they sounded their protest against the footfalls of the unseen stranger. Barks of alarm were mixed with whines of hysteria, distorted bits of humanness absorbed from these families of two-legged creatures, the ankles and knees they lived among. They could not see the storm, only feel its electricity. Long ago, before man, their ancestors had felt the earth tremble on the steppes, sniffed the terror of prairie fires racing on the rising wind. One dog in a house had an acutely threatening bark. Obviously a big fellow, the bark boomed from deep in its throat, reverberant with the naked wish to sink its teeth into the unseen interloper, vocal cords twisting with the strain of that wish. He pictured it springing through the wallboard, the wallpaper, the decorative paneling, the flimsy tissue of the modern tract house. An image spurring him on towards home and to the welcome sight of the morning paper, every Washington man's semi-precious jewel—to be taken along with the first cup of coffee—waiting for him in his front walk. Droplets of water gleamed on its protective sheathing of plastic. Confirmation of its preciousness.

The nervous quality of the weather was reflected in the headlines. A twister had cut through the heart of a town in Oklahoma, killing six persons and leveling the business section. A photograph showed the tornado's path through the town, neatly cut and as severe as if a prodigious grinding wheel had pressed down upon the earth and chewed its way straight across this unlucky spot of civilization, in seconds reducing it to flattened rubble. Virginia's and Maryland's turn today, so the weather warnings told. Such predictions, rendered in somber tones, accompanied him on the car radio on the way to work, sustaining an appealing sense of wild weather, a titanic force—never felt so outrageously as in Washington, D.C.—beyond the control of government. A demented mood in himself, as well as in the weather, was reinforced by the heat within the offices at National Center. Weeks before air-conditioning was formally due to be turned on, let alone heat scheduled to be turned *off,* but governmental inflexibility was such— beyond the massed power of all official action to alter—that office workers must be subjected to a baking flow of circulating air, even while clouds of swirling grey mist outside were warm as soup. The effect was suffocating. Light-headed, David could not concentrate on a single page of printed matter. Hailstones smote the glass, the world went white, and for several minutes he was watching the hard popcorn of ice pelt away with harmless fury. On such a day it seemed not the least odd that one of his co-workers in the office, Albertson—young, but whose eyes had already caught a fatal lustrelessness—wandered over with word of the phone calls that had come in for David earlier this morning. "One around seven-thirty, 'nother about eight. Maybe the same guy. Sounded kinda old. It was before the secretaries arrived . . . ." Going on with unneeded explanation, as if ashamed for his earliness.

"I see."

"Well, who do you think it was, uh?" A disappointed Albertson because David was not showing more interest. *Two* calls that early were an excursion beyond Supportability's norm. Mystery redoubled. Big doings seemingly afoot, and doggone it, here was the principal actor not cooperating. At first, only a few days before, when rumors began to sweep through about the possibility of his testifying, David had felt himself avoided, leprous, virtually shunned by his fellow workers. Such feelings seemed to have worn off as it became apparent that occasional contact with one David Morgan (GS-13) was causing no one suddenly to bleed or to shrivel. Common sense reasserting itself. Few in Supportability could sustain serious belief that one of those hypothetical mighty arms of The System was going to strain to punish anyone dumped here whatever his transgression.

Right now though curiosity was coming to a flood over one David Morgan's presence in this corner of government where diversion was scant. As close to Celebrity as his fellows would ever know. A number of them, tipped off by Albertson about the calls, and already having speculated amongst themselves, drifted over to his desk (Supportability, with the starvation of its funds, did not offer even the privacy of office dividers to inhibit such approaches). Not an army of them, indeed mostly singly, sidling up with that tentativeness that marked them. An amiable bunch too, wry without being bitter. With the kind of wit that flourishes in the ranks of the defeated. Yet there was shyness too, guilt for not having troubled themselves to know their colleague better, having taken for granted the outsized misdemeanors that had plopped David Morgan into Supportability, without bothering to learn the specifics. They hung back still, their questions more circuitous than penetrating. "What'cha suppose it all means, eh?" Collins, a shrewd older man with hatred sometimes, whisky always, on his breath. Yet with a quirkily fierce loyalty too towards his fellow damned. "The Press getting wind? Someone trying to stop you maybe?" This was Albertson again, a softer fellow. Yet eyes for one rare moment shining. "What about Jack Anderson? Someone tip him off?" The face beamed too with an expectancy that matched those eyes. For a moment eagerness consuming. Up here rumor was preferred, more fun than facts any day. "Oh, I don't know," David said to a loose ring of curious faces, passing a look over each one honestly. Owing them that. There was shyness on his part too, a genuineness that these other members of Supportability, belatedly becoming known to him, appreciated. They had more than a normal taste for honesty, with mirthful deprecation, self and otherwise, being the much-handled currency of this place. Experts at it. Nay, connoisseurs. "Truly, I doubt it will be anything big."

They nodded. Filters sensitive for the right tones. Supportability was an unbroken wasteland of humiliation and they knew every stone in its demoralized territory. Knew also to mistrust everything, including their own excitement. After the *thunder*—did not the old saying have it right?—*don't always come the rain*. "So let's . . . just see," David concluded lamely. They liked even the lameness. In the end they drifted away, the thing incomplete. It was not merely that David was still comparatively new in Supportability—his several years here, and some months to boot, nothing compared to the lifetime sentences the others had drawn—nor that none of them had taken the trouble to absorb him into their clannish group. In some deeper way, it was as if he still did not belong. There was an unsettledness to his circumstances. It was not necessarily that they sensed that he was fated to rebound to some former state of responsibility and esteem. Clearly, their hungry looks—more curious than pitying (and there was something of the vulture in Supportability's crew too, unhealthily savoring the disasters of human ambition)—betrayed imaginings of one David Morgan sinking still further. Yet even if they could not picture what might lie below Supportability in the sloughs of Defense, the point was that David Morgan gave the impression of being still in transit, of destinations unreached. The fact that he seemed to have motion, however slight—blurred his image. Worse things might yet befall him, but the very shadow of such possibilities set him apart. For nothing was ever going to happen to the rest of them or to Mother Supportability again. Congress, which, in some forgotten fitfulness of passion had conceived its bastard offspring, long since ceased to acknowledge parentage.

Thus they returned to their newspapers and their and crossword puzzles and doodlings over their minor stock market speculations. David himself started reading, although knowing somehow he was not going to get far. Bare minutes later one of the secretaries, the toothy girl Marge, and behind her Albertson again—he like some damp leaf too swirled up by the storm—arrived at his desk in ludicrous tandem with word of yet another phone call. "It's an *Admiral?*" said Marge. "Snowdon you figure?" The name plucked from air, but Albertson was glowing once more. Such a *day*. "Who knows?" David waited, disappointing them again, until delayed instincts of politeness forced them to move back. He picked up the receiver, unsurprised at finding Admiral Waters on the other end. A Muddy though whose voice was altered, faint; these wild winds seemed to have blown away a portion of his tonal scale, stripping off all bark of authority. An old man's voice, querulous, echoing down deserted corridors, across once windy bridges of warships long in mothballs or palmed off on the Turks or melted down to razor blades.

"*Irish* . . . is that you, *Irish*? Speak up, old shipmate."

"No sir, this is David. Irish's son."

"*David*. Forgive me, my boy. Something in your voice played a trick." It seemed in keeping too, this day when nature was making off with comfort, sense, life itself in some regions, that the old man should confuse son and father. To be expected also that the old man was giving a long and not very coherent account of the visit he had just made to the White House. Seeming to be about the Corridor, (what else?) David, if listening sympathetically, was also—forgivably, having heard so much of this before—only partially attentive. Thinking vaguely of shining worlds beyond Supportability, or perhaps merely wishing for somehing better than this plastic pressed into his ear. Then Muddy said something, a phrase out of his norm, and inescapably David found little hairs standing up on the back of his neck. But poor Muddy knew no more how to answer David's questions, all at once tautly focused, than he truly understood just what had transpired on his visit. For which he had only helpless apology. "David, coming right down to it, I can't say with any confidence exactly what the young man was telling me. Rattling on too fast for these old ears to catch it all."

"That's all right, sir."

"Those fellows . . . speak a different language too from the one in which I was brought up." The pause that followed was not of David's making—in the bureaucratic world, in which David's tactics were honed, all would agree it remained the other fellow's move—but he felt still he ought to dispel this silence whose lengthening was like a small cruelty. "Admiral, I may or may not have the picture. Except I gather that it was important for you to call me."

An old man's recollection was struggling at the other end of the line. "Let me repeat it exactly David—'*it might be a good idea.*' His very words." David detected a sigh. "You would think that he could say straight out instead of this '*might*' business. Should not someone making a recommendation have some conviction as to whether or not it's a good idea? Mealy-mouthed. But I'm doing poorly at conveying the flavor of this . . . encounter. Bear in mind that this young fellow was very excited. At the same time, he was roundabout; he spoke in parables. Like Christ is supposed to have spoken. Not quite to the point. Though he doesn't make me think of Christ otherwise. Indeed, my word—his name, by the way, is Webster—sounded one jump ahead of a fit. What gets into people in this city, David?" There was another silence, which only the Admiral could break. David sensed imperfect recollection still valiantly striving. "Now here's a clue, David. This young man kept repeating that you were 'a key' to it. Don't ask me what 'it' is. Or '*the key*'."

"Key?" David repeated absently and Muddy's frustration turned testy. "A *key*. Such as for a door, David. I'm simply passing it on." "Sorry. My thoughts wandered."

"No, David. Apology must be mine. I had no right to bark at you."

"Anyway. You got the impression I should call this Webster?"

"I can't say." Muddy said unhappily. "Or he might well call you. I was hoping," the old Admiral's voice seemed to thicken with wistfulness, "that you might have an idea."

For a moment his consuming yearning for his Corridor seemed to tremble amongst the Admiral's words. To his credit he conveyed no hint of it. The pride of the man. "I see," David said. "Well, I've taken up enough of your busy day. Time for your mother and I to be heading out for our walk."

"Not much of a day for a walk, I'm afraid."

Of the intricacies of Washington's politics, the sourness and silliness of its human maneuverings, their viciousness too, Muddy Waters undeniably had lamentable lack of understanding. But concerning his city's streets and weather—what a man must do to conquer these—his grasp was rock firm. "I guarantee you won't get many walks if you sit around waiting for a good day. Anyway, good-bye my boy, and bless."

So, gazing out the window once more. A harmless habit, and a restful one. But perhaps it wasn't so harmless after all. At the least, a waste of time. But then, didn't he have worlds to waste? Upon that thought, he turned guiltlessly to his regular reading habit. This week's novel was *Howard's End*. Ever more he found consolation with works of the past, those treasures that lie about in such profusion, all but forgotten, sparkling gems awaiting if one just bothers to take a stroll down those dimming and uncrowded paths that lead back into the interior of time. How strongly and gracefully Forster got his people moving in ordinary and yet wonderful ways! The Schlegel sisters were warm, sensitive, enchanting. The author had him smelling cut fields of hay baking under the summer sun. He hated to come to the end, why he put the book down though there were only a few pages to go. Greyness was still dominant but there were signs of clearing. The wind, earlier so fitful, was steadying from the north. Soon it would be blowing like fury and the temperature plummet. The Potomac would become an angry white-capped brown sea, coppery in the weak sun, and the Jefferson Memorial would gleam softly like a pearl, cleansed, under those emerging pale skies. Though changing, the day's strangeness did not depart. So it was again, quite in tune, when Linda Lou, one of the new clerk-typists came hurrying to tell him the White House was on the phone. He looked down at his wide phone keyboard, many lines capable of being displayed and yet only one—never more in these offices of Supportability—actually blinking its orange light. The young woman, still in her teens, black and hired some months back during the latest cycle of renascent social uplift, was merry, not yet infected with the soul weariness of the place. But her street sense of humor had not the subtlety to read the deadpan look that the nice but odd Mr. Morgan offered to her own lively and expectant one. "The White House? How can a *'house'* call? It would have to be a person wouldn't it?" Her jaw dropped, recovered. "*Course* it's a person. Jist don't know *who*. Won't say." She stared with instant sullen suspicion.

"Maybe then it's the President." Have some fun. Washington, as the wise knew, best not taken too seriously. A lesson come too late.

"It ain't the *President!* Hey, man, you're putting me on." The little circle of commotion around his desk was drawing them back. Ever curious, the people of this quiet backwater. Linda Lou grinning again. Brash. Knowing better herself, after so little time, than to take Washington seriously. First of all, it was a living. That much was serious. "You gonna pick that phone up?"

"Oh, I guess maybe I will," he conceded, at last, reaching for the phone with exaggerated casualness. But even Collins was impressed. Eyes narrowed, regarding this new, if still tarnished, planet now lately swum into his ken with fresh surmising. "Who do you figure, Davey?" Never Davey before. He shrugged. "Who knows?" Unable to repress a smile. He hoped it was not a sly one, not caring for himself sly. They moved away, out of courtesy and respect, as he pressed down the button with the twitchy light. Nestling his ear to the receiver, trying to picture what some character, bound to be named Webster, looked like.

* * *

The phone rang that night and it was Tessa. "David, dear, I suppose you know what is on my mind. I'm keeping my voice down because I don't want Muddy to hear. It seems all very complicated and I don't pretend to understand. Not even after reading the newspapers. And Muddy says very little. But I gather that you are, somehow, a part of this . . . David?"

"So I seem to be, anyway."

"You sound far away and forlorn. Muddy himself is down."

"I am truly sorry about that."

"I shouldn't be holding you. No doubt you have lots of studying for tomorrow."

"No studying is necessary. If I'm not prepared by now . . . ."

"No? Of course I'm not surprised that you have such a solid grasp of your subject. For all that it hasn't done much for you. My question is, is there anything you can do to help Muddy . . . in this matter that is so close to his heart? I'm speaking from ignorance, to be sure, and while not pleading well, I take it that if you just didn't *show up* . . . that might do the trick." She stopped cold at his laugh. "David! I see nothing humorous."

"Nothing at all Mother. But yes, I agree. That just might do the trick."

"David?" Timidly, "I'm not asking anything, am I, that Muddy himself—?"

"Mother. All the Admiral said was that he couldn't puzzle it all out. But he thought I ought to know."

"You gathered though that he still has . . . his hopes. So what did you tell him?"

"I listened. And thanked him. Always."

"I see." She said nothing for a moment. Then her voice sounded especially small, shrunk to a whisper, "Is this then, my son, one of those matters of . . . *principle?*"

"Perhaps. Though I wouldn't lay on it quite so grand a word."

"Oh dear, it *is*. I was afraid of that."

"I wish I could tell you something that might please you more."

"Your business isn't to please me." Her voice rallied. "Do what you believe you must do. Good night, dear son. And don't you be worrying about either of us old people."

▲▲▲▲▲

West Gate at two o'clock David had been told, repeating it to himself. *West*. Even as he was still wondering why he was showing up at all. He looked up at the sun to dope out West and so decided that it must be the gate towards the side of the White House next to that graceless and yet winning old grey structure of a thousand chimneys that had been built first as the Department of War and was now the Executive Office Building. He was early and to kill time he walked the length of Pennsylvania Avenue in front of Lafayette Park. Protesters were carrying placards and chanting. Then, because he might be taken for a protester himself, he chose to distance himself from them and to walk around the White House, taking the long curve on the side towards the Washington Monument with its wide spaces of grass and forgotten memorials. Here it was quiet, colder in the shadows. He realized then how far around it was to get back and that if he didn't hurry he was going to be late. He didn't run though. He settled for a rapid walk, glancing around to see if he was being noticed, followed. Still he was too conscious of the suspiciousness of his pace, seeming flight.

Out of the corner of his eye popped a horse's head, huge, startling, only yards away. The horse was coal black, black as the boots and uniform of the imposing Park Policeman on its back. He felt the policeman's eyes upon him, the horse's head turning too to keep looking as he passed—two great liquid, violet, depthless eyes—but nothing happened. Horse and the policeman remained a motionless team except for the horse's tail switching back and forth. His nerves drew still tighter as he moved up the Treasury Department side. He kept his eyes down; dissociating himself physically and spiritually from the protesters whose clottings had notably thickened in the mere ten minutes of his circuit. At the guardhouse adjacent to the West Gate he announced his business. Surprised at his voice, high, altered, strange. "I have an appointment with Mr. Webster."

The gatehouse was larger than he had first realized and was full of surveillance equipment, metal detectors, monitor scopes, boxes with rhythmical lights. Full of low noise too, guard chatter, hard and special laughter. He sensed he was being photographed, but could not guess how. The blue shirted guards were impersonal to the point of coldness. Fitter, less bellied men than the gunless bargain basement Rent-A-Cops of Crystal City. He listened to one guard calling over to the White House, a voice faint on the other end of the line. Moments later, an identifying badge attached to his coat lapel, he was walking across the lawn and through the tree shadows towards a door pointed out to him. Squirrels scampered, quick, quivering, busy at squirrels' lives. It was temptingly lovely, haunting, these hundred yards or so of grounds, but it was too short a traverse and too soon he was announcing himself to another guard, looking bored but alert, this one seated at a desk.

He had been waiting, under the guard's eye, for some minutes in a large but darkened anteroom. The furniture was handsome and the walls covered with paintings. Restless, he had to get up and move about. He examined the paintings and saw that they were originals. One he made out on closer inspection was by Winslow Homer. The fact brought added apprehension, a sense of the casual majesty of the place. Simultaneously he felt, here in the cool silence, the unpleasantness of his perspiration-dampened shirt. In the reflection of the glass covering one painting he tugged his tie straight within the lost shape of his limp collar. His new jacket, so proud this morning. Al's pride too, bought especially for his congressional command appearance, already seemed intimidated, slackly askew in the grip of Washington's power and the agitation of his own exertions. He was caught at that moment still checking his reflection. The grinning intruder seemed astonishingly young at first and then with a closer look David saw he was not quite so young after all. "Donnie Webster here. Welcome and *welcome.*"

"David Morgan."

"Who else, eh?" They shook hands. "Just admiring the sea prints," David said.

"I guess they're okay," Donnie Webster said with a short laugh that was no laugh. "Never really looked." He led David into his office and shut the door. David noticed the time, 2:15, on an antique grandfather clock. "So. Better get right to it, uh?"

"I guess. Though I'm still not sure why I'm here."

"Not sure?" Donnie Webster seemed to find that vaguely funny. His fingers drummed the rhythm of a message without words. "Due with the Committee at 3:00?"

"Yes. They told me that I could be a little later, if I wanted."

"Bet on that. Lots of waiting in that committee game," Donnie agreed cheerily. He regarded David for a moment with an even, knowing gaze. "So. The Man of the Hour."

"Hardly that."

"Absolutely. In Washington every day brings some new Man of the Hour. You are today's in spades. Guarantee it, Brother." Today's Man of the Hour couldn't think of anything to say to that. David watched Donnie Webster's eyebrows slowly rise.

"I beg your pardon?" Oddly, his thoughts, in spite of everything, were wandering.

"Hey, my friend, we don't have much time. You've thought about what I had to say on the phone?"

"Some. But I still intend to testify before the Committee."

Donnie's reaction was explosive. "Jesus Christ on a crutch! Shit, man. *Why?* Say, didn't mean to whomp the words right out of you. Little over-reaction on my part. Apologize. Go on."

"I simply believe that the way the Navy is going is futile. As a taxpayer too—"

"Okay, okay . . . ." Donnie ran his hand sufferingly through his hair. "You got your case. All the angels swearing it. Know what being *right* in this town gets you?"

David shook his head with weary impatience. "That and five bucks buys you a drink at the Mayflower, or whatever . . . etc. etc."

"You got it. By the way, seen the old dude recently?"

"Admiral Waters? I talked with him on the phone. As you know."

"Hot as ever for his Memorial Corridor? Nice old guy. Means a lot to him, eh?"

"Yes to both items," not hiding his annoyance, "but I fail to see what that has to do with what we're talking about."

"Okay. No time for temper. And *please,* fella, don't make me explain this town to you. Listen. We'll probably never see each other again. Know you'll be glad of that. But right this steaming minute we've both got flaming good reasons to make a deal." David felt himself moving along on a swift narrow river and unable to see around the next bend. "Getting down to cases." Donnie went on, looking down at some scrawled notes on his desk. "Check me on this, but a while ago you apparently were all hot and bothered to find a slot here in the White House."

"That's a bit strong. Others were pushing me. My mother was somehow entranced with the notion. As for myself I—" Donnie held up a hand. "Yep, yep . . . gone with the wind. But enough of personal history. Besides, I gotta tell you. You were savvy not to push that one. You'd die in this zoo."

"Oh? Who says?"

"I do. You're not phony enough. But enough of personnel management and history. Let's get on with it." Donnie looked down again at his notes. "But, if I get it right, you're still hot to be head honcho of that . . . that place out at Wolf's Lake."

David's heart skipped a beat. *What the hell.* Nevertheless he found himself making proper correction. "*Wolf* Lake."

"Wolf's Lake, shmake. Have it your way," Donnie conceded amiably. His voice registered satisfaction. "Don't be so surprised. We do our homework, fellow. Nice spot?"

"Very beautiful."

"Good job too? That head one, whatever they call it, the big cheese?"

"Technical Director. Yes. A great job." Through the window David could see the lawn and a squirrel. Possibly the same one he had watched on the way in. Sunlight blazed through the fineness of its tail, each hair stiffened, glowing. A marvel of life.

"So. Your chance to go onward and upward. Or reward for one of our senior Simple Servants for long and faithful service? Hey, sorry about that last dig. Actually I'm a fan."

Was any of this real?

Donnie Webster snapped his fingers. "Reveille my friend. Time is short. It's *yours*, baby. But I can see that you've doped that out." Yet that wasn't the same, not nearly so, as comprehending the matter whole. Instead, all sort of loose ends seemed to be blowing in a strong wind. He reached for one at random. "Wolf Lake actually happens to have a Technical Director already. Far as I know, the incumbent is very content there."

"Incumbent?" A Donnie tickled at that one. "You call them that too? Okay. Enough. Maybe he is happy as a clam. He'll be happy too wherever we bounce him."

"You'd be *forcing* him out?" Thinking with sympathy of old Jason Butler.

"Mr. Morgan, *David*. Now we're getting down into the grass. Forget the fucking details. Trust me." Gazing, entranced, at the excruciatingly troubled features of one Donnie Lee Webster. David asked himself how it could actually bother him that he was making life difficult for this man about whom every single facet was unappealing. More, loathsome.

"Listen, I don't know what's going through your mind right now. Probably a lot of things?" Donnie Webster's tone was ingratiatingly understanding. "But let's guess at the main one. You can't stand giving up your chance to be a hero."

"That's not it at all!" Donnie wasted not a second in letting David know that he saw right through his outrage. "For *one* single day. Then what do you do for an encore? This town is chock-a-block with ex-heroes. Guys who shoot their wad and spend the rest of their lives trying to figure what to do next. And no matter what trolley you've derailed, next year the Navy will gin up a new way to pry the funding for its same old dumb ship class. Fresh Admirals will troop up the hill with the same old tired flipcharts and you won't be around to stop them." The clock read two forty-five. It began to chime the fact. As if politeness required, David let the little bells run their course. Donnie waited too. "Well?"

"Sorry. I still can't make heads or tails out of this."

"Thinking about *what*? What, *man*? Whether to grab the chance of a lifetime?"

David was hearing every tick of the old grandfather clock. Donnie Webster leaned back, hands behind his head. Regarding one David Morgan as if his was all the time in the world. "Okay, fellow. A few more things to get off my chest. Hoping I wouldn't have to get to these, and you're not going to like them . . . ."

"*Oh?*"

"First off. You got problems, buddy-o. Face 'em. Financial problems. Capital 'P'. Not to put too fine a point on it, but you know better than I that you're up to your hamhocks. Behind in more accounts than Carter's got pills. About to have to sell your daughter's horsey, breaking her heart by the way . . . hey, don't be so surprised. A person's credit report is the easiest things to get hold of, when you know how. Like I say, we do our homework."

There was, in the matter-of-fact pride of that last, not a trace of irony. Donnie Lee Webster held up his hand. Not done. "Okay, moving on. Let it all hang out. This next no secret to you either. Your wife has a tussle with the bottle . . . *whoa fella! Down.*"

David obeyed. His heart pounded.

"Okay. Hated to say that last. Private family stuff, I know. But no disgrace. Not around this town. If we hung out to dry every Congressman who's on the sauce, you couldn't get a bill passed to buy a net for the House dogcatcher. Okay, okay. You want to know where I'm heading. Fair enough. But let's first unclench those fists. Okay? That's better. Now just a moment more. A little philosophy and then your boy here is through."

Donnie Lee Webster the Philosopher. David stared.

"More often than not, when a family starts getting really fucked up in this town, just like in Valdosta or anywhere else, it can be that old Daddy Bear is not paying enough attention. He's too busy and Momma feels neglected and consoles herself with the juice and the kids get out of control . . . and well, it all becomes a domestic mess with a capital 'M'. *Wait* . . . just one more minute for the wrap. So, what better therapy for this family to move to somewhere nice and old Dad now making at last the bucks he needs to dig himself out of that hole. I guess I didn't mention that, you'll jump up to the grade for the job, 15 or 16, whatever—and lo! Our guy gets to be that caring Dad of the story books with time at last to devote to straightening out the domestic shit storm that his life has become. Maybe he *can't* do it. But at least it's a *chance*. So why the foot dragging? Why pass up the chance to relax, to make the wife and kids happy? Okay . . . *okay* . . . . Maybe it sounds dull. Especially if it goes on too long and our champ starts getting antsy. His life tidied up, he hankers to come back to the Big City, get back in the swim. No sweat. Who says there are no second acts in American lives? Bullshit. Whenever our man decides it, he just hops onto his white horse and comes clomping back into town, all those good deeds still waiting to be done."

David Morgan kept on staring.

Donnie threw up his hands. "*Don't* move. *Stay.* Be right back."

Sara Jane Whipley, her office some yards away, was meeting with a select advisory group of women concerned about the pace of assimilation of women into positions of governmental power. The kind of meeting, of which there were too few, Sara Jane genuinely enjoyed. Even the designation of the group. Speed

Women in Government—acronym SWIG—did not bother her. The members, each woman successful in her field, including business, education, and science, she liked and admired. Intelligent, individualistic women. Success gave them extra helpings of confidence that had freed them from tendencies towards the shrill and ideological harangues that animated many of their less capable sisters. The meetings, therefore, were something of a treat, serious but enlivened by wit and humor. The women had gotten to know one another and their get-togethers were distinguished by affectionate warmth as well as prideful accomplishment. Some of them, like Sara Jane, were also part of DACOWITS, Defense Advisory Committee or Women in the Service. They traveled, rode ships, visited bases, knew fun and camaraderie. It was the reason why Donnie's showing up at her door, gesturing frantically, face contorted with upset over something (bound to be some new trifle), was especially vexing. Excusing herself, she stepped out into the corridor. "Dammit Donnie, can't you see I'm in conference."

"Sorry, baby, this is business. Ultra serious. Need help."

"*Scheiss*. What now?"

"Shh." He explained it to her in a hoarsened voice, urgent tones ground out under pressure as Sara Jane began to shake her head. Not entirely adversely judgmental. "Your guy sounds like some kind of an idealist," she said. "You could have a problem."

"I *do* have a problem." Their talk burned on in whispers.

"Donnie. *Some* people can't be bought," she hissed. "Yeah, but he's not one of them. I need help. Big time. Get your dinking lists. Hey, *please*. Sara girl, don't piss-ant me on this one." He repeated the name of the place. *Wolf Lake*. Making sure he had it right.

It was a bewildered, and at least partially intimidated, David Morgan who shortly found himself escorted to another office and was confronted by a grim, dark-haired woman who radiated paralyzing efficiency. She whipped in carrying a sheaf of printout pages and was now talking in a special jargon and at a speed which could scarcely be understood. Not the least of David's puzzlement was the woman's obvious, and yet unaccountable, cold dislike for him. Her computer sheets crackled with anger as she flipped through them. Consisting of multiple summaries of government positions available for women, sorted out by expertise, location, level of advancement, the works, Sara Jane received updates every week. *This,* beyond idealism, beyond meetings, monitoring programs, kicking ass, the bread and butter of her job. Her finger paused in running down one column. "Ah *super*. *Yes*. There does happen to be something open at Wolf Lake for your wife. But only a thirteen. Best I can do."

"I'm sorry. I don't understand. You're offering my *wife* a job at *Wolf Lake*? Thirteen?" The number weirdly reverberant. "*I'm* only a thirteen."

"Jesus." She looked back over her shoulder at Donnie who was hovering twitchingly in the background. "Haven't you even discussed this with him?"

Donnie turned red. "Actually, haven't. Not yet. Things have been moving too fast. I was going—"

Sara Jane glared but, turning back to David, her tone was momentarily less acid. She explained: "Often, these days, we know that satisfying a wife's own professional aspirations may be a critical factor in a husband's acceptance of a governmental position. Especially when a major relocation is involved. Thus we try to accommodate both parties to make the move mutually attractive." She went on to describe the particular position in detail, the tasks involved. "As I say," Sara Jane concluded almost apologetically, "best we can do."

Of the many ideas and replies struggling for visibility in David's surprised, indeed overwhelmed, consciousness, only one made it to the surface initially. *"Comptroller?"*

"Comptroller," Sara Jane glanced down again, impatiently, at her papers. Reading off: *"Responsible for Wolf Lake's Station's financial management."*

"But my wife—"

"Just a *housewife*? What you were about to say?" Sara Jane commented with deceptive sweetness, "therefore unqualified, right?"

"Well, yes. As a matter of fact. I'm afraid it's altogether honestly so."

He could not have foreseen, certainly had no experience with, the fierce weathers that swirled in the mind of Sara Jane Whipley. Even less than he understood the mysteries of the jet stream, and the influence it had on sunshine and rain, could he suspect the banked fires of fury, the legacy of centuries of resentment, that smoldered behind that direct gaze and composed, businesslike face. He was to know it now in the quick breaking of a storm, words pouring out of Sara Jane in an unopposable blast of anger. It blew for a few minutes with the power of the ages, carried the sting of Sahara sands, this woman of a million grievances whose time had come. Force then spent, if not bitterness, Sara Jane concluded her tirade, "This woman, your wife, who has for some twenty years no doubt successfully managed a household, budgeted the money, helped educate your children, tinkered with electrical appliances, practiced domestic economies, decorated rooms, made clothes, been other things besides . . . ." Sara Jane had finally to catch her breath. And if, in that pause, David had time to reflect that, throughout this hail of words, he had caught only imperfect glimpses of his Aliason (and, more frequently, glimpses of someone not Aliason at all) it was something he chose not this minute to point out. Sara Jane's breath came back. "Now you're implying that she can't fulfill the responsibilities of some piddling half ass little research station out in the middle of nowhere. A woman"—and here Sara Jane's candidate Comptroller, neé Aliason became transformed, uplifted, from an unknown abstraction, and took off, became the embodiment of Modern Woman, shining, soaring, free—"competent as your wife is bound to be, can't learn to master what some probably tired hack of a time-serving *male* sitting on his duff has been managing to do out there—?"

"Oh, no," David said, "not saying any of that." For an instant he did not even know why he had interrupted. Only knew, like Saul toppled from his horse on the way to Tarsus, that a blazing light—more force than illumination—had struck. *Shut up, Morgan.* Meeting Sara Jane's unremitting glare with noddings of solemn affirmation.

"Well, *God damn. At last.*" Sara Jane was depleted. Pulled out the stops on this one.

"*Absolutely.* I'm confident that she'll do a bangup job." Groveling now, David Morgan, even as need for groveling was past. "One more thing though." His mind going a mile a minute. "There are numerous Civil Service procedures, which naturally I know pretty well. The various forms certifying the individual's qualifications for the job, and so on. What I'm saying is that there are a lot of hoops to go through still. Though I imagine you are familiar with them." Sara Jane paused in the making of a notation on her list to roll her eyes. *"Am I?* Tell me about them." Bringing eyes down from heaven, she said sharply. "Don't worry. We'll take it from here." He had the renewed sense, in that last look before she departed, computer sheets under her arm like a tucked football, of a powerful, no doubt eternal, contempt.

"That's right, buddy. Trust us," Donnie followed up. Rubbing his hands with controlled glee. "So we got a deal, eh?"

David waited out the grandfather clock bonging three. All kinds of thoughts were rushing at him. One stood out. "Admiral Waters gets his Corridor?"

"Man, the works." Donnie's jubilation was radiant. "I'll be pushing that hummer of Show Biz *per-son-al-lee*. Count on me. This is a town of its word." Which, of course, for its darker compacts and in stranger ways than David Morgan would ever know, was absolutely true. "Now," Donnie said, pointing his finger dramatically, "*your* turn. But you've doped that out."

"Yes." But just what do I do *now*? Uncertainty must have been written all over his face because Donnie's advice was sudden and blunt. Coming with a harsh laugh. "Get lost!" Then, taking further account of David's look, he spoke almost sweetly. "You simply disappear, my friend. Without a trace. Above all, you were *never here*. You can swear it on a stack of bibles because we never logged you in. When you don't show up, the Committee flunkies will start running amok. Fanning out with their subpoenas and bloodhounds. Thing is, they have awfully little time. That's our edge."

"But—"

"Hey, w*here* you go, *what* you do, *your* problem. As I said on the phone, they've got to have that committee vote this afternoon or, latest, by mid-morning tomorrow. Duke can't even hold them off a day. It's scheduled to go to the floor and nothing can stop that. Got him by his cowpoke gonads." While he was talking, Donnie pressed a button and a secretary appeared to receive instructions about a vehicle. "Side court and pronto, kiddo."

"I guess then I ought *not* to be going home," David mused aloud.

"Bingo! *Jesus,* my friend, last place you go." Donnie's exuberance was not contagious. David had a vivid picture of an army of agents swarming. A Wanted Man.

Donnie offered practical suggestions, with David having the feeling that this was not a new kind of event for him to be orchestrating. "Just stay away from the obvious places. Hey, don't look so gloomy. This is a big town. By noon tomorrow you're home free. Okay. I see what's bothering you. Getting started. Campbell's gonna help you there."

"Campbell?"

Donnie looked as if he could have responded with a great deal but chose to say the minimum. "Good man. Old pro." Donnie's arm was on his elbow, pushing him gently along. The little bells of the clock once more chiming swiftly. David thought of jolly mice making that sound, scampering across festive bits of metal. Yet a sound sinisterly vibrant all the same in the close air. Donnie's expression had settled into one of contentment. Nodding approvingly over his own last words. "Campbell will let you out wherever you want. Keep your head down too going out the gate. No point in taking a chance at being spotted. Also, a bunch of shitbirds out there protesting and you never know what they'll be tossing."

"What are they protesting?" Donnie found the question hilariously inconsequential. "Haven't the least. Don't keep up with them." His voice faded away to soured mutter. "Everyone doing their thing. Is this a great country or what . . . . ?"

They passed through a door at the end of the corridor which opened onto an asphalt driveway. High hedges shielded the area, ideal if not actually created for surreptitious departures. A bulky black man in a chauffeur's uniform was holding the door open on a gleaming limousine. "Don't be sad, fella, Donnie said." You're doing the right thing."

They shook hands. "Well, thank you," David said.

"Hey, old buddy, thank *you.*"

▲▲▲▲▲

As he scrunched in the back of the limousine the last view David had was of Donnie peering down through the car's window. Mouthing words unheard through extra thicknesses of bulletproof glass. *Keep your head down.* From that happy man there was a wave, or even a sort of salute, and then the limousine was moving out silently, on fine lubricated bearings, soft and mighty tires. David's upward angled view was of trees and sky toppling backwards. He was hearing shouts, but as from a distance. *Not* from a distance. In seconds feeling tremors, as of hands slapping the side of the car, rocking it, then a thump. The Protestors registering. The limousine kept going, a ship moving ahead steadily through a ripple of turbulence, and now, from buildings whose upper stories he could glimpse, he knew they were traveling up Pennsylvania Avenue. Smoothly they slowed for lights, smoothly accelerated. Unexpectedly he liked it where he was. It was roomy, vacuumed and scented, a peaceful refuge. He suspected that he was going to miss this embryonic place and hoped that this present voyage, wherever it was leading, would not end too soon. Sensing Georgetown, the cobbles of M Street, glimpsing the grander sky of the Key Bridge above the Potomac. Next it was the curves and the climbs and the trees and the shadows of the George Washington Parkway. A local radio station was softly playing popular tunes over the high fidelity speakers close to his head. All he could see of the driver was the back of a bull neck, its corrugations like hardened muscle. He had developed resentment at that stolidly complacent neck. "Where may I take you, sir?" First words that Campbell had spoken.

"I'm afraid I haven't yet thought about it enough."

"That's all right. Happens with some folk. Natural, I guess. The uncertainty. We'll 'jes drive a while." Communication made him more conscious of the sunken oddness of his position, deepening his fixation upon the back of Campbell's head. It was like poured chocolate but with taut wire-like curled grey hair. The rolled flesh was sinister with physical power. Perhaps, David thought, he might have been a boxer, some champion's sparring partner. Yet having had a sample of that genially relaxed, yet scornful, voice David wished for more of its sound. "I guess there's no good reason why I can't sit up normally now."

"Don't see no reason why not. Up to you, sir."

He untangled himself and sat up, relaxing against the soft upholstery. The smear of a broken egg, the cause of that thump earlier, was drying on the flawless hood. "Do you do this sort of thing often?" That cannon ball hard head cocked ever so slightly. "And what sort of thing would that be, sir?", Campbell responded softly, at peace with his work. "Now . . . and . . . then . . . yes sir, you could say that."

David decided that further questions along this line might be intrusive, improper probes of that discretion which was likely one of the man's prides. Bread and butter as well. He settled back, watched his driver take the exit to Dulles Airport and head west into the bare pale beginnings of spring. The first low line of dark mountains appeared in the distance and the fine, thrilling sight of the Dulles terminal came into view, winning in its isolation, a grand aerodynamic form posed for flight. A plane shot off roaring into the blue sky, the sun catching it and fleetingly turning it into a boil of fire. Campbell drove past the terminal, easing by the line of cars for departing passengers, circling back towards Washington. He stretched his powerful shoulders. "Made up your mind yet, sir?"

"I guess you're wanting to know where to drop me off."

He replied: "Would be helpful. Getting on that time. Off at four. Gotta return this mother to the barn." "I see. You're Civil Service?" Campbell chuckled. "I'm something."

David began to feel differently about Campbell, touched by guilt. This man too had his hours, times he came and went, a home waiting for him somewhere. He worked for a living, likely had flaming assholes amongst his bosses too. One for sure. Unspoken, they had a bonding sense of their government's busy and calculating folly. So, Morgan, let's get with it. "Some place in Arlington, say. No place special."

Campbell directed his grand vehicle over towards Leesburg Pike, heading east, past Tyson's Corner Shopping Center, Bloomingdale's and the rest, where Aliason came to buy. Campbell seemed to be considering something. "Always figured," he said at last, "that Clarendon is no place special." The road grew crowded again, traffic correspondingly slow. They passed older shopping centers, boarded up stores, an automobile dealership and a used car lot, pathetic plastic flags spinning in the wind. Dust from Metro construction rose and flew. Beneath metal coverings on the street the earth trembled with its resistance to the power of machines grinding away within. He noticed an old brick building, a survivor from a row of earlier stores, before glamour, when buying was necessity; this crossroads once a clot of frontier civilization in a long vanished forest. Clarendon. The limousine slowed to a crawl as with an instinct of its own. "I'll just hop out," he said. "Please don't get out to open the door."

"That would be best, sir." A Campbell never having the least intention otherwise. David felt the cool windy air as soon as he stepped out of the limousine. Suddenly assailed by sounds after the insulation of his noble cocoon, the dull roar of traffic, the clang of distant hammers, the restlessness of stone in transition. He said good-bye to Campbell but any reply—he had hoped to hear something, words of luck at least—was drowned out in racket. David saw him lean forward in the familiar motion of someone reaching to try another radio station which up until then the tact of his training had constrained him from changing. That massive head at once bobbing with evidently livelier music. The limousine was moving off with matching swiftness, weaving purposefully for advantage through the traffic. A man sniffing home. For which sensible wish David felt envy.

The failing light was grey-blue. The twilight air was turning sharply chill and against it the generated body heat of several hours of walking was no defense. Unprepared for wandering the streets, he had brought no topcoat. His cramped feet in their narrow shoes, handsome for his White House appearance but not so fine for hiking, had his toes scrunched together in the way that women of fashion must know. Al, too, bless her. At each step, he felt a toenail of a smaller toe methodically slicing into the flank of a larger. This wasn't going to do. He needed shelter, surcease from walking. He had chosen to walk downhill, at first mainly because it was easier. Asphalt and concrete covered land sloping irresistibly towards the river. Now he found himself consciously seeking those wide waters for another reason. He sensed their quiet and their peace. The Indian before and now himself, the shy deer too once at dusk. He had made it to concentrated Rosslyn, intensely urban, high buildinged, anonymous. The street swung left and ahead a lighted shape standing high and blunt against the blue-black sky was the Key Bridge Marriott. He recalled a two day course in underwater acoustics there by Urich a long time ago . . . a place pleasantly remembered. Now warmth. He crossed, dashing, several bad and dangerous streets, not meant to be dared by man unarmed, lacking proper allocation of civilization's steel. A tall youth in a drooping doorman's red uniform swung Marriott's doors open for him with a flourish.

The elevator made several stops at intermediate floors, each time taking aboard festive groups. The *maitre d'* at the rooftop lounge escorted him to a cramped corner space that did not seem to belong to any other coherent grouping, yet was not quite his own either. People were stepping over his legs in their comings and goings and there were chair-shoving rearrangements to accommodate shifting social needs. Soon though he had his drink in his hand and a dish of peanuts set out on a small black table. However tiny, the round shiny table uniquely his. With his first sip he felt better. Eased was the nervous conviction that every second person must know his face, was looking through him clear as glass, straight to his secret. As he figured it, he would remain as long as he could, nursing his drink and then aim to drowse away the night in one of those big soft out of the way chairs in the lobby.

On a dismal hunch, he opened his wallet. Only a handful of dollars left, along with some loose coin in his pocket. He was afraid to use his credit card, his identity bold on its plastic. Fortunately it was Happy Hour, drinks half price, and a side table by the entrance was set with plates of cheese and crackers and bits of meat somethings in a sauce bubbling over the blue flame of a chafing dish. Whatever the "somethings", they were going to be supper. Have to hold him through breakfast as well! Assessing the longness of the night ahead, he felt intimations of greater loneliness coming. This fugitive business, like anything else a man must do, demanded learning.

The crowd was lessening. Groupings of people were identifiable, not everyone indeterminably pressed together. On his right he observed that a couple whom he had assumed were part of a larger group were in fact by themselves. The departure of the people adjacent to them emphasized their isolation, an enveloping quiet. The woman was young, too blonde but not unhandsome for that, and not half the age of her grey-flecked escort in the fine-striped suit. Almost too obviously they represented typical doomed romance, blighted by factors easy to guess. A common story yet somehow seeming more intense in Washington (or perhaps merely more frequently seen) than elsewhere. Perhaps too it seemed still shallower with the shallowness of politics, diminished further by its worn predictability. Patronage on one side, opportunism on the other, last taste of youth for one, touches of power and its perks for the other. Fair trade, the cynic would say. That was not the way it looked. Not with their vulnerable humanity, for better or worse, offered up to a stranger's inspection. David noted the profile of an offending bump on the young woman's cheek that not all her makeup could smooth away. They were saying little, gazing down at the darkly luminous river and across to Georgetown University's towers rising from the hill above. Once they held hands, a brief squeezing that whitened the women's knuckles followed by an abrupt letting go, likely for the no doubt too many other lives shadowing their own and not going to go away. He saw her shake her head, be coaxed to a small smile. A moment later she picked up her purse and departed and the Man of Importance, after draining the last of his drink in somber isolation, left as well.

The woman on his left returned from a second trip to the Ladies. Again maneuvering around his table and with the same shy expression of apology. She did it more familiarly this time, as if the experience repeated was making them neighbors. The couple of melancholy mismatch no longer available, he turned his curiosity to the family of which the woman with the betrayingly small bladder was the mother. He overheard snatches of conversation, confirming his guess that they were on a standard tourist's mission, coinciding with their children's Spring Break. He was struck by the family's dignity, radiating from their subdued voices, the feel of a family at peace with itself. Sensibly able to contain both excitement and yearning. They were talking over the events of the day. They had been to the Capitol, gotten tickets to the galleries, finished the day off at the Air and Space Museum. Tomorrow, he gathered, going to the Smithsonian. Perhaps there would be a few hours for the zoo as well, the mother was telling her son, but she could not promise. The boy had his mother's black hair. His bare legs swung over the edge of his chair. About eleven, David estimated, beyond the age when most young boys cheerfully accept the wearing of short pants.

"A *few* hours," the daughter declared with good-humored scorn, "are not much for the National Zoo. It's one of the world's largest, you realize." She was several years older than her brother, yet not quite a teenager. Very much in between, and quite unbothered about it. Her dress was short, simply cut, but of rich brown velvet trimmed with old-fashioned lace. It heralded unfairly an unarrived, and plausibly never to come, prettiness. Her pale unstockinged legs did not swing, and her youthfully rounded features seemed unlikely to firm themselves into a likeness of her mother's. But even a mouthful of metal braces did not diminish her air of unselfconscious authority. Family conversation shifted to the challenge of identifying a scattering of flood lit monuments. Vessels of grandeur, they seemed afloat in isolated puddles of brightness amidst the broad and dark expanse of federal Washington. Discussion flared into dispute between brother and sister, their mother a gentle-toned referee. "That is the Jefferson Memorial," the daughter declared with finality. "I've looked at the map."

"*Lincoln,*" insisted the boy, whose elements of the argument had contracted to amiable but relentless repetition. David turned back towards the watery remains of what must be his last drink. He was surprised to hear the woman's voice, soft but determined, directed to his left ear. "Excuse me, sir, sorry to trouble you. Please settle something for us. Which of those two . . . buildings is the Jefferson Memorial?" Her finger pointed to the one, then the other. "The far one," David assured one and all, "is the Jefferson Memorial." A joyous snicker burst from the girl. "*Told* you." The map-reader, a student of them early. Suspecting that it was a skill that would define her character long.

"Thank you, sir. Now that's enough silly arguing. We'll be going in to dinner soon. I don't want stomachs getting upset." Her admonition did not hold, however, and more mild jangles erupted, also of the sort whose settlement demanded local knowledge. The ice having been broken, the two children sought out directly their newfound authority's judgments. Twisting around to fire off repeated questions at the accommodating stranger close by. "Children," said the mother, "please don't bother the gentleman further."

"No bother, I assure you." The father was the most distant of the four family figures, located at the other side of the low cocktail table. He had turned away, seeming to have formed his own communion with the dark bright river and night's bemusing scene. He spoke now, prefacing his words with his wife's name, or some shortened nickname, that David did not catch. "Let's invite the gentleman to join us. Done us a kindness."

"Oh yes, please do. We'll learn that much more about Washington from a man who knows it so well." No trace of irony was in that clear and elusively accented voice. He made no protests. Nursing the small calculation, shortly proven correct, that the invitation might include a welcome offer of that one more beer that he was in no position to furnish himself.

"Jess Hunter here." The voice was a gentle rumble. A big hand extended surprisingly far with friendliness. A wave of the other caught a waiter's eye. Introductions all around, rearranging of chairs, a cooperative shifting of the table by the two men to retain in the new accommodation the coziness of the old. The children in turn gave him firm handshakes and the regard of curious but not unlikable stares. The girl's braces gleamed with multi-faceted borrowings from the dim light. She added, pleasingly, a small curtsey. He was for some seconds the object of fascinated attention. Something new in their sightseeing sated lives. Their very first authentic Washington inhabitant. Reshufflings completed, he found himself on the side of the table with the mother. The children were closer to their father on the other side. Discussion continued communal as the family described itself, its visit; David was the interested listener, putting in a word now and then, just enough to keep things rolling. The family's day came freshly alive with its retelling.

Theirs was a small town with some forgettable name in southeastern Ohio. Its setting, he learned from the shy but strong pride with which they revealed their community's characteristics, partook not at all of the stripped landscape and flattened expanses of corn and cows and smoking industries that for most people defined their mighty home state. Their own county, they stressed, abutted West Virginia and that made the difference. There were vestiges of mountains, steep terrain, chasms with clear rushing rivers, forests alive. Business was a lumberyard: not large but prosperous enough. Ruling over it, it hardly need be said, Jess was king. It remained to be seen though, whether the boy would follow in his father's footsteps. Just as apparently it had to be decided by Fall whether the boy was going to enroll in junior football. A family's normal and not especially trying choices. A question too was whether it would be best next year if the girl were to go away to boarding school. If she did, Mrs. Hunter said with a wistful glance, she would miss her daughter. So naturally was David drawn into discussion that it was as if he had become a member of the family, lending his own warmth and light. Subtly they conveyed respect to one of Washington's wise. Talk dwindled, as with relaxed people before a dying fire. One of the children asked how it was that he knew so much about Washington. He explained that he had lived here a long time.

"How marvelous that must be." The tremor in the mother's voice was genuine. He was encouraged to talk about the city as he knew it, at the same time deprecating his own knowledge; no more, after all, than what any long time resident ought to know about his city. Nor was Washington Paris, where History was to be found at every street number, graven in every stone. Still, he insisted loyally, many obscure byways meandering off grander avenues were touched by admirable associations that were closer to the American heart than might be realized. He weighed, risked (anxious not to appear odd)—coming off successfully, he felt—bringing up the inspirational and cultural profit to be gained from old cemeteries. Just wandering around them, not morbidly, but . . . for example— and there was to this particular grave site, she should know, a steady trickle of pilgrimage still—St. Gauden's memorial to the wife of Henry Adams tucked away in Rock Creek Park . . . . Clasping her hands together in front of her, she did not let him finish. "Oh, yes, poor Mrs. Adams. That lovely lady."

Yes. All the while thinking about the Hunters. Curiosity increasing, not lessening. The black hair, to begin with, her accent—perhaps because of the slightly measured quality to her speech, the perfection of her English, the obvious product of some splendidly applied will, was it even detectable—from somewhere in Europe. Not anywhere obvious though, seemingly from darker frontiers, where once the Roman had held back the barbarian tribes. Some elusively recalled land of permanent defeats, he sensed, one of recurrent tides of conquest that bred in its people not optimism but character. Some poor and bony land in the sun, a joke of a modern nation perhaps, but with its ancient mountains soaked in blood. Natural to wonder then how she and Jess had met. Perhaps Jess was a young soldier stationed overseas. Way it often happened. The serviceman and his foreign bride. Such encounters enriching America. Passingly he thought of them in bed, not pruriently, not imagining details, merely speculating in the way everyone occasionally and inadmissibly wonders about the couplings of others. Feeling kinship with that act that keeps human existence going, its animal ordinariness, the surpassing strangeness. He almost jumped at the sound of Jess's voice. As if his host had caught him at a keyhole. "Work for the government?" Genially asked, not like his questioner had found him out at anything. Jess pronounced 'government' as if it had only two syllables. "Yes . . . yes," David stammered, "I confess that I do."

"Why 'confess'?" the mother spoke up warmly, "it must be exciting and rewarding." She had seen his flinch. Jess seemed to wait for that tic of feeling to pass. His drawl amiable as ever. "Figured." Figures, does Jess. The man had him pegged, nothing more, yet funny how he felt it. He waited for Jess to say something else—it seemed inevitable—to offer, if only by implication, some comparative value judgment on the sweetness of fresh cut wood, say, the song of a great rotary saw, on the usefulness of what he, Jess was doing as opposed to what were the customary products of Washington. At the least, David expected some sensible lament about the ways of 'guvment'. How Washington was making the trees ever harder to cut, chain saws too goldarned safe to be operable, eager beaver ignoramuses at desks ginning up preposterous regulations on the perils and penalties of sawdust . . . . As if the lungs of good men getting on with their job had not been sucking in that aromatic grand and nourishing dust for a long time!

There was none of this. Jess merely went on with some slight and private nodding of his head and reached for his beer with the same rocking awkwardness that seemed to be due to his suit jacket being too tightly buttoned. An item of clothing likely not worn too often. He was not a tall man but large. Not fat either; no more so, anyway, than Jackie Gleason was properly a fat man. Bulk that was all husky energy, the clasp of a hand that could bend horseshoes. Jess said something low to his children that had them giggling and their three heads drew closer. The woman's voice, unexpectedly directed solely at himself, startled. "You are out *late* for someone who has a home here," she observed. She contemplated his aloneness with decent concern. "Perhaps though you have appointments still to come this evening, and they prevent you from going home just yet."

He accepted the convenience of the excuse offered. Yes, that was it. Loose threads of government trailing right on demandingly into a person's night. He appreciated her deepening frown over the stressful ways of a city mysterious to her, but deflected further curiosity. They talked easily, softly. The enveloping mood of personal communication wove itself around them. Jess and the children seemed off on a separate island, voices and laughter—a kind of teasing game was in progress between father and children—clear but faint. The luminosity of the city, reradiating in thin wavering lines of color across the river's dark surface from Georgetown's lively shore, was dimming. The figures of Jess and his children grew darker, became silhouettes. He was conscious of the woman's hands, lying in her lap. Pale creatures, vital but resting. Her voice was steady, direct. He noted, to be remembered if he lived a thousand years, her high brow, the framing hair, whites of unblinking and steadily regarding eyes. He heard, he could swear, chimes. Bells sweet and sad floating across red tile rooftops of towns ancient and useful. Each distant note clear. *Thrift. Self-discipline. Seriousness. Endurance. Common Sense. Loyalty. An ancient racial remembrance of the wisdom of defeat. Warmth.* Not a word or a phrase of any of these did she utter; yet every pore breathed them. Out of the ordinary clay of life, and without once naming them: Poetry. Music. Beyond the world's fixation on its throbbing genitals, its soppy and graceless entwinings, an existence expressing the overwhelming importance—by differentials as towering as the blind and microscopic sperm measured against the heft and worth of the humans that grew out of those tiny fishtailings—of the quality of the lives builded from those awkward startings.

Sounds of people grew less. Jess and the kids drifting away. Belatedly he saw what was obvious, that her face was not merely strong, but beautiful. Any man would fall in love with her. One more just had. The waiter, an insubstantial intruder, brought another beer. David's head felt light. Despite his vigorous nibblings, his body was still craving Al's usual generous supper. Occasionally the woman's glance, worlds in it, went away momentarily towards her children, but the spell of solitude reclosed itself; dimness gave it form, soft, palpable. Still as if in a dream he watched the maitre d' arrive to inform that their table would be ready soon. Afar, Jess was fishing in his pocket and the girl was smoothing her dress over her knees. The woman was starting to get underway too. But first wanting to know something. "I realize that, going on as I have, I have been impolite. Not given you a chance to tell me what it is exactly that you do for the government?"

"Ah yes . . . . Good question." He made a move to stand up himself, wrestled with dizziness, plopped back. "First off, I cannot tell you 'exactly'. Prickly word. Nor dwell on the circumstances of my present exile which, I still hope against hope, will prove to be a mere transient. Where I count, where my heart dwells, is in satisfying the curiosity of a special naval community about the oceans. In a nutshell—apt metaphor—for mine is the province of nuts, I explore how well the oceans transmit acoustic energy for the detection of submarines. I have long been concerned, and will be concerned again I trust—alluding to the prison of my current situation!—with the entire *benthos*. 'Benthos', a term I will come back to shortly. I am speaking of all the seas of the world, from the sun-warmed glittering surfaces of the multi-hued tropics to the eternal icy blackness of the Arctic's abyssal plain. I measure, *used* to measure, the vertical migrations of the phytoplankton in the Mediterranean, which live out their lives in accordance with an iso-luminous curve. Drawn towards the surface by evening's skimpy starlight from hundreds of feet down, their ghostly massings bring ruinous reverberations to those sonars in which we have invested so much. Yet we ought to be able to depend upon those expensive devices for the detection of submarines at times *other* than broad daylight, don't you concur? Antisubmarine warfare a round-the-clock business. I fret too even about the light winds that tickle the surface of a sea so prettily, and yet have their own unhappy effects upon our fragile acoustics. I worry . . . ." He paused only for the quickest of breaths. Her eyes upon him—what *were* their color?—did not waver.

"I worry . . . but shit and vinegar, it's not important what I . . . my worries . . . . Let's say simply that I'm always thinking about submarines, brood too much upon them, those silent creations of precision machinery purring through dark cold seas. Better I know the abyssal plains four thousand fathoms deep and the little spiky worms that we startle with our lights, capturing on film their hasty burrowings into the monolithic silts, than the bugs that ravage my lawn."

"But . . . ." Her tongue went to her lips in the solemnity of her concentration. The 'benthos' . . . you were going to define . . . ." But her mad lecturer was off again.

"Yep, the good old *benthos*. Greek word . . . back to it in a minute. Anyway, scientifically speaking, I deal in the measurement of sound in the sea, the phenomenology of its propagation. Dealing in energies of near infinitesimal magnitude and of such esoteric nature that the untrained mind, straining for comfortably analog interpretations, cannot grasp the idea of acoustic signals traveling a mile a second in waves of compression and rarefaction hundreds of feet long, alternately reflecting off bottom and surface across the breadth of entire oceans. Energies no greater than those radiated in the glow of the tiniest flashlight bulb"—he flicked his fingernail on the glossy table—"whispers of sound not exceeding this, a bare watt of energy, yet moving across thousand of miles. I deal in the discrimination . . . ." Jess and the kids were now squeezing past their scrunched knees like patrons departing from inboard seats part way through a movie in a darkened theater. Yet carefully, as if out of courteous respect for the rapt attentiveness of those still viewing.

"Best come 'long, Varn," Jess said softly, "gotta be going in to eat now." "*Varn*"? Was that what Jess had said? Short, perhaps for Varna? The ancient city on the Black Sea? Or had he merely said, "hon"? David would never know. "Oh yes," said the lady, at once right back to the present, "my goodness, yes." She picked up her purse.

"I have listened to," David Morgan rolled on, faster, babbling, the lady standing now, "the song of the humpbacked whale wailing across the Pacific deeps.... In my business, I must...." His head was still going round but he was at last managing to stand up. She was touching his arm, looking into his eyes with unwavering attention. "But tell me, David, this business of yours, does it *pay?*" Jess interrupted, but as easily as ever. "Our new friend can join us for supper, if he cares. You can keep up your talk at the table."

"Oh, yes, please. Heavens. Where are my manners?"

Old Jess, David thought wryly. A man unbothered by this skinny smitten fellow. The strengths of Jess's sawmill, his easy pride, were packed solid through that barrel figure. Able to handle with his pinkie some adoring helpless fellow, a harmless raver, nothing in his pockets but words. David declined the invitation, shaking hands with Jess and each of the children. The lady touched his arm one last time. "Now, sir, truly you must *cancel* all your meetings for tonight," she said, "go straight home and stop fretting about your work and get a good night's sleep."

Don't leave. He still felt her hand's touch as the family walked away towards the dining room. She was not so tall as he had thought, watching her reach back to adjust the waistband of her skirt. Then she and the rest of the Hunters disappeared around a corner into eternity. He lingered over the last of his beer and delayed until his waiter did not see him emptying his pockets of coin onto the table to make up what must pass for a tip. Nor the waiter witness his finger sliding back, out of that pitiful sprinkle of bright metal with its mixture of dust and pennies, a quarter for one mandatory phone call.

* * *

He retrieved the saved quarter from his pocket. Al picked up the phone in the midst of its first ring. "Darling! *Where are you?*"

"Easy. I'm O.K."

"I can *hear* that. Oh, but *everything's* blown up on the news. A big report and news flashes on top of that. It's dreadful. You're mentioned on it everywhere. The Covert Mystery Witness. Government vehicles came by looking for you. Reporters have called. You didn't tell me this would happen."

"Let's just say it's happened."

"But still. How long will you be gone? Where will you spend the night?"

"No—"

"These are not *Twenty* Questions! This is *One* Question."

"Dear. I can't talk much longer."

"*Why?*" she wailed. But then she recovered with the thought, "Is it because you're afraid that they're listening in and can trace it? Is that why you won't tell me where you are?"

"Such is possible. I don't know much about these matters."

"You sound awfully tired." He heard a clicking on the line. It was probably only imagination but he had better end this. "Must cut it off now."

"Don't hang up yet. *Please don't.* You're all I've got. This line is my only link...." He let a little more of this go on before pressing a finger down on that wildish pulse. "Halt. This is only one night we're talking about. And sweet—"

"Oh I know, I *know.*" And now she was surprising him. "Please don't worry. I shall be your rock...." He blew a kiss whose sound had a crisp metallic echo.

Hanging up softly, he warily checked over his fellow callers along the line of booths. Only then did he exit his booth, and go down a hall to the men's room. Pass up no chance, he said to himself, repeating lore which seemed more or less to apply. In a few minutes he was circling the lobby discreetly, several times looking back abruptly. But he detected no one whose preoccupations, whether innocent or not, appeared to concern him any more than had those of his companions of the phone booths moments earlier.

▲▲▲▲▲

His plan worked well enough overall, though not as expected. He had not anticipated how uneasiness over possible discovery would impel him to keep shifting hotels during the night. His last turned out to be the lobby of a Hyatt, fancily pretentious but seen most clearly at a bleak pre-dawn hour through reddened eyes of truth. Merely a Holiday Inn dressed up in extra chrome. Sprawled in an out of the way chair, dozing when he dared, rereading the back pages of abandoned newspapers when he did not, he was conscious of the skeptical and increasingly hostile stares of the night clerks towards the rumpled stranger cadging free shelter. He awoke with a start, his body reacting to a jolt of sound like a physical impact. For a second he was sure that the clerks had taken some direct and positive action to eject him. But it was only the cleaning people. Except not *only*. For what a relentless patrol of sweepers and scrubbers they were! Operating as a team, swiftly dragging their mechanical contraptions about, they were a veritable panzer force of vacuums and washers and rotary polishers. Snapping their cords like angry whips. An ample black woman, whose thrusting vacuum had first jarred his sleeping feet, was pulling her arm back to ram her infernal machine once again through whatever impeded her route to any offending scraps or dust located beneath his chair. Her expression bearing down on him was scornful, pitiless. He hopped up and departed with a foolish smile and a plenitude of hasty apologetic nods right and left.

Beyond the glass doors that were holding in Hyatt's precious warmth, he stepped into the coldest air that had ever smacked him. The concrete sidewalks themselves felt like a form of gritty ice underfoot. Sodium vapor lamps made circles of dead light in bitter emptiness. Orange frost gleamed on tiny patches of wiry grass. Between the sharp black summits of Rosslyn's high buildings, stars were framed in angles against dawn's first touch of blue. A wind moaned protest at its enforced detours. Fortunately the weather was clear. At least he could walk and he did so with excessive briskness, as if he might stay ahead of furies bent on turning him to ice. He grew aware of the steepness of Arlington's hills. Nature had tossed the land in cataclysmic jumbles but, of all the soon-to-rouse drivers traveling over its prehistoric past, few could sense the earth's ancient violence in the asphalt contours into which men had smoothed and rounded them. With his striding though, for all his unstoppable shivering, came exhilaration. Absurdly exaggerated as his fears had been to begin with, for the first time in eighteen hours he had shed most of his hunted feeling. No longer feeling that every pair of human eyes was looking him over. A police car's brakes squeaked commandingly in response to a sharp halt at a traffic light. Its cops glanced neither right nor left. Taxis, bare of passengers, cruised past the lone and odd possibility of fare that he represented. One driver put down his window. "Taxi? *Como?*" "*Nada,*" called back merrily the Spanish student of long ago. A dark face made no reply except to express his dashed monetary hopes in an irritable burst of his engine's power. The sky was now a paler blue with the sure coming of day. Far out in the Atlantic, about Bermuda now he estimated, the sun was just risen. Its first rays, parallel to the horizon, would be skimming off the fine dark green of Bermuda's lagoon, leaping like flying fish shaking sparklets of gold. In a twinkling that the eye could miss, night dulled waters would alchemize into emerald and new born light would touch ordinary pastel houses with magical glow. Those gold and rose tints would enliven even the plain functional structure of the Navy's Research Facility whose look he had once known as well as the dimples in the aluminum siding of his own home. Ah, the stories from old Tudor Hill! Ones fascinating to men of low frequency sound at least, and despite present circumstances he shook his head amusedly; this constant hunger for faith in the meaning of his own experience. A franchise donut shop was brightly lighted from within and through its clear face lucky people were two deep at its counters. Out its wide swinging doors—they too of heavy glass and, such were the numbers of people entering and leaving, never coming quite fully shut—he caught scents of coffee and spicy sweetness, richly blended. He had not forgotten that he did not have the price of a donut but he paused to take in that small but excruciating feast of morning. At last he plunged on. At his back, beside him, all around, engines groaned; trucks clanged and rumbled. Man's rousing day blowing out the fragile night. Sounds that for all their dismaying power were reassurance. Just as those splendid smells, undirected at him but pouring out their appeal to join the brightness of dawn, had told in sweeter fashion that this roaring world had not come awake with one of its myriad small ciphers named David Morgan remotely on its mind.

▲ ▲ ▲ ▲ ▲

He made it home tired and without incident and after telling the tale of his adventure—some of it but not all—he slept away a fair part of what was left of the day. Later on with the evening news—delivered between a bulletin concerning an unidentified decomposing body, possibly that of an indicted (and, since the indictment, missing) Congressman feared a suicide, and reports on a march by farmers protesting restrictions on goat dairy products—there followed a featured "In-Depth Study" on the vote by the House shipbuilding subcommittee. The announcer commenced his story against the inevitable footage of a warship, smoke pouring, cutting a white wake through a blue sea. That was succeeded by a segment of grainy, harshly black and white film of a World War II U-boat wallowing on the surface, crew tumbling up out of its hatches with hands raised in surrender.

"By a close vote, the long-delayed legislation approving the Navy's controversial Sea Eagle program moved out of the key House subcommittee and onto the floor where the House gave it swift passage. In seacoast cities around the nation, where the multi-billion dollar program means years of prosperity to thousands of workers, the word touched off impromptu celebrations. Amidst under-utilized cranes, huge and still, and by gaunt empty building ways awaiting the return of the riveter's hammer, there were scenes of pandemonium reminiscent of locker room high jinks by Super bowl victors . . . ."

The TV camera then showed, through an unsteady lens, as if the violent hilarity of the events recorded was causing the earth itself to shake, a conga line of workers snaking their way around industrial buildings. The camera hastened by, but did not choose to miss entirely, two male workers and a struggling woman upended, held by her ankles, skirt over her head, exposing shiny yellow underpants. Both men were grinning, others cheering. An interviewer handed his microphone to a woman in bulging slacks whose hips for a few seconds stopped gyrating to the blaring rock music. Her face was red, ecstatic. "What do ah think about all this? Jus great. Jus guh-ray-*ray*-it. For our families, our country . . . for jus everyone." Her lips now moved with feelings too strong for words. Then, in a burst of feeling, connection made. "Honey. It's *life*".

"In the offices of the Pentagon celebration was more muted, but quiet jubilation was nevertheless to be read in the senior officials whom our newscaster visited. The Secretary of the Navy expressed his gratification at the wisdom of the Committee's action in breaking the lock on this shipbuilding program vital to assuring control of the seas. The Chief of Naval Operations spoke for the administration's leadership, and we quote, 'An inspiring day for all who have feared up to now the capacity of our Navy to defeat the submarines. Sea Eagle expresses the American people's faith in Sea Power. It is a victory for the reasoned processes of our democracy.' " "On Capitol Hill some people were decidedly unhappy over the outcome, none more so than Congressman Abner Duke, who has led a long uphill fight against acquisition of the Sea Eagle frigates. Ab Duke is a blunt-spoken westerner who maintains that Sea Eagle is a woefully deficient warship by the Navy's own definition of what it is supposed to do. A pain in the neck to some, Ab Duke is a hero to many. We encountered the Congressman, who has gained a national reputation in the course of his unprecedented struggle, coming down the Capitol steps." David and Aliason watched, holding hands. Against the background of the Capitol, with grey swift-moving clouds scudding above the green bronze of Liberty's towering sculpture, Abner Duke came into view. His head was lowered against the swirling wind and he was holding his hat. Saplings were bending and the waters of a fountain's basin were whipped like the sea. *"Excuse me, Mr. Congressman. We can see you're in a hurry, but wanted to ask a few questions."*

"Shoot."

"First, sir, how would you characterize your reaction to today's vote?"

"Disappointed as hell. Worse, sad for my country."

"Would you mind briefly reviewing for our viewers the essence of the arguments against Sea Eagle?" Ab Duke glared straight into the camera. "Damn right, I mind. Don't you do your homework? Don't even answer. Seriously, where in heck *have* you guys in the press been? Anyway, the damned ship is supposed to detect submarines, but with the ears it's got it couldn't hear a bull snorting next to it in a barn. The whys I leave to the experts. But I suggest you dig into it further if you take any pride in how you earn your pay."

"Now we understand that there was a key witness . . . ."

"Correct." Bitingly.

"Who apparently didn't show up before your subcommittee."?

"Nope. Gone hiyaku."

"Do you think that he would have made a crucial difference on the fate of Sea Eagle?"

"Sure would have. He had the goods on those fakers who are pushing this dog. Forgive me," and Ab Duke's face spread with a grin at a small joke he could not resist, "or should I say *bird?* Anyway, the guy knew where all the bodies were buried."

"What do you think happened?"

"No idea. Maybe he got cold feet. Maybe the other side got to him. Anyway, he didn't show and that's what counts."

"Are you suggesting the possibility of . . . ?"

"Hey, not suggesting anything." He laughed. But, do I have a problem keeping my thoughts clean in this dirty town? You bet."

"Mr. Congressman, one more question. May we conclude that you've given up the fight against Sea Eagle?"

"Damnation no! I'll be back after those guys' tails next year. And nipping at the heels of that tragic mistake as long as she's afloat. Or *I* am. Hey fellows, gotta run. My anniversary. Promised the wife I'd get home on time for once. If I don't, I'm gonna get skinned." The camera followed the Congressman as he strode away, a short figure rapidly growing smaller. The scene shifted to the newsroom for the anchorman's final judgment.

"Despite Ab Duke's vow to keep up the fight, experts familiar with the ways of Pentagon funding processes are skeptical that the Sea Eagle program, once launched even for a year, will be turned off short of completion of the Navy's procurement of the by now full sixty-six units planned. Moving now to the local scene, protesting farmers in a traffic jamming tractorcade . . . ." There had been no mention of David Morgan by name.

The blustery weather glimpsed on the early news intensified. It brought still stronger winds hurling rain against the house, clattering off the sheets of aluminum siding like handfuls of thrown gravel. Yet a comfortable sound to David Morgan who, obedient to the tug of long-time habits unaffected by the last night's unique break with them, had settled himself once more into his study. In the latest issue of the *Journal of Underwater Acoustics* he encountered a report of a doctoral student's investigations of the interaction of DIANA's main acoustic lobes with the ocean bottoms The Hawaii Institute of Geophysics, where the author was enrolled, had sweet talked the Navy into a few hours' scientific sea tests with the prototypal DIANA. The investigator, no student of ASW but understanding that one of DIANA's main purposes was to exploit an acoustic path for long-range submarine detection by sound waves bouncing off the bottom, found it difficult to believe that the frequency chosen had not been calculated to *minimize* signal loss when it grazed the bottom. "Instead," the author noted—there was a winning innocence in the straightforwardness of his commentary—"it appears that this particular peak frequency penetrates the bottom sediments to an optimum degree, and hence suffers *higher losses*, thus confounding the designer's intent, by dissipating the energy of its powerful sonic pulses in unsought travel through the abyssal muds."

Ah, thought David, out of the mouths of babes . . . . The gladness of the young rescarcher—Maimonides Ho (ought to fit in well with that name, David thought, amongst the ranks of distinguished oceanographers which obviously he would soon be joining)—was palpable at his discovery, the good things to be made of it. Yet it was an admirably technical article too, quantifying the number of meters of bottom that could be penetrated versus the incident angle of the arriving sound. Manifested with the advent of DIANA "a marvelous new tool" had been created by which researchers could gain, with comparative simplicity and ease, knowledge which formerly they could only painfully extract through the near infinite tediousness of samples individually obtained by lowering coring tubes at the end of thousands of fathoms of wire and grindingly winching them back up again. At one's fingertips, with keyboard and console, a whole brave new world conferred. Square miles of ocean bottom to be read in a single ping. The young Mister Ho (clearly soon to be Doctor) did not go so far as to urge that naval ships equipped with DIANA be diverted indefinitely from their naval mission in order to carry out bottom surveys, but it was the gleam in his eye. The floor of the sea tabulated; in its undisturbed ooze a fair part of the long story of the earth. Among the finer of its layers, mere millimeters thick, the ash of volcanic explosions from islands that had vanished millions of years before man. DIANA might reveal the secrets of the dark and unknown slime of abyssal plains; caress seamounts man would never see. And in manganese modules, and the other concentrations of mineral wealth that DIANA could illuminate, was treasure for the plunder of commerce. David admired how boldly, with what "chutzpah", Mr. Ho dangled his vision before the powers who could make things happen. A young man who would go far, already deciphering the world's sensitive codes, unerringly knowing the right buttons to push. David shook his head at himself, though only partially regretful. Still: *True, I've never thought big....* Rain like shot rattled his window, roused him from reverie. He got ready for bed, went into the bedroom where Al was reading. Sitting up but scrunched down too, under the little table lamp with its insufficient cone of light. One of their persistent false economies. Perhaps they might, before long, each have first-rate lamps. Daring to touch new possibilities in his life. "I'd have thought you'd be fast asleep. It's been quite a day."

"For you *too*." It seemed that she must insist that for herself as well that books, not sleep, was the proper reaction. "Reading, reading, far into the night," she said, as if reciting a poem. "As I am wont to do." She smiled. "'Wont.' Did I use it correctly? I did?"

There was a pleasure in her sigh. "Thinking actually, more than I've been reading. Trying to decide what we'll take. What we must throw away. I won't sleep a wink."

"I shouldn't worry. Our weight allowance will be generous." A long time, he reflected, since they'd had a move for which someone else was paying. She was concerned for their books. "I know they're heavy, but promise me that we won't leave any behind. Some, you've probably forgotten, are from my school days. They still have my notes in the margin." She cocked her head at that, "Still?" Silly, isn't it? Why wouldn't they still be there? But there they are, like old friends waiting, my little insights and girlish exclamations. Then there are our paperbacks. Some tattered and grubby, but it's always nice to be able to give an old favorite to a friend who may be visiting. A gift of yourself, isn't it? She did not relinquish the subject soon or lightly. "Don't humor me on this. They're our *library*, when you come down to it." Are indeed, he nodded. But much more was on her mind than books. Tonight, the world. Later on she tapped him while he lay half asleep, restless with the light from her reading. "David?" In pregnant silence she went on rehearsing her ill-formed question. But no preparation was adequate for her awkward trespass on this dim and slippery terrain that lay so far outside her experience. "This has all happened . . . so much and so fast. In time I know you will explain it to me. But I wanted to . . . be sure that this good fortune isn't all the result of . . . one of those awful 'horsetrades' you're always condemning, or even worse, possibly because of your having"—her voice lowered, no dirty word half so hard to utter—*"compromised yourself."* His reply, though muffled by his pillow, was clear. "What else, sweetheart?"

"Oh." Shocked silence followed her soft wounded cry. Still seeking meaning, she grabbed for a phrase presumably yet more shameful. "I mean, you didn't actually *'sell out'*?" He rolled over to look up into eyes of concern and impulsively leapt out of bed. The extraordinary events of the last thirty-six hours, the question itself, could not be accommodated by any ordinary answer. Words had bounds. Absurdly, a skinny middle-aged man wearing only pajama top he dashed round the room waving his arm like a sword, slashing, parrying, a berserk duelist, slaying invisible foes.

The bedroom and the mysteries behind its doors are a staple of human curiosity; a rich tapestry of voyeuristic wonder where imagination plays freely. But the general focus, natural enough, upon sex is awry. Given the simple and immutable nature of human equipment—the universality of desire and humankind's clinical knowledge of copulation—all the endless ways by which people dress it up and give it variety, trying to make it "different," can only culminate, at bottom, in trivial and unsurprising variations. Pathetic too, missing the point. The strangeness of the bedroom has little to do with anything as commonplace as naked human bodies. Its tension and drama, its wonders, and its sorrows, roam the whole wilderness of emotions that human beings customarily keep hidden, tucked away deeper than their lustings. There people may let slip rarer revelations, face the merciless mirrors of themselves, admit death, dare ask who they are, what they may become. Strange things can happen when masks fall, simple things don the oddest garb. Simple and precious as honesty.

"Ha!" He jabbed on, Hamlet skewering a phantom Polonius behind a drape. Wide eyes followed her madman about the room. Yet without a word. For there is great tolerance up here too—and there can be matching affection—in one's private theater of nonsense. "Matter of fact"—he halted, breathless from his antic exertions—"that's exactly it . . . took their thirty pieces of silver and ran." He started moving about again, a slower dance, so that he still did not have to meet her eyes fully. "Come back to bed, sweet nut," she ordered tenderly and stroked him after he had obeyed. "Darling. What's bothering me most is that I don't want you to regret this. Above all, I don't want to feel that you've done this only for me."

"Put that idea out of your mind. For *us*."

Which, for a little while, must do. There was the sound of her heavy book plopping shut. "Are you still awake? Good. Because here's another thing going round and round. It's how to react to this new life out here. It's all going to be so *strange*. And marvelous and beautiful and dreamlike, but somehow I'm afraid it's going to seem . . . *tainted*." He half rose, propped himself up on one elbow. "Sweetie. Accept that the cudgel of fate has swung, but gentle as a baby, and knocked us into paradise. You're another Dorothy, whirled off from humdrum old Annandale to some new Oz of our own but without the Wicked Witch of the West. Nor," he found himself chanting with easy fun to which she responded with a smile that grew, ". . . *lions and tigers and bears*."

"Oh, but there *are* bears. Don't tell me there are not. Grizzlies, in fact. I've been reading up." She wagged a finger. "But what about *you?*"

"The station runs itself. I will have worlds of time to do all kinds of good things. More time with the kids. Working with Boat. Be a Dad. Fish."

"Time too," she reminded, "to get on with your work about the submarine."

"Yes," he said, "that too." Funny how far that was out of mind.

"I'm worrying too about my new job. *Financial* management! Your Aliason and her checkbook," she said . . . . "It's all so preposterous."

"Relax. You'll have trusty assistants. Don't open your mouth too much and nobody will know what you don't know. Besides, you'll have your big kahuna here to protect and guide you. You're forgetting too—indeed, of course you've never known, how could you? the near infinite tolerance of Civil Service." She lingered over that. Biting her lip, but prettily. "It's all awfully sad though, isn't it, *that?*"

"Yes." In truth, few things sadder.

She picked up her book again. First kissing his ear, the most accessible part of him. "I want to read a little more. Sure the light won't bother you?" But sleep, for all his tiredness, was not easy. Misdeed was not troubling, but powerful imaginings were roaming his mind. Giants stomping along dark ways. The wind shaking the house, the lashing rain, was a reminder of lowland Washington's nearness to the sea, a sea floor itself not so far back, and of the greater storm bound to be raging out there upon it. Waves were pounding Ocean City, stealing its sand. Wind was whistling through taut wire, howling by masts swinging in sickening arcs of large ships slowed to mere steerageway. A bluish chunk of moon was fleeing through tattered clouds . . . . Sometimes the house groaned; this was tract house, after all, thin timbered, aluminum-sided, shallow-founded. Not your old solid homes, but these new ones, spawning ghosts, that set imagined footsteps creaking up stairs. Half in sleep again, thinking about nuclear submarines out there in the black sea, sinister but secure, calm in their chosen depths. Picturing their crews—knowing them from voyages upon patrol as a junior engineer maintaining their inertial navigations systems—moving about in their standard jumpsuits, intent at their control boards, or studying at the cleared tables in the bright, broad mess deck. This space which was their social center and where for weeks on end there was no day or night, only this core of light and activity. Young faces, best of America, so it was said, and truth there. He remembered the treasures of food, the golden flaky French pastries prepared by naval cooks who had taken finishing courses in their trade from chefs at the Hotel Pierre and the Waldorf and other places famed for luxury dining. Nothing too good, so the theory—so the practice—for those manning these prodigious men-of-war upon whose alertness and invisibility so much of the survival strategy of the United States depended. A "first class Navy," Surface Admirals grumbled enviously, whereas their own Navy, they could not help seeing, was second-class. But it had not come about from luck, or merely greater cleverness in the bureaucratic scramble for funds. The physics of energy were destiny. History had tolled.

* * *

Donnie Lee Webster had been right as rain. His instincts for this sort of thing never sharper. There was no Follow-Up. No posse, no hounds of process, came baying after one citizen Morgan who had failed his civic duty: violated the law, in fact. A *subpoena* was sacred, right? But apprehension swiftly faded. David realized again, as Donnie knew far better, that the governmental system rushes on, is always in a hurry, has scant curiosity in the past . . . unless there be political profit in it. He was too unimportant, the matter too fleetingly of the moment, and no one—least of all some outraged committee staffer whose duty it would have become—was going to win points pursuing vengeance on some pip-squeak no-show. There were too many of those types around, it happened too often and, besides, what person could not plead a sudden nosebleed, lapse of memory, whatever . . . ? Nor are juries of ordinary citizens inclined to convict some hapless nobody when a detestable Congress is the plaintiff. Probably though it was Abner Duke himself who had given the signal to call off the dogs. Win some, lose some—mostly the latter—and get on with things that might still be won. In a twinkling, the disappointing David Morgan had become as trivial as one more pebble tossed into the muddy waters of Washington Tidal Basin and as soon forgotten, say, as one Fannie Fox, the Argentina Firecracker who around that time had dazzled the mighty Wilbur Mills, living her own brief, and different, moment of Tidal Basin infamy.

9

Moving day had come. Sooner even than those Morgans had guessed it would happen, bringing on more than the usual hecticness of such days. Moving men tromping in and out, uncovering clottings of dust where furniture had stood. Outside, a sad little Boat kept his spirits diverted, with him and his pals fashioning clumpy structures out of the abundant brown paperboard packing material stacked on the lawn. Material sturdy for unfolding and molding into tunnels down which his gang rolled and tumbled themselves on a minor hillside, the tannish paperboard walls flexing and vibrating but not giving way. In the midst of all this Tony Ghezzi, Al's pal through thick and thin, dropped by to say goodbye. That loyal and generous soul bearing a full hot meal, including soup and salad and dessert, dishes and silverware too, for a family that was not going to be able to do much to feed itself this day. "And I shan't be able to touch a bite of it," Aliason said regretfully after Tony had departed. Pleased nonetheless to watch David and Boat dig in while standing side by side at an area briefly cleared out of the disorder of the kitchen counter. She was dressed smartly, ready to depart.

"All set, are you?", he said, "about the correct entrance, how to identify yourself, where to turn off on Pennsylvania . . . . ?" They had gone over all this earlier, but he remained apprehensive. "All set," she said, tightening her grip on her purse, symbol and reassurance, "stop worrying. How do I look?"

"Super," he said, "though perhaps grandly attired for grabbing a bite there in the White House cafeteria amongst the working stiffs."

"Or maybe not too. Sara Jane spoke of the 'dining room,' whatever that means." Whatever indeed, his knowledge of the labyrinthine ways and hierarchy of the White House being no more than his own fleeting and soiled acquaintance of weeks ago. Still, Sara Jane's late, almost last minute, call inviting Al both tickled and mystified him.

"Tell me, light of my life," he said, "did you get the impression that it's standard for the formidable Mrs. Whipley to favor all of her . . . let's say nominees, with a luncheon?"

"I have no idea. She just said that she would enjoy our getting together."

He watched her head for the car. Something of steel in her form's confident sway and something not. Suspecting that maybe she had taken a snort, maybe only a single one; but taken right, at the cliff edge of danger, strength measured and accepted along with the peril. He did not linger over the possibility. This thing would be there still, pursuing them across the continent. Right now too busy, the moving supervisor coming at him with more questions. And then, with all he had to do, before he realized it several hours had passed and Al was back. Returning radiant. Yet thinly, below her surface cheerfulness, there was something opaque, capable of becoming combative if touched. "Yes, it did turn out to be a true luncheon as well," she replied to his initial question, "and a very nice one. So, Mister Smarty, I actually made it to the White House Mess *before* you."

"You did indeed. And did it go well?" "Of course. But why would you ask that?"

"Naturally curious. It has to do with our future." The glint in her eyes was not all amusement. "You needn't be so skeptical. We talked about all sorts of things. And of course the job *is* mine. Why shouldn't it be?" Sensibly he withdrew from this encounter.

In their bedroom, now all dust rolls and emptiness and with the moving men thumping away just beyond the closed door against which he was braced to prevent its being opened inadvertently, she was stripping off her finery and reaching for the saved casual slacks and blouse kept unpacked for travel. Down to bra and panties. "I *did* like her. I think she liked me too. We giggled over some things; yes, girl fashion, and she shared with me a secret. Taking off herself on an adventure of her own. A 'fling' she called it."

"Who's the unlucky guy?"

"She didn't say and I didn't ask. Someone, I gathered, in the White House. Maybe not so unlucky as you think. She was an excited girl. So what do we know?"

His own turn to head off. To this one last thing that had to be done. Goodbye to Billy. Put off out of a general reluctance, mixed with shame, but also there being so little time. But even now, the two of them settled with cups of coffee in the Alpine Restaurant in Arlington, one of their old haunts—Billy not even going to get a meal out of this, only coffee—and looking at Billy's long face, he had still not worked out what he was going to say. Yet, unexpectedly, it went easier than David had thought because Billy did not press for understanding of the topsy-turvy changes in the Morgan family's life, his pal David's professional life in particular. There was only a dominant pall of mournfulness in Billy because his friend was going far away. And even as David's guilt lingered amidst the sad desultoriness of their conversation, calling forth from himself the unasked explanation, easier to provide in a cryptically passing allusion, no light lit up Billy's gloomy eyes.

"*What?* What in heck are you talking about Davey?"

"*Lord Jim*," David repeated, "he also *jumped*. Remember? *Como?*"

"Oh right," perhaps remembering, but if he did, still not caring. A Billy whom David could not leave in this mood. Bringing forth from his friend at least a minimal brightening with the invitation to pay a visit to Wolf Lake. "You and the family will have a whole floor of our roomy quarters to rattle around in."

"Hey. Now there's a thought." Which thought David took with him on the ride home, even as it struck him not likely to happen. One more of life's appealing pledges that seldom blossom for reasons that you can never quite put your finger on. Thoughts of Billy, others as well, were shoved aside in his arrival home at the last stages of moving out. A pair of brawny furniture lifters shouldering him out of the way through the front door with their near last load of a cushionless sofa and Aliason hugging an inconsolably weeping Boat.

"So, this is just about it," Al pronounced brightly, not even listening to David's reply to her question about how farewell *et al* had gone with Billy, and gazing around at the all at once somehow exciting emptiness of all these rooms in the imminence of their abandonment. "Well, just don't stand there, sweetheart. Grab a broom and start sweeping. Boat will pitch in too. Won't you, Boat?" With Boat dumbly, obediently, taking up a broom, moving no faster to his father's ironic exhortations which Al nevertheless took up excitedly. "That's right, dear ones." Eager to go. Was she ever! Taking up David's words like a refrain. *Shake the dust of Annandale* . . . . Thence on to Beth.

Beth waiting at the stable, having prepared the unknowing King for transformational journey from Eastern Horse to Western Horse. King blessedly saved from being sold in the nick of time. His shiny new trailer awaiting, along with Beth's sack of grooming tools and just acquired thick compendium on the lodging establishments and pastures in the United States serving the needs of travelers *cum* horse. His daughter heretofore not renowned for putting her nose in any book, but who had nevertheless demanded this one in order to lay out for her father a track zig-zagging across a dozen states to ensure the optimum healthfulness of King's grasses en route. King and Beth there in the long shadows of the westering sun.

Abruptly, shattering the precarious tranquility that is modern motoring at the best of times, a car that had been following that of the Morgan's trailering progress, impatient at its leisurely pace and the succession of curves and hills that had delayed passing, saw its chance. It was red, sporty, muscled, and left them in a snarling wake of noise and blue smoke. "Goodness!" Aliason exclaimed, "*Some* people. Please, you drive carefully at least." He watched the powerful sports car climb the next hill, a vision of purpose and beauty. Perhaps because he thought vaguely that he had recognized the man and the woman, the latter driving, that he felt an extra pull of envy at that zestful freedom. Not trying long though to figure out who they might be. Washington a stream of faces, too many to keep straight. Try no more. Farewell.

Anyway better late than never. Sara Jane's own show finally on the road. At the wheel of Donnie Lee's red Jaguar, the boy's pride, letting the feel of the car's power give her pleasure. A rare surrender to a shallow sensation, but it absorbed her impatience at the station wagon ahead, all the pokier and harder to pass for the horse trailer it was towing. At a mercifully straight stretch of road she had pulled out swiftly, catching a glimpse of a standard American family, complete with a boy and girl typically making faces as she zoomed by. The low sun drew her, fine wheels hummed a song. Donnie Lee had been dozing, his mouth slackly open. Having felt through his sleep her swerve, the surge of power, he stirred. The coarse word of decision with which she had irritably initiated the act of passing penetrated his relaxed consciousness. "Nearly there?"

"Hardly. Miles and miles to go, my boy."

His eyelids trembled with the flitting shadows and the smiting sunlight. He caught sight of a historical marker and raised his head too late to catch its message.

"*Ewell's Line of March to Antietam,*" she read off helpfully.

"How in gosh all heck did you get all that, Sara Jane?"

"Truth is, Donnie, I've read it before."

"War Between the States, right?" The very one, she confirmed, and Donnie drifted back into silence. Their route took them through little towns with old brick homes and stone fences, over narrow bridges and streams running over gray rocks. In fields, horses and cows were motionless, toy figures. The last rays of the sun, infinite lines of cooling gold visibly shrinking against the surging shadows, lit up the rich green of Virginia's astonishing Spring. From the radio, music heretofore soft rose to tumultuous climax; it groaned sweet and grand, through the convertible's windy swirl. Donnie sat up, suddenly alert. "Hey, Sara girl. What's the good old clock say?" She told him.

"That so?" He yawned ostentatiously. "Thinking like, it's about time for *New Rome.*"

It was. And for a bit of teasing she couldn't resist. "Why Donnie I wouldn't have guessed you ever paid attention to such fluff."

"Well, hardly, like ever." He made his voice gruff with unsuccessful deprecation. "It's just that I got tipped off that it might be, you know, worth my tuning in tonight...."

"Why Donnie, that's great." Sincerely wishing him well at the start of this weekend. Her big weekend too, after all. "Yeah, well, we'll see. So, Sara, girl, if you don't mind passing up your symphonies for a min...." She let him do the necessary fiddling, with Beethoven replaced by an announcer providing a summary of the day's political happenings. A woman commentator, who most of Washington—if not Sara Jane—knew as Lark Bright, followed with *"Doings and Delectables,"* which turned out to be five minutes of gossipy tidbits. Lark then signed off, but not before promising that after the next commercial the show would return with its popular weekly feature, PIP, *"Personality in Power—An In-Depth Profile."*

"And that's to be our boy here?", Sara Jane said.

"Reckon, maybe...." Though he was shruggngly casual about the whole thing, she felt his body tensing as for several minutes they listened to a commentator—evidently a *Rich* Bright now—describe Donnie's background, how he had met the President at a Johnston County barbecue and how, when the latter had been simply a junior state representative, Donnie had begun to serve in useful ways and eventually thrown in his lot with him. *"Two destinies merging...."* Campaigns were recounted, cities passing in a blur, in that dizzying ever-upward spiral that improbably had landed them both in the White House. *"Donnie Lee Lamar Webster licked stamps, made ten thousand calls, sawed lumber, hammered platforms together, hooked up speakers, carried coats... in short, performed all the indispensable chores of a typical campaign operation. Now—"* Rich Bright's voice lowered with the trained ability of his trade to invest his words with suspense—*"came the big chance, the workings of fate."*

Sara Jane's lips curled deliciously. "You actually did all those things, Donnie?"

"Bet your sweet ass. And lots more I'll never spill." Listeners were left to ponder the workings of fate during another commercial break, after which Rich Bright described Donnie's position on the White House staff. Rich changed the pitch of his voice to yet another one of his identities, this one judicious and sympathetic:

"Quick, affable, with unshed still the undergraduate's enthusiasm for campus politics, a fierce Loyalist, a touch of cynicism too has lately come to Donnie Lee—as he is known everywhere amongst Washington's heavy hitters—along with a few grey hairs in those curly locks. Maturity as well has come to this young man whose oft fatigue-reddened eyes reveal more somber cares of State than many in our jealous backbiting town will concede. America's leadership of the Free World, the tremendous pressures of defending our country, the need to grasp endless subtleties of foreign policy, are not a burden borne by Presidents alone. If they could not rely upon the knowledge of dedicated subordinates, the greatest of our Chief Executives would find their job tragically impossible. Donnie Lee: One of those special few.

"It is no secret that the President is favorably aware of what our PIP is accomplishing. In his critical role in breaking the shipbuilding logjam—so serious it could have caused the closing of a great construction yard and denied our Fleet the Men-of-War to defeat the submarine—his adroit handling of the myriad strands of the dispute revealed a rare grasp of the issues and equal skill at mediation. A total professional, he understands that the essence of government is ACTION. Act he did, in ways both visible... and behind the scenes. Insiders say that he is slated for a significantly expanded role in the decision processes at the highest levels of national security. Salute a rising new star."

After Sara Jane made sure that there was no more, she switched the radio off to welcome quietness. Donnie had not stirred but she was in no doubt that he was all glorious wakefulness. Could tell too that he was dying for her to speak. Thence complying. But first with a sigh below his threshold of detection. "So, Donnie. What did you think of all that?"

"Okay, I guess." He covered a little yawn, more exaggerated casualness. "There were some mistakes. Nothing big, but like, that barbecue wasn't Johnston County, but over in Sidney Lanier...." "Ah.... They really should be more careful in their research, Donnie"

When she spoke again moments later he did not see her smile, at first private, that grew irrepressibly. "But gee, Donnie, you'd think that in all that talk about solving the shipbuilding crisis that they'd at least give our Sara Jane here credit for a little assist."

"Huh?" Something in him struggled to extricate itself from a pleasant haze.

"I mean, face it Donnie, if I hadn't forced the job for that poor A-hole's wife down his throat, why the whole shipbuilding program of America might have come to a screeching halt there in Ab Duke's subcommittee."

"Hey!" Crossly. "Now come on, Sara Jane, you just cut all that out. Ah *mean* it." He drew himself up straighter. "There was a whole doggoned lot more to it than that."

"Sure there was." Giving his crotch a friendly pat; Donnie's cynicism shallower than she supposed, even as his self-evaluation lately seemed higher. She could not hear it herself—the kind of sensitivity to the upper registers that goes first—but it was easy to imagine Donnie listening to mighty music. Maybe too that high white note, as Scott Fitzgerald had put it (never better), trumpeting amongst the stars.

The sun had set and in the bluing sky first stars were out. Pale green gems in serene cloudless heavens. She felt Donnie shift position and relax. Snug again in dreams. And a little later when she reached over to him, fingers more bold, his murmur of pleasure had no residue of rancor. Expectation palpable. Their own rising star. They were truly in the mountains at last, those dark savage peaks of the East whose formidability can still surprise. West Virginia had returned to forbidding and gratifying wilderness. From Cass to the Greenbrier Valley the turn of the century logger's scars had healed. The road opened out onto a rocky ridge and for seconds there was a view of the western sky, night's blue but with a faintness of retreating daylight, last pale intimation of the vanished sun now dozens of horizons below the one she could just make out, range upon range of gloom-ridden mountains, swells of the earth frozen in dark time. She pictured the sun speeding westward, bright over much of the vastness of the United States, high up still over California, shining on the hoods of cars beginning rush hour on the Santa Monica Freeway, clogging Sepulveda Boulevard, highways known well in younger times. In between, in Kentucky, Iowa, the Dakotas, Montana... she saw a calming golden light falling, touching the frowns and smiles of those millions of people who—the faith and ardent conceit of her own circle—must truly care what government was doing back here. *But oh no,* she said to herself again, tell me I'm not thinking crap like that, pro or con. Not this weekend anyway, by God.

▲▲▲▲▲

The drive settled into wearisome miles, its destination farther than Sara Jane remembered it beyond these lightless hills, rounded and soft in the moonlight. Asking herself again why she was doing this. The twisting road had finally left all signs behind. The headlights swept by great tree trunks pressing close, bored a tunnel through buttery darkness, speared glowing eyes by the side of the road. Of these, she took little notice, zipping along, driving skills sharpened by years as Independent Woman, pressing down on the accelerator with each little length of straightaway, greedy for seconds. They might have been more pleasurable miles if Donnie had been better company, but his head was heavy on her shoulder. Sated with triumph, periodically he snored, short stutters in a rhythm that had her hands reflexively tightening on the wheel. She shifted her position, not used to sitting this long. She turned the radio back on, softly not to disturb Donnie, taking her mind off the persistent distress in her rear. Speedy notes cascaded in intricate harmony; over hills and through the stars, the sublime majesty of Bach. At once her lungs were sucking in memory of college days, concentrated in one fine moment that had begun with her swinging down the outside steps after a history lecture, floating with secret joy. Passing the School of Music she had heard a harpsichord coming from a basement window and had halted to listen, leaning dizzily against old sun-warmed brick on a sparkling Fall day when the hopes of her life were at their highest.

Yet for all its power the music was incidental. Straining her heart sac were the words of her professor. Matt Wilson was a homely man with a pipe and stained teeth and—beyond the yellow walls of the lecture hall and the segments of time cut out on the big electric clock above his head—a mind that soared on easy wings. Moderately well known, he had written a number of books which had drifted off into shadows of respected obscurity. Setting him uniquely apart was his teaching, out of a nature that held in exquisite balance a sense of man's noble strivings joined to the variety of institutions by which he sought to order his existence. Matt Wilson's talk kept his classes gripped to catch every nuance in his soft voice. Such talk! Nowhere did it flourish more than at his Sunday teas. Amidst dogs and children, the few of his many who were still left at home, the fire crackling and with Letty Wilson ever the generous hostess, the glorious talk went on. Neither barking dogs nor exuberant children were ever serious distraction. They were the normal and beautiful music of ordinary life, part of the solid earth in which Matt Wilson's knowledge and humanity were rooted. Street lights came on in that old college town, shining on wet flattened leaves, casting shadows of gothic towers towards an immense world beyond the surrounding prairie. But that cluttered living room of a standard professor's quarters, students sitting all over the floor, was the center of the universe.

They talked of populist democracy and Andrew Jackson and his fight with Biddle over the national bank. Sara Jane had never lost the image that Matt Wilson had implanted of old Sam Houston, walking with a cane and his life daily threatened in a Texas turned fiercely towards the Confederacy, a lion holding fast for the Union. Matt Wilson talked too of Thomas Reed, the Speaker of the House at the turn of the century, one of the great forgotten men of American history. Matt Wilson saw frequent parallels in history, but never strained for them. He suggested, but characteristically did not insist, that the dissipation of U.S. strength in peripheral wars might prove as fateful as Napoleon's wasteful adventuring in Spain during the Peninsular Wars. He was a master of stimulating trivia—no doubt one of his scholarly defects, along with his weakness for heroes— and he breathed life to every story. He recounted Harriet Beecher Stowe's hard go of it as a young wife in frontier Cincinnati in the 1830's, washing clothes in the muddy Ohio. He forgave much for grit. Ed Doheny may have warmed his oily hands on the Teapot Dome, but fifty years earlier he had made it alone across a desert swarming with Apaches to save a man's life. Kate Sprague, for all the scarlet blazes she set on the Washington scene, ended as a butter and egg lady. Not in Matt Wilson's eyes, a dreadful descent. No fall at all if one proved dependable in getting fresh eggs to those who counted on them. Yet all these were mere grace notes. The consuming passion of Matt Wilson's life was the mystery of the forces that surged across the vast and unruly land that was America. In the smarmy streams of politics, in which she feared she swam too well, a part of her never stopped wishing that she might find some oasis of companionship, share again those fine insights of graduate days. Late at night, her mind going round, she dreamed of shedding all clichés and jargon, saying again true and keen things and have the right someone listening. Interpretation. Contemplation. Depth. Beautiful words all; she yearned for their rich weave.

Her heart was drinking in last notes, caressing memory. All this from one Bach concerto. Suddenly she felt herself stirred in quite a different way, one both exceedingly familiar and yet, in the erratic infrequency of its occurrence these days, stunningly unexpected. *Oh no.* In the deep and secret machinery of her femaleness, meant soon to get another kind of workout, cramps were assaulting her. Pain twisted through her organs as if in redoubled vengeance for the long wait for this arousal. *Shit!* Immediately Sara Jane's mind took charge. Politics had trained a temperament to meet crises, how to rejuggle a fluid host of possibilities and set them down in sure new order of priority. That the weekend was shot, and that they would be heading back to Washington tomorrow, was the major message drumming through her mind, mocking instincts not recovering quite so fast from their disappointment. The realization not getting in the way of an even more urgent consideration. Hoping like hell Bessie Hank's Sundries was still open.

Which place, a few miles up the way and not far from their destination, had been sitting alongside this road more years than Sara Jane had been traveling it.

A low building, drab inside as it was out, it served not the masses but the loner, the hunter, the random passer-by. An occasional tourist family, not put off by anything so unchic, might not forbear to stop there if desperate for a few sodas to shush the kids. *Thank God.* Open. The bare light bulb outside, besieged by insects, the sense of equally harsh lights within, would not in ordinary circumstances be anyone's shining idea of salvation but Sara Jane was ready to kiss its worn and creaky boards. The crunch of gravel jolted Donnie awake. Yawning good-naturedly. "So, kid. Whatch'a stopping for? Anyway," he offered amiably, I'll go in with you."

"You will not!" Slamming the door shut. There were no other customers and possibly there had not been for some time. Bessie Hanks, an ample woman of indeterminate age and rough cut manner, did not stay open at these late hours primarily for business reasons. Hope of conversation kept her. Which accounted both for the lighting up of her face at Sara Jane's bursting through the door and the precipitous downcasting of her expression at realizing that there would be no enjoyable talk with this determined, emphatically modern, woman. No chitchatting about weather, no congenial imaginations measuring the night skies for rain. Not with this cookie. Scant chance either for Bessie to embellish her storied, if fraudulent, claim to kinship with that branch of Hanks that used to dwell just one range yonder before young Nancy trekked off to Illinois to marry Abraham Lincoln's father and become History. For such windy bullshit encounters Bessie lived. Taking in with ill-concealed resentment this city lady's breathless request for one specific item. Shifting her tobacco with juicy relish. "Fer you?" "I think that hardly matters." Chasms of time, planetary distances, divided two women. Bessie squinted a matching disdain. "Ain't got that kind. Only...."

"*Any* kind will do." Sara Jane reached into her purse as Bessie glumly set a bulky package on the counter. A woman beyond uplift, Bessie, though Sara Jane's loyalty to all variants of her sex refused to admit any such conclusion. "May I please use your ladies room?" Bessie jerked her thumb backwards indicating a door beyond her cluttered dusty shelves. "Only hit's fer men too. Reckon better latch it." You bet. "Thank you." Saved.

By the time she was on her way out Sara Jane was thinking steps ahead. "Might I also purchase gas? I'll be getting going early tomorrow and I'm low."

"Pump's closed. Closed at six."

"What time do you open in the morning?" Bessie inexplicably directed her bulk to the window to peer out at the car in front. Shaking her head. "Odd."

"*What?*"

"License number. 'Morrow's an even day fur rationing," she pointed out with complacent satisfaction. "Gotta wait 'till day after. 'Cept it be Sunday and store's closed."

Shit! Shit redux. Giving herself then an added lash: Serves me right. Cloistered in the White House, oblivious to what the rest of the country was putting up with. After they resumed their journey she drove more slowly. No need for hurry now. It took Donnie a few minutes to screw up his nerve against a smoldering barrier of silence. "Okay to ask . . . ?"

"Of course it's all right." She told him plainly, a woman of her times. She reached over to rub that curly, not unlikable, and now understandably subdued head. "Sorry, Donnie. Truly am." She sensed him struggling for some expression of gallantry and possibly, by his lights, finding it. "Hey baby, could happen to anyone."

"Well," not holding back a dry laugh, "I agree with you there."

"Seriously, it doesn't matter. Really."

"Truly?" For a moment, mere airy flattering seconds, she had thought that he had actually meant something else. Something helpful. Even something theoretical, she would have settled for. But no . . . . Through the lens of refocusing good sense the absurdity of the notion leapt forth. Least of all Donnie who, if she read him right—confident she did—would be one with ancient man in knowing well the curse of menstrual blood. Whose single drop could burn through a marble floor, pass sizzling to the very center of the earth, craze a hawk, set a thousand cattle to bawling. Not hard to guess then how it could shrivel some poor guy's pecker. She shook her head, a private rueful smile. Not Donnie. Not *Donnie's*. Well, almost there. Off on yet another road, narrower and more winding still. "Been thinking," he said. Evidently most cheerfully. "It can still be a great time. We'll talk, uh?"

"Donnie, *of course*. Why shouldn't we talk?"

"No, you don't get me. I mean *really* talk. Serious stuff. You know, like . . . what was the name of that prof you used to think was so great?"

"Professor Wilson?" Amazed. She could not remember herself ever mentioning Matt Wilson to Donnie, but obviously she had. Her fingers squeezed the wheel. Crushing its leather. She spoke slowly, deliberately, working at control. "It was a wonderful time in my life, Donnie. Yes, special. I'm asking you, please not to pee on it."

"Uh, huh. But you made it sound so great. That's what I'm needing too. You'd probably never guess, but I'm really insecure about all that crap I'm supposed to know. Heck"—once again that appealing boyishness in the candor of his confessions—"even with my counting of electoral votes, and all that stuff, I don't really understand where it all comes from . . . how it's written down in the—"

"Constitution."

His voice took on exultancy with the possibilities of new seeing. "I want to sit back and think about what all our wheeling and dealing really means. Talk with someone like you who's studied it." As they unloaded the car Donnie was briefly silent, but once inside the cabin, which to Sara Jane had never looked so small—no romantic nook but a cramped stony prison—his checked spirits rebubbled forth. "Thinking about tomorrow. You remember all those nature trails around here you said you knew?"

"Yes." Numbly. Yet reminding herself not to give in to that fatal numbness. The Antarctic explorer, Scott, and the noble Oates, knew how you must fight it. But it was hard. "I *had* supposed that hiking was one of the nice things we might do."

"But we can hold off hiking. In fact, hoping it rains all day. Forecast sounds like it might. We can make a fire. You like fires don't you?"

"Donnie." It was a cry. "Everyone likes fires, for Christ's sake." A cry quite unheard. "Hey, I guess they do, at that. Well, we can have ourselves a roarer."

There had to be ways, even desperate ones of cooling the errant passion of his runaway vision. Ways to divert the energies of this poor sweet maddening dope. A most practical physical one occurred to her. Simple as they come. Unilateral action, as her city of Washington would put it. Except that in the icy caldrons of its calculation, it was grotesque. God save us. God save Sara Jane. Decidedly, not up to it.

"Hey. We can start tonight. Don't have to hold off until tomorrow. What's your opinion, on all this Decline of the West stuff? I'll make us a little drinky-poo for openers."

"Donnie dear. I'm not up to talking about anything. Bear with me, but I'm dreadfully tired." Dear God. Far off, beyond heartbreaking numbers of mountain ridges, her apartment beckoned. She pictured the comfort of its books and a rare quiet weekend, some salvageable remnant of it anyway, that still might be. The first thing she must see about—eyes shut for sleep but all the lights of her mind on bright—was gasoline. Sweet fuel. Power for happiness. Slip out early then and talk Bessie Hanks out of ten illegal gallons. That the plan. For which she would listen reverently to Bessie's heretofore-interrupted monologues on the ramified genealogy of the Hanks clan, of wagons across mountains, rattling on into legend by the banks of the Sangamon, the whole nine yards.... Shamelessly she would bribe. For ten lousy gallons of gasoline Sara Jane, priorities straight once more, would risk much.

* * *

A traveler on his own special road. Tawney Gray needed no signs to guide him on this last zig of his career. A whisper, a mere cocked eyebrow, was enough to tell all. He'd had it. It occurs rarely in government but there are mishaps—big enough and in plain sight of too many of the important, earning the grander title of "Royal Fuckups"—that exceed the generous threshold of the forgivable. Henceforth, so long as anyone was alive to remember, Tawney's name and SUNRISE and its cockeyed central gem, CORRIDA, all of it lit up by the blazing Near Miss of the Duke Hearings, were infamously crowned. Say, like, *wasn't that Morgan jerk once one of Tawney's boys?* They couldn't force Tawney to retire—even Presidents were powerless to storm the impregnable bastions of Civil Service regulations—but they could threaten transfer and make it some place far away. His seniors didn't even have to say where banishment would be. Tawney could not be other than keenly aware. In southern Mississippi, sited deep in the wide wetlands drained by the lonely Pearl River of sinister history, where a grab-bag of Navy shore activities were being relocated. In the swampland, a relic of the Golden Age of Space, men had once tested mighty rocket motors that took Americans to the moon. Canals barged the rockets to this remote place where, should they blow up, there was nothing to disturb but egrets and the alligators for miles around. Those stirring times and their needs were past, but it was a mighty Senator's intent to keep the place open and that was that. Whatever the price, or the deal—another naval ship, say, or only another airplane perhaps (such horsetrades are never written down)—the Senator had merely to crook his finger and the Navy agreed to transfer whole organizations to fill up its cobwebbed deserted buildings and thereby justify keeping it open. Indeed, more than typically unresistant, the Navy showed itself eager to trot on down there. Soon claiming the idea as its bright own and thence leading the Senator's fight to make it come to pass. Tumbling all over itself.

A strange area, lunar in mood as it once was moonstruck in objective. The towns are small and have hayseed names like Picayune. Interstate signs point to far off places like Hattiesburg. Here are not city lights, fine restaurants, limousines filled with gay people bound for the best of theaters. Here will not be met the massed company of the highly educated, knowing the latest jokes and wise with self-knowledge and paths of power. In Picayune people dress, talk differently, and take other routes toward fulfillment. Fulfillment, in fact, not an everyday word down there. Survival nearer to their hearts. The roads through these vast coastal swamps are depressingly straight and seem, in the moist shimmering heat of summer, to rise up in the distance in a way that awes and frightens. Mighty Interstate 10 floods in hurricanes and lesser rains too and in Slidell, home of the world's largest truckers' stop, many a girl type finds it worthwhile to drive up from New Orleans to provide the truck drivers services other than the standard lube jobs on their parked eighteen wheelers. Along the prodigally wide road to the base itself—it is a moribund place still, owning the kind of road to nowhere that only the mightiest governments build, eerily shy of traffic— flattened nutria are the sole punctuation along its empty miles. For a man such as Tawney Gray, loving his boat, dependent upon the special peace that it alone could bring, if he had to be banished to such a region his thoughts must inevitably shift to the question of where he would be able to sail his lovely toy. The answer that came, an echo as grimly inaccurate as all his other broodings; Lake Pontchatrain! God save us! Lake of mud, shallow, lusterless, confined, full of choppy mean little waves, delightless . . . not for such did Tawney's heart beat.

Tawney though did not have to advance his thinking far on a future home to his boat. As soon as he had absorbed the fateful letter—not a long one but typed on logoed elegant paper, with the dread named location leaping off the page with the force of a black panther—he exhaled a whistle of despair no less heartfelt than when the Concierge once breathed the guillotine to the doomed. With a hand that moved as swiftly as his lips had grown pale, he reached for a pen to draft his request for retirement.

Tawney's Retirement Party was the biggest in memory, for all its hasty setting up. People flew in from far away, every last living recipient of EAR's financial largesse. Sentiment the least part of their motivation, because Tawney's relief, EAR's new incumbent, would be there and one had best get one's oar in early. Even if Tawney were history, there would be other projects, funding to come. A broad world out there to be supported, a world that must go on. Yet another gathering of the clan. The liquor gushed. Acousticians and signal processors not always dull fellows. Once in a while theirs too a night to howl. There was the inevitable Roast. Messages from the Important Who Could Not Make It were read. Admiral Snowdon's was especially warm in its expression of the Navy's gratitude for wise service rendered. A generously signed scroll of tribute was unrolled before the surprisingly moist-eyed honoree. All agreed, one hell of a party. Good old Tawney.

All the same, sure as shit time for him to go.

▲ ▲ ▲ ▲ ▲

At last, Tessa said to herself, *at last*. Her benediction fervent. The day of the Corridor's dedication ceremony finally at hand. Many months after its approval, an interval of waiting time that only government could explain. It was bitter cold. The façade of the Pentagon's Mall Entrance was colorfully decorated and in the gusting wind bunting strained and snapped. A wooden stand draped in red, white, and blue, with a rosette of the Great Seal of the United States tacked to its front of raw lumber, had been erected for the principals. Facing the stand were rows of chairs, mostly unfilled. Only the duty bound were here this day. By the standards of Pentagon ceremonies, this was not a big one and, like the funerals of the very old, the honoree had outlived his friends. Her program clutched in her thinly gloved hand, Tessa sat beside Muddy who, in turn, was seated next to the Secretary of Defense. On Tessa's other side sat the Chief of Naval Operations. He struck her as a surprisingly young-looking man and, although she couldn't remember his name, she was sure that she had known his father. On the end sat a plumpish Navy Chaplain with a face both blue and red at the same time; his shoulders were hunched with misery. A droplet clung trembling on the tip of his nose. Tessa sympathized with the poor man, waiting to offer his prayer. The cold penetrated her boots, came up through the metal of the folding chair she sat upon, crept into her spine. She pictured ice crystals forming in her bones. Yet Muddy, as she glanced over at him fondly—wishing him well on his long-dreamed day—was oblivious to the weather, the whip of fine sleet in the air. His head, under his dark homburg, kept nodding jerkily, trying to catch ragged notes of music, a speaker's words of praise.

The band started playing again. Its notes were tinny: the notes had ice in them too. The bandsmen in their pathetically bright uniforms Tessa observed sympathetically. How could their stiff fingers move, frozen cheeks blow? Snatches of melody she retrieved from out of the swirling wind. She sat down after some music, rose again for a prayer of invocation. She did it in a copycat mode, without reference to her program, the way her non-Catholic friends dumbly followed her own movements when she dragooned them into accompanying her to Mass. Poor Muddy looked quite stricken with feeling. His squeaking noises, now more clearly than ever sounding like a trapped mouse, grew frantic. By this time she had deciphered them, the anguish of his frustration. He whispered hoarsely in her ear, "Can't hear a damned thing, Tess." She put her hand over his. "There, I'll listen *for* you."

"Will you, my dear?" For a bit he seemed reassured. She strained for words, which the electronic speaker amplifiers were delivering best to distant and empty spaces in the North parking lot. A pair of fat black crows, perched high up in the bare shivering limbs, cawed in irritated rebuttal. "Eh? What was that he just said? Did I hear 'Destroyer'?"

"Just relax." She patted his hand. "He's saying nice things. *Lovely* words."

But Muddy could not contain his concern for long. "What about Choiseul? I gave them all the dope. Delivered a whole box of it. Thought these pantywaists should see a real sea chest. You're sure he mentioned Makassar Straits too?"

"Absolutely." Like every woman successful with her man, Tessa had a capacity for lying in a good cause. But too much practice at exaggeration had perhaps made her more than usually careless. For she did not have to add: "Loads."

Muddy gave her an odd look, but at least he was quiet for a few more minutes. Only a few though. "Yes indeed, I gave 'em' all the information they would need. Starting with my commission as a midshipman. Had it brought to that young fellow right over there wearing the wings. God knows what he did with it. You can't lay everything on an aide, Tess. Sometimes there's no one like an Admiral to not know what's going on. Har."

There was clapping now, glove-muffled, and one last forlorn piece by the gallant band. In little clusters, people were offering congratulations, shaking hands. The naval aide stepped forward and offered Tessa his arm. A plastic tag told his name. Lieutenant Anson. "You must be proud of the Admiral this day, Mrs. Waters."

"I am proud of him every day." He was, she guessed, not used to the old, fearing all sorts of parts inside her ready to break. She was grateful though for his steadying arm as they made towards the Pentagon steps. "I *can* walk a bit faster," she said.

"Very well." The timbre of a spirit standing by for greater challenges was in his voice. His lengthening stride tugged her along. *"Let's,* my little lady." Her sigh was inward, telling herself that he means well. Inside, past the guards, Muddy took over. He pointed out a wide yellowish corridor so long that, wherever it ended, was beyond the power of her eyes to tell. She marveled: this her very first visit to the Pentagon. Poor David, this was his kind of world too, a life amongst telephones and paper. In Irish's day Washington was a place that naval officers shunned. Those worth their salt, anyway. Muddy was going on, voluble in a way that she had never experienced. "You're taking up this whole corridor?" she asked. He smiled indulgently. "Heavens no, my dear. Just a portion of its length. But," he took a deep breath of pure happiness; "it will fill a sizeable piece of it at that." He did not add, to her relief, his usual "by Jove." Progress on small fronts.

In the spacious offices of the Secretary of Defense their little party was served coffee and cakes. The best part of this day, picturing herself recounting it to Miriam, who would enjoy reliving memorially the presence of the massy ornamental silver, the gift of cities, the wardroom cups with the ceramic blue flags and gold stars, and the impeccable stewards, their fine olive skins and snowy jackets. Cream of the Orient's cream still. Sinful in this day and age to think this way, but still the truth. She was enjoying chatting with the Secretary of the Navy, Mr. Menson, about Old Annapolis. He loved its quaintness, he said, the cobbled streets .... She noticed though that Mr. Menson's eyes were red, almost sorrowfully so, and she sensed the closing down of what must have been for him rare moments of relaxation. The poor man's coffee cup rattled as he set it down. Equally she felt the ending of the mood of congratulation and peace which had for a few minutes revolved around her and Muddy. Reading *finis* in another form, in the expression on one aide's face whose smile, until just seconds ago, seemed frozen as a gargoyle's.

The looks these aides passed. Once you started catching them .... Signals that were like basketball players passing the ball, flick here, then flick over there, the ball sailing over the heads of the dwarf players around them—a team of giant centers, lords of their game, not in confrontation with one another, but in a cooperative dominance—one side of the room to the other. One tall, no longer smiling, aide was holding up his arm to reveal the largest wristwatch she had ever seen; he tapped it vigorously and the ball appeared to go arching over to the equally capable Lieutenant Anson whose lips were forming their own silent, urgent message. Faces were starting to twist in what persons more experienced in such matters than Tessa could diagnose as an aide's special kind of suffering, precious minutes leaking away, schedules sagging perilously. *Something was happening.* Tessa glimpsed yellow lights on a phone face blinking. Rhythmic, ripples of nervous light. She saw a secretary scurrying, then a generalized extraordinary acceleration of movement. As if an army were breaking camp, she felt the swift folding of invisible tents. Vividly she remembered, from seventy years ago, a violent storm coming down on a traveling circus set up in a field outside of her town, men running, stakes being pulled, a great billowing brown canvas heaving convulsively, animals in their cages bawling, and upon the trampled grass rain drops spattering out of black rolling clouds. "Excuse me, Junior," she said to the Chief of Naval Operations. Recalling his name at last. Salty Murdock's son, "Junior", of course, Junior then, Junior now. She had danced with Salty, another charmer dead these many years. "What on earth is going on?"

Junior Murdock spun around, his face the sickly green of a man who has just learned of a new attack on the Navy's budget. From unexpected quarters—old enemies joining faint friends—that very morning a cunning assault on Navy programs had begun across a wide front. Through a metaphorical dike trickles of money, once well contained, were turning into rushing torrents, hemorrhages of lost dollars from a dozen holes whose flow, if not staunched, would bleed their great loved Navy white. Abner Duke might be leaving Congress, but mischievous disciples lived on. Junior Murdock's lips moved queerly. "... *attacked. Getting it on all sides.*" Tessa's eyes flew open wide. *"The Russians?"* The head of the Navy's Number One Admiral jerked. This ancient lady, he has gathered vaguely, and not comfortably, evidently knew him as a boy. One more of these sweet old nuts still around malingering on beyond her time. Yet she sounded utterly serious. Then seconds later, his release from any such preposterous misapprehension, plus the cleverness of this wrinkled fossil who has quite taken him in, forces an explosively uproarious laugh that has him wiping his eyes. *Good God! Thank God!* He needed that. He gazes down gratefully. "That's pretty good. Would that it were the Ruskis. Least of our problems."

Tessa observed Junior Murdock's behavior with astonishment, unable to get over that extraordinary laugh with nothing to provoke it. *My word,* what a peculiar boy Salty and Jane got themselves. She took out a last cigarette but this time no aide bounded over to supply flame. Lieutenant Anson noticed her fiddling with her light and she saw him dismiss her need with a cold flash of those alert eyes. So, *our time is up,* she told herself. People were reaching for their coats as their group drifted doorward, irresistibly sucked that way, in the tug of mysterious destinies . . . . Coats, opening doors, limousines, and she knew not what other details—a whole unified symphony of logistical synchronization, all these important lives polarized in a single direction—seemed mere extensions of the fingertips of these incomparable orchestrating aides. Muddy alone oblivious. Embarked on discussion of the evolving shapes and colors of naval pennants down through the centuries, he went on even as his gloves were thrust in his gesturing hand. The object of his tutorial was an unidentified little man whose desire to join this senior crowd heading for the Hill was visible in his fixed beaverish smile and busy eyes, pitifully anxious not to be left behind. Evincing the special desperation of a world where simple absence can be failure. The tenderness she felt for Muddy, his lasting innocence, had not departed from her as they waited on the Mall steps for their limousine, one of a line of long black ones, to advance to where they stood. The wind off the frozen Potomac howled around the huge geometric impediment of stone, swirling out of skies like dirty grey ice. Yet for all that it mattered, Muddy might have been breathing in the orchid air of the South Pacific. This morning had restored him. Yet even as she observed him she saw small lines of reflective vexation reforming. "You know, Tess, I don't believe that I was quite finished talking to that young fellow when we were broken off."

She minimized the possibility of any rudeness. "After all, those busy people did have to be getting on to whatever they had to do." Icy air rushed into her mouth as she spoke. She felt it smite in every dental filling. The line of limousines was slowly advancing, each one taking aboard its designated clot of Important People, but their own transportation, which had been pointed out to them further down the line, was a few minutes away still. An evidently lesser aide—possibly at some stage of apprenticeship—was at their elbow and it was he presumably who would open the door when their vehicle finally crept up to them right at the bottom of the stone steps. Some residue of this morning's ceremony, shreds of unexhausted protocol, seemingly forbade their walking a few yards on down the line and hopping into that oasis of warmth that their chauffer was enjoying so contentedly. Such a detail, however, was outside of the orbit of Muddy's concentration, which presently reached its conclusion. "We *were* hurried." His recollection of events was clearing, bringing forlorn echoes of a once formidable capacity for outrage. "Indeed we were . . . hustled right out of there, Tess." Ah Muddy. "Taken right by the arm, by Jove. Just getting to the point, interesting one, by the way, and regarding which this chap—nice fellow, can't remember his name, only that he was deuced anxious to hear more of how the Roman imperial eagle evolved from an Etruscan form—had no chance to learn more. He was as shocked as I was to be hauled away like that. You recall, Tess, my telling you just a little while ago that a flag officer mustn't hand too much over to his subordinates?" He wagged his finger knowingly. "I wonder if I ought not to do something more though," he mused. "Perhaps drop a note to Junior Murdock. He's not likely to learn of it otherwise."

"*Jesus, Mary and Joseph.* The only thing more you ought to be doing right now Muddy, is figure out how to get us out of this cold and into that car faster." Muddy appeared not to hear. His eyes were fixed distantly. She pictured him, in his easy and unconscious pose, on the bridge of his ship, just as she once used to imagine Irish. The picture softened her. It must be good for men, looking out at all that blue water for so much of their lives. It kept their thoughts clean (well, fairly clean, she amended that, for men at least), their ways simple. A decent bunch, naval officers, on the whole, boy scouts at heart all their lives. Muddy's preoccupation with officious aides and negligent admirals, the possibilities of setting them right, did not last. He was humming a Navy tune, scratchily—but hardly doing worse with it than the poor cold-cursed band had managed a while ago—as he helped her into the limousine. "A fine day, eh Tess? Calls for celebration, wouldn't you say?"

But Tessa's own thoughts were wandering. The limousine seats, the warmth toasty as a fire, lulled. The heavy car glided past monuments and buildings she no longer knew. She felt strange, close to slipping off again into the mystery at whose edge, for all the impatient practicality of her nature, she suspected that she had always dwelled too closely. Filling her mind were memories of her childhood prairie home, the look of broad snowy fields bereft of human footprints, patches of trees thickening by the river banks. It was Muddy's voice, good old Muddy's talk, running on like a dull but comforting stream that drew her back. "So what shall it be, my girl? '*Where do we go from here? Anywhere from Harlem to a Jersey City Pier.*' Remember that one? A bite of lunch, maybe even a bottle of champagne . . . eh?" He glanced towards the driver, who must be told something. Her fingers dug into his arm and he turned in surprise. But her look, though oddly bright, was certainly Tessa. And her laugh back in all its richness. "Any place, Muddy, goddamit, so long as it's warm."

▲ ▲ ▲ ▲ ▲

The altar was rich with flowers; great candles had the brasses gleaming. The organ was thrumming and massed voices were lifted in stirring hymn. Amongst the overflowing congregation, Tiny Gray's lips moved along in humbler replica of holy song, her voice not being one to lift her into any choir. Yet transcendent feelings could still be hers. Snobs to the contrary, a paucity of talent is no barrier to the grandest of emotions.

Her rapt expression, however, was not solely a manifestation of love of God; for if that love was pure, it was also, well . . . complicated. The Reverend Henry Bruton, standing in that carved pulpit, was a man to arouse temporal as well as eternal passions. Hester Prynne had her troubles with just such a fellow as this. Pale, ethereal, educated abroad amidst medieval towers, blessed with elegance of gesture, his appeal was not cut from the ministry's ordinary cloth. A rarer bird, he vibrated at higher frequencies and well removed from those coarser perches where beefy Irishmen of God's earthly kingdom jostled. If he seemed too frail to generate, or to absorb, such powerful feelings, upon closer observation—and none had observed him more closely than Tiny—first impression was deceptive. The strongest flames, like naphtha fuel in sunlight, can be invisible. His voice could whisper, holding a whole congregation in thrall, freeze mice in their nibblings. It could also reverberate in the polished rafters, jar pigeons right off the fakery of the flying buttresses on the church walls outside. The Reverend waited for total hush. Tiny settled herself back against the polished wood of the pew.

"My text is from Ezekiel: '*Yea, Anaphor was wife to Bukob, but though she cleaved herself unto him and reckoned herself a good wife, she was not concerned with her husband's godlessness and sought not solace for the barrenness of his spirit'.*"

The Reverend had labored over his sermon and rehearsed it; the full-length mirror in his quarters not meant for the vanity of his dress but for the practice of his words. They flowed with the majesty of the Nile. Secular quotations were set like jewels in the darker surface of God's wisdom. In truth, he did not approve of the practice—a kind of *peccadillo* now endemic amongst his profession—of employing the words of poets and philosophers to supplement the Scriptures. He excused his own bowing to the times, however, because—well, even God's own troops had to face it—sometimes those ancient gospel spinning Bedouins could get bogged down in the sands. Thus in addition to keeping in his stable, saddled and ready, Buber and Camus to help him handle the tangled greyness of the modern spirit, he had also corralled Donne and Hardy from out of their pastures for the darker colors of his palette. Bobbie Burns roped in skillfully too for his sprightly way of catching the bitter sweetness of life. Ah, yes. No one better.

It made not a bit of difference to Tiny Gray which Masters the Reverend chose, or with what artistry and intellect he blended their eloquent insights. Only the melody she absorbed and not the words. This particular morning though—so like many another Sunday in its pleasant aura of mindless inspiration—Something Happened. The first sign, there in the quiet, glades of her imagination, was tentative as the touch of a small bird that means to alight on a slender branch and then, finding it too frail to support its weight, flits away. It happened again, moments later, this time the shaking stronger, unmistakable. The disturbance was her own heart starting to pound. She pictured Tawney at home morose amidst the litter of his Sunday paper. At once, every fiber of her being was rigid with attention. "*Yea, and she concerned herself if not with his godlessness....*" Words, once comfortably far away, rolled through her like a river in flood. The Reverend was talking about *her*. She felt her skin being pulled away, soul laid bare, selfishness pitilessly exposed. Not merely had she been grossly negligent concerning poor Tawney's religious spirits, but as for the *cleaving*... well, and here she shut her eyes with pain. *Memory of man runneth not back.*

Her hands shook on the wheel as she drove home and she called out her husband's name as she burst through the front door. Tawney put aside his paper—by now reduced to the dreariness of the crossword puzzle—to contemplate the apparition of a Tiny who, if not truly bearable to him at her most docile, was decidedly less so in her present state of aggressive agitation. Her eyes wide with desperate sincerity and alarm. An alarm, which communicated itself to Tawney beneath his mask of calm. "And just what, my lady, is on your mind this bright Sunday morning?" he said with forced joviality. For countless years, and even with the continual propinquity that retirement had forced upon him, Tawney had been able to evade talks such as the one he now saw coming, the kind of Serious Dialogue with one's wife that all sensible men dread.

His idleness constantly on display, any pleas of busyness was patently passé. But Tawney, ever resourceful in such matters, had other tactics. Not all the years of his government experience in vain. For those occasions when a question used to be too sticky, decision awkward—or when he had found himself, as he was ever more frequently in those last years of his eminence, pressed for some lucid technical judgment—he would light up his pipe. Just as he was doing so now with full ceremony—unfolding the pouch with care, the act of tamping down made to seem a skill whose mystical aspects few were privileged to share ... now the downward sucked flame of the match was playing over the mixture—its topsy-turvy behavior strange for a flame, if you let yourself think about it, even hypnotic—the extinction of the match itself a flourish, the whole business a dragging out of time, working to grind away the sharper edges of another's impatience. He fiddled on, behind clouds of narcotic blue smoke, working away towards reenactment of that little, but ever gratifying, miracle which was going to be (with the smoke's clearing) an exasperated Tiny once more having thrown up her hands and gone off to do something else. But that little rock of a woman was staring at him with demoralizing patience, forcing further temporizing. "Well, well, my goodness ... *surely* not ... ?"

By most standards of dissimulation and obfuscation. Tawney would be given A for effort. His the sort of good try which, under ordinary circumstances, would have sufficed to derail Tiny's engine of unwanted good. But now, as determinedly as his mate had waited out his smoke, ominously she waited out the froth of his banter. Straightway she told him, *"Surely yes Tawney. The subject is the state of your immortal soul."*

"Tiny, for Jesus Christ's sake."

"Exactly!" She told him how the sermon had pierced her heart, bringing agonizing self-awareness. She reviewed their past, conceding it some initial youthful vigor and propagative value, but then bringing forth the overshadowing melancholy of its Spiritual Poverty. Theirs had not been a House of God. The past put in dismal perspective; she was now wagging her finger in summons of a new and brighter future. Tawney dodged and weaved, demurred, parried as best he could this passionate monologue. His defenses were like a child's dam, a thing of twigs and mud, against the torrent of her words. He grew pale, "My dear," at one point he managed to insert weakly, "allow me to observe that, while recent events in my life may have been disappointing, your imagination exaggerates my unhappiness."

"I'm not talking about *happiness*," she said scornfully. "We are going to change our lives. I shall be the wife and companion I haven't been in years. And you'll change with me, my darling love." Her grin, meant to be jolly and encouraging, was horrible. "Tiny." His voice was pleading. He had always ruled by bluff, and now there was nothing behind it. "Shouldn't we, may I offer, simply go on just as we have been? Surely there have been some good . . . features. Change," he croaked, "can be dangerous."

"Dangerous?" she flung back. "What danger can there be in salvation?"

"But dear . . . ." His pipe out cold. Only a steady hand can make that game go and such loony extremes of emotion such as Tiny's had never buffeted him before. Mercifully, properly, the civil service system itself did not *permit* it. It furnished barriers, trip wires against rashness, nooks to hide. Layers of subordinates, defense in depth. Indeed, leadership required such. A fellow otherwise could be stripped bare in minutes by people howling their unwanted Truths. In a flash Tawney saw the fundamental flaw in the whole idea of marriage. Its defect, that is, in structural terms. Marriage lacked *definition*. Had no wiring diagrams. Its hierarchical edifice was forever teetering, out of control. Everything was free form, perilously shifting. One of the principals, say, in a twinkling, on mere whim, could turn things quite upside down. In Crystal City, there had been uniforms, offices, titles, authority explicit. As for *marriage*; why marriage was just two people wandering about in their underwear. Or worse. Now, at a Pentagon conference, for instance—a meeting called ostensibly to settle something—the affair was conducted with protocol. No one shouting from unexpected directions, tugging at you during your morning shave, ramming argument maniacally through bathroom doors. Most comforting of all, it was understood that, however awesomely some conference was heralded as the arena of Final Decision, in truth nothing would be decided. There would always be *reclama, further* conferences. None of this "now or never" stuff: there was always another day. Yet here, good God, was his Tiny, *sans* Agenda right in his face, running amok. *Unilaterally*, deciding things beyond recall. There it was, no Ifs, Ands, or Buts . . . .

"No buts." She smiled with monstrous confidence. "It's all settled."

Tawney feebly waved his pipe, impotent as a rubber dagger, and with his last bit of resistance available, chose to address that one feature of Tiny's plan— already looming monstrously as The Plan—that concerned him the most: The peace of his days on his beloved boat. Precious last redoubt that must be saved above all. He took a deep breath before marshaling his arguments. Concluding with a seeming note of sad regret, a sly old dog still. "It's no disgrace my sweet, you're simply not a sailor."

"I respect your experience, and your wisdom there. I'm *not* a sailor." She glanced down at her hands and then looked up. A light possibly blessed, surely bright, shone from within. "But I can *make* myself into one."

Tawney was looking ahead, calculating. Reconciled that their last test was to be a trial of arms. Something else was bothering him though, a lower note of alarm, so to speak, lost back there in the bigger bang. Something to which he had perked up his ears earlier. In her forecast of changes to come, Tiny had declared that henceforth they would be doing *everything* together. Seeming at the time mere hyperbole, sufficiently ambiguous, it struck him now nevertheless as prudent to take a minute or so to check this one out. What the dickens was she getting at? His route was roundabout—ever a fellow for spiraling in on a thing—but just what, ahem, did this "everything" encompass? Her wide smile of old was one in which he recognized—a jarring note of unwanted nostalgia— a gold tooth tucked far back in a corner of her mouth. He had not noticed it for years, a bit of gold winking at him obscenely from out of a dark wet cavern. No ambiguity either in that grotesque smile. "*Everything*, my darling." It was the very mockery of lust.

He did not reveal his dismay. His whole life, after all, had been a training ground in avoidance of showing what he felt. Presently came a succession of sounds. Ordinary kitchen sounds, but so rare in this house, the rattling of pots and pans, the whirr of a blender. He deduced, needing no further enlightenment, that they represented first installment on one of the less wounding of the many vows that had tumbled out of her this dreadful morning. Good food again, a healthy diet, meals henceforth on schedule. The matter of sustenance restored to its ancient place in the hierarchy of importance, wreathed again in ceremony, the same communal sharing of nutrition that had built families through history apparently now going to prop this one up as well . . . . After a while, the aroma of forgotten spices preceding, Tiny emerged, aglow with the joy of creation. She perched coquettishly on the arm of his chair. "Two pennies for your thoughts."

"Nothing really. Merely planning our sailing trip. We want the weather to be right."

"Goodness yes. I appreciate your thinking of that. But let's not wait too long, dear. I'm dying to get out there on the waters!" A smallish smile had revisited Tawney. To a closer observation than Tiny, it might have appeared somewhat enigmatic. "I'm watching the weather forecasts." Despair, as the world knows, is a state that seldom hangs on indefinitely in the healthy. Where there is life there is hope. "Trust me, sweet."

▲ ▲ ▲ ▲ ▲

It was the second day of what was planned as a week's cruise. Not that Tawney imagined it would last a full week. Or even close to it. Not the least of his planning was the inclusion of visits to little ports along the Eastern Shore familiar to the regular sailor of Chesapeake Bay—St. Michaels, Crisfield . . . . The night before they drove down to Annapolis, where he kept his boat now, he had broken out the charts and gone over their intended track with an excited Tiny. Putting on her glasses to make out the fine print of strange place names, the unfamiliar symbology of the mariner's world. A frown of puzzlement settled on her forehead, but her eyes shone with great willingness. "So *many* places to explore."

"Indeed, sweet." So many places for her to call it quits.

A new and fonder light in Tiny's eyes—one that Tawney correctly diagnosed, though he discounted its danger—accompanied her next words. Her fingers curled in a little ball of resolve that once he had found adorable and her voice dropped into a mock accent, likewise meant to be cute, whose unappealing roots he had no wish to trace. "Ahm gonna do mah durndest, love." Ghost of Shirley Temple? "Don't get your hopes too high" he had cautioned once more. Giving her a small and rare pat. Yet an affection that had been methodical, just as everything else about this trip was calculated. At stake no less than this last enclave of his once far spread empire of pleasure.

Low dark clouds had been scudding by as the two prospective sharers in adventure carried their duffels down the wooden pier at McKenzie's boathouse. Wind ruffled Spa Creek, swift wild tracks of its gusts zigging and zagging across that dark and normally placid surface. Looking towards Trumpy's yard and the forest of aluminum masts that is one of the wonders of the affluent world, the eye saw that the forest was in motion. Small swells, echoes of the heavier seas outside, were lifting hulls in heaving rhythms. On his own boat the wind slapped the taut halyards against the mast. Tiny looked up apprehensively at that sky and then over at Tawney. Reassurance found in her husband's figure—his pipe easily in his mouth, removing the canvas covers from compass and wheel—she set about doing that one task that she remembered confidently, rigging the jib. Down the pier, dressed in yellow slicker, came the solitary figure of Angus McKenzie. No one else going out this day, he was lonely. Older now, his sailing days were done. But those veined eyes now glancing up towards the darkling sky had, in his youth, traveled with the fishing fleets out of Northern Scotland— out of Ullapool and John O'Groats—looked to the Hebrides, seen gales off the Faeroes that, *aye*, no man would forget. Angus removed his own pipe. "Shocking day. But I reckon ye've planned on it."

"We have." Tawney was short with his old friend. "We were counting on this trip," and he sprung to start unstrapping the mainsail cover atop the boom. Angus shrugged. "Aye. If ye be decided. Good luck." He walked back down the pier quite as slowly as he had come. Tiny, overhearing the conversation, shouted aft against the wind. *"Should* we go? Don't feel we have to on my account."

"Nonsense," he called cheerily, "the kind of weather you really learn to sail." Tiny cocked her ear to that and went back to conscientiously snapping the jib on upside down. To the screams of the gulls, wheeling in their storm-tossed rhythms of flight, and with the jib finally made right by a suitably disgusted Tawney, he had then set underway on the auxiliary motor, moving slowly past wave-splashed channel markers. Just as he had said; this trip indeed had been planned. Not for nothing had he been studying weather maps, looking for those eastward moving cross-hatched patches of gray spreading across the Western Plains, telling of a confluence of storms, the perfection of timing for all that gathering nastiness to be dumping itself upon the Middle-Atlantic States.

As noted, it was the second day and early morning, rocking at anchor in St. Michael's Bay. The previous day's sail had been a hard one, requiring much tacking into gusts up to forty knots: the rigging so taut that it sang and strummed. All day, until near dusk, they had fought their way to make it here to this protected anchorage. Through a hundred changes of course and accompanying shouts of *"Helm's Alee,"* he had kept Tiny scrambling from side to side, drawing the flapping sheet in, tightening it on the winch, and then, no sooner than her having made it fast, hurriedly having to fling it free again. *Wanderer* had bounced and rolled in vicious cross swells and Tiny, a top-heavy little figure, had bounced about too and several times been toppled, her feet slipping out from under and bringing her down in painful crashes; only the mesh webbing attached below the railings saved her from going over the side. She had taken dramamine pills but they proved unreliable salvation, several times she had lurched to the rail in reenactment of one of mankind's earliest forms of maritime disaster. Hounded by helpful directions from Tawney. "Not *that* side, goddammit! *Away* from the wind." Yet Tiny had managed better than he had expected. Turning into her bunk that evening, before starting the familiar ritual of her private prayers— whose drone had not abated by the time he fell asleep—she had even sent out little chirps of optimism.

"My dear," he said," it's too soon to be getting cocky though."

"Oh, I'm not cocky, dear. But actually I am looking forward to tomorrow."

"Good. So am I! Now get all the rest for it that you can." The second day's beginning was signaled by the early pressure of dawn's sunlight coming through the ports. Tawney caught the shriek of wind. He switched on the marine radio by his head for the local forecasts. From Tiny's bunk across the narrow passageway came small but poignant groans, clarifying into the focus of human's speech; words telling a story of the bruises of yesterday, of muscles tortured to a soreness that the dedicatedly non-physical life of that lady had never known. A detached observer, listening to that plaint and weighing that awesome marine forecast that he had just overheard, might have been genuinely mystified by Tawney's expression. A five hundred foot freighter in trouble off Hatteras, crabbers seeking the lee of Smith Island, yet he smiled. His chagrin that had attended what had been, up to now—he had to admit—at least a mild setback to what had been optimistic hopes for an early knockout blow, had all faded. Left was a devil's smile of pure dark radiance. *"Okay, rise and shine,"* suddenly shouted the devil, springing from his bunk with orders for a protean breakfast. "You can eat *all* that?" Tiny said finally, when her wits had gradually filtered back into her exhaustion-drugged senses. Her hair, in strings, bordered a pale and lifeless face. With each step, each motion of her arms, she gritted her teeth. The glass of fresh orange juice which, put in the round slot on the tiny table to keep it from skidding, sloshed its pulpy contents back and forth. Bluish vapors of frying bacon filled the little cabin; smells of melting butter and burning toast blended nauseously. Between theatrically hearty bites Tawney urged his shipmate to eat hearty too. "Oh, I *can't.*" Once again she flew out and up on deck to heave her guts out. Day was bright but the wind was incredibly strong, a roaring laughing storm. From his position in the wheel cockpit Tawney shouted to Tiny to hurry up. "Lots of miles to cover." Promises to keep. Tiny's stricken face appeared in the doorway. *"I can't find my dramamine."*

"Shake a leg, we've got to get underway."

"Tawney...." But her skipper's face was set like stone. The ocean sailor may scorn Chesapeake Bay, belittle its storms. It has not the fetch, the immense distances, nor the great depths out of which mighty swells can build. As it is so with the Mediterranean too, in theory. But the sailor of the Bay—as stout Odysseus himself long ago—knows better. Knows how that vicious twisting chop, those wild gusts, can challenge the best of sailors. *"Ready about!"* For the fiftieth time Tawney barked out that preparatory command on the tacking drill south, setting Tiny scrambling to fling off one sheet and gather in another one out of the wild wind. Then came the inevitable follow-up commands to which Tiny's soft muscles strained at the winch handle. "Another *foot* at least." Tawney's words were a constant lash. "We're sailing close-hauled, don't you see? I've got to point higher if we're going to make Crisfield." And she would nod and look up despairingly at the bowed sail, taut as a sheet of steel. In between tasks, fleeting periods of peace, she flopped motionless. A plump, helpless figure, like a pink jellyfish tossed up on the wet deck, and, to Tawney, a goad to imagination to find ways of rousing her to new activity. *"Up!* Get moving and have a go at straightening up things below. This tack should be a little longer and steadier than most."

Once more Tiny would haul herself upright, a stained, salt-soaked stringy-haired apparition of agony and willingness. Soon to stagger up topside, her face a freshly stricken green. There was nothing left to throw up, even the unlucky dramamine found too late, came back up as soggy ovaloids of yellow after the briefest of stays in a stomach whose turbulence matched the grander scale of violence raging outside. Blood came up with her slime. Tawney's commands never eased. *"Trim the jib!"* Up Tiny would scramble once more and snatch the winch handle out of its slot and get cranking. *"Make up those loose lines! Fake down that halyard.* Free that sheet from the stanchion!" Did a demon's smile tug at the corners of Tawney's mouth? And did the sun glitter off that angry sea, did the wind moan in the taut rigging, and do the seas still roll over Ahab's thousand fathoms grave?

"*Bear a hand there,*" he would shout, resurrecting sea phrases from an older time. "*Now go below and fetch me an orange!*" At last he was roaring; he snarled, he spat, swore obscenities dredged up from the vasty deep. He was Bligh and Sir Henry Morgan and all the pirate skippers rolled into one; the driving Yankee skipper too, spurring his clipper on to greed and glory. He roared at that flopped and drained figure. His face—she stared at it aghast—was grim as a Maine headland in winter. The gulls' harsh cries echoed his own. He was, this former infinitely careful protector of his rear in the realms of government, something else out here. King of Storm. Give him credit. Yet as morning departed and afternoon wore on—and greyness settled on the wasting sea—his smile was turning sardonic. He did not have to put on an act now; theatrical impulses were merging with more natural instincts. Genuine rage was supplanting that once confident burble of mean-spirited and self-satisfied mirth. A funny thing was happening on the way to Crisfield. No matter how often the sharp bark of his words sped, like yet another harpoon, hurtling into that pudgy ball of a female body—a body seeming scarcely human now in its disarray—there she was, up once again, valiantly, maddeningly, tugging, stretching . . . doing whatever it was that had to be done. Along with his surprised reaction there was at first even a bit of grudging admiration and then later, as the day wore on and as she kept managing to jerk herself back to life in response to his commands, it began to strike him as a miracle. But a miracle performed once is, well . . . a *miracle*. Repeated fifty times, and if it be not the miracle that one wishes, it can become an affront. To Tawney it was growing monstrous.

Again and again his gaze was drawn back to the sight of Tiny's hip and thigh, those ample soaked ballooning buttocks, taut with strain as she ground away at the winches, the whole mass quivering like a saucy and insulting salute. He would force himself to look away; then irresistibly his eyes would be drawn back to that looming ridge of her old-fashioned panties, mocking him for the time when that line encased the whole of that mortal, but otherwise quite unreal, mystery of sex that every high spirited lad of ardor and innocence craved. The sight mocked more than the sadness, the infinite uselessness, of dead desire. Blatantly, it proclaimed the fashionless—the irretrievable shapelessness—of the Tiny of today. The more he contemplated that loveless view and, as twilight fell across the storm-torn waters, he found his eyes almost stuck on that little ridge; now looming like a mountain, it seemed like a burning symbol of her unconquerability. Concentrating the fury of his frustration. He had this long day traveled through many moods and now he felt himself sliding down into the chilling clutches of fear. "Get the running lights switched on," he shouted, with sudden decision, sending her scurrying below once more, "we'll be sailing tonight." "*All night?*" His hoarsened voice wrestled with the wind, "We're not as far along as we should be." In truth, he had only the dimmest idea where they were; in concentrating upon his victim he had skimped on navigation. The lifelessness in Tiny's look gave him new heart.

Tawney did his best, did his *damnedest,* through that night. The gods—any small and mean-spirited ones at least who might be pleased to judge such matters—would swear to that. At some dim hour, when the wind showed signs of slackening slightly from its former gale force, abruptly he ordered the jib to be replaced with the Genoa, a gigantic billow of a sail unrivaled for awkwardness and—in the wildness of its furious flapping—danger in rigging under such conditions. He had to assist Tiny with it, but helping as little as possible, making her snap its confusing clips all by herself while the bow pounded into the swells and with each shuddering poured solid water.

He thought up numerous other things that night, coming up with a succession of small and demeaning tasks as long as he could. All at once, he could think of no more. Fatigue was wearing him down, his mind was wandering. Rigging the jenny had been an act of madness. He had made the boat overpowered, ceased to have it under control. The very business of sailing at all in such terrible weather and a night was even worse. All his good sailing habits, the core of his pride had been cast aside. He had abandoned all pretense of piloting, paying no attention to the beams of distant lighthouses, nor the quick flashing buoys that he kept passing close aboard either, hearing the dings of their bells but failing to note the numbers on their metal sides that their flashes lit up. Long hours since he had ceased to keep proper lookout, and many times during the night they found themselves passing great merchantmen close by. They did not notice them until very late—mountainous ore ships bound for the steel furnaces of Sparrows Point, blotting out half the sky with their bulk—monsters with one red and one green eye high up at which they stared paralyzed with fright bracing for the swells to come—mere seconds away—signaled by the great white wall of water which these blunt vessels, graceless giants of the new age of ships, piled up upon their bows. One ship roared out loud warning hoots of its whistle, causing Tawney almost to jump out of his skin as the great hull slid by them, its swift moving slab sides like the flank of some mysterious beast whose heat they could feel through the air warmed by its passage. The last hours of the night, as the blue-blackness melted to the dirty-grey of a storm-ravaged dawn, he found himself watching the moon, a lop-sided ping-pong ball bouncing off clumps of racing clouds, ducking into dark caverns, sprinting again wildly out through swirling tunnels of colliding mists. Feeling himself holding onto that moon as well, hanging onto it like the back of a plunging whale, all he had.

Fate, mostly luck—anything but careful seamanship—and navigation—brought *Wanderer* into Crisfield's harbor around mid-morning. Through glazed eyes he looked over at the familiar line of houses, old and white, which so often before had been welcome to his spirits. Now, under low grey clouds with bits of blue sky showing through, that shore scene was shifting, rearranging itself gently, with entry through the simply marked channel. Over *there*, that low place, no sign marking its purpose, were to be had the most golden flaky crab cakes, the freshest oysters, on earth. Evenings he used to smoke his pipe with the oystermen, with their faint accents of somewhere distant in time floating away on the soft sea air. To this windswept port of strong-smelling salty flats and marsh grasses, he had come treasured times for the joy of a special peace sweeter than his heart could tell.

As he glided now towards his intended place of anchorage, this worn man with the drawn face of exhaustion, the crust of drying salt was on his jacket, his slick rain hat, his hair, even on his eyelids, grainy little clumps weighing down those handsomely graying lashes. From those red eyes ran salty fluid, the slippery oil of the sea. Yet not all the sea's doing. Some was the salt of tears running down his face freely, coursing through gullies that had deepened overnight, reaching the corners of his mouth with bitter taste. Oh this happy and lost place! "Run the line first *under* the lifeline," he yelled at Tiny who was standing in the bow with the anchor, ready to let it go. "Yes. Oh dear me. I *do* see the consequences." Their voices were now very clear, above the muffled auxiliary, as they glided across the calm waters.

"Hurry it up. We'll overrun my spot if you don't," he barked. Scarcely a bark, mere croak, a last cracked growl of a defeated lion. Even as the picture of Tiny standing in a bight of the anchor line when she let go was a forlorn dream. Yet he saw it clearly, the line whipping out, wild and dangerous, snatching up one ankle and yanking her over the side in a crazy cartwheel—the image frozen in a kind of suspended animation, that chunky doll-like figure upended in mid-air, spread-eagled against the sky—a startled look on her face, a quite disbelieving Tiny with the taut line wrapped around her ankle and the anchor's merciless weight pulling her straight down to oblivion. But reality, in the form of a safely and accurately anchored *Wanderer*, and the sight of Tiny conscientiously flemishing down the extra anchor line, banished the image of her hurtling doomward that had for a moment been so winningly vivid. He rose from the wheel and moved stiffly towards an overdue visit to the head. He took a step without looking, missing the ladder down into the cabin, and pitched forward, striking his brow on the hatch coaming, his unconscious body ending up sprawled amidst the storm-tossed litter of the cabin floor. A moment's dizziness, had clouded his brain. Or perhaps, he simply wanted to die. Yet that plausible notion was contradicted by the human cry for help which he let out as suddenly he felt only air beneath his feet.

Die he did not. But it was hours later that he came to and by this time he was in his bunk, somehow in pajamas, and the doctor had come and gone. He learned about Dr. Oakton—"Doc Oke" as he was known on the waterfront—and the setting of his broken wrist and how Tiny had gotten the dinghy into the water and rowed for help, and, oh, learned a few dozen other things as well; how he must lie very still for another day or so. Learned all this from Tiny who was—to the extent his throbbing skull could tolerate it—a fount of information. "Wouldn't it be better if I were in a hospital?" he said weakly. A hospital, yes, that would be nicer, relief from the ministrations of the hovering Tiny who every minute had a fresh compress to put to his head or some medicine to push between his lips. "Not at all," she said. "The Doctor will be aboard tomorrow morning to check you over." Yet perhaps anywhere else but amongst this hearty race of boatmen Tawney might indeed have found himself in a hospital. But Doc Oke had patched men of bloodier wounds and sent them back to their boats with a dram of whiskey. "But . . . ." he began a feeble protest.

"Shh. I know you're hurting, dear. When you wake up we'll pray. I bought a little book of Sea Prayers when I was ashore." Her voice took on its recognized tones of certainty when addressing matters of salvation. "It's called 'Deliverance From the Sea'." An inward groan passed through his stricken form. Neither could it be kept entirely inward. The beginning of words, some rudimentary expression of more specific meaning tugged at his lips, irresistibly demanded escape; the words sought form for an otherwise pure animal anguish. The next morning arrived. Outside, so far as he could tell from the tiny port by his head, was a blue and golden world. The light was sparkling, jewel-like; a world cleansed and polished by storm. He stretched, insofar as bruised muscles and split forehead permitted, and his heart, as of old, his free heart, flew out the port to those pure horizons of gold. Then he realized where he was. Overhead, a bare eighteen inches above his nose, reflected sunlight off the water rippled across that surface of mahogany; golden light in rhythmic formal pattern danced across that polished wood, yellow and warm as a woman's hair.

He became aware of other things, smelled bacon frying, coffee perking, the sweetness of orange juice. And after a while these once glorious zesty foods—mocking memories too, like those wondrous ripples, recalling the joy of appetite—were borne to his chapped lips by an inexhaustible Tiny. "Tiny . . . ." Yet all demurrers were feeble against this whirlwind.

"Shh, the doctor will be here soon." And so the reliable Doc Oke was, pronouncing another day of rest would bring the patient up and around. Numbly Tawney watched, vaguely he listened, as Tiny put questions. Unaccountably, there was a guffaw from Doc Oke, a mutual wreathing of smiles. Then Doc was gone and Tiny's face was hovering over him again, a round pink moon, an over-large solicitous one with egg on its breath, dominant in his near sky. A moon too, rather—by its own lights justifiably so—proud. "I'll bet we'll have *many* a sail together. What do you think?" What he thought was unutterable. He dozed a little more then awoke, aware of Tiny's bustlings and regretting the limits of sleep.

"Try this, love. Open wide." She pushed a smoked oyster between his lips, wide or not. Now she was tugging at his sheets, tucking a blanket. He became aware of perfume. *Perfume!*. He realized too (a gradually dawning awareness) that the cabin had not merely been cleaned but spruced up. Fresh flowers were set in a coffee can. Tiny had changed into a flowered blouse; bracelets clicked on her plump wrists, earrings swayed from plump pink earlobes; out of the wet and tumble of the storm's disorder this summoned forth, phoenix-like, by a willpower he could not fathom. A power not to entrance, but to horrify. For, definitely, the horror, *the horror* . . . words remembered from somewhere, kept repeating themselves. He shook his head in hopeless negation of an olive thrust at his lips, a denial which aggressive fingers, steadying his hand to receive this morsel, were a gently firm corrective to the absurdity of refusal. "Good for you," insisted his ministering angel; helpfully those fingers remained close to retrieve the pit. "Good for *us*," she giggled. Now Tiny was unaccountably tugging at sheets again which needed no straightening, and simultaneously the smell of perfume was stronger. Alarmingly so, and his eyes flew open to confront Tiny's round pink face, the whole full moon of it, inches from his own. And if there happened to be any ambiguity in Tiny's glassy-eyed fixation, her mouth tugged grotesquely into some shape of mingled leer and smile—satisfactorily neither—there was no doubt whatsoever in the gropings of her hand working away at those covers but patently not to neaten them. *"Tiny. For Christ's sake . . . ."* "Shh. Don't agitate yourself, darling. Shortly you're going to feel so lovely. I've decided," and here her expression, losing its leer, grew resolute, yet with a glitter in her eyes, "that you shall look forward to our sails in *every* way."

"Tiny, *please* . . . ." She was actually trying to get into the bunk with him, even as she was doing a number of other things which, taken all in concurrency, seemed downright impossible. But as has been proven ever and anon—through countless forms of insurgent eroticism—extremes of awkwardness are not the same thing as impossibility. Where there is a will, there is a way . . . and one particular will, as he was experiencing it, was demonic. "I realize what's holding you back, dear. But you don't have to worry, I spoke to the doctor." For a moment more he put up a forlorn struggle. Fought with his aching body, his one good hand, his not quite immobile hips. All hurting, but nothing compared to the sensation—excruciatingly brutal as a two-by-four cracking down on his skull—*felt* when he made the error of jerking his bandaged head with its tender lump too sharply away from the lips of his ravenous succubus. "Oh, oh, *oh* . . . ."

Yet for all the medically optimistic manumission granted, Doc Oke's standards were by a heartier breed of man. "There," Tiny said soothingly. "*There*. It's all right." Drawing forth only peepings from this depleted man, meant to be screams but which were no more than whimpers. The golden ripples kept on dancing mockingly across that overhead of glossy mahogany and, out the port, through whose small round opening Tawney's gaze was fastened in desperate appeal, that constrained circle seemed to explode into a vast dome of limitless blue. A sky at once stunningly beautiful and pitiless. Heavens that had looked down unweeping on much worse than a speck of sailboat at peaceful anchor in a bay which, however appealing to those who love it is still—viewed by those who orbit the earth—but a thin wedge of placid silver water beside the wide dark Atlantic.

▲ ▲ ▲ ▲ ▲

Amidst the hustle and tumult of the Homecoming crowds, the whoops of reunion, cries of loving friends, two old people moved up the gentle slope of Chauvenet Walk. They were walking more slowly this Saturday than other couples heading towards Homecoming's traditional observance of the midshipmen's noon meal formation. The man was in distinguished grey and the woman holding onto his arm was dressed in a rich tweed suit of gold and brown, the colors of autumn leaves. Both were bundled up more warmly than this mild October day demanded of youth which was all around them. She was wearing a fox fur, ages out of fashion but an old favorite, and also a jaunty hat with a bright feather. Members of younger classes strode by them on strong legs, their overtaking steps hurried on by the low drum beat rolling out from the grey front of Bancroft Hall. "Good Lord, Muddy. Our *sixtyeth*. There ought to be a limit. Shouldn't the Alumni Association pass some kind of a law prohibiting reunions after a certain point?"

"I expect," thinking it over, "it's probably not necessary." Tessa laughed delightedly, rewarding him, as she often did, for wit not his own. "What you're saying is that it gets taken care of. One way or another."

"Hmm. Well, yes," Muddy conceded. Not caring for this kind of talk. "Oh dear." Ahead of them, was a mass of spectators viewing the formation. Their backs walled off all view. People were crowding onto benches and had even climbed up onto the roundish corrosion-greened antique cannons, straining to see over blocking heads. Children and slips of girls were perched on men's shoulders. "We won't get to see a doggoned thing," he said disappointedly. She squeezed his arm. "It makes no difference. We've seen lots of formations. All we'll ever need. Let's grab this bench. I'm a little out of breath."

"You didn't overdo last night, I hope." His manner became quickly anxious. "That dancing . . . ."

"That was fun. You were the best dancer in the class, you know."

"I used to think I was pretty good." He was holding his head quite straight and high; it was one of the last heads of those living that had worn a cocked hat and worn it well and he seemed to be listening to something faint and far away. The drum beat changed tempo, boomed louder. The Brigade Staff, Muddy deduced, was performing its maneuvers. He pictured the intricate and yet brisk steps involved in taking that triangular formation through a change in direction. Now, to a different drum beat, he pictured the First Company stepping off behind the staff. That as it had always been too. "Muddy." Tessa had her head leaning back against the stone of their bench and she was looking lazily towards the Severn which was full of white sails. "I was thinking of a few years back about David, and all that fuss about the Navy's ships and that submarine detecting gadget with the girl's name . . . ."

"I'd not call DIANA a gadget." He surprised himself by remembering the name though. "Well, some day please explain it to me," she said. "What it was all about."

"To tell the truth, Tess," he said with a candor that a few years before he could not have imagined would be his. "I never understood what was happening so well myself." After a bit, uncomfortable as ever with her pensive silences that seemed to desert him, he went on. "Of course, I daresay that I could get the full story. Young Fritz Kline who was my aide made flag recently and is now in Materiel . . . ."

"It's not worth the bother. Just wondering . . . ." What she was wondering came a moment later. "Do you suppose that David was right?" Muddy had pulled out a cigar whose unwrapping and lighting he did not hurry. "There is disagreement about that. Some of the experts apparently feel so. I gather that others believe that in time the system will—"

"*Muddy*! What I'm asking is: Did he *do* right?" She put her hand over his. "Sorry, didn't mean to bark at you."

"Well, let us consider. He did stand up for what he believed." He weighed that further, but still tentatively. "That surely has to be admirable." She nodded, perhaps growing sleepy. The sun was warm on the stone.

"Of course," he observed, wishing to move them off this ground as rapidly as possible, "he does seem to have come out of it decently." Correctly he believed that David's mother would also be keener to discuss the more tangible aspects of her son's well-being. Even as this was all unsought reminder that the young fellow's misfortunes were likely prospering for reasons not totally linked to merit. A matter tucked away, as far as it took, to keep from himself the truth that one proud old man could harbor a bit of the fox. But Tessa seemed to be talking almost to herself. "He does sound happy. Things don't seem to eat away at him as much. And Aliason is positively bubbly these days. They seem to have more money too. But it took them all so far away. I see those grandchildren of mine less than ever." He had been thinking about this. He spoke gently, unveiling an idea that he knew would please. "On our next trip I thought we might take in all of our grandchildren. A grand tour of the little buggers. Maybe we'll even go around the world. Drop by London and hoist one with Sir Bruce. See what the old devil's up to these days." His enthusiasm for the idea grew. "Come back by way of Singapore and Hong Kong. I'd like to see the Lombok Straits and then Palawan again. And Makassar Straits where the Japs pounded us in that first night action. They had much better binoculars for night vision, you know. But . . . back to the point. They've got cruises and tours that take you practically everywhere these days. Ah, those islands,

Tessa. We must see them together. Homeward bound we could check on my brood in San Francisco and then hop on up to visit David and Aliason. So, my girl, what would you think of getting a look at Shanghai again? Get a whiff of the honey barges on old Chefoo Creek. How about *that*? Going back to China?"

"That does sound nice," she replied vaguely. The drums had stopped.

The crowd was dispersing, drifting hither and yon. Music had begun at the bandstand over by the Chapel. A band of musicians was sprinkling light and lively marches on the air. Pleasantly bored, Muddy had begun to take notice of the semicircular stone bench, twin of the one they were sitting upon, on the opposite side of the walk. There was a bronze plaque, as there were on many of these benches, setting forth the circumstances of its donation. He could make out the larger words and read them aloud. "Commander Hilyar Gresham Oates III, U.S.N.—Perished in Gallant Battle on 3 March 1942—. Erected in Eternal Memory by his Classmates." It suddenly came to him. "Why, that's Wheatie' Oates! I had no idea that they had put something up for him."

"I don't believe that I knew him," Tessa stifled a yawn. It was perfect just sitting here. Relaxing after all the hubbub. "Perhaps not, my dear. He was a few classes behind Irish and me. Lost in the Java Sea in *Tolliver*. The old four-piper. Went down with practically all hands. "*Wheatie'* Oates. Well, what do you know?"

"Benches make nice memorials." She wanted to make brighter reply to his excitement, but one was not a hand. She sensed in him again deeper tugs of restlessness. "So, Muddy, what's it to be next?" The question was not an idle one, but reflected the fact that the Waters Corridor had finally become reality during just the past year. A "consummate reality", someone had said, which Muddy liked to repeat without knowing exactly what it meant. To the extent that it might mean that there was no room to fit anything more in the designated space, however, it was absolutely true. More than two years of planning and execution had culminated in one lengthy section of the fourth floor of the E-ring being converted, in the words of a Washington Post reporter,

> "... *into a unique, surprising, and living memorial honoring one of the Navy's most prestigious warriors of World War II. Quirky, cluttered, jam-packed, having more the aura of the Smithsonian's attic (which is itself the nation's attic), it will tell the browser probably more about one man's career and obscure naval engagements than likely he will want to know. But also, if the viewer will suspend a portion of his normal human critical faculties, something else will happen. He will be charmed. For it is also enjoyable, strangely innocent fun, a brush with courage and human gallantry that we pray that future generations may be able to apply in kinder and more creative ways. And through a maze of eclectic memorabilia and instructive up-to-date material, liberally mixed with one man's*

junk, the visitor will also learn a great deal about destroyers, the familiar 'tin—cans' of a class of naval officers, and how and why they are beloved as cavalrymen are said to have loved their steeds."

Though Muddy harrumphed a bit at that last, that about told it. For what had happened, a joy to Muddy and yet a curse to the virtue of economy in art, was that, not untypically to those who know Washington, a good deal more money had unexpectedly become available to the project at the last minute. It had grown into something precious, something all government managers love. A place to squirrel monies away, a *vehicle* for spending them. Not driblets of money either, but gobs of it, challenging imagination in ways to expend it—all, to be rid of it by 30 September, the sacred last day of the fiscal year, every last drop of this particular vial of the taxpayer's blood—and quite overwhelming the abilities of the project's artistic staff to apply it intelligently and tastefully. The result was a wholesale trampling upon sensibilities. For the Corridor's professionals had, logically enough, a comprehensive scheme, a Plan . . . . Too bad *that*. Into the ashcan, that admirable Plan. Several staffers quit in rage, one talented lady in tears. Which was O.K. by Muddy. He had weathered worse. Maybe knowing nothing about art, but knowing what he liked. Knowing when to toss in the kitchen sink. He bought a world more of material, haunted Army-Navy surplus stores, installed binnacles and engine order telegraphs rich with *verdi-gris*, recreating a fair representation of an old Farragut class's bridge. He commissioned a number of paintings of battle scenes with guns blazing orange, destroyers plunging through massive gray swells, destroyers shepherding landing craft towards smoking jungled shores. Destroyers were everywhere, doing everything, contributing mightily to the winning of the war. A wild card had been thrown in too, not even out of an American War. There was a painting of the royal Navy destroyer *Shark*, a sinking smoking wreck but with one pathetically small gun still firing at the German High Seas Fleet steaming by in the sinister twilight of Jutland. Her skipper, Loftus Jones, V.C., had been one of his youthful heroes. In the creation of the memorial to Muddy a subtle metamorphosis had taken place. It had been transformed into a shrine of Destroyerdom. Rightly and decently so.

But if one was going to create a proper shrine, it was not enough to present only a record of the past. The direction of the destroyer's future ought to be indicated as well. For this Muddy had to do research, could not rely simply upon memory. He had to learn more about the coming destroyer types too. And in these investigations he was surprised, and delighted, by the help that the great ship-building companies were willing to provide. No one else in Washington, to be sure, *except* Muddy would have been surprised at the extent of their help, the depth and variety of it they offered. Suffice to say, he was inundated with material. It could have, had he adopted it all, filled a wing of a fair-sized museum. So many paintings of glory, so many listings of weapons and configurations, writings of the wonders that they would perform . . . all persuading. He read all of this, swallowed all, understood little, believed much. And if a careful look at the oddness of the hull configuration of the ships to be, their scanty freeboard, and bows designed more for submerging beneath the waves than properly shrugging off the North Atlantic's mountains of blue water, did cause those old eyes to blink with his doubts . . . . Well, *no matter what*, it was still a *good* thing that young David Morgan—and those other know-it-alls—had not been allowed to prevail and so have ended, thirty years too soon, the life of *Sea Eagle*. Sixty plus ships, strangled in the cradle every one, when there were too few ships in the Navy already! Now there was to be this Indian Ocean Fleet too, the turbulent Mid-East with all of its own urgent new needs . . . . And anyway, what else *is* a Navy but ships?

Mixing with such thoughts—part recollection, part sea-foam of indignation—was another set of impressions. A midshipman and his girl had sat down on the stone bench—Wheatie's bench—opposite them. Their heads were close together and they were paying no attention to the old couple across from them. The midshipman was tall, a senior striper, and the girl, so far as his eyes could tell, was pretty. Of course, they all were pretty now. The sun burned with a bright spot on the curving gloss of her hair. He was conscious of her profile, its tender gravity, dedicated to that deep and excellent conversation that was surely taking place between them. An easy transport in Muddy's mind back sixty years and picturing that same scene being re-enacted among the young officers and young ladies he had known when he was young. Others had sat along these same walks, under the same trees—the girls then not one whit less desirable, though their dress had certainly changed a great deal—and, he liked to think, had engaged in the same kind of talk he imagined taking place now. Talk laden with the excitement and the shadows of the future . . . the foreknowledge of ships and distant voyages and strange ports, of saddening farewells and laughing passionate reunions after long months of deployments. It would not have occurred to Muddy that the talk of these young people could more compellingly be centered around how soon that the midshipman's obligated service would end and he set sail on some more remunerative career. Touching as well the girl's allied concerns over some promising position in public relations, say, that she was hoping for. Harmonizing two careers, something like that, or whatever the heck they called it these days. He refused to think in such terms. Wanting too much another picture, let imagination relive vivid and lovely years of his own life. A peep of sound from his beloved let him know that he had not yet replied to her question. "I have, as a matter of fact, been invited to be a member of the Presidential Blue Ribbon Commission on Military Pensions of Older Wars. It has some acronym, but I forget it." He stroked his chin. "It could be interesting, I suppose."

"*Another* study? Will it consider World War II widows' pensions?" Tessa asked with immediate sharpness. "It darned well better. There are a lot of us old crocks around, you know. I'll be glad to give your bunch an earful on that one."

Enough. Not comfortable with such proddings, enjoying this Homecoming too much, and with more to come. A class luncheon and football, Navy songs, the faint thunder of wars old and new. A good life, this one the Navy had given him for so long, and seemed so still, worth preserving for the unknown midshipman and the girl who had caught his attention over there on Wheatie's bench. It was pride and satisfaction, nourishment of his days, to reflect on his own part in assuring that for this young man too, and for countless others down through an unending stream of years, that when their time came there would be grey ships waiting for them to serve and eventually to command. Yes, even if many of them must be the much hooted at Sea Eagles. Maybe no prize—even Muddy in his heart of hearts knew that—but they were *ships*, by God, they floated, they'd get you there, could show the flag, get you back. Like a great religion, however flawed, whatever its bumbles, this must be preserved. His thoughts blurred, ran together, like water-colors in the rain. He thought of green spray, solid water, splatting on the windshield of his bridge in a Channel storm. He had his good reasons to doubt the world's sanity, certainly its stability, and his faith in the young had been sorely tried, but still he could not picture their lives other than as some worthy reenactment of his own. Once more he pictured his old destroyer, its beauty and grace, the swoop and dare of its lines, made for the cleaving of waves. He was handing it on, a tired rider but a tireless steed, for the adventure of men and the good uses of the nation.

"You're thinking," Tessa said accusingly. With tenderness too.

"Oh, just a bit!" he answered with false gruffness. It embarrassed him vaguely to be the recipient of such an observation. Thinking was such an ambivalent word; why, even occasionally a treacherous one. And at once, as if to dispel any impression that he might have gotten off that particular firm and practical track that was most his own, he amplified that initial confession and cleansed it of any cobwebs with gestures of vigorous purpose. "What I was thinking mostly was that we should take a walk. A good long walk. Around MacDonough and Luce Hall and past where the old Reina used to be moored. Don't even know what they call that little basin now. Then we'll stroll by the Maine mast and outboard of the athletic fields by the Bay. Remember, before the War there was a seawall and you could go crabbing. Just net 'em up by the bucket ful."

She looked at her man. "What I'd like to do most is just stay here and listen to the music." In her words a soft cry he did not hear.

"I thought you were my walker," he teased.

"At the moment, Muddy dear, I'm afraid I'm a sitter." The music, coming from not far away, was sweet and loud, Marches, old favorites, light airs, pieces everyone had heard and yet whose names too easily slipped the mind . . . perhaps one of the tunes Tessa heard was *The Monkeys have no Tails in Zamboanga* but she couldn't be sure. Too long since she heard that rollicking one with mugs banging down in some forgotten bar. Muddy knew them all, so much better. The music struck and reflected off a million leaves in a hail of silver notes coming from everywhere. On the dappled grass small children ran about, arms outstretched, tumbling happily, trying to catch the invisible elements of the exciting sound. The deeper notes, the thump of the drums, the plaint of horns, traveled further, bounced off Flagg's classical front of Bancroft Hall, the dormitories, the simpler splendor of the much newer Michelson Hall. Muddy reconciled to the intrusion of the latter's modernity. A boffin, Michelson, not a naval officer at all, even if one of the trail blazers for Einstein. But that was all right. Michelson had too, in his own way, bought renown to this holy place.

The pout of disappointment faded from his expression, and by and by those impulses departed too that had been tugging his limbs to activity. The midshipman had left again, though no doubt briefly, last seen trotting off in the direction of Bancroft Hall. For a little while at least the girl would be waiting there alone. She smiled shyly Muddy's way. Tessa had retreated to those deeper silences that were becoming more common with her, and Muddy could spin his fantasies undisturbed. There were worse ways for an old man to spend an hour in the autumn sun.

10

Admiral Sneedon Snowdon—*full* Admiral now—heard himself, Commander U.S. Naval Forces Europe, and his wife grandly announced as they entered Plantagenet House. No one doing this sort of thing better than the Brits. They entered a blaze of crystal and color, hanging banners and splendid uniforms. The great curving staircase was by Wren. A place of kings and solemn history. Music swelled and, even if it were not for them alone, the human heart can be forgiven that trip of vanity that has it, for a few seconds, responding as if it were so.

Her arm on her husband's, Ginger Snowdon gave an inward gasp. He felt that involuntary start and patted her hand in reassurance. No ill stroke of midnight, no crabbed hiccupping of the system, was going to snatch away their good fortune, this dream-like tour of London duty, their elegant quarters of Romany House, its gardens and the richness of romantic legend. She squeezed his hand in return, a special one for their own private story that every triumphant marriage has. A great deal of scrubbing and polishing, forced smiles beyond counting, a plenitude of public good works, had led up to this moment. This their first Queen's Birthday Ball, but there would be more. "Isn't that Sir Bruce Maxton?" she whispered, indicating the squarish man in the full dress uniform of the British Navy. Sneedon tautened his bearing, wishing to convey a dignity comparable to that of the famed sailor. Shortness and all, Sir Bruce impressed. Drake too had been a squat man, built like that special tribe of Devoners still. Sneedon, in truth, was a trifle anxious about his relations with Sir Bruce. The two of them had chatted at previous ceremonies and there had been that professional encounter some years back in the States, but none of those moments had the desired dimensions of fulfillment. He had made allowance for traditional British reserve, but could not help feeling that on the part of the older man something was withheld. He suspected that it was respect; vexingly too, for his own he gave to Sir Bruce ungrudgingly. Sir Bruce Maxton; midshipman at Jutland on the *Royal Oak*, two years with Cunningham in the Mediterranean, four years in the Battle of the Atlantic, peer of Peter Gretton and Johnny Walker as an escort commander, nine U-boats sunk. Truth to tell, Sir Bruce made him uneasy. His eyes bored unfairly right through a man.

Tonight appeared destined to be different though. Sir Bruce greeted him with warmth. He bowed to Ginger Snowdon who found herself looking into two glacier blue eyes, no higher off the ground than her own, and a red, cherubic face topped by iron gray stiff hair. A wild bush of hair, in fact—unruly, just like the man himself was once said to have been—beyond powers of brush and comb. Sir Bruce turned merry; there were devils dancing in his eyes and he told a funny, mildly naughty story about a virgin WREN and a midshipman in a lifeboat and Ginger was charmed. "Your husband, I gather, is to speak tonight," Sir Bruce said.

"Oh, *yes.*" A proud Ginger. "Good show. Ah, people are taking their seats."

Moments later, when the Snowdons had taken their places at the head table, she leaned over to confide a thought. "Sir Bruce is not very neat, is he?" "Downright rumpled, I should say." Sneedon had been thinking, in fact, that Sir Bruce looked as if his full dress uniform had been disinterred from the depths of a moldy sea chest. Yet he was forgiving. Sir Bruce had, after all, paid him this night the tribute of recognition. "You realize," he whispered back, "he doesn't wear his uniform often. It has to be a nuisance to break it out only on an occasion." Sneedon gave further thought, a professional rumination to Sir Bruce's special problem, which, he reflected, must some day be his own. "He has no stewards' mates now, you know, to help him keep things straight." "Still, I'm afraid too," Ginger said, "that he's already in his cups." "The warrior tradition," Sneedon observed tolerantly. Rather liking that, a touch of wise humanity that he had sensed himself lacking. One of those frills squeezed out by ambition. Bringing it back would round him out.

"*You* don't behave like that. Isn't there a *Lady* Maxton?" The matter persisted, irritatingly, to Ginger. "A man of that stature, I mean . . . after all." "I believe there was," Sneedon said, "but . . . shh." The first of the evening's speakers was making his remarks. Between the pair of them, however, the Snowdons had arrived at an accurate composite judgment of Sir Bruce's difficulties. For, indeed— just to begin with—the mere putting on of his uniform was becoming a damnable bother. Only someone with intimate knowledge of a flag officer's world can appreciate the detail it encompasses, the plethora of buttons, campaign ribbons, clutch pins, odd bits of brass, belts, cummerbunds, and assorted paraphernalia that such a life demands. All of which stuff has to be stowed systematically, made findable, kept polished, the gold maintained unfading . . . and so on, down through the years, even as eyesight is departing and fingers are stiffening. And, as Sneedon surmised, Sir Bruce was shorn of the kind of help indispensable to keeping straight what constituted a small and living museum embodied in failing flesh. With Sir Bruce having, in visible truth, arrived at the only sensible reaction possible, which was: *To hell with it.* Make do. Grab what you can find and don't fret that you'll no longer pass inspection. Prevailing in conflict, not shining at parade, had always been his business anyway. Hardly going to revise his priorities at this late stage.

The old sea dog's problem was at bottom merely another variant of the melancholy and solutionless dilemmas of age. Neither of the Snowdons, so much younger, could reasonably see beyond the obvious frustrations. Could not perceive the greater irritations fed by the lesser. Nor know the present and immediate truth, which was that Sir Bruce was unutterably bored. These affairs came around too often, always the bloody uniform once more to muddle into, speeches to be endured. The paltry ideas that he was fated to hear repeated were a heavy price for free drinks and the small chance of encountering a jolly comrade from days gone by. Worst of all, these affairs were so grimly tame; to Sir Bruce a disappointment so keen as to be felt like an affront. Trumpets blaring were a poor trade for bawdy song. The product, and the forger, of a Navy which, both through tradition and habits of victory, forgave virtually anything of its hell raisers ashore so long as they performed at sea, his was the raw material of his Navy's legend. The ancient Portsmouth waterfront pubs—tolerance personified—known for carting inert and bloodied bodies back aboard her majesty's ships since the timbers of the *Golden Hind* were green, had banded together once to declare him *persona non grata*, banning him for thirty days. From the Firth of Forth to Scapa Flow in the Orkneys, from Liverpool to the Clyde, a dozen waterfronts knew Sir Bruce. His visits to U.S. ports too had enlivened many an otherwise morose bar and left behind gildings of his renown. In far off Port Victoria in the Seychelles, though he had not seen the island of Mahe in forty years, his memory lived on in a fearsome concoction of coconut juice and rum known as the Sir Bruce.

In response to Ginger's question, there actually *was* a Lady Maxton, but she had, like several Lady Maxton's before her, given up on an impossible job. Sir Bruce wore his women out; grieved them until their tear ducts were dry as the Sahara. It was not that he did not care for women nor have a generous share of gallant and tender instincts. His problem was that he could never measure up to their marvelous and yet exacting standards. Not indefinitely and, good Lord, that was just what marriage appeared to mean. That is to say, a match up evidently supposed to go on and *on*, without relief. Which was, as many a man has had to face, a bit much. No archives kept track—least of all Sir Bruce—of that lovely and long passing multitude of his lady friends. Suffice to say, through the rich lawns of long summers, in stately homes as well as humble cottages, Sir Bruce had been a thunderous mower running amok. So that was another thing. Women, that is. There as well time playing cruel tricks. For while he grew relentlessly older, the women at these affairs seemed to grow younger, ever more desirable. He wanted them all still, exactly as he had in unwearying youth. Even tonight, there was another one that intrigued. What was her name, Cinnamon? Some spice anyway. No matter, the wife of that boy-faced American Admiral. She too was attractive enough, if you forgave the pinch around her mouth of many wives in high places, a chronic fretfulness beyond the woes of constipation. He could see that he had amused her, but . . . after all, what was to be done about it? Nothing! Sir Bruce shook his head over a heart staying young too long in its rattle-down cage. For comfort he thought of his dog, Invincible, last close companion and like himself damnably old. Things still stirred Invincible, the smell of roasty meat, the whine of a cat, a rub behind his ears, but he no longer leaped for the joy of them. At most, his tail would thump, his one good eye roll with remembrance of spirit . . . Well *damn*, Sir Bruce muttered, his own one good eye cocking for a moment as he surveyed Ginger Snowdon from several tables away, I'm an old dog too. Ginger herself had already put Sir Bruce out of mind, attention all on her husband. Almost time for his speech. She leaned over, all fond loyalty, "All memorized?" He patted the pocket of his jacket where his notes rustled. But he had to clear up one thing, "I don't memorize it, you realize, sweet." Her lips formed a kiss. "Still *better*." To the patter of applause, her face upturned, glowing with pride and excitement, she watched her husband rise to speak. Actually, as the accomplished speechmaker knows, and especially the experienced Toastmaster whose approved skills are to public address what the black belt is to the aspirant in karate, memorization is a small part of the art. The more important things, jewels each one, timing, expression, rhythm—the whole bag of the speechmaker's tricks—Sneedon had already gone over time and again, rehearsing with a care that only great and, paradoxically, uncritical self-love makes possible. But delivery itself was only a part of it. Melville noted that you cannot write a mighty novel on a flea, and doubtless would have bought the corollary that a mighty speech needs a mighty theme. Fortunately Sneedon had that too, being no less than the historic maritime supremacy of the Anglo-American alliance and the indispensability of keeping the sea lanes open.

"*Distinguished guests, dear friends . . . allies . . .*" He began with the obligatory funny story which drew moderate but encouraging laughter. Thereafter, he increased his tempo, warming to his ideas. There were a number of these, each selected with care and skillfully interwoven. It was his first major address since taking over Naval Forces in Europe and would be noticed by a wider audience than those in this hall. For the latter, of course, just throw in Solidarity, Friendship, Strength in the face of Adversity—all of the usual. But for his superiors back in Washington, other measures of effectiveness would apply. A senior Admiral in Europe could lend support to embattled programs. The eminence of his position offered a putatively independent voice from across the ocean, an extra pledge of loyalty not to be forgotten. Why . . . he spoke for the *Fleet*! And if the shore based Navy's regard for the Fleet was not all that it was supposed to be, Washington having to put up with the continual aggravation of a far flung scattering of ships never quite securely under its thumb, well, there were times too when it could be useful to summon forth and sprinkle those bright bits of mystique that still clung. The sea was, after all, the *Sea*! Real, not paper. So it had to be altogether a fine thing to have our boy Sneedon right out there at the water's edge, sketching in the threat with sure ominous strokes—the Soviet Navy still a *Bear*, count on that, despite all this fluff of glastnost and perestroika *et al*—and finer still, hard on the heels of his chilling assessment, be able to come up with a message of hope, prescribe anodynes going to save.

At this point his audience could be forgiven for feeling that he was becoming overly technical, losing them. A bit too much extolling of apparently marvelous new combat systems with strange sounding names that, however terrible that infestation of Russian submarines that he had described moments before, were evidently . . . *well, jolly well going to clean up on them!* This was a minor complaint though and forgotten in the general pleasure of things heard. Storied British tolerance at work. *Ideas*, and even the Admiral's constant stream of statistics (how Americans *did* love their numbers) were not too much of a bother. After all, it was a Birthday Party. Besides, something was so appealing in this boyish American who, many agreed, didn't really look like an Admiral at all. And even if he did have a tendency to go mucking about in thickets where no one could follow (that, too, being amusingly American) his manner of speech was unerringly falling into the British way. It happened to all Americans over there, a necessity for better communication, but many U.S. Navy officers adopted the accent only with reluctance. To others it was an insensible adaptation, taking on a sea coloration natural and inevitable. Either way, for most, upon their return to the States, it soon faded in the hard tumble of the American wash. A few though fell in love with the sound. Britain's voice becoming part of them. Sneedon did not know it yet, but that was to be he. Early along he felt sure that his speech was going to be a hit. Once he looked down at Ginger, but the adoration glowing on her upturned face was actually a bit unnerving. Even faith, rationally considered, ought to have limits. Thereafter, he kept his gaze lifted towards anonymous faces, addressing distant horizons, just as he was speaking to Loftier Realms of Understanding.

But loyalty apart, there was in fact no other direction Ginger Snowdon wanted to look; a glance anywhere else and she found herself, a celebrity this night, making eye contact with people paying her undesired attention. Most definitely she didn't want to look again towards Sir Bruce because the last time she had seen him change from one eye reluctantly cocked open, a defiant rooster, to both eyes firmly shut. Like a slow disturbing wink, it had struck her as an insult to Sneedon too. Towards the end though she could not keep herself from sneaking one more look. Yet with eyes still shut he appeared quite different, harmless, a sprawled old man, uniform in disarray, at peace with the world. Sir Bruce though was not dozing, nor at peace. It was a part of his own defense mechanism. With eyes closed he had the hope that he might somehow hear less. For these speeches truly got him down. The planners of these affairs ought to realize the utter impossibility of any human being holding forth for an hour and making every minute worthwhile. Tonight was typical, this time the latest of these American Admirals—what *was* this one's name?—Cinnamon's husband anyway. Their names scarcely worth learning, no sooner did you get one straight than there was a new one beaming away at you. And what had they *done* to get their stars? For sure not winning any wars lately. Oddest of all though was their thinking. So full of bright schemes, they were, so misunderstanding of war, going on about the Russians. Except that Americans insisted on calling them "Soviets", *whoever* in hell they were. Well, damn them too. Kipling bang-on. Truce of the Bear indeed! Be having to take on the bloody lot sure as shooting some day.

Though pinned with his eyes shut, Sir Bruce's thoughts were anything but idle. Far from his being able to take aboard any less of the speaker's words, here in his self-imposed darkness that boyish voice seemed to have acquired added volume. Every phrase reverberated, like melancholy organ music throbbing through a deserted castle that once had bustled with life. Words known of old, recognizable but perversely twisted, were like a torment of swarming demons. Thus if Ginger had been watching Sir Bruce more closely she would have formed another picture than one of relaxed age, sturdy grandeur secure within itself, an old man willing to bless passing events over which he no longer had any say. She would have detected suffering flitting across that storm-beaten face. For while Sir Bruce was no expert on Temperance, and while difficult to imagine anyone consulting him for wise words on, say, Domestic Fidelity, there were still a few matters about which he knew a great deal. Amongst them was the business of killing submarines. Tonight he had been forced to listen to nonsense.

God Save. Over at last. Actually, not the worst speech he had been forced to hear. Sir Bruce clapping away hard as anyone. A good sport. More important things than brooding upon yet another one of these strangely innocent Americans. They drove ships hither and yon and showed the flag and that was apparently how they got their broad stripes. And by doing such stunningly odd things too as passing out propitiatory gifts of candy, so Sir Bruce had heard, to the crews of the Russian ships they had boarded during the Cuban Missile Crisis. They truly had. Amazing. Passingly, wistfully, he thought of his old pal Muddy Waters. Stout chap. Had a card from him some time ago. Gotten married again apparently. Maybe coming over, anxious to introduce his new bride. Well, maybe better speed that one up, old boy. Ah well . . . good thoughts of his friend Muddy yielding to gloomier ones. Tides of folly running strong and nothing one could do about them. Yet amongst things he *could* do something about was to hasten to the gents and then back for the final toasts and the consoling mercy of a cigar. And afterwards, and lastly, a grateful tossing off of his uniform and a brandy nightcap beside a contented Invincible, tail busy as his head of fleas was being scratched. Pushing his way through the crowds, that picture was beckoning foremost in Sir Bruce's thoughts.

The people impeding Sir Bruce were the same crowding around Sneedon in congratulation, Ginger holding her man's arm. But though the moment was pleasing, all such praise was dross compared to some small nugget from Sir Bruce, now spotted caught in the mob and seemingly unable to make his way over to him. Sneedon disengaged himself from well wishers and, tugging Ginger—a lady accustomed to being tugged across busy rooms—maneuvered himself to intercept Sir Bruce for the meeting which (it did not occur to him otherwise) must be Sir Bruce's momentarily balked intent as well. Thus a few seconds later Sir Bruce, his looked forward to solitary pumping of bilges having nothing to do with human company, was surprised to find his way blocked by the American Admiral whose expectant smile made a pair with his wife's. The fair Cinnamon again, unreachable as the stars. A phalanx of shining teeth mocking. *Ye Gods.*

"Good evening again, Sir Bruce." "Again, it is." Afterwards—become memorialized as *The Incident of* Sir Bruce—its villain would recall it with rare defensiveness. Because truly he had not *sought* the encounter. As God was his witness—no other to the purity of his intention—he had gone out of his way to avoid it. Then, most inopportunely, here was the fool blocking his pathway. It was fate. Later, Sir Bruce rethought that. He did not believe in fate. He believed only in his own will and the power to shape matters, a battle, the jollity of a pub, a game of darts, as he chose. This was something else. Temptation thrust upon him. Deliciously irresistible. "I hope you liked my little talk, Sir Bruce," Sneedon said.

Sir Bruce cocked an eye. "Interesting, give you that." Ginger was at the moment the more alert of the Snowdon team, but could not think how to signal alarm for what she saw in Sir Bruce's red eyes. Those two devils loose again and dancing a jig. His feet also doing their own shuffle, the universal human response for delay in the purpose for which he had been bound. But that he could hold. "Interesting?" Snowdon repeated. Yearning for a warmer word.

"Interesting, I say, how you'll have all those submarines getting bashed."

"I didn't mean it to sound quite that simple," Sneedon said apologetically, "I chose not to overcomplicate things for the general audience."

"On the contrary, most reassuring," declared Sir Bruce. "Convoys safely shepherded our way, bringing over oranges and fresh eggs and other tasties we poor British cousins may be desperate for again in the next set-to. 'The sharks routed.' Bully good."

"Perhaps, I was a bit melodramatic but . . ." Sneedon's smile had turned sickly. "Not at all. Sharks indeed. Only one bother. Didn't catch how you were going to do the job. Though recall some sort of briefing the last time that I paid call on your Navy. Lots of pretty drawings of escorts with thirty mile range circles around them. Convergence zones, your chaps call them. Do the submarines of our foes just bounce off them?" Sneedon's smile had sunk out of sight. "I believe that I made clear the nature of those circles," he said. There was a little crowd now around, silent, polite, and attentive.

"Unfortunately missed it. Blasted ears can't keep track of all the grand new whatnots your labs keep churning out. Dinah and the lot . . . ."

"*DIANA.*" Sir Bruce bowed. "Whoever. One of those ladies of shaky virtue. Too many in that harem for an old sailor to keep straight. But do recall that one. Your boffins were over here peddling it not long ago. Extraordinary, really, I thought the sheer weight of all the bells and whistles would send your frigate to the bottom. But somehow that particular day your Yank pride and joy couldn't find an otter in a cistern. Have you ever actually seen Dinah doing its stuff? Do recommend. Bid adieu to your comfy office on Grosvenor Square and bounce your way out into the Channel. Nothing like salt air to clear the head."

"Unfortunately Sir Bruce, you were witness to tests of one of DIANA's earlier models. Since then the I.D. version is now in service. *Improved* DIANA."

"Improved DIANA, eh? Sounds like one of your American toothpastes. New and brighter ones popping up each year. Jolly good. Can't deny its need for improvement."

Sneedon had turned pale. "Sir Bruce, I beg your . . . ." But at last Sir Bruce emphatically did have to get on to the act from which he had been diverted. "Good luck and God bless." With a cheery wave he was gone. Around Sneedon voices grew loudly murmurous with disapproval. A spontaneous upwelling of support for the insulted honoree. Ginger's words came through first though most clearly. Saying it for all. "What a *horrid* man!" One of Sneedon's hosts patted him on the back. "Shameful, old man. Sort of thing simply not done." "Are you all right, darling?" Ginger asked.

"Perfect." He patted her hand, worked up a little laugh. "Not a scratch. See." But in spite of Sneedon's grand sportingness, Something, all agreed, Had To Be Done about Sir Bruce. Who had become Impossible. Other words of sympathy flowed from those who had been witness to the embarrassing scene. And they helped, were good for Sneedon's bruised spirits. And yet truly he did not greatly need their kind words. Sneedon knew instinctively, with the resilient heart of the public man—which he had become—he must expect such things. Just as The Political Man, the ultimate evolution of the Public Man, the kind who will stand on street corners, by factory gates, spreading his Faith out for the multitude to trample upon, must of course put up with that and much more. Shaking hands with the calloused hands of workers streaming out of sooted factories is a perilous act of faith and nerve. Serious men spit your way, knowing that you can do them no good. Some yell that you know nothing, are a fraud, yet one more pain-in-the-ass pretender distinguished only by brass and ambition.

Yet perhaps still harder to take may be certain small encounters. Some sensible woman will be crossing a parking lot with a load of groceries and momentarily you distract her in hurried stride towards her aging station wagon. Although she is too much the lady to say so, plainly you are a bother and your vans laden with banners and loudspeakers are so much nonsense. The trouble is, for such a seeking man, the lady may look like someone he once knew, and those eyes that regard him with such blank contempt might belong to someone who once cared about him, and vice versa, a long time ago. But such men—and though Sneedon Snowdon didn't know it yet, he was one of them, heart and soul—must shrug that off, let appalling things, even truth, indeed truth foremost, roll off like water from the oily feathers of a duck's back. And if there are rebuffs, there are compensations. Restoratives more magical than bottles of Dr. Good. The mindless roar of multitudes, grander than Beethoven for him who craves it. What are the grumbles of one noxious old man beside this? *"Marvelous speech, old man."*

Sneedon's smile was stronger than ever and Ginger's fears were eased by seeing his color return. Needing reassurance herself, for a moment recalling that time in Hawaii when the loonies had surged out of the fishpond. No connection, only knowledge reinforced that even the most carefully constructed lives cannot always escape being slapped with life's disagreeableness. But Sneedon's shoulders had already drawn well back to suck in that richer air that brightens the blood. Medication for the soul. Sips from Hyperion Springs.

▲ ▲ ▲ ▲ ▲

These travels levied upon David Morgan out at Wolf Lake came fairly often and, at first, surprisingly so. Gradually he understood. When powers-be in Washington looked around for someone to undertake certain kinds of trips, some meritless and others necessary, distant eyes kept lighting on the underemployed Director of the Wolf Lake Station. He was, as it is said, "available." Anyway, here was yet another one under his belt, and home once again. Always a quiet joy, and never more so than in these years moving by so fast and so well at Wolf Lake. The catching up on the news, Aliason's excited talk, her hands working away because words were never enough, the chance for him to plot some new deed with Boat . . . his own small tales to tell. To these she listened with all her flattering attentiveness of old; he was her traveler returned from far places and adventures, however mild. And she in turn would always, in the right weather and seasons, take him through her garden with pride in her patch of earth and the sun's work. There were cabbages big as those in Alaska, great blue-grey stiff flowers, growing and growing in these endless limpid twilights of the northern summer.

She was wispier, wirier, stronger. She was still caring of her appearance, but less fussily attentive to it. Some things she let go, these giving way before the press of better ones. Her hair she kept mostly pulled straight back, pioneer-woman fashion, but often still, just as now, the low sun shining through abundant stray wisps would fire them with gold and all the old enchantment. He followed her along the narrow path that led amongst her garden's riches. She stooped to pull up a tiny weed, an intruder in an otherwise perfect bed, and stuffed it in the pocket of her smock. She noticed her hands and held up the backs of them to full merciless view. His to call.

"Hands. They do the job. They're fine. Just love spots."

"Don't call them that." She took a deep, exceedingly private, breath. Her face turned away partially towards the mountains. Some still had snow upon them; whether she was even seeing them right now could not be told. Instead her expression mirrored something of those internal battles, the whole long interior struggle of her life. Not ever to be totally won, above all, not losing. On that most expressive of faces—an actress's face, but with all the moods that played there intensely real—she summoned a look of cheer and a sudden hug. "To heck with them, right?"

That had been a Friday evening. And Saturday morning, sweetest kernel of the week, was extra sweet after a trip. The world to which he returned at Wolf Lake did not close around him so fast as Washington's used to do. The threads that had been cut upon his departure took their time to reattach themselves. Obligation had not yet reasserted itself as he lazed through breakfast, taking in the morning news, time the slowest of rivers. Where the riches of the world seem to lie at one's feet and stretch away forever and all things be possible still. From the ashtray close by the hand that held her newspaper, Aliason's cigarette sent up its curl of smoke in hazy, sinuous grace, sunlight beaming in it. Its twisty smoke seemed natural, permanent, as inseparable a part of her life and its traditions as the Indian and his campfire. Tobacco a friend who must at the end betray, meanwhile a friend still.

"I believe that our local *Rocky Mountain Calls* is becoming a somewhat better paper," she was saying. "All the word about births and deaths and rancher's barbecues over at Massacre Creek, and what the falling price of beef will mean, and so on. More real news in it and not burdened with so many Causes. A long time since DIANA's even been mentioned. And what's the name of that other one?"

"AJAX, ARTEMIS . . . take your pick. Yes, he's letting go of those too." For a moment more she silently concluded, over the last of her coffee, the article she was reading. "Though he's off again on saving the eagles, I see. Are you going to offer some of the Navy's land as a special nesting sanctuary, as the editor suggests?"

"It's possible. I'll be seeing him this afternoon."

"He's driving *all* the way down here, just to talk about eagles?"

He grinned. "As a matter of fact, he's mainly wanting to see you. Easy there. You've seen the paper's series of articles about successful women at various jobs in the county. He'd like to interview you." Perhaps he only imagined that she grew pale. "You're joking. You're not going to let him?"

"Up to you, after all."

"I don't want to then. I just couldn't . . . go through anything like that. Lord. The things you never tell me. Until the last." She bounced back with a rueful smile. He watched her concentrating and guessed, correctly, concentration upon memory. "Actually, I did like the one of those young reporters who became the editor. And I guess still is." He gave her Andy Wirth's full and sonorously sounding name.

"That's the same one who brought about all the furor, isn't he? It was that other man I can't say I cared for. Nor the girl. I suppose I had nothing against her except that I felt she was too much Child of the Sixties. Those girls never seemed . . . quite *clean.*"

"Evidently she got herself cleaned up. They've been married, she and Andy, for some time. Have a new baby too, I hear."

He never minded going into his office on Saturday, not even so soon after returning from travel. A narrow, private path leading from the back of his quarters took him, in a few hundred yards, to the station's main road, deserted except for the leisurely cruise of the patrolman on his security rounds. An elderly quiet man, guardian only of the wind song in the pines. A few hundred yards more and David was mounting the steps of the administration building in front of which, out of a shaped bed of lawn and flowers—a brightly colorful small island in the curve of asphalt driveway—rose the same soaring flagpole and the flapping flag that he and Al had looked down on wistfully from that fine height in those moments of yearning that seemed to belong to a lifetime ago.

A number of other Wolf Lake Station employees were in their offices. Why numbers of them showed up on Saturdays was something that he still pondered. It seemed not necessarily any greater motivation, nor fondness for work, that animated the civil servant out here as opposed to his counterpart in Washington. Not credibly. In the end the virus would claim. In spite of wishing it not to be, David read the signs. Yet at the same time the Wolf Lake Station, in its metamorphosis as Naval Test Facility, was a comparative newcomer in these parts, prosperously reborn only a handful of decades ago. Thus while in theory, and generally in fact, familiarity with government's workings ought to breed the well chronicled contempt, still there was not everywhere visible, as in its parent city, that sheer blooming superabundance of government, aggregating into critical mass, capable of atomizing illusion. But also, for its people, it was something new, novelty, *boon*, this bit of federal largesse plopped down in their midst. An alternative to a hard life in a harsh world, work at something nicer, kindlier, than subsistence ranching, riding fence in blizzards, splitting firewood frozen hard as steel. Succor that kept its employees still glad. Over the Station too brooded the ghosts of trail gatherings, encampments of Calvary, trumpets stirring across a wild land, the safety of the stockade. A sort of second home. Here folks liked to meet.

One of his people, doubling as receptionist, put her head in to let him know that the man from the newspaper was here. David stepped out to greet Andy Wirth who, improbably, after much water over the dam, had become a friend. "Good afternoon, Doctor. Got that right?"

"No one in my world ever minds if you err in that direction. But no, I don't happen to be Doctor. Hello Andy." They shook hands. Andy Wirth looked different, more relaxed. Adapted might be the word. He wore a red-checked wool shirt, blue jeans, boots, the virtual uniform of these parts. He still had his beard but it was trimmed. A small, likely irreversible, incipience of portliness expressed an evident, and pleasing, softening of the former sharp edges of his nature. The possible interview with Aliason, the ostensible purpose of his visit—though it had never been more than tentative—did not seem to occupy other than a small part of his thoughts. His final attempt to persuade David to use his influence struck the latter as more than formal, but less than fervent. Andy though was an explainer. "Each week, you know, in the Friday edition we run a feature article on prominent and successful women in the tri-county area. You do subscribe, don't you?"

"Yes. And we like your articles," Andy nodded. Taking that in stride. "They have been fairly well received. Of course, features like this have been standard in most papers for years. But I suppose that, if you looked into it, up here in the Big Sky country"—an ambiguously deprecating expression twisted the corners of his fluidly expressive mouth—"there has been greater reluctance to recognize a woman's right to an independent identity. The tides of revolution . . . ." He paused, bemused by that pretentious phrase that he was unable to do anything more with. It bobbed around like one of those old wartime barrage balloons; out of place, silver, possibly beautiful, insufficiently useful. He started over again. "Anyway let's say that revolutions, like Spring up our way, arrive late." David let him ramble on; he was a good talker and his talk was undemanding. All at once Andy Wirth's eyes, bright with health and energy, narrowed. "Actually, it's you who interests me most."

"Moi?"

"You. For the much that's gone before. The turbulence of certain events with which we were both associated. And yet now everything's whisper quiet on that front, and you're way out here where it all began. It seems like such a strange coincidence."

David's heart skipped a beat. "That's all that it is, coincidence. Mine is a small world professionally and there are not all that many places to be assigned."

He looked at David with eyes that, along with their bright pulsing glows of enthusiasm, held a steady gleam of shrewdness. "Strange then maybe is the word. Somehow there must have been a coming to terms. Manumissions, explicit or understood. All I'm getting at is that it seems to me that in your case there's more than meets the eye."

"Rather less, I expect. Just look upon it as your government in action." Still able to be amused, even if warily, at the reporter's puzzlement. He took a last meaningless sip of coffee grown cold, talking to himself. *Well, I'm glad to talk the eagles over with you, if that's what you wish. But I won't help you in any fishing expedition, my friend.* Andy Wirth's conversation though was mostly just idling. Not truly the digger. Otherwise he might have been mucking about in big cities, in richer stuff, gaining some Pulitzer Prize that conceivably he had traded away for all this abundance of pure mountain air.

As it turned out though, David was to be spared further explanation of the roots of his altered circumstances. Down the corridor, and then flooding still more strongly through the outer reception area, came sounds of approaching footsteps and voices. One voice, at this moment bubbling and gay, full of an as yet undecipherable enthusiasm, he knew better, had known longer. Understanding every nuance in its approach. He heard the receptionist caution politely, "Your husband has a visitor with him right now, Mrs. Morgan."

"I'll just be a minute. He's *got* to see this." She entered with a rush, an entire bolt of material cradled in her arms. She was spreading it across his desk even as multiple introductions and explanations, all awkward, if none truly irritating, were going on at the same time. They sailed over her head, were lost in delight at her own purposes. Not even the realization of the identity of David's visitor, registering with fleeting dismay, slowed her down for more than seconds. "Look, darling," she cried, *"feel."* No ancient traveler returned from exotic lands bearing treasures ever beamed with more glowing expectation of appreciation than Aliason. "Don't you agree? Isn't it marvelous?" Afire with the fuel of government dollars.

"Well, yes." The material was heavy, rich, a luxuriant reddish brown flecked with gold. It lay as it had fallen, tumbling over the side of his desk with the soft, frozen appeal of a waterfall in winter. "And what does it make you think of? *Exactly.* It sings with autumn." The nature of his visitor on his mind, David deemed it prudent to get the answer on the record. "Sure the Station can afford these goodies? All within budget, etc.?"

"Oh yes. No *problema.*" Al pirouetted gaily, scooping up the material in both her arms without folding it, and now it was spilling over her arms and down the full length of her, toga-like, unpinned but unconsciously graceful, touching the floor as she drew away. "Lovely surroundings are very important, David," she declared . "It makes people feel better, and then they work better. I've decided that we must get in the habit of changing our drapes twice a year in all our offices, just as people do in their homes. We'll have something else for spring, some sort of cream and minty green. But for right now this is what we want. I think our financial troops will be very happy with this." Burdened with fabric, almost engulfed by it, she worked one hand free to shake Andy's own. "A pleasure meeting you again, Mr . . . Andy."

"A pleasure to me, too, ma'am."

"And I hope you and your bride remain happy out here."

"Not exactly a bride these days, you'd have to say, by this time."

"Don't say that. She can be your bride all her life, if you will make it so. Congratulations too on your new baby."

Charmed he was, David could see. More, dazzled. At the same time David was thinking of other occasions in which he had assumed that he could read people's faces, only later to find out that what was going on underneath their expressions was something else. It was with this fleeting, but still acute, doubt in mind that he chose to pronounce something between an apology and a benediction on the departing scene. Like a small circus folding and passing out of the room. "So, there you have it Andy. Live and in color. Giving you glimpses of the small stuff of the job. Well, anyway . . . ."

But Andy Wirth was buying no part of the apology. "No sirree. I realize that a whole lot of things go into leadership. I'm darned impressed. I can tell you." He will, David had the passing but suddenly sure thought, be yet another one of those men who will some day adopt a pipe. That too will become a part of him and at some future moment he will brandish it in reinforcement of similar pontifications.

David need not have worried. He could not know it, but beneath his visitor's expression of composed and sober professional attentiveness, a still more active, certainly more fervent, and uncritical process of admiration was racing along. An Andy Wirth trusting to first impressions. And these were so immensely favorable that he was already mentally composing an item for his paper. As it was to appear in his next weekly column—entitled *Fool's Gold*, being a *potpourri* of small items gathered round the countryside—it began and went skippingly on:

> *Another Nugget. Jounced me downlake on the sagging springs of the old pickup to visit the Navy's Wolf Lake Test Station, not so long ago the object of much controversy, and not a little mystification, to Lake Shore dwellers—as many will remember!—now quietly going about its secret business under the capable leadership of Mr. David Morgan. Came to enlist the Station's help in saving the eagles which, glad to say, is in hand. One drops by the Station sharing something of the citizen's suspicion that those who work for the government are overpaid and under—worked. Well, it would be hard to claim that a single visit to a small and remote outpost of our federal government ought to be justification for abandoning the prejudices of a lifetime. All I can report is the evidence of these eyes, which ought to give heart to every taxpayer. On a Saturday afternoon, when most of us are occupied with the pleasure of the Weekend, working on the demise of some lunker of the lake, or simply puttering around the house on the usual chores of grass and shingle, the corridors of the Test Station's Administration building resounded to the brisk steps of a surprising number of civil servants—yes, civil servants!—going about their government's business with no other motivation, so far as one could see, except that they had thought much about what their own activity was doing, believed in it, and found it good. I encountered a number of employees, amongst them the shy but very capable Mrs. Aliason*

Morgan, head of the Comptroller's Department and mistress of the mysteries of Finance. I was impressed by the evident care and devotion, in small matters as well as large, that this lady manifested in getting on with the government's business. Neither was it 'crisis time' in those busy corridors, which might plausibly have explained the number of people who were there. No, it was merely a routine Saturday. Interestingly, and hearteningly too, one major topic of a discussion in which I was fortunate enough to find myself an observer was how, while scrupulously yielding to the stringencies of budgets, leadership might ensure that offices could be decorated in a manner designed to raise spirits and enhance morale of those working there.

"*But enough. It suffices to affirm that no derided stereotypes of the government workers were to be found on this visit. . . . And speaking for the rest of us, the many whom those dedicated civil servants serve, I assert that there is far more reason than we generally realize to feel grateful for the kinds of caring that go on busily but unseen, beyond our ken . . . .*"

And so on, for yet another page, not a word of which could have offended the most thin-skinned civil servant anywhere.

Through what was an evident reverie on the part of his visitor, David kept his eyes on Andy Wirth with what was at first a certain gratitude for unexpected quietness from that energetically curious and loquacious reporter. As reverie lengthened, however, he grew more puzzled at that distant expression. David felt as if he were detecting the small, secret rustling of time itself. The coffee pot gave out some faint and happy gurgle. Through periodic sightings, checking against the window's straight edge, he could track the barest movement of cloud puffs in that all but windless sky. He noticed the black speck of a soaring eagle against the blue. On the verge of working his fingers to snap him out of his mood, David then saw the man's look change, return to the present. At once more acute, perceptive, conveying that its owner was ready to go. But with one thing more still on his mind. He was sure that he knew what it was going to be as Andy stood up and, before shaking hands, went over to the window. "There's one of our friends high up there now."

From the movement of his shoulders a deep breath could be read. "So. Moment of truth."

"Count on the Station," David confirming his earlier promise.

Andy Wirth shook his hand, overcome with gratefulness. His eyes brimmed. The richness of his emotions then appeared to coalesce, freshets of enthusiasm joining to make an irresistible flow. "Hey. Why do we want to get into this at all?"

"Who knows?" Andy Wirth knew. "They're beautiful. Few. Creatures of our ancient past. From before the world had names for places, before we counted the days. Right?" He slapped a fist into his palm. "And they'll be here after we're gone. After man is gone."

"That is our hope."

"Here are these great creatures that we admire because they're so damned different. Something we can never be. Untouchable. Like . . . like Drake, Sir Francis Drake. You've followed him, *the World Encompassed,* all of that, *Nombre de Dios Bay, the Golden Hind . . . ?*

"Yes."

"I can see that you don't like to talk about such things. Some things are at the core of a guy. It's like religion. Even though it's probable that you don't have any more of that than I, but still you don't want anyone touching your business there. Because it's *you.* Here are parts of you that you don't mind your wife poking around in, amazing parts maybe her own too and vice versa, but still, that's nothing compared to what I'm talking about. Am I right?"

Go home, Andy.

"Okay, let it go. What matters is, you're going to help. I don't want to bother you more today."

"You're not bothering me."

"Sure I am. Good luck to us both, and thanks again." There was a second handshake, this one quick, and he was gone.

▲ ▲ ▲ ▲ ▲

After Andy Wirth had departed, it took a few minutes for a certain frozen expression of amiable good will, not insincere but nevertheless forced, to gradually relax. Thereafter he worked until late afternoon, spending some time going over summaries of data from the dark and hidden places of the oceans, great mountain ranges of obscure and strategic decision, the Emperor Sea Mounts, the Mendocino Escarpment, and so on, about which, amongst a handful of the cognoscenti, more talk revolved than the world knew. Mostly he skimmed. The old absorption not there. Then remembering he had to get back to meet Beth's new young man who was coming by this evening.

His daughter had, with disciplined slimming down and the natural recession of her teenage acne, turned attractive and a succession of young men were coming by. This one had evidently, in the few weeks that David had been gone, become someone "rather special," according to Aliason. Every one of similar meetings with these various young men had at first seemed important to him too but gradually, with each new young man who came by, he felt that they were less so. Yet as he locked his safe and hurried out into the cool greyness that the waning day had become, he did so with a continuing sense of paternal duty, if no clearer grasp of his objective. In front of his quarters he paused to examine the characteristics of yet another example of the powerful country work vehicles now so frequently pulled up there. Part truck and part van, mostly ostentatious social statement, precise definition eluded him. It looked brand new, shiny, big, high-sitting, immensely sprung, with chunky balloon tires made for traversing boulders, chuck holes, roots . . . able to vanquish whatever impediments presumptuous Nature heaved up. Banks of lights, like bugs' eyes, were massed to destroy darkness in many colors. It expressed the power and the affluence of America, and something else as well. It was saying: *Get out of my way.*

"Hi darling," Aliason greeted him at the door. Kissing him eagerly, as if more than a few hours had passed. "Now, I want you to meet Ashton Burger. Ashton, Mr. Morgan."

"How do you do, Ashton?" A strong hand closed around his.

"Howdy." They really did say that out here. Thus the father found himself contemplating yet another young man who, in his most evident characteristics of dress, physique and manner might, with minor variations, have been the prototype of every one of Beth's recent callers. Windburned, sandy-haired, blue-eyed, wearing tight jeans, wide belt, showy buckle, pointed boots, with a turquoise and silver clip gathering a string tie over checkered shirt, his was an aggressive visual flamboyance that was counter-balanced by great and dumb shyness. This latter characteristic, if possibly in some respects a disadvantage to the young man, was all pleasure for Aliason. Gaily she carried the conversation along.

"David Ashton—I think though they call you Ash, don't they?—has a place over on Bear Creek just beyond the Bitterroot Ridge. Or I suppose," she halted with a burst of meaningless laughter, the strain of keeping things going sometimes overcoming her dedication to the task, "I guess it still is your father's place."

An odd grin of disbelief spread across Ash's pleasant and guileless features. "Hit's Pa's, all right." He had, young Ash, cleared his throat before speaking, as David was to notice he would do so each time in those few additional instances this evening where he was to utter even a word or two. "Anyhoo," Aliason sped along, "the Burgers breed quarter horses and enter them in races and other events. Beth has even ridden a champion belonging to their family who's been shown all over the West. What is that horse's name, Beth?"

"Belle's Beauty," Beth's expression, which had lapsed into suffering endurance, came bright for an instant. "And is she really a beauty?" *"Of course she is, mother."* Beth, who possessed some creditable, if not overpowering, sense of the necessity of these antique parlor introduction sessions, had a good instinct as well when it was time to cut them off. "We've really got to buzz now, folks. It's a lot of miles to the dance."

David, however, at this moment chose to interpose himself between the couple and their otherwise clear route of escape through the front doorway. He stood there antically, chatting on, "So, Ash, you evidently think that all of these horses are really here to stay. I mean, even in this age of myriad means of sophisticated personal locomotion?"

For a moment Ashton Burger looked into his tormentor's eyes with an expression as prodigiously puzzled as David kept his own solemnly earnest. Soon, having the young man gazing down at his comfortingly familiar boots, fingering the brim of his hat and letting it drift around in painfully low rotation.

"Or do you think that it may be that the horse will eventually have to serve, however reluctantly we may visit it upon him, as one of the staple food supplies for mankind's dwindling resources of protein? Will the world be contemplating great herds of horses grazing for the butcher, even as today we fatten our long horn cattle?"

Ash swallowed. He looked in desperate appeal towards Beth who now shrieked. "Daddy!" Amused, but not altogether. "Please stop this nonsense. And let us go."

Decisively she picked up her shawl and swung it round her shoulders. Looking good, David thought. He was glad she was in a dress tonight, for once forsaking her eternal jeans. It was a swinging flaring dress, chosen well for what it did to flatter a small but definite extra broadness of beam, a heft around her hips that years of horses and some factor of heredity, the latter certainly not evident in her mother, had probably already rendered eternal. He caught Ash's glance, adoring but something else as well. It was recognition that she was Eastern still, with the Easterner's kind of certainty, the Easterner's impatience. A girl sure of herself, in charge, at least until the young man discovered more. Her farewell kiss for her father was short and only partially sweet. "We're going. And don't ask when we'll be getting back."

With pleasant defiance she took her young man's hand and tugged him out the door, cutting short what—it was plain in Ash's demeanor—instincts of old-fashioned courtesy were still inclining him towards a more respectfully deferential exit. Down the walkway, through the cool air of dusk, tree and garden and lawn trapped the ancient silences of these mountains like a spell. Young voices carried. "Your Pa was just funning, wasn't he?" "I never know *what* my father is doing." The affectation in her voice, even her sigh, was distinct. "But yes, that's one of his little games." There was a shared chuckle over the eccentric and only moderately interesting ways of adults. Nothing to waste time dwelling upon. Ash's van started up, a throaty roar, it's big stiff tires mashing gravel as it got going.

"Anyway, so what do you think?", Aliason said.

He looked at her blankly. "About what?" *"Ash*, do you like him?"

"I hardly know him."

"Jesus' sakes. Must you always complicate the simplest of questions?"

"Well," he said, "I would judge, if it's what you're wondering, he appears quite capable of doing his own part in the begetting of fine, healthy grandchildren."

"That's not at all what I was wondering," she said, "certainly not this soon."

"Soon enough." He watched lines of anger recompose themselves into older settled lines of permanent worry. He stopped himself, once again mid-way in one of his foolish and wasteful games, not sure how to get out of this one. Dangerous games still. He watched the rigid set of those shoulders, the body carrying them, go out of the room. Not until hours later did she really speak to him again. Anger gone but her voice was dry. "Some mail for you sitting on the sideboard. I hope you'll get to it soon. It becomes messy if you just let it sit there."

He had noticed it when he got back from his trip. He no longer hastened to his mail; one more thing that he had ceased to believe in. Promise in mail.

"Most of it's yours, those little envelopes with glassy windows. But some are my bills too. I could use some help with my checkbook. There's a letter too from Admiral Waters. It's well down in the pile. He's waiting for an answer, poor dear."

Muddy's envelope was larger than most and it was thick with pages of what were sure to be massed sheets of plain white unadorned paper. The remembered tastes of government and the habits of thrift intertwined. The hand was unsteady but large with remembered authority from before the age of electronic word processors. The ink was the Navy's blue. An old man's rambling kind of message, composed with all the time in the world.

"My Dear David. It seems that I am writing again quite soon, even before receiving your reply to my last letter. I realize how busy you must be. Perhaps, even so, our letters will cross. However, I felt it necessary to write to apprise you of several matters, and to present you with a decision which must be yours to make. . . . " The matters of which he seemed to want to apprise David were numerous but unfocussed: The heat of Washington, his flower boxes, the birds that came to his window, the doubtful satisfactions of solitary cooking, old comrades passing, the disturbing state of U.S. defenses (although there was at least encouragement to be found in the steady building up of numbers of the *Sea Eagle* class in the U.S. Fleet), and recurrent battles with the stubborn management of his apartment, no less responsive evidently to the complaints of tenants concerning the quality of service than were other landlords of far humbler dwellings . . . . Anyway though, on that last, by golly, he judged that he had the rascals on the run. There definitely was going to be a spiffier entranceway "kept continually titivated," a more responsive doorman, and hallways vacuumed by the cleaning people at hours *other* than those when people wanted to sleep. A wry note of self appraisal followed. Out of his recent readings in history, he treasured the words of a certain scribe who chronicled the doings of some ruler of power and probity. *"This life is but a journey and a warfare."* So it must be, Muddy supposed, so it must be.

The decision to be made came at the end of the letter. The Admiral wished to plan on being buried with Tessa, if David consented. *"I visited her grave the other day and left flowers. The stone is now in place with the words requested. The grass has grown up and it looks nice. Please let me hear from you soon. My fond best wishes to Aliason and to your children. Yours faithfully, Malcolm Waters."*

He refolded the sheets of the letter. He had felt the pressure of her attention throughout his reading. She put down her book, "He writes an interesting letter, doesn't he?"

"Yes. But a windy one too."

"Of course, he's windy. The poor old man is dying for someone to listen to him. Well, what do you think of his request?"

"Sure, why not?" "You agree? Darling, that's wonderful. I hoped you would." Her voice, with its rush of gratitude, seemed to convey an appreciation of a profound decision momentarily hanging in doubt but which now was satisfactorily resolved. "Sure. What difference?"

"A lot of difference to an old man. You will reply right away?"

"I'm surprised that he asked. He didn't have to, you know. Not in legal terms."

For a moment, with conscious effort, as if it could be useful to gaining a stronger appreciation of the matter than he had given it, he summoned recollections of Tessa. He was seeing her at some long ago cocktail hour, laughing, scolding, eager to open the door to a friend. He remembered the quick and almost funny, and all but unattended, wedding with Muddy in the chambers of the municipal judge. He pictured his mother in her grave, frail dust. Not a thought, that last, one that hurt. He wondered at himself, if maybe it ought. Something he had said though, casual but somehow distressful, hung in the air with Al. "It *does* make a difference," she said. "If I go first, my evil cigarettes and me, you must promise that you will follow me down there eventually." "All right."

"No. Not *just 'all right',* I need more positive than that. No matter what happens afterwards, with you and someone else, and all that.... Promise." The evening ended thus, after a day of some shaky parts, on a high note of agreement. It had been a good while though, in truth, since this had not been the case. Many a difficult day now well handled. Something favorable usually happened, or it was something that they both contrived to make sure *did* happen, around which they could rally.

Aliason stayed up late that night, waiting for Beth. Though David would volunteer to share that chore (soon falling asleep on the couch, even while fulfilling his duty), it was almost always she who assumed it. A marvelous opportunity to read, deeply and without interruption, immersing herself in a book in the old-fashioned way. *That,* she and her books, not having changed. The night chill would creep into the room and she would get the fire going again and snuggle up to it. The books kept on coming, in their flood of old, scarcely a book club slighted anywhere. They carried messages from the present world and from all its past, gathered and hoarded. A messy dusty and lovely weight of ownership;

yet too, with the responsibility of sorting them out, ultimate disposition and all that, to be the task of unknown, certainly undesignated, descendants. For now though, in this place, and for this flicker of eternity, pleasure and light.

▲ ▲ ▲ ▲ ▲

Green hills enfolded the chalk blue waters of Ahabiyuk's harbor, presently full of anchored ships. The rotting piers jutting from the shore could handle but a small fraction of the Material in Aid pouring in and some ships had been waiting months to offload. A valentine's fringe of modern buildings, pale pinks and creams, rose close to the water's edge and, pressing against these towers of luxurious modernity like a halted mudslide, was the brown sprawl of shanty-towns. This David Morgan had seen from the air, as he had also been able to pick out the U.S. military base by its starkly cleared area, the sense of a Navy SEABEE battalion's patch of vanquished jungle, the disciplined regularity of the rows of tan buildings. Yet drawing the eye most, beyond the cuts of civilization, were waves of steep green mountains that had in them—so the background papers that David had been given to prepare himself for the trip—in addition to the insurgent guerillas, a handful of Sumatran tigers closing out their own last stand.

Winston, his fellow worker at EAR in former days, much moved up in affairs and now the head of the U.S. Combined Research Assistance Program to the indigenous government, had met him at the airport. In the ordinary course of events Winston would not have deigned to greet such a middling level visitor as David Morgan. The counterinsurgency though, if not going badly, was not being won either and there were signs of wavering back in Washington where Winston had not visited for a good while. One could never tell, in the case of one of these hurriedly cooked-up willy-nilly inspection trips from the mainland, what mistaken impressions might be carried away. Also, this fellow Morgan had been an odd duck, likely was one still. Years since all that fuss over DIANA and, so far as Winston knew at least, Brother Morgan had turned quiet as a mouse out there at Wolf Lake. Even so, wariness was the watchword of the successful administrator, caution the ticket. In Winston's nervousness David read with amusement a familiar reaction. His reputation dogging him like a lively shadow. On the drive to the waterfront, and, as they stood now looking across the harbor toward the anchored frigate *Esposito*—she, the very same, from the days of *CORRIDA*—David did his best to encourage in Winston a more relaxed frame of mind. His host opened up and explanations, almost compulsive—though not yet, and probably never to be, honestly confessional—tumbled forth. David nodded politely to Winston's recounting of what he already knew from reports.

"The Freedom Fighters, as they call themselves, have been damaging about a ship a week with their homemade mines. Limpets. Old-fashioned things. But then, it's an old-fashioned war. *C'nest pas?*" He pointed to clefts in the near hills. "Rivers flow out of the interior and swimmers come floating down them at night on rafts, or sometimes only clinging to teakwood logs. Swimming is a great tradition with these people. They were pearl divers and . . ." His voice trailed off. Winston was wearing a pure white linen suit, a Panama hat. Bought the place.

"Anyhow, the idea is to see if insonification of the harbor waters with a high energy source, e.g., DIANA"—he actually spoke the letters, "e.g."— "wouldn't . . . *deter* them. The steep harbor sides ought to be able to contain the intense reverberations and so . . ."

"Be bothersome presumably to any swimmer out there," David finished.

Winston's frustration burst forth. "Ought to scramble their brains! Disorient the heck out of them. So the theory. Anyway someone figured we ought to give it a try."

By not so much as the flick of an eyelid did David betray his knowledge that the "someone" behind the idea was Winston himself. "Anyway. There she is, our sonic source. Luckily we were able to get her here in a hurry. Apparently one of the less committed of Seventh Fleet's ships in the South China Sea."

Brown-skinned children scrambled chattering over the rocks of the shore. Peddler's carts tinkled, carrying cigarette lighters, tinny brass, junk of the Orient. David waited but apparently it was going to be necessary to coax Winston out of his afflicted silence. "Anyway," David observed neutrally, "whatever the worthy intentions, I gather it's not presently working out."

"Afraid not." Winston said tightly. The misery of his expression was alleviated by the murmured comfort of a purely technical reflection. "Between sea water and the human skull . . . there is an impedance mismatch . . . ." Winston looked down at his shoes, scuffing the gray earth of the road powdered by the passage of millions of bare feet. A small note of aggressiveness reasserted itself. "We shouldn't toss in the towel. I hope no one back in Washington is thinking of yanking *Esposito* out of here. The ship likes it. Crew's shacked up all over the town. The skipper's a real-gung ho type and working on getting home-ported out here. Of course, the infrastructure can't yet support such an influx. The acculturation of the enlisted families is another problem . . ." His voice faded again.

"No danger of her being yanked." David could not help grinning, his vow to behave himself slipping. "All kinds of folk in Washington want to send more DIANA's. Further justification for the class. Just get your naval commander to put that in a message." Conscience was struggling behind Winston's troubled eyes and winning. There was something more. Straining for casualness, looking away towards the harbor that was like a bowl of blue milk, he went on. Naval Intelligence, it seemed, was exploring the possibility that the rebel swimmers actually *liked* DIANA. Whatever "like" meant, *but hold on,* he was coming to that. It seemed that some of the mountain tribes might actually *revere* it. Suspicion that some of the swimmers were coming right up and stroking its great smooth surface while it was transmitting. And then there was the incontrovertible physical evidence that, by the use of hooks of bone embedded into the rubber sheathing, some swimmers were attaching woven baskets, weighted with pottery and decorative ivory, the kind of offerings that back in the mountains they customarily packed in with their dead, phallic shapes too, symbols of immortality, to accompany spirits into the world beyond. "Unbelievable."

"Yes." Yet another one to add to his store to believe in. Then couldn't resist. "Sex after death, maybe they are on to something." Winston blinked but he went on, pointing out that obviously the swimmers could just as easily have attached explosives. With a mixture of exasperation and amusement he told of anthropologists now drawn into the act. A specialist in primitive peoples was flying out from the University of Utah. "Costing the Program a piss-pot for two days consult," Winston complained, "but there's evidence that it may have something to do with virility. The dome is shaped, let's face it, like a gonad. A hell of a big ball. Or a pregnant bulbous womb . . . . Anyway, they've a name for it, Aggiki-Lomo, after one of their gods. So . . . ."

"So it would seem then that you wouldn't want any more DIANA's," David said, weighing at the same time a further crumbling of his good intentions, "in fact, especially hard to see any merit in lobbying to keep the fair ship *Esposito* out here at all."

Winston was spared having to reply by the return of his official vehicle and their hurriedly entering it under the irritated stare of a barefoot policeman in khaki shorts trying to keep traffic moving. Yet the matter, though it hovered demandingly after they had settled back in their seats, nevertheless traveled along with them unanswered on the poky ride. The streets were thronged with motor scooters, rickshaws, beggars, donkeys; high-pitched engines snarled and roared; the honking of horns was bad but lively music. A city prosperous and bustling with a not unhappy war for most of its people. They waited for a military convoy, green trucks and gun-bearing vehicles, to rumble by with lights on. A whiff of manure came through the window, counterpoint to gasoline vapors, the richness of molten asphalt. The trip had been suddenly called. The man Washington wanted sent out not at hand, David pressed into service as a distant second choice. This sort of tasking still being laid on just enough to be a welcome break in Wolf Lake's untaxing days. He was feeling the effects of a dozen time zones difference from half a world away and he leaned back lazily, surrendering to the local warmth. Winston could not realize it but David's business, heart of it really—confirmation of a few facts—had already been accomplished and there was little more to do but to wait for his plane to depart at dawn the next morning.

Winston's offices were crowded, the war clattering here as noisily as it honked in the streets. Desks were crammed together, reliable old-fashioned typewriters rat-a-tat-tatting like machine guns, secretaries slapping at their carriage returns with the vigor of the animal drivers in the streets. Xeroxes were humming, spitting paper. Status boards covered the walls, pins displaying progress of this and that. An unerased blackboard retained remnant equations on signal processing and search theory. Back in the reassuring ambience of his office, Winston's mood changed. He apologized humorously for the unfortunate acronym designating his Program. Now the genially expansive host, he set David up in an office with a view towards the mountains, hazier as morning moved into mid-day. Make yourself comfortable, Winston said, anything you want, holler, coffee at the other end of the Typing Pool, donuts too. If you want, we can set up an Exchange run . . . et cetera. A stream of helpfulness. Yet plainly not to be fully at ease until one David Morgan was out of his hair.

"Don't be concerned about me," David said. Looking forward to being left alone. Magazines were set out on a table; Defense journals, copies of *Aerospace*, *Caisson*, even the good old *Proceeding*, plus a thick government booklet explaining what the U.S. was doing out here. A document too detailing special research programs, all the excellent things hi-tech was contributing to the counter-insurgency. He skimmed the material, yet feeling he should be going through it more conscientiously, storing up the lore of this place and time, but his gaze kept being tempted to views of mountain, and sea. He thought of Honolulu, the Punchbowl, clouds and rainbows, Al and time long ago, with unappeasable longing. The palm tree is planted in most hearts, roots stronger in some. After a while he started pacing about his borrowed office. The tiredness that came with the long flight, the pressing power of associations, DIANA out there in the harbor doing her vigorous if forlorn thing, all were working away upon him, too vibrant in his senses. In one way a marvelous feeling, in another a messy one, taking him beguilingly by the hand where he might not wish to be led. Dissipating restlessness, he wandered the office spaces, making trips for coffee, finding excuse for conversation with the secretaries. An especially gabby lot out here, but then seemingly they had more to tell. A jolly black girl, Amelia, told him she was "having a *ball*" out here. "On my *second* extension, man."

"Good for you." He said it sincerely. "Well, ye . . . eh . . . ess *indeedy*." Her fingers were hitting the typewriter keys while she tossed off amusing stories. Yet his sense of powerful and yet non-specific memory would not lose itself in small talk. The feeling had begun, he decided, with the cooking smells that had poured in through the car window while proceeding through town. Rich, spicy, they had seemed to compound the whole world, poignant as only smells can be. This sensitivity, now awakened, had carried over with him into this modern building with its vapor of disinfectant polish, clean but unlovely whiffs of plastic on the ride up the elevator, then the usual office smells, the dry electricity of copiers, the winning freshness of just opened boxes of paper, washroom soap, the fragrance of perfumes blending. Every female a belle out here. One of the secretaries, he could not tell which, owned a markedly stronger perfume. It hung heavy in the office air like flowers in a closed garden; he had noticed it upon arrival and vaguely—all the while trying unsuccessfully to concentrate upon the dry literature of war—it had nagged him with its familiarity. Suddenly though while chatting with Amelia, as if borne to his nostrils on an invisible breeze, it was much stronger; rich, dense, a rolling wave of unambiguous knockout smell known before. *Viola Fletch.* She was coming from one of the private offices and frowning over papers. The frown too carried intact across oceans and jungles, across years. Only at the last instant did she look up and in stunned surprise drop her papers. "Mr. Morgan!" Reunion was with hugs and exclamations, friendly and fond. She asked a dozen questions, waiting for answers on none. Introducing him around proudly. "Former boss—*best* of bosses." She'd put on weight, but luxuriantly. Her hair was lustrous as ever, still making him think of some luscious fruit. Her lipstick was orange but did not clash. All this color set off vividly by a linen dress of glowing whiteness. Same tailor as Winston's?

In any event, the place agreed. Her jaws still moved, discreetly but apparently eternally, with their wad of gum. But something was different too, a touch of class. Anyway—she was rattling on—there was not time, not right here and now, to tell him all that she wanted to tell, to ask all that she wanted to hear. Her Chief needed something. She made a pout. A *flap.* But . . . to the point. She shook her massy head of hair by way of punctuation. Just here for the day? Gee, a real shame. Still, there were things he would have time for. Tasman's Tower. Vasco da Gama's wall. Lots of history here. Grand Anse Beach. The Post Exchange (best in the Far East, outside of Naha). The Raj Hotel. By now a local girl, proud of her town. He must see it and she was going to make sure he did. She had a vehicle and a driver (don't ask *how,* she said coyly) and she would meet him in ten minutes down in the lobby. "Okay?"

"Okay." When she left he noticed a dropped piece of paper she had missed. It was stamped, SECRET AND URGENT. "I imagine Viola may be wanting this," he said to Amelia.

"Just reckon she may," she smirked. "So you know our Vi. *My* goodness." She clucked her tongue. Sharply amused and full of stories, he could see, that it would not take much to encourage her to tell. "Well, well, well, and *all* that."

"So, how is Viola getting along?"

"Why just *super*-fine. Running the office and us girls and all good things."

"I see." He felt small as he leaned down to ask his next with a voice meant not to carry. "Just between you and me. How is her typing these days?"

"Ooh . . . ooh . . . *ooh* . . . *ee* . . ." A whoop of delighted laughter did not settle down all at once. "Our girl don't *have* to type. Got herself a *colonel!*" Which would explain some things, but not all. He poked his head into Winston's office to say goodbye.

"You're in good hands. Viola will give you the grand tour." Winston paused, tickled by recollection. "Used to work for you, didn't she? And you fired her, as

I recall. Quite a thing at the time." Winston nodded on, musing. Across time and half a world away the rarity of the event, sticking in memory. "And all for naught, eh?" Winston enjoying his own smile.

"I wonder if you have any idea how it all happened," David asked. That smile irked. "I mean, reentry into Civil Service, despite the required cross-checks, the SF171 form and all that?" The question was owed. A fight worthy once ought not to trail away into nothingness. But Winston was giving another one of his little shrugs. "Our cutie pie was on-site when I got here. You're asking me, of course, the Big One, Why Government Doesn't Work." He seemed to have sudden reason, by his own lights, for another too bright smile. "A war on, eh? All kinds of fish get through the net." They shook hands. Winston's own was damp, still nervous. For a fraction of a second his lips twisted slightly without sound, as a person's will when difficult to begin what he wants to say. "You know, Morgan, it wasn't really such a *bad* idea, bringing DIANA out here."

"It was pretty bad." David saw: he is still worried. Simply because I must file a report. Of course, most probably it would simply disappear, be unread even by those who had sent him out here. There was a residue of pleading in Winston's eyes, but a contrary stubbornness in his manner. "Anyway, if not DIANA, then perhaps MINERVA, which admittedly is a bit further downstream. There's always a teething period in these things."

Narcotic too in every governmental cliché. A man could grow numb with them. Millions had. Sometimes David felt himself succumbing. "So they say."

Winston's smile was weak but then bloomed, fed by an ironic thought that he took for granted David was bound to share. "After all," winking, "as you've pointed out, it's not as if it were useful for anything else. Like finding submarines." It was the wink, not the words, that offended. It stepped too boldly across some threshold, was bravado too lightly won, like someone else's medal snatched from a pawnshop. Winston had not earned irony.

"Isn't it time then, overdue, for you to speak up? Point out the nonsense of what Esposito's up to and have her sent home." Winston's face fell. "My God, Morgan, one can't say that. Not yet. *It's budget time . . .*" In Washington it was always budget time. City of a single season. Embers of old anger, thought dead by even David himself, glowed within from a sudden stirring of this wind. Where were you, my slippery fellow, when the rocks were molten? His last words were soft, but a sword flick all the same. "No? Then when shall it be?"

He turned, walked away, a small but deep cut inflicted. So let it sting. But then, bare minutes later, comfortably seated in Viola's official car, looking at the back of the dark head of Abu, their driver, both the matter and its emotion had slipped away. Languor swirled in on the warm breeze through the open windows. Abu, who obviously knew Viola well, responded to her directions given in the local *patois*. Scenes drifted by to the accompaniment of enthusiastic description. "Over there." She pointed to a tiny wooden storefront with a sign, emblazoned with flaming red dragons, big as the store itself, "HAMBURGER'S SEVENTH HEAVEN", which was apparently the only really *good* hamburger place in this part of the whole Southwest Pacific. "The *only* one," she repeated solemnly. "Can you believe it?" Incuriously he accepted that Viola had a car and driver. Figuring that he was bound to find out the how and why of it since, in her unpausing flow of commentary, she did not withhold anything. Soon recounting how she had been reinstated in Civil Service. One might have imagined a convoluted tale, with many twists and surprises of luck, but as Viola told it the whole thing had been simplicity itself, without trickery. "Easy," quoth she, ". . . as falling off a log." Why not? Thousands of logs in government fallen off of every day.

Oh, she did have a few complaints. "My goodness, who *doesn't?*" They had to put out a lot of reports and that could mean a late hour or two. But on the whole, she was happy. "I've got a GS-eleven and I should get a thirteen at my next review. We get per diem at eighty-eight dollars a day and all our income is tax-free. And we have full exchange and commissary privileges and medical and dental care out at Camp Leftwich." Her recital of benefits and perquisites went on, an easy droning background of words. They were out of the city and winding up a mountain through shadowy green forests. He had not remembered her as this much of a talker, but then maybe he'd never given her much chance.

Her voice was soft, bland, a pleasant match for the whine of the tires on the long climb. "And, oh. yeah. There's combat zone pay too." "Is it all that dangerous?" he asked. "I mean for those stationed in town."

"A bomb was rolled into the San Francisco Café a year ago. What a mess. That was the last bad thing to happen though." She giggled. "Of course, it's not really dangerous. But if they're gonna pass out all that green, what the heck, who's *not* gonna take it?" One more good thing. Piling up points out here. Bumping rights for when she got back to the States.

They had reached a summit where a lookout area was bordered by a rocky parapet. Getting out of the car, the shadow of a weathered stone tower fell across them. "That's Drake's Tower," she said, "after the sailor that went round the world." The view was breathtaking in all directions and Viola knew each one well. She admitted, when he complimented her on the skill of her pitch, to coming here often. A standard stop on the VIP tour. "And you," he gestured with a flourish, "are the VIP guide."

"Well, one of them." She was embarrassed, sought to erase an imputation not yet defined. "Hey, but you're a *friend*." The harbor appeared small from here, far below and far off, the crowding ships like tiny toys. Beyond was the ocean, spreading out with an immensity of pale blue that went on until it vaguely joined the sky. The island, Viola said, which the writer Conrad had in mind for his novel *Victory* was only a hundred miles out that way. She hadn't read the story herself, though meaning to, but it was about this guy whose business had tumbled down about his ears and who kept staring out from the end of an empty pier. "Then this girl came over. But they had enemies. Dick said it was awful sad."

Inland the mountains rose one behind the other, fading into gray, rain-softened dimness. Back in there, she said, were supposed to be headhunters, tribes who had never seen a white man. She indicated a valley, which was part of the front, marked by the permanent haze of gun smoke. "The front?" he repeated. "Oh yeah. Listen and you can hear the mortars. Now, shh . . . No, not that one. That's a one-oh-five. *There.* That's a mortar." Faint and far off, they were a trembling in the air, innocent as the blood rustling in one's ear. "*Hear them?*" she whispered. "How are we doing?, he asked."

"On time? Oh, you mean the *fighting*. It's kind of hard to tell. But Dick says it's important to make a stand. If not here, it's bound to be somewhere else. I guess you figure the same way." Struck though mostly by how little he thought about such things lately. Stands, and the like. Viola relaxed, yawned, made appropriate gratified noises, an opulent and clothed Venus stretching lazily towards the burning day. Straining blouse and skirt and jacket, underwear too surely feeling its limits. The act without grace but its naturalness fascinated. An animal magnificence. She patted her tummy. "So. You want to try shopping now?" She ticked off the Exchanges. One for each of the Services. An extra one for the Joint Staff.

"It's a thought." Maybe he should bring something back for the family. Coming this far.

"They do carry good stuff. 'Course, you can't get the island beads any more."

"Beads?" "Yeah. They're famous. But kind of poisonous, the jequirity ones, if you nibble at them, and kids do, because they got bright, pretty colors. They were selling them for a while though like hot cakes and then this Congressman came out and made a stink so . . ."

"So none of the fabled beads unfortunately are now to be had at the PX."

"That's right! You must of heard. Anyway, they're hard to get anywhere now." He allowed as how he could forego the beads and she looked at him thoughtfully. Guessing that maybe he'd just as soon pass up Exchange hopping. "Anyway there's cute little shops near the Raj." On the speedy exhilarating ride back down, whipping through a succession of curves without guardrails, she told him about Dick. Her colonel, an expert on small arms. It seemed that out here the soldiers needed special rifles because the regular sizes got tangled up in the jungle vines and he was helping evaluate new kinds of rifles. A really sweet guy but with problems at home. A divorce could be in the cards, soon as some things could be straightened out. "Hope so," she said, "because I sure think it's love."

"Good luck." Her small wry laugh, popping out of sober silence was winning. "Luck's what I'll need. Not so many of these romances out here really work out. They don't travel so good, know what I mean?" The great shadowing trees of the rain forest, like a colonnade, were being left behind them. The grit and the colors of the city lay ahead. "Anyhoo," for some seconds her gum had been given thoughtful reprieve, "time will tell." Everyone came to the Raj at this quickening hour of the late afternoon, she said. They had a round white table under an umbrella set out on a broad veranda that overlooked fine gardens and an entranceway of baroque grandeur. Lush and yet tamed flowers rose out of a flawless lawn. They had a narrow but framed view of stone piers, tawny battlements made for defending against arrows, a small crane swinging its load of cargo in dreamy motion over the rusty stack of a freighter wavering in the heat. Though the Raj swarmed with modern foreign military uniforms, its ornate columns and wooden latticework, and the barefoot natives in red fezzes and khaki shorts bringing them drinks, kept alive stronger still the flavor of a century gone. He thought of planters, traders, ship captains, scoundrels and dreamers, and the sandalwood and cinnamon and all the fine-scented plunder of the East for which they had dared. He thought how Al could sit here forever-sipping iced tea, fingering a long spoon graceful as a swan. He noticed Viola getting looks. She was the exotic, her red hair and fine whiteness vivid amongst the olive dark faces, the glossy black hair. David found himself observing her differently. Experience, the years conferring a part of what education had not, leagues of confidence had lengthened her stride through the time and space she'd traveled since that final teary day at EAR. She held her head up, like someone. Dimly at least she too had doped out things about the world. He let her order their drinks. In foreign phrases she rattled off the names of the local nibblers, both tart and sweet. By the end of their second round—the drink was fruity with vague consolation of healthfulness, smoking icy vapors from a frosty glass—he realized that a troubled expression had encroached upon her normal placidity. "I got a question." Biting her lip. "Shoot."

"It's real personal, I'm afraid." "Think about it then for a moment first," he offered conventional caution. "Because you could regret asking it afterwards."

She shook her head. "Not with the kind of person you are." There was still a ludicrous mismatch between her moods and her expression. Pout was not what was called for, but her out-thrust lower lip made it that. Anyway, the problem was Dick. More precisely, his tastes. He was . . . "into art." She wrinkled her nose like a rabbit sniffing cabbage. "But not your ordinary kind. Erratic art." The cocktail chairs were wicker, none too steady. Ditto notoriously for their little table. Twin factors heightening the risk of toppling over if amusement strikes too hard. He barely recovered. "*What* kind of art?" She colored, angrily. "Please don't tease me. I can't stand that. You know what I mean."

"I daresay I do at that." "*Course you do!*" Distantly bells chimed, a muezzin called. In the softening light east and west joined. "I think I oughta tell you what . . . the stuff is like."

No words rose this time to stop her. With euphemisms and allusions, hands waving out of tune with her words, she described the curios of this place and the predilections of her colonel. "And that's not the *worst* of it." Her eyes met his with pleading.

"He didn't invent it, you know," she said, "and it's not that it affects him. He's normal as the day is long." She smiled sadly and a stray beam of departing sunlight caught the gold of an inner tooth. "Guess I'd know *that*." An additional thought struggled for a moment before escaping. "I mean, I'm a real straight forward kind of person myself, not . . ." Fancy, he completed silently. "What's bothering you, I suppose, is that you're afraid that he may grow too fond of it. That it may somehow," he felt his modest talent for useful summarization faltering, "change him?" She turned defensive, cashed reserves of loyalty. "He's not the only one. VIP's and all, are shipping the stuff back to CONUS hidden in their household stuff. It's antique and they're not making any more."

Barefoot children were scrambling for coins outside the gate, their high voices carrying. Shadows were deep and pure as jewels upon the flowered lawn. Such variety of counsel, he mused, as a man gets called upon to give. "I'll tell you what I think, Viola. Though hardly an expert on the subject, I gather that it seldom does any real harm." She drew in a great breath and exhaled. Were she draped in diaphanous cloth, instead of her shiny PX blouse, her bosom was probably one whose pink only the brush of Rubens could have done justice. Her concern, and therefore her relief, was apparently even greater than he had supposed. "The way I figured it too. I guess you got to take that view. Sorry to load you up with my problem, but thanks for the advice." He borrowed from her emerging smile. "Well, for what it's worth . . ." His voice sank into the quietness. Seconds passed. "So," she said almost briskly, "you doing okay?"

"Oh fine." He shook the ice in his glass. "I expect I've had enough."

"Not your drink. I was thinking of you, Mr. Morgan." Those large dark liquid eyes were staring into his own. A man could fall into them and drown. He realized how he must look to her, face drawn from too many hours of flight, needing a shave, his paleness standing out absurdly in this land that was a hymn to the sun. He felt himself strengthless, a bird stripped of plumage in the winds of this too swift trip. Yet for a time one David Morgan had been the most important person in her life. "I'm doing all right," he said. "You're a happy guy?", she asked.

"Very." But added, "though happiness isn't the same thing as contentment, of course."

She merely blinked—smaller weathers of the soul did not touch her—and leaned towards him. "You probably don't think I remember those Washington times. But I thought it was great the way you were always fighting to change things. I got to say too, here and now, I was proud to do your typing." He thought that she was going to giggle but it was too solemn a moment. Even as she seemed honor bound to add the obvious postscript. "Even if I was a lousy typist. *Am*." He was not going to cheapen the truth with false denial and looked away.

"And you didn't change nothin'. You sure didn't stop . . . that DIANA. The Navy went right ahead and bought scads of them." "Scads," he seconded, "cheaper by the dozen."

"They got one out here now, you know." "Tell me about it." Her eyes moistened. Wanting to offer consolation without knowing how. "Don't worry about me," he said.

"Anyway, I wanted you to know, I was hoping I'd get the chance some day to say these things. Well golly," her smile was radiant in the dusk, "my red letter day." A red-letter day calling for a final drink. Enjoyed while lone stars brightened in the deepening blue, and graceful robed figures, silent as the moths, lit the candles on the tables. She insisted on picking up the check. *Her* treat. After Abu had dropped them off at her building and been dismissed by her, he escorted her up to the door of her apartment where she invited him in. "I think not. But thanks for a lovely day." Beyond the open doorway her apartment expanded into a pale brightness of gold and silver colors, a carpet white as a polar bear, oriental rugs vivid as blood. A sensuous and yet not unappealing vulgarity. There were tables with the legs of dragons, piles of cushions, ornate mirrors. Luxuriance without elegance. Through a far window the evening sky was all but dead, rose and gold cooling,

"I could fix something simple after all those spices. The commissary takes good care of us. Maybe just a hamburger. Got hot dogs too. Whatever." "I'm not truly hungry, thanks."

"Gee. But it's silly. You got hours 'till your plane." She was looking up at him from that always surprising shortness of stature that one fails to note in a woman until she has kicked off her shoes and is before him flat-footed in stockinged-feet. The colonel far way, he and his rifle tangled up in the snarl of those jungle vines. He tried to picture the man, expert in guns, reader of Conrad, confident that stands had to be made. But the colonel would not come into focus and he did not try. There was a small Viola sound, a mere shifting of gum, girl and her wad reunited after brief separation. A pop recalling him to the trembling moment. Her gaze was steady, gently wistful. "Really, I do have to run." He amplified his excuses needlessly, said other foolish things to those kindness-intending eyes. "No? You're sure?"

"Yes," he said. No. Not sure at all. He had read somewhere that, perhaps keenest and most lucid amongst the many regrets besetting a man facing his life's end, are likely to be recall of such chances missed. Those unambiguous opportunities, clear and beautiful as a full moon, that even the densest of fellows can see were a sweetness freely offered and freely to be taken, and which only a fool lets pass by. There had already been a few such instances before, not only Daisy Ketcham, even in a carnal history as undistinguished and a nature as physically unexalted as David Morgan's own, that were there stored in memory. Seeds of latent self-rebuke in long gestation awaiting that time when they must come back fully alive in wreathings of regret and for which one David Morgan, with whatever vitality he could spare from the business of dying, would be kicking himself.

This was not to be one of those occasions. Not with this self-described, and accurately so, "straightforward" female with her ardor and her warmth and her knowingness. With something lovely too in the simple, touching earthy practicality of her caring, at some point in the proceedings offering him, with good and explicit purpose, a glimpse into her Dick's shunned closet of antique replicas of human parts both explicit and fanciful. Suggesting to him shyly, considerately, for all her abomination of what the closet sheltered, after a knowledgeable and rueful downward glance, that "maybe a look or two might . . . you know, Mr. Morgan, help . . . ." Thanking her for her thoughtfulness but as it turned out her concern was premature, needing no help. Not at first, and not the second or the third time either. Not for this winning sweetness and glory, natural and simple as grass and earth, this time to be savored long of an ardent and affectionate and tireless lover at last asleep in his arms, one plump arm thrown across him and breathing deeply, punctuated by dainty snores, the relaxed sleep of the generous and the just. With David Morgan, himself dozing more fitfully, scatterings of thought flitting through languor, such as the amused reflection at those long ago idling imaginings back in Crystal City days of the precise shade of her private hair. Getting his answer, startling and unexpected, in the apparition of a pad trimmed to the shape of a heart and with framing tufts in a fiery mélange of dyed purple and yellow and fire engine red. For a second she had flinched in embarrassment at what he was seeing, having forgotten what was no doubt another one of her colonel's tastes, and hoping "he was not turned off, like you know." Assuring her that he was not. Truer words never spoken. He waited for guilt, feeling that it was due, but the closest he could come was only light sorrow for lost simplicity, the skein of complexity that often still beset him and Al, none of which should matter a rats ass, least of all impede the great and good thing. Viola awoke, bouncing up merrily, determined that he must have something better sticking to his ribs on his long homeward flight than . . . "One of those doggoned old Military Airlift Command's dreary box lunches." Assuring it too with frying him up another savory burger and microwave defrosted French fries fare, far removed from Al's gourmet best, but gratefully received. Plus a companionable cup of coffee with refills too at her shiny kitchen table while waiting for the cab she had called.

"Well, thanks a whole lot, Viola." She gave him an impish look, wagged a finger.

"You don't thank someone for *that*," she said, "you got to know *that*, Mr. Morgan."

"Yes." He weighed that unexpected touch of sophistication, was pleased to respond to it with a wink. "That was just for the burgers." She gave him a gentle dig. "Oh, yeah, right."

The taxicab's horn was musical, soft as the aromatic night air drifting in from the sea. He rose. "Sorry I have to go. Truly. But maybe we'll be seeing each other again."

"Don't reckon it," she said mournfully. Her robe, a silken splendor of boldly colored dragons rampant, was carelessly drawn over her pink and pale softness. Her makeup vanquished this long and busy day, he read upon that pale shiny skin bumps, tiny hairs, childhood scars, life unretouched. Reddened eyes, dark circled, drew him in to a farewell embrace and a bouquet of smells, fading perfumes, dried sweat, the milkiness of the female, hamburger oils in her clotted hair, even a whiff of the barnyard . . . thinking all this while taking aboard Viola's telling him that he must please, *please* pass on her best wishes to Mrs. Morgan.

"Indeed, I shall." Al to get the full dump, right? "Anyway, you take care, Viola. It really could happen. You never know, we might bump into each other again."

"I wish."

His plane's departure was delayed and it was near dawn when he woke up from a doze on a hard airport bench, and saw his plane still not ready. Men were working under floodlights, figures in greasy white overalls toiling on an engine under one wing. He ached for home. Wanting to be away from this terminal of sullen strangers. America's latest Struggle for Freedom, however possibly worthy, he was glad to leave for others to wage. Already he grudged the extra day he must spend in Honolulu to keep the Pacific Naval Command informed. Reasonably they wanted a report to justify the trouble and expense of his trip, and he would give them a mildly factual one, shorn of the kind of editorial content that was still simmering away in him. It came easier all the time, going through the motions. Easing the boredom of waiting, he wandered about and did something rare. He bought a cigar, one of Fidel's best smuggled far, and he smoked it for its remembered consolation, for its present peace, down to gummy stump. A tired man in a rumpled suit that would be lots more rumpled before the trip was done.

The called passengers shuffled aboard, a line snaking through the soft warm dawn across the asphalt and up the aluminum ladder. The plane took off, rising over taupe waters flickering with fishermen's lanterns. In the center of the harbor, glimpsed for some seconds over one wing as the plane banked, he detected something different from the sprinkle of those tiny and appealing lights. Only later, on the long murmurous flight over the Pacific, did he figure it out. Encircled as if in its own pool of light, shining through the pale green illuminated waters, like a puddle of dissolving emerald, it was apparent that he had been witness to *Esposito's* floodlit monitoring vigilance against those vexing tides of secret swimmers pressing their unwelcome suit upon DIANA. All that light hopefully some protection. Vividly luminous images kept stirring his imagination, making him think of a great pale lily pad upon dark waters, a grunting frog in the center, or a candle floating in its special little boat upon a swimming pool. His nation's striving touching him still.

Images, benign and lulling, aiding sleep. Which is what he did for hours, mercifully undreaming, until he felt the high mid-Pacific sun blazing across the wing's silver surface. Waking up then to thoughts of this thing that had been, even as it already seemed far off, receding now in time and space more with each hour of the plane's five hundred mile an hour thunderous crawl across the silver blue ocean. Wistful already for that experience that could not come again but, in the treasuring of it feeling something achieved, appeased, mysteriously larger and grander than its transient joy. Something was eased in him, tautness released, something repaid. To be kept tucked away in a corner of his mind, even if only unconsciously, for the good feeling it kept radiating within him.

And then in behavior most conscious, when he got back to Wolf Lake, taking up again the reins of its Directorship, but ever so *lightly*, even more negligently than before. This fondly regarded place but which—his gratifying secret—pretty much truly did run itself. An inward thing, this further loosening of the bands of his caring and responsibility, not to be read by a single one of the hundreds of staff and employees under him, going about the business of the Wolf Lake Acoustic Facility no less well even as its irrelevancy deepened year by year. Correspondingly, David Morgan directing ever more of his heart and energies to the well-being of his family, the continued strengthening of Al, who by God was coming along still, defying the well told myths of the "geographical cure", a transformation making for the quiet joy of her husband and a peace blessing her family. By now having taken up flying, his Al, something she had so longed dreamed of doing, and now ardently pursuing her lessons at a little airstrip in a neighboring valley. Her instructor, and a severe taskmaster, a grumpy old Navy flier, nevertheless pronouncing her progress as excellent and indicating himself soon ready, over the unexpressed fears of a deeply apprehensive husband, to clear his pupil to solo.

▲ ▲ ▲ ▲ ▲

Lately, he had taken more to watching golf on television. More time to watch, ever less to do. Sneaking away in the middle of the day even, totally shirking his Wolf Lake duties. He didn't watch just the big tournaments but lesser ones too, those many sponsored in various nebulous, name-lending ways by marginal celebrities . . . the Jamie Farr Something or Other *(Jamie Farr?)*, sponsoring names who didn't, not a one, have a worthwhile body turn, couldn't even decently shift their weight, hackers all . . . . How did *they* get there? No matter, putting aside envy to enjoy. He wasn't just watching either, as once he used to, only when the weather was bleak, when ice glazed the ground and his own local fairways were hard as iron and the only tournaments going on were in southern places, warm desert lands, in Arizona or Southern California or Blue

Hawaii. He watched too when the weather was fine and the mountain tops were clear and he could just as well have been out hiking with Boat. But consoling himself with the realization that these days Boat was no longer so glad to head off with him every weekend to climb. A fellow couldn't be climbing mountains all the doggoned time, his son had let him know annoyedly. Translation: Discovering girls.

He got to know the newer players through television, learned their history, where they came from, their wives. Names too that never made headlines but who kept coming back week after week to try. Joe Newton, Harry Crocker, Albert Neeter . . . others too, all serious, no jokes with the crowd from these scowlers at fate, staring down at their mischief-making clubs to make sure they were straight. And, of course, there were the new giants, the Normans and the like, becoming ever more sharply individualized with each shot that he watched them play. With each fly of the ball, or roll of the putt, one learned a little more about them. He had gotten to like Ben Crenshaw, never thinking that he would, but as time went on he found himself seeing beneath the floppy blond hair, his scowly ways. Forgiving him such because of his intensity, his tremendous love of the game, his immersion in the history of golf. No longer the Boy Wonder, no longer a boy, tracks around his eyes. Ben went down the fairways, they told, hearing not the murmurs of the gallery but the voices of ghosts, remembering Hogan's famous two iron at Oakland Hills, the curling put that Bobby Jones sank to tie at Merion in '29. Maybe that was Ben's trouble. David figuring that at least he understood the curse of memory too. Having too much of it himself.

Came the British Open this year. Played on an old and famous seaside links close by an ancient town with a cathedral soaring high. Most of the world's best were playing, but some of the near best amongst the American golfers had not come. The high cost deterred them, it was said, and one of the young hotshots said, heck, he would have to finish at least *twelfth* just to make expenses. They showed themselves as men who played mostly for the money, keeping score with dollars. Resenting too the random bounces of the British links. Just as well that they stayed home. Because Nicklaus had come, and Trevino, and Watson, of course, and Arnold Palmer, showing up once more. Enough. And enough of the lesser known pros had come too, amongst them that Albert Neeter whose name he recalled as not having done badly in some of the lesser tournaments earlier in the year.

David had always loved the British Open best. The courses were so different, sandy humpy expanses by the edge of misty seas. The winds blew across them and the shiny grasses of their roughs were high and the ball took crazy and cruel kicks. Courses created by nature rather than molded by man's bulldozers. The holes each had names and even some of the bunkers too, like *Ye Slough of Despond* and other such somber designations, expressing the meanness of fate, or punishment that fit the crime. After the first two rounds this time, while there were some big names fairly well up there amongst the leaders, actually none of the famous were playing all that well (there were shots of them tramping around in the tall grass and thick purple heather looking for balls), and the television's attention more and more was focussed on other challenging entrants. The latest colorful muscle boy from Australia, say, the wiry master from Japan. And there was yet to be one more interview with Arnold Palmer, not playing so badly this time, but seen standing there in the Press Tent and having, as always, to answer silly questions with undeserved seriousness. *Arnie, why have you entered? Why do you keep on?* And so on. Arnie frowned a little and paused before answering, as if having to think of answers so obvious that he had never had to consider them before. A wrinkled smile, "why, to win." He did not add, "of course." The unfailing grace of the man.

Reluctantly, and without much conviction, more of the media's attention was devoted to Albert Neeter. Sure to fold, of course, these unknowns high up on the board always did blow to eighty on the last day, didn't they? But no getting around the scoreboard that showed him still just one stroke away from the lead at the start of the fourth round. There was a hastily done profile of Neeter, giving his start as a caddie, the driving ranges he had run in various towns near Kansas City, Missouri, working himself up to head professional at the Fair View Municipal Course. He had won a State Open and several seasons played well enough to get his Tournament Players Tour Card, but not until this season won enough dollars even to make expenses. This was the year, the viewer gathered, he had chosen to make the big push. He was not a young man, seeming in his late thirties, and his answers to the patronizing questions were given slowly, stiffly, in an angular way. But he was not self deprecating, made no humorous remarks about himself, and a listener could sense the determination of the man. He felt that he belonged here, that he had a real chance to win.

They showed pictures of his wife, his children and his home; the latter white-painted, wooden, old-fashioned, roomy but humble. His wife's name was Ellie and in a sea of tweedy fashion she was the one in the shapeless blue dress and an old cardigan and shoes all wrong, heels bound to be sinking into the wetted English grasses. She might have been pretty once, though never in the way of the Trophy wives of the younger hot-shot pros, those smoothly groomed, Products of Care—the new breed of pros married *rich*—upon whom the TV cameras liked to concentrate, revealing them in their cutesy ways, fingers crossed, eyes shut tight in fear and prayer at tense shots, bursting forth photogenically in wide smiles of joy at their man's successful execution. Justified believers in their good luck. Ellie Neeter plainly had little faith in luck. Her dark hair was pulled back, it was grey-streaked, and she seldom smiled. She had cooked too many hamburgers, eaten too many as well, and her fists were clenched all through the final round except when her hands were on her son, the youngest of four, whom they had brought over on this trip so that he might get a chance to" . . . see some castles and all the nice old scenes." They couldn't afford to bring over but one child, she explained further to the interviewer, and "well . . . he is the right age to appreciate these things the most . . . ." The camera dissected Ellie Neeter, gave her no mercy, showed every line around tired and dark circled eyes. She never closed those eyes but kept them staring wide at every hop and break of her husband's ball each one of the seventy-two holes. A woman looking beyond those treacherous green fairways too, constantly thinking as well—one was bound to believe it—of the piggy bank they had cracked for this one. The interviewer wanted more color, you couldn't blame him—networks did not grow rich nor sell oceans of beer on such as the Albert Neeters—and he was digging for whatever he could get out of lean ore. "I daresay, actually, it's none of this 'Albert' stuff around home. It must be 'Al' back there?"

"Oh no." Those serious eyes had widened further, almost in alarm, but wholly in honesty. "It's always been *Albert.*" The camera dissected Albert Neeter's swing, along with Ellie's wrinkles. There were slow motion shots of his takeaway, his position at the top, juxtaposed with critiques of the magnificence of Tom Watson's swing, the latter's tremendous extension, the coiling and unleashing of power like a beautiful whip cracking, the ball flying out like a stone flung from a sling-shot. Beside it the swing of Albert Neeter was downright creaky, a thing of rags and patches. He seemed to take the club back painfully. He positioned the toe of the club at the ball, requiring himself, in the course of his swing, to change both the plane and the arc of his swing. He brought the club back outside, he swayed, he was flat-footed; grace was not here. Everything done the hard way. Not a swing carved from gold, tuned and refined by the great teachers, every nuance shaped, loveliness sucked in, as it were, from a hundred gorgeous courses. It was a swing *built*, adapted to ordinariness, meant for the physical skills of a man whose muscles and reflexes were far from those of a panther. "Put together in a bicycle shop," one of the commentators said, getting a laugh from his fellows.

The British commentator a famed golfer from the past, observed quietly though, "But getting the job done. Hanging in there, chaps, is he not?"

"But for now long? That's the question." Which to answer, the camera now concentrated upon Albert Neeter with ghoulish intensity. Following him into cavernous bunkers, into rough after rough where methodically he kept swatting himself out; you saw him hacking his way through grass tough as wire. It followed him up onto those great rolling, multi-plateau greens where somehow, and shakily to be sure, he was nevertheless holing putt after curving putt for his scrambled pars. The commentators had less to say; they were awed, fascinated. More, they were puzzled, disconcerted. Their momentarily central actor was not obeying the script. They seemed a little annoyed too. The script called for crumbling, humiliation; how well the networks knew the mob's craving for disaster's blood, and how well to give it what it wanted. Simple goodness did not pay. David sat at the television, glued. He had, at the start of the day's watching, taken a beer out of a plastically bound six-pack in the refrigerator, intending to have just one. But as the long day's coverage wore on he went back for one after another, ritually, nervously, crushing each can when he had finished it. Today, the true American with his six-pack. "A gutsy round," said the British commentator. Not a man who used the word lightly. For the script was still changing. Its theme now was *miracle*. One by one the mighty made their charges and fell back, Nicklaus, Trevino, Aoki . . . no finishing kick in any of those splendid legs today. And yet you were sure, even to the end, that the new script was going to be torn up and blown away, its scraps wheeling off into those grim grey skies along with the sea gulls, storm-driven, which the camera caught along with the flight of the ball; the birds soared and wheeled above the tiny figures of men striding down the rolling carpets of green. You could not believe it even as Albert Neeter walked down the middle of the seventy-second fairway, his ball safely on the green's middle, not too far away from the pin and two putts to win, with the crowd clapping and roaring its approval of this stocky homely man now transformed in size and heroic dignity. You were sure that he was going to blow it still, and when his first put went boldly three feet past you were convinced that conventional sad wisdom was right, that he was going to jerk the next one by. A tester, as they say; a knee-knocker. All the nasty little clichés in one. You knew otherwise, in fact, right up until his last putt rolled to the edge and paused there for a fraction of a second, seeming to take a look in first. Then it rolled over and disappeared.

Albert Neeter did not look skyward nor sink to his knees. Neither did he reach into the cup and then fling his ball to the crowd. It was too splendid a moment to be used cheaply, the kind that comes to a man but once, for most men not at all. He simply stood there, a smile widening on that face that hadn't cracked one since the first hole of the tournament, and then out of the crowd, violating the protocol of these events, in the same drear blue dress she had worn on at least two other days and in heels woundingly sharp for golf greens, Ellie Neeter flew into his arms. The two stood there, tears running down their cheeks, saying nothing, just holding tightly. Ten thousand people were packed around the green, their incipient surge held back by the helmeted bobbies, and yet for two people, a man and a woman, as private a moment as there ever was. David was well into his last beer, the six-packed destroyed. There was a long silence from the commentators, letting the scene speak for itself. The Britisher finally broke it in a strained voice that cracked a little. "Chaps. Well, he hung in there all the way, did he not?" *Did he ever,* David's eyes blurred and he guessed that many another pair of eyes were swimming too. A good man had hung in there.

He got up shakily. Having sat too long, swilled too many beers. Too much, period. He had to get out to walk, breathe fresh air, feel sunshine. He did not call out his intention to Al who was busy in the kitchen, but headed out and across the lawn to the lake. Standing there watching the water fade from gold to silver as the sun dropped below the mountains. It was where she found him some minutes later, easy to guess where he had gone. Coming up behind him quietly, giving the barest touch. "You're not letting yourself get cold?" she said. One of life's features out here, the quick falling chill of evening.

"Not at all." He did not turn around.

"I gather the tournament's over and that nice guy, the long shot won." Through the long afternoon she had followed the progress of the last round intermittently, popping in and out, but enough to get the drift. Not truly understanding golf, still impatient at its dawdling pace, a fan mostly for his sake. "That he did."

"How are you doing?", she said. Still talking to the back of his head. The pull of her hand on his elbow did not turn him. She marched around to face him.

"Oh dear," she said, "what I was afraid of. Am I seeing what I think I am?"

"Don't make too much of them. Or it."

"They are nothing to be ashamed of. It was very moving, I realize, that older man's triumph. And his frumpy wife. What was his name?"

He told her. "They called him a journeyman," she mused, "didn't they? Funny old-fashioned word. I'd hate it if you had won and they called you a journeyman."

"You won't have to face that."

She snuggled close beside him. "But that's not it, is it?", she said softly.

He did not reply. She waited to say: "But you know, darling, it wouldn't have made any difference. Not a particle's. Not in the long run."

They walked along the shore. Gazing out, they were all in shadows now, the chill was deeper. She took his hand. "I read something somewhere that I think is true. That helps us, we women, that is. Why maybe it is that we live longer. Because we are not bothered by . . . *things*. Like where we stand, what we've accomplished. It should bother me, I suppose, I should be conflicted with guilt, that I'm a joke as Comptroller . . . no *please*, sweet, don't pretend otherwise . . . but still every now and then something comes along in the course of my day, even at the office, and I sort of hold my head a little higher for something I've done. It may be nothing at all by male standards; in fact, be so small that no one in the world knows of it but me, no more than just having saved the Station on paper clips, but still I go around clasping it to my bosom, my secret pride."

"I'm glad that you can."

"Unlike you men, unlike *you*, my man," she laughed, lightening the moment, "who can't be content unless he's stopped a speeding locomotive in its tracks, fed a nation, changed the world . . . ." He nodded, toyed with bits of irony which might be the first reviving spark of humor. "I hear you, my lamb. But, since I haven't stopped any locomotives in their tracks, I'm scouring my mind for one of those lesser triumphs of which you speak."

"Why . . . well, right here under your nose you've got a happy and well run Wolf Lake Test Station. Not to mention all those people living along the shore no longer up in arms."

"So it is told."

"Tsk." She made the sound, for herself, at what he felt was most likely a vexing insufficiency of further worthy examples. After some seconds it burst forth.

"Viola!"

"What?" He almost jumped. Not almost. Did.

"My goodness. What was *that* for? But obviously you do remember her."

"Miss Fletch."

"That nice but airhead secretary you worked away so hard at to get fired for incompetence. That was *not* nothing, you will agree. A worthy accomplishment that may have set an example . . . to oh, how many others who may have been . . . *emboldened* . . . to no longer be willing to put up with inferior government performance. That may have been a small thing, but still, it was *something*."

"A beacon, yea," he said, "that lit up the skies." It was near dark. The past was in him. Closed in like the blue black sky and eternity's chill. He felt wryness, another stunted off-shoot of true laughter. He was thinking of Donnie Lee Webster and that fateful afternoon and his urging that one David Morgan dedicate himself henceforth more to the well-being of his family. David had not before passed on to Al the details of that particular segment of that afternoon's tautly compelling exchange. Doing so now.

"The man was absolutely right," she said, ticking off all the good things that had accrued to the family, the boon to mind and spirits, the wellbeing of their children, that had flowed from their coming out here. "Not to mention the salvation of your effed up wife."

"Out of the months of A—holes," he pronounced, "wisdom, eh?"

"Who cares where it comes from?"

True enough. But thinking how, after all, doing right by one's loved ones ought to be only the least common denominator of a man. And not to be achieved at the cost of scamping on all the rest of what it was that a man should be and do. She seemed to read what was contained in his silence. Old worries and new. Might he not, she suggested, ever so gently, want to get back seriously to his work on the submarine. A good thing still to at last turn that crammed file drawer's collection of jottings into that masterfully finished work that had once been so close to his heart. A coyote howled off in the darkness.

"That's all history now."

He sensed her not knowing what to make of that. Not sure himself.

"Still. You've got to have *something*. Everyone must."

"Yes." Thinking of what that might be. Returning to this lesser idea that he had long had in mind. Through thick and thin, whatever befell, hanging on like a distant candle's light in the darkness, small, fluttering, wavering, yet apparently inextinguishable. Still there, after all, this notion of taking on the challenge of Government itself, the hopelessness of Civil Service . . . .

"About which, hon," he said, "I'll admit I don't have all the answers. But it's a story that ought to be told. Maybe some good even come of it."

She sighed. It was like a little inchoate cry in the dark. She took his arm, quickening the steps of them both towards the house. It was truly cold. The light of their windows beckoned.

"Yes, sweet, I do hear you," she said, "but does anybody give a darn?"

11

It had been one of his rare trips back to Washington and his business, which had been slight, taken care of he was able to indulge this wish that had been in him for some time. Drawing out his travel one extra day, Uncle's nickel after all, and driving down to visit his boyhood home. It was a pleasant stroll along the streets of old Annapolis The day was pretty and David had walked through the old market, gazed at the snuggled boats in the inner harbor. Debris clotted thick the base of the harbor's sheltering concrete walls, lapped by corrupted waters. Grimy plastic cups and cans bobbed in the brown scum but doing no harm. The cooler air borne on the breeze was the undefiled salt and shore-side grasses of the distant bay. Across placid water stood Hennessy's Ship Chandlery, recalling his quest for those pesky light bulbs. A different Hennessy's, no longer a faded wooden structure with weathered shingles; this one sleek with prosperity. But its nautical grays and blues still beckoned in the waterfront's pallid hazy sunshine. A quiet hour. Sparse traffic glided slowly up Main Street. Three black youths looking of an age that ought to have them still in school were lounging on a bench. They rose in unison, hopping up on powerful internal springs; at the same time with paradoxically slow and lazy grace. Linked in rhythm, they were in file as their feet hit the decorative brick paving. Without transition they went into a shuffle that had them borne backwards as with desperate jerky gestures they seemed to struggle against invisible fluid force. From captivating start they spun into dance, vigorous, stunningly skillful.

"Well, hi," David said to them with a self-conscious—he hoped not foolish—grin. Taking for granted that the dance was for him, and that it also must call for a donation of money. Except he couldn't figure out how to present it to their whirling figures. What did you do? Just *stop* them in the midst of their splendid spasmodic motion, tapping idiotically on some nimbly twitching shoulder? In a blur uncertainty was resolved and the youths had slid past, were behind him, receding swiftly, magically. He walked on with feelings glad and strange, images of beauty undiminished by irony. Offered, as was now apparent, simply to air and sun.

Part way up Main Street he stopped at a small café. Despite its French name and weathered poster of the Eiffel Tower, the clemency too of its gritted tables thrust out onto the sidewalk, it was a far piece from Paris and had given up pretending. Yet from its mild elevation, with a glimpse of the distant Bay and its heartening blue, Tessa would have known her town still. After a beer he continued up Main Street and veered over to State Circle where mid-way along its curve was the little scripted sign marking the start of Cornhill Street. Halfway down, close to Tessa's former home, he was struck oddly by the sight of two women coming up the hill. The oddness was their tininess. They had the form and the dress of adult figures, but their height was that of children. They were miniatures. He paused for a few seconds to check out his impressions, subject them to the test of sober reason, shaking off his one beer. His first idea was that the women were more distant than originally estimated. But now, counting off door fronts and noting which one the women were opposite, he saw that they could not be far away. Next, because he was on a down slope, testing the hypothesis that he was the victim of optical illusion, the eye's natural tendency being to align itself with the horizontal plane, and hence anyone located below that instinctively sought level can appear compressed in vertical stature. That was not it either.

For another moment he had a different thought born of the visual evidence that the women were moving so slowly, that . . . perhaps they weren't moving at all. Maybe merely a pair of those amazingly lifelike statues of the kind one is startled to encounter in many urban settings. The sort of thing created in plastic or weathered bronze placed in natural poses in parks and arcades—representations of people reading newspapers, hailing cabs—so realistic that the sharpest eyed observer has to look twice. Could someone whimsically have set up a pair of impeccably molded figures? Yet no, again. Even though Tessa had taught him that Annapolis did serve up its moments of whimsy. Because one of the figures, the lady in the black suit, definitely *had* moved. Her cane waggled. Compressed now in a handful of seconds he had other thoughts, trying to confer plausibility to the unaccountable. So maybe this . . . maybe *that* . . . But, *not so* . . . . To all of this and that. *These were real people, adults, even if dwarfs.* Beyond doubt too he was almost upon them and wondering whether to squeeze by on the sidewalk or to step out into the street and give proper room. In the last seconds of dreamlike closure of distance, perspective reasserted itself. They were the product of no special deformity, simply two elderly women who had undergone bone loss, the normal contractions of age. The one in black was Miriam Gearing. *My* God, he thought, *how long people lived.* Forever! He could not believe it. His impulse was to slip on by but the honor of memory opposed that temptation. Choice was taken from him by Miriam's eyes popping wide in recognition. Peeps of joy preceding coherent speech. "*David!* God bless. You are back. This is my friend, Alice Navarro, whom your dear mother knew." Alice Navarro smiled faintly. Where Miriam was chunky, Alice Navarro was excruciatingly thin. Her suit of pale linen with red piping fell from her shoulders like clothes on a wire hanger. Her hand in his was bone. "How do you do, Mrs. Navarro?"

"I'm still here, thank you."

"Oh, you know how it is with us old Navy widows, David," Miriam gushed, "we're doing a lot better than *that*. You know what they call us. 'Battleships. Formidable but still obsolete'. Or is it the other way around, Alice?"

"Close enough." Alice Navarro's sensible if disturbingly husky voice had its calming effect. "Alice. Listen, David used to be embroiled in controversies. They were *Something*. He caused quite a stir." Alice Navarro's eyes were shiny, lights of a tiny excess of vitality hoarded for mirth. "Tell me, David, are you still causing stirs?" "Nary a ripple."

"Oh, but he did, Alice. It was so sad. Writing about bollixed naval ships that couldn't find submarines. Oh, and the *lies* that people told." "Haven't they always, sweet?"

"Alice. These were *Naval Academy men*. A lie was once such a dreadful thing. Remember how midshipmen killed themselves over being caught in even a little fib?"

Alice Navarro shuddered. "I had always assumed those were just stories."

"Indeed not, Alice. Even the tiniest white lie was dreadful. I remember hearing of a Duty Officer, sword and all, bursting into a room and asking a midshipman if he'd been eating while lying there on his bed. Or is it bunk? Anyway against regulations, at that time at least. But who knows these days? The flustered midshipman hopped up and said no, even though a bag of potato chips was right beside him." She let the enormity sink in. "Of course, since the Duty Officer had not actually *seen* the midshipman pick up a chip, he couldn't place him on report. But minutes afterwards the young man realized the terrible thing he'd done and ran down to the Main Office and confessed. And right after that he opened the closet where the Duty Officer keeps his pistol . . . ." She wrinkled her brow, wringing flakes of thickish power from the crevices. "Tell me, David, why would the Duty Officer in Bancroft Hall need a pistol?"

"I can only guess. You realize, I didn't attend the Academy." "I'm sorry David dear. I'd quite forgotten that." She reached for his arm consolingly, but only succeeded in bumping it. "Doesn't matter. Many fine young men, I'm sure, did not. Anyway, that boy straightway grabbed that gun and put it to his temple. The shame too much to bear."

He gazed down the hazy sunlit port street with its cobbles. The emptiness concentrated the focus upon himself, rendering escape subtly but tenaciously impossible. "They didn't all do that, of course," Miriam added. Alice Navarro laughed. "I'm relieved to hear it. That could have made it awfully difficult to man our ships." "Alice, you're such a cynic still. But they did indeed punish them most severely. Snipped the gold buttons off their uniforms, and the tailor shop sewed on black ones and that's the way they'd banish them home." Her tone became wistful. "I don't know that they're doing that anymore. But there's every bit as much lying going around as there used to be. Isn't that so, David?"

"I can't say. I don't keep track of those things the way that I once did."

"I think you know." She wagged her finger playfully in his face. "I see it in your little smile. I can tell. You're still bumping into those devils up there in Washington, I bet." She waved aside further quibbles. By gum, if you knew, you *knew*. Her hand held him in a grip of certainty by which, as if he were a post, she hauled her guileless baby-like face inches from his own. Her eyes were solemn, centroid of a total and desperate sincerity. Liars deserved what they got. "Know what we ought to do to them?" He blinked. *"Them?"*

"*Shoot* 'em. That's what I'd do. Every one of those blasted deceivers." He was conscious of her earnest eyes, her unrelenting grip, breath redolent of spearmint mouthwash, yet not unpleasant. "What do you think of *that*, Alice? Wouldn't that do it?"

"Do something." Across the thin but curly top of Miriam Gearing's white hair he caught Alice Navarro's wink. She looked away towards State Circle and their interrupted destination. "What I think too, pet, is that I'm feeling chill."

"That we don't want. Alice has had a little bout of . . . well, no matter what, she's bounced back. Can we not invite David to share tea with us?"

"Naturally David is invited. I doubt though he will find our ancient company all that thrilling." "It would be lovely, ladies. Unfortunately, I have to be getting on."

Alice Navarro gave him her hand in its sackishly loose glove. "Good luck to you, David Morgan. I miss your mother. My last years are duller without her." Miriam gave him a kiss that just reached his neck. "Then another day, dear. Let us know when you are coming next." At the bottom of Cornhill, before he turned off into Market Square, he looked back. As he had seen them first, they seemed not to be moving. Perhaps catching their breath before proceeding around the at last attained mercifully level arc of State Circle. No longer did he see them as absurdly sized, merely respectably small. Centered in his vision between the vertical edges of the street's last two dwellings, centuries old, framed by time.

▲ ▲ ▲ ▲ ▲

Winter. But winter as few in the U.S. ever know it. Winter as the Russians approve, frozen lakes able to bear the crossing of armies of tanks. A bitter blazingly white world. But mail still came through, Christmas cards pouring in from everywhere. From Hawaii, a Pacific Ocean Research Corporation card with a note from Artie Perrozzi. Prospects golden. Analysts now in Taipei, Singapore, no end of good things to do for the Navy around the Pacific Rim. Yesterday Ford Island, tomorrow the world. From Billy Jencks a newsy card. Billy still taking pains to keep up to date—though far removed from it all now and, as usual lately, getting it mostly wrong—with his old first love, antisubmarine warfare. ". . . oh, and finally, I hear DIANA has at last truly fallen on her sword. Spilled her guts all over the place." David could hear his voice, pictured him fondly. "Vindication, eh? Lord knows, our careers didn't prosper afterwards (make that mine!) but there's the satisfaction of being right. I *know*. I know . . . . Still, I bet we sleep better than all those guys who pushed that turkey . . ." Ah, Billy. Haven't you figured it yet? *They sleep like babes.* On the back of Billy's card was a note that he almost missed, wishing he had. Mention of a small piece in the Washington Post that Daisy Ketcham was dead. Her body found in the courtyard below her balcony from which she had evidently fallen. There were no witnesses and her death was unexplained. *Right. Daisy, Daisy . . . .*

From Charlie Wicker, that splendid engineer, rusting in exile, the unsurprising news that he was not enjoying his retirement. He scrawled: "I feel autumnal. Is DIANA getting anywhere? Just curious." Amongst the many cards, with the usual reindeer and Santas, one stood out, elegant with a reproduction of the great rosette of Chartres Cathedral. Light filtered through the wondrous stained glass, ennobling the words of Hallmark's current poet laureate. In Tiny Gray's fine, fervent hand, *"Deus Meus et Omnia!"* The cards piled up. Muddy's showed a scene of the Naval Academy Chapel in blue twilight with a formation of midshipmen outside in the snow caroling to the brightness within. The card was a large one with lots of room for writing which Muddy put to full use. David had come full circle, grown to love that ancient man. Muddy had recently visited Tessa's grave, a heartfelt memorial act, but with a purpose as well. Wanting ". . . to determine if the lack of a liner was a regrettable decision. Tessa's wish was to keep things economical and a liner was to her a frill. Fortunately, there's still no sinkage." Awkward possibilities trembled unspokenly. *"Sinkage?"* Aliason said, making a face. David explained. "A liner encases the coffin. Otherwise, seepage can cause rotting of the coffin and then the earth tumbles in . . ."

She put her hands to her ears. "Stop." This was Christmas Eve. She tramped through the snow to the mailbox once more, hopes that the postman brings. One card only today. A hand she saw seldom, but knew well. An undistinguished card, she pictured it grabbed from the least of some drugstore's stock. Marty, as usual, on the go. This card read alone, held with gloved, awkward fingers that shook with cold. "Love. *But never forget who you are.*" She didn't forget. In daylight, the hour changed from evening, not in deference to Christmas Eve but due to the depth of the snow on the roads, they drove twenty-two miles to the regular meeting at Aspen Meadows. There, gathered in a featureless church basement from out of all this snow and great lonely skies, was the same clutch of humanity, the hubbub from its people welling up as if from a party, the sober gaiety of a special comradeship. Tobacco smoke thick as ever, not all vices relinquished.

Talking today was Jimmy B., a rancher and a favorite as a speaker. A giant of a man who used to twist grown steers to the ground; his face was splotched but his eyes clear. He talked in his high plainsman's drawl, smiling with winning self-deprecation. Once owned forty thousand acres and four thousand head, herds of antelope besides. Wasn't enough. Wanted to be the biggest rancher in the state. Got himself elected state senator but that didn't satisfy either. He burned to be governor. Inside he was hollow and liquor bridged the gap between what he was and what he wanted to be. He had busted up bars and knew the insides of jails from Laramie to Ketcham. Six cars he wrecked, lost his cattle, saw his land auctioned off. His wife left him, though now she was back, but his sons hated him unto this day. He hit rock bottom the morning he was found senseless in an icy pasture, lying there all night without so much as a parka. Body so full of liquor it kept him from freezing as solid as the brick hard cow turds in which he sprawled. Doctors claimed that it didn't work that way, but Jimmy B. knew better. His veins were filled with antifreeze. Didn't know why they even bothered to thaw his carcass out. He would pause, drawing his audience along comfortably with his silences. They were looking at a miracle. Here he had discovered his Higher Power. Always figured that he was some kind of a rustic atheist—pronouncing it with an old fashioned pause between the first and the second syllable—even from boyhood roaming the wilderness and gazing up into the impenetrable blue sky and seeing nothing up there but deeper blue. He'd had some scary times out on the range and come through them on his own and as sure as crap wasn't about to thank some phantom up there in the sky.

Here in the fellowship it made no difference. If he wanted to be an atheist, fine; the program asked only that he be a sober one. He confessed that he still didn't know much about God, but he was damned sure that there was Something Out There that had saved his worthless ass. It had been nine years and two days since he'd had a drink and, with the help of the Fellowship, he wouldn't have one tomorrow. Heads nodded. This was a region for tales, the heritage of campfires and stories told over and over. They had taken in Aliason's tale too, paid no less rapt attention to the slender airy easterner who had made her story part of their own. They finished with the Lord's Prayer; hands tightening upon each other's like lion's claws. Afterwards, Aliason thanked the speaker, by now a friend. Today she and David did not linger. Christmas awaited. The crystalline structure of each unmelted snowflake was intact, the tires biting into the snowy roadway with a sound like hard gritty sand crackling underneath. "It really is like a religion though, isn't it?", he reflected aloud "an unvarying ritual."

"*Not* a religion," she said impatiently, "Don't you *listen?*"

"But still it unfolds always with exactly the same words. So, it's possible to see it as sort of like a mass." There was an irresistible feeling of power in his vehicle's mastery over the snowy road that communicated itself to the driver like grand knowledge. With Aliason gazing off at passing fence stakes, an endless count of them, toying with the wish to bang one of those stakes down on someone's skull. "*You don't know what you're talking about. You can't ever know. Be grateful and shut up.*"

He went over to his office late that afternoon. Habit, but also a chance to be apart. The phone rang and it was Washington. He picked it up, knowing who it had to be this late on Christmas Eve. He pictured the scattered office lights in the Pentagon's face of dark stone, the isolated cars in the ice-sheathed vastness of North Parking. "Hello, Julius." A big man now, Julius, no longer at the right hand of the throne he had coveted. His the throne itself.

"David?" Julius's voice was altered, hard, urgent. The microwave relay, zipping from hill-top to hill-top through the crackling air of winter, seemed to have dried it. Still he got right to the point. DIANA in trouble on the Hill and it might never be procured in the numbers needed. New resistance in the area of foreign military sales . . . Australians doubtful, somebody feeding them bum dope and, now the Greeks . . .

"Greeks? Like those folks, Julius, to beware of bearing gifts . . . ?" "Hey, not funny." Anyway, it seemed that DIANA was only part of the problem. It was the successor, AJAX, coming along so nicely, or so Julius claimed to believe, that was worrying him most. He had just heard that both systems were being tested at one thirty second of maximum power. If word ever leaked out that those systems were slipping into the fleet after a degraded test program, the bleep was going to hit the fan. Was there anything to the rumor? At David's confirmation that there was a whole lot, an anguished oath burst from Julius. "*Why*, David, for Christ's sake?"

"Hey, Julius. Where have you been all this time? This is Wolf Lake. Remember? Its people once up in arms. Why do you think they're happy now?"

"I think, Mr. Technical Director, you've taken a lot on yourself. Where are your priorities?" David toyed with that one for a moment but then thought of his waiting bowl of eggnog. Made the old-fashioned way, only the yolks kept, with rum and protean gobs of whipped cream. A sanitized cup for Al. Friends coming over tonight. Picturing the log fire, the inviting brown sprinkle of nutmeg across the nog's creamy surface, he felt unaccustomedly kindly towards Julius, whose outrage was now peaking with the sudden fullness of his understanding. "*Those systems are expected to operate at full power in the detection mode in the fleet.*" And detect naught. Softly he responded: "Julius. What diff really?" He pretended a yawn. "Send a message directly to crank it up 15 decibles. Let your command put it on record." Julius' bluster became pleading. "Hey, Dave. I'm on the hot seat. The committee could spear me. How am I going to field this one?"

"Play the innocent. Take the line that a highly placed executive, yourself right?, with wide ranging responsibilities, can't, after all, be on top of what some renegade subordinate is up to thousands of miles away. *Lie.*"

"It's very sad to hear you talking that way." Julius's tone was sorrowful. "People respect you David. Your friends had hopes . . . ."

He cut off the sermon. "Come on Julius. You've got bigger probs than us renegade folk out here in the sticks. Like getting your story straight on all those whales and porpoises beaching themselves."

"There's not an iota of objective scientific proof linking that behavior to our transmissions."

"Right. Julius relax. One day at least. It's Christmas. *Adios.*"

All day he'd kept his eye on Aliason. Christmas always danger. She was too gay, brittleness palpable. Now it was late, guests departed. Candles still burning, their light the last downstairs except for the dying fire whose flickerings reflected off the decorations on the tree, the shiny wrappings of present, danced off sequined stockings that had seen beter days. So, what was that rhyme? Al could help there. Hers before it was theirs to share.

*"Bayberry candles
Burned to the socket
Bring luck through the year
And pence to the pocket."*

She cocked her ear. "Oh *yes,*" she confirmed joyously. But she had caught something else. Storms came up suddenly out here, winds pouring out of the mountains with a wild fury, driving fine snow that tore at all things living. The giant trees outside in the pale darkness swayed and their tops tossed as if they were saplings. Clumps of massy snow, dislodged from the trees, hit the roof with alarming thumps. Solid as those remembered coconuts that fell long ago on their rooftop in Honolulu. Later, easing into sleep, they savored the sense of malevolent force comfortably withstood. She squeezed him tightly, kissing the side of the head, first place her lips found. He slid his hand down but she stopped it with some kind of murmured message. Other images aroused by the storm had come to his mind. Those submarines would not stay in focus though. A great part of his life, too much of his talent, had gone into knowledge of them and yet he felt a pang that it was slipping away, becoming mere memory. The storm blew and shook the house, even these sturdily old government quarters. Childlike, awed, they held each other. He had a simple and stark sense of time, all things passing. Aliason's white flank, that fair strained flesh now splintering in threads of red and blue. A struggle for groceries, hopes for grandchildren, the son you pray for luck in war. What love might be. A lone rock amidst gray seas and two naked people clinging until the foaming swells sucked them away.

* * *

Rather than viewing the flow of human life as he once did, as a mighty novel, a meshing of countless plots, more and more David Morgan was feeling it in episodic lurchings of postscripts. One came to his attention first by way of brief filler on the latest hit TV show "Five Minutes." As reported, the government was demolishing the old National Center and, in the course of a routine last check around the deserted lower interior of National Center Two, there was discovery of an unaccountably undesignated space. Evidently, from vestigial markings on the exterior corridor walls, doors had once been in place but at some time in the past a barring structure of permanent wall had superseded earlier entry. From reference to old building prints, the mysterious space was impressive, amounting to many thousands of square feet. The contractor in charge of the eventual demolition had been reluctant to proceed without first reporting on the oddness of the circumstances. The General Services Administration had ordered that demolition be delayed until a duly constituted investigative team was authorized to break into the space to find out what was what. The reporter covering the story was young, bulldogish, voice atremble with outrage, taking as a model bad Mike Wallace, which is to say very bad indeed.

The Team was shown tramping across trashy corridors en route to their forcible entry, and thence one saw them shining flashlights into darkness that had obviously not been disturbed for years. One of the first men to enter, evidently of amateur archaeological bent, likened his feelings to those of the discoverers of the tomb of Tutankhamen as their torchlights had first flickered on the wonders within. It was the *pristineness* that got him, everything untouched, ready to hum, seemingly as hastily abandoned in the midst of its shiny electronic life as the dishes on the mess table of the *Mary Celeste*. Brand new equipment was still uncrated. Fallen to the floor (the scotch tape holding it having lost its stuff) was one of those computer printed cartoons, this one of a judicial Neptune carrying a formidable Trident labeled TRUTH in one hand and in the other bearing, like Moses his tablet, a sign—ADAMP—whose meaning no one had come forward to explain. The last face to appear on the "Five Minutes" filler item was a uniformed Navy spokesman who stated that the U.S. Navy deplored all forms of waste and would spare no effort to get "to the bottom of this mystery." The Secretary of the Navy himself was requesting suspension of the destructive process until all evidence could be gotten and wrongdoers . . . "ferreted out." Stay tuned, the announcer urged, for further announcements.

"Be dammed . . . ."

"You say something dear?" murmured Al.

She lowered her glasses, looking over the top of her book. Watching her man repeating to himself, but more carefully, lips all but unmoving, *well, well* . . . . Old ADAMP itself. Wondering how many persons left on earth could decipher those initials, and if sleuthing would go so far as to ferret out Billy Jencks for a few words.

"Nothing really, hon," waving her back to her reading. At the same time the television program was urging viewers to stay alert for further developments on this "breaking" story. Alert he was for the next few weeks, but there was nothing new on the tube and somehow he was sure that was going to be that

▲ ▲ ▲ ▲ ▲

Perhaps it was no more than his championing of the Eagles. Or afterwards, as the years went on, his taking up the Cause of the Wolves, however pitiful their numbers, against the wrath of the local ranchers. Or it could have been, too, even more plausibly, when the eyes of those in Washington turned rare looks westward towards Wolf Lake's mostly ignored little Naval Test Station, that gradually things came home to them. Such as that the Station Director's main energies seemed to be the favoring of neighboring critters and varmints. Or that practically any phone call would find him off fishing or golfing. What was it with this guy? Perhaps explanation was even simpler. Just high time. For the old boy to pack it in. And as for the circumstances of his posting out there, it was history writ on air. Faces change, administrations pass, nothing is meant to last forever, no more than earth and skies. Ditto for all those vows writ in blood. Blood dries, fades, goes flaky, turns to dust, and blows away in fickle winds. Gone too, long since, was Donnie Lee Webster—though any rejoicing by those who knew him must be muted because the likes of those volunteering to replace him are legion—at most a footnote in the journalistic memoirs of the times. Donnie's latest whereabouts unknown. Possibly by now at last engaged in honest labor, though that is to be doubted.

David Morgan's departure from Wolf Lake was regretted, but not unduly. Not so Aliason Morgan. She had become cherished for her generous nature, her big heart even amongst many such. A Twelfth Stepper too, as it is said in some circles. It went with the territory. One of her good deeds, in the small world department, focused on the sister of the retired Congressman Duke. Paying repeated visits to that afflicted soul, negotiating perilous mountain passes in the depths of winter. Not saving the poor lady, a far-gone case, though she tried mightily. When the Wolf Lakers thought of Aliason, regretting her departure as they did acutely, and remembering her spirit, it was of a woman who kept her hair too long for her age but forgivably so, that last, rich tresses, blowing in the prop wash of her little plane.

Anyway, those who live in Government quarters know that sooner or later they must move on. They are merely tenants and no matter how much they love a particular place, one grander than they could afford on their own, time and circumstance dictate that one day they will say goodbye to their temporary home. The moving van with its travel-grimed license plates of many States pulls up and upheaval begins. The utilitarian government-issue furniture, the great deal of it that normally is allocated to large quarters and is necessary to fill out its many extra rooms, that, of course, remains. The family identifies its own, and its treasures as well as its necessities are packed in cartons and loaded aboard by beefy silent men. And the huge van, slowly being maneuvered out of the front yard, is a ponderous thing, its initial progress as awkwardly careful as a great jet plane being towed from its hangar. At last though it gets itself headed fair and picks up speed and once again is lord of the Interstates, all eighteen wheels beating their way along the smoothed and dark singing tracks of a continent. Their shredded spun-off rubber are like crows' carcasses tossed in the gravel and hot dust beside the road. In its irresistible and heedless energy is the destiny and mystery of America.

A new family arrives and like mating birds coming upon an old nest, softening it with their own fresh down, scraps from here and there, make it their own. Filling it with their music and their quarrels, and pretty soon there is no sign, no recollection, of families who lived here before. Except this is not quite true. Marks on the wall, faint pencil marks of a child's progressing height, various minor scratches and bumps, the micrometer rain of everyday living, are a subtler record of who has preceded. Less dramatic than the unhealed slashes of Tarleton's saber on the banister at Carter's Grove, still they are touches of indecipherable time that the lick-and-a—promise refurbishing of Public Works does not erase.

And in the attic—these older quarters always have fine attics, for they are the standing residue of history, in Pensacola, at Leavenworth, at Kit Carson, and those other places where stockades once secured some vanished line, Wolf Lake too, encampment for the pursuers of Chief Joseph and the last of his Nez Percé— some things are left behind. The attic's dim recesses, corners where you must stoop under the angle of the rafters, hold junk of previous tenants; the unimportant, the forgotten, stuff that people cannot bring themselves to throw away. Lots of room up there and out of the general eye, doing no harm. A *potpourri;* old hats, single mittens, faded discount coupons, unfinished needlepoint—here half an eyeglass case, an intricate design for so small a piece— and at the bottom of all this a surprising number of handwritten notes pertaining to submarines. Stacks of travel folders too, the hyper-colored riches of the world, and tucked down deep, understandably so, a copy not overly thumbed, of *My Secret Life*. What man does not, sooner or later, need help? Here also are battered children's toys, crayon scrawls, a stampless stamp album, an unfinished log fort . . . a world of beginnings. One box is heavy and, digging for the source of its weight, one would find a thick manuscript tied with ribbon. Apparently a poem and, for all its heft, still incomplete. Love letters are tucked into these boxes too that should have been burned, not left to make some unknown finder blush. That is, should Times of Blushing return.

The Morgan children's books are in another box. Covers are torn off and the imprint of sticky fingers remains. A few, evidently loved, had been repaired; layers of scotch tape yellow and cracking cover the exposed fibers of their wounded backs. Several were Boat's favorites, ones he could never get enough of and whose images as he lay back on his pillow used to keep him awake long. Agate-bright eyes, reflecting the bright glow of his imagination, picturing those splendid creatures of the wild. Pointirex the deer, Dart the Chipmunk, and Orsa and Hug the great bears.

After the long years at Wolf Lake the Morgans settled in one of those retirement communities of the kind that were to become so popular. David Morgan took up volunteer work, tutoring natives of Third World countries English, helping out at the local Public Library. Books he knew. Aliason had at first a harder time adapting, feeling keenly her uprootedness from her beloved mountains. Yes, *yes*, she realized, they did have to give up their lovely quarters, all that was understood. Accepting too that they were no longer of an age, nor temperament, to wrest contentment from a harsh wilderness against which the Wolf Lake Station had put up for those lucky Morgans its dream-like protective wall. Even so, did that mean that they had to retreat this far? Why all the way back to the Washington, D.C. area? What in heck was waiting for them there?

To which questions, and against her flood of emotional objections, husband David had only imperfect reply. Amounting mostly to the D.C. area being home territory, one man's remembered battlefield. Here too was Arlington Cemetery as well, his mother's bones, and no less honored for the good things he had brought to Tessa's life, Muddy's beside. Also David's many siblings, a host of warrior cousins as well, borne to Arlington's green and stony hills.

Yet Aliason, for all that she had been dragged back here kicking, if not screaming, came to fare better in this kind of place than husband David with his permanent restlessness, all those sheets of paper, their blankness haunting. She had her meetings, of course, faithfully attended, with David pulled along to the Open ones. They were necessity, comfort, duty. But more important, she had regained joy. Which was her flying, the love of which she brought back from Wolf Lake unimpaired and which, after a patch of frustration, most of it administrative nitpicks, she was able to practice again. Thence several times a month seeking VFR days of blue skies, heading out old Route 7 to Leesburg Airport and renting a light plane. A favorite flight was to West Virginia where a tiny field's coffee shop served up home-made apple pie ala mode. Always she came back from her adventure refreshed and high spirited and David was glad for her and proud.

"You are something," he said, "a flying grandmother." "Pshaw," she always responded. "Well, all right then. In not too many years you'll find yourself the flying *great*-grandmother." "Oh that's not anything to be either," she said, "not these days."

"Come on, Al, why do you still keep putting yourself down?" She sighed. Why indeed? He went flying with her once. A windy fall day and they lurched and bumped across the glorious colors of the Appalachian ridges, rounded and softened these, once higher than the Rockies and which went on and on like the swells of some dark frozen sea. No airman at heart, he was pleased to have it over though with a male's pride keeping from her his own fears. The call he had so long dreaded came one afternoon from an airport official telling him that Al's plane was overdue and presumably down somewhere amongst the hills west of Purcellville. Low on fuel and not sure where she was, her plight had caught the attention of a nearby airline pilot who spotted her plane and directed her to follow his big passenger jet heading for Dulles Airport. Then he lost sight of her as her plane apparently ran out of gas and disappeared behind a wooded ridge. Her voice, the airline pilot reported, was throughout this time high with tension but also steady and, as the accident investigation subsequently revealed, her flight training did not desert her as she resisted the temptation to turn her aircraft abruptly and risk a stall. Also remembering to cut the ignition before plowing into a cornfield. Straight in unflinchingly, as she had been taught. But cornfields, contrary to folklore, can be tough and she was dead, probably within minutes after going in. The plane was not found for hours and by then David had made it to the crash scene and was present when they lifted her out of the crumpled fuselage.

There was not a mark on her except for a bruise on her forehead. A ruptured spleen gives no sign. He watched the experts carry her limp body out to the red and white rescue vehicle and the sight of that pale face, bloodless lips pressed tight, was his last and best farewell look before the undertakers did their usual and erased more than he wished of his girl who could soar but could not navigate.

Some months after Aliason's death David received a letter from Betty Morgan. By this time, Sean's widow. He had not seen her for several years, not since he and Al had invited her to visit them over the first Thanksgiving after Sean's own death. Sean who had died unexpectedly, his heart stopping suddenly while mowing the grass one summer's day and Betty had found him slumped over the wheel of his new tractor, engine still chugging away, when she stepped out into the sunshine to bring him a glass of lemonade. That Thanksgiving dinner had been warm, humorous, affectionate, and had done much to raise Betty's spirits. It reestablished bonds that had eased off from the closeness of their time together in the Islands. They drank a little too much, both Betty and David, but with no harm either except to the feelings of Aliason who was left somewhat out of the gaiety that radiated intermittently from the living room while she was busy with turkey stuffing and basting and the rest of it. But then, as ever, Al was the marvelous and conscientious cook and overall seemed not too much bothered because of the satisfaction she found in her preparations and the extravagant praise of her guest.

They had done a lot of serious talking too that long winy afternoon, Betty and he. It was talk, naturally enough given recent sad circumstances, of life and its transitoriness, how fast it went and how one should seize and love it. Every precious moment. The kind of things that everyone says on those occasions. But talk too—given the nature of Betty, that was also practical, down to earth—of the inevitably transformed leadership of her family. Whether she should move or stay put for a while. Anyway, what to do next? She brought up the subject of money too, investments for proper income, how to minimize taxes and so on, with David trying to sound to her like a wiser man than he was in such matters. Yet the problem of money seemed last and least; Betty was well off in that regard. Following Sean's retirement from the Navy, they had carried out their plan to settle on the Eastern Shore. Betty to raise her dogs, champions of glowing fur, and Sean becoming the busy and organized country squire, making themselves part of that quirky, eclectically talented hunting and outdoors society that had lodged itself for centuries along the secluded crab and oyster filled backwaters that sluggishly finger their way between the Big and Little Choptank west of Cambridge. But that society—though parts of it were hard drinking, carrying other dangers too—did not get to them. They lived with their same inner discipline. Gradually, not rushing it, they converted a decrepit, turn of the century farmhouse into rustic beauty on which, not long before Sean's death, *Country Homes* was readying a feature article. On occasional visits David and Al had watched it come to life.

They had not set out to create a showplace. They were merely making another home, as they had across time and around the world. Each time their dogs returned from their wild romps through the woods and the swamps, scaring up the deer, either Sean or Betty would wipe off those sopping muddy feet, each individual horny toe, with towels kept by the door. No matter how many times each day, they did it. Great bounding loveable red setters without a brain in their heads. At night the dogs would become still, their bear-like nails no longer clattering on the slippery hardwood floors or sliding the oriental carpets sideways in a single powerful turn of their eager restless bodies. In front of the fire the dogs' coats would gleam like gold; only their tails would move, thumping with dreams of chase, and in those moments anyone in Sean and Betty's company would believe that he was sharing a perfection of peace. Nor was it illusion. But such a world of labor to make it! Betty did not permit their land to be hunted, and in the winter, across the barren stubble fields of corn, thousands of geese found sanctuary. Some flocks were Snow Geese, pale as cream, haunting in their loveliness. Many times she ventured out onto the ice to rescue geese wounded by hunters. She tended wings, mended bad legs, and gradually a flock of lame and loyal ones, doing well but not up to the arduous springtime flights to the tundra of northern Canada.

But, the letter. In it Betty expressed sadness for David and regretted that she had been in Europe when Aliason had died. Not even having heard the news until many weeks later. Her turn now to offer words of advice, wisely not too many. Walk, she told him, amongst other things. *Walk a lot.* As for herself, doing all right. But, lonely though, guessing that would never go away. It was too unpopulated over where she was living still. Of course that was why they had settled there in the first place, the appeal of its distances and its silence. But when the sun went down no lights were to be seen coming on for miles up and down Arundel Creek. A jungle darkness, of time before man, welled up from that wilderness scene. So do drop down, she suggested at the end of her letter, and pay a visit when it suited. It would be nice for her, she wrote in her firm upright hand, hoping that it might be good for him too.

That was all, but he thought that he had detected something more. But exactly what? That was the question. A silly one too. Just *go*. Go and enjoy and stop all this cerebrating. But he didn't go. He was apprehensive of what he thought that he might have read between the lines. Had he detected . . . some kind of willingness? And, if so, willingness for what? And how just would it all come about? Well . . . ? Were they going to fly straight into each other's arms the instant that he walked through the arched antique wood front door and stay stuck to one another? She did like him, that much he knew. But the picture was ludicrously improbable. Whatever was possible in that classically lovely and self-contained woman of so many interests, yet who seemed to keep all things in perspective, he could not see it. That silvered lady would make sure each dog's paw was toweled off before anything else. And it was not as if either of them were spring chickens any more.

If what he was afraid of—the specifics and the surrounding conditionals—was a vague and uncertain thing, the *why* part of his reluctance, on the other hand, was clear. He did not measure up. As with golf too, holiest of games, he did not feel himself worthy, and it wrong to gain a prize through no virtue but that of having outlasted the impediment of other lives. Detecting in himself echoes of Billy's old attacks of conscience that no man ought to be automatic inheritor of luck. Better, he stay within his league, not be tempted beyond. There was a hierarchy in this sort of thing too.

He delayed a while, long enough that his point was made simply by silence, before sending Betty a reply. His letter was warm but distant and he did not hear from her again. Several years later he learned that she had remarried a somewhat younger man, evidently a sportsman of wealth who owned an estate that rivaled in luxury and beauty, in game and horses, its nearby neighbor the legendary Pokety Farm. He heard too eventually, in a roundabout way, that she did not appear especially happy, that her husband drank heavily and that she may have joined him in his fault. He doubted that last, believing in her iron, but since they had no further contact he learned nothing more.

As he had set out to do long ago, David Morgan has tried to do well by his children. Boat has made a good life far removed from mountains, living in a suburb of New Orleans. He contends in the pressured world of commodity trading, dealing in substances both real and yet abstract, gold futures, soybeans, sorghum, pork bellies . . . he who has never seen a pork belly and would not recognize a soybean if one popped into his mouth. But he can read a fateful twitching of a rival trader's nerve at fifty paces. He lives on the West Bank, close to the Mississippi, and late in the afternoon he and his wife take their drinks and walk over to the levee and watch from there the passing ships, the colors of sunset, the great tawny river surging by. He likes the thought of it going on down to the sea because the oceans dwell in him.

But Boat is modern man too, in him the hope and the peril of America, could care less about government or politics. From time to time he takes his family on explorations of adventure to the undersea world, to the Florida Keys, to the Pacific atolls, to the Bahamas and once—fortunately he has the money for it—to the Great Barrier Reef off Australia. *Hey now, this is what's important.* And when he comes back from such trips, that beautiful world tingles in him and he feels whole again, refreshed, clean as those crystal waters that contain that amazing concentration of life. Though he does not fully realize it, it is what he lives for. On shorter trips, in different company, he goes for tarpon, down to Bahia Honda, where the silver kings, the record breakers, the lunkers, begin to gather in April. He has learned how to do it well from guides, using live bait and letting the float and the little victim pinfish together drift out into the tidal estuaries and then socking it to the tarpon as it runs away, watching that great shining form leap shaking, ten feet out of the water, ablaze in the sunlight . . . one of life's splendid moments. Always he releases. But he feels the tug and the tremble of that vibrant amazing life in his arms long afterwards. It helps. He happened to mention to his father that the big sharks come also every April, pursuing the returning tarpon, and his father sent him a long letter, out of his own long ago Key West days, confirming the ways of those sharks. Exhorting his son to remember their family trips to a place called Cobham's Wharf, near Newport News, where the family would picnic and scrounge around at the base of those old crumbling cliffs for Miocene fossils, fragments of gelatinous oysters three feet long, the giant teeth of sharks forty feet long that dominated those warm soupy rich seas of ten million years ago. Those sharks! His father really went on about that, about those awesome creatures, seeming to demand that the son himself keep the sense of those prehistoric lives vivid in his consciousness, until at last Boat rebelled. *Now what the hell? I don't get it.* But saving the letter all the same.

Strengthening the son's doubts, or rather his certitudes, is the continuing rain of his father's words. They descended upon him first in the days of his youth, and keep coming still, through letters and phone calls, on into this new century—this New Millennia!—in which his father now is quite the old man. Going on still about the submarine. "You see, you *see* . . . ." But no one sees, knows what he is talking about, or cares. He cackles now, just like his own mother did towards the end. The old man likes to tell horror stories of government, remembers the old ones, collects new . . . repeats himself. Still claims that he's still going to write that book some day. *The book.* But he won't. Not the time left, too many threads to be drawn together for a no longer first rate mind—if ever he owned such—and only a pair of skinny old arms to put themselves around it. It is an old man's loneliness talking. He misses Boat's mother terribly. She made him a king. He blames himself still for not discouraging her from taking up flying, bowing to romantic follies, overworked visions of flying grandmothers who ought to keep both feet on the ground.

Boat's imagination is a different one now. Other things sing in him now and those creatures of his loved animal stories that his mother read to him have been subsumed into the froth of the world's turbulent flow, into amazement at all that has gone into the century's turning into a third millennia. They are merely parts of the strengths of a happy childhood, absorbed and carried over into the bloodstream of the man. But Orsa and Dart and Hug, and the rest, live on in shrinking numbers that know nothing of the names that children's' books authors have pinned on them. On stunning heights beyond Wolf Lake, beyond the timber line, and in steep valleys so remote that they have thus far defeated the blood-thirst of men, humbled even the wanderlust of the lonely backpacker, the habits of those splendid wild animals are little altered from the days before Asian man first crossed the land bridge into North America. Yet the animals are not unaware of the existence of man; they know him not by his presence, but his works. Glints of silver and straight white trails high across the blue sky count the passage of jet liners. But scant attention is paid to these. The senses of the creatures of the wild are not tuned to that foreign world of the skies. Planes do not bother them. But sometimes, through their hooves, the pads of their feet or through long glassy claws, they detect vibrations that cause them to tremble with fear. Signals from out of the unknown that seem to tell of the solid earth itself in trouble.

Which may well be the case.

From beyond the mountains, ridge upon ridge of storied purple ones, receding like great frozen waves in a mighty sea, comes a mysterious pulsing of energy. It is not sound, not as man ordinarily knows it, because it is below those frequencies that he can hear. It is below even what he can ordinarily *feel*, for this is sound that travels not through the air, but through the earth and its stone and its molten cores. This is no longer the domain of the acoustician but of the seismologist. Lord Rayleigh would be at home here. For today (and all this has taken place after David Morgan's time there), from the bottom of Wolf Lake, unseen in its depths but connected to the massive domed concrete structures of the test station's new power generators by an umbilical of insulated cable—cable a foot thick containing wires that constitute a treasure of copper and capable of carrying millions of amperes of current—ascend totally submerged towers of steel. They serve purposes of experiment with giant transducers of sound that are far larger than any known in the past. Transducers that dwarf DIANA as a whale does a minnow. Pyramidal in form, the towers rival in size those of Cheops in Egypt. And like those awesome structures of ancient man, they too more than hint of human vanity as well as grandeur, of the folly of excessive hopes, of taking a once reasonable idea and pursuing it to hell and gone. Striving to create systems for ships and structures that will never be built, never could be built. Playing at finding submarines which, if they can be defeated at all, must be defeated in very different ways. Best strangled in the cradle, least and last and worst taken on in the open seas. In some future age, when record of this one has vanished, men may go down into the lake and rediscover those rusting masses of metal, with their great suspended orbs of aluminum and rubber, like some odd male *genitalia* of science, ten stories high, swaying three hundred feet down in those gentle currents, silenced at last, no longer causing Pointirex to cock an ear to this odd vibrancy coming through the earth, nor Orsa's black nose to twitch in baffled alarm. Dead in those dim depths, their thick green mosses nibbled at by the beautiful rainbow trout, these objects will keep their sense of strangeness even after archaeologists have explained, if explain they can, their titanic mystery.

Oh yes, one thing more was abandoned in that attic of the Morgan's quarters too—wisely and well left behind—a cheap and ludicrous picture of a warship and a giant mythical eagle clutching a submarine, the former as fanciful a creation as were the fears of the local ranchers that the pathetic handful of real eagles surviving out their way actually were soaring off to their high and remote nests with infant calves and lambs in their talons.

* * *

David Morgan kept on going to Meetings long afterwards. Long after the time when Al was not there to go with him. He gave his dollar at the mid-way break, at the droning ritual call—*"We have no dues or fees but we do have expenses"*— and kept his hand in, another echo of the old days, volunteering now and then to take on the duty of making the coffee for the coming month of meetings. Yet he hardly ever opened his mouth at these meetings except when he would happen to meet a friend of Al's, one of her old comrades in arms, and warmed to some nice thing about her that in a way kept her alive. Ghosts nowhere else as strong as within the bright antiseptically white painted cinder block walls of church basements. More rarely he chatted with newcomers—"pigeons" they called them still—and only when David Morgan had been pointed out as someone having something worth saying. Mostly though his experience was akin to the comfort of the soothed unbeliever drowsing away in his church's backmost pew and letting the organ music surge through his mind like the dumb power of the sea.

Yet if no visions of saints or martyrs ever crowded his imagination, in reverie he would think back to Akron, Ohio, that surprisingly ordinary city of polluted skies and sooted brick buildings where he used to visit occasionally on the business of EAR. Something had happened there as quietly amazing as anything that ever went on in Ephesus or Tarsus or any of those other storied biblical hot spots. And yet of its own two saints, little appeared to survive but the folklore of their nicknames. Perhaps (indeed no doubt) there were photographs, likely whole books—the two men had not lived in a vacuum—and even some small secular shrines were extant that could be visited by the curious. It was more appealing though to think of the founders of the Fellowship without icons, not have to accept them as the object of guesses by unknown sculptors of the past whose doubtful creations one was stuck with in churches gone cold and dead. He preferred to imagine the pair faceless, disembodied, floating in the white mists of that city in the geographical nothingness of central Ohio, yet which region has its own hidden rivers born of vanished seas, lakes of Indian portages, not without the mystery and resonances of ancient times. Enough that the pair be known, even at their most publicly visible, simply as Bill W. and Dr. Bob as set forth in the old English lettering of certain distinctive garishly luminous bumper stickers. Marking the many cars—more than one could first believe, once a soul began to notice—by the friendship of the knowing, belonging to men and women who have their own acute reasons for remembering.

Though Aliason did not live to see it, it worked out mostly as she had hoped for Beth. Except that there was no college for her. In too much of a hurry to get on with life. Her Ashton seemingly the right man still, or is so far at this telling. It is no dream life, for all that it is composed so prominently of picturesque elements, and ranching is unrelentingly hard work even for the owners themselves. Her children are her mainstay and keep her going now that other things have cooled. Sometimes still, late in the afternoon when nothing at the moment commandingly has to be done, she will hop bareback aboard Bell's Beau, the big stallion out of Beauty's mare, and ride around the corral. At such times those working nearby take notice of a woman on a horse running faster and faster, almost wildly it seems, but under control. As she races around in a blur, it strikes onlookers that she grows younger too and, with the low golden sun—just starting to drop below the black bulk of Duke's peak—intensely shining through her flying hair she could be as young as any of her girls still. But whether the plumpish out of breath woman who hops down off her steaming horse has forgotten her years, even who she is for these minutes, cannot be read in those steady, illusionless eyes that look now towards the house and supper to be attended to for many.

It is a big house, timbered, sprawling, built in chunks added on with each step upward onto its greater prosperity by a family that has been here a long time. Strong in structure, it weathers fierce winters and six foot snows as if they are nothing. Aliason visited there only a few times, despite the lure of her grandchildren. It wanted charm, was too much a man's domain. And it had no books. David kept insisting to her that the human inventory holds thousands of things worse than a life that has chosen to express itself through action rather than reflection, but nevertheless, picturing it from her daughter's standpoint, she found that difficult to accept. In truth, picturing it from her *own* standpoint. Always having dreamed of Beth as some version of herself. Some Aliason of the mountains. So it goes.

At odd times her father, unmindful of time zone differences, sees to it that Beth is hit up with the same kind of crapola that he dumps on Boat. But mostly he just wants to talk, to have someone *listen*. At bottom he wants his kids' esteem. Things flip-flop. Whereas once it is the child who craves approval from the parent, ever more it shifts the other way. It was, of course, too late, ludicrously late, for the return of the age of obedience, but at least he could hope for some respect. The old hand still claws for much, misses most everything by a mile. He settled for—rather, circumstances, the facts, settled it for him—being a "character", presumably eccentrically lovable. That became his final fate, protracted, demeaning, frustrating besides which—when an unremarkable death would at last make its call—his passing would be trivial. Ending up as the old codger, an egghead's repetitive and forgetful Archie Bunker.

From barn and corral, in the act of tightening a saddle or cleaning a stall, Beth would be summoned to the main house. Putting down her pitchfork, stripping off her gloves, to come to the phone to hear What Next, *Yes, yes.* Always listening patiently to his reports, no matter how childishly he went on. But what was the point? Even she knew, from casual reading, that all those Russian submarines, once so feared, were now just rusting away in the Kola Peninsula. *What more the hell did he want?* And should people give up just because all public men were not paragons. Why that was just plain *silly;* then there was no hope at all. For herself, the far off capitols of her state and national government barely shone in her thoughts. Her political concerns were acute, but small and tightly focused. All very well, to revere the grandeur of a Churchill; for Beth Berger it must be enough to take a bead on the county's water commissioner, his fat belly that of the fair land itself, whose corrupt tenure went back to her parents' time. She had stood up to him, was digging into his dealings, one day would nail him. That enough. Hers were the balls of the family.

Yes, yes . . . still more. Sure, Pop . . . . Thinking only how she could end this without hurting his feelings. Finally returning to her work shaking her head, often with eyes swimming . . . on occasion laughing helplessly. *"Hopeless,"* she would sometimes be seen murmuring. What else was there to say?

Well, there was *one* thing more. Fed up, she finally said it.

"Come on, Dad, face it, for all your pissing and moaning, you have to admit that you got yourself one pretty darned good life out of Government."

Which, that last, stopped him cold. It sure did.

EPILOGUE

One thing more. Tawney Gray had gotten a seamount named for himself at last. News of it came in one of those Oceanographic bulletins that David Morgan was no longer around to skim. But there it was, Tawney's picture on the first page—the old boy himself—impossible to miss. Unlike his seamount. *For, as ardently and as long as he had sought it, the christening had come too late, the honor too small. Like an old-timer's election to the Hall of Fame after he has become too feeble to rejoice. A mere consolation prize.*

Chosen was one of those obscure and flattened mounts in the Indian Ocean west of the Wharton Basin, far off the beaten track. It was no spectacular peak, not one rising close to the surface, no great mountain sprung from an abyssal floor which, if the seas were drained, would cause men to gasp at some new Everest exposed, casting its immense shadow across the gleaming muds and their flopping fish. Neither Cobb nor Kermit Roosevelt Seamount this one, its topography fascinating to contemplate: Tawney's own was far removed from the underseas battlegrounds of fame. Indeed it lay almost beyond the borders of curiosity. Its undramatic summit was fifteen hundred fathoms down and the lives of the lightless creatures that knew it as home, even assuming that man's measurements and observations ever came their way, were not likely to be altered by this new designation that would appear for a fleeting instant of geological time on those updated hydrographic charts marking their long quenched and cave-pocked volcano.

THANKS

Grateful acknowledgment is made to the publishers of Nicholas Monsaratt's masterwork, THE CRUEL SEA, for the brief segment reprinted herein.

BVG